OXFORD WORLD'S CLASSICS

ALEXANDRE DUMAS

The Man in the Iron Mask

Edited with an Introduction and Notes by
DAVID COWARD

OXFORD
UNIVERSITY PRESS

OXFORD

UNIVERSITY PRESS

Great Clarendon Street, Oxford OX2 6DP

Oxford University Press is a department of the University of Oxford.
It furthers the University's objective of excellence in research, scholarship,
and education by publishing worldwide in

Oxford New York

Athens Auckland Bangkok Bogotá Buenos Aires Calcutta
Cape Town Chennai Dar es Salaam Delhi Florence Hong Kong Istanbul
Karachi Kuala Lumpur Madrid Melbourne Mexico City Mumbai
Nairobi Paris São Paulo Singapore Taipei Tokyo Toronto Warsaw

with associated companies in Berlin Ibadan

Oxford is a registered trade mark of Oxford University Press
in the UK and in certain other countries

Published in the United States
by Oxford University Press Inc., New York

British Library Cataloguing in Publication Data

Data available

Library of Congress Cataloging in Publication Data

Data available

ISBN 0–19–283842–3

7 9 10 8

Printed in Great Britain by
Clays Ltd, St Ives plc

ALEXANDRE DUMAS was born at Villers-Cotterêts in 1802, the son
of an innkeeper's daughter and of one of Napoleon's most remarkable generals. He moved to Paris in 1823 to make his fortune in the
theatre. By the time he was 28, he was one of the leading literary
figures of his day, a star of the Romantic Revolution, and known for
his many mistresses and taste for high living. He threw himself
recklessly into the July Revolution of 1830 which he regarded as a
great adventure. Quickly wearying of politics, he returned to the
theatre and by the early 1840s was producing vast historical novels
at a stupendous rate and in prodigious quantities for the cheap
newspapers which paid enormous sums of money to authors who
could please the public. His complete works were eventually to fill
over 300 volumes and his yarns made him the best-known Frenchman of his age. He earned several fortunes which he gave away,
or spent on women and travel, or wasted on grandiose follies like
the 'Château de Monte Cristo' which he built to symbolize his
success. In 1848 he stood unsuccessfully in the elections for the new
Assembly. By 1850, his creditors began to catch up with him and,
partly to escape them and partly to find new material for his novels,
plays, and travel books, he lived abroad for long periods, travelling
through Russia where his fame had preceded him, and Italy where
he ran guns in support of Garibaldi's libertarian cause. Without
guile and without enemies, he was a man of endless fascination who
lived long enough to see his talent desert him. He died of a stroke at
Puys, near Dieppe, in 1870.

DAVID COWARD is Senior Fellow and Emeritus Professor of French
Literature at the University of Leeds. He is the author of studies
of Marivaux, Marguerite Duras, Marcel Pagnol, and Restif de La
Bretonne. For Oxford World's Classics, he has edited eight novels
by Alexandre Dumas, including the whole of the Musketeer saga,
and translated Dumas *fils' La Dame aux Camélias*, Diderot's *Jacques
the Fatalist*, two selections of Maupassant short stories, and Sade's
Misfortunes of Virtue and Other Early Tales. Winner of the 1996
Scott-Moncrieff prize for translation, he reviews regularly for the
Times Literary Supplement.

OXFORD WORLD'S CLASSICS

For over 100 years Oxford World's Classics have brought readers closer to the world's great literature. Now with over 700 titles—from the 4,000-year-old myths of Mesopotamia to the twentieth century's greatest novels—the series makes available lesser-known as well as celebrated writing.

The pocket-sized hardbacks of the early years contained introductions by Virginia Woolf, T. S. Eliot, Graham Greene, and other literary figures which enriched the experience of reading. Today the series is recognized for its fine scholarship and reliability in texts that span world literature, drama and poetry, religion, philosophy and politics. Each edition includes perceptive commentary and essential background information to meet the changing needs of readers.

CONTENTS

CONTENTS

CONTENTS

INTRODUCTION

The Man in the Iron Mask is the final instalment of a saga of chivalry and valour which spans half a century of French history and runs to over a million and a quarter words. It began with *The Three Musketeers* (1844) in which d'Artagnan, Athos, Porthos, and Aramis foil the wicked Milady and the steely Cardinal Richelieu; was continued in *Twenty Years After* (1845) where Dumas's legendary heroes fight for right during the civil wars of the Fronde in 1648 and fail gloriously in an attempt to rescue Charles I from the clutches of the evil Cromwell; and reaches its climax in *The Vicomte de Bragelonne, or Ten Years After* (1848–50), which embroils the famous four in their last tilt. Dumas promised further adventures which, however, were never written.

The Vicomte de Bragelonne has more often than not been issued in English as three separate novels. The first part, *Bragelonne, or the Son of Athos*, introduces the languid Raoul who, though 'the principal hero of this tale', is unmanned by his love for Louise de la Vallière and plays little part in the action which tells how d'Artagnan, Porthos, and Athos, with some subtle manœuvring from Aramis, restore Charles II to the English throne in the summer of 1660. The second section, *Louise de la Vallière*, follows Louis XIV's growing love for Louise and his deepening antagonism towards Fouquet in the early summer of 1661. The sleuthings of d'Artagnan, who detects a threat to the King whom he continues to serve faithfully, and the sinister intrigues of Aramis, now Vicar-General of the Jesuits, are carried on into *The Man in the Iron Mask*. Porthos, who has been subverted by Aramis, and the increasingly vulnerable Athos are reduced to supporting roles but die appropriately honourable deaths. In the last pages, Dumas hurries time (which has for long periods stood still) and finally allows d'Artagnan to fall at the battle of Maestricht in 1673.

Readers will not perhaps have heard much of the battle of Maestricht and may not wish to. But they have always known

ix

d'Artagnan and what he stands for: the spirit of adventure. They may not have read any of the Musketeer novels, but they will nevertheless be familiar with Athos, Porthos, and Aramis and their cry 'All for one and one for all!'. It is quite likely too that their idea of France in the seventeenth century has been largely shaped by Dumas's habit of seeing history in terms of personalities and by his tendency to pour black-and-white judgements over people and events. Ruthless Richelieu, miserly Mazarin, and conniving Colbert were in reality rather Good Things for France, though Dumas has all three down as thoroughly Bad Hats. On the other hand, Fouquet, who amassed considerable ill-gotten gains, becomes a sorely tried innocent, and Charles II of England—as clear an example of a Catastrophic King as any one could wish—is a Merry Monarch. Even freer with English history than with French, Dumas arranges for Aramis to crouch beneath the scaffold on which Charles I is executed and sends d'Artagnan to Newcastle where he kidnaps General Monk and exports him to Holland in a wooden barrel.

For when history failed to live up to expectations or proved inconvenient or uncertain, Dumas simply improved it. Historians wince at the liberties he took and have some cause to believe that on occasions he got as close as any Frenchman has ever come to Sellar and Yeatman's *1066, And All That*. Yet Dumas went to considerable lengths to graft his tales of adventure on to history of which he had a remarkable grasp. He immersed himself in seventeenth-century memoirs which, in his history-conscious age, were being published in large numbers, some for the first time. From them, always with an eye to the juicier morsels which he instinctively knew would appeal to a sensation-hungry public, he formed a strong idea of events and the people who made them. He worked closely with Auguste Maquet, a failed novelist of scholarly disposition, who gave him leads to follow and suggested ways of inserting his fictitious yarnings into the weave of historical fact. Maquet's role as documentor and collaborator is a little clearer now than it was in 1845 when a journalist named Jacquot accused Dumas of running a 'fiction factory': how else to explain an output so prodigious that surely no one man could ever dictate, let alone write, all the books that Dumas signed? Dumas promptly sued for libel and won his case. He cheerfully acknowledged his debts to others—it was at Maquet's suggestion that he recast *The Count of Monte Cristo*, for example—but claimed, rightly, that his own genius, drive, and unerring sense of drama gave everything he wrote (and he did write it all, or nearly all) the 'Dumas touch'. He discussed story-lines with others and employed secretaries (who added punctuation and corrected his spelling) to copy the pages he filled so rapidly at sittings which sometimes lasted fourteen hours. But only he had the imaginative involvement, the compulsion, and the intuition to create characters and situations which, even in our own cynical times, have yet to lose their appeal and which, in his own day, made him not only France's best-selling author but the most famous living Frenchman in the world.

Dumas's novels were written for serialization in the new cheap papers and magazines which brought large rewards to novelists who had the knack. Balzac, who took too long to warm up his stories, failed miserably to deliver what was needed—action, strong characters, and suspense. Dumas was one of a select band of highly paid authors who supplied all three in vast quantities and on time. The pressures of deadlines and the need to cater for popular taste go some way to explaining why Dumas wrote in three colours, black, white, and gaudy, and why he rarely delayed matters by pontificating on historical themes or adding documentary detail—descriptions of dress, buildings, or court ritual—which would simply have bored the reader. Nor did he ever show more than a fleeting interest in using the past as a stick to beat the present. The business of keeping the reader enthralled and impatient to buy the next issue was more important than psychological subtleties and overall structures, and Dumas aimed instead for pace and high impact. His reader, who finds something interesting on every page, always knows who to cheer and who to boo. Literary critics carp at Dumas's sprawling, unmade-beds of novels; historians complain of oversimplification and anachronisms (in *The Three Musketeers* Dumas cheerfully thinks of transporting Milady to Botany Bay a century and a half before Captain Cook set foot there); and both may prefer historical novelists with a better grasp of fact and a stronger grip on form. But few story-tellers have spun better yarns and no one has ever made history as exciting.

If Walter Scott, much admired by Dumas as the creator of the historical novel, was wary of involving famous figures in episodes of his invention, Dumas fearlessly cast kings and queens in major roles. The ploy sometimes misfires, for Dumas tended to divide humanity into Cavaliers, who are dashing fellows of generous spirit (Fouquet, for instance), and Roundheads who, like Colbert, are miserly, base plotters, grim of purpose and bent on treasons, stratagems, and spoils. And when there are not sufficient infamous to balance the famous, Dumas simply invents villains like de Wardes. If a touch of humour is need, he does not hesitate to turn La Fontaine and Molière into ripe caricatures. Nor was he as true to the spirit of the age as he liked to believe. His Louise is a more melting creature than the Louise de la Vallière of reality and, like Raoul—and there was a Raoul de Bragelongne who was her childhood sweetheart—she reflects more of the sentimental values of Dumas's own Romantic age than those of the seventeenth century. Meanwhile, under Dumas's guidance, with embellishments sanctioned by imaginative licence, they scamper through the corridors of history, knocking on doors, upsetting applecarts, and rousing the neighbourhood.

When *The Man in the Iron Mask* begins, the King's scheme to unseat Fouquet is well under way, Aramis has succeeded in speaking to the masked prisoner and is committed to a mysterious course of action which his recent appointment as Vicar-General of the Jesuit Order gives him the means to implement, and d'Artagnan, now commander of the Musketeers, scents multiple plots but as yet is uncertain how to act . . .

But a summary of the plot so far is as necessary as a handle on a cabbage. Ever attentive to the needs of freshly recruited readers, Dumas regularly inserts brief reminders of who has been doing what (and to whom, and when and where). But such matters are in any case made redundant by the incessant urgency of the narrative. The suspense starts on the first page with the secret meeting between Aramis and Mme de Chevreuse, and thereafter the pace never slackens. Although it takes the first thirty chapters to follow the huge cast of characters through a single day, Dumas's expanded time does not seem artificial. Events come thick and fast and interlinked situations develop on a number of fronts. At the simplest level, we are drawn into the most royal of soap operas. At the highest, we are offered an infinitely varied gallery of simple but forcefully drawn characters who are moved through time and space with such control that only finicky readers will notice minor inconsistencies. Dumas moves us along on a high tide of excitement, makes us party to devilish plotting and brilliant counter-attacks, and carries us through a variety of moods: humour with Porthos, sadness with Raoul, tenderness with Louise, and despair with Athos. Our emotions are fully engaged because we are never in doubt that Dumas himself participated vicariously in the story he tells; it comes as no surprise to learn that his son found him sobbing at his desk on the day he killed off Porthos. For above all, it is the Musketeer spirit, though wrinkled now by the passing years, which draws us on. As long as the four indomitables are around, anything is possible.

They drew their life from Dumas, a loud, unpredictable, larger-than-life and endlessly fascinating man who invested his heroes with aspects of his own personality and values. D'Artagnan's cheerful resourcefulness is an echo of Dumas's own boundless energy, optimism, and sense of adventure. Porthos is as good a trencherman as his gormandizing creator and displays the Herculean powers attributed to Dumas's own father who was known for his feats of strength. Aramis, the least likeable of the quartet, reflects his intellectual cynicism and Athos his Romantic sensibilities. They represent what is best in male friendship which, however, across the span of years, is gravely tested. They follow their destinies and they change, but they grow old in ways which are perfectly consistent with their characters. D'Artagnan matures with the responsibilities of leadership, but still retains his dash and flair. Aramis's secretive soul grows darker and his motives larger and more complex. Porthos never quite grows up, but he remains forever the good-hearted Titan. Athos, the noblest of them all, always vulnerable to his feelings, meets his match only in the spectacle of Raoul's unhappiness, a human problem which is beyond the reach of his flashing blade. Dumas both understood and loved them. As they near 60, they might buckle a more intermittent swash, but their spirit is untarnished.

D'Artagnan remains faithful to an ideal of honour which is stronger than his loyalty to kings and ministers who abuse their power—hence his opposition to Colbert and his stormy interviews with Louis XIV who may be a king but acts without nobility of heart. Athos also groans under the royal yoke and looks forward two centuries to a time when kings will be shorn of their absolutist privileges and will exude a spirit of democratic monarchy which coincides rather obviously with Dumas's own rather confused political allegiances. Aramis may appear to be bent only on personal ambition and , in embroiling the good-hearted Porthos in his schemes, to act as ruthlessly as the hated Richelieu once had done, but his motive is simple and honourable: he too is offended by injustice. The masked prisoner has been doomed to a ghastly fate by the political expediency of a regime which has lost its moral credibility. The Mask's claim to the throne is legitimized not by the law of primogeniture but by the cruelty with which he has been treated. The Mighty Porthos may express few opinions but by his actions he encapsulates the loyalty, honour, and courage on which the Musketeer code is built. The new generation of men (to which the oversensitive Raoul belongs) is weak and ineffectual by comparison.

Even so, *The Man in the Iron Mask* has a distinctly autumnal quality. Dumas's Invincibles suddenly become mortal: they outlive the day when companionship and courage were enough to solve simple problems. They have lost none of their capacity for action and now have the advantage of money and experience. But they have been undermined from within by age and regret and, from without, are assailed by irresistible forces. The political stakes are higher—to save Fouquet and give

France a worthy king—but the result has been decided in advance by events; we know that Fouquet cannot be saved and that Louis XIV will rule. Their enemy is not human; it is history itself. D'Artagnan never finally revolts against Louis XIV who, after the arrest of Fouquet, begins at last to behave like a true king. Aramis casts himself as the Agent of Providence and, like the Count of Monte Cristo, learns the taste of defeat. Athos is strong against everything except the death of those he loves, but he too must finally bow to God's will. Porthos's glorious end is prefigured by bouts of mortal weakness and he dies because his physical powers fail him. The Musketeers are defeated by no man, but by change and decay. Yet if they fade away, they leave behind them trails of glory.

Dumas's heroes can be explained in many ways—as an extension of their creator's personality, as a reflection of his growing awareness that life gets the better of our dreams, or even as a lament for the vigour and values of the ageing generation of writers who had given France a new direction in the Revolution of 1830. What is certain, however, is that he did not entirely invent them. Charles de Batz-Castelmore d'Artagnan (?1615–73) was a Gascon who arrived in Paris in 1640, enlisted in the King's service, became a lieutenant of the Royal Guard in 1651, and six years later moved into the Musketeers which he was commanding in 1667. It was he who was given the delicate task of arresting Fouquet in 1661 and Lauzun in 1671. Appointed acting Governor of Lille in 1672, he was killed in action the following year, leaving two sons by a marriage which had ended by mutual consent in 1665. Much less is known about Armand de Sillègue d'Athos, a Béarnais, who was born near Sauveterre in the Oloron valley. A nephew of the Tréville who commanded the Musketeers briefly in the 1640s, he seems to have died in a duel in 1645. Henri d'Aramitz also hailed from the Oloron valley. He too was a nephew of Tréville and served in the Musketeers between 1640 and 1655. Isaac de Porteau was born at Pau in about 1617. After enlisting in the King's Guard in the early 1640s, he became a Musketeer in 1643. There is nothing to suggest that they were in any way remarkable or even that they knew each other. It is more than likely that only d'Artagnan was alive in 1660 when Dumas recalled them for their final adventure.

Dumas found them not in the history books but in their already dashing adventures as written by Gatien Courtilz de Sandras (1644–1712). A soldier of fortune and author of libellous pamphlets which earned him several stays in the Bastille, Courtilz published a number of fabricated pseudo-memoirs, including the *Mémoires de M. d'Artagnan* (1700) from which Dumas borrowed wholesale for *The Three Musketeers*. Having made Courtilz's heroes his own, Dumas proceeded to put them through their paces, slotting them into history and turning them into archetypes who, as Swinburne wrote, will never lose their appeal 'while the boy's heart beats in man'. Their adventures lit up the skies and occupied the printing presses of the world. The first translation of *The Man in the Iron Mask* was published in Philadelphia within a year of its serialization in *Le Siècle*, and Routledge of London issued the first complete English text of *The Vicomte de Bragelonne*, running to 700,000 words, in 1857. This anonymous version, subsequently lightly amended by the American Henry Llewellyn Williams (and frequently announced as 'a new translation'), was republished many times either in full or in three separate parts. At the height of the Dumasmania which afflicted the English-speaking world between 1890 and the First World War, *The Man in the Iron Mask* was reprinted some thirty times in England and about as frequently in the United States. The drama was transferred to the stage (Norman Forbes Robinson produced a spectacular *Prisoner of the Bastille* at the Adelphi in 1899) where it kept interest high. The vogue picked up again after the War on both sides of the Atlantic before being overtaken by the cinema which gave Dumas's story of the Masked Prisoner a new lease of life. Douglas Fairbanks played the ageing d'Artagnan with athletic gusto in the splendid 1929 silent film and among his more notable successors have been Warren Williams (1939), Louis Jourdan (in a version for television made in 1976), and, in *The Fifth Musketeer* (1977), Cornel Wilde. Cinema fashions may change, but d'Artagnan, played seriously or, more often, with tongue in cheek, still makes good box office.

But who is d'Artagnan? Surely not the obscure Musketeer of history nor the adventurer invented by Courtilz. Before Dumas, there was no d'Artagnan legend and after Dumas had done with him d'Artagnan passed into our cultural mythology. If Tarzan expresses the city-dweller's longing for natural freedom and Dracula is the shape of our fear of the dark, d'Artagnan symbolizes thrills, youth, and adventure. The cornerstone of a vast epic of honour and courage, he is a figure of high romance, a Hero, a myth.

He is not, however, the only mythical force at work in *The Man in the Iron Mask*. The gratifyingly elusive tale of the mysterious masked captive is not so much a product of history as of historians who have argued about his identity for nearly three hundred years. The brief entries in the unofficial register kept by the Deputy Governor of Bastille, Étienne du Junca, tell as much of the tale as is certain.

On 18 September 1698, M. de Saint-Mars, formerly Governor of the prisons of Pignerol in Piedmont, Exiles in the Alps, and the island of Sainte-Marguerite off the coast of Cannes, arrived in Paris to take command of the Bastille. He brought with him, 'in his litter', a long-term prisoner 'whom he kept masked at all times and whose name is not spoken'. On 19 November 1703, the unknown prisoner, after a short illnesss, 'still masked with a mask of black velvet ... died this day at half past ten of the evening ...; he that had been so long a captive, was buried on Tuesday, at four of the afternoon, 20th November, in the cemetery of Saint Paul in this parish. In the register of deaths was entered a name, also unknown.' A marginal note in du Junca's hand adds: 'I have since learnt that he was named in the Register as M. de Marchiel and that 40 livres were paid for his funeral.' The entry in the burial register for 19 November records the death of 'Marchioly, aged forty-five years, or thereabouts, [who] departed this life in the Bastille'.

These bald entries establish the secret existence of an unknown, masked prisoner. The correspondence between Saint-Mars and the King's ministers is so discreet that no positive identification is possible, though it reveals that the man was guarded in conditions of exceptionally tight security. None of his gaolers or fellow prisoners (who for a time included Courtilz de Sandras) ever spoke of him—a sure proof, say the mystery-mongers, that there was something to hide. The secret was well guarded; nothing leaked out for over thirty years, by which time almost everyone who might have been able to throw light on the mystery was dead. By 1745, however, the hunt had begun. An anonymous author identified the Mask as the Duke de Vendômois, the illegitimate son of Louis XIV and Louise de la Vallière. Voltaire scented a scandal and, alluding knowingly to unimpeachable sources of information, claimed that the prisoner was no less than Louis XIV's older brother. This startling suggestion made by the most combative intellectual of the age, turned a minor historical oddity into a sensational quest. Others argued that the unknown prisoner was the Duke of Monmouth, son of Charles II by Lucy Walters, or an Italian named Ercolo Antonio Matthioli, secretary to the Duke of Mantua, who had once duped the King of France, unless, that is, he were Muhammad IV, or the Duke de Beaufort whose naval service was cunningly buried in the code-name 'Marchiali' which, deciphered, reads 'hic amiral' ('here lies the Admiral'). Gibbon doubted that any well-known public figure could have been removed from circulation without being missed, and inclined to believe that the mask hid the face of the son of Mazarin and Anne of Austria, while Benjamin Franklin thought the man was the bastard of Anne and the Duke of Buckingham.

Witnesses spoke, or rather whispered, not of what they had seen but of what they had heard, and what they had heard always came on the very best authority. The dramatist Crébillon told Casanova that Louis XIV had told him, personally, that the story of the masked prisoner was nothing but a tale. According to J. Anquetil (*Memoirs of the Court of France during the reign of Louis XIV*, Edinburgh, 1791, i. 163), Lenglet du Fresnoy, a cleric who had himself been several times sent to the Bastille for uttering subversive writings, 'had often seen this man. About the year 1754, he related to me nearly all that is commonly told of his moderate stature, the sprightliness and elegance of his wit and the respect with which he was treated by the Governor. From this conversation, he inferred that he had travelled through almost all Europe. He talked very well of public affairs, politics, history and religion. When I pressed the Abbé to tell me whom he took him to be, he replied; "Would you have me sent a ninth time to the Bastille?"' A Mme Cassis of Cannes was said to have visited the Mask in his cell where she shook his hand: it was a woman's hand. There were reports that peasants had sighted the prisoner when Saint-Mars transferred him in 1687 from Exiles to Sainte-Marguerite and thence to the Bastille in 1698: he was tall and short, young and old, robust and frail, and had hair that was black or quite possibly white. Some swore that they had seen a silver plate bearing a message etched with a knife which had been thrown from the poor prisoner's window, or claimed to have examined the very tweezers which he used to pluck his beard beneath the mask which was fitted with a hinged chin-piece to allow the wearer to eat of the finest food, which he did off gold plates. The mask, made of cloth, seems to have turned into a mask of *vair*—the same fur of which Cinderella's slipper was made before it was turned into *verre* (glass) by printer's error—and thence became horrifying *fer* (iron). The mask itself was discovered as often as the grave was opened; inside the coffin, when there was a coffin, was found a decapitated body, or simply a stone. It was said that the tomb had been connected by a dark tunnel to the Bastille itself...

When the Bastille fell in 1789, a Dutch journal reported the discovery of a note bearing the number 64389000, the name 'Kersadion', and the words: 'Fouquet arriving from the Island of Sainte-Marguerite in an Iron Mask'. The suggestion that the Mask was Fouquet, who died in 1680, was startling enough, but there was far better to come. In 1790, Soulavie, in his apocryphal memoirs of the Duke de Richelieu, published the death-bed confession of an unnamed courtier who had, in a sequestered house in Burgundy, brought up a male child, born eight hours after Louis XIV, who was not merely his brother but his twin. Playwrights capitalized on this highly theatrical fancy as did, in a minor way, constitutional revolutionaries; the inhumanity of Louis XIV towards his brother clearly made him and his Bourbon successors unfit to sit on the throne which must needs revert, legitimately, to Philippe Égalité, the Mask's true descendant. But the victim's lineage was to be hotly disputed. Staunch royalists in the Vendée warned the faithful against the idea, bruited by his emissaries, that Napoleon had usurped the throne with a view to returning it to the Bourbons; on the contrary, one pamphlet said in 1801, Bonaparte 'is simply waiting for peace to be restored, at which time he will show his hand and base his claim to the throne upon his descendance from the children of the Iron Mask'. Las Cases later recalled in the *Mémorial de Sainte-Hélène* (at 12 July 1816) that Napoleon knew that he had been connected with the Mask, dismissed the story as fanciful but had never denied it, finding the idea politically useful. (The connection had been made through an absurd variant which seems to have been widely current. The governor of Sainte-Marguerite, a M. de Bonpart so the story went, had a daughter who fell in love with the Mask and eventually married him. Their children drifted and finally settled in Corsica where they Italianized their name to Buonaparte.) Having been appropriated by the Revolution and the Empire, the legend turned royalist after the restoration of the monarchy. In the 1830s Charles Naundorff, a clockmaker who claimed to be the lost prince, Louis XVII, and therefore true heir to the throne, offered to prove his title by revealing the identity of the Mask which he could only have known through his father Louis XVI, who told him the secret as he had been told by his father Louis XV. As late as 1911, a priest in the diocese of Marseilles, tracing his descent from yet another son of the Mask, went about calling himself Henri de Valois and, as such, laid claim to the French throne at a time when France had long since been a Republic.

Meanwhile, Literature refused to be denied its share of the spoils. By the 1820s the Romantic imagination, which had a particular weakness for prisons and prisoners, was warming to the subject. Vigny lamented his fate in one of his grim poems in 1821, and variants of the 'King's twin' theory were turned into melodramas in Paris and London in the 1830s. In 1847–8 Hugo wrote two acts of *The Twins* but gave up when he heard that Dumas had beaten him to it.

But historians, some more serious than others, also began rummaging through dusty archives and came up with new solutions, some well documented, and others so peculiar as to make the protestations of the Sons of the Mask appear unremarkable. A retired soldier named Taulès found in 'Kersadion' a not altogether convincing anagram of Awedick, the name of an obscure Armenian patriarch who had incurred the wrath of the Jesuits. On surer ground, Delort (1825) plumped for Matthiolo, the double-dealing secretary of the Duke of Mantua, and Paul Lacroix (1836) for Fouquet. By the time Dumas wrote up the affair in volume viii of his *Crimes célèbres* (1840), he was able to list fourteen solutions of which he selected the 'twin' theory for its dramatic impact. His view did not convince the scholars who continued to trawl for facts. In 1869 Marius Topin rejected fifty-two names before championing Matthioli. Colonel Iung (1873) preferred an obscure soldier named Bulonde. Jules Lair (1890) made an impressive case for Eustache Dauger who, he speculated, was a minor courtier arrested in 1669 for his part in a conspiracy to overthrow Louis XIV, and who later served as Fouquet's valet at Pignerol. Oddest of all was the eccentric theory put forward by Auguste Loquin in 1890. The Mask was Molière who did not die on stage in 1673 as most people believe but was jailed at the behest of the Jesuits whom he had offended. He subsequently escaped—the body buried in 1703 was that of an unknown man—and made his way to Genoa as a variant of the M. de Bonpart whom we have already met. He settled at a later date in Corsica, gave his name an Italian ring, and, at the rather advanced age of 150 or so, became the father or perhaps the grandfather of Napoleon.

In 1903 an English Catholic, Monsignor Barnes, brought forward further incontrovertible proof to support his candidate, the abbé Prignani. By the time Maurice Duvivier rehearsed all the arguments once more in 1932, he estimated that over one thousand identifications had been made, mostly by lunatics. Duvivier demolished the case for Matthioli and positively identified Dauger as Eustache Dauger de Cavoye, gaoled for his part in the 'Affaire des Poisons', though it has subsequently emerged that Dauger de Cavoye died in Paris, in the prison of Saint-Lazare, in about 1683. Georges Mongrédien reviewed the evidence again in 1952 and judged both the Matthioli and the Dauger solutions to be historically viable, while Pierre-Jacques Arrèse renewed the case for Fouquet in 1970. Marcel Pagnol (1973) shrewdly remarked that seekers of the true Mask generally favour candidates who resemble themselves in some way; historians opt for obscure historical figures, politicians select politically convenient candidates, Monsignor Barnes chose a cleric and Colonel Iung a general. Pagnol, who was a maker of myths like Dumas, accordingly opted for the 'twin' theory, adding a complicated coda suggesting that Dauger's real name was James de la Cloche, and that James de la Cloche was Louis XIV's twin brother who was brought up secretly in Jersey. In 1987 a similar thesis was advanced by Harry Thompson who concluded that Dauger de Cavoye was Louis XIV's illegitimate half-brother. After 300 years of ingenuity and diligence, historians agree only that there was a Mask and that he was 'Eustache Dauger'—though who Dauger was, and whether Dauger was his real name, remain unanswered questions.

Any suggestion that there was no mystery to uncover has always been regarded at best as unsporting, and at worst as obtuse. It is, of course, quite possible that the man was simply one of many prisoners who mouldered forgotten in Louis XIV's jails. But whether or not there was an important masked prisoner, the persistence of the quest is to be explained as much by the trappings of the tale as by the search for Truth. The legend became a myth by association with the Bastille which, even in the eighteenth century, symbolized injustice and tyranny. Moreover, the sadistic idea of enclosing a prisoner within a claustrophobic iron mask starts a *frisson* of horror. It is probably this rather than the innumerable efforts to establish his true identity that explains the very memorable, grisly glamour which has made the Mask a star of stage and screen and the hero of many speculative novels, the most recent of which is Peter Hoyle's *The Man in the Iron Mask* (1986) which deals with an old man's obsession with the mysterious prisoner.

The legend has held historians, enquirers both informed and uninformed, novelists, playwrights, and generations of open-mouthed readers in its thrall. Tom Sawyer, that connoisseur of stylish 'evasions', was of a mind to make Jim write a message 'on the bottom of a tin plate with a fork and throw it out of the window to let the world know where he was captivated', just as the Iron Mask had done in Dumas's romance (*Huckleberry Finn*, chap. 35). Mark Twain had visited the Château d'If and seen for himself not only the 'authentic' dungeon where Edmond Dantès languished in *The Count of Monte Cristo*, but also the cell where Dumas's Iron Mask had lain, though he was never there except in the imagination of the guide. Twain would not have given a fig to know beyond question who the man was and why he had been so cruelly punished. 'Mystery! That was the charm. That speechless tongue, those prisoned features, that heart so freighted with unspoken troubles, and that breast so oppressed with its piteous secret had been there. These dank walls had known the man whose dolorous story is a sealed book forever! There was fascination in the spot' (*Innocents Abroad*, 1869, chap. 11). If the imaginative involvement of Tom and his creator was complete, it was surely because no story-teller has ever exploited the tale with more panache than Dumas. But then, few have had the advantage of being able to graft a fourteen-carat legend on to a solid-gold myth. Why, to get the Musketeers *and* the Mask in one book is like having two puddings.

SELECT BIBLIOGRAPHY

The Vicomte de Bragelonne was serialized in *Le Siècle* between 20 October 1847 and, with a few breaks, 12 January 1850, and was published in France in book form by Michel Lévy (26 vols., Paris, 1848–50). The final section containing *The Man in the Iron Mask* was first translated by Thomas Williams in 1851 for T. B. Peterson of Philadelphia. The version reproduced in this edition is taken from the classic anonymous translation, many times reprinted, of the complete text issued by Routledge in 1857. Readers wishing to follow the complex printing history of Dumas's writings in French may usefully consult Frank W. Reed's *A Bibliography of Dumas père* (London, 1933), and Douglas Munro's *Dumas: A Bibliography of Works Published in French, 1825–1900* (New York and London, 1981). *Alexandre Dumas père: A Bibliography of Works Translated into English to 1910* (New York and London, 1978), also by Douglas Munro, is the best guide to British and American editions.

Dumas's autobiography (*Mes Mémoires* (1852–5), ed. Pierre Josserand (5 vols., Paris, 1954–68); English translation (London, 1907–9)) is entertaining but highly romanced and does not proceed beyond 1832. The best French biographies are those of Henri Clouard, *Alexandre Dumas* (Paris, 1955); André Maurois, *Les Trois Dumas* (Paris, 1957; English translation, London, 1958); and Claude Schopp, *Dumas, le génie de la vie* (Paris, 1985). Gilles Henry, *Le Secret de Monte Cristo, ou Les Aventures des ancêtres de Dumas* (Paris, 1982) throws new light on the Davy–Dumas family, and Isabelle Jan, *Dumas romancier* (Paris, 1973) offers the fullest study of the novels.

Among the many books in English devoted to Dumas, good introductions are provided by A. Craig Bell, *Alexandre Dumas* (London, 1950) and Richard Stowe, *Dumas* (Boston, 1976). Michael Ross's *Alexandre Dumas* (Newton Abbot, 1981) gives a sympathetic account of Dumas's life. The most balanced and comprehensive guide, however, is F. W. J. Hemmings's excellent *The King of Romance* (London, 1979).

Enquiries into the identity of the Mask are numerous. The most reliable are those by Maurice Duvivier (*Le Masque de fer*, Paris, 1932) and Georges Mongrédien (*Le Masque de fer*, Paris, 1952), while Marcel Pagnol's *Le Secret du Masque de fer* (Éditions de Provence, 1973; first edn., 1965) is entertaining and often acute. The most recent study in English is Harry Thompson's *The Man in the Iron Mask: A Historical Detective Investigation* (London, 1987).

A CHRONOLOGY OF
ALEXANDRE DUMAS

1762   25 March: Birth at Saint-Domingo of Thomas-Alexandre, son of the French-born Marquis Davy de la Pailleterie and a mulatto, Marie-Cessette Dumas. He returns to France with his father in 1780 and, after enlisting in 1786, rises rapidly through the ranks.

1792   28 November: Marriage of Colonel Dumas and Marie-Louise-Elizabeth Labouret, daughter of an inn-keeper, at Villers-Cotterêts.

1801   1 May: General Dumas returns to France from prison in Italy.

1802   24 July: Birth at Villers-Cotterêts of Alexandre Dumas who, after his father's death in 1806, is brought up in straitened circumstances by his mother. He attends local schools and has a happy childhood.

1819   Dumas, now a lawyer's office-boy, falls in love with Adèle Dalvin who rejects him. Meets Adolphe de Leuven, with whom he collaborates in writing unsuccessful plays.

1822   Visits Leuven in Paris, meets Talma, the leading actor of the day, and resolves to become a playwright.

1823   Moves to Paris. Enters the service of the Duke d'Orléans. Falls in love with a seamstress, Catherine Labay.

1824   27 July: Birth of Alexandre Dumas *fils*.

1825   22 September: Dumas's first play, *La Chasse et l'amour* (*The Chase and Love*), written in collaboration with Leuven and Rousseau, makes no impact.

1826   Publication of a collection of short stories, Dumas's first solo composition, which sells four copies.

1827   A company of English actors, which includes Kean, Kemble, and Mrs Smithson, performs Shakespeare in English to enthusiastic Paris audiences: Dumas is deeply impressed. Liaison with Mélanie Waldor.

1828–9 Dumas enters Parisian literary circles through Charles Nodier.

1829   11 February: First of about fifty performances of *Henri III et sa cour* (*Henry III and His Court*) which makes Dumas famous and thrusts him into the front line of the Romantic revolution in literature. Dumas meets Victor Hugo.

1830   30 March: First performance of *Christine* (written in 1828). May: Start of an affair with the actress Belle Krelsamer. Active in the July Revolution: Dumas single-handedly captures a gunpowder magazine at Soissons and is sent by Lafayette to promote the National Guard in the Vendée (August).

1831   5 March: birth of Marie, his daughter by Belle Krelsamer. 17 March: Dumas acknowledges Alexandre, his son by Catherine Labay. First performances of *Napoléon Bonaparte* (10 January), *Antony* (3 May), *Charles VII et ses grands vassaux* (*Charles VII and the Barons*) (20 October), and *Richard Darlington* (10 December).

1832   6 February: Start of his affair with the actress Ida Ferrier. 15 April: Dumas succumbs to the cholera which kills 20,000 Parisians. 29 May: First performance of *La Tour de Nesle* (*The Tower of Nesle*): Gaillardet accuses Dumas of plagiarism. July: Suspected of republicanism, Dumas leaves Paris for Switzerland. After the spectacular failure of his next play, *Le Fils de l'émigré* (*The Son of the Emigré*) (28 August), he begins to take an interest in the literary possibilities of French history.

1833   Serialization of a book of impressions of Switzerland, the first of his travelogues.

1834–5   October: Dumas travels in the Midi. From the Riviera, he embarks on the first of many journeys to Italy.

1836   31 August: Dumas returns triumphantly to the theatre with *Kean*.

1837   Becomes a *chevalier* of the Legion of Honour.

1838   Death of Dumas's mother. Travels along the Rhine with Gérard de Nerval who introduces him to Auguste Maquet in December.

1840   1 February: Dumas marries Ida Ferrier, travels to Italy and publishes *Le Capitaine Pamphile*, the best of his children's books.

1840–2   Dividing his time between Paris and Italy, Dumas increasingly abandons the theatre for the novel.

1842   June: Publication of *The Chevalier d'Harmental*, the first of
many romances written in association with Maquet.

1844   March–July: Serialization of *The Three Musketeers* in *Le Siècle*.
August: First episode of *The Count of Monte Cristo* published in
Le Journal des Débats. 15 October: Amicable separation from
Ida Ferrier. Publication of *Louis XIV and his Century*.

1845   21 January: Start of serialization of the second D'Artagnan
story, *Twenty Years After*, in *Le Siècle*. February: Wins his libel
suit against the journalist Jacquot, author of *Fabrique de
romans: Maison Alexandre Dumas et Cie* (*A Fiction Factory: The
Firm of Alexandre Dumas and Company*), in which Jacquot
accused Dumas of publishing other men's work under his own
name.

1846   Separates from Ida Ferrier. Brief liaison with Lola Montès.
November–January: Travels with his son to Spain and North
Africa.

1847   30 January: Loses a lawsuit brought by newspaper proprietors
for failure to deliver copy for which he had accepted large
advances. 11 February: Questions are asked in the National
Assembly about Dumas's appropriation of the Navy vessel, *Le
Véloce*, during his visit to North Africa. 20 February: Opening
of the 'Théâtre historique'. 7 March: Completion of the
'Château de Monte Cristo' at Marly-le-Roi. 20 October–12
January 1850: Serialization of *The Vicomte de Bragelonne* in *Le
Siècle*.

1843   Dumas puts up, unsuccessfully, as a parliamentary candidate
and votes for Louis-Napoleon in the December elections.

1850   Beginning of a nine-year liaison with Isabella Constant. 20
March: The 'Théâtre historique' is declared bankrupt. The
Château de Monte Cristo is sold off for 30,000 francs.

1851   Michel Lévy begins to bring out the first volumes of Dumas's
complete works which will eventually be complete in 301
volumes. 7 December: Using Louis-Napoleon's *coup d'état* as
an excuse, Dumas flees to Belgium to avoid his creditors.

1852   Publication of the first volumes of *Mes Mémoires*. Dumas
declared bankrupt with debts of 100,000 francs.

1853   November: Dumas returns to Paris and founds a periodical,
Le Mousquetaire (last issue 7 February 1857) for which he
writes most of the copy himself.

1857   23 April: Founds a literary weekly, *Le Monte Cristo* which, with one break, survives until 1862.

1858   15 June: Dumas leaves for a tour of Russia and returns in March 1859.

1859   11 March: Death of Ida Ferrier. Beginning of a liaison with Emilie Cordier which lasts until 1864.

1860   Meets Garibaldi in Turin and just misses the taking of Sicily (June). He returns to Marseilles where he buys guns for the Italian cause and is in Naples just after the city falls in September. Garibaldi stands, by proxy, as godfather to Dumas's daughter by Emilie Cordier. 11 October: Founds *L'Indipendente*, a literary and political periodical published half in French and half in Italian.

1861   22 March: First performance of Dumas's five-act drama, based on *The Man in the Iron Mask*, *Le Prisonnier de la Bastille*, at the Théâtre du Cirque.

1863   The works of Dumas are placed on the Index by the Catholic Church.

1864   April: Dumas returns to Paris.

1865   Further travels through Italy, Germany, and Austria.

1867   Publishes *Le Terreur prussienne* (*The Prussian Terror*), a novel designed to warn France against the coming Prussian threat. Begins a last liaison, with Adah Menken, an American actress (d. 1868).

1869   10 March: Dumas's last play, *Les Blancs et les Bleus* (*The Whites and the Blues*).

1870   5 December: Dumas dies at Puys, near Dieppe, after a stroke in September.

1872   Dumas's remains transferred to Villers-Cotterêts.

1883   Unveiling of a statue to Dumas in Paris.

THE MAN IN
THE IRON MASK

TWO OLD FRIENDS

WHILST every one at court was busily engaged upon his own affairs, a man mysteriously entered a house situated behind the Place de Grève. The principal entrance of this house was in the Place Baudoyer; it was tolerably large, surrounded by gardens, enclosed in the Rue Saint-Jean*by the shops of tool-makers, which protected it from prying looks, and was walled in by a triple rampart of stone, noise, and verdure, like an embalmed mummy in its triple coffin. The man we have just alluded to walked along with a firm step, although he was no longer in his early prime. His dark cloak and long sword plainly revealed one who seemed in search of adventures; and, judging from his curling moustaches, his fine and smooth skin, which could be seen beneath his sombrero, it would not have been difficult to pronounce that the gallantry of his adventures was unquestionable. In fact, hardly had the cavalier entered the house, when the clock struck eight; and ten minutes afterwards a lady, followed by a servant armed to the teeth, approached and knocked at the same door, which an old woman immediately opened for her. The lady raised her veil as she entered; though no longer beautiful or young, she was still active and of an imposing carriage. She concealed beneath a rich toilette and the most exquisite taste, an age which Ninon de l'Enclos*alone could have smiled at with impunity. Hardly had she reached the vestibule, than the cavalier, whose features we have only roughly sketched, advanced towards her, holding out his hand.

"Good-day, my dear Duchesse,"*he said.

"How do you do, my dear Aramis," replied the Duchesse.

He led her to a most elegantly furnished apartment, on whose high windows were reflected the expiring rays of the setting sun, which filtered through the dark crests of some adjoining firs. They sat down side by side. Neither of them thought of asking for additional light in the room, and they buried themselves as it were in the shadow, as if they wished to bury themselves in forgetfulness.

"Chevalier," said the Duchesse, "you have never given me a single sign of life since our interview at Fontainebleau, and I confess that your presence there on the day of the Franciscan's death,*and your initiation in certain secrets, caused me the liveliest astonishment I ever experienced in my whole life."

"I can explain my presence there to you, as well as my initiation," said Aramis.

"But let us, first of all," said the Duchesse, "talk a little of ourselves, for our friendship is by no means of recent date."

"Yes, madame; and if Heaven wills it, we shall continue to be friends, I will not say for a long time, but for ever."

"That is quite certain, Chevalier, and my visit is a proof of it."

"Our interests, Duchesse, are no longer the same as they used to be," said Aramis smiling, without apprehension in the gloom in which the room was cast, for it could not reveal that his smile was less agreeable and less bright than formerly.

"No, Chevalier, at the present day we have other interests. Every period of life brings its own; and, as we now understand each other in conversing, as perfectly as we formerly did without saying a word, let us talk, if you like."

"I am at your orders, Duchesse. Ah! I beg your pardon, how did you obtain my address, and what was your object?"

"You ask me why? I have told you. Curiosity in the first place. I wished to know what you could have to do with the Franciscan, with whom I had certain business transactions, and who died so singularly. You know that on the occasion of our interview at Fontainebleau, in the cemetery, at the foot of the grave so recently closed, we were both so much overcome by our emotions that we omitted to confide to each other what we may have had to say."

"Yes, madame."

"Well then, I had no sooner left you than I repented, and have ever since been most anxious to ascertain the truth. You know that Madame de Longueville* and myself are almost one, I suppose?"

"I am not aware," said Aramis discreetly.

"I remembered, therefore," continued the Duchesse, "that neither of us said anything to the other in the cemetery; that you did not speak of the relationship in which you stood to the Franciscan, whose burial you had superintended, and that I did not refer to the position in which I stood to him; all which seemed very unworthy of two such old friends as ourselves, and I have sought an opportunity of an interview with you in order to give you some information that I have recently acquired, and to assure you that Marie Michon,* now no more, has left behind her one who has preserved her recollection of events."

Aramis bowed over the Duchesse's hand, and pressed his lips

upon it. "You must have had some trouble to find me again," he said.

"Yes," she answered, annoyed to find the subject taking a turn which Aramis wished to give it; "but I knew you were a friend of M. Fouquet's, and so I inquired in that direction."

"A friend! oh!" exclaimed the Chevalier. "I can hardly pretend to be that. A poor priest who has been favoured by so generous a protector, and whose heart is full of gratitude and devotion to him, is all that I pretend to be to M. Fouquet."

"He made you a bishop?"

"Yes, Duchesse."

"A very good retiring pension for so handsome a musketeer."

"Yes; in the same way that political intrigue is for yourself," thought Aramis. "And so," he added, "you inquired after me at M. Fouquet's?"

"Easily enough. You had been to Fontainebleau with him, and had undertaken a voyage to your diocese, which is Belle-Île-en-Mer, I believe."

"No, madame," said Aramis. "My diocese is Vannes."

"I meant that. I only thought that Belle-Île-en-Mer——"

"Is a property belonging to M. Fouquet, nothing more."

"Ah! I had been told that Belle-Île was fortified; besides, I know how great the military knowledge is you possess."

"I have forgotten everything of the kind since I entered the Church," said Aramis, annoyed.

"Suffice it to know that I learnt you had returned from Vannes, and I sent to one of our friends, M. le Comte de la Fère, who is discretion itself, in order to ascertain it, but he answered that he was not aware of your address."

"So like Athos," thought the bishop; "that which is actually good never alters."

"Well, then, you know that I cannot venture to show myself here, and that the Queen-Mother has always some grievance or other against me."

"Yes, indeed, and I am surprised at it."

"Oh! there are various reasons for it. But, to continue, being obliged to conceal myself, I was fortunate enough to meet with M. d'Artagnan, who was formerly one of your old friends, I believe?"

"A friend of mine still, Duchesse."

"He gave me some information, and sent me to M. Baisemeaux, the governor of the Bastille."

Aramis was somewhat agitated at this remark, and a light flashed from his eyes in the darkness of the room, which he could not conceal from his keen-sighted friend. "M. de Baisemeaux!" he said; "why did d'Artagnan send you to M. de Baisemeaux?"

"I cannot tell you."

"What can this possibly mean?" said the Bishop, summoning all the resources of his mind to his aid, in order to carry on the combat in a befitting manner.

"M. de Baisemeaux is greatly indebted to you, d'Artagnan told me."

"True, he is so."

"And the address of a creditor is as easily ascertained as that of a debtor."

"Very true; and so Baisemeaux indicated to you——"

"Saint-Mandé, where I forwarded a letter to you."

"Which I have in my hand, and which is most precious to me," said Aramis, "because I am indebted to it for the pleasure of seeing you here." The Duchesse, satisfied at having successfully alluded to the various difficulties of so delicate an explanation, began to breathe freely again, which Aramis, however, could not succeed in doing. "We had got as far as your visit to M. Baisemeaux, I believe?"

"Nay," she said, laughing, "further than that."

"In that case we must have been speaking about the grudge you have against the Queen-Mother."

"Further still," she returned,—"further still; we were talking of the connection——"

"Which existed between you and the Franciscan," said Aramis, interrupting her eagerly; "well, I am listening to you very attentively."

"It is easily explained," returned the Duchesse. "You know that I am living at Brussels with M. de Laicques?"*

"I have heard so."

"You know that my children have ruined and stripped me of everything."

"How terrible, dear Duchesse."

"Terrible indeed; this obliged me to resort to some means of obtaining a livelihood, and, particularly, to avoid vegetating the remainder of my existence away, I had old hatreds to turn to account, old friendships to serve; I no longer had either credit or protectors."

"You, too, who had extended protection towards so many persons," said Aramis softly.

"It is always the case, Chevalier. Well, at the present time I am in the habit of seeing the King of Spain* very frequently."

"Ah!"

4

"Who has just nominated a general of the Jesuits," according to the usual custom."

"Is it usual, indeed?"

"Were you not aware of it?"

"I beg your pardon; I was inattentive."

"You must be aware of that—you who were on such good terms with the Franciscan."

"With the general of the Jesuits, you mean?"

"Exactly. Well, then, I have seen the King of Spain, who wished to do me a service, but was unable. He gave me recommendations, however, to Flanders, both for myself and for Laicques too; and conferred a pension on me out of the funds belonging to the order."

"Of Jesuits?"

"Yes. The general—I mean the Franciscan—was sent to me; and, for the purpose of conforming with the requisitions of the statutes of the order, and of entitling me to the pension, I was reputed to be in a position to render certain services. You are aware that that is the rule?"

"No, I did not know it," said Aramis.

Madame de Chevreuse paused to look at Aramis, but it was perfectly dark. "Well, such is the rule, however," she resumed. "I ought, therefore, to seem to possess a power of usefulness of some kind or other. I proposed to travel for the order, and I was placed on the list of affiliated travellers. You understand it was a formality, by means of which I received my pension, which was very convenient for me."

"Good heavens! Duchesse, what you tell me is like a dagger thrust into me. *You* obliged to receive a pension from the Jesuits?"

"No, Chevalier; from Spain."

"Except as a conscientious scruple, Duchesse, you will admit that it is pretty nearly the same thing."

"No, not at all."

"But surely, of your magnificent fortune there must remain——"

"Dampierre* is all that remains."

"And that is handsome enough."

"Yes; but Dampierre is burdened, mortgaged, and almost fallen to ruin, like its owner."

"And can the Queen-Mother know and see all that, without shedding a tear?" said Aramis with a penetrating look, which encountered nothing but the darkness.

"Yes, she has forgotten everything."*

"You have, I believe, attempted to get restored to favour?"

"Yes; but, most singularly, the young King inherits the

antipathy that his dear father had for me. You will, too, tell me that I am indeed a woman to be hated, and that I am no longer one who can be loved."

"Dear Duchesse, pray arrive soon at the circumstance which brought you here; for I think we can be of service to each other."

"Such has been my own thought. I came to Fontainebleau with a double object in view. In the first place, I was summoned there by the Franciscan whom you knew. By the bye, how did you know him?—for I have told you my story, and have not yet heard yours."

"I knew him in a very natural way, Duchesse. I studied theology with him at Parma. We became fast friends; and it happened, from time to time, that business, or travels, or war, separated us from each other."

"You were, of course, aware that he was the general of the Jesuits?"

"I suspected it."

"But by what extraordinary chance did it happen that you were at the hotel where the affiliated travellers had met together?"

"Oh!" said Aramis in a calm voice, "it was the merest chance in the world. I was going to Fontainebleau to see M. Fouquet, for the purpose of obtaining an audience of the King. I was passing by unknown; I saw the poor dying monk in the road, and recognised him immediately. You know the rest—he died in my arms."

"Yes; but bequeathing to you so vast a power that you issue your sovereign orders and directions like a monarch."

"He certainly did leave me a few commissions to settle."

"And for me?"

"I have told you—a sum of twelve thousand livres was to be paid to you. I thought I had given you the necessary signature to enable you to receive it. Did you not get the money?"

"Oh! yes, yes. You give your orders, I am informed, with so much mystery, and such a majestic presence, that it is generally believed you are the successor of the defunct chief."

Aramis coloured impatiently, and the Duchesse continued, "I have obtained my information," she said, "from the King of Spain himself; and he cleared up some of my doubts on the point. Every general of the Jesuits is nominated by him, and must be a Spaniard, according to the statutes of the order. You are not a Spaniard, nor have you been nominated by the King of Spain."

Aramis did not reply to this remark, except to say, "You see, Duchesse, how greatly you were mistaken, since the King of Spain told you that."

6

"Yes, my dear Aramis; but there was something else which I have been thinking of."

"What is that?"

"You know, I believe, something about most things; and it occurred to me that you know the Spanish language."

"Every Frenchman who has been actively engaged in the Fronde* knows Spanish."

"Yo have lived in Flanders?"

"Three years."

"And have stayed at Madrid?"

"Fifteen months."

"You are in a position, then, to become a naturalised Spaniard when you like."

"Really?" said Aramis, with a frankness which deceived the Duchesse.

"Undoubtedly. Two years' residence and an acquaintance with the language are indispensable. You have upwards of four years—more than double the time necessary."

"What are you driving at, Duchesse?"

"At this—I am on good terms with the King of Spain."

"And I am not on bad terms," thought Aramis to himself.

"Shall I ask the King," continued the Duchesse, "to confer the succession to the Franciscan's post upon you?"

"Oh, Duchesse!"

"You have it already, perhaps?" she said.

"No, upon my honour."

"Very well, then, I can render you that service."

"Why did you not render the same service to M. de Laicques, Duchesse? He is a very talented man, and one you love besides."

"Yes, no doubt; but, at all events, putting Laicques aside, will you have it?"

"No, I thank you, Duchesse."

She paused. "He is nominated," she thought; and then resumed aloud, "If you refuse me in this manner, it is not very encouraging for me, supposing I should have something to ask of you."

"Oh! ask, pray ask."

"Ask! I cannot do so, if you have not the power to grant what I want."

"However limited my power and ability, ask all the same."

"I need a sum of money to restore Dampierre."

"Ah!" replied Aramis coldly—"money? Well, Duchesse, how much would you require?"

"Oh! a tolerably round sum."

"So much the worse—you know I am not rich."

"No, no; but the order is—and if you had been the general——"

"You know I am not the general, I think."

"In that case you have a friend who must be very wealthy— M. Fouquet."

"M. Fouquet! He is more than half ruined, madame."

"So it is said, but I would not believe it."

"Why, Duchesse?"

"Because I have, or rather Laicques has, certain letters in his possession, from Cardinal Mazarin,* which establish the existence of very strange accounts."

"What accounts?"

"Relative to various sums of money borrowed and disposed of. I cannot very distinctly remember what they are; but they establish the fact that the Surintendant, according to these letters, which are signed by Mazarin, had taken thirty millions of francs from the coffers of the State. The case is a very serious one."

Aramis clenched his hands in anxiety and apprehension. "Is it possible," he said, "that you have such letters as you speak of, and have not communicated them to M. Fouquet?"

"Ah!" replied the Duchesse, "I keep such little matters as these in reserve. The day may come when they may be of service; and they can then be withdrawn from the safe custody in which they now are."

"And that day has arrived?" said Aramis.

"Yes."

"And you are going to show those letters to M. Fouquet?"

"I prefer to talk about them with you, instead."

"You must be in sad want of money, my poor friend, to think of such things as these—you, too, who held M. de Mazarin's prose effusions in such indifferent esteem."

"The fact is, I am in want of money."

"And then," continued Aramis in cold accents, "it must have been very distressing to you to be obliged to have recourse to such a means. It is cruel."

"Oh! if I had wished to do harm instead of good," said Madame de Chevreuse, "instead of asking the general of the order, or M. Fouquet, for the five hundred thousand francs I require——"

"Five hundred thousand francs!"

"Yes; no more. Do you think it much? I require at least as much as that to restore Dampierre."

"Yes, madame."

"I say, therefore, that, instead of asking for this amount, I

8

should have gone to see my old friend the Queen-Mother; the letters from her husband, the Signor Mazarini,* would have served me as an introduction, and I should have begged this mere trifle of her, saying to her, 'I wish, madame, to have the honour of receiving you at Dampierre. Permit me to put Dampierre in a fit state for that purpose.'"

Aramis did not reply a single word. "Well," she said, "what are you thinking about?"

"I am making certain additions," said Aramis.

"And M. Fouquet subtractions. I, on the other hand, am trying the art of multiplication. What excellent calculators we are! How well we could understand one another!"

"Will you allow me to reflect?" said Aramis.

"No, for with such an opening between people like ourselves, 'yes,' or 'no' is the only answer, and that an immediate one."

"It is a snare," thought the Bishop; "it is impossible that Anne of Austria could listen to such a woman as this."

"Well?" said the Duchesse.

"Well, madame, I should be very much astonished if M. Fouquet had five hundred thousand francs at his disposal at the present moment."

"It is no use speaking of it then," said the Duchesse, "and Dampierre must get restored how it can."

"Oh! you are not embarrassed to such an extent as that, I suppose."

"No; I am never embarrassed."

"And the Queen," continued the Bishop, "will certainly do for you, what the Surintendant is unable to do."

"Oh! certainly. But tell me, do you not think it would be better, that I should speak, myself, to M. Fouquet, about these letters?"

"Nay, Duchesse, you will do precisely whatever you please in that respect. M. Fouquet either feels, or does not feel himself to be guilty; if he really be so, I know he is proud enough not to confess it; if he be not so, he will be exceedingly offended at your menace."

"As usual, you reason like an angel," said the Duchesse as she rose from her seat.

"And so, you are now going to denounce M. Fouquet to the Queen," said Aramis.

"'Denounce!' Oh! what a disagreeable word. I shall not 'denounce,' my dear friend; you now know matters of policy too well to be ignorant how easily these affairs are arranged. I shall merely side against M. Fouquet, and nothing more; and, in a war of party against party, a weapon of attack is always a weapon."

"No doubt."

"And, once on friendly terms again with the Queen-Mother, I may be dangerous towards some persons."

"You are at perfect liberty to be so, Duchesse."

"A liberty of which I shall avail myself."

"You are not ignorant, I suppose, Duchesse, that M. Fouquet is on the best of terms with the King of Spain."

"I suppose so."

"If, therefore, you begin a party warfare against M. Fouquet, he will reply in the same way; for he, too, is at perfect liberty to do so, is he not?"

"Oh! certainly."

"And as he is on good terms with Spain, he will make use of that friendship as a weapon of attack."

"You mean that he will be on good terms with the general of the order of the Jesuits, my dear Aramis."

"That may be the case, Duchesse."

"And that, consequently, the pension I have been receiving from the order will be stopped."

"I am greatly afraid it might be."

"Well; I must contrive to console myself in the best way I can; for after Richelieu, after the Frondes, after exile, what is there left for Madame de Chevreuse to be afraid of?"

"The pension, you are aware, is forty-eight thousand francs."

"Alas! I am quite aware of it."

"Moreover, in party contests, you know, the friends of the enemy do not escape."

"Ah! you mean that poor Laicques will have to suffer."

"I am afraid it is almost inevitable, Duchesse."

"Oh! he only receives twelve thousand francs pension."

"Yes, but the King of Spain has some influence left; advised by M. Fouquet, he might get M. Laicques shut up in prison for a little while."

"I am not very nervous on that point, my dear friend; because, thanks to a reconciliation with Anne of Austria, I will undertake that France should insist upon M. Laicques's liberation."

"True. In that case you will have something else to apprehend?"

"What can that be?" said the Duchesse, pretending to be surprised and terrified.

"You will learn; indeed, you must know it already, that having once been an affiliated member of the order, it is not easy to leave it; for the secrets that any particular member may have acquired are unwholesome, and carry with them the germs of misfortune for whoever may reveal them."

The Duchesse paused and reflected for a moment, and then said, "That is more serious, I will think over it."

And, notwithstanding the profound obscurity, Aramis seemed to feel a burning glance, like a hot iron, escape from his friend's eyes, and plunge into his heart.

"Let us recapitulate," said Aramis; determined to keep himself on his guard, and gliding his hand into his breast, where he had a dagger concealed.

"Exactly, let us recapitulate; good accounts make good friends."

"The suppression of your pension———"

"Forty-eight thousand francs, and that of Laicques twelve, make, together, sixty thousand francs; that is what you mean, I suppose?"

"Precisely; and I was trying to find out what would be your equivalent for that?"

"Five hundred thousand francs, which I shall get from the Queen."

"Or, which you will not get."

"I know a means of procuring them," said the Duchesse thoughtlessly.

This remark made the Chevalier prick up his ears; and from the moment his adversary had committed this error, his mind was so thoroughly on its guard, that he seemed every moment to gain the advantage more and more; and she, consequently, to lose it. "I will admit, for argument's sake, that you obtain the money," he resumed, "you will lose the double of it, having a hundred thousand francs' pension to receive instead of sixty thousand, and that for a period of ten years."

"Not so, for I shall only be subjected to this reduction of my income during the period of M. Fouquet's remaining in power, a period which I estimate at two months."

"Ah!" said Aramis.

"I am frank, you see."

"I thank you for it, Duchesse; but you would be wrong to suppose, that after M. Fouquet's disgrace the order would resume the payment of your pension."

"I know a means of making the order pay, as I know a means of forcing the Queen-Mother to concede what I require."

"In that case, Duchesse, we are all obliged to strike our flags to you. The victory is yours, and the triumph also is yours. Be clement, I entreat you."

"But is it possible," resumed the Duchesse, without taking

notice of the irony, "that you really draw back from a miserable sum of five hundred thousand francs, when it is a question of sparing you—I mean your friend—I beg your pardon, I ought rather to say your protector—the disagreeable consequences which a party conquest produces."

"Duchesse, I will tell you why; supposing the five hundred thousand francs were to be given you, M. Laicques will require his share, which will be another five hundred thousand francs, I presume? and then, after M. de Laicques' and your own portions have been arranged, the portions which your children, your poor pensioners, and various other persons will require, will start up as fresh claims; and these letters, however compromising they may be in their nature, are not worth from three to four millions. Can you have forgotten the Queen of France's diamonds?—they were surely worth more than these bits of waste paper signed by Mazarin, and yet their recovery did not cost a fourth part of what you ask for yourself."

"Yes, that is true; but the merchant values his goods at his own price, and it is for the purchaser to buy or refuse."

"Stay a moment, Duchesse; would you like me to tell you why I will not buy your letters."

"Pray tell me?"

"Because the letters you say are Mazarin's are false."

"What an absurdity."

"I have no doubt of it, for it would, to say the least, be very singular, that after you had quarrelled with the Queen through M. Mazarin's means, you should have kept up any intimate acquaintance with the latter; it would look as if you had been acting as a spy; and upon my word, I do not like to make use of the word."

"Oh! pray say it."

"Your great complaisance would seem very suspicious, at all events."

"That is quite true; but what is not less so, is that which the letter contains."

"I pledge you my word, Duchesse, that you will not be able to make use of it with the Queen."

"Oh! yes, indeed; I can make use of everything with the Queen."

"Very good," thought Aramis. "Croak on, old owl—hiss, viper that you are!"

But the Duchesse had said enough, and advanced a few steps towards the door. Aramis, however, had reserved an exposure which she did not expect—the imprecation of the slave behind the car of the conqueror. He rang the bell, candles immediately appeared in the adjoining room, and the Bishop found himself completely encircled by lights, which shone upon the worn, haggard face of the Duchesse, revealing every feature but too clearly. Aramis fixed a long and ironical look upon her pale, thin, withered cheeks—upon her dim, dull eyes—and upon her lips, which she kept carefully closed over her blackened and scanty teeth. He, however, had thrown himself into a graceful attitude, with his haughty and intelligent head thrown back; he smiled so as to reveal his teeth, which were still brilliant and dazzling. The old coquette understood the trick that had been played her. She was standing immediately before a large mirror, in which her decrepitude, so carefully concealed, was only made more manifest. And, thereupon, without even saluting Aramis, who bowed with the ease and grace of the musketeer of early days, she hurried away with trembling steps, which her very precipitation only the more impeded. Aramis sprang across the room, like a zephyr, to lead her to the door. Madame de Chevreuse made a sign to her servant, who resumed his musket; and she left the house where such tender friends had not been able to understand each other, only because they had understood each other too well.

2

WHEREIN MAY BE SEEN THAT A BARGAIN WHICH CANNOT BE
MADE WITH ONE PERSON, CAN BE CARRIED OUT
WITH ANOTHER

ARAMIS had been perfectly correct in his supposition; for hardly had she left the house in the Place Baudoyer, than Madame de Chevreuse proceeded homeward. She was, doubtless, afraid of being followed, and by this means thought she might succeed in throwing those who might be following her off their guard; but scarcely had she arrived within the door of the hotel, and hardly had assured herself that no one who could cause her any uneasiness was on her track, when she opened the door of the garden, leading into another street, and hurried towards the Rue Croix des Petits Champs, where M. Colbert*resided.

We have already said that evening, or rather night, had closed in; it was a dark, thick night, besides; Paris had once more sunk into its calm, quiescent state, enshrouding alike within its indulgent mantle the high-born Duchesse carrying out her political intrigue, and the simple citizen's wife, who, having been detained late by a supper in the city, was making her way slowly homewards, hanging on the arm of a lover, by the shortest possible route. Madame de Chevreuse had been too well accustomed to nocturnal political intrigues to be ignorant that a minister never denies himself, even at his own private residence, to any young and beautiful woman who may chance to object to the dust and confusion of a public office, or to old women, as full of experience as of years, who dislike the indiscreet echo of official residences. A valet received the Duchesse under the peristyle, and received her, it must be admitted, with some indifference of manner; he intimated, after having looked at her face, that it was hardly at such an hour that one so advanced in years as herself could be permitted to disturb Monsieur Colbert's important occupations. But Madame de Chevreuse, without feeling or appearing to be annoyed, wrote her name upon a leaf of her tablets,—a name which had but too frequently sounded so disagreeably in the ears of Louis XIII. and of the great Cardinal.* She wrote her name in the large, ill-formed characters of the higher classes of that period, folded the paper in a manner peculiarly her own, handed it to the valet without uttering a word, but with so haughty and imperious a gesture that the fellow, well accustomed to judge of people from their manners and appearance, perceived at once the quality of the person before him, bowed his head, and ran to M. Colbert's room. The minister could not control a sudden exclamation as he opened the paper; and the valet gathering from it the interest with which his master regarded the mysterious visitor returned as fast as he could to beg the Duchesse to follow him. She ascended to the first floor of the beautiful new house very slowly, rested herself on the landing-place, in order not to enter the apartment out of breath, and appeared before M. Colbert, who, with his own hands, held both the folding-doors open. The Duchesse paused at the threshold, for the purpose of well studying the character of the man with whom she was about to converse. At the first glance, the round, large, heavy head, thick brows, and ill-favoured features of Colbert, who wore, thrust low down on his head, a cap like a priest's, seemed to indicate that but little difficulty was likely to be met with in her negotiations with him, but also that she was to expect as little interest in the discussion of particulars; for there was scarcely any indication that the rough and uncouth nature of the man was susceptible to the impulses of a refined revenge, or of an exalted ambition. But when, on closer inspection, the Duchesse perceived the small piercingly black eyes, the longitudinal wrinkles of his high and massive forehead, the imperceptible twitching of the lips, on which were apparent traces of rough good humour, Madame de Chevreuse altered her opinion of him, and felt she could say to herself: "I have found the man I want."

"What is the subject, madame, which procures me the honour of a visit from you?" he inquired.

"The need I have of you, monsieur," returned the Duchesse, "as well as that which you have of me."

"I am delighted, madame, with the first portion of your sentence; but, as far as the second portion is concerned——"

Madame de Chevreuse sat down in the arm-chair which M. Colbert advanced towards her. "Monsieur Colbert, you are the Intendant of Finances, and are ambitious of becoming the Surintendant?"*

"Madame!"

"Nay, do not deny it; that would only unnecessarily prolong our conversation, and that is useless."

"And yet, madame, however well disposed and inclined to show politeness I may be towards a lady of your position and merit, nothing will make me confess that I have ever entertained the idea of supplanting my superior."

"I said nothing about supplanting, Monsieur Colbert. Could I accidentally have made use of that word? I hardly think that likely. The word 'replace' is less aggressive in its signification, and more grammatically suitable, as M. de Voiture* would say. I presume, therefore, that you are ambitious of replacing M. Fouquet."

"M. Fouquet's fortune, madame, enables him to withstand all attempts. The Surintendant in this age plays the part of the Colossus of Rhodes; the vessels pass beneath him and do not overthrow him."

"I ought to have availed myself precisely of that very comparison. It is true, M. Fouquet plays the part of the Colossus of Rhodes; but I remember to have heard it said by M. Conrart,* a member of the academy, I believe, that when the Colossus of Rhodes fell from its lofty position, the merchant who had cast it down—a merchant, nothing more, M. Colbert—loaded four hundred camels with the ruins. A merchant! and that is considerably less than an Intendant of Finances."

"Madame, I can assure you that I shall never overthrow Monsieur Fouquet."

"Very good, Monsieur Colbert, since you persist in showing so much sensitiveness with me, as if you were ignorant that I am Madame de Chevreuse, and also that I am somewhat advanced in years; in other words, that you have to do with a woman who has had political dealings with the Cardinal de Richelieu, and who has no time to lose; as, I repeat, you do not hesitate to commit such an imprudence, I shall go and find others who are more intelligent and more desirous of making their fortunes."

"How, madame, how?"

"You give me a very poor idea of negotiators of the present day. I assure you that if, in my earlier days, a woman had gone to M. de Cinq-Mars,* who was not, moreover, a man of very high order of intellect, and had said to him about the Cardinal what I have just now said to you of M. Fouquet, M. de Cinq-Mars would by this time have already set actively to work."

"Nay, madame, show a little indulgence, I entreat you."

"Well, then, you do really consent to replace M. Fouquet."

"Certainly I do, if the King dismisses M. Fouquet."

"Again, a word too much; it is quite evident that if you have not yet succeeded in driving M. Fouquet from his post, it is because you have not been able to do so. Therefore, I should be the greatest simpleton possible if, in coming to you, I did not bring you the very thing you require."

"I am distressed to be obliged to persist, madame," said Colbert, after a silence which enabled the Duchesse to sound the depth of his dissimulation, "but I must warn you that, for the last six years, denunciation after denunciation has been made against M. Fouquet, and he has remained unshaken and unaffected by them."

"There is a time for everything, Monsieur Colbert; those who were the authors of those denunciations were not called Madame de Chevreuse, and they had no proofs equal to the six letters from M. de Mazarin, which establish the offence in question."

"The offence!"

"The crime, if you like it better."

"The crime! committed by M. Fouquet!"

"Nothing less. It is rather strange, M. Colbert, but your face, which just now was cold and indifferent, is now positively the very reverse."

"A crime!"

"I am delighted to see it makes an impression upon you."

"It is because that word, madame, embraces so many things."

"It embraces the post of Surintendant of Finance for yourself, and a letter of exile, or the Bastille, for M. Fouquet."

"Forgive me, Madame la Duchesse, but it is almost impossible that M. Fouquet can be exiled; to be imprisoned or disgraced, that is already a great deal."

"Oh, I am perfectly aware of what I am saying," returned Madame de Chevreuse coldly. "I do not live at such a distance from Paris as not to know what takes place there. The King does not like M. Fouquet, and he would willingly sacrifice M. Fouquet if an opportunity were only given him."

"It must be a good one, though."

"Good enough, and one I estimate to be worth five hundred thousand francs."

"In what way?" said Colbert.

"I mean, monsieur, that holding this opportunity in my own hands, I will not allow it to be transferred to yours except for a sum of five hundred thousand francs."

"I understand you perfectly, madame. But since you have fixed a price for the sale, let me now see the value of the articles to be sold."

"Oh, a mere trifle; six letters, as I have already told you, from M. de Mazarin; and the autographs will most assuredly not be regarded as too highly priced, if they establish, in an irrefutable manner, that M. Fouquet has embezzled large sums of money from the treasury, and appropriated them to his own purposes."

"In an irrefutable manner, do you say?" observed Colbert, whose eyes sparkled with delight.

"Perfectly so; would you like to read the letters?"

"With all my heart. Copies, of course?"

"Of course, the copies," said the Duchesse, as she drew from her bosom a small packet of papers flattened by her velvet bodice. "Read," she said.

Colbert eagerly snatched the papers and devoured them.

"Excellent!" he said.

"It is clear enough, is it not?"

"Yes, madame, yes; M. Mazarin must have handed the money to M. Fouquet, who must have kept it for his own purposes; but the question is, what money?"

"Exactly,—what money? if we come to terms I will join to these six letters a seventh, which will supply you with the fullest particulars."

Colbert reflected. "And the originals of those letters?"

"A useless question to ask; exactly as if I were to ask you, Monsieur Colbert, whether the money-bags you will give me will be full or empty."

"Very good, madame."

"Is it concluded?"

"No; for there is one circumstance to which neither of us has given any attention."

"Name it!"

"M. Fouquet can be utterly ruined, under the circumstances you have detailed, only by means of legal proceedings."

"Well?"

"A public scandal, for instance; and yet, neither the legal proceedings nor the scandal can be commenced against him."

"Why not?"

"Because he is Procureur-Général of the Parliament;*because, too, in France, all public administrations, the army, justice itself, and commerce, are intimately connected by ties of good fellowship, which people call *esprit de corps*. In such a case, madame, the Parliament will never permit its chief to be dragged before a public tribunal; and never, even if he be dragged there by royal authority, never, I say, will he be condemned."

"Well, Monsieur Colbert, I do not see what I have to do with that."

"I am aware of that, madame; but I have to do with it, and it consequently diminishes the value of what you have brought to show me. What good can a proof of crime be to me without the possibility of obtaining a condemnation?"

"Even if he be only suspected, M. Fouquet will lose his post of Surintendant."

"Is that all!" exclaimed Colbert, whose dark, gloomy features were momentarily lighted up by an expression of hate and vengeance.

"Ah, ah! Monsieur Colbert," said the Duchesse, "forgive me, but I did not think you were so impressionable. Very good; in that case, since you need more than I have to give you, there is no occasion to speak of the matter at all."

"Yes, madame, we will go on talking of it; only, as the value of your commodities has decreased, you must lower your pretensions."

"You are bargaining, then?"

"Every man who wishes to deal loyally is obliged to do so."

"How much will you offer me?"

"Two hundred thousand francs," said Colbert.

The Duchesse laughed in his face, and then said suddenly, "Wait a moment, I have another arrangement to propose; will you give me three hundred thousand francs?"

"No, no."

"Oh, you can either accept or refuse my terms; besides, that is not all."

"More still! you are becoming too impracticable to deal with, madame."

"Less so than you think, perhaps, for it is not money I am going to ask you for."

"What is it, then?"

"A service. You know that I have always been most affectionately attached to the Queen, and I am desirous of having an interview with Her Majesty."

"With the Queen?"

"Yes, Monsieur Colbert, with the Queen, who is, I admit, no longer my friend, and who has ceased to be so for a long time past, but who may again become so if the opportunity be only given her."

"Her Majesty has ceased to receive any one, madame. She is a great sufferer, and you may be aware that the paroxysms of her disease* occur with greater frequency than ever."

"That is the very reason why I wish to have an interview with Her Majesty; for in Flanders there is a great variety of these kinds of complaints."

"What, cancers—a fearful, incurable disorder?"

"Do not believe that, Monsieur Colbert. The Flemish peasant is somewhat a man of nature, and his companion for life is not alone a wife, but a female labourer also; for while he is smoking his pipe, the woman works: it is she who draws the water from the well; she who loads the mule or the ass, and even bears herself a portion of the burden. Taking but little care of herself, she gets knocked about, first in one direction, and then in another, and very often is beaten by her husband, and cancers frequently arise from contusions."

"True, true," said Colbert.

"The Flemish women do not die the sooner on that account. When they are great sufferers from this disease they go in search of remedies, and the Béguines of Bruges are excellent doctors for every kind of disease. They have precious waters of one sort or another; specifics of various kinds; and they give a bottle of it and a wax candle to the sufferer, whereby the priests are gainers, and Heaven is served by the disposal of both their wares. I will take the Queen some of this holy water, which I will procure from the Béguines* of Bruges; Her Majesty will recover, and will burn as many wax candles as she may think fit. You see, Monsieur Colbert, to prevent my seeing the Queen is almost as bad as committing the crime of regicide."

"You are, undoubtedly, Madame la Duchesse, a woman of exceedingly great abilities, and I am more than astounded at their display; still I cannot but suppose that this charitable consideration towards the Queen in some measure covers a slight personal interest for yourself."

"I have not given myself the trouble to conceal it, that I am aware of, Monsieur Colbert. You said, I believe, that I had a slight personal interest? On the contrary, it is a very great interest, and I will prove it to you, by resuming what I was saying. If you procure me a personal interview with Her Majesty, I will be satisfied with the three hundred thousand francs I have claimed; if not, I shall keep my letters, unless, indeed, you give me, on the spot, five hundred thousand francs for them."

And rising from her seat with this decisive remark, the old Duchesse plunged M. Colbert into a disagreeable perplexity. To bargain any further was out of the question; and not to bargain was to pay a great deal too dearly for them. "Madame," he said, "I shall have the pleasure of handing you over a hundred thousand crowns; but how shall I get the actual letters themselves?"

"In the simplest manner in the world, my dear Monsieur Colbert—whom will you trust?"

The financier began to laugh silently, so that his large eyebrows went up and down like the wings of a bat, upon the deep lines of his yellow forehead. "No one," he said.

"You surely will make an exception in your own favour, Monsieur Colbert?"

"In what way, madame?"

"I mean that if you would take the trouble to accompany me to the place where the letters are, they would be delivered into your own hands, and you would be able to verify and check them."

"Quite true."

"You would bring the hundred thousand crowns with you at the same time, for, I, too, do not trust any one?"

Colbert coloured to the tips of his ears. Like all eminent men in the art of figures, he was of an insolent and mathematical probity. "I will take with me, madame," he said, "two orders for the amount agreed upon, payable at my treasury. Will that satisfy you?"

"Would that the orders on your treasury were for two millions, monsieur. I shall have the pleasure of showing you the way, then?"

"Allow me to order my carriage."

"I have a carriage below, monsieur."

Colbert coughed like an irresolute man. He imagined, for a moment, that the proposition of the Duchesse was a snare; that perhaps some one was waiting at the door; and that she whose secret had just been sold to Colbert for a hundred thousand crowns, had already offered it to Fouquet for the same sum. As he still hesitated a good deal, the Duchesse looked at him full in the face.

"You prefer your own carriage?" she said.

"I admit that I do."

"You suppose that I am going to lead you into a snare or trap of some sort or other?"

"Madame la Duchesse, you have the character of being somewhat inconsiderate at times, and, as I am clothed in a sober, solemn character, a jest or a practical joke might compromise me."

"Yes; the fact is, you are afraid. Well, then, take your own carriage, as many servants as you like, only think well of what I am going to say. What we two may arrange between us, we are the only persons who know it; if a third had witnessed, we might as well have told the whole world of it. After all, I do not make a point of it; my carriage shall follow yours, and I shall be satisfied to accompany you in your own carriage to the Queen."

"To the Queen!"

"Have you forgotten that already? Is it possible that one of the clauses of the agreement, of so much importance to me, can have escaped you already? How trifling it seems to you, indeed; if I had known it I should have asked double what I have done."

"I have reflected, madame, and I shall not accompany you."

"Really—and why not?"

"Because I have the most perfect confidence in you."

"You overpower me. But provided I receive the hundred thousand crowns?"

"Here they are, madame," said Colbert, scribbling a few lines on a piece of paper, which he handed to the Duchesse, adding, "You are paid."

"The trait is a fine one, Monsieur Colbert, and I will reward you for it," she said, beginning to laugh.

Madame de Chevreuse's laugh was a very sinister sound; every man who feels youth, faith, love, life itself throbbing in his heart, would prefer tears to such a lamentable laugh. The Duchesse opened the front of her dress and drew forth from her bosom, somewhat less white than it once had been, a small packet of papers, tied with a flame-coloured ribbon, and, still laughing, she said, "There, Monsieur Colbert, are the originals of Cardinal Mazarin's letters; they are now your own property," she added, refastening the body of her dress; "your fortune is secured, and now accompany me to the Queen."

"No, madame; if you are again about to run the chance of Her Majesty's displeasure, and it were known at the Palais Royal that I had been the means of introducing you there, the Queen would never forgive me while she lived. No; there are certain persons at the palace who are devoted to me, who will procure you an admission without my being compromised."

"Just as you please, provided I enter."

"What do you term those religious women at Bruges who cure disorders."

"Béguines."

"Good; you are one."

"As you please, but I must soon cease to be one."

"That is your affair."

"Excuse me, but I do not wish to be exposed to a refusal."

"That is again your own affair, madame. I am going to give directions to the head valet of the gentleman in waiting on Her Majesty to allow admission to a Béguine, who brings an effectual remedy for Her Majesty's sufferings. You are the bearer of my letter, you will undertake to be provided with the remedy, and will give every explanation on the subject. I admit a knowledge of a Béguine, but I deny all knowledge of Madame de Chevreuse. Here, madame, then, is your letter of introduction."

3

THE SKIN OF THE BEAR

COLBERT handed the Duchesse the letter, and gently drew aside the chair behind which she was standing. Madame de Chevreuse, with a very slight bow, immediately left the room. Colbert, who had recognised Mazarin's handwriting, and had counted the letters, rang to summon his secretary, whom he enjoined to go in immediate search of M. Vanel, a counsellor of the Parliament. The secretary replied that, according to his usual practice, M. Vanel had just that moment entered the house, in order to render to the Intendant an account of the principal details of the business which had been transacted during the day in the sitting of the Parliament. Colbert approached one of the lamps, read the letters of the deceased Cardinal over again, smiled repeatedly as he recognised the great value of the papers Madame de Chevreuse had just delivered to him and, burying his head in his hands for a few minutes, reflected profoundly. In the meantime, a tall, large-made man entered the room; his spare thin face, steady look, and hooked nose, as he entered Colbert's cabinet, with a modest assurance of manner, revealed a character at once supple and decided,—supple towards the master who could throw him the prey, firm towards the dogs who might possibly be disposed to dispute it with him. M. Vanel carried a voluminous bundle of papers under his arm, and placed it on the desk on which Colbert was leaning both his elbows, as he supported his head.

"Good-day, M. Vanel," said the latter, rousing himself from his meditation.

"Good-day, monseigneur," said Vanel naturally.

"You should say monsieur, and not monseigneur," replied Colbert gently.

"We give the title of monseigneur to ministers," returned Vanel, with extreme self-possession, "and you are a minister."

"Not yet."

"You are so in point of fact, and I call you monseigneur accordingly; besides, you are my seigneur for me, and that is sufficient; if you dislike my calling you monseigneur before others, allow me, at least, to call you so in private."

Colbert raised his head as if to read, or to try to read, upon Vanel's face how much actual sincerity entered into this protestation of devotion. But the counsellor knew perfectly well how to sustain the weight of his look, even were it armed with the full authority of the title he had conferred. Colbert sighed; he could not read anything in Vanel's face, and Vanel might possibly be honest in his professions, but Colbert recollected that this man, inferior to himself in every other respect, was actually his superior through the fact of his having a wife unfaithful to him. At the moment he was pitying this man's lot, Vanel coldly drew from his pocket a perfumed letter, sealed with Spanish wax, and held it towards Colbert, saying, "A letter from my wife, monseigneur."

Colbert coughed, took, opened, and read the letter, and then put it carefully away in his pocket, while Vanel turned over the leaves of the papers he had brought with him with an unmoved and unconcerned air. "Vanel," he said suddenly to his protégé, "you are a hard-working man, I know; would twelve hours' daily labour frighten you?"

"I work fifteen hours every day."

"Impossible. A counsellor need not work more than three hours a day in Parliament."

"Oh! I am working up some returns for a friend of mine in the department of accounts, and, as I still have time left on my hands, I am studying Hebrew."

"Your reputation stands high in the Parliament, Vanel."

"I believe so, monseigneur."

"You must not grow rusty in your post of counsellor."

"What must I do to avoid it?"

"Purchase a high place. Mean and low ambitions are very difficult to satisfy."

"Small purses are the most difficult to fill, monseigneur."

"What post have you in view?" said Colbert.

"I see none—not one."

"There is one, certainly, but one need be almost the King himself to be able to buy it without inconvenience; and the King will not be inclined, I suppose, to purchase the post of Procureur-Général."

At these words, Vanel fixed his at once humble and dull look upon Colbert, who could hardly tell whether Vanel had comprehended him or not. "Why do you speak to me, monseigneur," said Vanel, "of the post of Procureur-Général to the Parliament; I know no other post then the one M. Fouquet fills."

"Exactly so, my dear counsellor."

"You are not over fastidious, monseigneur; but before the post can be bought, it must be offered for sale."

"I believe, Monsieur Vanel, that it will be for sale before long."

"For sale! What, M. Fouquet's post of Procureur-Général?"

"So it is said."

"The post which renders him so perfectly inviolable, for sale! Oh! oh!" said Vanel, beginning to laugh.

"Would you be afraid, then, of the post?" said Colbert gravely.

"Afraid! no, but——"

"Nor desirous of obtaining it?"

"You are laughing at me, monseigneur," replied Vanel; "is it likely that a counsellor of the Parliament would not be desirous of becoming Procureur-Général?"

"Well, Monsieur Vanel, since I tell you that the post, as report goes, will be shortly for sale——"

"I cannot help repeating, monseigneur, that it is impossible; a man never throws away the buckler, behind which he maintains his honour, his fortune, his very life."

"There are certain men mad enough, Vanel, to fancy themselves out of the reach of all mischances."

"Yes, monseigneur; but such men never commit their mad acts for the advantage of the poor Vanels of the world."

"Why not?"

"For the very reason that those Vanels are poor."

"It is true that M. Fouquet's post might cost a good round sum. What would you bid for it, Monsieur Vanel?"

"Everything I am worth."

"Which means?"

"Three or four hundred thousand francs."

"And the post is worth——"

"A million and a half at the very lowest. I know persons who have offered one million seven hundred thousand francs, without being able to persuade M. Fouquet to sell. Besides, supposing it were to happen that M. Fouquet wished to sell, which I do not believe, in spite of what I have been told——"

"Ah! you have heard something about it, then; who told you?"

"M. de Gourville, M. Pélisson, and others."*

"Very good; if, therefore, M. Fouquet did wish to sell——"

"I could not buy it just yet, since the Surintendant will only sell for ready money, and no one has a million and a half to throw down at once."

Colbert suddenly interrupted the counsellor by an imperious gesture; he had begun to meditate. Observing his superior's serious attitude, and his perseverance in continuing the conversation on this subject, Vanel awaited the solution without venturing to precipitate it. "Explain fully to me the privileges which this post confers."

"The right of impeaching every French subject who is not a prince of the blood; the right of quashing all proceedings taken against any Frenchman, who is neither king nor prince. The Procureur-Général is the King's right hand to punish the guilty; he is the means whereby also he can evade the administration of justice. M. Fouquet, therefore, will be able, by stirring up the Parliaments, to maintain himself even against the King; and the King could as easily, by humouring M. Fouquet, get his edicts registered in spite of every opposition and objection. The Procureur-Généralship can be made a very useful or very dangerous instrument."

"Vanel, would you like to be Procureur-Général?" said Colbert suddenly, softening both his look and his voice.

"I!" exclaimed the latter; "I have already had the honour to represent to you that I want about eleven hundred thousand francs to make up the amount."

"Borrow that sum from your friends."

"I have no friends richer than myself."

"You are an honest and honourable man, Vanel."

"Ah! monseigneur, if the world were to think as you do!"

"I think so, and that is quite enough; and if it should be needed, I will be your security."

"Do not forget the proverb, monseigneur."

"What is that?"

"That he who becomes responsible for another, has to pay for his responsibility."

"Let that make no difference."

Vanel rose, quite bewildered by this offer which had been so suddenly and unexpectedly made to him. "You are not trifling with me, monseigneur?" he said.

"Stay; you say that M. Gourville has spoken to you about M. Fouquet's post."

"Yes; and M. Pélisson also."

"Officially so, or only by their own suggestion?"

"These were their very words: 'These Parliamentary people are as proud as they are wealthy; they ought to club together two or three millions among themselves, to present to their protector and great luminary, M. Fouquet.' "

"And what did you reply?"

"I said that, for my own part, I would give ten thousand francs if necessary."

"Ah! you like M. Fouquet, then?" exclaimed Colbert, with a look full of hatred.

"No; but M. Fouquet is our chief. He is in debt—is on the high road to ruin; and we ought to save the honour of the body of which we are members."

"Exactly; and that explains why M. Fouquet will be always safe and sound so long as he occupies his present post," replied Colbert.

"Thereupon," said Vanel, "M. Gourville added, 'If we were to do anything out of charity to M. Fouquet, it could not be otherwise than most humiliating to him; and he would be sure to refuse it. Let the Parliament subscribe among themselves to purchase, in a proper manner, the post of Procureur-Général; in that case, all would go on well, the honour of our body would be saved, and M. Fouquet's pride spared.' "

"That is an opening."

"I considered it so, monseigneur."

"Well, Monsieur Vanel, you will go at once, and find out either M. Gourville or M. Pélisson. Do you know any other friend of M. Fouquet?"

"I know M. de la Fontaine very well."

"La Fontaine, the rhymester?"

"Yes; he used to write verses to my wife, when M. Fouquet was one of our friends."

"Go to him, then, and try to procure an interview with the Surintendant."

26

"Willingly—but the sum itself?"

"On the day and the hour you arrange to settle the matter, Monsieur Vanel, you shall be supplied with the money; so, do not make yourself uneasy on that account."

"Monseigneur, such munificence! You eclipse kings even— you surpass M. Fouquet himself."

"Stay a moment—do not let us mistake each other. I do not make you a present of fourteen hundred thousand francs, Monsieur Vanel; for I have children to provide for—but I will lend you that sum."

"Ask whatever interest, whatever security you please, monseigneur; I am quite ready. And when all your requisitions are satisfied, I will still repeat, that you surpass kings and M. Fouquet in munificence. What conditions do you impose?"

"The repayment in eight years, and a mortgage upon the appointment itself."

"Certainly. Is that all?"

"Wait a moment. I reserve to myself the right of repurchasing the post from you at one hundred and fifty thousand francs profit for yourself, if, in your mode of filling the office, you do not follow out a line of conduct in conformity with the interests of the King and with my projects."

"Ah! ah!" said Vanel, in a slightly altered tone.

"Is there anything in that which can possibly be objectionable to you, Monsieur Vanel?" said Colbert coldly.

"Oh! no, no," replied Vanel quickly.

"Very good. We will sign an agreement to that effect, whenever you like. And now, go as quickly as you can to M. Fouquet's friends, obtain an interview with the Surintendant; do not be too difficult in making whatever concessions may be required of you; and when once the arrangements are all made——"

"I will press him to sign."

"Be most careful to do nothing of the kind; do not speak of signatures with M. Fouquet, nor of deeds, nor even ask him to pass his word. Understand this, otherwise you will lose everything. All you have to do is to get M. Fouquet to give you his hand on the matter. Go, go."

4

AN INTERVIEW WITH THE QUEEN-MOTHER

THE Queen-Mother was in her bedroom at the Palais-Royal, with Madame de Motteville and the Senora Molena.* The King, who had been impatiently expected the whole day, had not made his appearance; and the Queen,* who had grown quite impatient, had often sent to inquire about him. The whole atmosphere of the court seemed to indicate an approaching storm; the courtiers and the ladies of the court avoided meeting in the antechambers and the corridors, in order not to converse on compromising subjects. Monsieur had joined the King early in the morning for a hunting party; Madame remained in her own apartments, cool and distant to every one; and the Queen-Mother, after she had said her prayers in Latin, talked of domestic matters with her two friends in pure Castilian. Madame de Motteville, who understood the language perfectly, answered her in French. When the three ladies had exhausted every form of dissimulation and of politeness, as a circuitous mode of expressing that the King's conduct was making the Queen and the Queen-Mother pine away from sheer grief and vexation, and when, in the most guarded and polished phrases, they had fulminated every variety of imprecation against Mademoiselle de la Vallière,* the Queen-Mother terminated her attack by an exclamation indicative of her own reflections and character. "*Estos hijos!*" said she to Molena—which means, "These children!" words full of meaning in a mother's lips—words full of terrible significance in the mouth of a queen who, like Anne of Austria hid many curious and dark secrets in her soul.

"Yes," said Molena, "these children! for whom every mother becomes a sacrifice."

"Yes," replied the Queen; "a mother has sacrificed everything, certainly." She did not finish her phrase; for she fancied, when she raised her eyes towards the full-length portrait of the pale Louis XIII., that light had once more flashed from her husband's dull eyes, and that his nostrils were inflated by wrath. The portrait seemed animated by a living expression—speak it did not, but it seemed to menace. A profound silence succeeded the Queen's last remark. La Molena began to turn over the ribbons and lace of a large work-table. Madame de Motteville, surprised at the look of mutual intelligence which had been exchanged between the confidante and her mistress, cast down her eyes like a discreet woman, and, pretending to be observant of nothing that was passing, listened with the utmost attention instead. She heard nothing, however, but a very significant "hum" on the part of the Spanish duenna, who was the perfect representation of extreme caution—and a profound sigh on that of the Queen. She looked up immediately.

"You are suffering?" she said.

"No, Motteville, no; why do you say that?"

"Your Majesty almost groaned just now."

"You are right; I did sigh, in truth."

"Monsieur Vallot* is not far off, I believe he is in Madame's apartment."

"Why is he with Madame?"

"Madame is troubled with nervous attacks."

"A very fine disorder, indeed! There is little good in M. Vallot being there, when another physician instead would cure Madame."

Madame de Motteville looked up with an air of great surprise, as she replied, "Another doctor instead of M. Vallot?—whom do you mean?"

"Occupation, Motteville, occupation. If any one is really ill, it is my poor daughter."

"And your Majesty, too."

"Less so this evening, though."

"Do not believe that too confidently, madame," said de Motteville. And, as if to justify her caution, a sharp acute pain seized the Queen, who turned deadly pale, and threw herself back in the chair, with every symptom of a sudden fainting fit. Molena ran to a richly-gilded tortoiseshell cabinet, from which she took a large rock-crystal smelling-bottle, and immediately held it to the Queen's nostrils, who inhaled it wildly for a few minutes, and murmured:—

"It will hasten my death—but Heaven's will be done!"

"Your Majesty's death is not so near at hand," added Molena, replacing the smelling-bottle in the cabinet.

"Does your Majesty feel better now?" inquired Madame de Motteville.

"Much better," returned the Queen, placing her finger on her lips, to impose silence on her favourite.

"It is very strange," remarked Madame de Motteville, after a pause.

"What is strange?" said the Queen.

"Does your Majesty remember the day when this pain attacked you for the first time?"

"I remember only that it was a grievously sad day for me, Motteville."

"But your Majesty had not always regarded that day a sad one."

"Why?"

"Because three and twenty years before, on that very day, his present Majesty, your own glorious son, was born*at the very same hour."

The Queen uttered a loud cry, buried her face in her hands, and seemed utterly lost for some minutes; but whether from recollections which arose in her mind, or from reflection, or even from sheer pain, it was of course uncertain. La Molena darted almost a furious look at Madame de Motteville, which was so full of bitter reproach that the poor woman, perfectly ignorant of its meaning, was, in her own exculpation, on the point of asking an explanation of its meaning; when, suddenly Anne of Austria arose and said, "Yes, the 5th of September; my sorrow began on the 5th of September. The greatest joy, one day; the deepest sorrow the next;—the sorrow," she added, "the bitter expiation of a too excessive joy."

And, from that moment, Anne of Austria, whose memory and reason seemed to have become entirely suspended for a time, remained impenetrable, with vacant look, mind almost wandering, and hands hanging heavily down, as if life had almost departed.

"We must put her to bed," said La Molena.

"Presently, Molena."

"Let us leave the Queen alone," added the Spanish attendant.

Madame de Motteville rose; large and glistening tears were fast rolling down the Queen's pallid face; and Molena, having observed this sign of weakness, fixed her black vigilant eyes upon her.

"Yes, yes," replied the Queen. "Leave us, Motteville; go."

The word "us" produced a disagreeable effect upon the ears of the French favourite; for it signified that an interchange of secrets, or of revelations of the past, was about to be made, and that one person was *de trop* in the conversation which seemed likely to take place.

"Will Molena, alone, be sufficient for your Majesty to-night?" inquired the Frenchwoman.

"Yes," replied the Queen. Madame de Motteville bowed in submission, and was about to withdraw, when, suddenly, an old female attendant, dressed as if she had belonged to the Spanish court of the year 1620, opened the doors, and surprised the Queen in her tears. "The remedy!" she cried, delightedly, to the Queen, as she unceremoniously approached the group.

"What remedy?" said Anne of Austria.

"For your Majesty's sufferings," the former replied.

"Who brings it?" asked Madame de Motteville eagerly; "Monsieur Vallot?"

"No; a lady from Flanders."

"From Flanders? Is she Spanish?" inquired the Queen.

"I don't know."

"Who sent her?"

"M. Colbert."

"Her name?"

"She did not mention it."

"Her position in life?"

"She will answer that herself."

"Her face?"

"She is masked."

"Go, Molena; go and see!" cried the Queen.

"It is needless," suddenly replied a voice, at once firm and gentle in its tone, which proceeded from the other side of the tapestry hangings; a voice which made the attendants start, and the Queen tremble excessively. At the same moment, a masked female appeared through the hangings, and, before the Queen could speak a syllable, she added, "I am connected with the order of the Béguines of Bruges, and do, indeed, bring with me the remedy which is certain to effect a cure of your Majesty's complaint." No one uttered a sound, and the Béguine did not move a step.

"Speak," said the Queen.

"I will, when we are alone," was the answer.

Anne of Austria looked at her attendants, who immediately withdrew.

The Béguine, thereupon, advanced a few steps towards the Queen, and bowed reverently before her. The Queen gazed with increasing mistrust at this woman, who, in her turn, fixed a pair of brilliant eyes upon her, through her mask.

"The Queen of France must, indeed, be very ill," said Anne of Austria, "if it is known at the Béguinage of Bruges that she stands in need of being cured."

"Your Majesty is not irremediably ill."

"But, tell me, how do you happen to know I am suffering?"

"Your Majesty has friends in Flanders."

"Since these friends, then, have sent you, mention their names."

31

"Impossible, madame, since your Majesty's memory has not been awakened by your heart."

Anne of Austria looked up, endeavouring to discover through the concealment of the mask, and through her mysterious language, the name of her companion, who expressed herself with such familiarity and freedom; then, suddenly, wearied by a curiosity which wounded every feeling of pride in her nature, she said, "You are ignorant, perhaps, that royal personages are never spoken to with the face masked."

"Deign to excuse me, madame," replied the Béguine humbly.

"I cannot excuse you. I may, possibly, forgive you, if you throw your mask aside."

"I have made a vow, madame, to attend and aid all afflicted or suffering persons without ever permitting them to behold my face. I might have been able to administer some relief to your body and to your mind, too; but, since your Majesty forbids me, I will take my leave. Adieu, madame, adieu."

These words were uttered with a harmony of tone and respect of manner that deprived the Queen of all her anger and suspicion, but did not remove her feeling of curiosity. "You are right," she said, "it ill becomes those who are suffering to reject the means of relief which Heaven sends them. Speak, then; and may you, indeed, be able, as you assert you can, to administer relief to my body——"

"Let us first speak a little of the mind, if you please," said the Béguine; "of the mind, which, I am sure, must also suffer."

"My mind?"

"There are cancers so insidious in their nature that their very pulsation is invisible. Such cancers, madame, leave the ivory whiteness of the skin untouched, and marble not the firm, fair flesh, with their blue tints; the physician who bends over the patient's chest hears not, though he listens, the insatiable teeth of the disease grinding its onward progress through the muscles, as the blood flows freely on; the knife has never been able to destroy, and rarely even, temporarily, to disarm the rage of these mortal scourges; their home is in the mind, which they corrupt; they fill the whole heart until it breaks. Such, madame, are the cancers, fatal to queens; are you, too, free from their scourge?"

Anne slowly raised her arm, dazzling in its perfect whiteness, and pure in its rounded outlines, as it was in the time of her earlier days.

"The evils to which you allude," she said, "are the condition of the lives of the high in rank upon earth, to whom Heaven has imparted mind. When those evils become too heavy to be borne,

Heaven lightens their burden by penitence and confession. There we lay down our burden, and the secrets which oppress us. But, forget not, that the same gracious Heaven, in its mercy, apportions to their trials the strength of the feeble creatures of its hand; and my strength has enabled me to bear my burden. For the secrets of others, the silence of Heaven is more than sufficient; for my own secrets, that of my confessor is just enough."

"You are as courageous, madame, I see, as ever, against your enemies. You do not acknowledge your confidence in your friends."

"Queens have no friends; if you have nothing further to say to me,—if you feel yourself inspired by Heaven as a prophetess— leave me, I pray you, for I dread the future."

"I should have supposed," said the Béguine resolutely, "that you would rather have dreaded the past."

Hardly had these words escaped her lips, than the Queen rose up proudly. "Speak," she cried, in a short, imperious tone of voice; "explain yourself briefly, quickly, entirely; or, if not——"

"Nay, do not threaten me, your Majesty," said the Béguine gently; "I came to you full of compassion and respect. I came here on the part of a friend."

"Prove that to me! Comfort, instead of irritating me."

"Easily enough; and your Majesty will see who is friendly to you. What misfortune has happened to your Majesty during these three and twenty years past——"

"Serious misfortunes, indeed; have I not lost the King?"

"I speak not of misfortunes of that kind. I wish to ask you if, since the birth of the King, any indiscretion on a friend's part has caused your Majesty the slightest serious anxiety or distress?"

"I do not understand you," replied the Queen; setting her teeth hard together in order to conceal her emotion.

"I will make myself understood, then. Your Majesty remembers that the King was born on the 5th of September, 1638, at a quarter past eleven o'clock."

"Yes," stammered out the Queen.

"At half-past twelve," continued the Béguine, "the Dauphin, who had been baptised by Monseigneur de Meaux in the King's and in your own presence, was acknowledged as the heir of the crown of France. The King then went to the chapel of the old Château de Saint-Germain, to hear the *Te Deum* chanted."

"Quite true, quite true," murmured the Queen.

"Your Majesty's confinement took place in the presence of Monsieur, His Majesty's late uncle, of the princes, and of the ladies attached to the court. The King's physician, Bouvard, and

Honoré,* the surgeon, were stationed in the antechamber; your Majesty slept from three o'clock until seven, I believe!"

"Yes, yes; but you tell me no more than every one else knows as well as you and myself."

"I am now, madame, approaching that which very few persons are acquainted with. Very few persons, did I say, alas! I might almost say two only, for formerly there were but five in all, and, for many years past, the secret has been well preserved by the deaths of the principal participators in it. The late King sleeps now with his ancestors. Péronne, the midwife, soon followed him, Laporte*is already forgotten."

The Queen opened her lips as though about to reply; she felt beneath her icy hand, with which she kept her face half concealed, the beads of perspiration upon her brow.

"It was eight o'clock," pursued the Béguine; "the King was seated at supper, full of joy and happiness; around him on all sides arose wild cries of delight and drinking of healths; the people cheered beneath the balconies; the Swiss guards, the musketeers, and the royal guards wandered through the city, borne about in triumph by the drunken students. Those boisterous sounds of the general joy disturbed the Dauphin, the future King of France, who was quietly lying in the arms of Madame de Hausac,* his nurse, and whose eyes, as he opened them, and stared about, might have observed two crowns at the foot of his cradle. Suddenly, your Majesty uttered a piercing cry, and Dame Péronne immediately flew to your bedside. The doctors were dining in a room at some distance from your chamber; the palace, deserted from the frequency of the irruptions made into it, was without either sentinels or guards, The midwife, having questioned and examined your Majesty, gave a sudden exclamation as if in wild astonishment, and taking you in her arms, bewildered almost out of her senses from sheer distress of mind, despatched Laporte to inform the King that Her Majesty the Queen wished to see him in her room. Laporte, you are aware, madame, was a man of the most admirable calmness and presence of mind. He did not approach the King as if he were the bearer of alarming intelligence and wished to inspire the terror which he himself experienced; besides, it was not a very terrifying intelligence which awaited the King. Therefore, Laporte appeared with a smile upon his lips, and approached the King's chair, saying to him, —'Sire, the Queen is very happy, and would be still more so to see your Majesty.' On that day Louis XIII. would have given his crown away to the veriest beggar for a 'God bless you.' Animated, light-hearted, and full of gaiety, the King rose from the table, and said to those

around him, in a tone that Henry IV. might have adopted,—
'Gentlemen, I am going to see my wife.' He came to your bedside,
madame, at the very moment Dame Péronne presented to him a
second prince, as beautiful and healthy as the former, and said,—
'Sire, Heaven will not allow the kingdom of France to fall into the
female line.' The King, yielding to a first impulse, clasped the
child in his arms, and cried, 'Oh! Heaven, I thank thee!'"

At this part of her recital the Béguine paused, observing how
intensely the Queen was suffering; she had thrown herself back
in her chair, and with her head bent forward and her eyes fixed,
listened without seeming to hear, and her lips moving convulsively,
either breathing a prayer to Heaven or in imprecations against the
woman standing before her.

"Ah! do not believe that, because there could be but one
Dauphin in France," exclaimed the Béguine, "or that if the Queen
allowed that child to vegetate, banished from his royal parents'
presence, she was on that account an unfeeling mother. Oh! no,
no; there are those alive who know the floods of bitter tears she
shed; there are those who have known and witnessed the passionate
kisses she imprinted on that innocent creature in exchange for a
life of misery and gloom to which State policy condemned the
twin brother of Louis XIV."

"Oh! Heaven!" murmured the Queen feebly.

"It is admitted," continued the Béguine, quickly, "that when
the King perceived the effect which would result from the
existence of two sons, both equal in age and pretensions, he
trembled for the welfare of France, for the tranquillity of the State;
and it is equally well known that the Cardinal de Richelieu, by
the direction of Louis XIII., thought over the subject with deep
attention and, after an hour's meditation in His Majesty's cabinet,
he pronounced the following sentence:—'One prince is peace and
safety for the state; two competitors are civil war and anarchy.'"

The Queen rose suddenly from her seat, pale as death, and her
hands clenched together:—"You know too much," she said, in a
hoarse, thick voice, "since you refer to secrets of State. As for the
friends from whom you have acquired this secret, they are false
and treacherous. You are their accomplice in the crime which is
being now committed. Now, throw aside your mask, or I will have
you arrested by my captain of the guards. Do not think that this
secret terrifies me! You have obtained it, you shall restore it to
me. Never shall it leave your bosom, for neither your secret nor
your own life belong to you from this moment."

Anne of Austria, joining gesture to the threat, advanced a
couple of steps towards the Béguine. "Learn," said the latter,

"to know and value the fidelity, the honour, and secrecy of the friends you have abandoned." And, then, suddenly she threw aside her mask.

"Madame de Chevreuse!" exclaimed the Queen.

"With your Majesty, the sole living confidante of this secret."

"Ah!" murmured Anne of Austria; "come and embrace me, Duchesse. Alas! you kill your friend in thus trifling with her terrible distress."

And the Queen, leaning her head upon the shoulder of the old Duchesse, burst into a flood of bitter tears. "How young you are still!" said the latter, in a hollow voice, "you can weep!"

5

TWO FRIENDS

THE Queen looked steadily at Madame de Chevreuse, and said: "I believe you just now made use of the word 'happy' in speaking of me. Hitherto, Duchesse, I had thought it impossible that a human creature could anywhere be found less happy than the Queen of France."

"Your afflictions, madame, have indeed been terrible enough. But by the side of those great and grand misfortunes to which we, two old friends separated by men's malice, were just now alluding, you possess sources of pleasure, slight enough in themselves it may be, but which are greatly envied by the world."

"What are they?" said Anne of Austria bitterly. "What can induce you to pronounce the word 'pleasure,' Duchesse—you, who just now, admitted that my body and my mind both stood in need of remedies."

Madame de Chevreuse collected herself for a moment, and then murmured, "How far removed kings are from other people."

"What do you mean?"

"I mean that they are so far removed from the vulgar herd that they forget that others stand in need of the bare necessaries of life. They are like the inhabitant of the African mountain, who, gazing from the verdant tableland, refreshed by the rills of melted snow, cannot comprehend that the dwellers in the plains below him are perishing from hunger and thirst in the midst of their lands, burned up by the heat of the sun."

The Queen slightly coloured, for she now began to perceive the drift of her friend's remark. "It was very wrong," she said, "to have neglected you."

"Oh! madame, the King I know has inherited the hatred his father bore me. The King would dismiss me if he knew I were in the Palais-Royal."

"I cannot say that the King is very well disposed towards you, Duchesse," replied the Queen; "but I could—secretly, you know——"

The Duchesse's disdainful smile produced a feeling of uneasiness in the Queen's mind. "Duchesse," she hastened to add, "you did perfectly right to come here, even were it only to give us the happiness of contradicting the report of your death."

"Has it been said, then, that I was dead?"

"Everywhere."

"And yet my children did not go into mourning."

"Ah! you know, Duchesse, the court is very frequently moving about from place to place; we see M. Albert de Luynes* but seldom, and many things escape our minds in the midst of the preoccupations which constantly beset us."

"Your Majesty ought not to have believed the report of my death."

"Why not? Alas! we are all mortal; and you may perceive how rapidly I, your younger sister, as we used formerly to say, am approaching the tomb."

"If your Majesty had believed me dead, you ought, in that case, to have been astonished not to have received any news of me."

"Death not infrequently takes us by surprise, Duchesse."

"Oh! your Majesty, those who are burdened with secrets such as we have just now discussed, must, as a necessity of their nature, satisfy their craving desire to divulge them, and they feel they must gratify that desire before they die. Among the various preparations for their final journey, the task of placing their papers in order is not omitted."

The Queen started.

"Your Majesty will be sure to learn, in a particular manner, the day of my death."

"In what way?"

"Because your Majesty will receive the next day, under several coverings, everything connected with our mysterious correspondence of former times."

"Did you not burn them?" cried Anne in alarm.

"Traitors only," replied the Duchesse, "destroy a royal correspondence."

"Traitors, do you say?"

"Yes, certainly, or rather they pretend to destroy, instead of

37

which they keep or sell it. Faithful friends, on the contrary, most carefully secrete such treasures, for it may happen that some day or other they would wish to seek out their Queen in order to say to her: 'Madame, I am getting old; my health is fast failing me; in the presence of the danger of death, for there is the danger for your Majesty that this secret may be revealed; take, therefore, this paper, so fraught with danger for yourself, and trust not to another to burn it for you.'"

"What paper do you refer to?"

"As far as I am concerned, I have but one, it is true, but that is indeed most dangerous in its nature."

"Oh! Duchesse, tell me what it is."

"A letter, dated Tuesday, the 2nd of August, 1644, in which you beg me to go to Noisy-le-Sec, to see that unhappy child. In your own handwriting, madame, there are those words, 'that unhappy child!' "

A profound silence ensued; the Queen's mind was wandering in the past; Madame de Chevreuse was watching the progress of her scheme. "Yes, unhappy, most unhappy," murmured Anne of Austria; "how sad the existence he led, poor child, to finish it in so cruel a manner."

"Is he dead!" cried the Duchesse suddenly, with a curiosity whose sincere accents the Queen instinctively detected.

"He died of consumption, died forgotten, died withered and blighted, like the flowers a lover has given to his mistress, which she leaves to die secreted in a drawer where she had hid them from the gaze of others."

"Died!" repeated the Duchesse with an air of discouragement, which would have afforded the Queen the most unfeigned delight, had it not been tempered in some measure by a mixture of doubt.

"Died—at Noisy-le-Sec?"

"Yes, in the arms of his tutor, a poor, honest man, who did not long survive him."

"That can easily be understood; it is so difficult to bear up under the weight of such a loss and such a secret," said Madame de Chevreuse, the irony of which reflection the Queen pretended not to perceive. Madame de Chevreuse continued: "Well, madame, I inquired some years ago at Noisy-le-Sec about this unhappy child. I was told that it was not believed he was dead, and that was my reason for not having at first been grieved with your Majesty; for, most certainly, if I could have thought it were true, never should I have made the slightest allusion to so deplorable an event, and thus have re-awakened your Majesty's legitimate distress."

"You say that it is not believed that the child died at Noisy?"

"No, madame."

"What did they say about him, then?"

"They said—but, no doubt, they were mistaken——"

"Nay, speak, speak!"

"They said, that, one evening, about the year 1645, a lády, beautiful and majestic in her bearing, which was observed notwithstanding the mask and the mantle which concealed her figure —a lady of rank, of very high rank no doubt—came in a carriage to the place where the road branches off; the very same spot, you know, where I awaited news of the young Prince when your Majesty was graciously pleased to send me there."

"Well, well?"

"That the boy's tutor or guardian took the child to this lady."

"Well, what next?"

"That both the child and his tutor left that part of the country the very next day."

"There, you see there is some truth in what you relate, since, in point of fact, the poor child died from a sudden attack of illness, which makes the lives of all children, as doctors say, suspended as it were by a thread."

"What your Majesty says is quite true; no one knows it better than you—no one believes it more than myself. But yet, how strange it is——"

"What can it now be?" thought the Queen.

"The person who gave me these details, who had been sent to inquire after the child's health——"

"Did you confide such a charge to any one else? Oh, Duchesse!"

"Some one as dumb as your Majesty, as dumb as myself; we will suppose it was myself, madame; this 'some one,' some months after, passing through Touraine——"

"Touraine!"

"Recognised both the tutor and the child, too! I am wrong; he thought he recognised them, both living, cheerful, happy, and flourishing, the one in a green old age, the other in the flower of his youth. Judge after that what truth can be attributed to the rumours which are circulated, or what faith, after that, placed in anything that may happen in the world? But I am fatiguing your Majesty; it was not my intention, however, to do so, and I will take my leave of you, after renewing to you the assurance of my most respectful devotion."

"Stay, Duchesse; let us talk a little about yourself."

"Of myself, madame; I am not worthy that you should bend your looks upon me."

"Why not, indeed? Are you not the oldest friend I have? Are you angry with me, Duchesse?"

"I, indeed! what motive could I have? If I had reason to be angry with your Majesty, should I have come here?"

"Duchesse, age is fast creeping on us both; we should be united against that death whose approach cannot be far off."

"You overpower me, madame, with the kindness of your language."

"No one has ever loved or served me as you have done, Duchesse."

"Your Majesty is too kind in remembering it."

"Not so. Give me a proof of your friendship, Duchesse."

"My whole being is devoted to you, madame."

"The proof I require is, that you should ask something of me."

"Ask——"

"Oh, I know you well,—no one is more disinterested, more noble, and truly royal."

"Do not praise me too highly, madame," said the Duchesse, somewhat anxiously.

"I could never praise you as much as you deserve to be praised."

"And yet, age and misfortune effect a terrible change in people, madame."

"So much the better; for the beautiful, the haughty, the adored Duchesse of former days might have answered me ungratefully, 'I do not wish for anything from you.' Heaven be praised! The misfortunes you speak of have indeed worked a change in you, for you will now, perhaps, answer me, 'I accept.'"

The Duchesse's look and smile soon changed at this conclusion, and she no longer attempted to act a false part.

"Speak, dearest, what do you want?"

"I must first explain to you——"

"Do so unhesitatingly."

"Well, then, your Majesty can confer the greatest, the most ineffable pleasure upon me."

"What is it?" said the Queen, a little distant in her manner, from an uneasiness of feeling produced by this remark. "But do not forget, my good Chevreuse, that I am quite as much under my son's influence as I was formerly under my husband's."

"I will not be too hard, madame."

"Call me as you used to do; it will be a sweet echo of our happy youth."

"Well, then, my dear mistress, my darling Anne——"

"Do you know Spanish still?"

40

"Yes."

"Ask me in Spanish then."

"Will your Majesty do me the honour to pass a few days with me at Dampierre?"

"Is that all?" said the Queen stupefied. "Nothing more than that?"

"Good heavens! can you possibly imagine that in asking you that, I am not asking you the greatest conceivable favour. If that really be the case, you do not know me. Will you accept?"

"Yes, gladly. And I shall be happy," continued the Queen, with some suspicion, "if my presence can in any way be useful to you."

"Useful!" exclaimed the Duchesse, laughing; "oh, no, no, agreeable—delightful, if you like; and you promise me then?"

"I swear it," said the Queen, whereupon the Duchesse seized her beautiful hand, and covered it with kisses. The Queen could not help murmuring to herself, "She is a good-hearted woman, and very generous too."

"Will your Majesty consent to wait a fortnight before you come?"

"Certainly; but why?"

"Because," said the Duchesse, "knowing me to be in disgrace, no one would lend me the hundred thousand francs which I require to put Dampierre into a state of repair. But when it is known that I require that sum for the purpose of receiving your Majesty at Dampierre properly, all the money in Paris will be at my disposal."

"Ah!" said the Queen, gently nodding her head in sign of intelligence, "a hundred thousand francs! you want a hundred thousand francs to put Dampierre into repair?"

"Quite as much as that."

"And no one will lend you them?"

"No one."

"I will lend them to you, if you like, Duchesse."

"Oh, I hardly dare accept such a sum."

"You would be wrong if you did not. Besides, a hundred thousand francs is really not much. I know but too well that you never set a right value upon your silence and your secrecy. Push that table a little towards me, Duchesse, and I will write you an order on M. Colbert; no, on M. Fouquet, who is a far more courteous and obliging man."

"Will he pay it, though?"

"If he will not pay it, I will; but it will be the first time he will have refused me."

The Queen wrote and handed the Duchesse the order, and afterwards dismissed her with a warm and cheerful embrace.

6

HOW JEAN DE LA FONTAINE WROTE HIS FIRST TALE

ALL these intrigues are exhausted; the human mind, so variously complicated, has been enabled to develop itself at its ease in the three outlines with which our recital has supplied it. It is not unlikely that, in the future we are now preparing, a question of politics and intrigues may still arise, but the springs by which they work will be so carefully concealed that no one will be able to see aught but flowers and paintings, just as at a theatre, where a colossus appears upon the scene walking along moved by the small legs and slender arms of a child concealed within the framework.

We now return to Saint-Mandé,* where the Surintendant was in the habit of receiving his select society of epicureans. For some time past, the host had met with some terrible trials. Every one in the house was aware of and felt the minister's distress. No more magnificent or recklessly improvident *réunions*. Money had been the pretext assigned by Fouquet, and never *was* any pretext, as Gourville said, more fallacious, for there was not the slightest appearance of money.

M. Vatel* was most resolutely painstaking in keeping up the reputation of the house, and yet the gardeners who supplied the kitchens complained of a ruinous delay. The agents for the supply of Spanish wines frequently sent drafts which no one honoured; fishermen, whom the Surintendant engaged on the coast of Normandy, calculated that if they were paid all that was due to them, the amount would enable them to retire comfortably for the rest of their lives; fish, which, at a later period, was the cause of Vatel's death, did not arrive at all. However, on the ordinary day of reception, Fouquet's friends flocked in more numerously than ever. Gourville and the Abbé Fouquet* talked over money matters —that is to say, the Abbé borrowed a few pistoles from Gourville; Pélisson, seated with his legs crossed, was engaged in finishing the peroration of a speech with which Fouquet was to open the Parliament; and this speech was a masterpiece, because Pélisson wrote it for his friend—that is to say, he inserted everything in it which the latter would most certainly never have taken the trouble to say of his own accord. Presently Loret and La Fontaine would enter from the garden, engaged in a dispute upon the facility of making verses. The painters and musicians, in their turn, also, were hovering near the dining-room. As soon as eight o'clock struck the supper would be announced, for the Surintendant never kept any one waiting. It was already half-past seven, and the appetites of the guests were beginning to be declared in a very emphatic manner. As soon as all the guests were assembled, Gourville went straight up to Pélisson, awoke him out of his reverie, and led him into the middle of a room, and closed the doors. "Well," he said, "anything new?"

Pélisson raised his intelligent and gentle face, and said, "I have borrowed five-and-twenty thousand francs of my aunt, and I have them here in good sterling money."

"Good," replied Gourville, "we only want one hundred and ninety-five thousand livres for the first payment."

"The payment of what?" asked La Fontaine.

"What! absent as usual! Why, it was you who told us that the small estate at Corbeli was going to be sold by one of M. Fouquet's creditors; and you, also, who proposed that all his friends should subscribe; more than that, too, it was you who said that you would sell a corner of your house at Château-Thierry, in order to furnish your own proportion, and you now come and ask—'*The payment of what?*'"

This remark was received with a general laugh, which made La Fontaine blush. "I beg your pardon," he said "I had not forgotten it; oh, no! only——"

"Only you remembered nothing about it," replied Loret.

"There is the truth; and the fact is, he is quite right; there is a great difference between forgetting and not remembering."

"Well, then," added Pélisson, "you bring your mite in the shape of the price of the piece of land you have sold?"

"Sold? no!"

"Have you not sold the field, then?" inquired Gourville in astonishment, for he knew the poet's disinterestedness.

"My wife would not let me," replied the latter, at which there were fresh bursts of laughter.

"And yet you went to Château-Thierry for that purpose," said some one.

"Certainly, I did, and on horseback."

"Poor fellow!"

"I had eight different horses, and I was almost jolted to death."

"You are an excellent fellow! And you rested yourself when you arrived there?"

43

"Rested! Oh! of course I did, for I had an immense deal of work to do."

"How so?"

"My wife had been flirting with the man to whom I wished to sell the land. The fellow drew back from his bargain, and so I challenged him."

"Very good; and you fought?"

"It seems not."

"You know nothing about it, I suppose?"

"No, my wife and her relations interfered in the matter. I was kept a quarter of an hour with my sword in my hand; but I was not wounded."

"And your adversary?"

"Oh! he just as much, for he never came on to the field."

"Capital!" cried his friends from all sides; "you must have been terribly angry."

"Exceedingly so; I had caught cold; I returned home, and then my wife began to quarrel with me."

"In real earnest?"

"Yes, in real earnest; she threw a loaf of bread at my head, a large loaf."

"And what did you do?"

"Oh! I upset the table over her and her guests; and then I got upon my horse again, and here I am."

Every one had great difficulty in keeping his countenance at the exposure of this heroi-comedy, and when the laughter had somewhat ceased, one of the guests present said to him, "Is that all you have brought us back?"

"Oh, no! I have an excellent idea in my head."

"What is it?"

"Have you noticed that there is a good deal of sportive, jesting poetry written in France?"

"Yes, of course," replied every one.

"And," pursued La Fontaine, "only a very small portion of it is printed."

"The laws are strict, you know."

"That may be, but a rare article is a dear article and that is the reason why I have written a small poem, excessively free in its style, very broad, and extremely cynical in its tone."

"The deuce you have!"

"Yes," continued the poet, with cold indifference, "and I have introduced in it the greatest freedom of language I could possibly employ."

Peals of laughter again broke forth, while the poet was thus announcing the quality of his wares. "And," he continued, "I have tried to exceed everything that Boccacio, Arétin, and other masters of their craft, have written in the same style."

"Its fate is clear," said Pélisson; "it will be scouted and forbidden."

"Do you think so?" said La Fontaine simply; "I assure you, I did not do it on my own account so much as on M. Fouquet's."

This wonderful conclusion again raised the mirth of all present.

"And I have sold the first edition of this little book for eight hundred livres," exclaimed La Fontaine, rubbing his hands together. "Serious and religious books sell at about half that rate."

"It would have been better," said Gourville, "to have written two religious books instead."

"It would have been too long and not amusing enough," replied La Fontaine tranquilly; "my eight hundred livres are in this little bag, and I beg to offer them as my contribution."

As he said this, he placed his offering in the hands of their treasurer; it was then Loret's turn, who gave a hundred and fifty livres; the others stripped themselves in the same way; and the total sum in the purse amounted to forty thousand livres. The money was still being counted over when the Surintendant noiselessly entered the room; he had heard everything; and then this man, who had possessed so many millions, who had exhausted all the pleasures and honours that this world had to bestow, this generous heart, this inexhaustible brain, which had, like two burning crucibles, devoured the material and moral substance of the first kingdom in the world, was seen to cross the threshold with his eyes filled with tears, and pass his fingers through the gold and silver which the bag contained.

"Poor offering," he said, in a softened and affected tone of voice; "you will disappear in the smallest corner of my empty purse, but you have filled to overflowing that which no one can ever exhaust, my heart. Thank you, my friends—thank you." And as he could not embrace everyone present, who were all weeping a little, philosophers as they were, he embraced La Fontaine, saying to him, "Poor fellow! so you have, on my account, been beaten by your wife and censured by your confessor."

"Oh! it is a mere nothing," replied the poet; "if your creditors will only wait a couple of years, I shall have written a hundred other tales, which, at two editions each, will pay off the debt."

7

LA FONTAINE IN THE CHARACTER OF A NEGOTIATOR

FOUQUET pressed La Fontaine's hand most warmly, saying to him, "My dear poet, write a hundred other tales, not only for the eighty pistoles which each of them will produce you, but, still more, to enrich our language with a hundred other masterpieces of composition."

"Oh! oh!" said La Fontaine, with a little air of pride "you must not suppose that I have only brought this idea and the eighty pistoles to the Surintendant."

"Oh! indeed," was the general acclamation from all parts of the room. "M. de la Fontaine is in funds to-day."

"Heaven bless the idea, if it only brings us one or two millions," said Fouquet gaily.

"Exactly," replied La Fontaine.

"Quick, quick!" cried the assembly.

"Take care," said Pélisson in La Fontaine's ear; "you have had a most brilliant success up to the present moment, so do not go too far."

"Not at all, Monsieur Pélisson; and you, who are a man of decided taste, will be the first to approve of what I have done."

"We are talking of millions, remember," said Gourville.

"I have fifteen hundred thousand francs here, Monsieur Gourville," he replied, striking himself on the chest.

"The deuce take this Gascon from Château-Thierry!" cried Loret.

"It is not the pocket you should touch, but the brain," said Fouquet.

"Stay a moment, Monsieur le Surintendant," added La Fontaine; "you are not Procureur-Général—you are a poet."

"True, true!" cried Loret, Conrart, and every person present connected with literature.

"You are, I repeat, a poet, and a painter, a sculptor, a friend of the arts and sciences, but, acknowledge that you are no lawyer."

"Oh! I do acknowledge it," replied M. Fouquet smiling.

"If you were to be nominated at the Academy,* you would refuse, I think."

"I think I should, with all due deference to the academicians."

"Very good; if therefore you do not wish to belong to the

Academy, why do you allow yourself to form one of the Parliament?"

"Oh! oh!" said Pélisson, "we are talking politics."

"I wish to know whether the barrister's gown does or does not become M. Fouquet."

"There is no question of the gown at all," retorted Pélisson, annoyed at the laughter of those who were present.

"On the contrary, it is the gown," said Loret.

"Take the gown away from the Procureur-Général," said Conrart, "and we have M. Fouquet left us still, of whom we have no reason to complain; but, as he is no Procureur-Général without his gown, we agree with M. de la Fontaine, and pronounce the gown to be nothing but a bugbear."

"*Fugiunt risus leporesque*,"* said Loret.

"The smiles and the graces," said some one present.

"That is not the way," said Pélisson gravely, "that I translate *lepores*."

"How do you translate it?" said La Fontaine.

"Thus: The hares run away as soon as they see M. Fouquet." A burst of laughter, in which the Surintendant joined, followed this sally.

"But why hares?" objected Conrart, vexed.

"Because the hare will be the very one who will not be over-pleased to see M. Fouquet surrounded by all the attributes which his Parliamentary strength and power confer on him."

"Oh! oh!" murmured the poets.

"*Quo non ascendant*,"* said Conrart, "seems impossible to me, when one is fortunate enough to wear the gown of the Procureur-Général."

"On the contrary, it seems so to me without that gown," said the obstinate Pélisson; "what is your opinion, Gourville?"

"I think the gown in question is a very good thing," replied the latter; "but I equally think a million and a half is far better than the gown."

"And I am of Gourville's opinion," exclaimed Fouquet, stopping the discussion by the expression of his own opinion, which would necessarily bear down all the others.

"A million and a half," Pélisson grumbled out; "now I happen to know an Indian fable*——"

"Tell it me," said La Fontaine; "I ought to know it, too."

"Tell it, tell it," said the others.

"There was a tortoise, which was as usual well protected by its shell," said Pélisson; "whenever its enemies threatened it, it took refuge within its covering. One day some one said to it,

'You must feel very hot in such a house as that in the summer, and you are altogether prevented showing off your graces; there is a snake here, who will give you a million and a half for your shell.' "

"Good!" said the Surintendant, laughing.

"Well, what next?" said La Fontaine, much more interested in the apologue than its moral.

"The tortoise sold his shell and remained naked and defenceless. A vulture happened to see him and, being hungry, broke the tortoise's back with a blow of his beak and devoured it. The moral is, that M. Fouquet should take very good care to keep his gown."

La Fontaine understood the moral seriously. "You forget Eschylus," he said to his adversary.

"What do you mean?"

"Eschylus* was bald-headed, and a vulture—your vulture probably—who was a great amateur in tortoises, mistook at a distance his head for a block of stone, and let a tortoise, which was shrunk up in his shell, fall upon it."

"Yes, yes, La Fontaine is right," resumed Fouquet, who had become very thoughtful; "whenever a vulture wishes to devour a tortoise, he well knows how to break his shell; and but too happy is that tortoise which a snake pays a million and a half for his envelope. If any one were to bring me a generous-hearted snake like the one in your fable, Pélisson, I would give him my shell."

"*Rara avis interris!*"*cried Conrart.

"And like a black swan, is he not?" added La Fontaine; "well, then, the bird in question, black and very rare, is already found."

"Do you mean to say that you have found a purchaser for my post of procureur-général?" exclaimed Fouquet.

"I have, monsieur."

"But the Surintendant never said that he wished to sell," resumed Pélisson.

"I beg your pardon," said Conrart, "you yourself spoke about it, even——"

"Yes, I am a witness to that," said Gourville.

"He seems very tenacious about his brilliant idea," said Fouquet, laughing. "Well, La Fontaine, who is the purchaser?"

"A perfectly black bird, for he is a counsellor belonging to the Parliament, an excellent fellow."

"What is his name?"

"Vanel."

"Vanel!" exclaimed Fouquet, "Vanel, the husband of——"

"Precisely, her husband; yes, monsieur."

"Poor fellow!" said Fouquet, with an expression of great interest.

"He wishes to be everything that you have been, monsieur," said Gourville, "and to do everything that you have done."

"It is very agreeable; tell us all about it, La Fontaine."

"It is very simple. I see him occasionally, and a short time ago I met him, walking about on the Place de la Bastille, at the very moment when I was about to take the small carriage to come down here to Saint-Mandé."

"He must have been watching his wife," interrupted Loret.

"Oh, no!" said Fouquet, "he is far from being jealous. He accosted me, embraced me, and took me to the inn called L'Image Saint-Fiacre, and told me all about his troubles."

"He has his troubles, then?"

"Yes; his wife wants to make him ambitious."

"Well, and he told you——"

"That some one had spoken to him about a post in the Parliament; that M. Fouquet's name had been mentioned; that ever since, Madame Vanel dreams of nothing else but being called Madame le Procureuse-Générale, and that it makes her ill and keeps her awake every night she does not dream of it."

"The deuce!"

"Poor woman!" said Fouquet.

"Wait a moment. Conrart is always telling me that I do not know how to conduct matters of business; you will see how I managed this one."

"Well, go on."

" 'I suppose you know,' said I to Vanel, 'that the value of a post such as that which M. Fouquet holds is by no means trifling.' "

" 'How much do you imagine it to be?' he said."

" 'M. Fouquet, I know, has refused seventeen hundred thousand francs.' "

" 'My wife,' replied Vanel, 'had estimated it at about fourteen hundred thousand.' "

" 'Ready money?' I asked."

" 'Yes; she has sold some property of hers in Guienne, and has received the purchase-money.' "

"That's a pretty sum to touch all at once," said the Abbé Fouquet, who had not hitherto said a word.

"Poor Madame Vanel!" murmured Fouquet.

Pélisson shrugged his shoulders, as he whispered in Fouquet's ear, "That woman is a perfect fiend."

"That may be; and it will be delightful to make use of this fiend's money to repair the injury which an angel has done herself for me."

Pélisson looked with a surprised air at Fouquet, whose thoughts were from that moment fixed upon a fresh object in view.

"Well!" inquired La Fontaine, "what about my negotiation?"

"Admirable, my dear poet."

"Yes," said Gourville; "but there are some people who are anxious to have the steed who have not money enough to pay for the bridle."

"And Vanel would draw back from his offer if he were to be taken at his word," continued the Abbé Fouquet.

"I do not believe it," said La Fontaine.

"What do you know about it?"

"Why, you have not yet heard the *dénouement* of my story."

"If there is a *dénouement* why do you beat about the bush so much?"

"*Semper ad eventum.* Is that correct?" said Fouquet, with the air of a nobleman who condescends to barbarisms. To which the Latinists present answered with loud applause.

"My *dénouement*," cried La Fontaine, "is, that Vanel, that determined blackbird, knowing that I was coming to Saint-Mandé, implored me to bring him with me, and, if possible, to present him to M. Fouquet."

"So that——"

"So that he is here; I left him in that part of the grounds called Bel-Air. Well, M. Fouquet, what is your reply?"

"Well, it is not respectful towards Madame Vanel that her husband should run the risk of catching cold outside my house; send for him, La Fontaine, since you know where he is."

"I will go there myself."

"And I will accompany you," said the Abbé Fouquet; "I can carry the money bags."

"No jesting," said Fouquet seriously; "let the business be a serious one, if it is to be one at all. But first of all, let us show we are hospitable. Make my apologies, La Fontaine, to M. Vanel, and tell him how distressed I am to have kept him waiting, but that I was not aware he was there."

La Fontaine set off at once, fortunately accompanied by Gourville, for, absorbed in his own calculations, the poet would have mistaken the route, and was hurrying as fast as he could towards the village of Saint-Mandé. Within a quarter of an hour afterwards, M. Vanel was introduced into the Surintendant's cabinet. When Fouquet saw him enter, he called to Pélisson, and whispered a few words in his ear. "Do not lose a word of what I am going to say: let all the silver and gold plate, together with the jewels of every description, be packed up in the carriage. You will take the black horses; the jeweller will accompany you; and you will post-pone the supper until Madame de Bellière*'s arrival."

"Will it be necessary to inform Madame de Bellière of it?" said Pélisson.

"No; that will be useless; I will do that. So, away with you, my dear friend."

Pélisson set off, not quite clear as to his friend's meaning or intention, but confident, like every true friend, in the judgment of the man he was blindly obeying. It is that which constitutes the strength of such men; distrust only arises in the minds of inferior natures.

Vanel bowed low to the Surintendant, and was about to begin a speech.

"Do not trouble yourself, monsieur," said Fouquet politely; "I am told that you wish to purchase a post I hold. How much can you give me for it?"

"It is for you, monseigneur, to fix the amount you require. I know that offers of purchase have already been made to you for it."

"Madame Vanel, I have been told, values it at fourteen hundred thousand livres."

"That is all we have."

"Can you give me the money immediately?"

"I have not the money with me," said Vanel, frightened almost by the unpretending simplicity, amounting to greatness, of the man, for he had expected disputes, and difficulties, and opposition of every kind.

"When will you be able to have it?"

"Whenever you please, monseigneur"; for he began to be afraid that Fouquet was trifling with him.

"If it were not for the trouble you would have in returning to Paris, I would say at once; but we will arrange that the payment and the signature shall take place at six o'clock to-morrow morning."

"Very good," said Vanel, as cold as ice, and feeling quite bewildered.

"*Adieu*, Monsieur Vanel, present my humble respects to Madame Vanel," said Fouquet, as he rose; upon which Vanel, who felt the blood rushing up to his head, for he was quite con-founded by his success, said seriously to the Surintendant, "Will you give me your word, monseigneur, upon this affair?"

Fouquet turned round his head, saying "*Pardieu*, and you, monsieur?"

Vanel hesitated, trembled all over, and at last finished by hesitatingly holding out his hand. Fouquet opened and nobly extended his own; this loyal hand lay for a moment in Vanel's moist hypocritical palm, and he pressed it in his own, in order the better to convince himself of its truth. The Surintendant gently disengaged his hand as he again said "*Adieu.*" And then Vanel ran hastily to the door, hurried along the vestibules, and fled away as quickly as he could.

8

MADAME DE BELLIÈRE'S PLATE AND DIAMONDS

HARDLY had Fouquet dismissed Vanel, than he began to reflect for a few moments:—"A man never can do too much for the woman he has once loved. Marguerite wishes to be the wife of a procureur-général—and why not confer this pleasure upon her? And, now that the most scrupulous and sensitive conscience will be unable to reproach me with anything, let my thoughts be bestowed on her who has shown so much devotion for me. Madame de Bellière ought to be there by this time," he said, as he turned towards the secret door.

After he had locked himself in, he opened the subterranean passage, and rapidly hastened towards the means of communicating between the house at Vincennes and his own residence. He had neglected to apprise his friend of his approach, by ringing the bell, perfectly assured that she would never fail to be exact at the rendezvous; as, indeed, was the case, for she was already waiting. The noise the Surintendant made aroused her; she ran to take from under the door the letter that he had thrust there, and which simply said, "Come, marquise; we are waiting supper for you." With her heart filled with happiness Madame de Bellière ran to her carriage in the Avenue de Vincennes, and in a few minutes she was holding out her hand to Gourville, who was standing at the entrance, where, in order the better to please his master, he had stationed himself to watch her arrival. She had not observed that Fouquet's black horses had arrived at the same time, smoking and covered with foam, having returned to Saint-Mandé with Pélisson and the very jeweller to whom Madame de Bellière had sold her plate and her jewels. Pélisson introduced the goldsmith into the cabinet, which Fouquet had not yet left. The Surintendant thanked him for having been good enough to regard as a simple deposit in his hands the valuable property which he had every right to sell; and he cast his eyes on the total of the account, which amounted to thirteen hundred thousand francs. Then, going for a few moments to his desk, he wrote an order for fourteen hundred thousand francs, payable at sight, at his treasury, before twelve o'clock the next day.

"A hundred thousand francs profit!" cried the goldsmith. "Oh, monseigneur, what generosity!"

"Nay, nay, not so, monsieur," said Fouquet, touching him on the shoulder; "there are certain kindnesses which can never be repaid. The profit is about that which you would have made; but the interest of your money still remains to be arranged." And, saying this, he unfastened from his sleeve a diamond button, which the goldsmith himself had often valued at three thousand pistoles. "Take this," he said to the goldsmith, "in remembrance of me. And farewell; you are an honest man."

"And you, monseigneur," cried the goldsmith, completely overcome, "are the noblest man that ever lived."

Fouquet let the worthy goldsmith pass out of the room by a secret door, and then went to receive Madame de Bellière, who was already surrounded by all the guests. The Marquise was always beautiful, but now her loveliness was more dazzling than ever. "Do you not think, gentlemen," said Fouquet, "that Madame is more than usually beautiful this evening? And do you happen to know why?"

"Because Madame is really the most beautiful of all women," said some one present.

"No; but because she is the best. And yet——"

"Yet?" said the Marquise, smiling.

"And yet, all the jewels which Madame is wearing this evening are nothing but false stones." At this remark the Marquise blushed most painfully.

"Oh, oh!" exclaimed all the guests, "that can very well be said of one who has the finest diamonds in Paris."

"Well?" said Fouquet to Pélisson, in a low tone.

"Well, at last I have understood you," returned the latter; "and you have done excellently well."

"Supper is ready, monseigneur," said Vatel, with majestic air and tone.

The crowd of guests hurried, less slowly than is usually the case with ministerial entertainments, towards the banqueting-room, where a magnificent spectacle presented itself. Upon the buffets, upon the side-tables, upon the supper-table itself, in the midst of the flowers and light, glittered most dazzlingly the richest and most costly gold and silver plate that could possibly be seen—relics of those ancient magnificent productions which the Florentine artists, whom the Medici family had patronised, had sculptured, chased and cast for the purpose of holding flowers, at the time when gold yet existed in France. These hidden marvels, which had been buried during the civil wars, had timidly reappeared during the intervals of that war of good taste called La Fronde: at a time when noblemen fighting against noblemen, killed but did not pillage each other. All the plate present had Madame de Bellière's arms engraved upon it. "Look," cried La Fontaine, "here is a P. and a B."

But the most remarkable object present was the cover which Fouquet had assigned to the Marquise. Near her was a pyramid of diamonds, sapphires, emeralds, antique cameos, sardonyx stones, carved by the old Greeks of Asia Minor, with mountings of Mysian gold; curious mosaics of ancient Alexandria, mounted in silver; massive Egyptian bracelets lay heaped up in a large plate of Palissy ware, supported by a tripod of gilt bronze which had been sculptured by Benvenuto.* The Marquise turned pale, as she recognised what she had never expected to see again. A profound silence seemed to seize upon every one of the restless and excited guests. Fouquet did not even make a sign in dismissal of the richly-liveried servants who crowded like bees round the huge buffets and other tables in the room. "Gentlemen," he said, "all this plate which you behold once belonged to Madame de Bellière, who, having observed one of her friends in great distress, sent all this gold and silver, together with the heap of jewels now before her, to her goldsmith. This noble conduct of a devoted friend can well be understood by such friends as you. Happy indeed is that man who sees himself loved in such a manner. Let us drink to the health of Madame de Bellière."

A tremendous burst of applause followed his words; and made poor Madame de Bellière sink back dumb and breathless on her seat. "And then," added Pélisson, who was always affected by a noble action, as he was invariably impressed by beauty, "let us also drink to the health of him who inspired Madame's noble conduct; for such a man is worthy of being worthily loved."

It was now the Marquise's turn. She rose, pale and smiling; and as she held out her glass with her faltering hand, and her trembling fingers touched those of Fouquet, her look, full of love, found its reflection and response in that of her ardent and generous-hearted lover. Begun in this manner, the supper soon became a fête; no one tried to be witty, for no one failed in being so. La Fontaine forgot his Gorgny wine,* and allowed Vatel to reconcile him to the wines of the Rhône, and those from the shores of Spain. The Abbé Fouquet became so kind and good-natured that Gourville said to him, "Take care, Abbé; if you are so tender, you will be eaten."

The hours passed away so joyously, that, contrary to his usual custom, the Surintendant did not leave the table before the end of the dessert. He smiled upon his friends, delighted as a man is, whose heart becomes intoxicated before his head—and, for the first time, he had just looked at the clock. Suddenly, a carriage rolled into the courtyard, and, strange to say, it was heard high above the noise of the mirth which prevailed. Fouquet listened attentively, and then turned his eyes towards the antechamber. It seemed as if he could hear a step passing across it, and that this step, instead of pressing the ground, weighed heavily upon his heart. "M. d'Herblay Bishop of Vannes," the usher announced. And Aramis's grave and thoughtful face appeared upon the threshold of the door, between the remains of two garlands, of which the flame of a lamp had just burned the thread that had united them.

9

M. DE MAZARIN'S RECEIPT

FOUQUET would have uttered an exclamation of delight on seeing another friend arrive, if the cold air and averted aspect of Aramis had not restored all his reserve. "Are you going to join us at our dessert?" he asked. "And yet you would be frightened, perhaps, at the noise which our wild friends here are making."

"Monseigneur," replied Aramis respectfully, "I will begin by begging you to excuse me for having interrupted this merry meeting; and then, I will beg you to give me, as soon as pleasure shall have finished, a moment's audience on matters of business."

As the word "business" had roused the attention of some of the epicureans present, Fouquet rose, saying: "Business first of all, Monsieur d'Herblay; we are too happy when matters of business arrive only at the end of a meal."

As he said this, he took the hand of Madame de Bellière, who looked at him with a kind of uneasiness, and then led her to an adjoining *salon*, after having recommended her to the most reasonable of his guests. And then, taking Aramis by the arm, he led him towards his cabinet. As soon as Aramis was there, throwing aside the respectful air he had assumed, he threw himself into a chair, saying: "Guess whom I have seen this evening?"

"My dear Chevalier, every time you begin in that manner, I am sure to hear you announce something disagreeable."

"Well, and this time you will not be mistaken, either, my dear friend," replied Aramis.

"Do not keep me in suspense," added Fouquet phlegmatically.

"Well, then, I have seen Madame de Chevreuse."

"The old Duchesse, do you mean?"

"Yes."

"Her ghost, perhaps?"

"No, no; the old she-wolf herself."

"Without teeth?"

"Possibly, but not without claws."

"Well! what harm can she meditate against me? I am no miser with women who are not prudes. That is a quality that is always prized, even by the woman who no longer dares to provoke love."

"Madame de Chevreuse knows very well that you are not avaricious, since she wishes to draw some money out of you."

"Indeed! under what pretext?"

"Oh! pretexts are never wanting with her. Let me tell you what hers is; it seems that the Duchesse has a good many letters of M. de Mazarin's in her possession."

"I am not surprised at that, for the prelate was gallant enough."

"Yes, but these letters have nothing whatever to do with the prelate's love affairs. They concern, it is said, financial matters rather."

"And accordingly they are less interesting."

"Do you not suspect what I mean?"

"Not at all."

"Have you never heard speak of a prosecution being instituted for an embezzlement, or appropriation rather, of public funds?"

"Yes, a hundred, nay, a thousand times. Ever since I have been engaged in public matters I have hardly ever heard anything else but that. It is precisely your own case, when, as a bishop, people reproach you for your impiety; or, as a musketeer, for your cowardice; the very thing of which they are always accusing ministers of finance, is the embezzlement of public funds."

"Very good; but take a particular instance, for the Duchesse asserts that M. de Mazarin alludes to certain particular instances."

"What are they?"

"Something like a sum of thirteen millions of francs, of which it would be very difficult for you to define the precise nature of the employment."

"Thirteen millions!" said the Surintendant, stretching himself in his arm-chair, in order to enable him the more comfortably to

56

look up towards the ceiling. "Thirteen millions—I am trying to remember them out of all those I have been accused of having stolen."

"Do not laugh, my dear monsieur, for it is very serious. It is positive that the Duchesse has certain letters in her possession, and that these letters must be as she represents them, since she wished to sell them to me for five hundred thousand francs."

"Oh! one can have a very tolerable calumny got up for such a sum as that," replied Fouquet. "Ah! now I know what you mean," and he began to laugh heartily.

"So much the better," said Aramis, a little reassured.

"I remember the story of those thirteen millions, now. Yes, yes, I remember them quite well."

"I am delighted to hear it; tell me about them."

"Well, then, one day Signor Mazarin, Heaven rest his soul! made a profit of thirteen millions upon a concession of lands in the Valtelline; he cancelled them in the registry of receipts, sent them to me, and then made me advance them to him for war expenses."

"Very good, then, there is no doubt of their proper destination."

"No; the Cardinal made me invest them in my own name, and gave me a receipt."

"You have the receipt?"

"Of course," said Fouquet, as he quietly rose from his chair, and went to his large ebony bureau inlaid with mother-of-pearl and gold.

"What I most admire in you," said Aramis, with an air of great satisfaction, "is, your memory in the first place, then your self-possession, and, finally, the perfect order which prevails in your administration; you of all men, too, who are by nature a poet."

"Yes," said Fouquet, "I am orderly out of a spirit of idleness, to save myself the trouble of looking after things, and so I know that Mazarin's receipt is in the third drawer under the letter M; I open the drawer, and place my hand upon the very paper I need. In the night without a light I could find it."

And with a confident hand he felt the bundle of papers which were piled up in the open drawer. "Nay, more than that," he continued, "I remember the paper as if I saw it; it is thick, somewhat crumpled, with gilt edges; Mazarin had made a blot upon the figure of the date. Ah!" he said, "the paper knows we are talking about it, and that we want it very much, and so it hides itself out of the way." And as the Surintendant looked into the drawer, Aramis rose from his seat.

"This is very singular," said Fouquet.

57

"Your memory is treacherous, my dear monseigneur; look in another drawer."

Fouquet took out the bundle of papers, and turned them over once more; he then became very pale.

"Don't confine your search to that drawer," said Aramis; "look elsewhere."

"Quite useless; I have never made a mistake; no one but myself arranges any papers of mine of this nature; no one but myself ever opens this drawer, of which, besides, no one, with my own exception, is aware of the secret."

"What do you conclude, then?" said Aramis, agitated.

"That Mazarin's receipt has been stolen from me; Madame de Chevreuse was right, Chevalier; I have appropriated the public funds; I have robbed the state coffers of thirteen millions of money; I am a thief, Monsieur d'Herblay."

"Nay, nay, do not get irritated—do not get excited."

"But, why not, Chevalier? surely there is every reason for it. If the legal proceedings are well arranged, and a judgment is given in accordance with them, your friend the Surintendant can follow to Montfauçon*his colleague Enguerrand de Marigny, and his predecessor, Semblançay."

"Oh!" said Aramis, smiling, "not so fast as that."

"And why not? why not so fast? What do you suppose Madame de Chevreuse will have done with those letters, for you refused them, I suppose?"

"Yes; at once. I suppose that she went and sold them to M. Colbert."

"Well?"

"I said I supposed so; I might have said I was sure of it, for I had her followed, and when she left me, she returned to her own house, went out by a back door, and proceeded straight to the Intendant's house."

"Legal proceedings will be instituted then, scandal and dishonour will follow, and all will fall upon me like a thunderbolt, blindly, harshly, pitilessly."

Aramis approached Fouquet, who sat trembling in his chair, close to the open drawers; he placed his hand on his shoulder, and, in an affectionate tone of voice, said: "Do not forget that the position of M. Fouquet can in no way be compared to that of Semblançay or of Marigny."

"And why not, in Heaven's name?"

"Because the proceedings against those ministers were determined, completed, and the sentence carried out, whilst in your case the same thing cannot take place."

"Another blow, why not? A peculator is, under any circumstances, a criminal."

"Those criminals who know how to find a safe asylum are never in danger."

"What! make my escape! Fly!"

"No! I do not mean that; you forget that all such proceedings originate in the Parliament, that they are instituted by the Procureur-Général, and that you are Procureur-Général. You see that unless you wish to condemn yourself——"

"Oh!" cried Fouquet, suddenly, dashing his fist upon the table.

"Well! What? what is the matter?"

"I am Procureur-Général no longer."

Aramis at this reply became as livid as death; he pressed his hands together convulsively, and with a wild, haggard look, which almost annihilated Fouquet, he said, laying a stress upon every distinct syllable. "You are Procureur-Général no longer; do you say?"

"No."

"Since when?"

"Since the last four or five hours."

"Take care," interrupted Aramis coldly; "I do not think you are in the full possession of your senses, my friend; collect yourself."

"I tell you," returned Fouquet, "that a little while ago some one came to me, brought by my friends, to offer me fourteen hundred thousand francs for the appointment, and that I sold the appointment."

Aramis looked as if he had been thunder-stricken; the intelligent and mocking expression of his countenance assumed an aspect of such profound gloom and terror, that it had more effect upon the Surintendant than all the exclamations and speeches in the world. "You had need of money, then?" he said.

"Yes; to discharge a debt of honour." And in a few words, he gave Aramis an account of Madame de Bellière's generosity, and the manner in which he had thought it but right to discharge that act of generosity.

"Yes," said Aramis, "that is, indeed, a fine trait. What has it cost?"

"Exactly the fourteen hundred thousand francs—the price of my appointment."

"Which you received in that manner, without reflection. Oh! imprudent man."

"I have not yet received the amount, but I shall to-morrow."

"It is not yet completed, then?"

"It must be carried out, though; for I have given the goldsmith,

59

for twelve o'clock to-morrow, an order upon my treasury, into which the purchaser's money will be paid at six or seven o'clock."

"Heaven be praised!" cried Aramis, clapping his hands together, "nothing is yet completed, since you have not been paid."

"But the goldsmith?"

"You shall receive the fourteen hundred thousand francs from me, at a quarter before twelve."

"Stay a moment; it is at six o'clock, this very morning, that I am to sign."

"Oh! I will answer that you do not sign."

"I have given my word, Chevalier."

"If you have given it, you will take it back again, that is all."

"Can I believe what I hear?" cried Fouquet, in a most expressive tone. "Fouquet recall his word, after it has been once pledged?"

Aramis replied to the almost stern look of the minister by a look full of anger. "Monsieur," he said, "I believe I have deserved to be called a man of honour? As a soldier I have risked my life five hundred times; as a priest I have rendered still greater services, both to the State and to my friends. The value of a word, once passed, is estimated according to the worth of the man who gives it. So long as it is in his own keeping, it is of the purest, finest gold; when his wish to keep it has passed away, it is a two-edged sword. With that word, therefore, he defends himself as with an honourable weapon, considering that when he disregards his word he endangers his life, and incurs an amount of risk far greater than that which his adversary is likely to derive of profit. In such a case, monsieur, he appeals to Heaven and to justice."

Fouquet bent down his head, as he replied, "I am a poor, self-determined man, a true Breton born; my mind admires and fears yours. I do not say that I keep my word from a proper feeling only; I keep it, if you like, from custom, practice, what you will. But at all events, the ordinary run of men are simple enough to admire this custom of mine: it is my sole good quality, leave me such honour as it confers."

"And so you are determined to sign the sale of the very appointment which can alone defend you against all your enemies."

"Yes, I shall sign."

"You will deliver yourself up, then, bound hand and foot, from a false notion of honour, which the most scrupulous causists would disdain?"

"I shall sign," repeated Fouquet.

Aramis sighed deeply, and looked all round him with the impatient gesture of a man who would gladly dash something to pieces, as a relief to his feelings. "We have still one means left," he said; "and, I trust, you will not refuse to make use of that."

"Certainly not, if it be loyal and honourable; as everything is, in fact, which you propose."

"I know nothing more loyal than the renunciation of your purchaser. Is he a friend of yours?"

"Certainly; but——"

"'But!'—if you allow me to manage the affair, I do not despair."

"Oh! you shall be absolutely master to do what you please."

"Whom are you in treaty with? What man is it?"

"I am not aware whether you know the Parliament."

"Most of its members. One of the presidents, perhaps?"

"No; only a counsellor, of the name of Vanel."

Aramis became perfectly purple. "Vanel," he cried, rising abruptly from his seat; "Vanel! the husband of Marguerite Vanel."

"Exactly."

"Of your former mistress?"

"Yes, my dear fellow; she is anxious to be the wife of the Procureur-Général. I certainly owed poor Vanel that slight concession, and I am a gainer by it; since I, at the same time, can confer a pleasure on his wife."

Aramis walked up straight to Fouquet, and took hold of his hand. "Do you know," he said very calmly, "the name of Madame Vanel's new lover?"

"Ah! she has a new lover, then: I was not aware of it; no. I have no idea what his name is."

"His name is M. Jean-Baptiste Colbert; he is Intendant of the Finances; he lives in the Rue Croix-des-Petits-Champs, where Madame de Chevreuse has been this evening to take him Mazarin's letters, which she wishes to sell."

"Gracious Heaven!" murmured Fouquet, passing his hand across his forehead, from which the perspiration was starting.

"You now begin to understand, do you not."

"That I am utterly lost!—yes."

"Do you now think it worth while to be so scrupulous with regard to keeping your word?"

"Yes," said Fouquet.

"These obstinate people always contrive matters in such a way that we cannot but admire them all the while," murmured Aramis.

Fouquet held out his hand to him, and at the very moment a richly-ornamented tortoise-shell clock, supported by golden figures, which was standing on a console table opposite to the fireplace, struck six. The sound of a door being opened in the vestibule was heard, and Gourville came to the door of the cabinet to inquire if Fouquet would receive M. Vanel. Fouquet turned his eyes from the eyes of Aramis, and then desired that M. Vanel should be shown in to him.

10

MONSIEUR COLBERT'S ROUGH DRAFT

VANEL, who entered at this stage of the conversation, was nothing less for Aramis and Fouquet than the full stop which completes a phrase. But, for Vanel, Aramis's presence in Fouquet's cabinet had quite another signification; and, therefore, at his first step into the room, he paused as he looked at the delicate yet firm features of the Bishop of Vannes, and his look of astonishment soon became one of scrutinising attention. As for Fouquet, a perfect politician, that is to say, complete master of himself, he had already, by the energy of his own resolute will, contrived to remove from his face all traces of the emotion which Aramis's revelation had occasioned. He was no longer, therefore, a man overwhelmed by misfortune and reduced to resort to expedients; he held his head proudly erect, and indicated by a gesture that Vanel could enter. He was now the first minister of the State, and in his own palace. Aramis knew the Surintendant well; the delicacy of the feelings of his heart and the exalted nature of his mind could not any longer surprise him. He confined himself, then, for the moment—intending to resume later an active part in the conversation—to the performance of the difficult part of a man who looks on and listens, in order to learn and understand. Vanel was visibly overcome, and advanced into the middle of the cabinet, bowing to everything and everybody. "I am come," he said.

"You are exact, Monsieur Vanel," returned Fouquet.

"In matters of business, monseigneur," returned Vanel, "I look upon exactitude as a virtue."

"No doubt, monsieur."

"I beg your pardon," interrupted Aramis, indicating Vanel with his finger, but addressing himself to Fouquet; "this is the gentleman, I believe, who has come about the purchase of your appointment?"

"Yes, I am!" replied Vanel, astonished at the extremely haughty tone with which Aramis had put the question; "but in what way am I to address you, who do me the honour——"

"Call me monseigneur," replied Aramis dryly. Vanel bowed.

"Come, gentlemen, a truce to these ceremonies; let us proceed to the matter itself."

"Monseigneur sees," said Vanel, "that I am waiting your pleasure."

"On the contrary, I am waiting," replied Fouquet.

"What for, may I be permitted to ask, monseigneur?"

"I thought that you had perhaps something to say."

"Oh," said Vanel to himself, "he has reflected on the matter, and I am lost." But resuming his courage, he continued, "No, monseigneur, nothing, absolutely nothing more than what I said to you yesterday, and which I am again ready to repeat to you now."

"Come, now, tell me frankly, Monsieur Vanel, is not the affair rather a burdensome one for you?"

"Certainly, monseigneur; fourteen hundred thousand francs is an important sum."

"So important, indeed," said Fouquet, "that I have re-flected——"

"You have been reflecting, do you say, monseigneur?" exclaimed Vanel anxiously.

"Yes; that you might not yet be in a position to purchase."

"Oh, monseigneur!"

"Do not make yourself uneasy on that score, Monsieur Vanel; I shall not blame you for a failure in your word, which evidently may arise from inability on your part."

"Oh, yes, monseigneur, you would blame me, and you would be right in doing so," said Vanel; "for a man must either be very imprudent, or a perfect fool, to undertake engagements which he cannot keep; and I at least have always regarded a thing agreed upon as a thing actually carried out."

Fouquet coloured, while Aramis uttered a "Hum!" of impatience.

"You would be wrong to exaggerate such notions as those, monsieur," said the Surintendant; "for a man's mind is variable, and full of these very excusable caprices, which are, however, sometimes estimable enough; and a man may have wished for something yesterday of which he repents to-day."

Vanel felt a cold sweat trickle down his face. "Monseigneur!" he muttered.

Aramis, who was delighted to find the Surintendant carry on the debate with such clearness and precision, stood leaning his arm upon the marble top of a console, and began to play with a small gold knife, with a malachite handle. Fouquet did not hurry himself to reply; but, after a moment's pause, "Come, my dear Monsieur Vanel," he said, "I will explain to you how I am situated." Vanel began to tremble.

"Yesterday I wished to sell."

"Monseigneur did more than wish to sell, for you actually sold."

"Well, well, that may be so; but to-day I ask you the favour to restore me my word which I pledged you."

"I received your word as a perfect assurance that it would be kept."

"I know that, and that is the reason why I now entreat you; do you understand me? I entreat you to restore it to me."

Fouquet suddenly paused. The words "I entreat you," the effect of which he did not immediately perceive, seemed almost to choke him as he uttered it. Aramis, still playing with his knife, fixed a look upon Vanel which seemed as if he wished to penetrate to the inmost recesses of his heart. Vanel simply bowed, as he said, "I am overcome, monseigneur, at the honour you do me to consult me upon a matter of business which is already completed; but——"

"Nay, do not say *but*, dear Monsieur Vanel."

"Alas! monseigneur, you see," he said, as he opened a large pocket-book, "I have brought the money with me,—the whole sum, I mean. And here, monseigneur, is the contract of sale which I have just effected of a property belonging to my wife. The order is authentic in every way, the necessary signatures have been attached to it, and it is made payable at sight; it is ready money, in fact, and, in one word, the whole affair is complete."

"My dear Monsieur Vanel, there is not a matter of business in the world, however important it may be, which cannot be postponed in order to oblige a man who, by that means, might and would be made a devoted friend."

"Certainly," said Vanel awkwardly.

"And much more justly acquired would that friend become, Monsieur Vanel, since the value of the service he had received would have been so considerable. Well, what do you say? what do you decide?"

Vanel preserved a perfect silence. In the meantime, Aramis had continued his close observation of the man. Vanel's narrow face, his deeply-sunk orbits, his arched eyebrows, had revealed to the Bishop of Vannes the type of an avaricious and ambitious character. Aramis's method was to oppose one passion by another. He saw that Fouquet was defeated—morally subdued—and so he came to his rescue with fresh weapons in his hands: "Excuse me, monseigneur," he said; "you forget to show M. Vanel that his own interests are diametrically opposed to this renunciation of the sale."

Vanel looked at the Bishop with astonishment; he had hardly expected to find an auxiliary in him. Fouquet also paused to listen to the Bishop.

"Do you not see," continued Aramis, "that M. Vanel, in order to purchase your appointment, has been obliged to sell a property which belongs to his wife; well, that is no slight matter; for one cannot displace, as he has done, fourteen or fifteen hundred thousand francs, without some considerable loss, and very serious inconvenience."

"Perfectly true," said Vanel, whose secret Aramis had, with his keen-sighted gaze, wrung from the bottom of his heart.

"Inconveniences such as those are matters of great expense and calculation, and whenever a man has money matters to deal with, the expenses are generally the very first thing thought of."

"Yes, yes," said Fouquet, who began to understand Aramis's meaning.

Vanel remained perfectly silent; he, too, had understood him. Aramis observed his coldness of manner and his silence. "Very good," he said to himself, "you are waiting, I see, until you know the amount; but do not fear, I shall send you such a flight of crowns that you cannot but capitulate on the spot."

"We must offer M. Vanel a hundred thousand crowns at once," said Fouquet, carried away by his generous feelings.

The sum was a good one. A prince, even, would have been satisfied with such a bonus. A hundred thousand crowns at that period was the dowry of a king's daughter. Vanel, however, did not move.

"He is a perfect rascal," thought the Bishop; "well, we must offer the five hundred thousand francs at once," and he made a sign to Fouquet accordingly.

"You seem to have spent more than that, dear Monsieur Vanel," said the Surintendant. "The price of money is enormous. You must have made a great sacrifice in selling your wife's property. Well, what can I have been thinking of? I ought to have offered to sign you an order for five hundred thousand francs; and even in that case I shall feel that I am greatly indebted to you."

There was not a gleam of delight or desire on Vanel's face, which remained perfectly impassible, not a muscle of it changed in the slightest degree. Aramis cast a look almost of despair at Fouquet, and then, going straight up to Vanel and taking hold of him by the coat, in a familiar manner, he said, "Monsieur

Vanel, it is neither the inconvenience, nor the displacement of your money nor the sale of your wife's property even, that you are thinking of at this moment; it is something more important still. I can well understand it; so pay particular attention to what I am going to say."

"Yes, monseigneur," Vanel replied, beginning to tremble in every limb, as the prelate's eyes seem almost ready to devour him.

"I offer you, therefore, in the Surintendant's name, not three hundred thousand livres, nor five hundred thousand, but a million. A million,—do you understand me?" he added, as he shook him nervously.

"A million?" repeated Vanel, as pale as death.

"A million; in other words, at the present rate of interest, an income of seventy thousand francs."

"Come, monsieur," said Fouquet, "you can hardly refuse that. Answer,—do you accept?"

"Impossible," murmured Vanel.

Aramis bit his lips, and something like a white cloud seemed to pass over his face. The thunder behind this cloud could easily be imagined. He still kept his hold on Vanel. "You have purchased the appointment for fifteen hundred thousand francs, I think? Well, you will receive these fifteen hundred thousand francs back again; by paying M. Fouquet a visit and shaking hands with him on the bargain, you will have become the gainer of a million and a half. You get honour and profit at the same time, Monsieur Vanel."

"I cannot do it," said Vanel hoarsely.

"Very well," replied Aramis, who had grasped Vanel so tightly by the coat, that when he let go his hold, Vanel staggered back a few paces; "very well; one can now see clearly enough your object in coming here."

"Yes," said Fouquet, "one can easily see that."

"But——" said Vanel, attempting to stand erect before the weakness of these two men of honour.

"Does the fellow presume to speak!" said Aramis, with the tone of an emperor.

"Fellow!" repeated Vanel.

"The wretch, I meant to say," added Aramis, who had now resumed his usual self-possession. "Come, monsieur, produce your deed of sale,—you have it about you, I suppose in one of your pockets, already prepared, as an assassin holds his pistol or his dagger concealed under his cloak?"

Vanel began to mutter something.

"Enough!" cried Fouquet. "Where is this deed?"

Vanel tremblingly searched in his pockets, and as he drew out his pocket-book, a paper fell out of it, while Vanel offered the other to Fouquet. Aramis pounced upon the paper which had fallen out, as soon as he recognised the handwriting.

"I beg your pardon," said Vanel, "that is a rough draft of the deed."

"I see that very clearly," retorted Aramis, with a smile far more cutting than a lash of a whip would have been; "and what I admire most is, that this draft is in M. Colbert's handwriting. Look, monseigneur, look."

And he handed the draft to Fouquet, who recognised the truth of the fact; for, covered with erasures, with inserted words, the margins filled with additions, this deed—a living proof of Colbert's plot—had just revealed everything to its unhappy victim. "Well!" murmured Fouquet.

Vanel, completely humiliated, seemed as if he were looking for some deep hole where he could hide himself.

"Well!" said Aramis, "if your name were not Fouquet, and if your enemy's name were not Colbert—if you had not this mean thief before you I should say to you, 'Repudiate it'; such a proof of this absolves you from your word; but these fellows would think you were afraid; they would fear you less than they do; therefore sign the deed at once." And he held out a pen towards him.

Fouquet pressed Aramis's hand; but, instead of the deed which Vanel handed to him, he took the rough draft of it.

"No, not that paper," said Aramis hastily; "this is the one. The other is too precious a document for you to part with."

"No, no!" replied Fouquet; "I will sign under M. Colbert's own handwriting even; and I write, 'The handwriting is approved of.'" He then signed, and said, "Here it is, Monsieur Vanel." And the latter seized the paper, laid down his money, and was about to make his escape.

"One moment," said Aramis. "Are you quite sure the exact amount is there? It ought to be counted over, Monsieur Vanel; particularly since M. Colbert makes presents of money to ladies, I see. Ah, that worthy M. Colbert is not so generous as M. Fouquet." And Aramis, spelling every word, every letter of the order, to pay, distilled his wrath and his contempt, drop by drop, upon the miserable wretch, who had to submit to this torture for a quarter of an hour; he was then dismissed not in words, but by a gesture, as one dismisses or discharges a beggar or a menial.

As soon as Vanel had gone, the minister and the prelate, their eyes fixed on each other, remained silent for a few moments.

"Well," said Aramis, the first to break the silence; "to what can that man be compared, who, at the very moment he is on the point of entering into a conflict with an enemy armed from head to foot, thirsting for his life, presents himself for the contest quite defenceless, throws down his arms, and smiles and kisses his hands to his adversary in the most gracious manner. Good faith, M. Fouquet, is a weapon which scoundrels very frequently make use of against men of honour, and it answers their purpose. Men of honour ought, in their turn, also, to make use of dishonest means against such scoundrels. You would soon see how strong they would become, without ceasing to be men of honour."

"What they did would be termed the acts of a scoundrel," replied Fouquet.

"Far from that; it would be merely coquetting or playing with the truth. At all events, since you have finished with this Vanel; since you have deprived yourself of the happiness of confounding him by repudiating your word; and since you have given up, for the purpose of being used against yourself, the only weapon which can ruin you——"

"My dear friend," said Fouquet mournfully, "you are like the teacher of philosophy whom La Fontaine was telling us about the other day: he saw a child drowning, and began to read him a lecture divided into three heads."*

Aramis smiled as he said, "Philosophy—yes; teacher—yes; a drowning child—yes; but a child that can be saved—you shall see. But, first of all, let us talk about business. Did you not some time ago," he continued, as Fouquet looked at him with a bewildered air, "speak to me about an idea you had of giving a fête at Vaux?"

"Oh," said Fouquet, "that was when affairs were flourishing."

"A fête, I believe, to which the King invited himself of his own accord?"

"No, no, my dear prelate; a fête to which M. Colbert advised the King to invite himself."

"Ah—exactly; as it would be a fête of so costly a character that you would be ruined in giving it."

"Precisely so. In other times, as I said just now, I had a kind of pride in showing my enemies how inexhaustible my resources were; I felt it a point of honour to strike them with amazement, in creating millions under circumstances where they had imagined nothing but bankruptcies and failures would follow. But at the present day I am arranging my accounts with the State, with the

68

King, with myself; and I must now become a mean, stingy man; I shall be able to prove to the world that I can act or operate with my deniers as I used to do with my bags of pistoles; and from to-morrow my equipages shall be sold, my mansions mortgaged, my expenses contracted."

"From to-morrow," interrupted Aramis quietly, "you will occupy yourself, without the slightest delay, with your fête at Vaux, which must hereafter be spoken of as one of the most magnificent productions of your most prosperous days."

"You are mad, Chevalier d'Herblay."

"I!—you do not think that."

"What do you mean, then? Do you not know that a fête at Vaux, of the very simplest possible character, would cost four or five millions?"

"I do not speak of a fête of the very simplest possible character, my dear Surintendant."

"But, since the fête is to be given to the King," replied Fouquet, who misunderstood Aramis's idea, "it cannot be simple."

"Just so; it ought to be on a scale of the most unbounded magnificence."

"In that case, I shall have to spend ten or twelve millions."

"You shall spend twenty if you require it," said Aramis, in a perfectly calm voice.

"Where shall I get them?" exclaimed Fouquet.

"That is my affair, Monsieur le Surintendant; and do not be uneasy for a moment about it. The money will be placed at once at your disposal, as soon as you shall have arranged the plans of your fête."

"Chevalier! Chevalier!" said Fouquet, giddy with amazement, "whither are you hurrying me?"

"Across the gulf into which you were about to fall," replied the Bishop of Vannes. "Take hold of my cloak, and throw fear aside."

"Why did you not tell me that sooner, Aramis? There was a day when, with one million only, you could have saved me, whilst to-day——"

"Whilst to-day, I can give you twenty," said the prelate. "Such is the case, however——the reason is very simple. On the day you speak of, I had not the million which you had need of at my disposal; whilst now I can easily procure the twenty millions we require."

"May Heaven hear you, and save me!"

Aramis resumed his usual smile, the expression of which was so singular. "Heaven never fails to hear me," he said.

"I abandon myself to you unreservedly," Fouquet murmured.

"No, no; I do not understand it in that manner. I am unreservedly devoted to you. Therefore, as you have the clearest, the most delicate, and the most ingenious mind of the two, you shall have entire control over the fête, even to the very smallest details. Only——"

"Only?" said Fouquet, as a man accustomed to understand and appreciate the value of a parenthesis.

"Well, then, leaving the entire invention of the details to you, I shall reserve to myself a general superintendence over the execution."

"In what way?"

"I mean that you will make of me, on that day, a major-domo, a sort of inspector-general, or factotum—something between a captain of the guard and manager or steward. I will look after the people, and will keep the keys of the doors. You will give your orders, of course; but will give them to no one but to me; they will pass through my lips, to reach those for whom they are intended —you understand?"

"No, I am very far from understanding."

"But you agree?"

"Of course, of course, my friend."

"That is all I care about, then, thanks, and now go and prepare your list of invitations."

"Whom shall I invite?"

"Every one."

11

IN WHICH THE AUTHOR THINKS IT IS NOW TIME TO RETURN TO THE VICOMTE DE BRAGELONNE

OUR readers will have observed in this story, the adventures of the new and of the past generation being detailed, as it were, side by side. To the former, the reflection of the glory of earlier years, the experience of the bitter things of this world; to the former, also, that peace which takes possession of the heart, and that healing of the scars which were formerly deep and painful wounds. To the latter, the conflicts of love and vanity; bitter disappointments, and ineffable delights; life instead of memory. If, therefore, any variety has been presented to the reader in the different episodes of this tale, it is to be attributed to the numerous shades of colour which are presented on this double palette, where two pictures are seen side by side, mingling and harmonising their severe and pleasing tones. The repose of the emotions of the one is found in the bosom of the emotions of the other. After having talked reason with older heads, one loves to talk nonsense with youth. Therefore, if the threads of this story do not seem very intimately to connect the chapter we are now writing with that we have just written, we do not intend to give ourselves any more thought or trouble about it than Ruysdaël*took in painting an autumn sky, after having finished a spring-time scene. We wish our readers to do as much, and to resume Raoul*de Bragelonne's story at the very place where our last sketch left him.

In a state of frenzy and dismay, or rather without power or will of his own—without knowing what to do—he fled heedlessly away, after the scene in La Vallière's room. The King, Montalais, Louise, that chamber, that strange exclusion, Louise's grief, Montalais's terror, the King's wrath—all seemed to indicate some misfortune. But what? He had arrived from London because he had been told of the existence of a danger; and almost on his arrival, this appearance of danger was manifest. Was not this sufficient for a lover? Certainly it was; but it was insufficient for a pure and upright heart such as his. And yet Raoul did not seek for explanations in the very quarter where all jealous or less timid lovers would have done. He did not go straightway to his mistress and say, "Louise, is it true that you love me no longer? Is it true that you love another?" Full of courage, full of friendship as he was full of love; a religious observer of his word, and believing blindly the word of others, Raoul said within himself, "Guiche* wrote to put me on my guard; Guiche knows something; I will go and ask Guiche what he knows, and tell him what I have seen." The journey was not a long one. Guiche, who had been brought from Fontainebleau to Paris within the last two days, was beginning to recover from his wound, and to walk about a little in his room. He uttered a cry of joy as he saw Raoul, earnest in his friendship, enter his apartment. Raoul, too, had not been able to refrain from exclaiming aloud, when he saw de Guiche, so pale, so thin, so melancholy. A very few words, and a simple gesture which de Guiche made to put aside Raoul's arm, were sufficient to inform the latter of the truth.

"Ah! so it is," said Raoul, seating himself beside his friend; "one loves and dies."

"No, no, not dies," replied de Guiche smiling, "since I am now recovering, and since, too, I can press you in my arms."

"Ah! I understand."

"And I understand you, too. You fancy I am unhappy, Raoul?"

"Alas!"

"No; I am the happiest of men. My body suffers, but not my mind or my heart. If you only knew—— Oh! I am, indeed, the very happiest of men."

"So much the better," replied Raoul; "so much the better, provided it lasts."

"It is over. I have had enough happiness to last me to my dying day, Raoul."

"I have no doubt you have had; but she——"

"Listen; I love her because—but you are not listening to me."

"I beg your pardon."

"Your mind is preoccupied."

"Yes; your health, in the first place——"

"It is not that, I know."

"My dear friend, you would be wrong, I think, to ask me any questions—*you* of all persons in the world." And he laid so much weight upon the "you" that he completely enlightened his friend upon the nature of the evil, and the difficulty of remedying it.

"You say that, Raoul, on account of what I wrote to you."

"Certainly. We will talk over that matter a little, when you shall have finished telling me of all your own pleasures and pains."

"My dear friend, I am entirely at your service now."

"Thank you; I have hurried, I have flown here; I came here in half the time the Government couriers usually take. Now, tell me, my dear friend, what did you want?"

"Nothing whatever, but to make you come."

"Well, then, I am here."

"All is quite right, then."

"There must have been something else, I suppose?"

"No, indeed."

"De Guiche!"

"Upon my honour!"

"You cannot possibly have crushed all my hopes so violently, or have exposed me to being disgraced by the King for my return, which is in disobedience of his orders—you cannot, I say, have planted jealousy in my heart, merely to say to me, 'It is all right, be perfectly easy.'"

"I do not say to you, Raoul, 'Be perfectly easy,' but pray understand me; I never will, nor can I, indeed, tell you anything else."

"What sort of person do you take me for?"

"What do you mean?"

"If you know anything, why conceal it from me? If you do not know anything, why did you write so warningly?"

"True, true, I was very wrong, and I regret having done so, Raoul. It seems nothing to write to a friend and say 'Come,' but to have this friend face to face, to feel him tremble, and breathlessly and anxiously wait to hear what one hardly dare tell him, is very different."

"Dare! I have courage enough, if you have not," exclaimed Raoul, in despair.

"See how unjust you are, and how soon you forget you have to do with a poor wounded fellow such as your unhappy friend is. So, calm yourself, Raoul. I said to you, 'Come,'—you are here, so ask me nothing further."

"Your object in telling me to come was your hope that I should see with my own eyes, was it not? Nay, do not hesitate, for I have seen all."

"Oh!" exclaimed de Guiche.

"Or at least, I thought——"

"There now, you see you are not sure. But if you have any doubt, my poor friend, what remains for me to do?"

"I saw Louise much agitated—Montalais in a state of bewilderment—the King——"

"The King?"

"Yes. You turn your head aside. The danger is there, the evil is there; tell me, is it not so, is it not the King?"

"I say nothing."

"Oh! you say a thousand upon a thousand times more than nothing. Give me facts, for pity's sake, give me proofs. My friend, the only friend I have, speak—tell me all. My heart is crushed, wounded to death; I am dying of despair."

"If that really be so, as I see it is indeed, dear Raoul," replied de Guiche, "you relieve me from my difficulty, and I will tell you all, perfectly sure that I can tell you nothing but what is consoling, compared to the despair from which I now see you suffering."

"Go on,—go on; I am listening."

"Well, then, I can only tell you what you can learn from every person you meet."

"From every one, do you say? It is talked about, then?"

"Before you say people talk about it, learn what it is that people can talk about. I assure you solemnly, that people only talk about what may, in truth, be very innocent; perhaps a walk——"

"Ah! a walk with the King?"

"Yes, certainly, a walk with the King; and I believe the King has already very frequently before taken walks with ladies, without, on that account——"

"You would not have written to me, shall I say again,

73

if there had been nothing unusual in this promenade."

"I know that while the storm lasted, it would have been far better if the King had taken shelter somewhere else, than to have remained with his head uncovered before La Vallière; but the King is so very courteous and polite."

"Oh! de Guiche, de Guiche, you are killing me!"

"Do not let us talk any more, then."

"Nay; let us continue. This walk was followed by others, I suppose?"

"No—I mean yes; there was the adventure of the oak, I think. But I know nothing about the matter at all." Raoul rose; de Guiche endeavoured to imitate him, notwithstanding his weakness. "Well, I will not add another word; I have said either too much or not enough. Let others give you further information if they will, or if they can; my duty was to warn you, and that I have done. Watch over your own affairs now, yourself."

"Question others! Alas! you are no true friend to speak to me in that manner," said the young man in utter distress. "The first man I may meet may be either evilly disposed or a fool; if the former, he will tell me a lie to make me suffer more than I now do; if the latter, he will do far worse still. Ah! de Guiche, de Guiche, before two hours are over, I shall have been told ten falsehoods, and shall have as many duels on my hands. Save me then; is it not best to know the whole misfortune?"

"But I know nothing, I tell you; I was wounded, attacked by fever; my senses were gone, and I have only a very faint recollection of it all. But there is no reason why we should search very far, when the very man we want is close at hand. Is not d'Artagnan your friend?"

"Oh! true, true."

"Go to him, then. He will be able to throw some light on the subject." At this moment a lackey entered the room. "What is it?" said de Guiche.

"Some one is waiting for monseigneur in the Cabinet des Porcelaines."

"Very well. Will you excuse me, my dear Raoul? I am so proud since I have been able to walk again."

"I would offer you my arm, de Guiche, if I did not guess that the person in question is a lady."

"I believe so," said de Guiche, smiling, as he quitted Raoul.

Raoul remained motionless, absorbed in his grief, overwhelmed, like the miner upon whom a vault has just fallen in, who, wounded, his life-blood welling fast, his thoughts confused, endeavours to recover himself, to save his life and to preserve his reason. A few minutes were all that Raoul needed to dissipate the bewildering sensations which had been occasioned by these two revelations. He had already recovered the thread of his ideas, when, suddenly, through the door, he fancied he recognised Montalais's voice in the Cabinet des Porcelaines. "She!" he cried. "Yes, it is indeed her voice! She will be able to tell me the whole truth; but shall I question her here? She conceals herself even from me; she is coming no doubt from Madame. I will see her in her own apartment. She will explain her alarm, her flight, the strange manner in which I was driven out; she will tell me all that—after M. d'Artagnan, who knows everything, shall have given me fresh courage and strength. Madame, a coquette I fear, and yet a coquette who is herself in love, has her moments of kindness; a coquette who is as capricious and uncertain as life or death, but who tells de Guiche that he is the happiest of men. He at least is lying on roses." And so he hastily quitted the Comte's apartments, and reproaching himself as he went for having talked of nothing but his own affairs to de Guiche, he arrived at d'Artagnan's quarters.

12

BRAGELONNE CONTINUES HIS INQUIRIES

THE Captain was sitting buried in his leathern arm-chair, his spur fixed in the floor, his sword between his legs, and was occupied in reading a great number of letters, as he twisted his moustache. D'Artagnan uttered a welcome full of pleasure when he perceived his friend's son.* "Raoul, my boy," he said, "by what lucky accident does it happen that the King has recalled you?"

These words did not sound over agreeably in the young man's ears, who, as he seated himself, replied, "Upon my word, I cannot tell you; all I know is that I have come back."

"Hum!" said d'Artagnan, folding up his letters and directing a look full of meaning at him; "what do you say, my boy? that the King has not recalled you, and that you have returned? I do not understand that at all."

Raoul was already pale enough, and he began to turn his hat round and round in his hand.

"What the deuce is the matter that you look as you do, and what makes you so dumb?" said the Captain.* "Do people assume that sort of airs in England? I have been in England*and have come back again as lively as a chaffinch. Will you not say something?"

"I have too much to say."

"Ah! ah! how is your father?"

"Forgive me, my dear friend, I was going to ask you that."

D'Artagnan increased the sharpness of his penetrating gaze which no secret was capable of resisting. "You are unhappy about something," he said.

"I am, indeed; and you know very well what, Monsieur d'Artagnan."

"I?"

"Of course. Nay, do not pretend to be astonished."

"I am not pretending to be astonished, my friend."

"Dear Captain, I know very well that in all trials of *finesse*, as well as in all trials of strength, I shall be beaten by you. You can see that at the present moment I am an idiot, a perfect fool. I have neither head nor arm; do not despise, but help me. In two words, I am the most wretched of living beings."

"Oh! oh! why that?" inquired d'Artagnan, unbuckling his belt and softening the ruggedness of his smile.

"Because Mademoiselle de la Vallière is deceiving me."

"She is deceiving you," said d'Artagnan, not a muscle of whose face had moved; "those are big words. Who makes use of them?"

"Every one."

"Ah! if every one says so, there must be some truth in it. I begin to believe there is fire when I see the smoke. It is ridiculous, perhaps, but so it is."

"Therefore you do believe?" exclaimed Bragelonne, quickly.

"I never mix myself up in affairs of that kind; you know that very well."

"What! not for a friend, for a son!"

"Exactly.—If you were a stranger, I should tell you—I should tell *you* nothing at all. How is Porthos, do you know?"

"Monsieur," cried Raoul, pressing d'Artagnan's hand, "I entreat you in the name of the friendship you have vowed to my father!"

"The deuce take it, you are really ill—from curiosity."

"No, it is not from curiosity, it is from love."

"Good. Another grand word. If you were really in love, my dear Raoul, you would be very different."

"What do you mean?"

"I mean that if you were really so deeply in love that I could believe I was addressing myself to your heart—but it is impossible."

"I tell you I love Louise to distraction."

D'Artagnan could read to the very bottom of the young man's heart.

"Impossible, I tell you," he said. "You are like all young men; you are not in love, you are out of your senses."

"Well! suppose it were only that?"

"No sensible man ever succeeded in making much of a brain when the head was turned. I have completely lost my senses in the same way a hundred times in my life. You would listen to me, but you would not hear me; you would hear, but you would not understand me; you would understand, but you would not obey me."

"Oh! try, try."

"I go far. Even if I were unfortunate enough to know something, and foolish enough to communicate it to you—You are my friend you say?"

"Indeed, yes."

"Very good. I should quarrel with you. You would never forgive me for having destroyed your illusion, as people say in love affairs."

"Monsieur d'Artagnan, you know all; and yet you plunge me in perplexity and despair, in death itself."

"There, there, now."

"I never complain, as you know; but as Heaven and my father would never forgive me for blowing out my brains, I will go and get the first person I meet to give me the information which you withhold; I will tell him he lies, and——"

"And you would kill him. And a fine affair that would be. So much the better. What should I care for it. Kill any one you please, my boy, if it can give you any pleasure. It is exactly like a man with the toothache, who keeps on saying, 'Oh! what torture I am suffering I could bite a piece of iron in half.' My answer always is, 'Bite, my friend, bite; the tooth will remain all the same.'"

"I shall not kill any one, monsieur," said Raoul gloomily.

"Yes, yes! you now assume a different tone; instead of killing, you will get killed yourself, I suppose you mean? Very fine indeed! How much I should regret you! Of course I should go about all day saying, Ah! what a fine stupid fellow that Bragelonne was! as great a stupid as I ever met with. I have passed my whole life almost in teaching him how to hold and use his sword properly, and the silly fellow has got himself spitted like a lark. Go, then, Raoul, go and get yourself disposed of, if you like. I hardly know who can have taught you logic, but deuce take me if your father has not been regularly robbed of his money by whoever did so."

Raoul buried his face in his hands, murmuring, "No, no; I have not a single friend in the world."

THE MAN IN THE IRON MASK

"Oh! bah!" said d'Artagnan.

"I meet with nothing but raillery or indifference."

"Idle fancies, monsieur. I do not laugh at you, although I am a Gascon. And, as for being indifferent, if I were so, I should have sent you about your business a quarter of an hour ago, for you would make a man who was out of his senses with delight as dull as possible, and would be the death of one who was only out of spirits. How now, young man! do you wish me to disgust you with the girl you are attached to, and to teach you to execrate the whole sex who constitute the honour and happiness of human life."

"Oh! tell me, monsieur, and I will bless you."

"Do you think, my dear fellow, that I can have crammed into my brain all about the carpenter, and the painter, and the staircase, and a hundred other similar tales of the same kind?"

"A carpenter! what do you mean?"

"Upon my word I don't know; some one told me there was a carpenter who made an opening through a certain flooring."

"In La Vallière's room?"

"Oh! I don't know where."

"In the King's apartment, perhaps."

"Of course, if it were in the King's apartment, I should tell you, I suppose."

"In whose room, then?"

"I have told you for the last hour that I know nothing of the whole affair."

"But the painter, then? the portrait——"

"It seems that the King wished to have the portrait of one of the ladies belonging to the court."

"La Vallière's."

"Why, you seem to have only that name in your mouth. Who spoke to you of La Vallière?"

"If it be not her portrait, then, why do you suppose it would concern me?"

"I do not suppose it will concern you. But you ask me all sorts of questions and I answer you. You positively will learn all the scandal of the affair, and I tell you—make the best you can of it."

Raoul struck his forehead with his hand, in utter despair. "It will kill me!" he said.

"So you have said already."

"Yes, you're right," and he made a step or two as if he were going to leave.

"Where are you going?"

"To look for some one who will tell me the truth."

"Who is that?"

"A woman."

"Mademoiselle de la Vallière herself, I suppose you mean?" said d'Artagnan, with a smile. "Ah! a famous idea that! You wish to be consoled by some one, and you will be so at once. She will tell you nothing ill of herself, of course. So be off."

"You are mistaken, monsieur," replied Raoul; "the woman I mean will tell me all the evil she possibly can."

"You allude to Montalais, I suppose—her friend; a woman who, on that account, will exaggerate all that is either good or bad in the matter. Do not talk to Montalais, my good fellow."

"You have some reason for wishing me not to talk with Montalais?"

"Well, I admit it. And, in point of fact, why should I play with you as a cat does with a poor mouse? You distress me, you do indeed. And if I wish you not to speak to Montalais just now, it is because you will be betraying your secret, and people will take advantage of it. Wait, if you can."

"I cannot."

"So much the worse. Why, you see, Raoul, if I had an idea— but I have not got one."

"Promise that you will pity me, my friend, that is all I need, and leave me to get out of the affair by myself."

"Oh! yes, indeed, in order that you may get deeper into the mire! A capital idea, truly! go and sit down at that table and take a pen in your hand."

"What for?"

"To write and ask Montalais to give you an interview."

"Ah!" said Raoul, snatching eagerly at the pen which the captain held out to him.

Suddenly the door opened, and one of the musketeers approaching d'Artagnan, said, "Captain, Mademoiselle de Montalais is here, and wishes to speak to you."

"To me?" murmured d'Artagnan. "Ask her to come in; I shall soon see," he said to himself, "whether she wishes to speak to me or not."

The cunning Captain was quite right in his suspicions; for as soon as Montalais appeared, she exclaimed, "Oh, monsieur, monsieur, I beg your pardon, Monsieur d'Artagnan."

"Oh! I forgive you, mademoiselle," said d'Artagnan; "I know that at my age, those who are looking for me generally need me for something or another."

"I was looking for Monsieur de Bragelonne," replied Montalais.

"How very fortunate that is; he is looking for you too. Raoul, will you accompany Mademoiselle Montalais?"

"Oh! certainly."

"Go along, then," he said, as he gently pushed Raoul out of the cabinet; and then, taking hold of Montalais's hand, he said in a low voice: "Be kind towards him; spare him, and spare her too, if you can."

"Ah!" she said, in the same tone of voice, "it is not I who am going to speak to him."

"Who, then?"

"It is Madame who has sent for him."

"Very good," cried d'Artagnan, "it is Madame, is it?—In an hour's time, then, the poor fellow will be cured."

"Or else dead," said Montalais, in a voice full of compassion. "*Adieu*, Monsieur d'Artagnan," she said; and she ran to join Raoul, who was waiting for her at a little distance from the door, very much puzzled and uneasy at the dialogue, which promised no good augury for him.

13

TWO JEALOUSIES

LOVERS are very tender towards everything which concerns the person they are in love with. Raoul no sooner found himself alone with Montalais than he kissed her hand with rapture. "There, there," said the young girl sadly, "you are throwing your kisses away; I will guarantee that they will not bring you back any interest."

"How so?—Why?—Will you explain to me, my dear Aure?"

"Madame will explain everything to you. I am going to take you to her apartments."

"What!"

"Silence! and throw aside your wild and savage looks. The windows here have eyes, the walls have ears. Have the kindness not to look at me any longer; be good enough to speak to me aloud of the rain, of the fine weather and of the charms of England."

"At all events——" interrupted Raoul.

"I tell you, I warn you, that wherever it may be, I know not now, Madame is sure to have eyes and ears open. I am not very desirous, you can easily believe, to be dismissed or thrown into the Bastille. Let us talk, I tell you, or rather, do not let us talk at all."

Raoul clenched his hands, and tried to assume the look and gait of a man of courage, it is true, but of a man of courage on his way to the torture. Montalais glancing in every direction, walking along with an easy swinging gait, and holding up her head pertly in the air, preceded him to Madame's apartments, where he was at once introduced. "Well," he thought, "this day will pass away without my learning anything. Guiche showed too much consideration for my feelings; he had no doubt come to an understanding with Madame, and both of them, by a friendly plot, agreed to postpone the solution of the problem. Why have I not a determined inveterate enemy—that serpent de Wardes,* for instance; that he would bite, is very likely; but I should not hesitate any more. To hesitate, to doubt—better by far to die."

The next moment Raoul was in Madame's presence. Henrietta, more charming than ever, was half lying, half reclining in her armchair, her little feet upon an embroidered velvet cushion; she was playing with a little kitten with long silky fur, which was biting her fingers and hanging by the lace of her collar.

Madame seemed plunged in deep thought, so deep indeed, that it required both Montalais and Raoul's voices to disturb her from her reverie.

"Your Highness sent for me?" repeated Raoul.

Madame shook her head, as if she were just awakening, and then said, "Good morning, Monsieur de Bragelonne; yes, I sent for you; so you have returned from England?"

"Yes, madame, and am at your Royal Highness's commands."

"Thank you; leave us, Montalais;" and the latter immediately left the room.

"You have a few minutes to give me, Monsieur de Bragelonne, have you not?"

"My very life is at your Royal Highness's disposal," Raoul returned with respect, guessing that there was something serious in all these outward courtesies of Madame; nor was he displeased, indeed, to observe the seriousness of her manner, feeling persuaded that there was some sort of affinity between Madame's sentiments and his own. In fact, every one at court, of any perception at all, knew perfectly well the capricious fancy and absurd despotism of the Princess's singular character. Madame had been flattered beyond all bounds by the King's attentions; she had made herself talked about; she had inspired the Queen with that mortal jealousy which is the gnawing worm at the root of every woman's happiness; Madame, in a word, in her attempts to cure a wounded pride, had found that her heart had become deeply and passionately attached. We know what Madame had done to recall Raoul, who had been sent out of the way by Louis XIV. Raoul did not know of her letter to Charles II.,* although d'Artagnan had guessed its contents. Who will undertake to account for that seemingly inexplicable mixture of love and vanity, that passionate tenderness of feeling, that prodigious duplicity of conduct? No one can, indeed; not even the bad angel who kindles the love of coquetry in the heart of woman. "Monsieur de Bragelonne," said the Princess, after a moment's pause, "have you returned satisfied?"

Bragelonne looked at Madame Henrietta, and seeing how pale she was, not alone from what she was keeping back, but also from what she was burning to say, said: "Satisfied! what is there for me to be satisfied or dissatisfied about, madame?"

"But what are those things with which a man of your age, and of your appearance, is usually either satisfied or dissatisfied?"

"How eager she is," thought Raoul, almost terrified; "what is it that she is going to breathe into my heart?" and then, frightened at what she might possibly be going to tell him, and wishing to put off the opportunity of having everything explained, which he had hitherto so ardently wished for, yet had dreaded so much, he replied: "I left behind me, madame, a dear friend in good health, and on my return I find him very ill."

"You refer to M. de Guiche," replied Madame Henrietta, with the most imperturbable self-possession; "I have heard he is a very dear friend of yours."

"He is, indeed, madame."

"Well, it is quite true he has been wounded; but he is better now. Oh! M. de Guiche is not to be pitied," she said hurriedly; and then recovering herself, added: "But has he anything to complain of? Has he complained of anything? is there any cause of grief or sorrow that we are not acquainted with?"

"I allude only to his wound, madame."

"So much the better, then, for, in other respects, M. de Guiche seems to be very happy; he is always in very high spirits. I am sure that you, Monsieur de Bragelonne, would far prefer to be, like him, wounded only in body . . . for what, indeed, is such a wound, after all!"

Raoul started. "Alas!" he said to himself, "she is returning to it."

"What did you say?" she inquired.

"I did not say anything, madame."

"You did not say anything; you disapprove of my observation, then? you are perfectly satisfied, I suppose?"

Raoul approached closer to her. "Madame," he said, "your Royal Highness wishes to say something to me, and your instinctive kindness and generosity of disposition induce you to be careful and considerate as to your manner of conveying it. Will your Royal Highness throw this kind forbearance aside? I am able to bear everything; and I am listening."

"Ah!" replied Henrietta, "what do you understand, then?"

"That which your Royal Highness wishes me to understand," said Raoul, trembling, notwithstanding his command over himself as he pronounced these words.

"In point of fact," murmured the Princess . . . "it seems cruel, but since I have begun——"

"Yes, madame, since your Highness has deigned to begin, will you deign to finish——"

Henrietta rose hurriedly and walked a few paces up and down her room. "What did M. de Guiche tell you?" she said suddenly.

"Nothing, madame."

"Nothing! Did he say nothing? Ah! how well I recognise him in that."

"No doubt he wished to spare me."

"And that is what friends call friendship! But, surely, M. d'Artagnan, whom you have just left, must have told you?"

"No more than Guiche, madame."

Henrietta made a gesture full of impatience, as she said, "At least you know all that the court has known."

"I know nothing at all, madame."

"Not the scene in the storm?"

"No, madame."

"Not the *tête-à-tête* in the forest?"

"No, madame."

"Nor the flight to Chaillot?"*

Raoul, whose head drooped like a flower which has been cut down by the sickle, made an almost superhuman effort to smile, as he replied with the greatest gentleness: "I have had the honour to tell your Royal Highness that I am absolutely ignorant of everything, that I am a poor unremembered outcast, who has this moment arrived from England. There have been so many stormy waves between myself and those whom I left behind me here, that the rumour of none of the circumstances your Highness refers to has been able to reach me."

Henrietta was affected by his extreme pallor, his gentleness and his great courage. The principal feeling in her heart at that moment was an eager desire to hear the nature of the remembrance which the poor lover retained of her who had made him suffer so much. "Monsieur de Bragelonne," she said, "that which your friends have refused to do, I will do for you, whom I like and esteem very much. I will be your friend on this occasion. You hold your head high, as a man of honour should do; and I should regret that you should have to bow it down under ridicule, and in a few days, it may be, under contempt."

"Ah!" exclaimed Raoul, perfectly livid. "It is as bad as that, then?"

"If you do not know," said the Princess, "I see that you guess; you were affianced, I believe, to Mademoiselle de la Vallière?"

"Yes, madame."

"By that right, then, you deserve to be warned about her, as some day or another I shall be obliged to dismiss Mademoiselle de la Vallière from my service——"

"Dismiss La Vallière!" cried Bragelonne.

"Of course. Do you suppose that I shall always be accessible to the tears and protestations of the King? No, no! my house shall no longer be made a convenience for such practices; but you tremble, you cannot stand——"

"No, madame, no," said Bragelonne, making an effort over himself; "I thought I should have died just now, that was all. Your Royal Highness did me the honour to say that the King wept and implored you——"

"Yes, but in vain," returned the Princess; who then related to Raoul the scene that took place at Chaillot, and the King's despair on his return; she told him of his indulgence to herself, and the terrible word with which the outraged Princess, the humiliated coquette, had dashed aside the royal anger.

Raoul stood with his head bent down.

"What do you think of it all?" she said.

"The King loves her," he replied.

"But you seem to think she does not love him!"

"Alas, madame, I am thinking of the time when she loved me."

Henrietta was for a moment struck with admiration at this sublime disbelief; and then, shrugging her shoulders she said, "You do not believe me, I see. How deeply you must love her, and you doubt if she loves the King?"

"I do, until I have a proof of it. Forgive me, madame, but she has given me her word; and her mind and heart are too upright to tell a falsehood.'

"You require a proof! Be it so. Come with me, then."

14

A DOMICILIARY VISIT

THE Princess, preceding Raoul, led him through the courtyard towards that part of the building which La Vallière inhabited, and, ascending the same staircase which Raoul had himself ascended that very morning, she paused at the door of the room in which the young man had been so strangely received by Montalais. The opportunity had been well chosen to carry out the project which Madame Henrietta had conceived, for the château was empty. The King, the courtiers and the ladies of the court, had set off for Saint-Germain; Madame Henrietta was the only one who knew of Bragelonne's return, and, thinking over the advantages which might be drawn from this return, had feigned indisposition in order to remain behind. Madame was therefore confident of finding La Vallière's room and Saint-Aignan's apartment*perfectly empty. She took a pass-key from her pocket and opened the door of her maid-of-honour's apartment. Bragelonne's gaze was immediately fixed upon the interior of the room, which he recognised at once; and the impression which the sight of it produced upon him was one of the first tortures which awaited him. The Princess looked at him, and her practised eye could at once detect what was passing in the young man's heart.

"You asked me for proofs," she said, "do not be astonished, then, if I give you them. But if you do not think you have courage enough to confront them, there is still time to withdraw."

"I thank you, madame," said Bragelonne; "but I came here to be convinced. You promised to convince me,—do so."

"Enter then," said Madame, "and shut the door behind you."

Bragelonne obeyed, and then turned towards the Princess, whom he interrogated by a look.

"You know where you are, I suppose?" inquired Madame Henrietta.

"Everything leads me to believe I am in Mademoiselle de la Vallière's room."

"You are."

"But I would observe to your Highness that this room is a room, and is not a proof."

"Wait," said the Princess, as she walked to the foot of the bed, folded up the screen into its several compartments, and stooped down towards the floor. "Look here," she continued; "stoop down, and lift up this trap-door yourself."

"A trap-door!" said Raoul, astonished; for d'Artagnan's words began to return to his memory, and he had an indistinct recollection that d'Artagnan had made use of the same word. He looked, but uselessly so, for some cleft or crevice which might indicate an opening or a ring to assist in lifting up some portion of the planking.

"Ah, I forgot," said Madame Henrietta, "I forgot the secret spring; the fourth plank of the flooring,—press on the spot where you will observe a knot in the wood. Those are the instructions; press, Vicomte! press, I say, yourself!"

Raoul, pale as death, pressed his finger on the spot which had been indicated to him; at the same moment the spring began to work, and the trap rose of its own accord.

"It is ingenious enough, certainly," said the Princess; "and one can see that the architect foresaw that a very little hand only would have to make use of this spring, for see how easily the trap-door opened without assistance."

"A staircase!" cried Raoul.

"Yes, and a very pretty one, too," said Madame Henrietta. "See, Vicomte, the staircase has a balustrade intended to prevent the falling of timid persons who might be tempted to descend the staircase; and I will risk myself on it accordingly. Come, Vicomte, follow me!"

"But before following you, madame, may I ask where this staircase leads to?"

"Ah, true; I forgot to tell you. You know, perhaps, that formerly M. de Saint-Aignan lived in the very next apartment to the King?"

"Yes, madame, I am aware of that; that was the arrangement at least before I left; and more than once I have had the honour of visiting him in his old rooms."

"Well; he obtained the King's leave to change his former convenient and beautiful apartment for the two rooms to which this staircase will conduct us, and which together form a lodging for him, twice as small, and at ten times greater distance from the King,—a close proximity to whom is by no means disdained, in general, by the gentlemen belonging to the court."

"Very good, madame," returned Raoul; "but go on, I beg, for I do not understand yet."

"Well, then, it accidentally happened," continued the Princess, "that M. de Saint-Aignan's apartment is situated underneath the apartments of my maids of honour, and particularly underneath the room of La Vallière."

"But what was the motive of this trap-door and this staircase?"

"That I cannot tell you. Would you like us to go down to Monsieur de Saint-Aignan's rooms? Perhaps we shall be able to find the solution of the enigma there."

And Madame set the example by going down herself, while Raoul, sighing deeply, followed her. At every step Bragelonne took, he advanced farther into that mysterious apartment which had been witness to La Vallière's sighs, and still retained the sweetest perfume of her presence. Bragelonne fancied that he perceived, as he inhaled his every breath, that the young girl must have passed through there. Then succeeded to these emanations of herself, which he regarded as invisible though certain proofs, the flowers she preferred to all others,—the books of her own selection. Had Raoul preserved a single doubt on the subject, it would have vanished at the secret harmony of tastes, and connection of the mind with the use of the ordinary objects of life. La Vallière, in Bragelonne's eyes, was present there in every article of furniture, in the colour of the hangings, in every thing that surrounded him. Dumb, and completely overwhelmed, there was nothing further for him now to learn, and he followed his pitiless conductress as blindly as the culprit follows the executioner; while Madame, as cruel as all women of delicate and nervous temperaments are, did not spare him the slightest detail. But, it must be admitted that, notwithstanding the kind of apathy into which he had fallen, none of these details, even had he been left alone, would have escaped him. The happiness of the woman who loves, when that happiness is derived from a rival, is a living torture for a jealous man; but for a jealous man such as Raoul was, for one whose heart had for the first time been steeped in gall and bitterness, Louise's happiness was in reality an ignominious death, a death of body and soul. He guessed all; he fancied he could see them, with their hands clasped in each other's, their faces drawn close together, and reflected, side by side, in loving proximity, as they gazed upon the mirrors around them—so sweet an occupation for lovers, who, as they thus see themselves twice over, impress the picture more enduringly in their memories. He could guess, too, the stolen kiss snatched as they separated from each other's loved society. The luxury, the studied elegance, eloquent of the perfection of indolence, of ease; the extreme care shown, either to spare the loved object every annoyance or to occasion her a delightful surprise; that strength and power of love multiplied by the strength and power of royalty itself, seemed like a death-blow to

Raoul. If there be anything which can in any way assuage or mitigate the tortures of jealousy, it is the inferiority of the man who is preferred to yourself; whilst, on the very contrary, if there be an anguish more bitter than another, a misery for which language has no descriptive words, it is the superiority of the man preferred to yourself, superior, perhaps, in youth, beauty, grace. It is in such moments as these that Heaven almost seems to have taken part against the disdained and rejected lover.

One final pang was reserved for poor Raoul. Madame Henrietta lifted up a silk curtain, and behind the canvas he perceived La Vallière's portrait. Not only the portrait of La Vallière, but of La Vallière eloquent of youth, beauty and happiness, inhaling life and enjoyment at every pore, because at eighteen years of age love itself is life.

"Louise!" murmured Bragelonne,—"Louise! is it true, then? Oh, you have never loved me, for never have you looked at me in that manner." And he felt as if his heart were crushed within his bosom.

Madame Henrietta looked at him, almost envious of his extreme grief, although she well knew that there was nothing to envy in it, and that she herself was as passionately loved by de Guiche as Louise by Bragelonne. Raoul interpreted Madame Henrietta's look.

"Oh, forgive me, forgive me, madame; in your presence I know I ought to have greater mastery over myself. But Heaven grant that you may never be struck by a similar misery to that which crushes me at this moment, for you are but a woman, and would not be able to endure so terrible an affliction. Forgive me, I again entreat you, madame; I am but a man without rank or position, while you belong to a race whose happiness knows no bounds, whose power acknowledges no limit."

"Monsieur de Bragelonne," replied Henrietta, " a heart such as yours merits all the consideration and respect which a Queen's heart even can bestow. Regard me as your friend, monsieur; and as such, indeed, I would not allow your whole life to be poisoned by perfidy, and covered with ridicule. It was I, indeed, who, with more courage than any of your pretended friends—I except M. de Guiche—was the cause of your return from London; it is I, also, who have given you these melancholy proofs, necessary, however, for your cure, if you are a lover with courage in his heart, and not a weeping Amadis. Do not thank me; pity me even, and do not serve the King less faithfully than you have done."

Raoul smiled bitterly. "Ah! true, true; I was forgetting that; the King is my master."

"Your liberty, nay, your very life, is in danger."

A steady, penetrating look informed Madame Henrietta that she was mistaken, and that her last argument was not a likely one to affect the young man. "Take care, Monsieur de Bragelonne," she said, "for if you do not weigh well all your actions, you might throw into an extravagance of wrath, a prince, whose passions, once aroused, exceed the utmost limits of reason, and you would thereby involve your friends and family in the deepest distress; you must bend, you must submit, and must cure yourself."

"I thank you, madame; I appreciate the advice your Royal Highness is good enough to give me, and I will endeavour to follow it; but one final word, I beg."

"Name it."

"Should I be indiscreet in asking you the secret of this staircase, of this trap-door; a secret which, it seems, you have discovered?"

"Nothing is more simple. For the purpose of exercising a surveillance over the young girls who are attached to my service, I have duplicate keys of their doors. It seemed very strange to me that M. de Saint-Aignan should change his apartments. It seemed very strange that the King should come to see M. de Saint-Aignan every day, and, finally, it seemed very strange that so many things should be done during your absence that the very habits and customs of the court seemed to be changed. I do not wish to be trifled with by the King, nor to serve as a cloak for his love affairs; for, after La Vallière, who weeps incessantly, he will take a fancy to Montalais, who is always laughing; and then to Tonnay-Charente, who does nothing but sing all day; to act such a part as that would be unworthy of me. I have thrust aside the scruples which my friendship for you suggested. I have discovered the secret. I have wounded your feelings, I know; and I again entreat you to excuse me; but I had a duty to fulfil. I have discharged it. You are now forewarned; the tempest will soon burst; protect yourself accordingly."

"You naturally expect, however, that a result of some kind must follow," replied Bragelonne, with firmness; "for you do not suppose I shall silently accept the shame which is thrust upon me, or the treachery which has been practised against me."

"You will take whatever steps in the matter you please, Monsieur Raoul, only do not betray the source whence you derived the truth. That is all I have to ask, that is the only price I require for the service I have rendered you."

"Fear nothing, madame," said Bragelonne, with a bitter smile.

"I bribed the locksmith, in whom the lovers had confided. You can just as well have done so as myself can you not?"

"Yes, madame. Your Royal Highness, however, has no other advice or caution to give me except that of not betraying you."

"None other."

"I am about, therefore, to beg your Royal Highness to allow me to remain here for one moment."

"Without me?"

"Oh! no, madame. It matters very little; for what I have to do can be done in your presence. I only ask one moment to write a line to some one."

"It is dangerous, Monsieur de Bragelonne. Take care."

"No one can possibly know that your Royal Highness has done me the honour to conduct me here. Besides, I shall sign the letter I am going to write."

"Do as you please, then."

Raoul drew out his tablet, and wrote rapidly on one of the leaves the following words:—

"MONSIEUR LE COMTE.—Do not be surprised to find here this paper signed by me; the friend whom I shall very shortly send to call on you will have the honour to explain the object of my visit to you.

VICOMTE RAOUL DE BRAGELONNE."

He rolled up the paper, slipped it into the lock of the door which communicated with the room set apart for the two lovers, and satisfied himself that the paper was so apparent that Saint-Aignan could not but see it as he entered; he rejoined the Princess, who had already reached the top of the staircase. They then separated, Raoul pretending to thank Her Highness; Henrietta pitying, or seeming to pity, with all her heart, the poor wretched young man she had just condemned to such fearful torture. "Oh!" she said, as she saw him disappear, pale as death, and his eyes injected with blood, "if I had known this, I should have concealed the truth from that poor gentleman."

15

PORTHOS'S PLAN OF ACTION

THE numerous individuals we have introduced into this long story is the cause of each of them being obliged to appear only in his own turn, and according to the exigencies of the recital. The result is that our readers have had no opportunity of again meeting our friend Porthos since his return from Fontainebleau. The honours which he had received from the King had not changed the easy, affectionate character of that excellent-hearted man; he may perhaps have held up his head a little higher than usual, and a majesty of demeanour as it were may have betrayed itself since the honour of dining at the King's table had been accorded him. His Majesty's banqueting-room had produced a certain effect upon Porthos. Le Seigneur de Bracieux et de Pierrefonds delighted to remember that during that memorable dinner, the numerous array of servants, and the large number of officials who were in attendance upon the guests, gave a certain tone and effect to the repast, and seemed to furnish the room. Porthos undertook to confer upon Mouston a position of some kind or other, in order to establish a sort of hierarchy among his other domestics, and to create a military household, which was not unusual among the great captains of the age, since, in the preceding century, this luxury had been greatly encouraged by Messrs. de Tréville, de Schomberg, de la Vienville, without alluding to M. de Richelieu, M. de Condé, and de Bouillon-Turenne. And therefore why should not he, Porthos, the friend of the King, and of M. Fouquet, a baron, an engineer etc., why should not he indeed enjoy all the delightful privileges which large possessions and unusual merit invariably confer? Slightly neglected by Aramis, who we know was greatly occupied with M. Fouquet; neglected also, on account of his being on duty, by d'Artagnan; tired of Truchen and Planchet, Porthos was surprised to find himself dreaming, without precisely knowing why; but if any one had said to him, "Do you want anything, Porthos?" he would most certainly have replied "Yes." After one of those dinners, during which Porthos attempted to recall to his recollection all the details of the royal banquet, half joyful, thanks to the excellence of the wines; half melancholy, thanks to his ambitious ideas, Porthos was gradually falling off into a gentle doze, when his servant entered to announce that M. de Bragelonne wished to speak to him. Porthos passed into an adjoining room, where he found his young friend in the disposition of mind we are already aware of. Raoul advanced towards Porthos, and shook him by the hand; Porthos, surprised at his seriousness of aspect, offered him a seat. "Dear M. du Vallon," said Raoul, "I have a service to ask of you."

"Nothing could happen more fortunately, my young friend," replied Porthos; "I have had eight thousand livres sent me this morning from Pierrefonds; and if you want any money——"

"No, I thank you; it is not money."

"So much the worse, then. I have always heard it said that that is the rarest service, but the easiest to render. The remark struck me; I like to cite remarks that strike me."

"Your heart is as good as your mind is sound and true."

"You are too kind, I am sure. You will dine here, of course?"

"No; I am not hungry."

"Eh! not dine! What a dreadful country England is."

"Not too much so indeed—but——"

"Well. If such excellent fish and meat were not to be procured there, it would hardly be endurable."

"Yes, I came to——"

"I am listening. Only just allow me to take something to drink. One gets thirsty in Paris"; and he ordered a bottle of champagne to be brought; and, having first filled Raoul's glass, he filled his own, drank it down at a gulp, and then resumed,—"I needed that in order to listen to you with proper attention. I am now quite at your service. What have you to ask me, dear Raoul? What do you want?"

"Give me your opinion upon quarrels in general, my dear friend."

"My opinion! Well—but—— Explain your idea a little," replied Porthos, rubbing his forehead.

"I mean—are you generally good-humoured, or good-tempered, whenever any misunderstanding may arise between a friend of yours and a stranger, for instance?"

"Oh! in the best of tempers."

"Very good; but what do you do in such a case?"

"Whenever any friend of mine has a quarrel, I always act upon one principle."

"What is that?"

"That all lost time is irreparable, and that one never arranges an affair so well as when everything has been done to embroil the dispute as much as possible."

"Ah! indeed, that is the principle on which you proceed."

"Thoroughly; so soon as a quarrel takes place, I bring the two parties together."

"Exactly."

"You understand that by this means it is impossible for an affair not to be arranged."

"I should have thought that treated in this manner, an affair would, on the contrary——"

"Oh! not the least in the world. Just fancy now, I have had in my life something like a hundred and eighty to a hundred and ninety regular duels, without reckoning hasty encounters, or chance meetings."

"It is a very handsome number," said Raoul, unable to resist a smile.

"A mere nothing; but I am so gentle. D'Artagnan reckons his duels by hundreds. It is very true he is a little too hard and sharp— I have often told him so."

"And so," resumed Raoul, "you generally arrange the affairs of honour your friends confide to you."

"There is not a single instance in which I have not finished by arranging every one of them," said Porthos, with a gentleness and confidence which surprised Raoul.

"But the way in which you settle them is at least honourable, I suppose?"

"Oh! rely upon that; and at this stage, I will explain my other principle to you. As soon as my friend has confided his quarrel to me, this is what I do: I go to his adversary at once, armed with a politeness and self-possession which are absolutely requisite under such circumstances."

"That is the way, then," said Raoul bitterly, "that you arrange the affairs so safely."

"I believe you. I go to the adversary, then, and say to him, 'It is impossible, monsieur, that you are ignorant of the extent to which you have insulted my friend.'" Raoul frowned at this remark.

"It sometimes happens—very often, indeed," pursued Porthos —"that my friend has not been insulted at all; he has even been the first to give offence; you can imagine, therefore, whether my language is not well chosen." And Porthos burst into a peal of laughter.

"Decidedly," said Raoul to himself, while the formidable thunder of Porthos's laughter was ringing in his ears. "I am very unfortunate. De Guiche treats me with coldness, d'Artagnan with ridicule, Porthos is too tame, no one will settle this affair in my way. And I came to Porthos because I wish to find a sword instead of cold reasoning at my service. How my ill luck follows me."

Porthos, who had recovered himself, continued, "By a simple expression, I leave my adversary without an excuse."

"That is as it may happen," said Raoul distractedly.

"Not at all, it is quite certain. I have not left him an excuse; and then it is that I display all my courtesy, in order to attain the happy issue of my project. I advance, therefore, with an air of great politeness, and, taking my adversary by the hand, I say to him, 'Now that you are convinced of having given the offence, we are sure of reparation; between my friend and yourself, the future can only offer an exchange of mutual courtesies of conduct, and consequently, my mission is to give you the length of my friend's sword.'"

"What!" said Raoul.

"Wait a minute. 'The length of my friend's sword. My horse is waiting below; my friend is in such and such a spot, and is impatiently awaiting your agreeable society; I will take you with me; we can call upon your second as we go along'; and the affair is arranged."

"And so," said Raoul, pale with vexation, "you reconcile the two adversaries on the ground."

"I beg your pardon," interrupted Porthos. "Reconcile! What for?"

"You said that the affair was arranged."

"Of course! since my friend is waiting for him."

"Well! what then? If he is waiting——"

"Well! if he is waiting, it is merely to stretch his legs a little. The adversary, on the contrary, is stiff from riding; they place themselves in proper order, and my friend kills his opponent, and the affair is ended."

"Ah! he kills him, then?" cried Raoul.

"I should think so," said Porthos. "Is it likely I should ever have as a friend a man who allows himself to get killed? I have a hundred and one friends; at the head of the list stands your father, Aramis, and d'Artagnan, all of whom are living and well, I believe."

"Oh, my dear baron," exclaimed Raoul delightedly, as he embraced Porthos.

"You approve of my method, then?" said the giant.

"I approve of it so thoroughly, that I shall have recourse to it this very day, without a moment's delay,—at once, in fact. You are the very man I have been looking for."

"Good; here I am, then; you want to fight, I suppose?"

"Absolutely so."

"It is very natural. With whom?"

"With M. de Saint Aignan."

"I know him—a most agreeable man, who was exceedingly kind to me the day I had the honour of dining with the King. I shall certainly acknowledge his politeness in return, even if it had not happened to be my usual custom. So, he has given you offence?"

"A mortal offence."

"The deuce! I can say so, I suppose?"

"More than that, even, if you like."

"That is a very great convenience."

"I may look upon it as one of your arranged affairs, may I not?" said Raoul, smiling.

"As a matter of course. Where will you be waiting for him?"

"Ah! I forgot; it is a very delicate matter. M. de Saint-Aignan is a very great friend of the King's."

"So I have heard it said."

"So that if I kill him——"

"Oh! you will kill him, certainly; you must take every precaution to do so. But there is no difficulty in these matters now; if you had lived in our early days, oh! that was something like!"

"My dear friend, you have not quite understood me. I mean, that, M. de Saint-Aignan being a friend of the King, the affair will be more difficult to manage, since the King might learn beforehand——"

"Oh, no; that is not likely. You know my method: 'Monsieur, you have injured my friend, and——'"

"Yes, I know it."

"And then: 'Monsieur, I have horses below,' I carry him off before he can have spoken to any one."

"Will he allow himself to be carried off like that?"

"I should think so! I should like to see it fail. It would be the first time, if it did. It is true, though, that the young men of the present day—— Bah! I would carry him off bodily if that were all," and Porthos, adding gesture to speech, lifted Raoul and the chair he was sitting on off the ground, and carried them round the room.

"Very good," said Raoul, laughing. "All we have to do is to state the grounds of the quarrel to M. de Saint-Aignan."

"Well, but that is done, it seems."

"No, my dear M. du Vallon, the usage of the present day requires that the cause of the quarrel should be explained."

"Very good. Tell me what it is, then."

"The fact is——"

"Deuce take it! see how troublesome this is. In former days, we never had any occasion to say anything about the matter. People fought then for the sake of fighting; and I, for one, know no better reason than that."

"You are quite right, M. du Vallon."

"However, tell me what the cause is."

"It is too long a story to tell; only as one must particularise to some extent, and as, on the other hand, the affair is full of difficulties, and requires the most absolute secrecy, you will have the kindness merely to tell M. de Saint-Aignan that he has, in the first place, insulted me by changing his lodgings."

"By changing his lodgings? Good," said Porthos, who began to count on his fingers—"next?"

"Then in getting a trap-door made in his new apartments."

"I understand," said Porthos; "a trap-door; upon my word this is very serious; you ought to be furious at that. What the deuce does the fellow mean by getting trap-doors made without first consulting you? Trap-doors! *mordioux!* I haven't got any, except in my dungeons at Bracieux."

"And you will add," said Raoul, "that my last motive for considering myself insulted is, the portrait that M. de Saint-Aignan well knows."

"Is it possible? A portrait, too! A change of residence, a trap-door and a portrait! Why, my dear friend, with but one of these causes of complaint there is enough, and more than enough for all the gentlemen in France and Spain to cut each others' throats, and that is saying but very little."

"Well, my dear friend, you are furnished with all you need, I suppose?"

"I shall take a second horse with me. Select your own rendez-vous, and while you are waiting there, you can practise some of the best passes, so as to get your limbs as elastic as possible."

"Thank you. I shall be waiting for you in the wood of Vincennes, close to Minimes."*

"All's right, then. Where am I to find this M. de Saint-Aignan?"

"At the Palais-Royal."

Porthos rang a huge hand-bell. "My court suit," he said to the servant who answered the summons, "my horse, and a led horse to accompany me." Then, turning to Raoul, as soon as the servant had quitted the room, he said, "Does your father know anything about this?"

"No; I am going to write to him."

"And d'Artagnan?"

"No, nor d'Artagnan either. He is very cautious, you know, and might have diverted me from my purpose."

"D'Artagnan is a sound adviser though," said Porthos astonished that, in his own loyal faith in d'Artagnan, any one could have thought of himself so long as there was a d'Artagnan in the world.

"Dear M. du Vallon," replied Raoul, "do not question me any more, I implore you. I have told you all that I had to say; it is prompt action that I now expect, as sharp and decided as you know how to arrange it. That, indeed, is my reason for having chosen you."

"You will be satisfied with me," replied Porthos.

"Do not forget, either, that except ourselves, no one must know anything of this meeting."

"People always find these things out," said Porthos, "when a dead body is discovered in a wood. But I promise you everything, my dear friend, except concealing the dead body. There it is, and it must be seen, as a matter of course. It is a principle of mine, not to bury bodies. That has a smack of the assassin about it. Every risk must run its own risk."

"To work, then, my dear friend."

"Rely upon me," said the giant, finishing the bottle, while the servant spread out upon a sofa the gorgeously-decorated dress trimmed with lace.

Raoul left the room, saying to himself, with a secret delight, "Perfidious King! traitorous monarch! I cannot reach thee. I do not wish it; for kings are sacred objects. But your friend, your accomplice, your panderer—the coward who represents you—shall pay for your crime. I will kill him in thy name, and afterwards we will think of Louise."

16

THE CHANGE OF RESIDENCE, THE TRAP-DOOR, AND THE PORTRAIT

PORTHOS, intrusted to his great delight with this mission, which made him feel young again, took half an hour less than his usual time to put on his court suit. To show that he was a man acquainted with the usages of the highest society, he had begun by sending his lackey to inquire if Monsieur de Saint-Aignan were at home, and received in answer, that M. le Comte de Saint-Aignan, had had the honour of accompanying the King to Saint-Germain, as well as the whole court; but that Monsieur le Comte had just that moment returned. Immediately upon this reply, Porthos made as much haste as possible, and reached Saint-Aignan's apartments just as the latter was having his boots taken off. The promenade had been delightful. The King, who was in love more than ever, and of course happier than ever, behaved in the most charming manner to every one. Nothing could possibly equal his kindness. M. de Saint-Aignan, it may be remembered, was a poet, and fancied that he had proved that he was so, under too many a memorable circumstance, to allow the title to be disputed by any one. An indefatigable rhymester, he had, during the whole of the journey, overwhelmed with quatrains, sextains and madrigals, first the King, and then La Vallière. The King was, on his side, in a similarly poetical mood, and had made a distich; while La Vallière, like all women who are in love, had composed two sonnets. As one may see, then, the day had not been a bad one for Apollo; and, therefore, as soon as he had returned to Paris, Saint-Aignan, who knew beforehand that his verses would be sure to be extensively circulated in court circles, occupied himself, with a little more attention than he had been able to bestow during the promenade, with the composition, as well as with the idea itself. Consequently, with all the tenderness of a father about to start his children in life, he candidly interrogated himself whether the public would find these offspring of his imagination sufficiently elegant and graceful; and so, in order to make his mind easy on the subject, M. de Saint-Aignan recited to himself the madrigal he had composed, and which he had repeated from memory to the King, and which he had promised to write out for him on his return. All the time he was committing these words to memory, the Comte was engaged in undressing himself more completely. He had just taken off his coat, and was putting on his dressing-gown, when he was informed that Monsieur le Baron du Vallon de Bracieux de Pierrefonds was waiting to be received.

"Eh!" he said, "what does that bunch of names mean? I don't know anything about him."

"It is the same gentleman," replied the lackey, "who had the honour of dining with you, monseigneur, at the King's table, when His Majesty was staying at Fontainebleau."

"Introduce him, then, at once," cried Saint-Aignan.

Porthos in a few minutes entered the room. M. de Saint-Aignan had an excellent recollection of persons, and at the first glance, he recognised the gentleman from the country, who enjoyed so singular a reputation, and whom the King had received so favourably at Fontainebleau, in spite of the smiles of some of those who were present. He therefore advanced towards Porthos with all the outward signs of a consideration of manner which Porthos thought but natural, considering that he himself, whenever he called upon an adversary, hoisted the standard of the most refined politeness. Saint-Aignan desired the servant to give Porthos a chair; and the latter, who saw nothing unusual in this act of politeness, sat down gravely, and coughed. The ordinary courtesies having been exchanged between the two gentlemen, the Comte, to whom the visit was paid, said, "May I ask, Monsieur le Baron, to what happy circumstance I am indebted for the favour of a visit from you?"

"The very thing I am about to have the honour of explaining to you, Monsieur le Comte, but, I beg your pardon——"

"What is the matter, monsieur?" inquired Saint-Aignan.

"I regret to say that I have broken your chair."

"Not at all, monsieur," said Saint-Aignan; "not at all."

"It is the fact, though, Monsieur le Comte; I have broken it—so much so, indeed, that, if I do not move, I shall fall down, which would be an exceedingly disagreeable position for me in the discharge of the very serious mission which has been intrusted to me with regard to yourself."

Porthos rose, and just in time, for the chair had given way several inches. Saint-Aignan looked about him for something more solid for his guest to sit upon. "Modern articles of furniture," said Porthos while the Comte was looking about, "are constructed in a ridiculously light manner. In my early days, when I used to sit down with far more energy than is now the case, I do not remember ever to have broken a chair, except in taverns, with my arms."

Saint-Aignan smiled at this remark. "But," said Porthos as he settled himself down on a couch, which creaked, but did not give way beneath his weight, "that, unfortunately, has nothing whatever to do with my present visit."

"Why unfortunately? Are you the bearer of a message of ill omen, Monsieur le Baron?"

"Of ill omen—for a gentleman? Certainly not, Monsieur le Comte," replied Porthos nobly. "I have simply come to say you have seriously insulted a friend of mine."

"I, monsieur?" exclaimed Saint-Aignan—"I have insulted a friend of yours, do you say? May I ask his name?"

"M. Raoul de Bragelonne."

"I have insulted M. Raoul de Bragelonne!" cried Saint-Aignan. "I really assure you, that it is quite impossible; for M. de Bragelonne, whom I know but very slightly—nay, whom I know hardly at all—is in England; and, as I have not seen him for a long time past, I cannot possibly have insulted him."

"M. de Bragelonne is in Paris, Monsieur le Comte," said Porthos, perfectly unmoved; "and I repeat it is quite certain you have insulted him since he himself told me you had. Yes, monsieur, you have seriously insulted him, mortally insulted him, I repeat."

"It is impossible, Monsieur le Baron, I swear, quite impossible."

"Besides," added Porthos, "you cannot be ignorant of the circumstance, since M. de Bragelonne informed me that he had already apprised you of it by a note."

"I give you my word of honour, monsieur, that I have received no note whatever."

"This is most extraordinary," replied Porthos.

"I will convince you," said Saint-Aignan, "that I have received nothing in any way from him." And he rang the bell. "Basque," he said to the servant who entered, "how many letters or notes were sent here during my absence?"

"Three, Monsieur le Comte—a note from M. de Fiesque, one from Madame de Laferté, and a letter from M. de las Fuentès."

"Is that all?"

"Yes, Monsieur le Comte."

"Speak the truth before this gentleman—the truth, you understand. I will take care you are not blamed."

"There was a note also from—from——"

"Well, from whom?"

"From Mademoiselle de Laval——"

"That is quite sufficient," interrupted Porthos. "I believe you, Monsieur le Comte."

Saint-Aignan dismissed the valet, and followed him to the door, in order to close it after him; and when he had done so, looking straight before him, he happened to see in the keyhole of the adjoining apartment the paper which Bragelonne had slipped in there as he left. "What is this?" he said.

Porthos, who was sitting with his back to the room, turned round. "Oh, oh," he said.

"A note in the keyhole!" exclaimed Saint-Aignan.

"That is not unlikely to be the one we want, Monsieur le Comte," said Porthos.

Saint-Aignan took out the paper. "A note from M. de Bragelonne!" he exclaimed.

"You see, monsieur, I was right. Oh, when I say a thing——"

"Brought here by M. de Bragelonne himself," the Comte murmured, turning pale. "This is infamous! How could he possibly have come here?" And the Comte rang again.

"Who has been here during my absence with the King?"

"No one, monsieur."

"That is impossible! Some one must have been here."

"No one could possibly have entered, monsieur; since I keep the keys in my own pocket."

"And yet I find this letter in that lock yonder; some one must have put it there; it could not have come alone."

Basque opened his arms as if signifying the most absolute ignorance on the subject.

"Probably it was M. de Bragelonne himself who placed it there," said Porthos.

"In that case he must have entered here."

"How could that have been, since I have the key in my own pocket?" returned Basque perseveringly.

Saint-Aignan crumpled up the letter in his hand, after having read it. "There is something mysterious about this," he murmured, absorbed in thought. Porthos left him to his reflections; but after a while returned to the mission he had undertaken.

"Shall we return to our little affair?" he said, addressing Saint-Aignan as soon as the lackey had disappeared.

"I think I can now understand it, from this note, which has arrived here in so singular a manner. Monsieur de Bragelonne says that a friend will call."

"I am his friend, and am the one he alludes to."

"For the purpose of giving me a challenge?"

"Precisely."

"And he complains that I have insulted him?"

"Mortally so."

"In what way, may I ask; for his conduct is so mysterious, that it, at least, needs some explanation?"

"Monsieur," replied Porthos, "my friend cannot but be right; and, as far as his conduct is concerned, if it be mysterious, as you say, you have only yourself to blame for it." Porthos pronounced these words with an amount of confidence which, for a man who was unaccustomed to his ways, must have revealed an infinity of sense.

"Mystery, be it so; but what is the mystery about?" said Saint-Aignan.

"You will think it best, perhaps," Porthos replied with a low bow, "that I do not enter into particulars."

"Oh, I perfectly understand. We will touch very lightly upon it, then; so speak, monsieur, I am listening."

"In the first place, monsieur," said Porthos, "you have changed your apartments."

"Yes, that is quite true," said Saint-Aignan.

"You admit it," said Porthos with an air of satisfaction.

"Admit it! of course I admit it. Why should I not admit it, do you suppose?"

"You have admitted it. Very good," said Porthos lifting up one finger.

"But how can my having moved my lodgings have done M. de Bragelonne any harm? Have the goodness to tell me that, for I positively do not comprehend a word of what you are saying."

Porthos stopped him, and then said, with great gravity, "Monsieur, this is the first of M. de Bragelonne's complaints against you. If he makes a complaint, it is because he feels himself insulted."

Saint-Aignan began to beat his foot impatiently on the ground. "This looks like a bad quarrel," he said.

"No one can possibly have a bad quarrel with the Vicomte de Bragelonne," returned Porthos; "but at all events, you have nothing to add on the subject of your changing your apartments, I suppose?"

"Nothing. And what is the next point?"

"Ah, the next! You will observe, monsieur, that the one I have already mentioned is a most serious injury, to which you have given no answer, or rather have answered very indifferently. Is it possible, monsieur, that you have changed your lodgings? M. de Bragelonne feels insulted at your having done so, and you do not attempt to excuse yourself."

"What!" cried Saint-Aignan, who was getting annoyed at the perfect coolness of his visitor—"what! am I to consult M. de Bragelonne whether I am to move or not? You can hardly be serious, monsieur."

"Absolutely necessary, monsieur; but, under any circumstances, you will admit that it is nothing in comparison with the second ground of complaint."

"Well, what is that?"

Porthos assumed a very serious expression as he said, "How about the trap-door, monsieur?"

Saint-Aignan turned exceedingly pale. He pushed back his chair so abruptly that Porthos, simple as he was, perceived that the blow had told. "The trap-door," murmured Saint-Aignan.

"Yes, monsieur, explain that if you can," said Porthos, shaking his head.

Saint-Aignan held down his head as he murmured. "I have been betrayed, everything is known!"

"Everything," replied Porthos, who knew nothing.

"You see me perfectly overwhelmed," pursued Saint-Aignan, "overwhelmed to a degree that I hardly know what I am about."

"A guilty conscience, monsieur. Your affair is a bad one, and when the public shall learn all about it, and will judge——"

"Oh, monsieur!" exclaimed the Comte hurriedly, "such a secret ought not to be known, even by one's confessor."

"That we will think about," said Porthos; "the secret will not go far, in fact."

"Surely, monsieur," returned Saint-Aignan, "since M. de Bragelonne has penetrated the secret, he must be aware of the danger he as well as others run the risk of incurring."

"M. de Bragelonne runs no danger, monsieur, nor does he fear any either, as you, if it please Heaven, will find out very soon."

"This fellow is a perfect madman," thought Saint-Aignan. "What in Heaven's name does he want?" He then said aloud, "Come, monsieur, let us hush up this affair."

"You forget the portrait," said Porthos in a voice of thunder, which made the Comte's blood freeze in his veins.

As the portrait in question was La Vallière's portrait, and as no mistake could any longer exist on the subject, Saint-Aignan's eyes were completely opened. "Ah!" he exclaimed—"ah! monsieur, I remember now that M. de Bragelonne was engaged to be married to her."

Porthos assumed an imposing air, all the majesty of ignorance, in fact, as he said, "It matters nothing whatever to me, nor to yourself, indeed, whether or not my friend was, as you say, engaged to be married. I am even astonished that you should have made use of so indiscreet a remark. It may possibly do your cause harm, monsieur."

"Monsieur," replied Saint-Aignan, "you are the incarnation

of intelligence, delicacy and loyalty of feeling united. I see the whole matter now clearly enough."

"So much the better," said Porthos.

"And," pursued Saint-Aignan, "you have made me comprehend it in the most ingenious and the most delicate manner possible. I beg you to accept my best thanks."

Porthos drew himself up, unable to resist the flattery of the remark. "Only, now that I know everything, permit me to explain——"

Porthos shook his head as a man who does not wish to hear, but Saint-Aignan continued: "I am in despair, I assure you, at all that has happened; but how would you have acted in my place? Come, between ourselves, tell me what would you have done?"

Porthos drew himself up as he answered: "There is no question at all of what I should have done, young man; you have now been made acquainted with the three causes of complaint against you, I believe?"

"As for the first, my change of rooms, and I now address myself to you, as a man of honour and of great intelligence, could I, when the desire of so august a personage was so urgently expressed that I should move, ought I to have disobeyed?"

Porthos was about to speak, but Saint-Aignan did not give him time to answer. "Ah! my frankness, I see, convinces you," he said, interpreting the movement according to his own fancy. "You feel that I am right."

Porthos did not reply, and so Saint-Aignan continued: "I pass by that unfortunate trap-door," he said, placing his hand on Porthos's arm, "that trap-door, the occasion and the means of so much unhappiness, and which was constructed for—you know what. Well, then, in plain truth, do you suppose that it was I who, of my own accord, in such a place too, had that trap-door made?— Oh no! you do not believe it; and here, again, you feel, you guess, you understand the influence of a will superior to my own. You can conceive the infatuation, the blind, irresistible passion which has been at work. But, thank Heaven! I am fortunate enough in speaking to a man who has so much sensitiveness of feeling: if it were not so, indeed, what an amount of misery and scandal would fall upon her, poor girl! and upon him—whom I will not name."

Porthos, confused and bewildered by the eloquence and gestures of Saint-Aignan, made a thousand efforts to stem this torrent of words, of which, by the bye, he did not understand a single one; he remained upright and motionless on his seat, and that was all he could do. Saint-Aignan continued, and gave a new inflection to his voice, and an increasing vehemence to his gesture:

"As for the portrait, for I readily believe the portrait is the
principal cause of complaint, tell me candidly if you think me to
blame?—Who was it who wished to have her portrait? Was it I?—
Who is in love with her? Is it I?—Who wishes to gain her affection? Again, is it I?—Who took her likeness? I, do you think?
No! a thousand times no! I know M. de Bragelonne must be in a
state of despair; I know these misfortunes are most cruel. But, I,
too, am suffering as well; and yet there is no possibility of offering
any resistance. Suppose we were to struggle? We would be laughed
at. If he obstinately persists in his course, he is lost. You will tell
me, I know, that despair is ridiculous, but then you are a sensible
man. You have understood me. I perceive by your serious,
thoughtful, embarrassed air, even, that the importance of the
situation we are placed in has not escaped you. Return, therefore,
to M. de Bragelonne; thank him—as I have indeed reason to
thank him,—for having chosen as an intermediary a man of your
high merit. Believe me that I shall, on my side, preserve an
eternal gratitude for the man who has so ingeniously, so cleverly,
arranged the misunderstanding between us. And since ill luck
would have it that the secret should be known to four instead of to
three, why, this secret, which might make the most ambitious
man's fortune, I am delighted to share with you, monsieur, from
the bottom of my heart, I am delighted at it. From this very
moment you can make use of me as you please, I place myself
entirely at your mercy. What can I possibly do for you? What can
I solicit, nay, require even? You have only to speak, monsieur,
only to speak."

And, according to the familiarly friendly fashion of that period,
Saint-Aignan threw his arms round Porthos, and clasped him
tenderly in his embrace. Porthos allowed him to do this with the
most perfect indifference. "Speak," resumed Saint-Aignan, "what
do you require?"

"Monsieur," said Porthos, "I have a horse below, be good
enough to mount him, he is a very good one and will play you no
tricks."

"Mount on horseback! what for?" inquired Saint-Aignan,
with no little curiosity.

"To accompany me where M. de Bragelonne is awaiting us."

"Ah! he wishes to speak to me, I suppose? I can well believe
that; he wishes to have the details, very likely; alas! it is a very
delicate matter; but at the present moment I cannot, for the
King is waiting for me."

"The King must wait, then," said Porthos.

"What do you say? the King must wait!" interrupted the

finished courtier, with a smile of utter amazement, for he could not understand that the King could under any circumstances be supposed to have to wait.

"It is merely the affair of a very short hour," returned Porthos.

"But where is M. de Bragelonne waiting for me?"

"At the Minimes, at Vincennes."

"Ah, indeed! but are we going to laugh over the affair when we get there?"

"I don't think it likely," said Porthos, as his face assumed a stern hardness of expression.

"But the Minimes is a rendezvous where duels take place, and what can I have to do at the Minimes?"

Porthos slowly drew his sword, and said: "That is the length of my friend's sword."

"Why, the man is mad!" cried Saint-Aignan.

The colour mounted to Porthos's face, as he replied: "If I had not the honour of being in your own apartment, monsieur, and of representing M. de Bragelonne's interests, I would throw you out of the window. It will be merely a pleasure postponed, and you will lose nothing by waiting. Will you come with me to the Minimes, monsieur, of your own free will?"

"But——"

"Take care, I will carry you if you do not come quietly."

"Basque!" cried Saint-Aignan. As soon as Basque appeared, he said, "The King wishes to see Monsieur le Comte."

"That is very different," said Porthos; "the King's service before everything else. We will wait until this evening, monsieur."

And saluting Saint-Aignan with his usual courtesy, Porthos left the room, delighted at having arranged another affair. Saint-Aignan looked after him as he left; and then, hastily putting on his coat again, he ran off, arranging his dress as he went along, muttering to himself "The Minimes! the Minimes! We will see how the King will like this challenge; for it is for him after all, that is certain."

17

RIVAL POLITICS

ON his return from the promenade, which had been so prolific in
poetical effusions, and in which every one had paid his or her
tribute to the Muses, as the poets of the period used to say, the
King found M. Fouquet waiting for an audience. M. Colbert had
laid in wait for His Majesty in the corridor, and followed him like
a jealous and watchful shadow; M. Colbert, with his square head,
his vulgar and untidy, though rich, costume, somewhat resembled
a Flemish gentleman after he had been over-indulging in his
national drink—beer. Fouquet, at the sight of his enemy, remained perfectly unmoved, and during the whole of the scene
which followed scrupulously resolved to observe that line of
conduct which is so difficult to be carried out by a man of superior
mind, who does not even wish to show his contempt, from the
fear of doing his adversary too much honour. Colbert made no
attempt to conceal the insulting expression of the joy he felt. In
his opinion, M. Fouquet's was a game very badly played and
hopelessly lost, although not yet finished. Colbert belonged to that
school of politicians who think cleverness alone worthy of their
admiration, and success the only thing worth caring for. Colbert,
moreover, who was not simply an envious and jealous man, but
who had the King's interest really at heart, because he was
thoroughly imbued with the highest sense of probity in all matters
of figures and accounts, could well afford to assign as a pretext
for his conduct, that in hating and doing his utmost to ruin M.
Fouquet, he had nothing in view but the welfare of the state and
the dignity of the crown. None of these details escaped Fouquet's
observation; through his enemy's thick, bushy brows, and despite
the restless movement of his eyelids, he could, by merely looking
at his eyes, penetrate to the very bottom of Colbert's heart, and he
read to what an unbounded extent hate towards himself and
triumph at his approaching fall existed there. But, as, in observing
everything, he wished to remain himself impenetrable, he composed his features, smiled with that charmingly sympathetic smile
which was peculiarly his own, and saluted the King with the most
dignified and graceful ease and elasticity of manner. "Sire," he
said, "I perceive by your Majesty's joyous air that you have been
gratified with the promenade."

"Most gratified, indeed, Monsieur le Surintendant, most gratified. You were very wrong not to come with us, as I invited you to do."

"I was working, sire," replied the Surintendant, who did not even seem to take the trouble to turn aside his head even in the merest recognition of Colbert's presence.

"Ah! M. Fouquet," cried the King, "there is nothing like the country. I should be very delighted to live in the country always, in the open air and under the trees."

"I should hope that your Majesty is not yet weary of the throne," said Fouquet.

"No; but thrones of soft turf are very delightful."

"Your Majesty gratifies my utmost wishes in speaking in that manner, for I have a request to submit to you."

"On whose behalf, monsieur?"

"On behalf of the nymphs of Vaux, sire."

"Ah! ah!" said Louis XIV.

"Your Majesty, too, once deigned to make me a promise," said Fouquet.

"Yes, I remember it."

"The fête at Vaux, the celebrated fête, I think, it was, sire," said Colbert, endeavouring to show his importance by taking part in the conversation.

Fouquet, with the profoundest contempt, did not take the slightest notice of the remark, as if, as far as he was concerned, Colbert had not even thought or said a word.

"Your Majesty is aware," he said, "that I destine my estate at Vaux to receive the most amiable of princes, the most powerful of monarchs."

"I have given you my promise, monsieur," said Louis XIV., smiling; "and a King never departs from his word."

"And I have come now, sire, to inform your Majesty that I am ready to obey your orders in every respect."

"Do you promise me many wonders, Monsieur le Surintendant?" said Louis, looking at Colbert.

"Wonders? Oh! no, sire. I do not undertake that; I hope to be able to procure your Majesty a little pleasure, perhaps even a little forgetfulness of the cares of state."

"Nay, nay, M. Fouquet," returned the King; "I insist upon the word 'wonders.' You are a magician, I believe; we all know the power you wield; we also know that you can find gold even when there is none to be found elsewhere; so much so, indeed, that the people say you coin it."

Fouquet felt that the shot was discharged from a double

quiver, and that the King had launched an arrow from his own bow as well as one from Colbert's. "Oh!" said he laughingly, "the people know perfectly well out of what mine I procure the gold; and you know it only too well, perhaps; besides," he added, "I can assure your Majesty that the gold destined to pay the expenses of the fête at Vaux will cost neither blood nor tears; hard labour it may, perhaps, but that can be paid for."

Louis paused, quite confused. He wished to look at Colbert; Colbert, too, wished to reply to him; a glance as swift as an eagle's, a proud, loyal, king-like glance, indeed, which Fouquet darted at the latter, arresting the words upon his lips. The King, who had by this time recovered his self-possession, turned towards Fouquet, saying, "I presume, therefore, I am now to consider myself formally invited?"

"Yes, sire, if your Majesty will condescend so far as to accept my invitation."

"What day have you fixed?"

"Any day your Majesty may find most convenient."

"You speak like an enchanter who has but to conjure up the wildest fancies, Monsieur Fouquet. I could not say so much indeed."

"Your Majesty will do, whenever you please, everything that a monarch can and ought to do. The King of France has servants at his bidding who are able to do anything on his behalf, to accomplish everything to gratify his pleasures."

Colbert tried to look at the Surintendant, in order to see whether this remark was an approach to less hostile sentiments on his part; but Fouquet had not even looked at his enemy, and Colbert hardly seemed to exist as far as he was concerned. "Very good, then," said the King. "Will a week hence suit you?"

"Perfectly well, sire."

"This is Tuesday; if I give you until next Sunday week, will that be sufficient?"

"The delay which your Majesty deigns to accord me will greatly aid the various works which my architects have in hand for the purpose of adding to the amusement of your Majesty and your friends."

"By the bye, speaking of my friends," resumed the King; "how do you intend to treat them?"

"The King is master everywhere, sire; your Majesty will draw up your own list and give your own orders. All those you may deign to invite will be my guests, my honoured guests indeed."

"I thank you!" returned the King, touched by the noble thought expressed in so noble a tone.

Fouquet, therefore, took leave of Louis XIV., after a few words had been added with regard to the details of certain matters of business. He felt that Colbert would remain behind with the King, that they would both converse about him, and that neither of them would spare him in the least degree. The satisfaction of being able to give a last and terrible blow to his enemy seemed to him almost like a compensation for everything they were about to subject him to. He turned back again immediately, as soon indeed as he had reached the door and, addressing the King, said, "I was forgetting that I had to crave your Majesty's forgiveness."

"In what respect?" said the King graciously.

"For having committed a serious fault without perceiving it."

"A fault! You! Ah! Monsieur Fouquet, I shall be unable to do otherwise than forgive you. In what way or against whom have you been found wanting?"

"Against every sense of propriety, sire. I forgot to inform your Majesty of a circumstance that has lately occurred of some little importance."

"What is it?"

Colbert trembled; he fancied that he was about to frame a denunciation against him. His conduct had been unmasked. A single syllable from Fouquet, a single proof formally advanced, and before the youthful loyalty of feeling which guided Louis XIV., Colbert's favour would disappear at once; the latter trembled, therefore, lest so daring a blow might not overthrow his whole scaffold; in point of fact, the opportunity was so admirably suited to be taken advantage of, that a skilful, practised player like Aramis would not have let it slip. "Sire," said Fouquet, with an easy unconcerned air, "since you have had the kindness to forgive me, I am perfectly indifferent about my confession; this morning I sold one of the official appointments I hold."

"One of your appointments," said the King, "which?"

Colbert turned perfectly livid. "That which conferred upon me, sire, a grand gown and a stern air of gravity; the appointment of procureur-général."

The King involuntarily uttered a loud exclamation and looked at Colbert, who, with his face bedewed with perspiration, felt almost on the point of fainting. "To whom have you sold this appointment, Monsieur Fouquet?" inquired the King.

Colbert was obliged to lean against the side of the fireplace. "To a councillor belonging to the Parliament, sire, whose name is Vanel."

"Vanel?"

"Yes, sire, a friend of Colbert," added Fouquet; letting every word fall from his lips with the most inimitable nonchalance, and with an admirably assumed expression of forgetfulness and ignorance. And having finished, and having overwhelmed Colbert beneath the weight of this superiority, the Surintendant again saluted the King and quitted the room, partially revenged by the stupefaction of the King and the humiliation of the favourite.

"Is it really possible," said the King, as soon as Fouquet had disappeared, "that he has sold that office?"

"Yes, sire," said Colbert meaningly.

"He must be mad," the King added.

Colbert this time did not reply; he had penetrated the King's thought, a thought which amply revenged him for the humiliation he had just been made to suffer; his hatred was augmented by a feeling of bitter jealousy of Fouquet; and a threat of disgrace was now added to the plan he had arranged for his ruin. Colbert felt perfectly assured that for the future, between Louis XIV. and himself, hostile feelings and ideas would meet with no obstacles, and that at the first fault committed by Fouquet, which could be laid hold of as a pretext, the chastisement impending over him would be precipitated. Fouquet had thrown aside his weapons of defence, and hate and jealousy had picked them up. Colbert was invited by the King to the fête at Vaux; he bowed like a man confident in himself, and accepted the invitation with the air of one who almost confers a favour. The King was about to write down Saint-Aignan's name on his list of royal commands, when the usher announced the Comte de Saint-Aignan; as soon as the royal "Mercury"*entered, Colbert discreetly withdrew.

18

RIVAL AFFECTIONS

SAINT-AIGNAN had quitted Louis XIV. hardly a couple of hours before; but in the first effervescence of his affection, whenever Louis XIV. did not see La Vallière, he was obliged to talk of her. Besides, the only person with whom he could speak about her at his ease was Saint-Aignan, and Saint-Aignan had, therefore, become indispensable to him.

"Ah! is that you, Comte?" he exclaimed as soon as he perceived him, doubly delighted, not only to see him again, but also to get rid of Colbert, whose scowling face always put him out of humour. "So much the better, I am very glad to see you; you will make one of the travelling party, I suppose?"

"Of what travelling party are you speaking, sire?" inquired Saint-Aignan.

"The one we are making up to go to the fête, the Surintendant is about to give at Vaux. Ah! Saint-Aignan, you will, at last, see a fête, a royal fête, by the side of which all our amusements at Fontainebleau are petty, contemptible affairs."

"At Vaux! the Surintendant going to give a fête in your Majesty's honour? Nothing more than that!"

"'Nothing more than that,' do you say. It is very diverting to find you treating it with so much disdain. Are you, who express such an indifference on the subject, aware, that as soon as it is known that M. Fouquet is going to receive me at Vaux next Sunday week, people will be striving their very utmost to get invited to the fête. I repeat, Saint-Aignan, you shall be one of the invited guests."

"Very well, sire; unless I shall not in the meantime, have undertaken a longer and less agreeable journey."

"What journey do you allude to?"

"The one across the Styx,* sire."

"Bah!" said Louis XIV., laughing.

"No, seriously, sire," replied Saint-Aignan, "I am invited there; and in such a way, in truth, that I hardly know what to say, or how to act, in order to refuse it."

"I do not understand you. I know that you are in a poetical vein; but try not to sink from Apollo to Phœbus."*

"Very well; if your Majesty will deign to listen to me, I will not put your mind on the rack any longer."

"Speak."

"Your Majesty knows the Baron du Vallon?"

"Yes, indeed; a good servant to my father, the late King, and an admirable companion at table; for, I think, you are referring to the one who dined with us at Fontainebleau?"

"Precisely so; but you have omitted to add to his other qualifications, sire, that he is a most charming killer of other people."

"What! Does M. du Vallon wish to kill you?"

"Or to get me killed, which is the same thing."

"The deuce!"

"Do not laugh, sire, for I am not saying a word that is not the exact truth."

"And you say he wishes to get you killed?"

"That is that excellent person's present idea."

"Be easy; I will defend you, if he be in the wrong."

"Ah! there is an 'if'!"

"Of course; answer me as candidly as if it were some one else's affair instead of your own, my poor Saint-Aignan; is he right or wrong?"

"Your Majesty shall be the judge."

"What have you done to him?"

"To him, personally, nothing at all; but, it seems, I have to one of his friends."

"It is all the same. Is his friend one of the celebrated 'four'?"

"No! It is the son of one of the celebrated 'four,' instead."

"What have you done to the son? Come, tell me."

"Why, it seems I have helped some one to take his mistress from him."

"You confess it, then?"

"I cannot help confessing it, for it is true."

"In that case, you are wrong; and if he were to kill you, he would be acting perfectly right."

"Ah! that is your Majesty's way of reasoning, then?"

"Do you think it a bad way?"

"It is a very expeditious way, at all events."

"'Good justice is prompt'; so my grandfather, Henry IV., used to say."

"In that case, your Majesty will, perhaps, be good enough to sign my adversary's pardon, for he is now waiting for me at the Minimes, for the purpose of putting me out of my misery."

"His name, and a parchment!"

"There is a parchment upon your Majesty's table; and as for his name——"

"Well, what is it?"

"The Vicomte de Bragelonne, sire."

"'The Vicomte de Bragelonne'!" exclaimed the King, changing from a fit of laughter, to the most profound stupor; and then, after a moment's silence, while he wiped his forehead, which was bedewed with perspiration, he again murmured, "Bragelonne!"

"No other than he, sire."

"Bragelonne, who was affianced to——"

"Yes, sire."

"He was in London, however."

"Yes, but I can assure you, sire, he is there no longer."

"Is he in Paris, then?"

"He is at the Minimes, sire, where he is waiting for me, as I have already had the honour of telling you."

"Does he know all?"

"Yes; and many things besides. Perhaps your Majesty would like to look at the letter I have received from him;" and Saint-

Aignan drew from his pocket the note which we are already acquainted with. "When your Majesty has read the letter, I will tell you how it reached me."

The King read it in great agitation, and immediately said, "Well?"

"Well, sire; your Majesty knows a certain carved lock, closing a certain door of ebony-wood, which separates a certain apartment from a certain blue and white sanctuary?"

"Of course; Louise's boudoir."

"Yes, sire. Well, it was in the key-hole of that lock that I found that note."

"Who placed it there?"

"Either M. de Bragelonne, or the devil himself; but, inasmuch as the note smells of amber and not of sulphur, I conclude that it must be, not the devil, but M. de Bragelonne."

Louis bent down his head, and seemed absorbed in sad and melancholy reflections. Perhaps something like remorse was at the moment passing through his heart. "The secret is discovered," he said.

"Sire, I shall do my utmost, that the secret dies in the breast of the man who possesses it," said Saint-Aignan in a tone of bravado, as he moved towards the door; but a gesture of the King made him pause.

"Where are you going?" he inquired.

"Where I am waited for, sire."

"What for?"

"To fight, in all probability."

"You fight!" exclaimed the King. "One moment, if you please, Monsieur le Comte!"

Saint-Aignan shook his head as a rebellious child does, whenever any one interferes to prevent him throwing himself into a well, or playing with a knife.

"But yet, sire," he said.

"In the first place," continued the King, "I require to be enlightened a little."

"Upon that point, if your Majesty will be pleased to interrogate me," replied Saint-Aignan, "I will throw what light I can."

"Who told you that M. de Bragelonne had penetrated into that room?"

"The letter which I found in the keyhole told me so."

"Who told you that it was de Bragelonne who put it there?"

"Who but himself would have dared to undertake such a mission?"

"You are right. How was he able to get into your rooms?"

"Ah! that is very serious, inasmuch as all the doors were closed, and my lackey, Basque, had the keys in his pocket."

"Your lackey must have been bribed."

"Impossible, sire; for if he had been bribed, those who did so would not have sacrificed the poor fellow, whom, it is not unlikely, they might want to turn to further use by-and-by, in showing so clearly that it was he whom they had made use of."

"Quite true. And now I can only form one conjecture."

"Tell me what it is, sire, and we shall see if it is the same that has presented itself to my mind."

"That he affected an entrance by means of the staircase."

"Alas, sire, that seems to me more than probable."

"There is no doubt that some one must have sold the secret of the trap-door."

"Either sold it or given it."

"Why do you make that distinction?"

"Because there are certain persons, sire, who, being above the price of a treason, give, and do not sell."

"What do you mean?"

"Oh, sire! Your Majesty's mind is too clear-sighted not to guess what I mean, and you will save me the embarrassment of naming the person I allude to."

"You are right; you mean Madame! I suppose her suspicions were aroused by your changing your lodgings."

"Madame has keys of the apartments of her maids-of-honour, and she is powerful enough to discover what no one but yourself could do, or she would not be able to discover anything."

"And you suppose, then, that my sister-in-law must have entered into an alliance with Bragelonne, and has informed him of all the details of the affair?"

"Perhaps even better still, for she perhaps accompanied him there."

"Which way? through your own apartments?"

"You think it impossible, sire? Well, listen to me. Your Majesty knows that Madame is very fond of perfumes?"

"Yes, she acquired that taste from my mother."

"Vervain particularly."

"Yes, it is the scent she prefers to all others."

"Very good, sire! my apartments happen to smell very strongly of vervain."

The King remained silent and thoughtful for a few moments, and then resumed, "But why should Madame take Bragelonne's part against me?"

Saint-Aignan could very easily have replied, "A woman's

jealousy!" The King probed his friend to the bottom of his heart to ascertain if had learned the secret of his flirtation with his sister-in-law. But Saint-Aignan was not an ordinary courtier; he did not lightly run the risk of finding out family secrets; and he was too good a friend of the Muses not to think very frequently of poor Ovidius Naso,* whose eyes shed so many tears in expiation of his crime for having once beheld something, one hardly knows what, in the palace of Augustus. He therefore passed by Madame's secret very skilfully. But as he had shown no ordinary sagacity in indicating Madame's presence in his rooms in company with Bragelonne, it was necessary, of course, for him to repay with interest the King's *amour propre*, and reply plainly to the question which had been put to him of, "Why has Madame taken Bragelonne's part against me?"

"Why?" replied Saint-Aignan. "Your Majesty forgets, I presume, that the Comte de Guiche is the intimate friend of the Vicomte de Bragelonne?"

"I do not see the connection, however," said the King.

"Ah! I beg your pardon, then, sire; but I thought the Comte de Guiche was a very great friend of Madame's."

"Quite true," the King returned; "there is no occasion to search any further, the blow came from that direction."

"And is not your Majesty of opinion that, in order to ward it off, it will be necessary to deal another blow?"

"Yes, but not one of the kind given in the Bois de Vinçennes," replied the King.

"You forget, sire," said Saint-Aignan, "that I am a gentleman, and that I have been challenged."

"The challenge neither concerns nor was it intended for you."

"But it is I who have been expected at the Minimes, sire, during the last hour and more; and I shall be dishonoured if I do not go there."

"The first honour and duty of a gentleman is obedience to his sovereign."

"Sire!"

"I order you to remain."

"Sire!"

"Obey, monsieur!"

"As your Majesty pleases."

"Besides, I wish to have the whole of this affair explained; I wish to know how it is that I have been so insolently trifled with, as to have the sanctuary of my affections pried into. It is not you, Saint-Aignan, who ought to punish those who have acted in this manner, for it is not your honour they have attacked, but my own."

"I implore your Majesty not to overwhelm M. de Bragelonne with your wrath, for although in the whole of this affair he may have shown himself deficient in prudence, he has not been so in his feelings of loyalty."

"Enough! I shall know how to decide between the just and the unjust, even in the height of my anger. But take care that not a word of this is breathed to Madame."

"But what am I to do with regard to M. de Bragelonne? He will be seeking me in every direction, and——"

"I shall either have spoken to him, or taken care that he has been spoken to, before the evening is over."

"Let me once more entreat your Majesty to be indulgent towards him."

"I have been indulgent long enough, Comte," said Louis XIV., frowning severely; "it is now quite time to show certain persons that I am master in my own palace."

The King had hardly pronounced these words, which betokened that a fresh feeling of dissatisfaction was mingled with the remembrance of an old one, when the usher appeared at the door of the cabinet.

"What is the matter?" inquired the King, "and why do you presume to come when I have not summoned you?"

"Sire," said the usher, "your Majesty desired me to permit M. le Comte de la Fère to pass freely on any and every occasion, when he might wish to speak to your Majesty."

"Well, monsieur?"

"M. le Comte de la Fère is now waiting to see your Majesty."

The King and Saint-Aignan at this reply exchanged a look which betrayed more uneasiness than surprise. Louis hesitated for a moment, but, immediately afterwards, seeming to make up his mind, he said,—

"Go, Saint-Aignan, and find Louise; inform her of the plot against us; do not let her be ignorant that Madame will return to her system of persecutions against her, and that she has set those to work for whom it would have been far better to have remained neuter."

"Sire——"

"If Louise gets nervous and frightened, reassure her as much as you can; tell her that the King's affection is an impenetrable shield over her; if, which I suspect is the case, she already knows everything, or if she has already been herself subjected to an attack of some kind or other from any quarter, tell her, be sure to tell her, Saint-Aignan," added the King, trembling with passion, "tell her, I say, that this time, instead of defending her, I will avenge her, and that, too, so terribly, that no one will in future even dare to raise his eyes towards her."

"Is that all, sire?"

"Yes, all. Go as quickly as you can, and remain faithful; for you who live in the midst of this state of infernal torments have not, like myself, the hope of the paradise beyond it."

Saint-Aignan exhausted himself almost in protestations of devotion, took the King's hand, kissed it, and left the room radiant with delight.

19

KING AND NOBILITY

THE KING endeavoured to recover his self-possession as quickly as possible, in order to meet M. de la Fère with an undisturbed countenance. He clearly saw it was not mere chance that had induced the Comte's visit. He had some vague impression of its importance; but he felt that to a man of Athos's tone of mind, to one of his high order of intellect, his first reception ought not to present anything either disagreeable or otherwise than kind and courteous. As soon as the King had satisfied himself that, as far as appearances were concerned, he was perfectly calm again, he gave directions to the ushers to introduce the Comte. A few minutes afterwards Athos, in full court dress, and with his breast covered with the orders that he alone had the right to wear at the court of France, presented himself with so grave and solemn an air that the King perceived, at the first glance, that he was not deceived in his anticipations. Louis advanced a step towards the Comte, and, with a smile, held out his hand to him over which Athos bowed with the air of the deepest respect.

"Monsieur le Comte de la Fère," said the King rapidly, "you are so seldom here, that it is a real piece of good fortune to see you."

Athos bowed and replied, "I should wish always to enjoy the happiness of being near your Majesty."

The tone, however, in which this reply was conveyed, evidently signified, "I should wish to be one of your Majesty's advisers, to save you the commission of faults." The King felt it so and determined, in this man's presence, to preserve all the advantages which could be derived from his command over himself, as well as from his rank and position.

"I see you have something to say to me," he said.

"Had it not been so, I should not have presumed to present myself before your Majesty."

"Speak quickly, I am anxious to satisfy you," returned the King, seating himself.

"I am persuaded," replied Athos, in a slightly agitated tone of voice, "that your Majesty will give me every satisfaction."

"Ah!" said the King, with a certain haughtiness of manner, "you have come to lodge a complaint here, then."

"It would be a complaint," returned Athos, "only in the event of your Majesty—but if you will deign to permit me, sire, I will repeat the conversation from the very commencement."

"Do so, I am listening."

"Your Majesty will remember that at the period of the Duke of Buckingham's departure, I had the honour of an interview with you."

"At or about that period, I think I remember you did; only with regard to the subject of the conversation, I have quite forgotten it."

Athos started, as he replied, "I shall have the honour to remind your Majesty of it. It was with regard to a formal demand I had addressed to you respecting a marriage which M. de Bragelonne wished to contract with Mademoiselle de la Vallière."

"Ah!" thought the King, "we have come to it now. I remember," he said aloud.

"At that period," pursued Athos, "your Majesty was so kind and generous towards M. de Bragelonne and myself that not a single word which then fell from your lips has escaped my memory; and, when I asked your Majesty to accord me Mademoiselle de la Vallière's hand for M. de Bragelonne, you refused."*

"Quite true," said Louis dryly.

"Alleging," Athos hastened to say, "that the young lady had no position in society." Louis could hardly force himself to listen patiently.

"That," added Athos, "she had but little fortune." The King threw himself back in his arm-chair.

"That her extraction was indifferent." A renewed impatience on the part of the King.

"And little beauty," added Athos pitilessly. This last bolt buried itself deep in the King's heart, and made him almost bound from his seat.

"You have a good memory, monsieur," he said.

"I invariably have, on all occasions when I have had the distinguished honour of an interview with your Majesty," retorted the Comte, without being in the least disconcerted.

"Very good; it is admitted I said all that."

"And I thanked your Majesty for your remarks at the time, because they testified an interest in M. de Bragelonne which did him much honour."

"And you may possibly remember," said the King very deliberately, "that you had the greatest repugnance for this marriage."

"Quite true, sire."

"And that you solicited my permission, much against your own inclination?"

"Yes, sire."

"And, finally, I remember, for I have a memory nearly as good as your own; I remember, I say, that you observed at the time: 'I do not believe that Mademoiselle de la Vallière loves M. de Bragelonne.' Is that true?"

The blow told well, but Athos did not draw back. "Sire," he said, "I have already begged your Majesty's forgiveness; but there are certain particulars in that conversation which are only intelligible from the *dénouement*."

"Well, what is the *dénouement*, monsieur?"

"This," your Majesty then said, "that you would defer the marriage out of regard for M. de Bragelonne's own interests."

The King remained silent. "M. de Bragelonne is now so exceedingly unhappy that he cannot any longer defer asking your Majesty for a solution of the matter."

The King turned pale; Athos looked at him with fixed attention.

"And what," said the King, with considerable hesitation, "does M. de Bragelonne request?"

"Precisely the very thing that I came to ask your Majesty for at my last audience, namely, your Majesty's consent to his marriage."

The King remained perfectly silent. "The questions which referred to the different obstacles in the way are all now quite removed for us," continued Athos. "Mademoiselle de la Vallière, without fortune, birth or beauty, is not the less on that account the only good match in the world for M. de Bragelonne, since he loves this young girl."

The King pressed his hands impatiently together. "Does your Majesty hesitate?" inquired the Comte, without losing a particle either of his firmness or his politeness.

"I do not hesitate—I refuse," replied the King.

Athos paused a moment, as if to collect himself. "I have had the honour," he said in a mild tone, "to observe to your Majesty that no obstacle now interferes with M. de Bragelonne's affections, and that his determination seems unalterable."

"There is my will—and that is an obstacle, I should imagine!"

"That is the most serious of all," Athos replied quickly.

"Ah!"

"And may we, therefore, be permitted to ask your Majesty, with the greatest humility, for your reason for this refusal?"

"The reason!—a question to me!" exclaimed the King.

"A demand, sire!"

The King, leaning with both his hands upon the table, said in a deep tone of concentrated passion, "You have lost all recollection of what is usual at court. At court, please to remember, no one ventures to put a question to the King."

"Very true, sire; but if men do not question they conjecture."

"Conjecture! What may that mean, monsieur?"

"Very frequently, sire, conjecture with regard to a particular subject implies a want of frankness on the part of the King——"

"Monsieur!"

"And a want of confidence on the part of the subject," pursued Athos intrepidly.

"You are forgetting yourself," said the King, hurried away by his anger in spite of his control over himself.

"Sire, I am obliged to seek elsewhere for what I thought I should find in your Majesty. Instead of obtaining a reply from you, I am compelled to make one for myself."

The King rose. "Monsieur le Comte," he said, "I have now given you all the time I had at my disposal."

This was a dismissal.

"Sire," replied the Comte, "I have not yet had time to tell your Majesty what I came with the express object of saying, and I so rarely see your Majesty that I ought to avail myself of the opportunity."

"Just now you spoke of conjectures, you are now becoming offensive, monsieur."

"Oh, sire! offend your Majesty! I?—Never! All my life through have I maintained that kings are above other men, not only from their rank and power, but from their nobleness of heart and their true dignity of mind. I never can bring myself to believe that my sovereign, he who passed his word to me, did so with a mental reservation."

"What do you mean? What mental reservation do you allude to?"

"I will explain my meaning," said Athos coldly. "If, in refusing Mademoiselle de la Vallière to M. de Bragelonne, your

Majesty had some other object in view than the happiness and fortune of the Vicomte——"

"You perceive, monsieur, that you are offending me."

"If, in requiring the Vicomte to delay his marriage, your Majesty's only object was to remove the gentleman to whom Mademoiselle de la Vallière was engaged——"

"Monsieur! monsieur!"

"I have heard it said so in every direction, sire. Your Majesty's affection for Mademoiselle de la Vallière is spoken of on all sides."

The King tore his gloves, which he had been biting for some time. "Woe to those," he cried, "who interfere in my affairs. I have made up my mind to take a particular course, and I will break through every obstacle in my way."

"What obstacle?" said Athos.

The King stopped short, like a horse which, having taken the bit between his teeth and run away, finds it had slipped back again, and that his career was checked. "I love Mademoiselle de la Vallière," he said suddenly, with mingled nobleness of feeling and passion.

"But," interrupted Athos, "that does not preclude your Majesty from allowing M. de Bragelonne to marry Mademoiselle de la Vallière. The sacrifice is worthy of so great a monarch; it is fully merited by M. de Bragelonne, who has already rendered great service to your Majesty, and who may well be regarded as a brave and worthy man. Your Majesty, therefore, in renouncing the affection you entertain, offers a proof at once of generosity, gratitude and good policy."

"Mademoiselle de la Vallière does not love M. de Bragelonne," said the King hoarsely.

"Does you Majesty know that to be the case?" remarked Athos with a searching look.

"I do know it."

"Since a very short time, then; for, doubtlessly, had your Majesty known it when I first preferred my request, you would have taken the trouble to inform me of it."

"Since a very short time, truly, monsieur."

Athos remained silent for a moment, and then resumed: "In that case, I do not understand why your Majesty should have sent M. de Bragelonne to London. That exile, and most properly so, too, is a matter of astonishment to every one who regards your Majesty's honour with sincere affection."

"Who presumes to speak of my honour, Monsieur de la Fère?"

"The King's honour, sire, is made up of the honour of his whole nobility. Whenever the King offends one of his gentlemen, that is, whenever he deprives him of the smallest particle of his honour, it is from him, from the King himself, that that portion of honour is stolen."

"Monsieur de la Fère!" said the King haughtily.

"Sire, you sent M. de Bragelonne to London either before you were Mademoiselle de la Vallière's lover, or since you have become so."

The King, irritated beyond measure, especially because he felt that he was mastered, endeavoured to dismiss Athos by a gesture.

"Sire," replied the Comte, "I will tell you all; I will not leave your presence until I have been satisfied either by your Majesty or by myself; satisfied, if you prove to me that you are right,—satisfied, if I prove to you that you are wrong. Nay, sire, you cannot but listen to me. I am old now, and I am attached to everything that is really great and really powerful in your kingdom. I am a gentleman who shed my blood for your father and for yourself, without ever having asked a single favour either from yourself or from your father. I have never inflicted the slightest wrong or injury on any one in this world, and kings even are still my debtors. You cannot but listen to me, I repeat. I have come to ask you for an account of the honour of one of your servants whom you have deceived by a falsehood, or betrayed by a want of heart or judgment. I know that these words irritate your Majesty, but the facts themselves are killing us. I know you are endeavouring to find some means whereby to chastise me for my frankness; but I know also the chastisement I will implore God to inflict upon you when I relate to Him your perjury and my son's unhappiness."

The King during these remarks was walking hurriedly to and fro, his hands thrust into the breast of his coat, his head haughtily raised, his eyes blazing with wrath. "Monsieur," he cried suddenly, "If I acted towards you as the King, you would be already punished; but I am only a man, and I have the right to love in this world every one who loves me,—a happiness which is so rarely found."

"You cannot pretend to such a right as a man any more than as a king, sire; or, if you intended to exercise that right in a loyal manner, you should have told M. de Bragelonne so, and not have exiled him."

"I think I am condescending in discussing with you, monsieur!" interrupted Louis XIV., with that majesty of air and manner which he alone seemed able to give to his look and his voice.

"I was hoping that you would reply to me," said the Comte.

"You shall know my reply, monsieur."

"You already know my thoughts on the subject," was the Comte de la Fère's answer.

"You have forgotten you are speaking to the King, monsieur. It is a crime."

"You have forgotten you are destroying the lives of two men, sire. It is a mortal sin."

"Leave the room."

"Not until I have said this, 'Son of Louis XIII., you begin your reign badly, for you begin it by abduction and disloyalty! My race—myself too—are now freed from all that affection and respect towards you, which I made my son swear to observe in the vaults of Saint-Denis, in the presence of the relics of your noble forefathers. You are now become our enemy, sire, and henceforth we have nothing to do save with Heaven alone, our sole master. Be warned.'"

"Do you threaten?"

"Oh, no," said Athos sadly, "I have as little bravado as fear in my soul. The God of whom I spoke to you is now listening to me; He knows that for the safety and honour of your crown I would even yet shed every drop of blood which twenty years of civil and foreign warfare have left in my veins. I can well say, then, that I threaten the King as little as I threaten the man; but I tell you, sire, you lose two servants; for you have destroyed faith in the heart of the father, and love in the heart of the son; the one ceases to believe in the royal word, the other no longer believes in the loyalty of man, or the purity of woman; the one is dead to every feeling of respect, the other to obedience. *Adieu!*"

Thus saying, Athos broke his sword across his knee, slowly placed the two pieces upon the floor and, saluting the King, who was almost choking from rage and shame, he quitted the cabinet. Louis, who sat near the table, completely overwhelmed, was several minutes before he could collect himself; but he suddenly rose and rang the bell violently; "Tell M. d'Artagnan to come here," he said to the terrified ushers.

20

AFTER THE STORM

OUR readers will doubtlessly have been asking themselves how it happened that Athos, of whom not a word has been said for some time past, arrived so very opportunely at court. We will, without delay, endeavour to satisfy their curiosity.

Porthos, faithful to his duty as an arranger of affairs, had, immediately after leaving the Palais-Royal, set off to join Raoul at the Minimes in the Bois de Vincennes, and had related everything, even to the smallest details, which had passed between Saint-Aignan and himself. He finished by saying that the message which the King had sent to his favourite would not probably occasion more than a short delay, and that Saint-Aignan, as soon as he could leave the King, would not lose a moment in accepting the invitation which Raoul had sent him. But Raoul, less credulous than his old friend, had concluded from Porthos's recital, that if Saint-Aignan was going to the King, Saint-Aignan would tell the King everything; and that the King would, therefore, forbid Saint-Aignan to obey the summons he had received to the hostile meeting. The consequence of his reflections was, that he had left Porthos to remain at the place appointed for the meeting, in the very improbable case that Saint-Aignan would come there; and had endeavoured to make Porthos promise that he would not remain there more than an hour or an hour and a half at the very longest. Porthos, however, formally refused to do anything of the kind, but, on the contrary, installed himself in the Minimes as if he were going to take root there, making Raoul promise that when he had been to see his father, he would return to his own apartments, in order that Porthos's servant might know where to find him, in case M. de Saint-Aignan should happen to come to the rendezvous.

Bragelonne had left Vincennes, and had proceeded at once straight to the apartments of Athos, who had been in Paris during the last two days, the Comte having been already informed of what had taken place, by a letter from d'Artagnan. Raoul arrived at his father's; Athos, after having held out his hand to him, and embraced him most affectionately, made a sign for him to sit down.

"I know you come to me as a man would go to a friend,

Vicomte, whenever he is suffering; tell me, therefore, what it is that brings you now."

The young man bowed, and began his recital; more than once in the course of it his tears almost choked his utterance, and a sob, checked in his throat, compelled him to suspend his narrative for a few minutes. However, he finished at last. Athos most probably already knew how matters stood; as we have just now said that d'Artagnan had already written to him; but, preserving until the conclusion that calm, unruffled composure of manner which constituted the almost superhuman side of his character, he replied, "Raoul, I do not believe there is a word of truth in the rumours; I do not believe in the existence of what you fear, although I do not deny that persons most entitled to the fullest credit have already conversed with me on the subject. In my heart and soul I think it utterly impossible that the King could be guilty of such an outrage upon a gentleman. I will answer for the King, therefore, and will soon bring you back the proof of what I say."

Raoul, wavering like a drunken man between what he had seen with his own eyes and the imperturbable faith he had in a man who had never told a falsehood, bowed, and simply answered, "Go, then, Monsieur le Comte; I will await your return." And he sat down, burying his face in his hands. Athos dressed, and then left him, in order to wait upon the King; the result of that interview is already known to our readers.

When he returned to his lodgings, Raoul, pale and dejected, had not quitted his attitude of despair. At the sound, however, of the opening doors, and of his father's footsteps as he approached him, the young man raised his head. Athos's face was very pale, his head uncovered, and his manner full of seriousness; he gave his cloak and hat to the lackey, dismissed him with a gesture, and sat down near Raoul.

"Well, monsieur," inquired the young man, "are you quite convinced now?"

"I am, Raoul; the King loves Mademoiselle de la Vallière."

"He confesses it, then?" cried Raoul.

"Yes," replied Athos.

"And she?"

"I have not seen her."

"No; but the King spoke to you about her. What did he say?"

"He says that she loves him."

"Oh, you see—you see, monsieur!" said the young man with a gesture of despair.

"Raoul," resumed the Comte, "I told the King, believe me, all that you yourself could possibly have said; and I believe I did so in becoming language, though sufficiently firm."

"And what did you say to him, monsieur?"

"I told him, Raoul. that everything was now at an end between him and ourselves; that you would never serve him again. I told him that I, too, should remain aloof. Nothing further remains for me, then, but to be satisfied of one thing."

"What is that, monsieur?"

"Whether you have determined to adopt any steps."

"Any steps? Regarding what?"

"With reference to your disappointed affection, and—to your ideas of vengeance."

"Oh, monsieur, with regard to my affection, I shall, perhaps, some day or other, succeed in tearing it from my heart; I trust I shall do so, aided by Heaven's merciful help, and your wise exhortations. As far as vengeance is concerned, it occurred to me, only when under the influence of an evil thought, for I could not revenge myself upon the one who is actually guilty; I have, therefore, already renounced every idea of revenge."

"And so you no longer think of seeking a quarrel with M. de Saint-Aignan?"

"No, monsieur; I sent him a challenge; if M. de Saint-Aignan accepts it, I will maintain it; if he does not take it up, I will leave it where it is."

"And La Vallière?"

"You cannot, I know, have seriously thought that I should dream of revenging myself upon a woman?" replied Raoul, with a smile so sad that a tear started even to the eyes of his father, who had so many times in the course of his life been bowed beneath his own sorrows and those of others.

He held out his hand to Raoul, which the latter seized most eagerly.

"And so, Monsieur le Comte, you are quite satisfied that the misfortune is without a remedy?" inquired the young man.

"Poor boy!" he murmured.

"You think that I still live in hope," said Raoul, "and you pity me. Oh, it is indeed a horrible suffering for me to despise, as I ought to do, the one I have loved so devotedly. If I only had but some real cause of complaint against her, I should be happy, and should be able to forgive her."

Athos looked at his son with a sorrowful air, for the latter words which Raoul had just pronounced, seemed to have issued out of his own heart. At this moment the servant announced M. d'Artagnan. This name sounded very differently to the ears of Athos and of Raoul. The musketeer entered the room with a vague smile upon his lips. Raoul paused. Athos walked towards his friend with an expression of face which did not escape Bragelonne. D'Artagnan answered Athos's look by an imperceptible movement of the eyelid; and then, advancing towards Raoul, whom he took by the hand, he said, addressing both father and son, "Well, you are trying to console this poor boy, it seems."

"And you, kind and good as usual, are come to help me in my difficult task."

As he said this, Athos pressed d'Artagnan's hand between both his own; Raoul fancied he observed in this pressure something beyond the sense his mere words conveyed.

"Yes," replied the musketeer, smoothing his moustache with the hand that Athos had left free, "yes, I have come also."

"You are most welcome, chevalier; not from the consolation you bring with you, but on your own account. I am already consoled," said Raoul; and he attempted to smile, but the effect was far more sad than any tears d'Artagnan had ever seen shed.

"That is well and good then," said d'Artagnan.

"Only," continued Raoul, "you have arrived just as the Comte was about to give me the details of his interview with the King. You will allow the Comte to continue?" added the young man, as, with his eyes fixed on the musketeer, he seemed to read into the very depths of his heart.

"His interview with the King?" said d'Artagnan, in a tone so natural and unassumed that there was no means of suspecting that his astonishment was feigned. "You have see the King, then, Athos?"

Athos smiled as he said, "Yes, I have seen him."

"Ah, indeed, you were not aware, then, that the Comte had seen his Majesty?" inquired Raoul, half reassured.

"Yes, indeed, quite so."

"In that case, I am less uneasy," said Raoul.

"Uneasy—and about what?" inquired Athos.

"Forgive me, monsieur," said Raoul, "but knowing so well the regard and affection you have for me, I was afraid you might possibly have expressed somewhat plainly to His Majesty my own sufferings and your indignation, and that the King had consequently——"

"And that the King had consequently?" repeated d'Artagnan; "well, go on, finish what you were going to say."

"I have now to ask you to forgive me, Monsieur d'Artagnan," said Raoul. "For a moment, and I cannot help confessing it, I trembled lest you had come here, not as M. d'Artagnan, but as Captain of the Musketeers."

"You are mad, my poor boy," cried d'Artagnan, with a burst of laughter, in which an exact observer might perhaps have wished to have heard a little more frankness.

"So much the better," said Raoul.

"Yes, mad; and do you know what I would advise you to do?"

"Tell me, monsieur, for the advice is sure to be good as it comes from you."

"Very good, then; I advise you, after your long journey from England, after your visit to M. de Guiche, after your visit to Madame, after your visit to Porthos, after your journey to Vinçennes, I advise you, I say, to take a few hours' rest; go and lie down, sleep for a dozen hours, and when you wake up, go and ride one of my horses until you have tired him to death."

And drawing Raoul towards him he embraced him as he would have done his own child. Athos did the like; only it was very visible that the kiss was more affectionate, and the pressure of his lips still warmer with the father than with the friend. The young man again looked at both his companions, endeavouring to penetrate their real meaning, or their real feelings, with the utmost strength of his intelligence; but his look was powerless upon the smiling countenance of the musketeer, or upon the calm and composed features of the Comte de la Fère. "Where are you going, Raoul?" inquired the latter, seeing that Bragelonne was preparing to go out.

"To my own apartments," replied the latter in his soft and sad voice.

"We shall be sure to find you there, then, if we should have anything to say to you?"

"Yes, monsieur; but do you suppose it likely you will have something to say to me?"

"How can I tell?" said Athos.

"Yes, something fresh to console you with," said d'Artagnan, pushing nim towards the door.

Raoul, observing the perfect composure which marked every gesture of his two friends, quitted the Comte's room, carrying away with him nothing but the individual feeling of his own particular distress.

"Thank Heaven," he said, "since that is the case, I need only think of myself."

And wrapping himself in his cloak, in order to conceal from the passess by in the streets his gloomy and sorrowful face, he quitted them, for the purpose of returning to his own rooms, as he had promised Porthos. The two friends watched the young man as he walked away with a feeling akin to pity, only each expressed it in a very different way.

"Poor Raoul!" said Athos sighing deeply.

"Poor Raoul!" said d'Artagnan shrugging his shoulders.

21

HEU! MISER!*

"POOR Raoul!" had said Athos. "Poor Raoul!" had said d'Artagnan; and, in point of fact, to be pitied by both these men, Raoul indeed must have been most unhappy. And therefore when he found himself alone, face to face, as it were, with his own troubles, leaving behind him the intrepid friend and the indulgent father; when he recalled the avowal of the King's affection, which had robbed him of Louise de la Vallière, whom he loved so deeply, he felt his heart almost breaking, as indeed we all have at least once in our lives, at the first illusion destroyed, at our first affection betrayed. "Oh!" he murmured, "all is over, then. Nothing is now left me in this world. Nothing to look for, nothing to hope for. Guiche has told me so, my father has told me so, and M. d'Artagnan likewise. Everything is a mere idle dream in this life. That future, which I have been hopelessly pursuing for the last ten years, a dream! that union of our hearts, a dream! that life formed of love and happiness, a dream! Poor fool that I am," he continued after a pause, "to dream away my existence aloud, publicly, and in the face of others, my friends and my enemies—and for what purpose, too? in order that my friends may be saddened by my troubles, and that my enemies may laugh at my sorrows. And so my unhappiness will soon become a notorious disgrace, a public scandal; and who knows but that to-morrow I may not even be ignominiously pointed at."

And, despite the composure which he had promised his father and d'Artagnan to observe, Raoul could not resist uttering a few words of dark menace. "And yet," he continued, "if my name were de Wardes, and if I had the pliant character and strength of will of M. d'Artagnan, I should laugh, with my lips at least; I should convince other women that this perfidious girl, honoured by the affection I have wasted on her, leaves me only one regret, that of having been abused and deceived by her resemblance of a modest and irreproachable conduct; a few men might perhaps

fawn upon the King by laughing at my expense; I should put myself on the track of some of those jesters; I should chastise a few of
them, perhaps; the men would fear me, and by the time I had laid
three dying or dead at my feet, I should be adored by the women.
Yes, yes, that indeed would be the proper course to adopt, and
the Comte de la Fère himself would not object to it. Has not he
also been tried, in his earlier days, in the same manner as I have
just been tried myself?* Did he not replace affection by intoxication? He has often told me so. Why should not I replace love by
pleasure? He must have suffered as much as I suffer, even more
so perhaps. The history of one man is the history of all men, a
lengthened trial, more or less so at least, more or less bitter and
sorrowful. The voice of human nature is nothing but one prolonged
cry. But what are the sufferings of others compared to those from
which I am now suffering? Does the open wound in another's
breast soften the pain of the gaping wound in our own? Or does
the blood which is welling from another man's side staunch that
which is pouring from our own? Does the general anguish of our
fellow creatures lessen our own private and particular anguish?
No, no, each suffers on his own account, each struggles with his
own grief, each sheds his own tears. And besides," he went on,
"what has my life been up to the present moment? A cold,
barren, sterile arena, in which I have always fought for others,
never for myself. Sometimes for a king, sometimes for a woman.
The King has betrayed me, the woman disdained me. Miserable,
unhappy wretch that I am! Woman! Can I not make all expiate
the crime of one of their sex? What does that need? To have a
heart no longer, or to forget that I ever had one; to be strong, even
against weakness itself; to lean always, even when one feels that
the support is giving way. What is needed to attain, or succeed in
all that? To be young, handsome, valiant, rich, I am, or shall be,
all that. But honour?" he still continued, "and what is honour
after all? A theory which every man understands in his own way.
My father tells me, 'Honour is the respect of that which is due to
others, and particularly of what is due to oneself.' But Guiche,
and Manicamp, and Saint-Aignan particularly, would say to me:
'What's honour? Honour consists in studying and yielding to the
passions and pleasures of one's king.' Honour such as that, indeed,
is easy and productive enough. With honour like that, I can keep
my post at the court, become a gentleman of the chamber, and
accept the command of a regiment, which may have been presented to me. With honour such as that, I can be both duke and
peer.

"The stain which that woman has just stamped upon me, the

grief with which she has just broken my heart, the heart of the friend and playmate of her childhood, in no way affect M. de Bragelonne, an excellent officer, a courageous leader, who will cover himself with glory at the first encounter, and who will become a hundred times greater than Mademoiselle de la Vallière is to-day, the mistress of the King—for the King will not marry her —and the more publicly he will proclaim her as his mistress, the thicker will become the bandage of shame which he casts in her face, in the guise of a crown; and in proportion as others will despise her, as I despise her, I shall be gaining honours in the field. Alas! we had walked together side by side, she and I, during the earliest, the brightest and best portion of our existence, hand in hand along the charming path of life, covered with the flowers of youth; and then, alas! we reach a cross-road, where she separates herself from me, in which we have to follow a different route, whereby we become more and more widely separated from each other. And to attain the end of this path, oh, Heaven! I am now alone, in utter despair, and crushed to the very earth!"

Such were the sinister reflections in which Raoul indulged, when his foot mechanically paused at the door of his own dwelling. He had reached it without remarking the streets through which he had passed, without knowing how he had come; he pushed open the door, continued to advance, and ascended the staircase. The staircase, as in most of the houses in that period, was very dark, and the landings very obscure. Raoul lived on the first floor; he paused in order to ring. Olivain appeared, took his sword and cloak from his hands; Raoul himself opened the door which, from the ante-chamber led into a small *salon*, richly furnished enough for the *salon* of a young man, and completely filled with flowers by Olivain, who, knowing his master's tastes, had shown himself studiously attentive in gratifying them, without caring whether his master perceived his attention or not. There was a portrait of La Vallière in the *salon*, which had been drawn by herself and given by her to Raoul. This portrait, fastened above a large easy-chair covered with dark-coloured damask, was the first point towards which Raoul bent his steps—the first object on which he fixed his eyes. It was, moreover, Raoul's usual habit to do so; every time he entered his room, this portrait, before anything else, attracted his attention. This time, as usual, he walked straight up to the portrait, placed his knees upon the arm-chair, and paused to look at it sadly. His arms were crossed upon his breast, his head slightly thrown back, his eyes filled with tears, his mouth worked into a bitter smile. He looked at the portrait of one whom he so tenderly loved; and then all that he had said passed before his mind again, and all that he had suffered seemed again to assail his heart; and, after a long silence, he murmured for the third time, "Miserable, unhappy wretch that I am!"

He had hardly pronounced these words, when he heard the sound of a sigh and a groan behind him. He turned sharply round, and perceived in the angle of the *salon*, standing up, a bending veiled female figure, which he had been the means of concealing behind the door as he opened it, and which he had not perceived as he entered. He advanced towards this figure, whose presence in his room had not been announced to him; and as he bowed, and inquired at the same moment who she was, she suddenly raised her head, and removed the veil from her face, revealing her pale and sorrow-stricken features. Raoul staggered back as if he had seen a ghost.

"Louise!" he cried, in a tone of such utter despair, that one could hardly have thought that the human voice were capable of so desponding a cry, without some fibres of the human heart snapping.

22

WOUNDS UPON WOUNDS

MADEMOISELLE DE LA VALLIÈRE—for it was indeed she—advanced a few steps towards him. "Yes—Louise," she murmured.

But this interval, short as it had been, was quite sufficient for Raoul to recover himself. "You, mademoiselle?" he said; and then added, in an indefinable tone, "You here!"

"Yes, Raoul," the young girl replied, "I have been waiting for you."

"I beg your pardon. When I came into the room I was not aware——"

"I know—but I entreated Olivain not to tell you——" She hesitated; and as Raoul did not attempt to interrupt her, a moment's silence ensued, during which the sound of their throbbing hearts might have been heard, not in unison with each other, but the one beating as violently as the other. It was for Louise to speak, and she made an effort to do so.

"I wished to speak to you," she said. "It was absolutely necessary that I should see you—myself—alone. I have not hesitated adopting a step which must remain secret; for no one, except yourself, could understand my motive, Monsieur de Bragelonne."

"In fact, mademoiselle," Raoul stammered out, almost breathless from emotion, "as far as I am concerned, and despite the good opinion you have of me, I confess——"

"Will you do me the great kindness to sit down and listen to me?" said Louise, interrupting him with her soft, sweet voice.

Bragelonne looked at her for a moment; then, mournfully shaking his head, he sat, or rather fell down on a chair. "Speak," he said.

She cast a glance all around her. This look was a timid entreaty, and implored secrecy far more effectually than her expressed words had done a few minutes before. Raoul rose and went to the door, which he opened, "Olivain," he said, "I am not within for any one." And then, turning towards Louise, he added, "Is not that what you wished?"

Nothing could have produced a greater effect upon Louise than these few words, which seemed to signify, "You see that I still understand you." She passed a handkerchief across her eyes, in order to remove a rebellious tear which she could not restrain; and then, having collected herself for a moment, she said, "Raoul, do not turn your kind, frank look away from me. You are not one of those men who despise a woman for having given her heart to another, even though her affection might render him unhappy, or might wound his pride."

Raoul did not reply.

"Alas!" continued La Vallière, "it is only too true, my cause is a bad one, and I cannot tell in what way to begin. It will be better for me, I think, to relate to you, very simply, everything that has befallen me. As I shall speak but the pure and simple truth, I shall always find my path clear before me in the obscurity, hesitation and obstacles which I have to brave in order to solace my heart, which is full to overflowing, and wishes to pour itself out at your feet."

Raoul continued to preserve the same unbroken silence. La Vallière looked at him with an air that seemed to say, "Encourage me; for pity's sake, but a single word!" But Raoul did not open his lips; and the young girl was obliged to continue:—

"Just now," she said, "M. de Saint-Aignan came to me by the King's directions." She cast down her eyes as she said this; while Raoul, on his side, turned his away, in order to avoid looking at her. "M. de Saint-Aignan came to me from the King," she repeated, "and told me that you knew all;" and she attempted to look Raoul in the face, after inflicting this further wound upon him, in addition to the many others he had already received; but it was impossible to meet Raoul's eyes.

"He told me you were incensed with me—and justly so, I admit."

This time Raoul looked at the young girl, and a smile full of disdain passed across his lips.

"Oh!" she continued, "I entreat you, do not say that you have had any other feeling against me than that of anger merely. Raoul, wait until I have told you all—wait until I have said to you all that I had to say—all that I came to say."

Raoul, by the strength of his own iron will, forced his features to assume a calmer expression, and the disdainful smile upon his lip passed away.

"In the first place," said La Vallière, "in the first place, with my hands raised in entreaty towards you, with my forehead bowed to the ground before you, I entreat you, as the most generous, as the noblest of men, to pardon, to forgive me. If I have left you in ignorance of what was passing in my own bosom, never, at least, would I have consented to deceive you. Oh! I entreat you, Raoul —I implore you on my knees—answer me one word, even though you wronged me in doing so. Better, far better, an injurious word from your lips, than a suspicion from your heart."

"I admire your subtlety of expression, mademoiselle," said Raoul, making an effort to remain calm. "To leave another in ignorance that you are deceiving him is loyal; but to deceive him —it seems that that would be very wrong, and that you would not do it."

"Monsieur, for a long time I thought that I loved you better than anything else; and so long as I believed in my affection for you, I told you that I loved you. I could have sworn it on the altar; but a day came when I was undeceived."

"Well, on that day, mademoiselle, knowing that I still continued to love you, true loyalty of conduct ought to have obliged you to tell me you had ceased to love me."

"But on that day, Raoul—on that day, when I read in the depths of my own heart, when I confessed to myself that you no longer filled my mind entirely, when I saw another future before me than that of being your friend, your life-long companion, your wife—on that day, Raoul, you were not, alas! any more beside me."

"But you knew where I was, mademoiselle; you could have written to me."

"Raoul, I did not dare to do so. Raoul, I have been weak and cowardly. I knew you so thoroughly. I knew how devotedly you loved me, that I trembled at the bare idea of the grief I was going to cause you; and that is so true, Raoul, that at this very moment I am now speaking to you, bending thus before you, my heart crushed in my bosom, my voice full of sighs, my eyes full of tears, it is so perfectly true, that I have no other defence than my frankness, I have no other sorrow greater than that which I read in your eyes." Raoul attempted to smile.

"No!" said the young girl, with a profound conviction, "no, no; you will not do me so foul a wrong as to disguise your feelings before me now! You loved me; you were sure of your affection for me; you did not deceive yourself; you did not lie to your own heart—whilst I—I——" And pale as death, her arms thrown despairingly above her head, she fell upon her knees.

"Whilst you," said Raoul, "you told me you loved me, and yet you loved another."

"Alas! yes!" cried the poor girl; "alas, yes! I do love another; and that other—oh! for Heaven's sake let me say it, Raoul, for it is my only excuse—that other I love better than my own life, better than my own soul even. Forgive my fault, or punish my treason, Raoul, I came here in no way to defend myself, but merely to say to you: 'You know what it is to love!'—in that case I love! I love to that degree, that I would give my life, my very soul, to the man I love. If he should ever cease to love me, I shall die of grief and despair, unless Heaven come not to my assistance, unless Heaven does not show pity upon me. Raoul, I came here to submit myself to your will, whatever it might be—to die, if it were your wish I should die. Kill me, then, Raoul! if in your heart you believe I deserve death."

"Take care, mademoiselle!" said Raoul; "the woman who invites death is one who has nothing but her heart's blood to offer to her deceived and betrayed lover."

"You are right," she said.

Raoul uttered a deep sigh, as he exclaimed, "And you love without being able to forget!"

"I love without a wish to forget; without a wish ever to love any one else," replied La Vallière.

"Very well," said Raoul. "You have said to me, in fact, all you had to say; all I could possibly wish to know. And now, mademoiselle, it is I who ask your forgiveness, for it is I who have almost been an obstacle in your life; I, too, who have been wrong, for, in deceiving myself, I helped to deceive you."

"Oh!" said La Vallière, "I do not ask you so much as that, Raoul."

"I only am to blame, mademoiselle," continued Raoul; "better informed than yourself of the difficulties of this life, I should have enlightened you. I ought not to have relied upon uncertainty; I ought to have extracted an answer from your heart, whilst I hardly even sought an acknowledgement from your lips. Once more, mademoiselle, it is I who ask your forgiveness."

"Impossible, impossible!" she cried, "you are mocking me."

"How, impossible!"

"Yes, it is impossible to be good, and excellent, and perfect to such a degree as that."

"Take care!" said Raoul, with a bitter smile, "for presently you may say, perhaps, that I did not love you."

"Oh! you love me like an affectionate brother; let me hope that, Raoul."

"As a brother! undeceive yourself, Louise. I loved you as a lover, as a husband, with the deepest, the truest, the fondest affection."

"Raoul, Raoul!"

"As a brother! Oh, Louise, I loved you so deeply that I would have shed my blood for you, drop by drop; I would, oh! how willingly, have suffered myself to be torn in pieces for your sake, have sacrificed my very future for you. I loved you so deeply, Louise, that my heart feels crushed and dead within me,—that my faith in human nature is gone,—that my eyes seem to have lost their light; I loved you so deeply, that I now no longer see, think of, care for, anything, either in this world or in the next."

"Raoul—dear Raoul! spare me, I implore you!" cried La Vallière. "Oh! if I had but known."

"It is too late, Louise, you love, you are happy in your affection; I read your happiness through your tears—behind the tears which the loyalty of your nature makes you shed; I feel the sighs which your affection breathes forth. Louise, Louise, you have made me the most abjectly wretched man living; leave me, I entreat you. Adieu! adieu!"

"Forgive me! oh, forgive me, Raoul, for what I have done!"

"Have I not done more? Have I not told you that I loved you still?" She buried her face in her hands.

"And to tell you that—do you hear me, Louise?—to tell you that, at such a moment as this, to tell you that, as I have told you, is to pronounce my own sentence of death. Adieu!" La Vallière wished to hold out her hands to him.

"We ought not to see each other again in this world," he said; and as she was on the point of calling out in bitter agony at this remark, he placed his hand on her mouth to stifle the exclamation. She pressed her lips upon it, and fell fainting to the ground.

"Olivain," said Raoul, "take this young lady and bear her to the carriage which is waiting for her at the door." As Olivain lifted her up, Raoul made a movement as if to dart towards La Vallière, in order to give her a first and last kiss, but, stopping abruptly, he said, "No! she is not mine. I am not a thief like the King of France." And he returned to his room, whilst the lackey carried La Vallière, still fainting, to the carriage.

23

WHAT RAOUL HAD GUESSED

As soon as Raoul had quitted Athos and d'Artagnan, and as soon as the two exclamations which had followed his departure had escaped their lips, they found themselves face to face alone. Athos immediately resumed the earnest air that he had assumed at d'Artagnan's arrival.

"Well," he said, "what have you come to announce to me, my friend?"

"I?" inquired d'Artagnan.

"Yes; I do not see you in this way without some reason for it," said Athos, smiling.

"The deuce!" said d'Artagnan.

"I will place you at your ease. The King is furious, I suppose?"

"Well, I must say he is not altogether pleased."

"And you have come to arrest me, then?"

"My dear friend, you have hit the very mark."

"Oh! I expected it. I am quite ready to go with you."

"Deuce take it!" said d'Artagnan, "what a hurry you are in."

"I am afraid of delaying you," said Athos, smiling.

"I have plenty of time. Are you not curious, besides, to know how things went on between the King and me?"

"If you will be good enough to tell me, I will listen with the greatest pleasure," said Athos, pointing out to d'Artagnan a large chair, into which the latter threw himself, assuming the easiest possible attitude.

"Well, I will do so willingly enough," continued d'Artagnan, "for the conversation is rather curious, I must say. In the first place the King sent for me."

"As soon as I had left?"

"You were just going down the last steps of the staircase as the musketeers told me. I arrived. My dear Athos, he was not red in the face merely, he was positively purple. I was not aware, of course, of what had passed; only, on the ground, lying on the floor, I saw a sword broken in two."

"'Captain d'Artagnan,' cried the King, as soon as he saw me.

"'Sire,' I replied.

"'M. de la Fère has just left me; he is an insolent man.'

"'An insolent man!' I exclaimed, in such a tone that the King stopped suddenly short.

"'Captain d'Artagnan,' resumed the King with his teeth clenched, 'you will be good enough to listen to and hear me.'

"'That is my duty, sire.'

"'I have, out of consideration for M. de la Fère, wished to spare him, of whom I still retain some kind recollections, the discredit of being arrested in my palace. You will therefore take a carriage.' At this I made a slight movement.

"'If you object to arrest him yourself,' continued the King, 'send me my captain of the guards here.'

"'Sire,' I replied, 'there is no necessity for the captain of the guards, since I am on duty.'

"'I should not like to annoy you,' said the King kindly, 'for you have always served me well, Monsieur d'Artagnan.'

"'You do not "annoy" me, sire,' I replied; 'I am on duty, that is all.'

"'But,' said the King in astonishment, 'I believe the Comte is your friend.'

"'If he were my father, sire, it would not make me less on duty than I am.'

"The King looked at me; he saw how unmoved my face was, and seemed satisfied. 'You will arrest M. le Comte de la Fère, then?' he inquired.

"'Most certainly, sire, if you give me the order to do so.'

"'Very well; I order you to do so.'

"I bowed, and replied, 'Where is the Comte, sire?'

"'You will look for him.'

"'And I am to arrest him wherever he may be?'

"'Yes; but try that he may be at his own house. If he should have started for his own estate, leave Paris at once, and arrest him on his way thither.'

"I bowed; but as I did not move, he said, 'Well, what are you waiting for?'

"'For the order to arrest the Comte, signed by yourself.'

"The King seemed annoyed; for, in point of fact, it was the exercise of a fresh act of authority; a repetition of the arbitrary act, if, indeed, it is to be considered as such. He took hold of his pen slowly, and evidently in no very good temper; and then he wrote, 'Order for M. le Chevalier d'Artagnan, captain of my musketeers, to arrest M. le Comte de la Fère, wherever he is to be found.' He then turned towards me; but I was looking on without moving a muscle of my face. In all probability he thought he perceived something like bravado in my tranquil manner, for he signed hurriedly; and then handing me the order, he said, 'Go, monsieur!' I obeyed; and here I am.''

Athos pressed his friend's hand. "Well, let us set off," he said.

"Oh! surely," said d'Artagnan, "you must have some trifling matters to arrange before you leave your apartments in this manner."

"I?—not at all."

"Why not?"

"Why, you know, d'Artagnan, that I have always been a very simple traveller on this earth, ready to go to the end of the world by the order of my sovereign, ready to quit it at the summons of my Maker. What does a man who is thus prepared require in such a case?—a portmanteau, or a shroud. I am ready at this moment, as I have always been, my dear friend, and can accompany you at once."

"But Bragelonne——"

"I have brought him up in the same principles I laid down for my own guidance; and you observed, that as soon as he perceived you he guessed, that very moment, the motive of your visit. We have thrown him off his guard for a moment; but do not be uneasy, he is sufficiently prepared for my disgrace to be too much alarmed at it. So, let us go."

"Very well, 'let us go,''" said d'Artagnan quietly.

"As I broke my sword in the King's presence, and threw the pieces at his feet, I presume that will dispense with the necessity of delivering it over to you."

"You are quite right; and, besides that, what the deuce do you suppose I could do with your sword?"

"Am I to walk behind or before you?" inquired Athos, laughing.

"You will walk arm-in-arm with me," replied d'Artagnan, as he took the Comte's arm to descend the staircase; and in this manner they arrived at the landing. Grimaud, whom they had met in the anteroom, looked at them as they went out together in this manner, with some little uneasiness; his experience of affairs was quite sufficient to give him good reason to suspect that there was something wrong.

"Ah! is that you, Grimaud?'"* said Athos kindly. "We are going——"

"To take a turn in my carriage," interrupted d'Artagnan, with a friendly nod of the head.

Grimaud thanked d'Artagnan by a grimace, which was evidently intended for a smile, and accompanied both the friends to the door. Athos entered first into the carriage, d'Artagnan following him, without saying a word to the coachman. The departure had taken place so quietly, that it excited no disturbance or attention even in the neighbourhood. When the carriage had reached the quays, "You are taking me to the Bastille,* I perceive," said Athos.

"I?" said d'Artagnan, "I take you wherever you may choose to go; nowhere else, I can assure you."

"What do you mean?" said the Comte, surprised.

"Why, surely, my dear friend," said d'Artagnan, "you quite understand that I undertook the mission with no other object in view than that of carrying it out exactly as you liked. You surely did not expect that I was going to get you thrown into prison like that, brutally, and without any reflection. If I had not anticipated that, I should have let the captain of the guards undertake it."

"And so——?" said Athos.

"And so, I repeat again, we will go wherever you may choose."

"My dear friend," said Athos, embracing d'Artagnan, "how like you that is."

"Well, it seems simple enough to me. The coachman will take you to the barrier of the Cours-la-Reine;* you will find a horse there which I have ordered to be kept ready for you; with that horse you will be able to do three posts without stopping; and I, on my side, will take care not to return to the King, to tell him that you have gone away, until the very moment it will be impossible to overtake you. In the meantime you will have reached Havre, and from Havre across to England, where you will find the charming residence of which M. Monk* made me a present, without speaking of the hospitality which King Charles will not fail to show you. Well, what do you think of this project?"

Athos shook his head, and then said, smiling as he did so, "No, no; take me to the Bastille."

"You are an obstinate-headed fellow, dear Athos," returned d'Artagnan; "reflect for a few moments."

"Upon what?"

"That you are no longer twenty years of age. Believe me, I speak according to my own knowledge and experience. A prison is certain death to men of our time of life. No, no; I will never allow you to languish in prison in such a way. Why, the very thought of it makes my head turn giddy."

"Dear d'Artagnan," Athos replied, "Heaven most fortunately made my body as strong, powerful and enduring as my mind; and, rely upon it, I shall retain my strength up to the very last moment."

"But this is not strength of mind or character, it is sheer madness."

"No, d'Artagnan, it is the highest order of reasoning. Do not suppose that I should in the slightest degree in the world discuss the question with you, whether you would not be ruined in endeavouring to save me. I should have done precisely as you are doing if flight had been part of my plan of action; I should, therefore, have accepted from you what, without any doubt, you would have accepted from me. No! I know you too well even to breathe a word upon the subject."

"Ah! if you would only let me do it," said d'Artaganan, "how I would sent the King running after you."

"Still, he is the King; do not forget that, my dear friend."

"Oh! that is all the same to me; and King though he be, I would plainly tell him, 'Sire! imprison, exile, kill every one in France and Europe; order me to arrest and poniard even whom you like—even were it Monsieur, your own brother; but do not touch one of the four musketeers, or if so, *mordioux!*'"

"My dear friend," replied Athos, with perfect calmness. "I should like to persuade you of one thing; namely, that I wish to be arrested; that I desire above all things that my arrest should take place."

D'Artagnan made a slight movement of his shoulders.

"Nay; I wish it, I repeat, more than anything; if you were to let me escape, it would only be to return of my own accord, and constitute myself a prisoner. I wish to prove to this young man, who is dazzled by the power and splendour of his crown, that he can be regarded as the first and chiefest among men only on the condition of his proving himself to be the most generous and the wisest among them. He may punish me, imprison or torture me, it matters not. He abuses his opportunities, and I wish him to learn the bitterness of remorse, while Heaven teaches him what a chastisement is."

"Well, well," replied d'Artagnan, "I know, only too well, that when you have once said 'no,' you mean 'no.' I do not insist any longer; you wish to go to the Bastille?"

"I do wish to go there."

"Let us go then! To the Bastille!" cried d'Artagnan to the coachman. And throwing himself back in the carriage, he gnawed the ends of his moustache with a fury which, for Athos, who knew him well, signified a resolution either already taken or in course of formation. A profound silence ensued in the carriage, which continued to roll on, but neither faster nor slower than before. Athos took the musketeer by the hand.

"You are not angry with me, d'Artagnan?" he said.

"I!—oh, no! certainly not; of course not. What you do from heroism, I should have done from sheer obstinacy."

"But you are quite of opinion, are you not, that Heaven will avenge me, d'Artagnan?"

"And I know some persons on earth who will lend a helping hand." said the captain.

24

THREE GUESTS ASTONISHED TO FIND THEMSELVES AT
SUPPER TOGETHER

THE carriage arrived at the outside gate of the Bastille. A soldier on guard stopped it, but d'Artagnan had only to utter a single word to procure admittance, and the carriage passed on without further difficulty. Whilst they were proceeding along the covered way which led to the courtyard of the governor's residence, d'Artagnan, whose lynx eye saw everything, even through the walls, suddenly cried out, "What is that out yonder?"

"Well," said Athos quietly, "what is it?"

"Look yonder, Athos."

"In the courtyard?"

"Why, yes; make haste."

"Well, a carriage; very likely conveying a prisoner like myself."

"That would be too droll."

"I do not understand you."

"Make haste and look again, and look at the man who is just getting out of that carriage."

At that very moment a second sentinel stopped d'Artagnan, and while the formalities were being gone through, Athos could see at a hundred paces from him the man whom his friend had pointed out to him. He was, in fact, getting out of the carriage at the door of the governor's house. "Well," inquired d'Artagnan, "do you see him?"

"Yes; he is a man in a grey suit."

"What do you say of him?"

"I cannot very well tell; he is, as I have just told you, a man in a grey suit, who is getting out of a carriage; that is all."

"Athos, I will wager anything it is he."

"He—who?"

"Aramis."

"Aramis arrested? Impossible!"

"I do not say he is arrested, since we see him alone in his carriage."

"Well, then, what is he doing here?"

"Oh! he knows Baisemeaux, the governor," replied the musketeer slyly; "so we have arrived just in time."

"What for?"

"In order to see what we can see."

"I regret this meeting exceedingly. When Aramis sees me, he will be very much annoyed, in the first place, at seeing me, and in the next at being seen."

"Very well reasoned."

"Unfortunately, there is no remedy for it; whenever any one meets another in the Bastille, even if he wished to draw back to avoid him, it would be impossible."

"Athos, I have an idea; the question is, to spare Aramis the annoyance you were speaking of, is it not?"

"What is to be done?"

"I will tell you; or, in order to explain myself in the best possible way, let me relate the affair in my own manner; I will not recommend you to tell a falsehood, for that would be impossible for you to do; but I will tell falsehoods enough for both; it is so easy to do that with the nature and habits of a Gascon."

Athos smiled. The carriage stopped where the one we have just now pointed out had stopped; namely, at the door of the governor's house. "It is understood, then?" said d'Artagnan, in a low voice to his friend. Athos consented by a gesture. They ascended the staircase. There will be no occasion for surprise at the facility with which they had entered into the Bastille, if it be remembered that, before passing the first gate, in fact, the most difficult of all, d'Artagnan had announced that he had brought a prisoner of state. At the third gate, on the contrary, that is to say, when he had once fairly entered the prison, he merely said to the sentinel, "To M. Baisemeaux"; and they both passed on. In a few minutes they were in the governor's dining-room, and the first face which attracted d'Artagnan's observation was that of Aramis, who was seated side by side with Baisemeaux, and awaited the announcement of a good meal, whose odour impregnated the whole apartment. If d'Artagnan pretended surprise, Aramis did not pretend at all; he started when he saw his two friends, and his emotion was very apparent. Athos and d'Artagnan however, complimented him as usual, and Baisemeaux, amazed, completely stupefied by the presence of his three guests, began to perform a few evolutions around them all. "By what lucky accident——"

"We were just going to ask you," retorted d'Artagnan.

"Are we going to give ourselves up as prisoners?" cried Aramis, with an affectation of hilarity.

"Ah! ah!" said d'Artagnan; "it is true the walls smell deucedly like a prison. Monsieur de Baisemeaux, you know you invited me to sup with you the other day."

"I!" cried Baisemeaux.

"Yes, of course you did, although you now seem so struck with amazement. Don't you remember it?"

Baisemeaux turned pale and then red, looked at Aramis, who looked at him, and finished by stammering out, "Certainly—I am delighted—but upon my honour—I have not the slightest —Ah! I have such a wretched memory."

"Well! I am wrong, I see," said d'Artagnan, as if he were offended.

"Wrong, what for?"

"Wrong to remember anything about it, it seems."

Baisemeaux hurried towards him. "Do not stand on ceremony, my dear captain," he said; "I have the worst memory in the world. I no sooner leave off thinking of my pigeons and their pigeon-house, than I am no better than the rawest recruit."

"At all events, you remember it now," said d'Artagnan boldly.

"Yes, yes," replied the governor, hesitating; "I think I remember."

"It was when you came to the palace to see me; you told me some story or other about your accounts with M. de Louvière and M. de Tremblay."*

"Oh, yes! perfectly."

"And about M. d'Herblay's kindness towards you."

"Ah!" exclaimed Aramis, looking the unhappy governor full in the face, "and yet you just now said you had no memory, Monsieur de Baisemeaux."

Baisemeaux interrupted the musketeer in the midst of his revelations. "Yes, yes; you're quite right; how could I have forgotten; I remember it now as well as possible; I beg you a thousand pardons. But now, once for all, my dear M. d'Artagnan, be sure that at this present time, as at any other, whether invited or not, you are perfectly at home here, you and M. d'Herblay, your friend," he said, turning towards Aramis; "and this gentleman too," he added, bowing to Athos.

"Well, I thought it would be sure to turn out so," replied

d'Artagnan, "and that is the reason I came. Having nothing to do this evening at the Palais-Royal, I wished to judge for myself what your ordinary style of living was like; and as I was coming along, I met the Comte de la Fère."

Athos bowed. "The Comte, who had just left His Majesty. handed me an order which required immediate attention. We were close by here; I wished to call in, even if it were for no other object than that of shaking hands with you and of presenting the Comte to you, of whom you spoke so highly that evening at the palace when——"

"Certainly, certainly,—M. le Comte de la Fère."

"Precisely."

"The Comte is welcome, I am sure."

"And he will sup with you two, I suppose, whilst I, unfortunate dog that I am, must run off on a matter of duty. Oh! what happy beings you are, compared to myself," he added, sighing as loud as Porthos might have done.

"And so you are going away then?" said Aramis and Baisemeaux together, with the same expression of delighted surprise, the tone of which was immediately noticed by d'Artagnan.

"I leave you in my place," he said, "a noble and excellent guest." And he touched Athos gently on the shoulder, who, astonished also, could not prevent exhibiting his surprise a little; a tone which was noticed by Aramis only, for M. de Baisemeaux was not quite equal to the three friends in point of intelligence.

"What! are you going to leave us?" resumed the governor.

"I shall only be about an hour, or an hour and a half. I will return in time for dessert."

"Oh! we will wait for you," said Baisemeaux.

"No, no; that would be really disobliging me."

"You will be sure to return, though?" said Athos, with an expression of doubt.

"Most certainly," he said, pressing his friend's hand confidently; and he added in a low voice, "Wait for me, Athos; be cheerful and lively as possible, and above all, don't allude even to business affairs, for Heaven's sake."

And with a renewed pressure of the hand, he seemed to warn the Comte of the necessity of keeping perfectly discreet and impenetrable. Baisemeaux led d'Artagnan to the gate. Aramis, with many friendly protestations of delight, sat down by Athos, determined to make him speak; but Athos possessed every virtue and quality to the very highest degree. If necessity had required it, he would have been the finest orator in the world, but on other occasions he would rather have died than have opened his lips.

Ten minutes after d'Artagnan's departure, the three gentlemen sat down to table, which was covered with the most substantial display of gastronomic luxury. Large joints, exquisite dishes, preserves, the greatest variety of wines, appeared successively upon the table, which was served at the King's expense, and of which expense M. Colbert would have found no difficulty in saving two-thirds, without any one in the Bastille being the worse for it. Baisemeaux was the only one who ate and drank resolutely. Aramis allowed nothing to pass by him, but merely touched everything he took; Athos, after the soup, and three *hors d'œuvres*, ate nothing more. The style of conversation was such as could hardly be otherwise between three men so opposite in temper and ideas. Aramis was incessantly asking himself by what extraordinary chance Athos was at Baisemeaux's when d'Artagnan was no longer there, and why d'Artagnan did not remain when Athos was there. Athos sounded all the depths of the mind of Aramis, who lived in the midst of subterfuge, evasion and intrigue; he studied his man well and thoroughly, and felt convinced that he was engaged upon some important project. And then he, too, began to think of his own personal affair, and to lose himself in conjectures as to d'Artagnan's reason for having left the Bastille so abruptly, and for leaving behind him a prisoner so badly introduced and so badly looked after by the prison authorities. But we shall not pause to examine into the thoughts and feelings of these personages, but will leave them to themselves, surrounded by the remains of poultry, game, and fish, which Baisemeaux's generous knife and fork had so mutilated. We are going to follow d'Artagnan instead, who, getting into the carriage which had brought him, said to the coachman, "Return to the palace, and as fast as you can possibly make the horses go."

25

WHAT TOOK PLACE AT THE LOUVRE DURING THE SUPPER AT THE BASTILLE

M. DE SAINT-AIGNAN had executed the commission with which the King had entrusted him for La Vallière, as we have already seen in one of the preceding chapters; but, whatever his eloquence might have been, he did not succeed in persuading the young girl that she had in the King a protector powerful enough for her under any combination of circumstances, and that she had no need of any one else in the world when the King was on her side. In point of fact, at the very first word which the favourite mentioned of the discovery of the famous secret, Louise, in a passion of tears, abandoned herself in utter despair to a sorrow which would have been far from flattering to the King, if he had been a witness of it from one of the corners of the room. Saint-Aignan, in his character of ambassador, felt greatly offended at it, as his master himself would have been, and returned to inform the King what he had seen and heard; and it is there we shall now find him in a state of great agitation in the presence of the King, who was, if possible, in a state of greater agitation than he.

"But," said the King to the courtier, when the latter had finished his report, "what did she decide to do? Shall I at least see her presently before supper? Will she come to me, or shall I be obliged to go to her room?"

"I believe, sire, that if your Majesty wishes to see her, you will not only have to take the first step in advance, but will have to go the whole way."

"That I do not mind. Do you think she has still a fancy for that Bragelonne?" muttered the King between his teeth.

"Oh! sire, that is not possible; for it is you alone I am convinced Mademoiselle de la Vallière loves, and that, too, with all her heart. But you know that de Bragelonne belongs to that proud race who play the part of Roman heroes."

The King smiled feebly; he knew how true the illustration was, for Athos had just left him.

"As for Mademoiselle de la Vallière," Saint-Aignan continued, "she was brought up under the care of the Dowager Madame; that is to say, in the greatest austerity and formality. This young engaged couple coldly exchanged their little vows in the presence of the moon and the stars, and now, when they find they have to break those vows asunder, it plays the very deuce with them."

Saint-Aignan thought he should have made the King laugh; but quite on the contrary, from a mere smile Louis passed to the greatest seriousness of manner. He already began to experience that remorse which the Comte had promised d'Artagnan he would inflict upon him. He reflected that, in fact, these young persons had loved and sworn fidelity to each other; that one of the two had kept his word, and that the other was too conscientious not to feel her perjury most bitterly. And his remorse was not unaccompanied; for bitter pangs of jealousy began to beset the King's heart. He did not say another word, and instead of going to pay a visit to his mother, or the Queen, or Madame,* in order to amuse himself a little, and make the ladies laugh, as he himself used to say, he threw himself into the huge arm-chair in which his august father Louis XIII. had passed so many weary days and years in company with Baradas and Cinq-Mars.* Saint-Aignan perceived that the King was not to be amused at that moment; he tried a last resource, and pronounced Louise's name, which made the King look up immediately. "What does your Majesty intend to do this evening—shall Mademoiselle de la Vallière be informed of your intention to see her?"

"It seems she is already aware of that," replied the King. "No, no, Saint-Aignan," he continued, after a moment's pause, "we will both of us pass our time in thinking, and musing, and dreaming; when Mademoiselle de la Vallière shall have sufficiently regretted what she now regrets, she will deign, perhaps, to give us some news of herself."

"Ah! sire, is it possible you can so misunderstand her heart, which is so full of devotion?"

The King rose, flushed from vexation and annoyance; he was a prey to jealousy as well as to remorse. Saint-Aignan was just beginning to feel that his position was becoming awkward, when the curtain before the door was raised. The King turned hastily round; his first idea was that a letter from Louise had arrived; but, instead of a letter of love, he only saw his captain of musketeers standing upright and perfectly silent in the doorway. "M. d'Artagnan," he said, "ah! Well, monsieur?"

D'Artagnan looked at Saint-Aignan; the King's eyes took the same direction as those of his captain; these looks would have been clear to any one, and for a still greater reason they were so for Saint-Aignan. The courtier bowed and quitted the room, leaving the King and d'Artagnan alone.

"Is it done?" inquired the King.

"Yes, sire," replied the captain of the musketeers in a grave voice, "it is done."

The King was unable to say another word. Pride, however, obliged him not to pause at what he had done; whenever a sovereign has adopted a decisive course, even though it be unjust, he is compelled to prove to all who were witnesses of his having adopted it, and particularly to prove it to himself, that he was quite right in so adopting it. A good means for effecting that—an almost infallible means, indeed—is, to try and prove his victim to be in the wrong. Louis, brought up by Mazarin and Anne of Austria, knew better than any one else his vocation as a monarch; he therefore endeavoured to prove it on the present occasion. After a few moments' pause, which he had employed in making silently to himself the same reflections which we have just expressed aloud, he said in an indifferent tone: "What did the Comte say?"

"Nothing at all, sire."

"Surely he did not allow himself to be arrested without saying something?"

"He said he expected to be arrested, sire."

The King raised his head haughtily. "I presume," he said, "that M. le Comte de la Fère has not continued to play his obstinate and rebellious part?"

"In the first place, sire, what do you term rebellious?" quietly asked the musketeer. "A rebel, in the eyes of the King, is a man who not only allows himself to be shut up in the Bastille, but still more, who opposes those who do not wish to take him there."

"Who do not wish to take him there!" exclaimed the King. "What do you say, captain! Are you mad?"

"I believe not, sire."

"You speak of persons who did not wish to arrest M. de la Fère! Who are those persons, may I ask?"

"I should say those whom your Majesty entrusted with that duty."

"But it was you whom I entrusted with it," exclaimed the King.

"Yes, sire; it was I."

"And ye, you say, that, despite my orders, you had the intention of not arresting the man who had insulted me!"

"Yes, sire—that was really my intention. I even proposed to the Comte to mount a horse that I had had prepared for him at the Barrière de la Conférence."

"And what was your object in getting this horse ready?"

"Why, sire, in order that M. le Comte de la Fère might be able to reach Havre, and from that place make his escape to England."

"You betrayed me, then, monsieur?" cried the King, kindling with a wild pride.

"Exactly so."

There was nothing to say in answer to statements made in such a tone; the King was astounded at such an obstinate and open resistance on the part of d'Artagnan. "At least you had a reason, Monsieur d'Artagnan, for acting as you did," said the King proudly.

"I have always a reason for everything, sire."

"Your reason cannot be your friendship for the Comte, at all events,—the only one that can be of any avail, the only one that could possibly excuse you,—for I placed you perfectly at your ease in that respect."

"Me, sire!"

"Did I not give you the choice to arrest, or not to arrest, M. le Comte de la Fère?"

"Yes, sire, but——"

"But what?" exclaimed the King impatiently.

"But you warned me, sire, that if I did not arrest him, your captain of the guards should do so."

"Was I not considerate enough towards you, from the very moment I did not compel you to obey me?"

"To me, sire, you were, but not to my friend; for my friend would be arrested all the same, whether by myself or by the captain of the guards."

"And this is your devotion, monsieur! a devotion which argues and reasons. You are no soldier, monsieur!"

"I wait for your Majesty to tell me what I am."

"Well, then—you are a Frondeur."

"And since there is no longer any Fronde, sire, in that case——"

"But if what you say is true——"

"What I say is always true, sire."

"What have you come to say to me, monsieur?"

"I have come to say to your Majesty: 'Sire, M. de la Fère is in the Bastille.'"

"That is not your fault, it would seem."

"That is true, sire; but at all events he is there; and since he is there, it is important that your Majesty should know it."

"Ah! Monsieur d'Artagnan, so you set your King at defiance."

"Sire!——"

"Monsieur d'Artagnan! I warn you that you are abusing my patience."

"On the contrary, sire."

"What do you mean by 'on the contrary'?"

"I have come to get myself arrested too."

"To get yourself arrested,—you!"

"Of course. My friend will get wearied to death in the Bastille by himself, and I have come to propose to your Majesty to permit me to bear him company; if your Majesty will but give the word, I will arrest myself; I shall not need the captain of the guard for that, I assure you."

The King darted towards the table and seized hold of a pen to write the order for d'Artagnan's imprisonment. "Pay attention, monsieur, that this is for ever," cried the King in a tone of stern menace.

"I can quite believe that," returned the musketeer, "for when you have done such an act as that, you will never be able to look me in the face again."

The King dashed down his pen violently. "Leave the room, monsieur!" he said.

"Not so, if it please your Majesty."

"How is that?"

"Sire, I came to speak gently and temperately to your Majesty; your Majesty got into a passion with me; that is a misfortune; but I shall not the less on that account say what I had to say to you."

"Your resignation, monsieur,—your resignation!" cried the King.

"Sire, you know whether I care about my resignation or not, since at Blois, on the very day when you refused King Charles the million which my friend the Comte de la Fère gave him, I then tendered my resignation to your Majesty."

"Very well, monsieur—do it at once!"

"No, sire; for there is no question of my resignation at the present moment. Your Majesty took up your pen just now to send me to the Bastille,—why should you change your intention?"

"D'Artagnan! Gascon that you are! who is the King, allow me to ask,—you or myself?"

"You, sire, unfortunately."

"What do you mean by 'unfortunately'?"

"Yes, sire; for if it were I——"

"If it were you, you would approve of M. d'Artagnan's rebellious conduct, I suppose?"

"Certainly."

"Really!" said the King, shrugging his shoulders.

"And I should tell my captain of the musketeers," continued d'Artagnan, "I should tell him, looking at him all the while with human eyes, and not with eyes like coals of fire, 'M. d'Artagnan,

I had forgotten that I was the King, for I descended from my throne in order to insult a gentleman.'"

"Monsieur," said the King, "do you think you can excuse your friend by exceeding him in insolence?"

"Oh, sire! I should go much further than he did," said d'Artagnan, "and it would be your own fault. I should tell you what he, a man full of the finest sense of delicacy, did not tell you; I should say—'Sire, you have sacrificed his son, and he defended his son—you sacrificed himself; he addressed you in the name of honour, of religion, of virtue—you repulsed, drove him away, imprisoned him.' I should be harder than he was, for I should say to you—'Sire, it is for you to choose. Do you wish to have friends or lackeys—soldiers or slaves—great men or mere puppets? Do you wish men to serve you, or to bend and crouch before you? Do you wish men to love you, or to be afraid of you? If you prefer baseness, intrigue, cowardice, say so at once, sire, and we will leave you,—we, who are the only individuals who are left, nay, I will say more, the only models of the valour of former times; we who have done our duty, and have exceeded, perhaps, in courage and in merit, the men already great for posterity. Choose, sire! and that too without delay. Whatever remains to you of great nobles, guard it with a jealous eye; you will never be deficient in courtiers. Delay not—and send me to the Bastille with my friend; for, if you have not known how to listen to the Comte de la Fère, whose voice is the sweetest and noblest when honour is his theme; if you do not know how to listen to d'Artagnan, the frankest and honestest voice of sincerity, you are a bad King, and to-morrow will be a poor King. And learn from me, sire, that bad kings are hated by their people, and poor kings are driven ignominiously away.' That is what I had to say to you, sire; you were wrong to have driven me to do it."

The King threw himself back in his chair, cold as death and livid as a corpse. Had a thunderbolt fallen at his feet, he could not have been more astonished; he seemed as if his respiration had utterly ceased, and that he was at the point of death. The honest voice of sincerity, as d'Artagnan had called it, had pierced through his heart like a sword-blade.

D'Artagnan had said all he had to say. Comprehending the King's anger, he drew his sword, and, approaching Louis XIV., respectfully, he placed it on the table. But the King, with a furious gesture, thrust aside the sword, which fell on the ground and rolled to d'Artagnan's feet. Notwithstanding the perfect mastery which d'Artagnan exercised over himself, he, too, in his turn, became pale, and, trembling with indignation, said—"A king may disgrace a soldier,—he may exile him, and may even condemn him to death; but were he a hundred times a king he has no right to insult him by casting a dishonour upon his sword! Sire, a King of France has never repulsed with contempt the sword of a man such as I am! Stained with disgrace as this sword now is, it has henceforth no other sheath than either your heart or my own! I choose my own, sire; and you have to thank Heaven and my own patience that I do so." Then snatching up his sword, he cried, "My blood be upon your head!" and with a rapid gesture, he placed the hilt upon the floor and directed the point of the blade towards his breast. The King, however, with a movement far more rapid than that of d'Artagnan, threw his right arm round the musketeer's neck, and with his left hand seized hold of the blade by the middle, and returned it silently to the scabbard. D'Artagnan, upright, pale, and still trembling, let the King do all to the very end. Louis, overcome and softened by gentler feelings, returned to the table, took a pen in his hand, wrote a few lines, signed them, and then held it out to D'Artagnan.

"What is this paper, sire?" inquired the captain.

"An order for M. d'Artagnan to set the Comte de la Fère at liberty immediately."

D'Artagnan seized the King's hand, and imprinted a kiss upon it; he then folded the order, placed it in his belt, and quitted the room. Neither the King nor the captain had said a syllable.

"Oh, human heart! the guide and director of kings," murmured Louis, when alone, "when shall I learn to read in your inmost recesses, as in the leaves of a book! No, I am not a bad king—nor am I a poor king; but I am still a child, after all."

26

POLITICAL RIVALS

D'ARTAGNAN had promised M. de Baisemeaux to return in time for dessert, and he kept his word. They had just reached the finer and more delicate class of wines and liqueurs with which the governor's cellar had the reputation of being most admirably stocked, when the spurs of the captain resounded in the corridor, and he himself appeared at the threshold. Athos and Aramis had played a close game; neither of the two had been able to gain the slightest advantage over the other. They had supped, talked a good deal about the Bastille, of the last journey to Fontainebleau, of the intended fête that M. Fouquet was about to give at Vaux; they had generalised on every possible subject; and no one, excepting Baisemeaux, had, in the slightest degree, alluded to private matters. D'Artagnan arrived in the very midst of the conversation, still pale and much disturbed by his interview with the King. Baisemeaux hastened to give him a chair; d'Artagnan accepted a glass of wine, and set it down empty. Athos and Aramis both remarked his emotion; as for Baisemeaux, he saw nothing more than the captain of the King's musketeers, to whom he endeavoured to show every possible attention. But, although Aramis had remarked his emotion, he had not been able to guess the cause of it. Athos alone believed he had detected it. For him, d'Artagnan's return, and particularly the manner in which he, usually so impassible, seemed overcome, signified, "I have just asked the King something which the King has refused me." Thoroughly convinced that his conjecture was correct, Athos smiled, rose from the table, and made a sign to d'Artagnan, as if to remind him that they had something else to do than to sup together. D'Artagnan immediately understood him, and replied by another sign. Aramis and Baisemeaux watched this silent dialogue, and looked inquiringly at each other. Athos felt that he was called upon to give an explanation of what was passing.

"The truth is, my friends," said the Comte de la Fère, with a smile, "that you, Aramis, have been supping with a state criminal, and you, Monsieur de Baisemeaux, with your prisoner."

Baisemeaux uttered an exclamation of surprise, and almost of delight; for he was exceedingly proud and vain of his fortress; and, for his own individual profit,* the more prisoners he had, the happier he was; and the higher the prisoners were in rank, the prouder he felt. Aramis assumed an expression of countenance which he thought the position justified, and said, "Well, dear Athos, forgive me; but I almost suspected what has happened. Some prank of Raoul and La Vallière, I suppose?"

"Alas!" said Baisemeaux.

"And," continued Aramis, "you, a high and powerful nobleman as you are, forgetful that courtiers now exist,—you have been to the King, I suppose, and told him what you thought of his conduct."

"Yes, you have guessed right."

"So that," said Baisemeaux, trembling at having supped so familiarly with a man who had fallen into disgrace with the King; "so that, Monsieur le Comte——"

"So that, my dear governor," said Athos, "my friend d'Artagnan will communicate to you the contents of the paper which I perceive just peeping out of his belt, and which assuredly can be nothing else than the order for my incarceration."

Baisemeaux held out his hand with his accustomed eagerness. D'Artagnan drew two papers from his belt, and presented one of them to the governor, who unfolded it, and then read, in a low tone of voice, looking at Athos over the paper, as he did so, and pausing from time to time: "'Order to detain in my château of the Bastille, Monsieur le Comte de la Fère.' Oh! monsieur! this is indeed a very melancholy honour for me."

"You will have a patient prisoner, monsieur," said Athos, in his calm, soft voice.

"A prisoner, too, who will not remain a month with you, my dear governor," said Aramis; while Baisemeaux, still holding the order in his hand, transcribed it upon the prison registry.

"Not a day, or rather not even a night," said d'Artagnan, displaying the second order of the King, "for now, dear M. de Baisemeaux, you will have the goodness to transcribe also this order for setting the Comte immediately at liberty."

"Ah!" said Aramis, "it is a labour that you have deprived me of, d'Artagnan;" and he pressed the musketeer's hand in a significant manner, at the same moment as that of Athos.

"What!" said the latter, in astonishment, "the King sets me at liberty!"

"Read, my dear friend," returned d'Artagnan.

Athos took the order and read it. "It is quite true," he said.

"Are you sorry for it?" asked d'Artagnan.

"Oh, no, on the contrary; I wish the King no harm; and the greatest evil or misfortune that any one can wish Kings, is that they should commit an act of injustice. But you have had a difficult and painful task, I know. Tell me, have you not, d'Artagnan?"

"I? not at all," said the musketeer, laughing; "the king does everything I wish him to do."

Aramis looked fixedly at d'Artagnan, and saw that he was not speaking the truth. But Baisemeaux had eyes for nothing but d'Artagnan, so great was his admiration for a man who seemed to make the King do all he wished. "And does the King exile Athos?" inquired Aramis.

"No, not precisely; the King did not explain himself upon that subject," replied d'Artagnan; "but I think the Comte could not well do better, unless, indeed, he wishes particularly to thank the King——"

"No, indeed," replied Athos, smiling.

"Well, then, I think," resumed d'Artagnan, "that the Comte

cannot do better than return to his own château. However, my dear Athos, you have only to speak, to tell me what you want. If any particular place of residence is more agreeable to you than another, I am influential enough, perhaps, to obtain it for you."

"No, thank you," said Athos; "nothing can be more agreeable to me, my dear friend, than to return to my solitude beneath my noble trees, on the banks of the Loire.* If Heaven be the overruling physician of the evils of the mind, nature is the sovereign remedy. And so, monsieur," continued Athos, turning again towards Baisemeaux, "I am now free, I suppose?"

"Yes, Monsieur le Comte, I think so—at least, I hope so," said the governor, turning over and over the two papers in question, "unless, however, M. d'Artagnan has a third order to give me."

"No, my dear Monsieur Baisemeaux, no," said the musketeer; "the second is quite enough; we can stop there."

"Ah! Monsieur le Comte," said Baisemeaux, addressing Athos, "you do not know what you are losing. I should have placed you among the thirty-franc prisoners, like the generals—what am I saying?—I mean among the fifty-francs, like the princes; and you would have supped every evening as you have done to-night."

"Allow me, monsieur," said Athos, "to prefer my own simpler fare." And then, turning to d'Artagnan, he said, "Let us go, my dear friend. Shall I have that greatest of all pleasures for me—that of having you as my companion?"

"To the city gate only," replied d'Artagnan, "after which I will tell you what I told the King. I am on duty."

"And you, my dear Aramis," said Athos, smiling; "will you accompany me? La Fère is on the road to Vannes."

"Thank you, my dear friend," said Aramis, "but I have an appointment in Paris this evening, and I cannot leave without very serious interests suffering by my absence."

"In that case," said Athos, "I must say *adieu*, and take my leave of you. My dear Monsieur de Baisemeaux, I have to thank you exceedingly for your kind and friendly disposition towards me, and particularly for the specimen you have given me of the usual fare of the Bastille." And, having embraced Aramis, and shaken hands with M. de Baisemeaux, and having received their wishes for an agreeable journey from them both, Athos set off with d'Artagnan.

Whilst the *dénouement* of the scene of the Palais-Royal was taking place at the Bastille, let us relate what was going on at the lodgings of Athos and Bragelonne. Grimaud, as we have seen, had accompanied his master to Paris; and, as we have said, he was present when Athos went out; he had observed d'Artagnan gnaw the corners of his moustaches; he had seen his master get into the carriage; he had narrowly examined both their countenances, and he had known them both for a sufficiently long period to read and understand, through the mask of their impassibility, that something serious was the matter. As soon as Athos had gone, he began to reflect; he then, and then only, remembered the strange manner in which Athos had taken leave of him, the embarrassment —imperceptible for any one else but himself—of the master whose ideas were, to him, so clear and defined, and the expression of whose wishes was so precise. He knew that Athos had taken nothing with him but the clothes he had on him at the time; and yet he seemed to fancy that Athos had not left for an hour merely, or even for a day. A long absence was signified by the manner in which he pronounced the word "*Adieu.*" All these circumstances recurred to his mind, with feelings of deep affection for Athos, with that horror of isolation and solitude which invariably besets the minds of those who love; and all these combined, rendered poor Grimaud very melancholy, and particularly very uneasy. Without being able to account to himself for what he did, since his master's departure he wandered about the room, seeking as it were, for some traces of him, like a faithful dog, who is not exactly uneasy about his absent master, but at least is restless. Only as, in addition to the instinct of the animal, Grimaud subjoined the reasoning faculties of the man, Grimaud therefore felt uneasy and restless too. Not having found any indication which could serve as a guide, and having neither seen nor discovered anything which could satisfy his doubts, Grimaud began to imagine what could possibly have happened. Besides, the imagination is the resource, or rather the punishment of good and affectionate hearts. In fact, never does a good heart represent its absent friend to itself as being happy or cheerful. Never does the pigeon who travels in search of adventures inspire anything but terror to the pigeon who remains at home.

Grimaud soon passed from uneasiness to terror; he carefully went over, in his own mind, everything that had taken place; d'Artagnan's letter to Athos, the letter which had seemed to distress Athos so much after he had read it; then Raoul's visit to Athos, which resulted in Athos desiring him (Grimaud) to get his various orders and his court dress ready to put on; then his interview with the King, at the end of which Athos had returned home so unusually gloomy; then the explanation between the father and the son, at the termination of which Athos had embraced Raoul with such sadness of expression, while Raoul himself went away equally sad and melancholy; and, finally, d'Artagnan's arrival, biting, as if he were vexed, the end of his moustache, and his leaving again in the carriage, accompanied by the Comte de la Fère. All that composed a drama in five acts* very clearly, particularly for so analytical an examiner as Grimaud.

The first step he took was to search in his master's coat for M. d'Artagnan's letter; he found the letter still there, which contained the following:—

"MY DEAR FRIEND,—Raoul has been to ask me for some particulars about the conduct of Mademoiselle de la Vallière, during our young friend's residence in London. I am a poor captain of musketeers, and am sickened to death every day by hearing all the scandal of the barracks and bedside conversations. If I had told Raoul all I believe I know, the poor fellow would have died from it; but I am in the King's service, and cannot relate all I hear about the King's affairs. If your heart tells you to do it, set off at once; the matter concerns you more than myself, and almost as much as Raoul."

Grimaud tore, not a handful, but a finger-and-thumbful of hair out of his head; he would have done more if his head of hair had been in more flourishing circumstances.

"Yes," he said, "that is the key of the whole enigma. The young girl has been playing her pranks; what people say about her and the King is true, then; our young master has been deceived; he ought to know it. Monsieur le Comte has been to see the King, and has told him a piece of his mind; and then the King sent M. d'Artagnan to arrange the affair. Ah! gracious goodness!" continued Grimaud, "Monsieur le Comte, I now remember, returned without his sword."

This discovery made the perspiration break out all over poor Grimaud's face. He did not waste any more time in useless conjecture, but clapped his hat on his head, and ran to Raoul's lodgings.

Raoul, after Louise had left him, had mastered his grief, if not his affection; and, compelled to look forward on that perilous road on which madness and rebellion were hurrying him, he had seen, from the very first glance, his father exposed to the royal obstinacy; since Athos had himself been the first to oppose any resistance to the royal will. At this moment, from a very natural sympathy of feeling, the unhappy young man remembered the mysterious signs which Athos had made, and the unexpected visit of d'Artagnan; the result of the conflict between a sovereign and a subject revealed itself to his terrified vision. As d'Artagnan was on duty, that is, fixed to his post without possibility of leaving it, it was certainly not likely that he had come to pay Athos a visit merely for the pleasure of seeing him. He must have come to say something to him. This something, in such painful conjectures, was either a misfortune or a danger. Raoul trembled at having been so selfish as to have forgotten his father for his affection; at having, in a word, passed his time in idle dreams, or in an indulgence of despair, at a time when a necessity existed for repelling the imminent attack directed against Athos. The very idea nearly drove him wild; he buckled on his sword and ran towards his father's lodging. On his way there he encountered Grimaud, who, having set off from the opposite pole, was running with equal eagerness in search of the truth. The two men embraced each other most warmly.

"Grimaud," exclaimed Raoul, "is the Comte well?"

"Have you seen him?"

"No; where is he?"

"I am trying to find out."

"And M. d'Artagnan?"

"Went out with him."

"When?"

"Ten minutes after you had left."

"In what way did they go out?"

"In a carriage."

"Where did they go to?"

"I have no idea at all."

"Did my father take any money with him?"

"No."

"Or his sword?"

"No."

"I have an idea, Grimaud, that M. d'Artagnan came in order to——"

"Arrest Monsieur le Comte, do you not think, monsieur?"

"Yes, Grimaud."

"I could have sworn it."

"What road did they take?"

"The way leading towards the quays."

"To the Bastille, then?"

"Yes, yes."

"Quick, quick; let us run."

"Yes, let us not lose a moment."

"But where are we to go to?" said Raoul, overwhelmed.

"We will go to M. d'Artagnan's first, we may perhaps learn something there."

"No; if they kept me in ignorance at my father's, they will do the same everywhere. Let us go to—— Oh, good Heavens! why I must be mad to-day, Grimaud; I have forgotten M. du Vallon, who is waiting for and expecting me still."

"Where is he, then?"

"At the Minimes of Vincennes."

"Thank goodness, that is on the same side as the Bastille. I will run and saddle the horses, and we will go at once," said Grimaud.

"Do, my friend, do."

27

IN WHICH PORTHOS IS CONVINCED WITHOUT HAVING UNDERSTOOD ANYTHING

THE good and worthy Porthos, faithful to all the laws of ancient chivalry, had determined to wait for M. de Saint-Aignan until sunset; and, as Saint-Aignan did not come, as Raoul had forgotten to communicate with his second, and as he found that waiting so long was very wearisome, Porthos had desired one of the gatekeepers to fetch him a few bottles of good wine and a good joint of meat,—so that he at least might pass away the time with a glass of wine and a mouthful of something to eat. He had just finished when Raoul arrived, escorted by Grimaud, both riding at full speed. As soon as Porthos saw the two cavaliers riding at such a pace along the road, he did not for a moment doubt but that they were the men he was expecting, and he rose from the grass upon which he had been indolently reclining and began to stretch his legs and arms, saying, "See what it is to have good habits. The fellow has finished by coming after all. If I had gone away he would have found no one here, and would have taken an advantage from that." He then threw himself into a martial attitude, and drew himself up to the full height of his gigantic stature. But instead of Saint-Aignan, he only saw Raoul, who, with the most despairing gestures, accosted him by crying out, "Pray forgive me, my dear friend, I am most wretched."

"Raoul," cried Porthos, surprised.

"You have been angry with me?" said Raoul, embracing Porthos.

"I? What for?"

"For having forgotten you. But I assure you my head seems utterly lost. If you only knew!"

"You have killed him?"

"Who?"

"Saint-Aignan; or if that is not the case, what is the matter?"

"The matter is that Monsieur le Comte de la Fère has by this time been arrested."

Porthos gave a start that would have thrown down a wall.

"Arrested," he cried out; "by whom?"

"By d'Artagnan."

"It is impossible," said Porthos.

"My dear friend; it is perfectly true."

Porthos turned towards Grimaud, as if he needed a second confirmation of the intelligence. Grimaud nodded his head. "And where have they taken him to?"

"Probably to the Bastille."

"What makes you think that?"

"As we came along we questioned some persons, who saw the carriage pass; and others who saw it enter the Bastille."

"Oh, oh!" muttered Porthos.

"What do you intend to do?" inquired Raoul.

"I? Nothing; only I will not have Athos remain at the Bastille."

"Do you know," said Raoul, advancing nearer to Porthos, "that the arrest was made by order of the King?"

Porthos looked at the young man, as if to say, "What does that matter to me?" This dumb language seemed so eloquent of meaning to Raoul, that he did not ask another question. He mounted his horse again; and Porthos, assisted by Grimaud, had already done the same.

"Let us arrange our plan of action," said Raoul.

"Yes," returned Porthos, "that is the best thing we can do."

Raoul sighed deeply, and then paused suddenly.

"What is the matter?" asked Porthos; "are you faint?"

"No, only I feel how utterly helpless our position is. Can we three pretend to go and take the Bastille?"

"Well, if d'Artagnan were only here," replied Porthos, "I don't know about that."

Raoul could not resist a feeling of admiration at the sight of such a perfect confidence, heroic in its simplicity. These were truly the celebrated men who, by three or four, attacked armies, and assaulted castles! Those men who had terrified death itself, and who survived the wrecks of an age, and were still stronger than the most robust of the young.

"Monsieur," said he to Porthos, "you have just given me an idea; we absolutely must see M. d'Artagnan."

"Undoubtedly."

"He ought by this time to have returned home, after having taken my father to the Bastille. Let us go to his house."

"First inquire at the Bastille," said Grimaud, who was in the habit of speaking little, but that to the purpose.

Accordingly, they hastened towards the fortress, when one of those chances which Heaven bestows on men of strong will, caused Grimaud suddenly to perceive the carriage, which was entering by the great gate of the drawbridge. This was at the moment that d'Artagnan was, as we have seen, returning from his visit to the King. In vain was it that Raoul urged on his horse in order to join the carriage, and to see whom it contained. The horses had already gained the other side of the great gate, which again closed, while one of the sentries struck the nose of Raoul's horse with his musket; Raoul turned about, only too happy to find he had ascertained something respecting the carriage which had contained his father.

"We have him," said Grimaud.

"If we wait a little it is certain he will leave; don't you think so, my friend?"

"Unless, indeed, d'Artagnan also be a prisoner," replied Porthos, "in which case everything is lost."

Raoul returned no answer, for any hypothesis was admissible. He instructed Grimaud to lead the horses to the little street Jean-Beausire,* so as to give rise to less suspicion, and himself, with his piercing gaze, watched for the exit either of d'Artagnan or the carriage. Nor had he decided wrongly; for twenty minutes had not elapsed before the gate reopened and the carriage reappeared. A dazzling of the eyes prevented Raoul from distinguishing what figures occupied the interior. Grimaud averred that he had seen two persons, and that one of them was his master. Porthos kept looking at Raoul and Grimaud by turns, in the hope of understanding their idea.

"It is clear," said Grimaud, "that if the Comte is in the carriage, either he is set at liberty or they are taking him to another prison."

"We shall soon see that by the road he takes," answered Porthos.

"If he is set at liberty," said Grimaud, "they will conduct him home."

"True," rejoined Porthos.

"The carriage does not take that way," cried Raoul; and indeed the horses were just disappearing down the Faubourg St. Antoine.*

"Let us hasten," said Porthos; "we will attack the carriage on the road and tell Athos to flee."

"Rebellion," murmured Raoul.

Porthos darted a second glance at Raoul, quite worthy of the first. Raoul replied only by spurring the flanks of his steed. In a few moments the three cavaliers had overtaken the carriage, and followed it so closely that their horses' breath moistened the back of it. D'Artagnan, whose senses were ever on the alert, heard the trot of the horses, at the moment when Raoul was telling Porthos to pass the chariot so as to see who was the person accompanying Athos. Porthos complied, but could not see anything, for the blinds were lowered. Rage and impatience were gaining mastery over Raoul. He had just noticed the mystery preserved by Athos's companion, and determined on proceeding to extremities. On his part d'Artagnan had perfectly recognised Porthos, and Raoul also, from under the blinds, and had communicated to the Comte the result of his observation. They were desirous only of seeing whether Raoul and Porthos would push the affair to the uttermost. And this they speedily did, for Raoul, presenting his pistol, threw himself on the leader, commanding the coachman to stop. Porthos seized the coachman and dragged him from his seat. Grimaud already had hold of the carriage door. Raoul threw open his arms, exclaiming, "M. le Comte! M. le Comte!"

"Ah! it is you, Raoul," said Athos, intoxicated with joy.

"Not bad, indeed!" added d'Artagnan, with a burst of laughter, and they both embraced the young man and Porthos who had taken possession of them.

"My brave Porthos! best of friends," cried Athos, "it is still the same with you."

"He is still only twenty," said d'Artagnan, "brave Porthos!"

"Confound it," answered Porthos, slightly confused, "we thought that you were being arrested."

"While," rejoined Athos, "the matter in question was nothing but my taking a drive in M. d'Artagnan's carriage."

"But we followed you from the Bastille," returned Raoul, with a tone of suspicion and reproach.

"Where we had been to take supper with our good friend M. Baisemeaux. Do you recollect Baisemeaux, Porthos?"

"Very well, indeed."

"And there we saw Aramis."

"In the Bastille?"

"At supper."

"Ah!" said Porthos, again breathing freely.

"He gave us a thousand messages for you."

"And where is M. le Comte going?" asked Grimaud, already recompensed by a smile from his master.

"We were going home to Blois."

"How can that be?"

"At once?" said Raoul.

"Yes, right forward."

"Without any luggage?"

"Oh! Raoul would have been instructed to forward me mine, or to bring it with him on his return, *if* he returns."

"If nothing detains him longer in Paris," said d'Artagnan, with a glance firm and cutting as steel, and as painful (for it reopened the poor young fellow's wounds), "he will do well to follow you, Athos."

"There is nothing to keep me any longer in Paris," said Raoul.

"Then we will go immediately," replied Athos.

"And M. d'Artagnan?"

"Oh! as for me, I was only accompanying Athos as far as the barrier, and I return with Porthos."

"Very good," said the latter.

"Come, my son," added the Comte, gently passing his arm round Raoul's neck to draw him into the carriage, and again embracing him. "Grimaud," continued the Comte, "you will return quietly to Paris with your horse and M. de Vallon's, for Raoul and I will mount here and give up the carriage to these two gentlemen to return to Paris in; and then, as soon as you arrive, you will take my clothes and letters and forward the whole to me at home."

"But," observed Raoul, who was anxious to make the Comte converse, "when you return to Paris, there will not be a single thing there for you—which will be very inconvenient."

"I think it will be a very long time, Raoul, ere I return to Paris. The last sojourn we have made there has not been of a nature to encourage me to repeat it."

Raoul hung his head and said not a word more. Athos descended from the carriage and mounted the horse which had brought Porthos, and which seemed no little pleased at the exchange. Then they embraced, clasped each other's hands, interchanged a thousand pledges of eternal friendship. Porthos promised to spend a month with Athos at the first opportunity. D'Artagnan engaged to take advantage of his first leave of absence; and then, having embraced Raoul for the last time: "To you, my boy," said he, "I will write." Coming from d'Artagnan, who he knew wrote but very seldom, these words expressed everything. Raoul was moved even to tears. He tore himself away from the musketeer and departed.

D'Artagnan rejoined Porthos in the carriage: "Well," said he, "my dear friend, what a day we have had!"

"Indeed we have," answered Porthos.

"You must be quite worn out?"

"Not quite; however, I shall retire early to rest, so as to be ready to-morrow."

"And wherefore?"

"Why! to complete what I have begun."

"You make me shudder, my friend, you seem to me quite angry. What the devil have you begun which is not finished?"

"Listen; Raoul has not fought, but *I* must fight!"

"With whom? with the King?"

"How!" exclaimed Porthos astounded, "with the King?"

"Yes, I say, you great baby, with the King!"

"I assure you it is with M. Saint-Aignan."

"Look now, this is what I mean: you draw your sword against the King in fighting with this gentleman."

"Ah!" said Porthos, staring; "are you sure of it?"

"Indeed I am."

"What in the world are we to do then?"

"We must try to make a good supper, Porthos. The captain of the musketeers keeps a tolerable table. There you will see the handsome Saint-Aignan, and will drink his health."

"I!" cried Porthos, horrified.

"What!" said d'Artagnan, "you refuse to drink the King's health?"

"But body alive! I am not talking to you about the King at all; I am speaking of M. de Saint-Aignan."

"But since I repeat that it is the same thing."

"Ah, well, well!" said Porthos, overcome.

"You understand, don't you?"

"No," answered Porthos, "but 'tis all the same."

28

M. DE BAISEMEAUX'S 'SOCIETY'

THE reader has not forgotten that, on quitting the Bastille, d'Artagnan and the Comte de la Fère had left Aramis in close confabulation with Baisemeaux. When once these two guests had departed, Baisemeaux did not in the least perceive that the conversation suffered by their absence. He used to think that wine after supper, and that of the Bastille in particular, was excellent; and that it was a stimulant quite sufficient to make an honest man talk. But he little knew his greatness, who was never more impenetrable than at dessert. His greatness, however, perfectly understood M. de Baisemeaux, when he reckoned on making the governor discourse on the means which the latter regarded as efficacious. The conversation, therefore, without flagging in appearance, flagged in reality; for Baisemeaux not only had it nearly all to himself, but further, kept speaking only of that singular event—the incarceration of Athos—followed by so prompt an order to set him again at liberty. Nor, moreover, had Baisemeaux failed to observe that the two orders, of arrest and of liberation, were both in the King's hand. But then, the King would not take the trouble to write similar orders except under pressing circumstances. All this was very interesting, and, above all, very puzzling to Baisemeaux; but as, on the other hand, all this was very clear to Aramis, the latter did not attach to the occurrence the same importance as did the worthy governor. Besides, Aramis rarely put himself out of the way for anything, and he had not yet told M. de Baisemeaux for what reason he had now done so. And so at the very climax of Baisemeaux's dissertation, Aramis suddenly interrupted him.

"Tell me, my dear M. Baisemeaux," said he, "have you never any other diversions at the Bastille than those at which I assisted during the two or three visits I have had the honour to pay you?"

This address was so unexpected that the governor, like a vane which suddenly receives an impulsion opposed to that of the wind, was quite dumbfounded at it. "Diversions," said he, "but I take them continually, monseigneur."

"Oh, to be sure! And these diversions?"

"Are of every kind."

"Visits, no doubt?"

"No, not visits. Visits are not frequent at the Bastille."

"What, are visits rare, then?"

"Very much so."

"Even on the part of your society?"

"What do you term by my society—the prisoners?"

"Oh, no!—your prisoners, indeed! I know well it is you who visit them, and not they you. By your society I mean, my dear de Baisemeaux, the society of which you are a member."

Baisemeaux looked fixedly at Aramis, and then, as if the idea which had flashed across his mind were impossible, "Oh!" he said, "I have very little society at present. If I must own it to you, dear M. d'Herblay, the fact is, to stay at the Bastille appears, for the most part, distressing and distasteful to persons of the gay world. As for the ladies, it is never without a dread, which costs me infinite trouble to allay, that they succeed in reaching my quarters. And, indeed, how should they avoid trembling a little, poor things, when they see those gloomy dungeons, and reflect that they are inhabited by prisoners who——" And in proportion as the eyes of Baisemeaux concentrated their gaze on the face of Aramis, the worthy governor's tongue faltered more and more, until it ended by stopping altogether.

"No, you don't understand me, my dear M. Baisemeaux; you don't understand me. I do not at all mean to speak of society in general, but of a particular society—of *the* society, in a word,—to which you are affiliated."

Baisemeaux nearly dropped the glass of muscat which he was in the act of raising to his lips. "Affiliated!" cried he, "affiliated!"

"Yes, affiliated, undoubtedly," repeated Aramis, with the greatest self-possession. "Are you not a member of a secret society," my dear M. Baisemeaux?"

"Secret?"

"Secret or mysterious."

"Oh, Monsieur d'Herblay!"

"Consider now, don't deny it."

"But believe me."

"I believe what I know."

"I swear to you."

"Listen to me, my dear M. Baisemeaux; I say yes, you say no; one of us two necessarily says what is true, and the other, it inevitably follows, what is false."

"Well, and then?"

"Well, we shall come to an understanding presently."

"Let us see," said Baisemeaux; "let us see."

"Now drink your glass of muscat, dear Monsieur de Baisemeaux," said Aramis. "What the devil! you look quite scared."

"No, no; not the least in the world; no."

"Drink then." Baisemeaux drank, but he swallowed the wrong way.

"Well," resumed Aramis, "if I say you are not a member of a secret or mysterious society, which you like to call it, the epithet is of no consequence; if I say you are not a member of a society similar to that I wish to designate, well, then, you will not understand a word of what I am going to say, that is all."

"Oh! be sure, beforehand, that I shall not understand anything."

"Well, well!"

"Try now, let us see."

"That is what I am going to do."

"If, on the contrary, you are one of the members of this society, you will immediately answer me,—yes, or no."

"Begin your questions," continued Baisemeaux, trembling.

"You will agree, dear Monsieur de Baisemeaux," continued Aramis, with the same impassibility, "that it is evident a man cannot be a member of a society, it is evident that he cannot enjoy the advantages it offers to the affiliated, without being himself bound to certain little services."

"In short," stammered Baisemeaux, "that would be intelligible, if——"

"Well," resumed Aramis, "there is in the society of which I speak, and of which, as it seems, you are not a member."

"Allow me," said Baisemeaux, "I should not like to say absolutely."

"There is an engagement entered into by all the governors and captains of fortresses affiliated to the order." Baisemeaux grew pale.

"Now the engagement," continued Aramis firmly, "is of this nature."

Baisemeaux rose, manifesting unspeakable emotion; "Go on, dear M. d'Herblay; go on," said he.

Aramis then spoke, or rather recited the following paragraph in the same tone as if he had been reading it from a book. "The aforesaid captain or governor of a fortress shall allow to enter, when need shall arise, and on demand of the prisoner, a confessor affiliated to the order." He stopped. Baisemeaux was quite distressing to look at, being so wretchedly pale and trembling. "Is not that the text of the agreement?" quietly asked Aramis.

"Monseigneur!" began Baisemeaux.

"Ah! well you begin to understand, I think."

"Monseigneur," cried Baisemeaux, "do not trifle with my un-happy mind! I find myself nothing in your hands, if you have the malignant desire to draw from me the little secrets of my ad-ministration."

"Oh! by no means; pray undeceive yourself, dear M. Baise-meaux; it is not the little secrets of your administration, but those of your conscience that I aim at."

"Well, then, my conscience be it, dear M. d'Herblay. But have some consideration for the situation I am in, which is no ordinary one."

"It is no ordinary one, my dear monsieur," continued the inflexible Aramis, "if you are a member of this society; but it is quite a natural one if free from all engagements. You are answer-able only to the King."

"Well, monsieur, well! I obey only the King, and whom else would you have a French nobleman obey?"

Aramis did not yield an inch; but with that silvery voice of his, continued, "It is very pleasant," said he, "for a French nobleman, for a prelate of France, to hear a man of your mark express him-self so loyally, dear de Baisemeaux, and having heard you to believe no more than you do."

"Have you doubted, monsieur?"

"I? oh, no!"

"And so you doubt no longer?"

"I have no longer any doubt that such a man as you, monsieur," said Aramis, gravely, "does not faithfully serve the masters whom he voluntarily chose for himself."

"Masters!" cried Baisemeaux.

"Yes, masters I said."

"Monsieur d'Herblay, you are still jesting, are you not?"

"Oh, yes! I understand that it is a more difficult position to have several masters than one; but the embarrassment is owing to you, my dear Baisemeaux, and I am not the cause of it."

"Certainly not," returned the unfortunate governor, more embarrassed than ever; "but what are you doing? You are leaving the table?"

"Assuredly."

"Are you going?"

"Yes, I am going."

"But you are behaving very strangely towards me, mon-seigneur."

"I am behaving strangely,—how do you make that out?"

"Have you sworn, then, to put me to the torture?"

"No, I should be sorry to do so."

"Remain then."

"I cannot."

"And why?"

"Because I have no longer anything to do here; and, indeed, I have duties to fulfil elsewhere."

"Duties, so late as this?"

"Yes; understand me now, my dear de Baisemeaux; they told me at the place whence I came, 'The aforesaid governor or captain will allow to enter, as need shall arise, on the prisoner's demand, a confessor affiliated with the order.' I came; you do not know what I mean, and so I shall return to tell them that they are mistaken, and that they must send me elsewhere."

"What! you are——" cried Baisemeaux, looking at Aramis almost in terror.

"The confessor affiliated to the order," said Aramis, without changing his voice.

But, gentle as the words were, they had the same effect on the unhappy governor as a clap of thunder. Baisemeaux became livid, and it seemed to him as if Aramis's beaming eyes were two forks of flame, piercing to the very bottom of his soul. "The confessor!" murmured he; "you, monseigneur, the confessor to the order!"

"Yes, I; but we have nothing to unravel together, seeing that you are not one of the affiliated."

"Monseigneur!"

"And I understand, that not being so, you refuse to comply with its demands."

"Monseigneur, I beseech you, condescend to hear me."

"And wherefore?"

"Monseigneur, I do not say that I have nothing to do with the society."

"Ah, ah!"

"I say not that I refuse to obey."

"Nevertheless, M. de Baisemeaux, what has passed wears very much the air of resistance."

"Oh, no! monseigneur, no; I only wished to be certain."

"To be certain of what?" said Aramis, in a tone of supreme contempt.

"Of nothing at all, monseigneur." Baisemeaux lowered his voice and, bending before the prelate, said, "I am at all times and in all places at the disposal of my masters, but——"

"Very good. I like you better thus, monsieur," said Aramis, as he resumed his seat, and put out his glass to Baisemeaux, whose hand trembled so that he could not fill it. "You were saying 'but'——" continued Aramis.

"But," replied the unhappy man, "having no notice, I was far from expecting."

"Does not the Gospel say, 'Watch, for the moment is known only of God.' Do not the rules of the order say, 'Watch, for that which I will you ought always to will also.' And on what pretext is it that you did not expect the confessor, M. de Baisemeaux?"

"Because, monseigneur, there is at present in the Bastille no prisoner ill."

Aramis shrugged his shoulders, "What do you know about that?" said he.

"But, nevertheless, it appears to me——"

"M. de Baisemeaux," said Aramis, turning round in his chair, "here is your servant, who wishes to speak with you;" and, at this moment, de Baisemeaux's servant appeared at the threshold of the door.

"What is it?" asked Baisemeaux sharply.

"Monsieur," said the man, "they are bringing you the doctor's return."

Aramis looked at Baisemeaux with a calm and confident eye.

"Well," said he, "let the messenger enter."

The messenger entered, saluted, and handed in the report. Baisemeaux ran his eye over it, and raising his head said, in surprise, "No. 12 is ill."

"How was it then," said Aramis carelessly, "that you told me everybody was well in your hotel, M. de Baisemeaux?" And he emptied his glass without removing his eyes from Baisemeaux.

The governor then made a sign to the messenger, and when he had quitted the room said, still trembling, "I think there is in the article, 'on the prisoner's demand.'"

"Yes, it is so," answered Aramis. "But see what it is they want with you now."

At that moment, a sergeant put his head in at the door. "What do you want now?" cried Baisemeaux. "Can you not leave me in peace for ten minutes?"

"Monsieur," said the sergeant, "the sick man, No. 12, has commissioned the turnkey to request you to send him a confessor."

Baisemeaux very nearly sank on the floor; but Aramis disdained to reassure him, just as he had disdained to terrify him. "What must I answer?" inquired Baisemeaux.

"Just what you please," replied Aramis, compressing his lips; "that is your business. *I* am not governor of the Bastille."

"Tell the prisoner," cried Baisemeaux quickly—"tell the prisoner that his request is granted." The sergeant left the room.

"O monseigneur, monseigneur," murmured Baisemeaux, "how could I have suspected!—how could I have foreseen this!"

"Who requested you to suspect, and who besought you to foresee?" contemptuously answered Aramis. "The order suspects; the order knows; the order foresees—is not that enough?"

"What do you command?" added Baisemeaux.

"I?—nothing at all. I am nothing but a poor priest, a simple confessor. Have I your orders to go and see the sufferer?"

"Oh, monseigneur, I do not order; I pray you to go."

"'Tis well; then conduct me to him."

29

THE PRISONER

SINCE Aramis's singular transformation into a confessor of the order, Baisemeaux was no longer the same man. Up to that period the place which Aramis had held in the worthy governor's estimation was that of a prelate whom he respected, and a friend to whom he owed a debt of gratitude; but now he felt himself an inferior, and that Aramis was his master. He himself lighted a lantern, summoned a turnkey, and said, returning to Aramis, "I am at your orders, monseigneur." Aramis merely nodded his head, as much as to say "Very good"; and signed to him with his hand to lead the way. Baisemeaux advanced, and Aramis followed him. It was a beautiful starry night; the steps of the three men resounded on the flags of the terraces, and the clinking of the keys hanging from the jailer's girdle made itself heard up to the storeys of the towers, as if to remind the prisoners that liberty was out of their reach. It might have been said that the alteration effected in Baisemeaux had extended itself even to the prisoners. The turnkey, the same who on Aramis's first arrival had shown himself so inquisitive and curious, had now become not only silent, but even impassible. He held his head down, and seemed afraid to keep his ears open. In this wise they reached the basement of the Bertaudière, the two first storeys of which were mounted silently and somewhat slowly; for Baisemeaux, though far from disobeying, was far from exhibiting any eagerness to obey. On arriving at the door, Baisemeaux showed a disposition to enter the prisoner's chamber; but Aramis stopping him on the threshold said, "The rules do not allow the governor to hear the prisoner's confession."

Baisemeaux bowed, and made way for Aramis, who took the

173

lantern, and entered; and then signed to them to close the door behind him. For an instant he remained standing, listening whether Baisemeaux and the turnkey had retired; but as soon as he was assured by the sound of their dying footsteps that they had left the tower, he put the lantern on the table and gazed around. On a bed of green serge, similar in all respects to the other beds in the Bastille, save that it was newer, and under curtains half-drawn, reposed a young man. According to custom, the prisoner was without a light. At the hour of curfew, he was bound to extinguish his lamp, and we perceive how much he was favoured in being allowed to keep it burning even till then. Near the bed a large leathern armchair, with twisted legs, sustained his clothes. A little table—without pens, books, paper or ink—stood neglected in sadness near the window; while several plates, still unemptied, showed that the prisoner had scarcely touched his recent repast. Aramis saw that the young man was stretched upon his bed, his face half-concealed by his arms. The arrival of a visitor did not cause any change of position; either he was waiting in expectation, or was asleep. Aramis lighted the candle from the lantern, pushed back the armchair, and approached the bed with an evident mixture of interest and respect. The young man raised his head. "What is it?" said he.

"Have you not desired a confessor," replied Aramis.

"Yes."

"Because you are ill?"

"Yes."

"Very ill?"

The young man gave Aramis a piercing glance, and answered, "I thank you." After a moment's silence, "I have seen you before," he continued. Aramis bowed.

Doubtless, the scrutiny the prisoner had just made of the cold, crafty, and imperious character stamped upon the features of the Bishop of Vannes, was little reassuring to one in his situation, for he added, "I am better."

"And then?" said Aramis.

"Why, then—being better, I have no longer the same need of a confessor, I think."

"Not even of the haircloth, which the note you found in your bread informed you of?"

The young man started; but before he had either assented or denied, Aramis continued, "Not even of the ecclesiastic from whom you were to hear an important revelation?"

"If it be so," said the young man, sinking again on his pillow; "it is different, I listen."

Aramis then looked at him more closely, and was struck with the easy majesty of his mien, one which can never be acquired unless Heaven has implanted it in the blood or heart. "Sit down, monsieur," said the prisoner.

Aramis bowed and obeyed. "How does the Bastille agree with you?" asked the Bishop.

"Very well."

"You do not suffer?"

"No."

"You have nothing to regret?"

"Nothing."

"Not even your liberty?"

"What do you call liberty, monsieur?" asked the prisoner with the tone of a man who is preparing for a struggle.

"I call liberty the flowers, the air, light, the stars, the happiness of going whithersoever the nervous limbs of twenty years of age may wish to carry you." The young man smiled, whether in resignation or contempt it was difficult to tell. "Look," said he, "I have in that Japanese vase two roses gathered yesterday evening in the bud from the governor's garden; this morning they have blown and spread their vermilion chalice beneath my gaze; with every opening petal they unfold the treasures of their perfume, filling my chamber with a fragrance that embalms it. Look now, on these two roses; even among roses these are beautiful, and the rose is the most beautiful of flowers. Why then, do you bid me desire other flowers when I possess the loveliest of all?"

Aramis gazed t the young man in surprise. "If *flowers* constitute liberty," sadly resumed the captive, "I am free, for I possess them."

"But the air!" cried Aramis; "air so necessary to life!"

"Well, monsieur," returned the prisoner; "draw near to the window; it is open. Between heaven and earth the wind whirls on its storms of hail and lightning, wafts its warm mists or breathes in gentle breezes. It caresses my face. When mounted on the back of this armchair, with my arm around the bars of the window to sustain myself, I fancy I am swimming in the wide expanse before me." The countenance of Aramis darkened as the young man continued: "Light I have! what is better than light? I have the sun, a friend who comes to visit me every day without the permission of the governor or the jailer's company. He comes in at the window and traces in my room a square the shape of the window, and which lights up the hangings of my bed down to the border. This luminous square increases from ten o'clock to midday and decreases from one till three slowly, as if, having hastened to come, it sorrowed at leaving me. When its last ray disappears I have enjoyed its presence for five hours. Is not that sufficient? I have been told that there are unhappy beings who dig in quarries, and labourers who toil in mines, and who never behold it at all." Aramis wiped the drops from his brow. "As to the stars which are so delightful to view," continued the young man, "they all resemble each other save in size and brilliancy. I am a favoured mortal, for if you had not lighted that candle you would have been able to see the beautiful stars which I was gazing at from my couch before your arrival, and whose rays were playing over my eyes." Aramis lowered his head; he felt himself overwhelmed with the bitter flow of that sinister philosophy which is the religion of the captive. "So much, then, for the flowers, the air, the daylight, and the stars," tranquilly continued the young man; "there remains but my exercise. Do I not walk all day in the governor's garden, if it is fine—here if it rains? in the fresh air if it is warm; in the warm, thanks to my winter stove, if it be cold? Ah! monsieur, do you fancy," continued the prisoner, not without bitterness, "that men have not done everything for me that a man can hope for or desire?"

"Men!" said Aramis; "be it so; but it seems to me you forget Heaven."

"Indeed I have forgotten Heaven," answered the prisoner, with emotion; "but why do you mention it? Of what use is it to talk to a prisoner of Heaven?"

Aramis looked steadily at this singular youth who possessed the resignation of a martyr with the smile of an atheist. "Is not Heaven in everything?" he murmured in a reproachful tone.

"Say rather at the end of everything," answered the prisoner firmly.

"Be it so," said Aramis; "but let us return to our starting point."

"I desire nothing better," returned the young man.

"I am your confessor."

"Yes."

"Well, then, you ought, as a penitent, to tell me the truth."

"All that I wish is to tell it you."

"Every prisoner has committed some crime for which he has been imprisoned. What crime then have *you* committed?"

"You asked me the same question the first time you saw me," returned the prisoner.

"And then, as now, you evaded giving me an answer."

"And what reason have you for thinking that I shall now reply to you?"

"Because this time I am your confessor."

"Then if you wish me to tell what crime I have committed, explain to me in what a crime consists. For as my conscience does not accuse me, I aver that I am not a criminal."

"We are often criminals in the sight of the great of the earth, not alone for having ourselves committed crimes, but because we know that crimes have been committed."

The prisoner manifested the deepest attention. "Yes, I understand you," he said, after a pause; "yes, you are right, monsieur; it is very possible that in that light I am a criminal in the eyes of the great of the earth."

"Ah! then you know something," said Aramis, who thought he had pierced not merely through a defect in, but through the joints of the harness.

"No, I am not aware of anything," replied the young man; "but sometimes I think—and I say to myself——"

"What do you say to yourself?"

"That if I were to think any further I should either go mad, or I should divine a great deal."

"And then—and then?" said Aramis impatiently.

"Then I leave off."

"You leave off."

"Yes; my head becomes confused and my ideas melancholy; I feel *ennui* overtaking me; I wish——"

"What?"

"I don't know; but I do not like to give myself up to longing for things which I do not possess, when I am so happy with what I have."

"You are afraid of death?" said Aramis, with a slight uneasiness.

"Yes," said the young man, smiling.

Aramis felt the chill of that smile, and shuddered.

"Oh, as you fear death you know more about matters than you say," he cried.

"And you," returned the prisoner, "who bade me to ask to see you; you, who, when I did ask for you, came here promising a world of confidence; how is it that, nevertheless, it is you who are silent, and 'tis I who speak? Since, then, we both wear masks, either let us both retain them or put them aside together."

Aramis felt the force and justice of the remark, saying to himself, "This is no ordinary man; I must be cautious. Are you ambitious?" said he suddenly to the prisoner, aloud, without preparing him for the alteration.

"What do you mean by ambition?" replied the youth.

"It is." replied Aramis, "a feeling which prompts a man to desire more than he has."

"I said that I was contented, monsieur; but, perhaps, I deceive myself. I am ignorant of the nature of ambition; but it is not impossible I may have some. Tell me your mind; 'tis all I wish."

"An ambitious man," said Aramis, "is one who covets what is beyond his station."

"I covet nothing beyond my station," said the young man, with an assurance of manner which for the second time made the Bishop of Vannes tremble.

He was silent, but to look at the kindling eye, the knitted brow, and the reflective attitude of the captive, it was evident that he expected something more than silence—a silence which Aramis now broke. "You lied the first time I saw you," said he.

"Lied!" cried the young man, starting up on his couch, with such a tone in his voice, and such a lightning in his eyes, that Aramis recoiled, in spite of himself.

"I *should* say," returned Aramis, bowing, "you concealed from me what you knew of your infancy."

"A man's secrets are his own, monsieur," retorted the prisoner, "and not at the mercy of the first chance-comer."

"True," said Aramis, bowing still lower than before, "'tis true; pardon me, but to-day, do I still occupy the place of a chance-comer? I beseech you to reply, monseigneur."

This title slightly disturbed the prisoner; but nevertheless he did not appear astonished that it was given him. "I do not know you, monsieur," said he.

"Oh, if I but dared, I would take your hand and would kiss it."

The young man seemed as if he were going to give Aramis his hand; but the light which beamed in his eyes faded away, and he coldly and distrustfully withdrew his hand again. "Kiss the hand of a prisoner," he said, shaking his head, "to what purpose?"

"Why did you tell me," said Aramis, "that you were happy here? Why, that you aspired to nothing? Why, in a word, by thus speaking, do you prevent me from being frank in my turn?"

The same light shone a third time in the young man's eyes, but died ineffectually away as before.

"You distrust me?" said Aramis.

"And why say you so, monsieur?"

"Oh, for a very simple reason; if you know what you ought to know, you ought to mistrust everybody."

"Then be not astonished that I am mistrustful, since you suspect me of knowing what I know not."

Aramis was struck with admiration at this energetic resistance. "Oh, monseigneur! you drive me to despair," said he, striking the armchair with his fist.

"And, on my part, I do not comprehend you, monsieur."

"Well, then, try to understand me." The prisoner looked fixedly at Aramis. "Sometimes it seems to me," said the latter, "that I have before me the man whom I seek, and then——"

"And then your man disappears,—is it not so?" said the prisoner, smiling. "So much the better."

Aramis rose. "Certainly," said he; "I have nothing further to say to a man who mistrusts me as you do."

"And I, monsieur," said the prisoner, in the same tone, "have nothing to say to a man who will not understand that a prisoner ought to be mistrustful of everybody."

"Even of his old friends?" said Aramis. "Oh! monseigneur, you are *too* prudent!"

"Of my old friends?—you one of my old friends,—you?"

"Do you no longer remember," said Aramis, "that you once saw, in the village where your early years were spent——"

"Do you know the name of the village?" asked the prisoner.

"Noisy-le-Sec,* monseigneur," answered Aramis firmly.

"Go on," said the young man, with an immovable aspect.

"Stay, monseigneur," said Aramis; "if you are positively resolved to carry on this game, let us break off. I am here to tell you many things, 'tis true; but you must allow me to see that, on your side, you have a desire to know them. Before revealing the important matters I conceal, be assured I am in need of some encouragement, if not candour; a little sympathy, if not confidence. But you keep yourself intrenched in a pretended ignorance which paralyses me. Oh, not for the reason you think; for, ignorant as you may be, or indifferent as you feign to be, you are none the less what you are, monseigneur, and there is nothing,—nothing, mark me, which can cause you not to be so."

"I promise you," replied the prisoner, "to hear you without impatience. Only it appears to me that I have a right to repeat the question I have already asked—'Who *are* you?'"

"Do you remember, fifteen or eighteen years ago, seeing at Noisy-le-Sec a cavalier accompanied by a lady in black silk, with flame-coloured ribands in her hair?"

"Yes," said the young man; "I once asked the name of this cavalier, and they told me he called himself the Abbé d'Herblay. I was astonished that the Abbé had so warlike an air, and they replied that there was nothing singular in that, seeing that he was one of Louis XIII.'s musketeers."

"Well," said Aramis, "that musketeer and Abbé, afterwards Bishop of Vannes, is your confessor now."

"I knew it; I recognised you."

"Then, monseigneur, if you know that, I must further add a fact of which you are ignorant—that if the King were to know this evening of the presence of this musketeer, this Abbé, this bishop, this confessor, *here*—he, who has risked everything to visit you, would to-morrow see glitter the executioner's axe at the bottom of a dungeon more gloomy and more obscure than yours."

While hearing these words, delivered with emphasis, the young man had raised himself on his couch, and gazed more and more eagerly at Aramis.

The result of his scrutiny was that he appeared to derive some confidence from it. "Yes," he murmured, "I remember perfectly. The woman of whom you speak came once with you, and twice afterwards with another." He hesitated.

"With another woman, who came to see you every month,—is it not so, monseigneur?"

"Yes."

"Do you know who this lady was?"

The light seemed ready to flash from the prisoner's eyes. "I am aware that she was one of the ladies of the court," he said.

"You remember that lady well, do you not?"

"Oh, my recollection can hardly be very confused on this head," said the young prisoner. "I saw that lady once with a gentleman about forty-five years old. I saw her once with you, and with the lady dressed in black. I have seen her twice since with the same person. These four people, with my master, and old Perronnette, my jailer, and the governor of the prison, are the only persons with whom I have ever spoken, and, indeed, almost the only persons I have ever seen."*

"Then you were in prison?"

"If I am a prisoner here, there I was comparatively free, although in a very narrow sense—a house which I never quitted, a garden surrounded with walls I could not clear, these constituted my residence; but you know it, as you have been there. In a word, being accustomed to live within these bounds, I never cared to leave them. And so you will understand, monsieur, that not having seen anything of the world, I have nothing left to care for; and therefore, if you relate anything, you will be obliged to explain everything to me."

"And I will do so," said Aramis bowing, "for it is my duty, monseigneur."

"Well, then, begin by telling me who was my tutor."

"A worthy and, above all, an honourable gentleman, monseigneur; fit guide both for body and soul. Had you ever any reason to complain of him?"

"Oh, no; quite the contrary. But this gentleman of yours often used to tell me that my father and mother were dead. Did he deceive me, or did he speak the truth?"

"He was compelled to comply with the orders given him."

"Then he lied?"

"In one respect. Your father is dead."

"And my mother?"

"She is dead for you."

"But then she lives for others, does she not?"

"Yes."

"And I—and I, then" (the young man looked sharply at Aramis) "am compelled to live in the obscurity of a prison?"

"Alas! I fear so."

"And that, because my presence in the world would lead to the revelation of a great secret?"

"Certainly, a very great secret."

"My enemy must indeed be powerful, to be able to shut up in the Bastille a child such as I then was."

"He is."

"More powerful than my mother, then?"

"And why do you ask that?"

"Because my mother would have taken my part."

Aramis hesitated. "Yes, monseigneur; more powerful than your mother."

"Seeing, then, that my nurse and preceptor were carried off, and that I, also, was separated from them—either they were, or I am, very dangerous to my enemy?"

"Yes; a peril from which he freed himself, by causing the nurse and preceptor to disappear," answered Aramis quietly.

"Disappear!" cried the prisoner—"but how did they disappear?"

"In the surest possible way," answered Aramis;—"they are dead."

The young man turned visibly pale, and passed his hand tremblingly over his face. "From poison?" he asked.

"From poison."

The prisoner reflected a moment. "My enemy must indeed have been very cruel, or hard beset by necessity, to assassinate these two innocent people, my sole support; for the worthy gentleman and the poor nurse had never harmed a living being."

"In your family, monseigneur, necessity is stern. And so it is necessity which compels me, to my great regret, to tell you that this gentleman and the unhappy lady have been assassinated."

"Oh, you tell me nothing I am not aware of," said the prisoner, knitting his brows.

"How?"

"I suspected it."

"Why?"

"I will tell you."

At this moment the young man, supporting himself on his two elbows drew close to Aramis's face, with such an expression of dignity, of self-command, and of defiance even, that the Bishop felt the electricity of enthusiasm strike in devouring flashes from that seared heart of his, into his brain of adamant.

"Speak, monseigneur. I have already told you that by conversing with you, I endanger my life. Little value as it has, I implore you to accept it as a ransom of your own."

"Well," resumed the young man, "this is why I suspected that they had killed my nurse and my preceptor."

"Whom you used to call your father."

"Yes; whom I called my father, but whose son I well knew I was not."

"Who caused you to suppose so?"

"For the same reason that you, monsieur, are too respectful for a friend, he was also too respectful for a father."

"I, however," said Aramis, "have no intention to disguise myself."

The young man nodded assent, and continued:—"Undoubtedly I was not destined to perpetual seclusion," said the prisoner; "and that which makes me believe so, above all, now, is the care that was taken to render me as accomplished a cavalier as possible. The gentleman attached to my person taught me everything he knew himself—mathematics, a little geometry, astronomy, fencing, and riding. Every morning I went through military exercises, and practised on horseback. Well, one morning during summer, it being very hot, I went to sleep in the hall. Nothing up to that period, except the respect paid me, had enlightened me, or even roused my suspicions. I lived as children, as birds, as plants, as the air and the sun do. I had just turned my fifteenth year——"

"This, then, is eight years ago?"

"Yes, nearly; but I have ceased to reckon time."

"Excuse me; but what did your tutor tell you to encourage you to work?"

"He used to say that a man was bound to make for himself, in the world, that fortune which Heaven had refused him at his birth. He added, that, being a poor obscure orphan I had no one but myself to look to; and that nobody either did, or ever would, take any interest in me. I was then in the hall I have spoken of, asleep from fatigue in fencing. My preceptor was in his room on the first floor just over me. Suddenly I heard him exclaim: and then he called, 'Perronnette! Perronnette!' It was my nurse whom he called."

"Yes, I know it," said Aramis. "Continue, monseigneur."

"Very likely she was in the garden; for my preceptor came hastily downstairs. I rose, anxious at seeing him anxious. He opened the garden-door still crying out, 'Perronnette! Perronnette!' The window of the hall looked into the court; the shutters were closed; but through a chink in them I saw my tutor draw near a large well, which was almost directly under the windows of his study. He stooped over the brim, looked into the well, again cried out, and made wild and affrighted gestures. Where I was, I could not only see, but hear—and see and hear I did."

"Go on, I pray you," said Aramis.

"Dame Perronnette came running up, hearing the governor's cries. He went to meet her, took her by the arm, and drew her quickly towards the edge; after which, as they both bent over it together, 'Look, look,' cried he, 'what a misfortune!'

"'Calm yourself, calm yourself,' said Perronnette; 'what is the matter?'

"'The letter!' he exclaimed; 'do you see that letter?' pointing to the bottom of the well.

"'What letter?' she cried.

"'The letter you see down there; the last letter from the Queen.'

"At this word I trembled. My tutor—he who passed for my father, he who was continually recommending me modesty and humility—in correspondence with the Queen!

"'The Queen's last letter!' cried Perronnette, without showing more astonishment than at seeing this letter at the bottom of the well; 'but how came it there?'

"'A chance, dame Perronnette—a singular chance. I was entering my room, and on opening the door, the window, too, being open, a puff of air came suddenly and carried off this paper —this letter of Her Majesty's; I darted after it and gained the window just in time to see it flutter a moment in the breeze and disappear down the well.'

"'Well,' said dame Perronnette; 'and if the letter has fallen into the well, 'tis all the same as if it was burned, and as the Queen burns all her letters every time she comes——'

"And so you see this lady who came every month was the Queen," said the prisoner.

"'Doubtless, doubtless,' continued the old gentleman; 'but this letter contained instructions—how can I follow them?'

"'Write immediately to her; give her a plain account of the accident, and the Queen will no doubt write you another letter in place of this.'

"'Oh! the Queen would never believe the story,' said the good gentleman, shaking his head; 'she will imagine that I want to keep this letter instead of giving it up like the rest, so as to have a hold over her. She is so distrustful, and M. de Mazarin so—— This devil of an Italian is capable of having us poisoned at the first breath of suspicion.'"

Aramis almost imperceptibly smiled.

"'You know, dame Perronnette, they are both so suspicious in all that concerns Philippe.'

"Philippe was the name they gave me," said the prisoner.

"'Well, 'tis no use hesitating,' said dame Perronnette, 'somebody must go down the well.'

"'Of course; so that the person who goes down may read the paper as he is coming up.'

"'But let us choose some villager who cannot read, and then you will be at ease.'

"'Granted; but will not any one who descends guess that a paper must be important for which we risk a man's life? However, you have given me an idea, dame Perronnette; somebody shall go down the well, but that somebody shall be myself.'

"But at this notion dame Perronnette lamented and cried in such a manner, and so implored the old nobleman with tears in her eyes, that he promised her to obtain a ladder long enough to reach down, while she went in search of some stout-hearted youth, whom she was to persuade that a jewel had fallen into the well, and that this jewel was wrapped in a paper. 'And as paper,' remarked my preceptor, 'naturally unfolds in water, the young man would not be surprised at finding nothing, after all, but the letter wide open.'

"'But perhaps the writing will be already effaced by that time,' said dame Perronnette.

"'No consequence, provided we secure the letter. On returning it to the Queen, she will see at once that we have not betrayed her; and consequently, as we shall not rouse the distrust of Mazarin, we shall have nothing to fear from him.'

"Having come to this resolution they parted. I pushed back the shutter, and, seeing that my tutor was about to re-enter, I threw

184

myself on my couch, in a confusion of brain caused by all I had just heard. My governor opened the door a few moments after, and, thinking I was asleep, gently closed it again. As soon as ever it was shut, I rose, and, listening, heard the sound of retiring footsteps. Then I returned to the shutter, and saw my tutor and dame Perronnette go out together. I was alone in the house. They had hardly closed the gate before I sprang from the window and ran to the well. Then, just as my governor had leaned over, so leaned I. Something white and luminous glistened in the green and quivering ripples of the water. The brilliant disc fascinated and allured me; my eyes became fixed, and I could hardly breathe. The well seemed to draw me in with its large mouth and icy breath; and I thought I read, at the bottom of the water, characters of fire traced upon the letter the Queen had touched. Then, scarcely knowing what I was about, and urged on by one of those instinctive impulses which drive men upon their destruction, I lowered the cord from the windlass of the well to within about three feet of the water, leaving the bucket dangling, and at the same time taking infinite pains not to disturb that coveted letter, which was beginning to change its white tint for a greenish hue,— proof enough that it was sinking,—and then, with the rope weltering in my hands, slid down into the abyss. When I saw myself hanging over the dark pool, when I saw the sky lessening above my head, a cold shudder came over me, a chill fear got the better of me, I was seized with giddiness, and the hair rose on my head; but my strong will still reigned supreme over all the terror and disquietude. I gained the water, and at once plunged into it, holding on by one hand, while I immersed the other and seized the dear letter, which alas! came in two in my grasp. I concealed the two fragments in my body coat, and, helping myself with my feet against the sides of the pit, and clinging on with my hands, agile and vigorous as I was, and, above all, pressed for time, I regained the brink, drenching it as I touched it with the water that streamed off me. I was no sooner out of the well with my prize, than I rushed into the sunlight, and took refuge in a kind of shrubbery at the bottom of the garden. As I entered my hiding-place,the bell which resounded when the great gate was opened, rang. It was my preceptor come back again. I had but just time. I calculated that it would take ten minutes before he would gain my place of concealment, even, if, guessing where I was, he came straight to it; and twenty if he were obliged to look for me. But this was time enough to allow me to read the cherished letter, whose fragments I hastened to unite again. The writing was already fading, but I managed to decipher it all."

"And what read you there, monseigneur?" asked Aramis, deeply interested.

"Quite enough, monsieur, to see that my tutor was a man of noble rank, and that Perronnette, without being a lady of quality, was far better than a servant; and also to perceive that I must myself be high-born, since the Queen, Anne of Austria, and Mazarin, the prime minister, commended me so earnestly to their care."

Here the young man paused, quite overcome.

"And what happened?" asked Aramis.

"It happened, monsieur," answered he, "that the workman they had summoned found nothing in the well, after the closest search; that my governor perceived that the brink was all watery; that I was not so well dried by the sun as to escape dame Perronnette's observing that my garments were moist; and, lastly, that I was seized with a violent fever, owing to the chill and the excitement of my discovery, an attack of delirium supervening, during which I related the whole adventure; so that, guided by my avowal, my governor found under the bolster the two pieces of the Queen's letter."

"Ah!" said Aramis, "now I understand."

"Beyond this, all is conjecture. Doubtless the unfortunate lady and gentleman, not daring to keep the occurrence secret, wrote all to the Queen, and sent back to her the torn letter."

"After which," said Aramis, "you were arrested and moved to the Bastille."

"As you see."

"Then your two attendants disappeared?"

"Alas!"

"Let us not take up our time with the dead, but see what can be done for the living. You told me you were resigned?"

"I repeat it."

"Without any desire for freedom?"

"As I told you."

"Without ambition, sorrow, or thought?"

The young man made no answer.

"Well," asked Aramis, "why are you silent?"

"I think I have spoken enough," answered the prisoner; "and that now it is your turn. I am weary."

Aramis gathered himself up, and a shade of deep solemnity spread itself over his countenance. It was evident that he had reached the crisis in the part he had come to the prison to play.

"One question," said Aramis.

"What is it? speak."

"In the house you inhabited there were neither looking-glasses nor mirrors?"

"What are those two words, and what is their meaning?" asked the young man; "I have no sort of knowledge of them."

"They designate two pieces of furniture which reflect objects; so that, for instance, you may see in them your own lineaments, as you see mine now, with the naked eye."

"No; then there was neither a glass nor a mirror in the house," answered the young man.

Aramis looked round him. "Nor is there here either," he said; "they have again taken the same precaution."

"To what end?"

"You will know directly. Now, you have told me that you were instructed in mathematics, astronomy, fencing, and riding; but you have not said a word about history."

"My tutor sometimes related to me the principal deeds of the King, St. Louis, King Francis I., and King Henry IV."

"Is that all?"

"Very nearly."

"This also was done by design then; just as they deprived you of mirrors, which reflect the present, so they left you in ignorance of history, which reflects the past. Since your imprisonment, books have been forbidden you; so that you are unacquainted with a number of facts, by means of which you would be able to reconstruct the shattered edifice of your recollections and your hopes."

"It is true," said the young man.

"Listen, then; I will in a few words tell you what has passed in France during the last twenty-three or twenty-four years; that is, from the probable date of your birth; in a word, from the time that interests you."

"Say on." And the young man resumed his serious and attentive attitude.

"Do you know who was the son of Henry IV.?"

"At least I know who his successor was."

"How?"

"By means of a coin dated 1610, which bears the effigy of Henry IV.; and another of 1612, bearing that of Louis XIII. So I presumed that, there being only two years between the two dates, Louis was Henry's successor."

"Then," said Aramis, "you know that the last reigning monarch was Louis XIII.?"

"I do," answered the youth, slightly reddening.

"Well, he was a prince full of noble ideas and great projects, always, alas! deferred by the troubles of the times and the struggles that his minister Richelieu had to maintain against the great nobles of France. The King himself was of a feeble character; and died young and unhappy."

"I know it."

"He had been long anxious about having an heir; a care which weighs heavily on princes, who desire to leave behind them more than one pledge that their thoughts and works will be continued."

"Did the King, then, die childless?" asked the prisoner, smiling.

"No, but he was long without one, and for a long while thought he should be the last of his race. This idea had reduced him to the depths of despair, when suddenly, his wife, Anne of Austria——"

The prisoner trembled.

"Did you know," said Aramis, "that Louis XIII.'s wife was called Anne of Austria?"

"Continue," said the young man, without replying to the question.

"When suddenly," resumed Aramis, "the Queen announced an interesting event. There was great joy at the intelligence, and all prayed for her happy delivery. On the 5th of September, 1638, she gave birth to a son."

Here Aramis looked at his companion, and thought he observed him turning pale. "You are about to hear," said Aramis, "an account which few could now give; for it refers to a secret which they think buried with the dead or entombed in the abyss of the confessional."

"And you will tell me this secret?" broke in the youth.

"Oh!" said Aramis with unmistakable emphasis, "I do not know that I ought to risk this secret by entrusting it to one who has no desire to quit the Bastille."

"I hear you, monsieur."

"The Queen, then, gave birth to a son. But while the court was rejoicing over the event, when the King had shown the new-born child to the nobility and people and was sitting gaily down to table to celebrate the event, the Queen, who was alone in her room, was again taken ill, and gave birth to a second son."

"Oh!" said the prisoner, betraying a better acquaintance with the affair than he had owned to, "I thought that Monsieur was only born a——"

Aramis raised his finger: "Let me continue," he said.

The prisoner sighed impatiently, and paused.

"Yes," said Aramis, "the Queen had a second son, whom dame Perronnette, the midwife, received in her arms."

"Dame Perronnette!" murmured the young man.

"They ran at once to the banqueting-room, and whispered to the King what had happened; he rose and quitted the table. But this time it was no longer happiness that his face expressed, but something akin to terror. The birth of twins changed into bitterness the joy to which that of an only son had given rise, seeing that in France (a fact you are assuredly ignorant of) it is the oldest of the King's sons who succeeds his father."

"I know it."

"And that the doctors and jurists assert that there is ground for doubting whether he who first makes his appearance is the elder by the law of Heaven and of nature."

The prisoner uttered a smothered cry, and became whiter than the coverlet under which he hid himself.

"Now you understand," pursued Aramis, "that the King, who, with so much pleasure, saw himself repeated in one, was in despair about two; fearing that the second might dispute the first's claim to seniority, which had been recognised only two hours before; and so this second son, relying on party interests and caprices, might one day sow discord and engender civil war in the kingdom; by these means destroying the very dynasty he should have strengthened."

"Oh, I understand!—I understand!" murmured the young man.

"Well," continued Aramis; "this is what they relate, what they declare; this is why one of the Queen's two sons, shamefully parted from his brother, shamefully sequestered, is buried in the profoundest obscurity; this is why that second son has disappeared, and so completely, that not a soul in France, save his mother, is aware of his existence."

"Yes! his mother who has cast him off!" cried the prisoner in a tone of despair.

"Except, also," Aramis went on, "the lady in the black dress; and finally, excepting——"

"Excepting yourself—Is it not? You, who come and relate all this; you, who arouse in my soul curiosity, hatred, ambition, and, perhaps, even the thirst of vengeance; except you, monsieur, who, if you are the man whom I expect, whom the note I have received applies to; whom, in short, Heaven ought to send me, must possess about you——"

"What?" asked Aramis.

"A portrait of the King, Louis XIV., who at this moment reigns upon the throne of France."

"Here is the portrait," replied the Bishop, handing the prisoner a miniature in enamel, on which Louis was depicted, life-like, with a handsome, lofty mien. The prisoner eagerly seized the portrait, and gazed at it with devouring eyes.

"And now, monseigneur," said Aramis, "here is a mirror." Aramis left the prisoner time to recover his ideas.

"So high!—so high!" murmured the young man, eagerly comparing the likeness of Louis with his own countenance reflected in the glass.

"What do you think of it?" at length said Aramis.

"I think that I am lost," replied the captive; "the King will never set me free."

"And I—I demand," added the Bishop, fixing his piercing eyes significantly upon the prisoner, "I demand which of the two is the King; the one whom this miniature portrays, or whom the glass reflects?"

"The King, monsieur," sadly replied the young man, "is he who is on the throne, who is not in prison; and who, on the other hand, can cause others to be entombed here. Royalty is power; and you see well how powerless I am."

"Monseigneur," answered Aramis, with a respect he had not yet manifested, "the King, mark me, will, if you desire it, be he who, quitting his dungeon, shall maintain himself upon the throne, on which his friends will place him."

"Tempt me not, monsieur," broke in the prisoner bitterly.

"Be not weak, monseigneur," persisted Aramis; "I have brought all the proofs of your birth; consult them; satisfy yourself that you are a king's son; and then let us act."

"No, no; it is impossible."

"Unless, indeed," resumed the Bishop, ironically, "it be the destiny of your race, that the brothers excluded from the throne should be always princes void of courage and honesty, as was your uncle, M. Gaston d'Orléans,* who ten times conspired against his brother, Louis XIII."

"What!" cried the prince, astonished, "my uncle Gaston, 'conspired against his brother'; conspired to dethrone him?"

"Exactly, monseigneur; for no other reason. I tell you the truth."

"And he had friends—devoted ones."

"As much so as I am to you."

"And after all, what did he do?—Failed!"

"He failed, I admit; but always through his own fault; and, for the sake of purchasing—not his life—for the life of the King's brother is sacred and inviolable,—but his liberty, he sacrificed the lives of all his friends, one after another. And so, at this day, he is the very shame of history, and the detestation of a hundred noble families in this kingdom."

"I understand, monsieur; either by weakness or treachery, my uncle slew his friends."

"By weakness; which, in princes, is always treachery."

"And cannot a man fail, then, from incapacity and ignorance? Do you really believe it possible that a poor captive such as I, brought up, not only at a distance from the court, but even from the world—do you believe it possible that such a one could assist those of his friends who should attempt to serve him?" And as Aramis was about to reply, the young man suddenly cried out, with a violence which betrayed the temper of his blood, "We are speaking of friends; but how can *I* have any friends—I, whom no one knows; and have neither liberty, money, nor influence to gain any?"

"I fancy I had the honour to offer myself to your Royal Highness."

"Oh, do not style me so, monsieur; 'tis either treachery or cruelty! Bid me not think of ought else than these prison walls, which confine me; let me again love, or, at least, submit to my slavery and my obscurity."

"Monseigneur, monseigneur; if you again utter these desperate words—if, after having received proof of your high birth, you still remain poor-spirited in body and soul, I will comply with your desire, I will depart, and renounce for ever the service of a master, to whom so eagerly I came to devote my assistance and my life."

"Monsieur," cried the Prince, "would it not have been better for you to have reflected that, before telling me all that you have done, that you have broken my heart for ever?"

"And so I desired to do, monseigneur."

"To talk to me about power, grandeur, and even royalty. Is a prison the fitting place? You wish to make me believe in splendour, and we are lying hidden in night; you boast of glory, and we are smothering our words in the curtains of this miserable bed; you give me glimpses of absolute power, and I hear the step of the jailer in the corridor—that step, which, after all, makes you tremble more than it does me. To render me somewhat less incredulous, free me from the Bastille; let me breathe the fresh air; give me my spurs and trusty sword, then we shall begin to understand each other."

"It is precisely my intention to give you all this, monseigneur, and more; only, do you desire it?"

"A word more," said the Prince. "I know there are guards in

every gallery, bolts to every door, cannon and soldiery at every barrier. How will you overcome the sentries—spike the guns? How will you break through the bolts and bars?"

"Monseigneur,—how did you get the note which announced my arrival to you?"

"You can bribe a jailer for such a thing as a note."

"If we can corrupt one turnkey, we can corrupt ten."

"Well; I admit that it may be possible to release a poor captive from the Bastille; possible so to conceal him that the King's people shall not again ensnare him; possible, in some unknown retreat, to sustain the unhappy wretch in some suitable manner."

"Monseigneur!" said Aramis, smiling.

"I admit that, whoever would do thus much for me, would seem more than mortal in my eyes; but as you tell me I am a Prince, brother of a king, how can you restore me the rank and power which my mother and my brother have deprived me of? And as, to effect this, I must pass a life of war and hatred, how will you make me prevail in those combats—render me invulnerable by my enemies? Ah! monsieur reflect upon this; place me, to-morrow, in some dark cavern in a mountain's base; yield me the delight of hearing in freedom the sounds of river and plain, of beholding in freedom the sun of the blue heavens, or the stormy sky, and it is enough. Promise me no more than this, for, indeed, more you cannot give, and it would be a crime to deceive me, since you call yourself my friend."

Aramis waited in silence. "Monseigneur," he resumed, after a moment's reflection, "I admire the firm, sound sense which dictates your words; I am happy to have discovered my monarch's mind."

"Again, again! oh! for mercy's sake," cried the Prince, pressing his icy hands upon his clammy brow, "do not play with me! I have no need to be a king to be the happiest of men."

"But I, monseigneur, wish you to be a king for the good of humanity."

"Ah!" said the Prince, with fresh distrust inspired by the word; "ah! with what then has humanity to reproach my brother?"

"I forgot to say, monseigneur, that if you would allow me to guide you, and if you consent to become the most powerful monarch on earth, you will have promoted the interests of all the friends whom I devote to the success of your cause, and these friends are numerous."

"Numerous?"

"Less numerous than powerful, monseigneur."

"Explain yourself."

"It is impossible; I will explain, I swear before Heaven, on that day that I see you sitting on the throne of France."

"But my brother?"

"You shall decree his fate. Do you pity him?"

"Him, who leaves me to perish in a dungeon? No, I pity him not."

"So much the better."

"He might have himself come to this prison, have taken me by the hand and have said, 'My brother, Heaven created us to love, not to contend with one another. I come to you. A barbarous prejudice has condemned you to pass your days in obscurity, far from all men, and deprived of every joy. I will make you sit down beside me; I will buckle round your waist our father's sword. Will you take advantage of this reconciliation to put down or to restrain me? Will you employ that sword to spill my blood?' 'Oh! never,' I would have replied to him, 'I look on you as my preserver, and will respect you as my master. You give me far more than Heaven bestowed; for through you I possess liberty and the privilege of loving and being loved in this world.'"

"And you would have kept your word, monseigneur?"

"On my life! While now,—now that I have guilty ones to punish."

"In what manner, monseigneur?"

"What do you say to the resemblance that Heaven has given me to my brother?"

"I say that there was in that likeness a providential instruction which the King ought to have heeded; I say that your mother committed a crime in rendering those different in happiness and fortune whom nature created so similar in her womb; and I conclude that the object of punishment should be only to restore the equilibrium."

"By which you mean——"

"That if I restore you your place on your brother's throne, he shall take yours in prison."

"Alas! there is so much suffering in prison, especially to a man who has drunk so deeply of the cup of enjoyment."

"Your Royal Highness will always be free to act as you may desire; and if it seems good to you, after punishment, may pardon."

"Good. And now, are you aware of one thing, monsieur?"

"Tell me, my Prince."

"It is that I will hear nothing further from you till I am clear of the Bastille."

"I was going to say to your Highness that I should only have the pleasure of seeing you once again."

"And when?"

"The day when my Prince leaves these gloomy walls."

"Heavens! how will you give me notice of it?"

"By myself coming to fetch you."

"Yourself?"

"My Prince, do not leave this chamber save with me, or if in my absence you are compelled to do so, remember that I am not concerned in it."

"And so I am not to speak a word of this to any one whatever, save to you."

"Save only to me." Aramis bowed very low, the Prince offered his hand.

"Monsieur," he said, in a tone that issued from his heart, "one word more, my last. If you have sought me for my destruction; if you are only a tool in the hands of my enemies; if from our conference, in which you have sounded the depths of my mind, anything worse than captivity result, that is to say, if death befall me, still receive my blessing, for you will have ended my troubles, and given me repose from the tormenting fever that has preyed upon me these eight years."

"Monseigneur, wait the result ere you judge me," said Aramis.

"I say that, in such a case, I bless and forgive you. If, on the other hand, you are come to restore me to that position in the sunshine of fortune and glory to which I was destined by Heaven; if by your means I am enabled to live in the memory of man, and confer lustre on my race by deeds of valour, or by solid benefits bestowed upon my people; if, from my present depth of sorrow, aided by your generous hand, I raise myself to the very height of honour, then to you, whom I thank with blessings, to you will I offer half my power and my glory; though you would still be but partly recompensed, and your share must always remain incomplete, since I could not divide with you the happiness received at your hands."

"Monseigneur," replied Aramis, moved by the pallor and excitement of the young man, "the nobleness of your heart fills me with joy and admiration. It is not you who will have to thank me, but rather the nation whom you will render happy, the posterity whose name you will make glorious. Yes; I shall indeed have bestowed upon you more than life, as I shall have given you immortality." The Prince offered his hand to Aramis, who sank upon his knee and kissed it.

"It is the first act of homage paid to our future King," said he. "When I see you again, I shall say, 'Good-day, sire.'"

"Till then," said the young man, pressing his wan and wasted fingers over his heart,—"till then, no more dreams, no more strain upon my life—it would break! Oh, monsieur, how small is my prison—how low the window—how narrow are the doors! To think that so much pride, splendour, and happiness should be able to enter in and remain here!"

"Your Royal Highness makes me proud," said Aramis, "since you infer it is I who brought all this." And he rapped immediately on the door. The jailer came to open it with Baisemeaux, who, devoured by fear and uneasiness, was beginning, in spite of himself, to listen at the door. Happily, neither of the speakers had forgotten to smother his voice, even in the most passionate outbreaks.

"What a confessor!" said the governor, forcing a laugh; "who would believe that a mere recluse, a man almost dead, could have committed crimes so numerous, and so long to tell of?"

Aramis made no reply. He was eager to leave the Bastille, where the secret which overwhelmed him seemed to double the weight of the walls. As soon as they reached Baisemeaux's quarters, "Let us proceed to business, my dear governor," said Aramis.

"Alas!" replied Baisemeaux.

"You have to ask me for my receipt for one hundred and fifty thousand livres,"*said the Bishop.

"And to pay over the first third of the sum," added the poor governor, with a sigh, taking three steps towards his iron strong-box.

"Here is the receipt," said Aramis.

"And here is the money," returned Baisemeaux, with a threefold sigh.

"The order instructed me only to give a receipt; it said nothing about receiving the money," rejoined Aramis.

"*Adieu*, Monsieur le Gouverneur!"

And he departed, leaving Baisemeaux almost more than stifled with joy and surprise at this regal present, so liberally bestowed by the confessor extraordinary to the Bastille.

30

HOW MOUSTON HAD BECOME FATTER WITHOUT GIVING PORTHOS NOTICE THEREOF, AND OF THE TROUBLES WHICH CONSEQUENTLY BEFELL THAT WORTHY GENTLEMAN

SINCE the departure of Athos for Blois, Porthos and d'Artagnan were seldom together. One was occupied with harassing duties for the King; the other had been making many purchases of furniture, which he intended to forward to his estate, and by aid of which he hoped to establish in his various residences something of that court luxury which he had witnessed in all its dazzling brightness in His Majesty's society.* D'Artagnan, ever faithful, one morning during an interval of service, thought about Porthos, and being uneasy at not having heard anything of him for a fortnight, directed his steps towards his hotel, and pounced upon him just as he was getting up. The worthy Baron had a pensive—nay, more than pensive—a melancholy air. He was sitting on his bed, only half-dressed, and with legs dangling over the edge, contemplating a host of garments, which with their fringes, lace, embroidery, and slashes of ill-assorted hues, were strewed all over the floor. Porthos, sad and reflective, as La Fontaine's hare,* did not observe d'Artagnan's entrance, which was moreover screened at this moment by M. Mouston, whose personal corpulency, quite enough at any time to hide one man from another, was effectually doubled by a scarlet coat which the attendant was holding up for his master's inspection, by the sleeves, that he might the better see it all over. D'Artagnan stopped at the threshold and looked at the pensive Porthos; and then, as the sight of the innumerable garments strewing the floor caused mighty sighs to heave from the bosom of that excellent gentleman, d'Artagnan thought it time to put an end to these dismal reflections, and coughed by way of announcing himself.

"Ah!" exclaimed Porthos, whose countenance brightened with joy; "ah, ah! Here is d'Artagnan. I shall then get hold of an idea."

At these words Mouston, doubting what was going on behind him, got out of the way, smiling kindly at the friend of his master, who thus found himself freed from the material obstacle which had prevented his reaching d'Artagnan. Porthos made his sturdy knees crack again in rising, and crossing the room in two strides, found himself face to face with his friend, whom he folded to his breast with a force of affection that seemed to increase with every day. "Ah!" he repeated, "you are always welcome, dear friend; but just now you are more welcome than ever."

"But you seem in the dumps here?" exclaimed d'Artagnan. Porthos replied by a look expressive of dejection. "Well, then, tell me all about it, Porthos, my friend, unless it is a secret."

"In the first place," returned Porthos, "you know I have no secrets from you. This, then, is what saddens me."

"Wait a minute, Porthos; let me first get rid of all this litter of satin and velvet."

"Oh, never mind," said Porthos contemptuously; "it is all trash."

"Trash, Porthos! Cloth at twenty livres an ell! gorgeous satin! regal velvet!"

"Then you think these clothes are——"

"Splendid, Porthos, splendid! I'll wager that you alone in France have so many; and suppose you never had any more made, and were to live a hundred years, which wouldn't astonish me, you could still wear a new dress the day of your death, without being obliged to see the nose of a single tailor from now till then."

Porthos shook his head.

"Come, my friend," said d'Artagnan, "this unnatural melancholy in you frightens me. My dear Porthos, pray get out of it then; and the sooner the better."

"Yes, my friend, so I will; if indeed it is possible."

"Perhaps you have received bad news from Bracieux?"

"No; they have felled the wood, and it has yielded a third more than the estimate."

"Then has there been a falling off in the pools of Pierrefonds?"

"No; my friend; they have been fished, and there is enough left to stock all the pools in the neighbourhood."

"Perhaps your estate at Vallon has been destroyed by an earthquake?"

"No, my friend; on the contrary, the ground was struck by lightning a hundred paces from the château, and a fountain sprang up in a place entirely destitute of water."

"What in the world is the matter, then?"

"The fact is, I have received an invitation for the fête at Vaux," said Porthos, with a lugubrious expression.

"Well! do you complain of that? The King has caused a hundred mortal heartburnings among the courtiers by refusing invitations. And so, my dear friend, you are really going to Vaux?"

"Indeed I am!"

"You will see a magnificent sight."

"Alas! I doubt it, though."

"Everything that is grand in France will be brought together there!"

"Ah!" cried Porthos, tearing out a lock of his hair in despair.

"Eh! good Heavens, are you ill?" cried d'Artagnan.

"I am as well as the Pont-Neuf! It isn't that."

"But what is it then?"

"'Tis that I have no clothes!"

D'Artagnan stood petrified. "No clothes, Porthos; no clothes!" he cried, "when I see at least fifty suits on the floor."

"Fifty, truly; but not one which fits me!"

"What! not one that fits you? But are you not measured, then, when you give an order?"

"To be sure he is," answered Mouston; "but unfortunately *I* have grown stouter."

"What! *you* stouter?"

"So much so that I am now bigger then the baron. Would you believe it, monsieur?"

"*Parbleu!* it seems to me that is quite evident."

"Do you see, stupid?" said Porthos, "that is quite evident!"

"But still, my dear Porthos," resumed d'Artagnan, becoming slightly impatient, "I don't understand why your clothes should not fit you, because Mouston has grown stouter."

"I am going to explain it," said Porthos. "You remember having related to me the story of the Roman general Antony,* who had always seven wild boars kept roasting, each cooked up to a different point; so that he might be able to have his dinner at any time of the day he chose to ask for it. Well, then, I resolved, as at any time I might be invited to court to spend a week, I resolved to have always seven suits ready for the occasion."

"Capitally reasoned, Porthos—only a man must have a fortune like yours to gratify such whims. Without counting the time lost in being measured, the fashions are always changing."

"That is exactly the point," said Porthos, "in regard to which I flattered myself I had hit on a very ingenious device."

"Tell me what it is; for I don't doubt your genius."

"You remember what Mouston once was, then?"

"Yes; when he used to call himself Mousqueton."

"And you remember, too, the period when he began to grow fatter?"

"No' not exactly. I beg your pardon, my good Mouston."

"Oh! you are not in fault, monsieur," said Mouston graciously. "You were in Paris, and as for us, we were at Pierrefonds."

"Well, well, my dear Porthos; there was a time when Mouston began to grow fat. Is that what you wished to say?"

"Yes, my friend; and I greatly rejoice over the period."

"Indeed, I believe you do," exclaimed d'Artagnan.

"You understand," continued Porthos, "what a world of trouble it spared me."

"No, I do not, though."

"Look here, my friend. In the first place, as you have said, to be measured is a loss of time, even though it occur only once a fortnight. And then, one may be travelling; and then you wish to have seven suits always with you. In short, I have a horror of letting any one take my measure. Confound it! either one is a nobleman or not. To be scrutinised and scanned by a fellow who completely analyses you, by inch and line—'tis degrading! Here, they find you too hollow; there too prominent. They recognise your strong and weak points. See, now, when we leave the measurer's hands, we are like those strongholds whose angles and different thicknesses have been ascertained by a spy."

"In truth, my dear Porthos, you possess ideas entirely your own."

"Ah! you see when a man is an engineer."

"And has fortified Belle-Isle*—'tis natural, my friend."

"Well, I had an idea, which would doubtless have proved a good one, but for Mouston's carelessness."

D'Artagnan glanced at Mouston, who replied by a slight movement of his body, as if to say, "You will see whether I am at all to blame in all this."

"I congratulated myself, then," resumed Porthos, "at seeing Mouston get fat; and I did all I could, by means of substantial feeding, to make him stout—always in the hope that he would come to equal myself in girth, and could then be measured in my stead."

"Ah!" cried d'Artagnan. "I see—that spared you both time and humiliation."

"Consider my joy, when, after a year and a half's judicious feeding—for I used to feed him up myself—the fellow——"

"Oh! I lent a good hand myself, monsieur," said Mouston humbly.

"That's true. Consider my joy when, one morning I perceived Mouston was obliged to squeeze in, as I once did myself, to get through the little secret door that those fools of architects had made in the chamber of the late Madame du Vallon,* in the château of Pierrefonds. And, by the way, about that door, my friend, I should like to ask you, who know everything, why these wretches of architects, who ought by rights to have the compasses in their eye, came to make doorways through which nobody but thin people could pass?"

"Oh, those doors," answered d'Artagnan, "were meant for gallants, and they have generally slight and slender figures."

"Madame du Vallon had no gallant!" answered Porthos majestically.

"Perfectly true, my friend," resumed d'Artagnan; "but the architects were imagining the possibility of your marrying again."

"Ah! that is possible," said Porthos. "And now I have received an explanation how it is that doorways are made too narrow, let us return to the subject of Mouston's fatness. But see how the two things apply to each other. I have always noticed that ideas run parallel. And so, observe this phenomenon, d'Artagnan. I was talking to you of Mouston, who is fat, and it led us on to Madame du Vallon——"

"Who was thin?"

"Hum! Is it not marvellous?"

"My dear friend, a savant of my acquaintance, M. Costar,* has made the same observation as you have, and he calls the process by some Greek name which I forget."

"What! my remark is not then original?" cried Porthos, astounded. "I thought I was the discoverer."

"My friend, the fact was known before Aristotle's days,—that is to say, nearly two thousand years ago."

"Well, well, 'tis no less true," said Porthos, delighted at the idea of having concurred with the sages of antiquity.

"Wonderfully—but suppose we return to Mouston. It seems to me, we have left him fattening under our very eyes."

"Yes, monsieur," said Mouston.

"Well," said Porthos, "Mouston fattened so well, that he gratified all my hopes, by reaching my standard; a fact of which I was well able to convince myself, by seeing the rascal one day in a waistcoat of mine, which he had turned into a coat—a waistcoat, the mere embroidery of which was worth a hundred pistoles."

"'Twas only to try it on, monsieur," said Mouston.

"From that moment, I determined to put Mouston in communication with my tailors, and to have him measured instead of myself."

"A capital idea, Porthos; but Mouston is a foot and a half shorter than you."

"Exactly! They measured him down to the ground, and the end of the skirt came just below my knee."

"What a wonder you are, Porthos! Such a thing could happen only to you."

"Ah! yes; pay your compliments; there is something to do it upon. It was exactly at that time—that is to say nearly two years and a half ago—that I set out for Belle-Isle, instructing Mouston (so as always to have, in every event, a pattern of every fashion) to have a coat made for himself every month."

"And did Mouston neglect complying with your instructions? Ah! that would not be right, Mouston."

"No, monsieur, quite the contrary, quite the contrary."

"No, he never forgot to have his coats made; but he forgot to inform me that he had got stouter!"

"But it was not my fault, monsieur! your tailor never told me."

"And this to such an extent, monsieur," continued Porthos, "that the fellow in two years has gained eighteen inches in girth, and so my last dozen coats are all too large, from a foot to a foot and a half!"

"But the rest; those which were made when you were of the same size?"

"They are no longer the fashion, my dear friend. Were I to put them on, I should look like a fresh arrival from Siam; and as though I had been two years away from court."

"I understand your difficulty. You have how many new suits? nine? thirty-six? and yet not one to wear. Well, you must have a thirty-seventh made, and give the thirty-six to Mouston."

"Ah, monsieur!" said Mouston, with a gratified air. "The truth is that monsieur has always been very generous to me."

"Do you mean to think that I hadn't that idea, or that I was deterred by the expense? But it wants only two days to the fête; I received the invitation yesterday; made Mouston post hither with my wardrobe, and only this morning discovered my misfortune; and from now till the day after to-morrow there isn't a single fashionable tailor who will undertake to make me a suit."

"That is to say, one covered all over with gold, isn't it?"

"I wish it so! all over!"

"Oh, we shall manage it. You won't leave for three days. The invitations are for Wednesday, and this is only Sunday morning."

"'Tis true; but Aramis has strongly advised me to be at Vaux twenty-four hours beforehand."

"How, Aramis?"

"Yes, it was Aramis who brought me the invitation."

"Ah! to be sure, I see. You are invited on the part of M. Fouquet."

"By no means! by the King, dear friend. The letter bears the following as large as life: 'M. le Baron du Vallon is informed that the King has condescended to place him on the invitation list——'"

"Very good; but you leave with M. Fouquet?"

"And when I think," cried Porthos, stamping on the floor, "when I think I shall have no clothes, I am ready to burst with rage! I should like to strangle somebody or destroy something."

"Neither strangle anybody nor destroy anything, Porthos; I will manage it all; put on one of your thirty-six suits and come with me to a tailor."

"Pooh! my agent has seen them all this morning."

"Even M. Percerin?"

"Who is M. Percerin?"

"Only the King's tailor!"

"Oh, ah, yes," said Porthos, who wished to appear to know the King's tailor, but now heard his name mentioned for the first time; —"to M. Percerin's, by Jove! I thought he would be too much engaged."

"Doubtless he will be; but be at ease, Porthos; he will do for me what he won't do for another. Only you must allow yourself to be measured."

"Ah!" said Porthos, with a sigh, "'tis vexatious, but what would you have me do?"

"Do? as the others do; as the King does."

"What! do they measure the King too? does *he* put up with it?"

"The King is a beau, my good friend, and so are you, too, whatever you may say about it."

Porthos smiled triumphantly. "Let us go to the King's tailor," he said; "and since he measures the King, I think, by my faith, I may well allow him to measure me."

31

WHO MESSIRE JEAN PERCERIN* WAS

THE King's tailor, Messire Jean Percerin, occupied a rather large house in the Rue St Honoré, near the Rue de l'Arbre Sec. He was a man of great taste in elegant stuffs, embroideries, and velvet, being hereditary tailor to the King. The preferment of his house reached as far back as the time of Charles IX.; from whose reign dated, as we know, fancies in *bravery* difficult enough to gratify. The Percerin of that period was a Huguenot, like Ambrose Paré,* and had been spared by the Queen of Navarre,* the beautiful Margot, as they used to write and say, too, in those days; because, in sooth, he was the only one who could make for her those wonderful riding-habits which she loved to wear, seeing that they were marvellously well suited to hide certain anatomical defects, which the Queen of Navarre used very studiously to conceal. Percerin, being saved, made, out of gratitude, some beautiful black bodices, very inexpensive indeed for Queen Catherine,* who ended by being pleased at the preservation of a Huguenot, on whom she had long looked with aversion. But Percerin was a very prudent man; and having heard it said that there was no more dangerous sign for a Protestant than to be smiled upon by Catherine; and having observed that her smiles were more frequent than usual, he speedily turned Catholic with all his family; and having thus become irreproachable, attained the lofty position of master tailor to the crown of France. Under Henry III.,* gay King as he was, this position was as good as the height of one of the loftiest peaks of the Cordilleras. Now Percerin had been a clever man all his life and, by way of keeping up his reputation beyond the grave, took very good care not to make a bad death of it; and so contrived to die very skilfully; and that at the very moment he felt his powers of invention declining. He left a son and daughter, both worthy of the name they were called upon to bear; the son, a cutter as unerring and exact as the square rule; the daughter apt at embroidery, and at designing ornaments. The marriage of Henry IV. and Marie de Medici,* and the exquisite court-mourning for the aforementioned Queen, together with a few words let fall by M. de Bassompière,* king of the beaux of the period, made the fortune of the second generation of Percerins. M. Concino Concini,* and his wife Galligai, who subsequently shone at the French court, sought to Italianise the fashion, and introduced some Florentine tailors; but Percerin, touched to the quick in his patriotism and his self-esteem, entirely defeated these foreigners, and that so well that Concini was the first to give up his compatriots, and held the French tailor in such esteem that he would never employ any other; and thus wore a doublet of his on the very day that Vitry blew out his brains with his pistol at the Pont du Louvre.

And this is the doublet, issuing from M. Percerin's workshop, which the Parisians rejoiced in hacking into so many pieces with the human flesh it covered. Notwithstanding the favour Concino Concini had shown Percerin, the King, Louis XIII., had the generosity to bear no malice to his tailor and to retain him in his service. At the time that Louis the Just afforded this great example of equity, Percerin had brought up two sons, one of whom made his debut at the marriage of Anne of Austria, invented that admirable Spanish costume in which Richelieu danced a saraband, made the costumes for the tragedy of *Mirame*, and stitched on to Buckingham's mantle those famous pearls which were destined to be scattered about the pavement of the Louvre. A man becomes easily notable who has made the dresses of M. de Buckingham, M. de Cinq-Mars, Mademoiselle Ninon, M. de Beaufort, and Marion de Lorme. And thus Percerin the third had attained the summit of his glory when his father died. This same Percerin III., old, famous and wealthy, yet further dressed Louis XIV.; and having no son, which was a great cause of sorrow to him, seeing that with himself his dynasty would end, he had brought up several hopeful pupils. He possessed a carriage, a country house, men-servants, the tallest in Paris; and, by special authority from Louis XIV., a pack of hounds. He worked for MM. de Lyonne and Letellier, under a sort of patronage; but politic man as he was, and versed in state secrets, he never succeeded in fitting M. Colbert. This is beyond explanation; it is a matter for intuition. Great geniuses of every kind live upon unseen, intangible ideas; they act without themselves knowing why. The great Percerin (for, contrary to the rule in dynasties, it was, above all, the last of the Percerins who deserved the surname of Great) the great Percerin was inspired when he cut a robe for the Queen, or a coat for the King; he could mount a mantle for Monsieur, the clock of a stocking for Madame; but, in spite of his supreme talent, he could never hit the measure of M. Colbert. "That man," he used often to say, "is beyond my art; my needle can never hit him off." We need scarcely say that Percerin was M. Fouquet's tailor, and that the Surintendant highly esteemed him. M. Percerin was nearly eighty years old, nevertheless still fresh, and at the same time, so dry, the courtiers used to say, that he was positively brittle. His renown and his fortune were great enough for M. le Prince, that king of fops, to take his arm when talking over the fashions; and for those least eager to pay never to dare to leave their accounts in arrear with him; for Master Percerin would for the first time make clothes upon credit, but the second never, unless paid for the former order.

It is easy to see at once that a tailor of such standing, instead of running after customers, made difficulties about obliging any fresh ones.

And so Percerin declined to fit *bourgeois*, or those who had but recently obtained patents of nobility. A story used to circulate that even M. de Mazarin, in exchange for Percerin supplying him with a full suit of ceremonial vestments as cardinal, one fine day slipped letters of nobility into his pocket.

It was to the house of this great lord of tailors that d'Artagnan took the despairing Porthos; who, as they were going along, said to his friend, "Take care, my good d'Artagnan, not to compromise the dignity of a man such as I am with the arrogance of this Percerin, who will, I expect, be very impertinent; for I give you notice, my friend, that if he is wanting in respect to me I will chastise him."

"Presented by me," replied d'Artagnan, "you have nothing to fear, even though you were what you are not."

"Ah! 'tis because——"

"What? Have you anything against Percerin, Porthos?"

"I think that I once sent Mouston to a fellow of that name."

"And then?"

"The fellow refused to supply me."

"Oh, a misunderstanding, no doubt, which 'tis pressing to set right. Mouston must have made a mistake."

"Perhaps."

"He has confused the names."

"Possibly. That rascal Mouston never can remember names."

"I will take it all upon myself."

"Very good."

"Stop the carriage, Porthos; here we are."

"Here! how here? We are at the Halles;*and you told me the house was at the corner of the Rue de l'Arbre Sec."

"'Tis true, but look."

"Well, I do look, and I see——"

"What?"

"*Pardieu!* that we are at the Halles!"

"You do not, I suppose, want our horses to clamber up on top of the carriage in front of us?"

"No."

"Nor the carriage in front of us to mount on the one in front of it. Nor that the second should be driven over the roofs of the thirty or forty others which have arrived before us."

"No, you are right, indeed. What a number of people! And what are they all about?"

"'Tis very simple. They are waiting their turn."

"Bah! Have the comedians of the hotel de Bourgogne* shifted their quarters?"

"No; their turn to obtain an entrance to M. Percerin's house."

"And are we going to wait too?"

"Oh, we shall show ourselves more ready and less proud than they."

"What are we to do then?"

"Get down, pass through the footmen and lackeys, and enter the tailor's house, which I will answer for our doing, if you go first."

"Come then," said Porthos.

They both alighted and made their way on foot towards the establishment. The cause of the confusion was, that M. Percerin's doors were closed, while a servant, standing before them, was explaining to the illustrious customers of the illustrious tailor that just then M. Percerin could not receive anybody. It was bruited about outside still, on the authority of what the great lackey had told some great noble whom he favoured, in confidence, that M. Percerin was engaged upon five dresses for the King, and that, owing to the urgency of the case, he was meditating in his office on the ornaments, colours, and cut of these five suits. Some, contented with this reason, went away again, happy to repeat it to others; but others, more tenacious, insisted on having the doors opened, and amongst these last three Blue Ribands,* intended to take parts in a ballet, which would inevitably fail unless the said three had their costumes shaped by the very hand of the great Percerin himself. D'Artagnan, pushing on Porthos, who scattered the groups of people right and left, succeeded in gaining the counter, behind which the journeymen tailors were doing their best to answer queries. (We forgot to mention that at the door they wanted to put off Porthos like the rest, but d'Artagnan, showing himself, pronounced merely these words—"The King's order," and was let in with his friend.) The poor fellows had enough to do, and did their best, to reply to the demands of the customers in the absence of their master, leaving off drawing a stitch to turn a sentence; and when wounded pride, or disappointed expectation, brought down upon them too cutting rebukes, he who was attacked made a dive and disappeared under the counter. The line of discontented lords formed a very remarkable picture. Our captain of musketeers, a man of sure and rapid observation, took it all in at a glance; but having run over the groups, his eye rested on a man in front of him. This man, seated upon a stool, scarcely showed his head above the counter, which sheltered him. He was about forty years of age, with a melancholy aspect, pale face, and soft luminous eyes. He was looking at d'Artagnan and the rest, with his chin resting upon his hand, like a calm and inquiring amateur. Only on perceiving, and doubtless recognising, our captain, he pulled his hat down over his eyes. It was this action, perhaps, that attracted d'Artagnan's attention. If so, the gentleman who had pulled down his hat produced an effect entirely different from what he had desired. In other respects his costume was plain, and his hair evenly cut enough for customers, who were not close observers, to take him for a mere tailor's apprentice, perched behind the board, and carefully stitching cloth or velvet. Nevertheless, this man held up his head too often to be very productively employed with his fingers. D'Artagnan was not deceived,—not he; and he saw at once that if this man was working at anything, it certainly was not at velvet.

"Eh!" said he, addressing this man, "and so you have become a tailor's boy, Monsieur Molière?"*

"Hush, M. d'Artagnan!" replied the man softly, "you will make them recognise me."

"Well, and what harm?"

"The fact is, there is no harm, but——"

"You were going to say there is no good in doing it either, is it not so?"

"Alas! no; for I was occupied in looking at some excellent figures."

"Go on—go on, Monsieur Molière. I quite understand the interest you take in it—I will not disturb your study."

"Thank you."

"But on one condition; that you tell me where M. Percerin really is."

"Oh! willingly; in his own room. Only——"

"Only that one can't enter it?"

"Unapproachable."

"For everybody?"

"For everybody. He brought me here so that I might be at my ease to make my observations, and then he went away."

"Well, my dear Monsieur Molière, but you will go and tell him I am here."

"I!" exclaimed Molière, in the tone of a courageous dog, from which you snatch the bone it has legitimately gained; "I disturb myself! Ah! Monsieur d'Artagnan, how hard you are upon me!"

"If you won't go directly and tell M. Percerin that I am here, my dear Molière," said d'Artagnan, in a low tone, "I warn you of one thing; that I won't exhibit to you the friend I have brought with me."

Moliére indicated Porthos by an imperceptible gesture, "This gentleman, is it not?"

"Yes,"

Moliére fixed upon Porthos one of those looks which penetrate the minds and hearts of men. The subject doubtless appeared very promising to him, for he immediately rose and led the way into the adjoining chamber.

32

THE PATTERNS

DURING all this time the crowd was slowly rolling away, leaving at every angle of the counter either a murmur or a menace, as the waves leave foam or scattered sea-weed on the sands, when they retire with the ebbing tide. In about ten minutes Molière reappeared, making another sign to d'Artagnan from under the hangings. The latter hurried after him, with Porthos in the rear and, after threading a labyrinth of corridors, introduced him to M. Percerin's room. The old man, with his sleeves turned up, was gathering up in folds a piece of gold-flowered brocade, so as the better to exhibit its lustre. Perceiving d'Artagnan, he put the silk aside, and came to meet him, by no means radiant with joy, and by no means courteous, but take it altogether, in a tolerably civil manner.

"The captain of the musketeers will excuse me, I am sure, for I am engaged."

"Eh! yes, on the King's costumes; I know that, my dear Monsieur Percerin. You are making three, they tell me."

"Five, my dear monsieur, five."

"Three or five, 'tis all the same to me, my dear monsieur; and I know that you will make them most exquisitely."

"Yes, I know. Once made, they will be the most beautiful in the world, I do not deny it; but that they may be the most beautiful in the world, they must first be made; and to do this, captain, I am pressed for time."

"Oh, bah! there are two days yet; 'tis much more than you require, Monsieur Percerin," said d'Artagnan, in the coolest possible manner.

Percerin raised his head with the air of a man little accustomed to be contradicted, even in his whims; but d'Artagnan did not pay the least attention to the airs which the illustrious tailor began to assume.

"My dear M. Percerin," he continued, "I bring you a customer."

"Ah! ah!" exclaimed Percerin crossly.

"M. de Baron du Vallon de Bracieux de Pierrefonds," continued d'Artagnan. Percerin attempted a bow, which found no favour in the eyes of the terrible Porthos, who, from his first entry into the room had been regarding the tailor askance.

"A very good friend of mine," concluded d'Artagnan.

"I will attend to monsieur," said Percerin, "but later."

"Later? but when?"

"When I have time."

"You have already told my valet as much," broke in Porthos discontentedly.

"Very likely," said Percerin; "I am nearly always pushed for time."

"My friend," returned Porthos sententiously, "there is always time when one chooses to find it."

Percerin turned crimson, a very ominous sign indeed in old men blanched by age. "Monsieur is very free to confer his custom elsewhere."

"Come, come, Percerin," interposed d'Artagnan, "you are not in a good temper to-day. Well, I will say one more word to you, which will bring you on your knees; monsieur is not only a friend of mine, but more, a friend of M. Fouquet's."

"Ah! ah!" exclaimed the tailor, "that is another thing." Then turning to Porthos, "Monsieur le Baron is attached to the Surintendant?" he inquired.

"I am attached to myself," shouted Porthos, at the very moment that the tapestry was raised to introduce a new speaker in the dialogue. Molière was all observation, d'Artagnan laughed, Porthos swore.

"My dear Percerin," said d'Artagnan, "you will make a dress for the Baron. 'Tis I who ask you."

"To you I will not say nay, captain."

"But that is not all; you will make it for him at once."

"'Tis impossible before eight days."

"That then is as much as to refuse, because the dress is wanted for the fête at Vaux."

"I repeat that it is impossible," returned the obstinate old man.

"By no means, dear Monsieur Percerin, above all if *I* ask you," said a mild voice at the door, a silvery voice which made d'Artagnan prick up his ears. It was the voice of Aramis.

"Monsieur d'Herblay!" cried the tailor.

"Aramis," murmured d'Artagnan.

"Ah! our Bishop," said Porthos.

"Good morning, d'Artagnan; good morning, Porthos; good-morning, my dear friends," said Aramis. "Come, come, M. Percerin, make the Baron's dress; and I will answer for it you will gratify M. Fouquet." And he accompanied the words with a sign, which seemed to say, "Agree, and dismiss them."

It appeared that Aramis had over Master Percerin an influence superior even to d'Artagnan's, for the tailor bowed in assent, and turning round upon Porthos, "Go and get measured on the other side," said he rudely.

Porthos coloured in a formidable manner. D'Artagnan saw the storm coming, and, addressing Molière, said to him in an undertone, "You see before you, my dear monsieur, a man who considers himself disgraced if you measure the flesh and bones that Heaven has given him; study this type for me, Master Aristophanes, and profit by it."

Molière had no need of encouragement, and his gaze dwelt upon the Baron Porthos. "Monsieur," he said, "if you will come with me, I will make them take your measure without the measurer touching you."

"Oh!" said Porthos, "how do you make that out, my friend?"

"I say that they shall apply neither line nor rule to the seams of your dress. It is a new method we have invented for measuring people of quality, who are too sensitive to allow low-born fellows to touch them. We know some susceptible persons who will not put up with being measured,—a process which, as I think, wounds the natural dignity of man; and if perchance Monsieur should be one of these——"

"*Corbœuf!* I believe I am, too!"

"Well, that is a capital coincidence, and you will have the benefit of our invention."

"But how in the world can it be done?" asked Porthos, delighted.

"Monsieur," said Molière, bowing, "if you will deign to follow me, you will see."

Aramis observed this scene with all his eyes. Perhaps he fancied from d'Artagnan's liveliness that he would leave with Porthos, so as not to lose the conclusion of a scene so well begun. But, clear-sighted as he was, Aramis deceived himself. Porthos and Molière left together alone. D'Artagnan remained with Percerin. Why? From curiosity, doubtless; probably to enjoy a little longer the society of his good friend Aramis. As Molière and Porthos disappeared, d'Artagnan drew near the Bishop of Vannes, a proceeding which appeared particularly to disconcert him.

"A dress for you also, is it not, my friend?"

Aramis smiled. "No," said he.

"You will go to Vaux, however?"

"I shall go, but without a new dress. You forget; dear d'Artagnan, that a poor Bishop of Vannes is not rich enough to have new dresses for every fête."

"Bah!" said the musketeer, laughing, "and do we write no more poems now, neither?"*

"Oh! d'Artagnan," exclaimed Aramis, "I have long given over all these follies."

"True," repeated d'Artagnan, only half convinced. As for Percerin, he had relapsed into his contemplation of the brocades.

"Don't you perceive," said Aramis, smiling, "that we are greatly boring this good gentleman, my dear d'Artagnan?"

"Ah! ah!" murmured the musketeer, aside; "that is, I am boring you, my friend." Then aloud, "Well, then, let us leave; I have no further business here; and if you are as disengaged as I, Aramis——"

"No, not I—J wished——"

"Ah! you had something particular to say to M. Percerin? Why did you not tell me so at once?"

"Something particular, certainly," repeated Aramis, "but not for you, d'Artagnan. But, at the same time, I hope you will believe that I can never have anything so particular to say that a friend like you may not hear it."

"Oh, no, no! I am going," said d'Artagnan, imparting to his voice an evident tone of curiosity; for Aramis's annoyance, well dissembled as it was, had not a whit escaped him; and he knew that, in that impenetrable mind, everything, even the most apparently trivial, was designed to some end; an unknown one; but one which, from the knowledge he had of his friend's character, the musketeer felt must be important.

On his part, Aramis saw that d'Artagnan was not without suspicion, and pressed him. "Stay, by all means," he said, "this is what it is." Then turning towards the tailor, "My dear Percerin," said he, "I am even very happy that you are here, d'Artagnan."

"Oh, indeed," exclaimed the Gascon, for the third time, even less deceived this time than before.

Percerin never moved. Aramis roused him violently by snatching from his hands the stuff upon which he was engaged. "My dear Percerin," said he, "I have near at hand, M. Lebrun,* one of M. Fouquet's painters."

"Ah, very good," thought d'Artagnan; "but why 'Lebrun'?"

Aramis looked at d'Artagnan, who seemed to be occupied with an engraving of Mark Antony. "And you wish to have made for him a dress, similar to those of the Epicureans?" answered Percerin. And while saying this in an absent manner, the worthy tailor endeavoured to recapture his piece of brocade.

"An Epicurean's dress?" asked d'Artagnan, in a tone of inquiry.

"I see," said Aramis, with a most engaging smile, "it is written that our dear d'Artagnan shall know all our secrets this evening. Yes, my friend, you have surely heard speak of M. Fouquet's Epicureans, have you not?"

"Undoubtedly. Is it not a kind of poetical society, of which La Fontaine, Loret, Pelisson, and Molière are members, and which holds its sittings at St Mandé?"

"Exactly so. Well, we are going to put our poets in uniform, and enroll them in a regiment for the King."

"Oh, very well; I understand; a surprise M. Fouquet is getting up for the King. Be at ease; if that is the secret about M. Lebrur, I will not mention it."

"Always agreeable, my friend. No; Monsieur Lebrun has nothing to do with this part of it; the secret which concerns him is far more important than the other."

"Then, if it is so important as all that, I prefer not to know it," said d'Artagnan, making a show of departure.

"Come in, M. Lebrun, come in," said Aramis, opening a side-door with his right hand, and holding d'Artagnan with his left.

"I' faith, I, too, am quite in the dark," quoth Percerin.

Aramis took an "opportunity," as is said in theatrical matters.— "My dear M. Percerin," Aramis continued, "you are making fine dresses for the King, are you not? One in brocade, one in hunting-cloth, one in velvet, one in satin, and one in Florentine stuffs?"

"Yes; but how—do you know all that, monseigneur?" said Percerin, astounded.

"It is all very simple, my dear monsieur; there will be a hunt, a banquet, concert, promenade, and reception. These five kinds of dress are required by etiquette."

"You know everything, monseigneur!"

"And a great many more things, too," murmured d'Artagnan.

"But," cried the tailor, in triumph, "what you do not know, monseigneur—prince of the church though you are—what nobody will know—what only the King, Mademoiselle de la Vallière, and myself do know, is the colour of the materials, and the nature of the ornaments, and the cut, the *ensemble*, the finish of it all!"

"Well," said Aramis, "that is precisely what I have come to ask you, dear Percerin."

"Ah, bah!" exclaimed the tailor, terrified, though Aramis had pronounced these words in his sweetest and most honeyed voice. The request appeared, on reflection, so exaggerated, so ridiculous,

THE MAN IN THE IRON MASK

so monstrous, to M. Percerin, that, first he laughed to himself, then aloud, and finished with a shout. D'Artagnan followed his example, not because he found the matter so "very funny," but in order not to allow Aramis to cool.

"At the outset I appear to be hazarding an absurd question, do I not?" said Aramis. "But d'Artagnan, who is incarnate wisdom itself, will tell you that I could not do otherwise than ask you this."

"Let us see," said the attentive musketeer, perceiving with his wonderful instinct that they had only been skirmishing till now, and that the hour of battle was approaching.

"Let us see," said Percerin incredulously.

"Why, now," continued Aramis, "does M. Fouquet give the King a fête?—Is it not to please him?"

"Assuredly," said Percerin. D'Artagnan nodded assent.

"By delicate attentions? by some happy device? by a succession of surprises, like that of which we were talking of?—the enrolment of our Epicureans."

"Admirable."

"Well, then; this is the surprise we intend. M. Lebrun here is a man who draws most exactly."

"Yes," said Percerin; "I have seen his pictures, and observed that the dresses were highly elaborated. That is why I at once agreed to make him a costume—whether to agree with those of the Epicureans, or an original one."

"My dear monsieur, we accept your offer, and shall presently avail ourselves of it; but just now M. Lebrun is not in want of the dresses you will make for himself, but of those you are making for the King."

Percerin made a bound backwards, which d'Artagnan,—calmest and most appreciative of men—did not consider overdone; so many strange and startling aspects wore the proposal which Aramis had just hazarded. "The King's dresses! Give the King's dresses to any mortal whatever! Oh! for once, monseigneur, your grace is mad!" cried the poor tailor in extremity.

"Help me now, d'Artagnan," said Aramis, more and more calm and smiling. "Help me now to persuade monsieur, for *you* understand, do you not?"

"Eh! eh!—not exactly, I declare."

"What! you do not understand that M. Fouquet wishes to afford the King the surprise of finding his portrait on his arrival at Vaux; and that the portrait, which will be a striking resemblance, ought to be dressed exactly as the King will be on the day it is shown?"

"Oh! yes, yes;" said the musketeer, nearly convinced, so

plausible was this reasoning. "Yes, my dear Aramis, you are right; it is a happy idea. I will wager it is one of your own, Aramis."

"Well, I don't know," replied the Bishop; "either mine, or M. Fouquet's." Then, scanning Percerin, after noticing d'Artagnan's hesitation, "Well, Monsieur Percerin," he asked, "What do you say to this?"

"I say that——"

"That you are doubtless free to refuse. I know well—and I by no means count upon compelling you, my dear monsieur. I will say more; I even understand all the delicacy you feel in taking up with M. Fouquet's idea; you dread appearing to flatter the King. A noble spirit, M. Percerin, a noble spirit!" The tailor stammered. "It would, indeed, be a very pretty compliment to pay the young prince," continued Aramis; "but as the Surintendant told me, 'If Percerin refuse, tell him that it will not at all lower him in my opinion, and I shall always esteem him, only——'"

"Only?" repeated Percerin, rather troubled.

"'Only,'" continued Aramis, "'I shall be compelled to say to the King,'—you understand, my dear Monsieur Percerin, that these are M. Fouquet's words—'I shall be constrained to say to the King, "Sire, I had intended to present your Majesty with your portrait, but owing to a feeling of delicacy, slightly exaggerated perhaps, although creditable, M. Percerin opposed the project."'"

"Opposed!" cried the poor tailor, terrified at the responsibility which would weigh upon him; "I to oppose the desire, the will of M. Fouquet when he is seeking to please the King! Oh, what a hateful word you have uttered, monseigneur. Oppose! Oh, 'tis not I who said it. Heaven have mercy on me. I call the captain of the musketeers to witness it! Is it not true, Monsieur d'Artagnan, that I have opposed nothing?"

D'Artagnan made a sign indicating that he wished to remain neutral. He felt that there was an intrigue at the bottom of it, whether comedy or tragedy; he was at his wit's end at not being able to fathom it, but in the meantime wished to keep clear.

But already Percerin, goaded by the idea that the King should be told he had stood in the way of a pleasant surprise, had offered Lebrun a chair, and proceeded to bring from a wardrobe four magnificent dresses, the fifth being still in the workmen's hands, and these masterpieces he successively fitted upon four lay figures, which, imported into France in the time of Concini, had been given to Percerin II. by Marshal d'Onore, after the discomfiture of the Italian tailors, ruined in their competition. The painter set to work to draw and then to paint the dresses. But

Aramis, who was closely watching all the phases of his toil, suddenly stopped him.

"I think you have not quite got it, my dear Lebrun," he said; "your colours will deceive you, and on canvas we shall lack that exact resemblance which is absolutely requisite. Time is necessary for attentively observing the finer shades."

"Quite true," said Percerin, "but time is wanting, and on that head, you will agree with me, monseigneur, I can do nothing."

"Then the affair will fail," said Aramis quietly, "and that because of a want of precision in the colours."

Nevertheless Lebrun went on copying the materials and ornaments with the closest fidelity—a process which Aramis watched with ill-concealed impatience.

"What in the world, now, is the meaning of this imbroglio?" the musketeer kept saying to himself.

"That will certainly never do," said Aramis; "M. Lebrun, close your box and roll up your canvas."

"But, monsieur," cried the vexed painter, "the light is abominable here."

"An idea, M. Lebrun, an idea! If we had a pattern of the materials, for example, and with time, and a better light——"

"Oh, then," cried Lebrun, "I would answer for the effect."

"Good!" said d'Artagnan, "this ought to be the knotty point of the whole thing; they want a pattern of each of the materials. *Mordioux!* will this Percerin give it now?"

Percerin, beaten in his last retreat, and duped, moreover, by the feigned good-nature of Aramis, cut out five patterns and handed them to the Bishop of Vannes.

"I like this better. That is your opinion, is it not?" said Aramis to d'Artagnan.

"My dear Aramis," said d'Artagnan, "my opinion is that you are always the same."

"And consequently, always your friend," said the Bishop, in a charming tone.

"Yes, yes," said d'Artagnan, aloud; then, in a low voice, "If I am your dupe, double Jesuit that you are, I will not be your accomplice; and to prevent it, 'tis time I left this place." "*Adieu*, Aramis," he added aloud, "*adieu*; I am going to rejoin Porthos."

"Then wait for me," said Aramis, pocketing the patterns, "for I have done, and shall not be sorry to say a parting word to our friend."

Lebrun packed up, Percerin put back the dresses into the closet, Aramis put his hand on his pocket to assure himself the patterns were secure,—and they all left the study.

33

WHERE, PROBABLY, MOLIÈRE FORMED HIS FIRST IDEA OF THE BOURGEOIS GENTILHOMME*

D'ARTAGNAN found Porthos in the adjoining chamber, but no longer an irritated Porthos, or a disappointed Porthos, but Porthos radiant, blooming, fascinating, and chatting with Molière, who was looking upon him with a species of idolatry, and as a man would who had not only never seen anything better, but not even ever anything so good. Aramis went straight up to Porthos and offered him his delicate white hand, which lost itself in the gigantic hand of his old friend,—an operation which Aramis never hazarded without a certain uneasiness. But the friendly pressure having been performed not too painfully for him, the Bishop of Vannes passed over to Molière.

"Well, monsieur," said he, "will you come with me to Saint-Mandé?"

"I will go anywhere you like, monseigneur," answered Molière.

"To Saint-Mandé!" cried Porthos, surprised at seeing the proud Bishop of Vannes fraternising with a journeyman tailor. "What, Aramis, are you going to take this gentleman to Saint-Mandé?"

"Yes," said Aramis, smiling, "our work is pressing."

"And besides, my dear Porthos," continued d'Artagnan, "M. Molière is not altogether what he seems."

"In what way?" asked Porthos.

"Why, this gentleman is one of M. Percerin's chief clerks, and is expected at Saint-Mandé to try on the dresses which M. Fouquet has ordered for the Epicureans."

"'Tis precisely so," said Molière.

"Yes, monsieur."

"Come, then, my dear M. Molière," said Aramis, "that is, if you have done with M. du Vallon."

"We have finished," replied Porthos.

"And you are satisfied?" asked d'Artagnan.

"Completely so," replied Porthos.

Molière took his leave of Porthos with much ceremony, and grasped the hand which the captain of the musketeers furtively offered him.

"Pray, monsieur," concluded Porthos, mincingly, "above all, be exact."

"You will have your dress after to-morrow, Monsieur le Baron," answered Molière. And he left with Aramis.

Then d'Artagnan, taking Porthos's arm, "What has this tailor done for you, my dear Porthos," he asked, "that you are so pleased with him?"

"What has he done for me, my friend! done for me!" cried Porthos enthusiastically.

"Yes, I ask you what he has done for you?"

"My friend, he has done that which no tailor ever yet accomplished; he has taken my measure without touching me."

"Ah, bah! tell me how he did it."

"First, then, they went, I don't know where, for a number of lay figures, of all heights and sizes, hoping there would be one to suit mine; but the largest—that of the drum-major of the Swiss guard—was two inches too short, and half a foot too slender."

"Indeed!"

"It is exactly as I tell you, d'Artagnan; but he is a great man, or at the very least a great tailor, is this M. Molière. He was not at all put at fault by the circumstance."

"What did he do, then?"

"Oh! it is a very simple matter. I'faith, 'tis an unheard of thing that people should have been so stupid as not to have discovered this method from the first. What annoyance and humiliation they would have spared me!"

"Not to speak of the dresses, my dear Porthos."

"Yes, thirty dresses."

"Well, my dear Porthos, come, tell me M. Molière's plan."

"Molière? You call him so, do you? I shall make a point of recollecting his name."

"Yes; or Poquelin, if you prefer that."

"No; I like Molière best. When I wish to recollect his name, I shall think of Volière (an aviary); and as I have one at Pierrefonds——"

"Capital!" returned d'Artagnan; "and M. Molière's plan?"

"'Tis this; instead of pulling me to pieces, as all these rascals do—of making me bend in my back, and double my joints—all of them low and dishonourable practices——"

D'Artagnan made a sign of approbation with his head.

"'Monsieur,' he said to me," continued Porthos, "'a gentleman ought to measure himself. Do me the pleasure to draw near this glass,' and I drew near the glass. I must own I did not exactly understand what this good M. Volière wanted with me."

"Molière."

"Ah! yes, Molière—Molière. And as the fear of being measured still possessed me, 'Take care,' said I to him, 'what you are going to do with me; I am very ticklish, I warn you.' But he, with his soft voice (for he is a courteous fellow, we must admit, my friend), he, with his soft voice, 'Monsieur,' said he, 'that your dress may fit you well, it must be made according to your figure. Your figure is exactly reflected in this mirror. We shall take the measure of this reflection.'"

"In fact," said d'Artagnan, "you saw yourself in the glass; but where did they find one in which you could see your whole figure?"

"My good friend, it is the very glass in which the King sees himself."

"Yes; but the King is a foot and a half shorter than you are."

"Ah! well, I know not how that may be; it would no doubt be a way of flattering the King; but the looking-glass was too large for me. 'Tis true that its height was made up of three Venetian plates of glass, placed one above another, and its breadth of the three similar pieces in juxtaposition."

"Oh Porthos! what excellent words you have command of. Where in the world did you make the collection?"

"At Belle-Isle. Aramis explained them to the architect."

"Ah! very good. Let us return to the glass, my friend."

"Then, this good M. Volière——"

"Molière."

"Yes—Molière—you are right. You will see, now, my dear friend, that I shall recollect his name too well. This excellent M. Molière set to work tracing out lines on the mirror with a piece of Spanish chalk, following in all the make of my arms and my shoulders, all the while expounding this maxim, which I thought admirable. It is necessary that a dress do not incommode its wearer."

"In reality," said d'Artagnan, "that is an excellent maxim, which is, unfortunately, seldom carried out in practice."

"That is why I found it all the more astonishing, when he expatiated upon it."

"Ah! he expatiated!"

"*Parbleu!*"

"Let me hear his theory."

"'Seeing that,' he continued, 'one may, in awkward circumstances, or in a troublesome position, have one's doublet on one's shoulder, and not desire to take one's doublet off——'"

"True," said d'Artagnan.

"'And so,' continued M. Volière——"

"Molière."

"Molière, yes. 'And so,' went on M. Molière, 'you want to

draw your sword, monsieur, and you have your doublet on your back, what do you do?'

"'I take it off,' I answered.

"'How so?'

"'I say that the dress should be so well made that it can in no way encumber you, even in drawing your sword.'

"'Ah, ah!'

"'Throw yourself on guard,' pursued he.

"I did it with such wondrous firmness that two panes of glass burst out of the window.

"''Tis nothing, nothing,' said he. 'Keep your position.'

"I raised my left arm in the air, the forearm gracefully bent, the ruffle drooping, and my wrist curved, while my right arm, half extended, securely covered my waist with the elbow, and my breast with the wrist."

"Yes," said d'Artagnan, "'tis the true guard—the academic guard."

"You have said the very word, dear friend. In the meanwhile, Volière——"

"Molière."

"Hold! I should certainly, after all, prefer to call him—what did you say his other name was?"

"Poquelin."

"I prefer to call him Poquelin."

"And how will you remember this name better than the other?"

"You understand, he calls himself Poquelin, does he not?"

"Yes."

"I shall recall to mind Madame Coquenard."*

"Good."

"I shall change *Coc* into *Poc, nard* into *lin*; and instead of Coquenard I shall have Poquelin."

"'Tis wonderful,' cried d'Artagnan, astounded. "Go on, my friend, I am listening to you with admiration."

"This Coquelin sketched my arm on the glass."

"I beg your pardon—Poquelin."

"What did I say, then?"

"You said Coquelin."

"Ah! true. This Poquelin, then, sketched my arm on the glass; but he took his time over it; he kept looking at me a good deal. The fact is, that I was very handsome."

"'Does it weary you?' he asked.

"'A little,' I replied, bending a little in my hands, 'but I could yet hold out an hour.'

"'No, no, I will not allow it; the willing fellows will make it a duty to support your arms, as of old, men supported those of the prophet.'

"'Very good,' I answered.

"'That will not be humiliating to you?'

"'My friend,' said I, 'there is, I think, a great difference between being supported and being measured.'"

"The distinction is full of sense," interrupted d'Artagnan.

"Then," continued Porthos, "he made a sign; two lads approached; one supported my left arm, while the other, with infinite address, supported my right."

"'Another, my man,' cried he. A third approached. 'Support Monsieur by the waist,' said he. The *garçon* complied."

"So that you were at rest?" asked d'Artagnan.

"Perfectly; and Pocquenard drew me in the glass."

"Poquelin, my friend."

"Poquelin—you are right. Stay, decidedly I prefer calling him Volière."

"Yes, and then it was over, wasn't it?"

"During that time Volière drew me on the mirror.'

"''Twas delicate in him."

"I much like the plan; it is respectful, and keeps every one in his place."

"And there it ended?"

"Without a soul having touched me, my friend."

"Except the three *garçons* who supported you."

"Doubtless; but I have, I think, already explained to you the difference there is between supporting and measuring."

"'Tis true," answered d'Artagnan, who afterwards said to himself, "I'faith, I greatly deceive myself, or I have been the means of a good windfall to that rascal Molière, and we shall assuredly see the scene hit off to the life in some comedy or other." Porthos smiled.

"What are you laughing at?" asked d'Artagnan.

"Must I confess? Well, I was laughing over my good fortune."

"Oh, that is true; I don't know a happier man than you. But what is this last piece of luck that has befallen you?"

"Well, my dear fellow, congratulate me."

"I desire nothing better."

"It seems I am the first who has had his measure taken in that manner."

"Are you sure of it?"

"Nearly so. Certain signs of intelligence which passed between Volière and the other *garçons* showed me the fact."

"Well, my friend, that does not surprise me from Molière," said d'Artagnan.

"Volière, my friend."

"Oh, no, no, indeed; I am very willing to leave you to say Volière; but myself I shall continue to say Molière. Well, this, I was saying, does not surprise me, coming from Molière, who is a very ingenious fellow, and inspired you with this grand idea."

"It will be of great use to him by-and-by, I am sure."

"Won't it be of use to him, indeed! I believe you it will, and not a little so; for you see, my friend Molière is of all known tailors the man who best clothes our barons, comtes, and marquises—according to their measure."

On this observation, neither the application nor depth of which shall we discuss, d'Artagnan and Porthos quitted M. Percerin's house and rejoined their carriage, wherein we will leave them, in order to look after Molière and Aramis at Saint Mandé.

34

THE BEEHIVE, THE BEES, AND THE HONEY

THE Bishop of Vannes, much annoyed at having met d'Artagnan at M. Percerin's, returned to Saint Mandé in no very good humour. Molière, on the other hand, quite delighted at having made such a capital rough sketch, and at knowing where to find its original again, whenever he should desire to convert his sketch into a picture, Molière arrived in the merriest of moods. All the first storey of the left wing was occupied by the most celebrated Epicureans in Paris, and those on the freest footing in the house—every one in his compartment, like the bees in their cells, employed in producing the honey intended for that royal cake which M. Fouquet proposed to offer his Majesty Louis XIV. during the fête at Vaux. Pélisson, his head leaning on his hand, was engaged in drawing out the plan of the prologue to the *Fâcheux*, a comedy in three acts, which was to be put on the stage by Poquelin de Molière, as d'Artagnan called him, or Coquelin de Volière, as Porthos styled him. Loret, with all the charming innocence of a gazetteer—the gazetteers of all ages have always been so artless!—Loret was composing an account of the fêtes of Vaux, before those fêtes had taken place; La Fontaine sauntering about from one to the other, a wandering, absent, boring, unbearable shade, who kept buzzing and humming at everybody's shoulder a thousand poetic abstractions. He so often disturbed Pélisson, that the latter, raising his head, crossly said,

"At least, La Fontaine, supply me with a rhyme, since you say you have the run of the gardens of Parnassus."

"What rhyme do you want?" asked the *Fabler*, as Madame de Sevigné*used to call him.

"I want a rhyme to *lumière*."

"*Ornière*," answered La Fontaine.

"Ah, but my good friend, one cannot talk of *wheel-ruts* when celebrating the delights of Vaux," said Loret.

"Besides, it doesn't rhyme," answered Pélisson.

"How! doesn't rhyme!" cried La Fontaine in surprise.

"Yes; you have an abominable habit, my friend,—a habit which will ever prevent your becoming a poet of the first order. You rhyme in a slovenly manner."*

"Oh, oh, you think so, do you, Pélisson?"

"Yes, I do, indeed. Remember that a rhyme is never good so long as one can find a better."

"Then I will never write anything again but in prose," said La Fontaine, who had taken up Pélisson's reproach in earnest. "Ah! I often suspected I was nothing else but a rascally poet! Yes, 'tis the very truth."

"Do not say so; your remark is too sweeping, and there is much that is good in your *Fables*."

"And to begin," continued La Fontaine, following up his idea, "I will go and burn a hundred verses I have just made."

"Where are your verses?"

"In my head."

"Well, if they are in your head you cannot burn them."

"True," said La Fontaine; "but if I do not burn them——"

"Well, what will happen if you do not burn them?"

"They will remain in my mind, and I shall never forget them."

"The deuce!" cried Loret; "what a dangerous thing! One would go mad with it."

"The deuce! the deuce!" repeated La Fontaine; "what can I do?"

"I have discovered the way," said Molière, who had entered just at this point of the conversation.

"What way?"

"Write them first and burn them afterwards."

"How simple it is! Well, I should never have discovered that. What a mind that devil Molière has!" said La Fontaine. Then, striking his forehead, "Oh, thou wilt never be aught but an ass, Jean la Fontaine!" he added.

"*What* are you saying there, my friend?" broke in Molière, approaching the poet, whose aside he had heard.

"I say I shall never be aught but an ass," answered La Fontaine, with a heavy sigh and swimming eyes. "Yes, my friend," he added, with increasing grief, "it seems that I rhyme in a slovenly manner."

"Oh, 'tis wrong to say so."

"Nay, I am a poor creature."

"Who said so?"

"*Parbleu!* 'twas Pélisson; did you not, Pélisson?"

Pélisson, again lost in his work, took good care not to answer.

"But if Pélisson said you were so," cried Molière, "Pélisson has seriously offended you."

"Do you think so?"

"Ah! I advise you, as you are a gentleman, not to leave an insult like that unpunished."

"How?" exclaimed La Fontaine.

"Did you ever fight?"

"Once only, with a lieutenant in the light horse."

"What wrong had he done you?"

"It seems he had run away with my wife."*

"Ah, ah!" said Molière, becoming slightly pale; but, as at La Fontaine's declaration, the others had turned round, Molière kept upon his lips the rallying smile which had so nearly died away, and continuing to make La Fontaine speak——,

"And what was the result of the duel?"

"The result was that on the ground my opponent disarmed me, and then made an apology, promising never again to set foot in my house."

"And you considered yourself satisfied?" said Molière.

"Not at all! on the contrary, I picked up my sword. 'I beg your pardon, monsieur,' I said, 'I have not fought because you were my wife's friend, but because I was told I ought to fight. So, as I have never known any peace save since you made her acquaintance, do me the pleasure to continue your visits as heretofore, or, *morbleu!* let us set to again.' And so," continued La Fontaine, " he was compelled to resume his friendship with Madame, and I continue to be the happiest of husbands."

All burst out laughing. Molière alone passed his hand across his eyes. Why? Perhaps to wipe away a tear, perhaps to smother a sigh. Alas! we know that Molière was a moralist, but he was not a philosopher.*"'Tis all the same," he said, returning to the topic of the conversation, "Pélisson has insulted you."

"Ah! truly! I had already forgotten it."

"And I am going to challenge him on your behalf."

"Well, you can do so if you think it indispensable."

"I do think it indispensable, and I am going——"

"Stay," exclaimed La Fontaine, "I want your advice."

"Upon what? this insult?"

"No; tell me really now whether *lumière* does not rhyme with *ornière*?"

"I should make them rhyme—ah! I knew you would—and I have made a hundred thousand such rhymes in my time."

"A hundred thousand!" cried La Fontaine, "four times as many as La Pucelle, which M. Chaplain* is meditating. Is it also on this subject too that you have composed a hundred thousand verses?"

"Listen to me, you eternally absent creature," said Molière.

"It is certain," continued La Fontaine, "that *légume*, for instance, rhymes with *posthume*."

"In the plural, above all."

"Yes, above all in the plural, seeing that then it rhymes not with three letters, but with four; as *ornière* does with *lumière*."

"Put *ornières* and *lumières* in the plural, my dear Pélisson," said La Fontaine, clapping his hand on the shoulder of his friend, whose insult he had quite forgotten, "and they will rhyme."

"Hem!" cried Pélisson.

"Molière says so, and Molière is a judge of it; he declares he has himself made a hundred thousand verses."

"Come," said Molière, laughing, "he is off now."

"It is like *rivage*, which rhymes admirably with *herbage*."

"I would take my oath of it."

"But——" said Molière.

"I tell you all this," continued La Fontaine, "because you are preparing a *divertissement* for Vaux, are you not?"

"Yes, the *Fâcheux*."

"Ah, yes, the *Fâcheux*; yes, I recollect. Well, I was thinking a prologue would admirably suit your *divertissement*."

"Doubtless it would suit capitally."

"Ah! you are of my opinion?"

"So much so that I asked you to write this prologue."

"You asked *me* to write it?"

"Yes, you; and on your refusal begged you to ask Pélisson, who is engaged upon it at this moment."

"Ah! that is what Pélisson is doing, then? I'faith, my dear Molière, you might indeed often be right."

"When?"

"When you call me absent. It is a wretched defect. I will cure myself of it, and do your prologue for you."

"But seeing that Pélisson is about it!——"

"Ah, true, double rascal that I am! Loret was indeed right in saying I was a poor creature."

"It was not Loret who said so, my friend."

"Well, then, whoever said so, 'tis the same to me! And so your *divertissement* is called the *Fâcheux*! Well, then, can you not make *heureux* rhyme with *fâcheux*?"

"If obliged, yes."

"And even with *capriceux*."

"Oh, no, no."

"It would be hazardous, and yet why so?"

"There is too great a difference in the cadences."

"I was fancying," said La Fontaine, leaving Molière for Loret— "I was fancying——"

"What were you fancying?" said Loret, in the middle of a sentence. "Make haste."

"You are writing the prologue to the *Fâcheux*, are you not?"

"No! *mordieu!* it is Pélisson."

"Ah, Pélisson!" cried La Fontaine, going over to him. "I was fancying," he continued, "that the nymph of Vaux——"

"Ah beautiful!" cried Loret. "The nymph of Vaux! Thank you, La Fontaine; you have just given me the two concluding verses of my paper."

"Well, if you can rhyme so well, La Fontaine," said Pélisson, "tell me now in what way you would begin my prologue?"

"I should say, for instance, 'Oh! nymph, who——' After 'who' I should place a verb in the second person singular of the present indicative; and should go on thus: 'this grot profound.'"

"But the verb, the verb?" asked Pélisson.

"To admire the greatest king of all kings round," continued La Fontaine.

"But the verb, the verb," obstinately insisted Pélisson. "This second person singular of the present indicative?"

"Well, then; 'quittest':—

"O, nymph, who quittest now this grot profound,
    To admire the greatest king of all kings round."

"You would put 'who quittest,' would you?"

"Why not?"

"'Gentlest,' after 'you who'?"

"Ah! my dear fellow," exclaimed La Fontaine, "you are a shocking pedant."

"Without counting," said Molière, "that the second line, 'king of all kings round,' is very weak, my dear La Fontaine."

"Then you see clearly I am nothing but a poor creature—a shuffler, as you said."

"I never said so."

"Then, as Loret said."

"And it was not Loret either; it was Pélisson."

"Well, Pélisson was right a hundred times over. But what annoys me more than anything, my dear Molière, is that I fear we shall not have our Epicurean dresses."

"You expected yours, then, for the fêtes?"

"Yes, for the fête, and then for after the fête. My housekeeper told me that my own is rather faded."

"*Diable!* your housekeeper is right; rather more than faded!"

"Ah! you see," resumed La Fontaine, "the fact is, I left it on the floor of my room, and my cat——"

"Well; your cat——"

"She kittened upon it, which has rather altered its colour."

Molière burst out laughing; Pélisson and Loret followed his example. At this juncture, the Bishop of Vannes appeared, with a roll of plans and parchments under his arm. As if the angel of death had chilled all gay and sprightly fancies—as if that wan form had scared away the Graces to whom Xenocrates* sacrificed—silence immediately reigned through the study, and every one resumed his self-possession and his pen. Aramis distributed the notes of invitation, and thanked them in the name of M. Fouquet. "The Surintendant," he said, "being kept to his room by business, could not come and see them, but begged them to send him some of the fruits of their day's work, to enable him to forget the fatigue of his labour in the night."

At these words all settled to work. La Fontaine placed himself at a table, and set his rapid pen running over the vellum; Pélisson made a fair copy of his prologue; Molière gave fifty fresh verses, with which his visit to Percerin had inspired him; Loret, his article on the marvellous fêtes he predicted; and Aramis, laden with booty like the king of the bees, that great black drone, decked with purple and gold, re-entered his apartment, silent and busy. But before departing, "Remember, gentlemen," said he, "we all leave to-morrow evening."

"In that case I must give notice at home," said Molière.

"Yes; poor Molière," said Loret, smiling; "he loves his home."

"'*He* loves,' yes," replied Molière, with his sad, sweet smile. "'He loves,' that does not mean, they love *him*."

"As for me," said La Fontaine, "they love me at Château Thierry, I am very sure."

Aramis here re-entered after a brief disappearance. "Will any one go with me?" he asked. "I am going by Paris, after having passed a quarter of an hour with M. Fouquet. I offer my carriage."

"Good," said Molière, "I accept it. I am in a hurry."

"I shall dine here," said Loret. "M. de Gourville has promised me some craw-fish."

"He has promised me some whitings. Find a rhyme for that, La Fontaine."

Aramis went out laughing, as only he could laugh, and Molière followed him. They were at the bottom of the stairs, when La Fontaine opened the door, and shouted out—

> "He has promised us some whitings,
> In return for all our writings."

The shouts of laughter reached the ears of Fouquet, at the moment Aramis opened the door of the study. As to Molière, he had undertaken to order the horses, while Aramis went to exchange a parting word with the Surintendant. "Oh, how they are laughing there!" said Fouquet with a sigh.

"And do not you laugh, monseigneur?"

"I laugh no longer, now, M. d'Herblay."

"The fête is approaching."

"Money is departing."

"Have I not told you that was my business?"

"Yes, you promised me millions."

"You shall have them the day after the King's entrée into Vaux."

Fouquet looked closely at Aramis, and passed his icy hand across his moistened brow. Aramis perceived that the Surintendant either doubted him, or felt he was powerless to obtain the money.

"Why doubt me?" said Aramis. Fouquet smiled and shook his head.

"Man of little faith!" added the Bishop.

"My dear M. d'Herblay," answered Fouquet, "if I fall——"

"Well; if you fall?"

"I shall, at least, fall from such a height that I shall shatter myself in falling." Then, giving himself a shake as though to escape from himself, "Whence come you," said he, "my friend?"

"From Paris—from Percerin."

"And what have you been doing at Percerin's, for I suppose you attach no such great importance to our poet's dresses."

"No.—I went to prepare a surprise."

"Surprise!"

"Yes; which you are to give the King."

"And will it cost much?"

"Oh! a hundred pistoles you will give Lebrun."

"A painting?—Ah! all the better! And what is this painting to represent?"

"I will tell you; then at the same time, whatever you may say of it, I went to see the dresses for our poets."

"Bah! and they will be rich and elegant?"

"Splendid! There will be few great monseigneurs with so good. People will see the difference there is between the courtiers of wealth and those of friendship."

"Ever generous and graceful, dear prelate!"

"In your school."

Fouquet grasped his hand. "And where are you going?" he said.

"I am off to Paris, when you shall have given me a certain letter."

"For whom?"

"M. de Lyonne."*

"And what do you want with Lyonne?"

"I wish to make him sign a *lettre de cachet*."

"*Lettre de cachet!** Do you desire to put somebody in the Bastille?"

"On the contrary—to let somebody out."

"And who?"

"A poor devil—a youth, a lad who has been Bastilled these ten years, for two Latin verses he made against the Jesuits."

"'Two Latin verses!' and for 'two Latin verses,' the miserable being has been in prison for ten years!"

"Yes."

"And has committed no other crime?"

"Beyond this he is as innocent as you or I."

"On your word?"

"On my honour."

"And his name is——?"

"Seldon."*

"Yes.—But it is too bad. You knew this, and never told me!"

"'Twas only yesterday his mother applied to me, monseigneur."

"And the woman is poor."

"In the deepest misery."

"Oh! Heaven!" said Fouquet, "you sometimes bear with such unjustice on earth that I understand why there are wretches who doubt in your existence. Stay, M. d'Herblay." And Fouquet, taking a pen, wrote a few rapid lines to his colleague Lyonne. Aramis took the letter and made ready to go.

"Wait," said Fouquet. He opened his drawer, and took out ten government notes which were there, each for a thousand francs. "Stay," he said; "set the son at liberty, and give this to the mother; but, above all, tell her not——"

"What, monseigneur?"

"That she is ten thousand livres richer than I. She would say, I am but a poor surintendant! Go! and I hope that God will bless those who are mindful of His poor!"

"So also do I hope," replied Aramis, kissing Fouquet's hand.

And he went out quickly, carrying off the letter for Lyonne and the notes for Seldon's mother, and taking up Molière, who was beginning to lose patience.

35

ANOTHER SUPPER AT THE BASTILLE

SEVEN o'clock sounded from the great clock of the Bastille, that famous clock, which like all the accessories of the state prison, the very use of which is a torture, recalled to the prisoners' minds the destination of every hour of their punishment. The timepiece of the Bastille,* adorned with figures, like most of the clocks of the period, represented St Peter in bonds. It was the supper hour of the unfortunate captives. The doors grating on their enormous hinges, opened for the passage of the baskets and trays of provisions, the delicacy of which, as M. de Baisemeaux has himself taught us, was regulated by the condition in life of the prisoner. We understand on this head the theories of M. de Baisemeaux, sovereign dispenser of gastronomic delicacies, head cook of the royal fortress, whose trays, full laden, were ascending the steep staircases, carrying some consolation to the prisoners in the bottom of honestly-filled bottles. This same hour was that of M. le Gouverneur's supper also. He had a guest to-day, and the spit turned more heavily than usual. Roast partridges flanked with quails and flanking a larded leveret; boiled fowls; ham fried and sprinkled with white wine; *cardons* of Guipuzcoa and *la bisque écrevisses*: these together with the soups and hors-d'œuvre, constituted the governor's bill of fare. Baisemeaux, seated at table, was rubbing his hands and looking at the Bishop of Vannes, who, booted like a cavalier, dressed in grey, and sword at side, kept talking of his hunger and testifying the liveliest impatience. M. de Baisemeaux de Montlezun was not accustomed to the unbending movements of his greatness, my Lord of Vannes, and this evening Aramis, becoming quite sprightly, volunteered confidence on confidence. The prelate had again a little touch of the musketeer about him. The Bishop just trenched on the borders only of licence in his style of conversation. As for M. de Baisemeaux, with the facility of vulgar people, he gave himself up entirely upon this point of his guest's freedom. "Monsieur," said he, "for indeed to-night I dare not call you monseigneur."

"By no means," said Aramis; "call me monsieur; I am booted."

"Do you know, monsieur, of whom you remind me this evening?"

"No! faith," said Aramis, taking up his glass; "but I hope I remind you of a capital guest."

"You remind me of two, monsieur. François, shut the window; the wind may annoy his greatness."

"And let him go," added Aramis. "The supper is completely served, and we shall eat it very well without waiters. I like extremely to be *tête-à-tête* when I am with a friend." Baisemeaux bowed respectfully. "I like extremely," continued Aramis, "to help myself."

"Retire, François," cried Baisemeaux. "I was saying that your greatness puts me in mind of two persons; one very illustrious, the late Cardinal, the great Cardinal de la Rochelle, who wore boots like you."

"Indeed," said Aramis; "and the other."

"The other was a certain musketeer, very handsome, very brave, very adventurous, very fortunate, who, from being abbé, turned musketeer, and from musketeer turned abbé." Aramis condescended to smile. "From abbé," continued Baisemeaux, encouraged by Aramis's smile—"from abbé, bishop—and from bishop——"

"Ah! stay there, I beg," exclaimed Aramis.

"I say, monsieur, that you gave me the idea of a cardinal."

"Enough, dear M. Baisemeaux. As you said, I have on the boots of a cavalier, but I do not intend, for all that, to embroil myself with the church this evening."

"But you have wicked intentions, however, monseigneur."

"Oh, yes, wicked I own, as everything mundane is."

"You traverse the town and the streets in disguise?"

"In disguise, as you say."

"And do you still make use of your sword?"

"Yes, I should think so; but only when I am compelled. Do me the pleasure to summon François."

"Have you no wine there?"

"'Tis not for wine, but because it is hot here and the window is shut."

"I shut the windows at supper-time so as not to hear the sounds of the arrival of couriers."

"Ah, yes. You hear them when the window is open?"

"But too well, and that disturbs me. You understand."

"Nevertheless, I am suffocated. François," François entered. "Open the windows, I pray you, Master François," said Aramis. "You will allow him, dear M. Baisemeaux?"

"You are at home here," answered the governor. The window was opened. "Do you not think," said M. de Baisemeaux, "that you will find yourself very lonely now M. de la Fère has returned to his household gods at Blois? He is a very old friend, is he not?"

"You know it as I do, Baisemeaux, seeing that you were in the musketeers with us."

"Bah! with my friends I reckon neither bottles of wine nor years."

"And you do right; but I do more than love M. de la Fère, dear Baisemeaux, I venerate him."

"Well, for my part, though 'tis singular," said the governor, "I prefer M. d'Artagnan to him. There is a man for you, who drinks long and well! That kind of people allow you at least to penetrate their thoughts."

"Baisemeaux, make me tipsy to-night; let us have a debauch as of old, and if I have a trouble at the bottom of my heart, I promise you, you shall see it as you would a diamond at the bottom of your glass."

"Bravo!" said Baisemeaux, and he poured out a great glass of wine and drank it off at a draught, trembling with joy at the idea of being, by hook or by crook, in the secret of some high archiepiscopal misdemeanour. While he was drinking he did not see with what attention Aramis was noting the sounds in the great court. A courier came in about eight o'clock as François brought in the fifth bottle, and, although the courier made a great noise, Baisemeaux heard nothing.

"The devil take him," said Aramis.

"What! who?" asked Baisemeaux. "I hope 'tis neither the wine you drink nor he who is the cause of your drinking it."

"No; it is a horse, who is making noise enough in the court for a whole squadron."

"Pooh! some courier or other," replied the governor, redoubling his numerous bumpers. "Yes; and may the devil take him, and so quickly that we shall never hear him speak more! Hurrah! hurrah!"

"You forget me, Baisemeaux! my glass is empty," said Aramis, showing his dazzling goblet.

"Upon honour, you delight me. François, wine!"

François entered. "Wine, fellow, and better."

"Yes, monsieur, yes; but a courier has just arrived."

"Let him go to the devil, I say."

"Yes, monsieur, but——"

"Let him leave his news at the office; we will see to it to-morrow. To-morrow, there will be time to-morrow; there will be daylight," said Baisemeaux, chanting the words.

"Ah, monsieur," grumbled the soldier François, in spite of himself, "monsieur——"

"Take care," said Aramis, "take care!"

"Of what? dear M. d'Herblay," said Baisemeaux, half intoxicated.

"The letter which the courier brings to the governor of a fortress is sometimes an order."

"Nearly always."

"Do not orders issue from the ministers?"

"Yes; undoubtedly; but——"

"And what do these ministers do but countersign the signature of the King?"

"Perhaps you are right. Nevertheless, 'tis very tiresome when you are sitting before a good table, *tête-à-tête* with a friend—Ah! I beg your pardon, monsieur; I forgot it is I who engage you at supper, and that I speak to a future cardinal."

"Let us pass over that, dear Baisemeaux, and return to our soldier, to François."

"Well, and what has François done?"

"He has demurred."

"He was wrong, then?"

"However, he *has* demurred, you see; 'tis because there is something extraordinary in this matter. It is very possible that it was not François who was wrong in demurring, but you, who will be wrong in not listening to him."

"Wrong? I to be wrong before François? that seems rather hard."

"Pardon me, merely an irregularity. But I thought it my duty to make an observation which I deem important."

"Oh! perhaps you are right," stammered Baisemeaux. "The King's order is sacred; but as to orders that arrive when one is at supper, I repeat that the devil——"

"If you had said as much to the great cardinal—hem! my dear Baisemeaux, and if his order had any importance."

"I do it that I may not disturb a Bishop. *Mordieux!* am I not, then, excusable?"

232

"Do not forget, Baisemeaux, that I have worn the soldier's coat, and I am accustomed to see everywhere obedience."

"You wish, then——"

"I wish that you should do your duty, my friend; yes, at least before this soldier."

"'Tis mathematically true," exclaimed Baisemeaux. François still waited: "Let them send this order of the King's up to me," he repeated, recovering himself. And he added in a low tone, "Do you know what it is? I will tell you something about as interesting as this. 'Beware of fire near the powder magazine'; or 'Look close after such a one, who is clever at escaping.' Ah! if you only knew, monseigneur, how many times I have been suddenly awakened from the very sweetest and deepest slumber, by messengers arriving at full gallop to tell me, or rather bring me a slip of paper, containing these words: 'Monsieur de Baisemeaux, what news?' 'Tis clear enough that those who waste their time writing such orders never slept in the Bastille. They would know better; the thickness of my walls, the vigilance of my officers, the number of rounds we go. But, indeed, what can you expect, monseigneur? It is their business to write and torment me when I am at rest, and to trouble me when I am happy," added Baisemeaux, bowing to Aramis. "Then let them do their business."

"And do you do yours," added the Bishop smiling.

François re-entered; Baisemeaux took from his hands the minister's order. He slowly undid it, and as slowly read it. Aramis pretended to be drinking, so as to be able to watch his host through the glass.

Then, Baisemeaux having read it: "What was I just saying?" he exclaimed.

"What is it?" asked the Bishop.

"An order of release! There, now; excellent news indeed to disturb us!"

"Excellent news for him whom it concerns, you will at least agree, my dear governor!"

"And at eight o'clock in the evening!"

"It is charitable!"

"Oh! charity is all very well, but it is for that fellow who says he is so weary and tired, but not for me who am amusing myself," said Baisemeaux, exasperated.

"Will you lose by him, then? And is the prisoner who is to be set at liberty a high payer?"

"Oh, yes, indeed! a miserable, five-franc rat!"

"Let me see it," asked M. d'Herblay. "It is no indiscretion?"

"By no means; read it."

233

"There is 'Urgent,' on the paper; you have seen that, I suppose?"

"Oh, admirable! 'Urgent!'—a man who has been there ten years! It is *urgent* to set him free to-day, this very evening, at eight o'clock!—*urgent!*" And Baisemeaux, shrugging his shoulders with an air of supreme disdain, flung the order on the table and began eating again. "They are fond of these dodges!" he said, with his mouth full; "they seize a man some fine day, maintain him for ten years, and write to you, ' Watch this fellow well,' or 'Keep him very strictly.' And then, as soon as you are accustomed to look upon the prisoner as a dangerous man, all of a sudden, without cause or precedent they write—'Set him at liberty'; and actually add to their missive—'urgent.' You will own, my lord, 'tis enough to make any one shrug his shoulders!"

"What do you expect? It is they who write," said Aramis, "and it is for you to execute the order."

"Good! good! execute it! Oh, patience! You must not imagine that I am a slave."

"Gracious Heaven! my very good M. Baisemeaux, who ever said so? Your independence is known."

"Thank Heaven!"

"But your heart also is known."

"Ah! don't speak of it!"

"And your obedience to your superiors. Once a soldier you see, Baisemeaux, always a soldier."

"And so I shall strictly obey; and to-morrow morning at day-break, the prisoner referred to shall be set free."

"To-morrow?"

"At dawn."

"Why not this evening, seeing that the *lettre de cachet* bears, both on the direction and inside, '*urgent!*'"

"Because this evening we are at supper, and our affairs are urgent too!"

"Dear Baisemeaux, booted though I be, I feel myself a priest, and charity has higher claims upon me than hunger and thirst. This unfortunate man has suffered long enough, since you have just told me that he has been your prisoner these ten years. Abridge his suffering. His good time has come; give him the benefit quickly. God will repay you in Paradise with years of felicity."

"You wish it?"

"I intreat you."

"What! in the very middle of our repast?"

"I implore you; such an action is worth ten Benedicites."

"It shall be as you desire, only our supper will get cold."

"Oh! never heed that."

Baisemeaux leaned back to ring for François, and by a very natural motion turned round towards the door. The order had remained on the table; Aramis seized the opportunity when Baisemeaux was not looking to change the paper for another, folded in the same manner, and which he took from his pocket. "François," said the governor, "let the major come up here with the turnkeys of the Bertaudière." François bowed and quitted the room, leaving the two companions alone.

36

THE GENERAL OF THE ORDER

THERE was now a brief silence, during which Aramis never removed his eyes from Baisemeaux for a moment. The latter seemed only half decided to disturb himself thus in the middle of supper, and it was clear he was seeking some pretext, whether good or bad, for delay, at any rate till after dessert. And it appeared also that he had hit upon a pretext at last.

"Eh! but it is impossible," he cried.

"How impossible?" said Aramis. "Give me a glimpse of this impossibility."

"'Tis impossible to set a prisoner at liberty at such an hour. Where can he go to, he, who is unacquainted with Paris?"

"He will go wherever he can."

"You see, now, one might as well set a blind man free!"

"I have a carriage, and will take him wherever he wishes."

"You have an answer for everything. François, tell the major to to go and open the cell of M. Seldon, No. 3, Bertaudière."*

"Seldon!" exclaimed Aramis, very naturally. "You said Seldon, I think?"

"I said Seldon, of course. 'Tis the name of the man they set free."

"Oh! you meant to say Marchiali?"*said Aramis.

"Marchiali? oh, yes, indeed. No, no, Seldon."

"I think you are making a mistake, Monsieur Baisemeaux."

"I have read the order."

"And I also."

"And I saw 'Seldon' in letters as large as that," and Baisemeaux held up his finger.

"And I read 'Marchiali' in characters as large as this," said Aramis, also holding up two fingers.

"To the proof; let us throw a light on the matter," said Baise-meaux, confident he was right. "There is the paper, you have only to read it."

"I read 'Marchiali,'" returned Aramis, spreading out the paper. "Look."

Baisemeaux looked, and his arms dropped suddenly.

"Yes, yes," he said, quite overwhelmed; "yes, Marchiali. 'Tis plainly written Marchiali! Quite true!"

"Ah!"

"How? the man of whom we have talked so much? The man whom they are every day telling me to take such care of?"

"There is 'Marchiali,'" repeated the inflexible Aramis.

"I must own it, monseigneur. But I understand absolutely nothing about it."

"You believe your eyes, at any rate."

"To tell me very plainly there is 'Marchiali.'"

"And in a good handwriting, too."

"'Tis a wonder! I still see this order and the name of Seldon, Irishman. I see it. Ah! I even recollect that under this name there was a blot of ink."

"No, there is no ink; no, there is no blot."

"Oh! but there was, though; I know it, because I rubbed the powder that was over the blot."

"In a word, be it how it may, dear M. Baisemeaux," said Aramis, "and whatever you may have seen, the order is signed to release Marchiali, blot or no blot."

"The order is signed to release Marchiali," repeated Baisemeaux mechanically, endeavouring to regain his courage.

"And you are going to release this prisoner. If your heart dictates to you to deliver Seldon also, I declare to you I will not oppose it the least in the world." Aramis accompanied the remark with a smile, the irony of which effectually dispelled Baisemeaux's confusion of mind, and restored his courage.

"Monseigneur," he said, "this Marchiali is the very same prisoner whom the other day a priest, confessor of *our order*, came to visit in so imperious and so secret a manner."

"I don't know that, monsieur," replied the Bishop.

"'Tis no such long time ago, dear Monsieur d'Herblay."

"It is true. But *with us*, monsieur, it is good that the man of to-day should no longer know what the man of yesterday did."

"In any case," said Baisemeaux, "the visit of this Jesuit confessor must have given happiness to this man."

Aramis made no reply, but recommenced eating and drinking. As for Baisemeaux, no longer touching anything that was on the table, he again took up the order and examined it in every way. This investigation, under ordinary circumstances, would have made the ears of the impatient Aramis burn with anger; but the Bishop of Vannes did not become incensed for so little, above all, when he had murmured to himself that to do so was dangerous. "Are you going to release Marchiali?" he said. "What mellow and fragrant sherry this is, my dear governor."

"Monseigneur," replied Baisemeaux, "I shall release the prisoner Marchiali when I have summoned the courier who brought the order, and above all, when, by interrogating him, I have satisfied myself."

"The order is sealed, and the courier is ignorant of the contents. What do you want to satisfy yourself about?"

"Be it so, monseigneur; but I shall send to the ministry, and M. de Lyonne will either confirm or withdraw the order."

"What is the good of all that?" asked Aramis coldly.

"What good?"

"Yes; what is your object, I ask?"

"The object of never deceiving oneself, monseigneur, nor being wanting in the respect which a subaltern owes to his superior officers, nor infringing the duties of that service which one has voluntarily accepted."

"Very good; you have just spoken so eloquently that I cannot but admire you. It is true that a subaltern owes respect to his superiors; he is guilty when he deceives himself, and he should be punished if he infringe either the duties or laws of his office." Baisemeaux looked at the Bishop with astonishment.

"It follows," pursued Aramis, "that you are going to ask advice, to put your conscience at ease in the matter?"

"Yes, monseigneur."

"And if a superior officer gives you orders, you will obey?"

"Never doubt it, monseigneur."

"You know the King's signature well, M. de Baisemeaux?"

"Yes, monseigneur."

"Is it not on this order of release?"

"It is true, but it may——"

"Be forged, you mean?"

"That is evident, monseigneur."

"You are right. And that of M. de Lyonne?"

"I see it plain enough on the order; but for the same reason that the King's signature may have been forged, so also, even more likely, may M. de Lyonne's."

"Your logic has the stride of a giant, M. de Baisemeaux," said Aramis; "and your reasoning is irresistible. But on what special grounds do you base your idea that these signatures are false?"

"On this: the absence of counter-signatures. Nothing checks His Majesty's signature; and M. de Lyonne is not here to tell me he has signed."

"Well, Monsieur de Baisemeaux," said Aramis, bending an eagle glance on the governor, "I adopt so frankly your doubts, and your mode of clearing them up, that I will take a pen, if you will give me one."

Baisemeaux gave him a pen.

"And a sheet of white paper," added Aramis.

Baisemeaux handed some paper.

"Now, I—I, also—I, here present—incontestably, I—am going to write an order to which I am certain you will give credence, incredulous as you are!"

Baisemeaux turned pale at this icy assurance of manner. It seemed to him that that voice of the Bishop's, but just now so playful and so gay, had become funereal and sad; that the wax-lights changed into the tapers of a mortuary chapel, and the glasses of wine into chalices of blood.

Aramis took a pen and wrote. Baisemeaux, in terror read over his shoulder.

"A.M.D.G." wrote the Bishop; and he drew a cross under these four letters, which signify *ad majorem Dei gloriam*, "to the greater glory of God"; and thus he continued, "It is our pleasure that the order brought to M. de Baisemeaux de Montlezun, governor, for the King, of the castle of the Bastille, be held good and effectual, and be immediately carried into operation.

"(Signed) D'HERBLAY,
"General of the Order, by the grace of God."

Baisemeaux was so profoundly astonished, that his features remained contracted, his lips parted, and his eyes fixed. He did not move an inch, nor articulate a sound. Nothing could be heard in that large chamber but the buzzing of a little moth, which was fluttering about the candles. Aramis, without even deigning to look at the man whom he had reduced to so miserable a condition, drew from his pocket a small case of black wax; he sealed the letter, and stamped it with a seal suspended at his breast, beneath his doublet, and when the operation was concluded, presented— still in silence—the missive to M. de Baisemeaux. The latter, whose hands trembled in a manner to excite pity, turned a dull and meaningless gaze upon the letter. A last gleam of feeling played over his features, and he fell, as if thunderstruck, on a chair.

"Come, come," said Aramis, after a long silence, during which the governor of the Bastille had slowly recovered his senses, "do not lead me to believe, dear Baisemeaux, that the presence of the General of the Order is as terrible as His, and that men die merely from having seen Him. Take courage; rouse yourself; give me your hand, and obey."

Baisemeaux, reassured, if not satisfied, obeyed, kissed Aramis's hand, and rose. "Immediately?" he murmured.

"Oh, there is no pressing haste, my host; take your place again, and do the honours over this beautiful dessert."

"Monseigneur, I shall never recover such a shock as this; I who have laughed, who have jested with you! I who have dared to treat you on a footing of equality!"

"Say nothing about it, old comrade," replied the Bishop, who perceived how strained the cord was, and how dangerous it would have been to break it; "say nothing about it. Let us each live in our own way; to you, my protection and my friendship; to me, your obedience. Having exactly fulfilled these two requirements, let us live happily."

Baisemeaux reflected; he perceived, at a glance, the consequences of this withdrawal of a prisoner by means of a forged order; and, putting in the scale the guarantee offered him by the official order of the General, did not consider it of any value.

Aramis divined this. "My dear Baisemeaux," said he, "you are a simpleton. Lose this habit of reflection when I give myself the trouble to think for you."

And at another gesture he made, Baisemeaux bowed again. "How shall I set about it?" he said.

"What is the process for releasing a prisoner?"

"I have the regulations."

"Well, then, follow the regulations, my friend."

"I go with my major to the prisoner's room, and conduct him, if he is a personage of importance."

"But this Marchiali is not an important personage," said Aramis, carelessly.

"I don't know," answered the governor; as if he would have said, "It is for you to instruct me."

"Then, if you don't know it, I am right; so act towards Marchiali as you act towards one of obscure station."

"Good; the regulations so provide. They are to the effect that the turnkey, or one of the lower officials, shall bring the prisoner before the governor, in the office."

"Well, 'tis very wise, that; and then?"

"Then we return to the prisoner the valuables he wore at the time of his imprisonment, his clothes and papers, if the minister's order has not otherwise directed."

"What was the minister's order as to this Marchiali?"

"Nothing; for the unhappy man arrived here without jewels, without papers, and almost without clothes."

"See how simple it all is. Indeed, Baisemeaux, you make a mountain of everything. Remain here, and make them bring the prisoner to the governor's house."

Baisemeaux obeyed. He summoned his lieutenant, and gave him an order, which the latter passed on, without disturbing himself about it, to the next whom it concerned.

Half an hour afterwards they heard a gate shut in the court; it was the door to the dungeon, which had just rendered up its prey to the free air. Aramis blew out all the candles which lighted the room but one, which he left burning behind the door. This flickering glare prevented the sight from resting steadily on any object. It multiplied tenfold the changing forms and shadows of the place, by its wavering uncertainty. Steps drew near.

"Go and meet your men," said Aramis to Baisemeaux.

The governor obeyed. The sergeant and turnkeys disappeared. Baisemeaux re-entered, followed by a prisoner. Aramis had placed himself in the shade; he saw without being seen. Baisemeaux, in an agitated tone of voice, made the young man acquainted with the order which set him at liberty. The prisoner listened without making a single gesture, or saying a word.

"You will swear ('tis the regulation that requires it)" added the governor, "never to reveal anything that you have seen or heard in the Bastille."

The prisoner perceived a crucifix; he stretched out his hands, and swore with his lips. "And now, monsieur, you are free; whither do you intend going?"

The prisoner turned his head, as if looking behind him for some protection, on which he ought to rely. Then was it that Aramis came out of the shade: "I am here," he said, "to render the gentleman whatever service he may please to ask."

The prisoner slightly reddened, and without hesitation passed his arm through that of Aramis. "God have you in His holy keeping," he said, in a voice the firmness of which made the governor tremble as much as the form of the blessing astonished him.

Aramis, on shaking hands with Baisemeaux, said to him: "Does my order trouble you? Do you fear their finding it here, should they come to search?"

"I desire to keep it, monseigneur," said Baisemeaux. "If they found it here it would be a certain indication I should be lost, and in that case you would be a powerful and a last auxiliary for me."

"Being your accomplice, you mean?" answered Aramis, shrugging his shoulders. "*Adieu*, Baisemeaux," said he.

The horses were in waiting, making the carriage shake again with their impatience. Baisemeaux accompanied the Bishop to the bottom of the steps. Aramis caused his companion to mount before him, then followed, and without giving the driver any further order, "Go on," said he. The carriage rattled over the pavement of the courtyard. An officer with a torch went before the horses, and gave orders at every post to let them pass. During the time taken in opening all the barriers, Aramis barely breathed, and you might have heard his "sealed heart knock against his ribs." The prisoner, buried in a corner of the carriage, made no more sign of life than his companion. At length a jolt more severe than the others announced to them that they had cleared the last water-course. Behind the carriage closed the last gate, that in the Rue St Antoine. No more walls either on the right or left; heaven every-where, liberty everywhere, and life everywhere. The horses, kept in check by a vigorous hand, went quietly as far as the middle of the faubourg. There they began to trot. Little by little, whether they warmed over it, or whether they were urged, they gained in swiftness, and once past Bercy, the carriage seemed to fly, so great was the ardour of the courses. These horses ran thus as far as Villeneuve St George's, where relays were waiting. Then four in-stead of two whirled the carriage away in the direction of Mehun, and pulled up for a moment in the middle of the forest of Senarl. No doubt, the order had been given the postilion beforehand, for Aramis had no occasion even to make a sign.

"What is the matter!" asked the prisoner, as if waking from a long dream.

"The matter is, monseigneur," said Aramis, "that before going further, it is necessary your Royal Highness and I should converse."

"I will wait an opportunity, monsieur," answered the young Prince.

"We could not have a better, monseigneur; we are in the middle of a forest, and no one can hear us."

"The postilion?"

"The postilion of this relay is deaf and dumb, monseigneur."

"I am at your service, M. d'Herblay."

"Is it your pleasure to remain in the carriage?"

"Yes, we are comfortably seated, and I like this carriage, for it has restored me to liberty."

"Wait, monseigneur; there is yet a precaution to be taken."

"What?"

"We are here on the highway; cavaliers or carriages travelling like ourselves might pass, and seeing us stopping deem us in some difficulty. Let us avoid offers of assistance which would embarrass us."

"Give the postilion orders to conceal the carriage in one of the side avenues."

"'Tis exactly what I wished to do, monseigneur."

Aramis made a sign to the deaf and dumb driver of the carriage, whom he touched on the arm. The latter dismounted, took the leaders by the bridle, and led them over the velvet sward and the mossy grass of a winding alley, at the bottom of which, on this moonless night the deep shades formed a curtain blacker than ink. This done, the man lay down on a slope near his horses, who, on either side, kept nibbling the young oak shoots.

"I am listening," said the young Prince to Aramis; "but what are you doing there?"

"I am disarming myself of my pistols, of which we have no further need, monseigneur."

37

THE TEMPTER

"My prince," said Aramis, turning in the carriage towards his companion, "weak creature as I am, so unpretending in genius, so low in the scale of intelligent beings, it has never yet happened to me to converse with a man without penetrating his thoughts through that living mask which has been thrown over our mind, in order to retain its expression. But to-night, in this darkness, in the reserve which you maintain, I can read nothing on your features, and something tells me that I shall have great difficulty in wresting from you a sincere declaration. I beseech you, then, not for love of me, for subjects should never weigh as anything in the balance which princes hold, but for love of yourself, to retain every syllable, every inflexion which, under our present grave circumstances, will all have a sense and value as important as any ever uttered in the world."

"I listen," repeated the young prince, "decidedly, without either eagerly seeking or fearing anything you are about to say to me." And he buried himself still deeper in the thick cushions of the carriage, trying to deprive his companion not only of the sight of him, but even of the very idea of his presence.

Black was the darkness which fell wide and dense from the summits of the intertwining trees. The carriage, covered in by this vast roof, would not have received a particle of light, not even if a ray could have struggled through the wreaths of mist which were rising in the avenue of the wood.

"Monseigneur," resumed Aramis, "you know the history of the government which to-day controls France. The King issued from an infancy imprisoned like yours, obscure as yours, and confined as yours; only, instead of ending, like yourself, this slavery in a prison—this obscurity in solitude—these straitened circumstances in concealment, he was fain to bear all these miseries, humiliations, and distresses, in full daylight, under the pitiless sun of royalty; or an elevation so flooded with light, where every stain appears a miserable blemish and every glory a stain. The King has suffered; it rankles in his mind; and he will avenge himself. He will be a bad king. I say not that he will pour out blood, like Louis XI. or Charles IX.,* for he has no mortal injuries to avenge; but he will devour the means and substance of his people; for he has himself undergone wrongs in his own interest and money. In the first place, then, I quite acquit my conscience when I consider openly the merits and faults of this Prince; and if I condemn him, my conscience absolves me."

Aramis paused. It was not to listen if the silence of the forest remained undisturbed, but it was to gather up his thoughts from the very bottom of his soul—to leave the thoughts he had uttered sufficient time to eat deeply into the mind of his companion.

"All that Heaven does, Heaven does well," continued the Bishop of Vannes; "and I am so persuaded of it that I have long been thankful to have been chosen depositary of the secret which I have aided you to discover. To a just Providence was necessary an instrument, at once penetrating, persevering, and convinced, to accomplish a great work. I am this instrument: I possess penetration, perseverance, conviction: I govern a mysterious people, who have taken for their motto, the motto of God, 'Patiens quia æternus.'"*
The Prince moved. "I divine, monseigneur, why you are raising your head, and are surprised at the people I have under my command. You did not know you were dealing with a king—oh! monseigneur, king of a people very humble, much disinherited; humble, because they have no force save when creeping; disinherited, because never, almost never in this world, do my people reap the harvest they sow nor eat the fruit they cultivate. They labour for an abstract idea; they heap together all the atoms of their power, to form one man; and round this man, with the sweat of their labour they create a misty halo, which his genius shall in

turn render a glory gilded with the rays of all the crowns in Christendom. Such is the man you have beside you, monseigneur. It is to tell you that he has drawn you from the abyss for a great purpose, and that he desires, for this sublime purpose, to raise you above the powers of the earth—above himself."

The Prince lightly touched Aramis's arm. "You speak to me," he said, "of that religious order whose chief you are. For me, the result of your words is, that the day you desire to hurl down the man you shall have raised, the event will be accomplished; and that you will keep under your hand your creation of yesterday."

"Undeceive yourself, monseigneur," replied the Bishop. "I should not take the trouble to play this terrible game with your Royal Highness, if I had not a double interest in gaining it. The day you are elevated, you are elevated for ever; you will overturn the footstool, as you rise, and will send it rolling so far, that not even the sight of it will ever again recall to you its right to gratitude."

"Oh, monsieur!"

"Your movement, monseigneur, arises from an excellent disposition. I thank you. Be well assured, I aspire to more than gratitude! I am convinced that, when arrived at the summit, you will judge me still more worthy to be your friend; and then, monseigneur, we two will do such great deeds, that ages hereafter shall long speak of them."

"Tell me plainly, monsieur—tell me without disguise—what I am to-day, and what you aim at my being to-morrow."

"You are the son of King Louis XIII., brother of Louis XIV., natural and legitimate heir to the throne of France. In keeping you near him, as Monsieur has been kept—Monsieur, your younger brother—the King reserved to himself the right of being legitimate sovereign. The doctors only could dispute his legitimacy. But the doctors always prefer the King who is to the king who is not. Providence has willed that you should be persecuted; and this persecution to-day consecrates you King of France. You had then a right to reign, seeing that it is disputed; you had a right to be proclaimed, seeing that you have been concealed; and you possess royal blood, since no one has dared to shed yours, as your servants' has been shed. Now see, then, what this Providence, which you have so often accused of having in every way thwarted you, has done for you. It has given you the features, figure, age, and voice of your brother; and the very causes of your persecution are about to become those of your triumphant restoration. To-morrow, after to-morrow—from the very first, regal phantom, living shade of Louis XIV., you will sit upon his throne, whence the will of

Heaven, confided in execution to the arm of man, will have hurled him, without hope of return."

"I understand," said the Prince, "my brother's blood will not be shed, then."

"You will be sole arbiter of his fate."

"The secret of which they made an evil use against me?"

"You will employ it against him. What did he do to conceal it? He concealed you. Living image of himself, you will defeat the conspiracy of Mazarin and Anne of Austria. You, my Prince, will have the same interest in concealing him who will, as a prisoner, resemble you, as you will resemble him as king."

"I fall back on what I was saying to you. Who will guard him?"

"Who guarded you?"

"You know this secret—you have made use of it with regard to myself. Who else knows it?"

"The Queen-Mother and Madame de Chevreuse."

"What will they do?"

"Nothing, if you choose."

"How is that?"

"How can they recognise you, if you act in a manner that no one can recognise you?"

"'Tis true; but there are grave difficulties."

"State them, Prince."

"My brother is married; I cannot take my brother's wife."

"I will cause Spain to consent to a divorce; it is in the interest of your new policy; it is human morality. All that is really noble and really useful in this world will find its account therein."

"The imprisoned King will speak."

"To whom do you think he should speak—to the walls?"

"You mean by walls, the men in whom you put confidence."

"If need be, yes. And besides, your Royal Highness——"

"Besides?"

"I was going to say, that the designs of Providence do not stop on such a fair road. Every scheme of this calibre is completed by its results, like a geometrical calculation. The King, in prison, will not be for you the cause of embarrassment that you have been for the King enthroned. His soul is naturally proud and impatient; it is, moreover, disarmed and enfeebled, by being accustomed to honours, and by the licence of supreme power. The same Providence which has willed that the concluding step in the geometrical calculation I have had the honour of describing to your Royal Highness should be your accession to the throne, and the destruction of him who is hurtful to you, has also determined that the conquered one shall soon end both his own and your sufferings. Therefore, his soul and body have been adapted for but a brief agony. Put into prison as a private individual, left alone with your doubts, deprived of everything, you have exhibited a solid, enduring principle of life in withstanding all this. But your brother, a captive, forgotten, and in bonds, will not long endure the calamity; and Heaven will resume his soul at the appointed time—that is to say, *soon*."

At this point in Aramis's gloomy analysis, a bird of night uttered from the depths of the forest that prolonged and plaintive cry which makes very creature tremble.

"I will exile the deposed King," said Philippe, shuddering; "it will be more humane."

"The King's good pleasure will decide the point," said Aramis. "But has the problem been well put? Have I brought out the solution according to the wishes or the foresight of your Royal Highness?"

"Yes, monsieur, yes; you have forgotten nothing—except indeed two things."

"The first?"

"Let us speak of it at once, with the same frankness we have already conversed in. Let us speak of the causes which may bring about the ruin of all the hopes we have conceived. Let us speak of the risks we are running."

"They would be immense, infinite, terrific, insurmountable, if, as I have said, all things did not concur in rendering them of absolutely no account. There is no danger either for you or for me, if the constancy and intrepidity of your Royal Highness are equal to that perfection of resemblance to your brother which nature has bestowed upon you. I repeat it, there are no dangers, only obstacles; a word, indeed, which I find in all languages, but have always ill understood, and, were I king, would have obliterated as useless and absurd."

"Yes, indeed, monsieur; there is a very serious obstacle, an insurmountable danger, which you are forgetting."

"Ah!" said Aramis.

"There is conscience, which cries aloud; remorse, which never dies."

"True, true," said the Bishop; "there is a weakness of heart of which you remind me. You are right, too, for that indeed is an immense obstacle. The horse afraid of the ditch, leaps into the middle of it, and is killed! The man who tremblingly crosses his sword with that of another leaves loopholes, whereby his enemy has him in his power."

"Have you a brother?" said the young man to Aramis.

"I am alone in the world," said the latter, in a hard, dry voice.

"But, surely, there is some one in the world whom you love?" added Philippe.

"No one!—Yes, I love you."

The young man sank into so profound a silence, that the mere sound of his respiration seemed like a roaring tumult for Aramis. "Monseigneur," he resumed, "I have not said all I had to say to your Royal Highness; I have not offered you all the salutary counsels and useful resources which I have at my disposal. It is useless to flash bright visions before the eyes of one who seeks and loves darkness; useless, too, is it to let the magnificence of the cannon's roar be heard in the ears of one who loves repose and the quiet of the country. Monseigneur, I have your happiness spread out before me in my thoughts; listen to my words; precious they indeed are in their import and their sense, for you who look with such tender regard upon the bright heavens, the verdant meadows, the pure air. I know a country instinct with delights of every kind, an unknown paradise, a secluded corner of the world—where alone, unfettered and unknown, in the thick covert of the woods, amidst flowers, and streams of rippling water, you will forget all the misery that human folly has so recently allotted you. Oh! listen to me my Prince. I do not jest. I have a heart, and mind, and soul, and can read to the depths of your own. I will not take you, incomplete for your task, in order to cast you into the crucible of my own desires, or my caprice, or my ambition. Everything or nothing. You are chilled and galled, sick at heart, almost overcome by the excess of emotion, which but one hour's liberty has produced in you. For me, that is a certain and unmistakable sign that you do not wish to continue at liberty. Would you prefer a more humble life, a life more suited to your strength? Heaven is my witness, that I wish your happiness to be the result of the trial to which I have exposed you."

"Speak, speak," said the Prince, with a vivacity which did not escape Aramis.

"I know," resumed the prelate, "in the Bas-Poiton," a canton, of which no one in France suspects the existence. Twenty leagues of country is immense, is it not? Twenty leagues, monseigneur, all covered with water and herbage, and reeds of the most luxuriant nature; the whole studded with islands covered with woods of the denses foliage. These large marshes, covered with reeds as with a thick mantle, sleep silently and calmly beneath the sun's soft and genial rays. A few fishermen with their families indolently pass their lives away there, with their large rafts of poplars and alders, the flooring formed of reeds, and the roof woven out of thick rushes. These barks, these floating-houses, are wafted to and fro by the changing winds. Whenever they touch a bank, it is but by chance; and so gently too, that the sleeping fisherman is not awakened by the shock. Should he wish to land, it is merely because he has seen a large flight of landrails or plovers, of wild ducks, teal, widgeon, or woodcocks, which fall an easy prey to his nets or his gun. Silver shad, eels, greedy pike, red and grey mullet, fall in masses into his nets; he has but to choose the finest and largest, and return the others to the waters. Never yet has the foot of man, be he soldier or simple citizen, never has any one, indeed, penetrated into that district. The sun's rays there are soft and tempered; in plots of solid earth, whose soil is rich and fertile, grows the vine, which nourishes with its generous juice, its black and white grapes. Once a week a boat is sent to fetch the bread which has been baked at an oven—the common property of all. There—like the seigneurs of early days—powerful, because of your dogs, your fishing-lines, your guns, and your beautiful reed-built house, would you live, rich in the produce of the chase, in the plenitude of perfect security. There would years of your life roll away, at the end of which, no longer recognisable, for you would have been perfectly transformed, you would have succeeded in acquiring a destiny accorded to you by Heaven. There are a thousand pistoles in this bag, monseigneur—more, far more, than sufficient to purchase the whole marsh of which I have spoken; more then enough to live there as many years as you have days to live; more than enough to constitute you the richest, the freest, and the happiest man in the country. Accept it, as I offer it you—sincerely, cheerfully. Forthwith, without a moment's pause, I will unharness two of my horses, which are attached to the carriage yonder, and they, accompanied by my servant—my deaf and dumb attendant—shall conduct you—travelling throughout the night, sleeping during the day—to the locality I have mentioned; and I shall, at least, have the satisfaction of knowing that I have rendered to my prince the service that he himself most preferred. I shall have made one man happy; and Heaven for that will hold me in better account than if I had made one man powerful; for that is far more difficult. And now, monseigneur, your answer to this proposition? Here is the money. Nay, do not hesitate. At Poiton, you can risk nothing, except the chance of catching the fevers prevalent there; and even of them, the so-called wizards of the country may cure you, for the sake of your pistoles. If you play the other game you run the chance of being assassinated on a throne, or of being strangled in a prison. Upon my soul, I assure you, now I begin to compare them together, I should hesitate which of the two I should accept."

"Monsieur," replied the young Prince, "before I determine, let me alight from this carriage, walk on the ground, and consult that still voice within me, which Heaven bids address us all. Ten minutes is all I ask, and then you shall have your answer."

"As you please, monseigneur," said Aramis, bending before him with respect; so solemn and august in its tone and address had been the voice which had just spoken.

38

CROWN AND TIARA

ARAMIS was the first to descend from the carriage; he held the door open for the young man. He saw him place his foot on the mossy ground with a trembling of the whole body, and walk round the carriage with an unsteady and almost tottering step. It seemed as if the poor prisoner was unaccustomed to walk on God's earth. It was the 15th of August, about eleven o'clock at night; thick clouds, portending a tempest, overspread the heavens, and shrouded all light and prospect beneath their heavy folds. The extremities of the avenues were imperceptibly detached from the copse by a lighter shadow of opaque grey, which, upon closer examination, became visible in the midst of the obscurity. But the fragrance which ascended from the grass, fresher and more pene-trating than that which exhaled from the trees around him; the warm and balmy air which enveloped him for the first time for many years past; the ineffable enjoyment of liberty in an open country, spoke to the Prince in so seducing a language that, not-withstanding the great caution, we would almost say the dissimula-tion of his character, of which we have tried to give an idea, he could not restrain his emotion, and breathed a sigh of joy. Then, by degrees, he raised his aching head and inhaled the perfumed air, as it was wafted in gentle gusts across his uplifted face. Crossing his arms on his chest, as if to control this new sensation of delight, he drank in delicious draughts of that mysterious air which penetrates at night-time through lofty forests. The sky he was contemplating, the murmuring waters, the moving creatures, was not this reality? Was not Aramis a madman to suppose that he had aught else to dream of in this world? Those exciting pictures of country life, so free from cares, from fears, and troubles, that ocean of happy days which glitters incessantly before all youthful imaginations, are real allurements wherewith to fascinate a poor unhappy prisoner, worn out by prison life, and emaciated by the close air of the Bastille. It was the picture, it will be remembered, drawn by Aramis, when he offered the thousand pistoles which he had with him in the carriage to the Prince, and the enchanted Eden, which the deserts of Bas-Poiton hid from the eyes of the world. Such were the reflections of Aramis as he watched, with an anxiety impossible to describe, the silent progress of the emotions of Philippe, whom he perceived gradually becoming more and more absorbed in his meditations. The young Prince was offering up an inward prayer to Heaven to be divinely guided in this trying moment, upon which his life or death depended. It was an anxious time for the Bishop of Vannes, who had never before been so perplexed. His iron will, accustomed to overcome all obstacles, never finding itself inferior or vanquished on any occasion, to be foiled in so vast a project for not having foreseen the influence which a view of nature in all its luxuriance would have on the human mind. Aramis, overwhelmed by anxiety, contemplated with emotion the painful struggle which was taking place in Philippe's mind. This suspense lasted the whole ten minutes which the young man had requested. During this space of time, which appeared an eternity, Philippe continued gazing with an imploring and sorrowful look towards the heavens; Aramis did not remove the piercing glance he had fixed on Philippe. Suddenly the young man bowed his head. His thoughts returned to the earth, his looks perceptibly hardened, his brow contracted, his mouth assuming an expression of fierce courage; and then again his look became fixed, but this time it wore a worldly expression, hardened by covetousness, pride, and strong desire. Aramis's look then became as soft as it had before been gloomy. Philippe, seizing his hand in a quick, agitated manner, exclaimed,—

"Let us go where the crown of France is to be found!"

"Is this your decision, monseigneur?" asked Aramis.

"It is."

"Irrevocably so?"

Philippe did not even deign to reply. He gazed earnestly at the Bishop, as if to ask him if it were possible for a man to waver after having once made up his mind.

"These looks are flashes of fire, which portray character," said Aramis, bowing over Philippe's hand; "you will be great, monseigneur; I will answer for that."

"Let us resume our conversation. I wished to discuss two points with you; in the first place, the dangers or the obstacles we may meet with. That point is decided. The other is the conditions you intend imposing upon me. It is your turn to speak M. d'Herblay."

"The conditions, monseigneur?"

"Doubtless. You will not allow so mere a trifle to stop me, and you will not do me the injustice to suppose that I think you have no interest in this affair. Therefore, without subterfuge or hesitation, tell me the truth?"

"I will do so, monseigneur. Once a king——"

"When will that be?"

"To-morrow evening—I mean in the night."

"Explain yourself."

"When I shall have asked your Highness a question."

"Do so."

"I sent to your Highness a man in my confidence, with instructions to deliver some closely-written notes carefully drawn up, which will thoroughly acquaint your Highness with the different persons who compose and will compose your court."

"I perused all the notes."

"Attentively?"

"I know them by heart."

"And understood them? Pardon me, but I may venture to ask that question of a poor, abandoned captive of the Bastille. It will not be requisite in a week's time to further question a mind like yours, when you will then be in full possession of liberty and power."

"Interrogate me, then, and I will be a scholar repeating his lesson to his master."

"We will begin with your family, monseigneur."

"My mother, Anne of Austria! all her sorrows, her painful malady. Oh! I know her—I know her."

"Your second brother?" asked Aramis, bowing.

"To these notes," replied the Prince, "you have added portraits so faithfully painted that I am able to recognise the persons, whose characters, manners, and history, you have so carefully portrayed. Monsieur, my brother, is a fine dark young man, with a pale face; he does not love his wife, Henrietta, whom I, Louis XIV., loved a little, and still flirt with, even although she made me weep on the day she wished to dismiss Mademoiselle de la Vallière from her service in disgrace."

"You will have to be careful with regard to watchfulness of the latter," said Aramis; "she is sincerely attached to the actual King. The eyes of a woman who loves are not easily deceived."

"She is fair, has blue eyes, whose affectionate gaze will reveal her identity. She halts slightly in her gait; she writes a letter every day, to which I shall have to send an answer by M. de Saint-Aignan."

"Do you know the latter?"

"As if I saw him, and I know the last verses he composed for me, as well as those I composed in answer to his."

"Very good. Do you know your ministers?"

"Colbert, an ugly, dark-browed man, but intelligent enough; his hair covering his forehead; a large, heavy, full head; the mortal enemy of M. Fouquet."

"As for the latter, we need not disturb ourselves about him."

"No; because necessarily you will require me to exile him, I suppose?"

Aramis, struck with admiration at the remark, said, "You will become very great, monseigneur."

"You see," added the Prince, "that I know my lesson by heart, and with Heaven's assistance, and yours afterwards, I shall seldom go wrong."

"You have still a very awkward pair of eyes to deal with, monseigneur."

"Yes, the captain of the musketeers, M. d'Artagnan, your friend."

"Yes; I can well say 'my friend.'"

"He who escorted La Vallière to Le Chaillot; he who delivered up Monk, fastened in an iron box, to Charles II.; he who so faithfully served my mother; he to whom the crown of France owes so much that it owes everything. Do you intend to ask me to exile him also?"

"Never, sire. D'Artagnan is a man to whom, at a certain given time, I will undertake to reveal everything; but be on your guard with him; for if he discovers our plot before it is revealed to him, you or I will certainly be killed or taken. He is a bold, enterprising man."

"I will think over it. Now, tell me about M. Fouquet; what do you wish to be done with regard to him?"

"One moment more, I entreat you, monseigneur; and forgive me, if I seem to fail in respect in questioning you further."

"It is your duty to do so, and more than that, your right also."

"Before we pass to M. Fouquet, I should very much regret forgetting another friend of mine."

"M. du Vallon, the Hercules of France, you mean; oh! as far as he is concerned, his fortune is safe."

"No; it is not he whom I intended to refer to."

"The Comte de la Fère, then."

"And his son, the son of all four of us."

"That poor boy, who is dying of love for La Vallière, whom my brother so disloyally deprived him of? Be easy on that score; I shall know how to restore him. Tell me only one thing, Monsieur d'Herblay: do men, when they love, forget the treachery that has been shown them? Can a man ever forgive the woman who has betrayed him? Is that a French custom, or is it one of the laws of the human heart?"

"A man who loves deeply, as deeply as Raoul loves Mademoiselle de la Vallière, finishes by forgetting the fault or crime of the woman he loves; but I do not know if Raoul will be able to forget."

"I will see after that. Have you anything further to say about your friend?"

"No; that is all."

"Well, then, now for M. Fouquet. What do you wish me to do for him?"

"To continue him as Surintendant, as he has hitherto acted, I entreat you."

"Be it so; but he is the first minister at present."

"Not quite so."

"A King, ignorant and embarrassed as I shall be, will, as a matter of course, require a first minister of state."

"Your Majesty will require a friend."

"I have only one, and that is yourself."

"You will have many others by-and-by, but none so devoted, none so zealous for your glory."

"You will be my first minister of state."

"Not immediately, monseigneur; for that would give rise to too much suspicion and astonishment."

"M. de Richelieu, the first Minister of my grandmother, Marie de Medici, was simply Bishop of Luçon, as you are Bishop of Vannes."

"I perceive that your Royal Highness has studied my notes to great advantage; your amazing perspicacity overpowers me with delight."

"I am perfectly aware that M. de Richelieu, by means of the Queen's protection, soon became Cardinal."

"It would be better," said Aramis, bowing, "that I should not be appointed first minister until after your Royal Highness had procured my nomination as Cardinal."

"You shall be nominated before two months are past, Monsieur d'Herblay. But that is a matter of very trifling moment; you would not offend me if you were to ask more than that, and you would cause me serious regret if you were to limit yourself to that."

"In that case I have something still further to hope for, monseigneur."

"Speak! speak!"

"M. Fouquet will not keep long at the head of affairs, he will soon get old. He is fond of pleasure, consistently so with his labours, thanks to that amount of youthfulness which he still retains; but this youthfulness will disappear at the approach of the first serious annoyance, or at the first illness he may experience. We will spare him the annoyance because he is an agreeable and noble-hearted man, but we cannot save him from ill-health. So it is determined. When you shall have paid all M. Fouquet's debts, and restored the finances to a sound condition, M. Fouquet will be able to remain the sovereign ruler in his little court of poets and painters, but we shall have made him rich. When that has been done, and I shall have become your Royal Highness's Prime Minister, I shall be able to think of my own interests and yours."

The young man looked at his interrogator.

"M. de Richelieu, of whom we were speaking just now, was very blamable in the fixed idea he had of governing France alone, un-aided. He allowed two kings, King Louis XIII. and himself, to be seated upon the same throne, whilst he might have installed them more conveniently upon two separate and distinct thrones."

"Upon two thrones?" said the young man, thoughtfully.

"In fact," pursued Aramis, quietly, "a cardinal, Prime Minister of France, assisted by the favour and by the countenance of His Most Christian Majesty the King of France, a cardinal to whom the King his master lends the treasures of the state, his army, his counsel—such a man would be acting with twofold injustice in applying these mighty resources to France alone. Besides," added Aramis, "you will not be a King such as your father was; delicate in health, slow in judgment, whom all things wearied; you will be a king governing by your brain and by your sword; you will have in the government of the state no more than you could manage un-aided; I should only interfere with you. Besides, our friendship ought never to be, I do not say impaired, but in any way affected, by a secret thought. I shall have given you the throne of France, you will confer on me the throne of St Peter. Whenever your loyal, firm, and mailed hand shall have joined in ties of intimate associa-tion the hand of a pope such as I shall be, neither Charles the Fifth, who owned two-thirds of the habitable globe, nor Charle-magne, who possessed it entirely, will be able to reach to half your stature. I have no alliances, I have no predilections; I will not throw you into persecutions of heretics, nor will I cast you into the troubled waters of family dissension. I will simply say to you: The whole universe is our own; for me the minds of men, for you their bodies. And as I shall be the first to die, you will have my inheritance. What do you say of my plan, monseigneur?"

"I say that you render me happy and proud, for no other reason than that of having comprehended you thoroughly. Monsieur d'Herblay, you shall be Cardinal, and when Cardinal, my Prime Minister; and then you shall point out to me the necessary steps to be taken to secure your election as Pope, and I will take them. You can ask what guarantees from me you please."

"It is useless. I shall never act except in such a manner that you are the gainer; I shall never ascend the ladder of fortune, fame, or position, until I shall have first seen you placed upon the round of the ladder immediately above me; I shall always hold myself sufficiently aloof from you to escape incurring your jealousy, sufficiently near to sustain your personal advantage and to watch over your friendship. All the contracts in the world are easily violated because the interest included in them inclines more to one side than to another. With us, however, it will never be the case; I have no need of any guarantees."

"And so—my brother—will disappear?"

"Simply. We will remove him from his bed by means of a plank which yields to the pressure of the finger. Having retired to rest as a crowned sovereign, he will awaken in captivity. Alone you will rule from that moment, and you will have no interest dearer and better than that of keeping me near you."

"I believe it. There is my hand on it, Monsieur d'Herblay."

"Allow me to kneel before you, sire, most respectfully. We will embrace each other on the day we shall both have on our temples, you the crown, and I the tiara."

"Still embrace me this very day also, and be, for and towards me, more than great, more than skilful, more than sublime in genius; be kind and indulgent—be my father."

Aramis was almost overcome as he listened to his voice; he fancied he detected in his own heart an emotion hitherto unknown to him; but this impression was speedily removed. "His father!" he thought; "yes, his Holy Father."

And they resumed their places in the carriage, which sped rapidly along the road leading to Vaux-le-Vicomte.

39

THE CHÂTEAU DE VAUX-LE-VICOMTE

THE château of Vaux-le-Vicomte,* situated about a league from
Mélun, had been built by Fouquet in 1655, at a time when there
was a scarcity of money in France; Mazarin had taken all that
there was, and Fouquet expended the remainder. However, as
certain men have fertile faults and useful vices, Fouquet, in scat-
tering broadcast millions of money in the construction of this
palace, had found a means of gathering, as the result of his
generous profusion, three illustrious men together: Levan, the
architect of the building; Lenôtre, the designer of the gardens; and
Lebrun,* the decorator of the apartments. If the Château de Vaux
possessed a single fault with which it could be reproached, it was
its grand, portentous character. It is even at the present day
proverbial to calculate the number of acres of roofing, the reparation of which would, in our age, be the ruin of fortunes cramped
and narrowed as the epoch itself. Vaux-le-Vicomte, when its
magnificent gates, supported by caryatides, have been passed
through, has the principal front of the main building opening upon
a vast, so-called court of honour, enclosed by deep ditches,
bordered by a magnificent stone balustrade. Nothing could be
more noble in appearance than the forecourt of the middle, raised
upon the flight of steps, like a king upon his throne, having around
it four pavilions forming the angles, the immense Ionic columns of
which rose majestically to the whole height of the building. The
friezes ornamented with arabesques, and the pediments which
crowned the pilasters, conferred richness and grace upon every
part of the building, while the domes which surmounted the whole
added proportion and majesty. This mansion, built by a subject,
bore a far greater resemblance to those royal residences which
Wolsey fancied he was called upon to construct, in order to present
them to his master from the fear of rendering him jealous. But if
magnificence and splendour were displayed in any one particular
part of this palace more than another—if anything could be preferred to the wonderful arrangement of the interior, to the
sumptuousness of the gilding, and to the profusion of the paintings
and statues, it would be the park and gardens of Vaux. The *jets
d'eau*, which were regarded as wonderful in 1653, are still so, even
at the present time; the cascades awakened the admiration of

kings and princes; and as for the famous grotto, the theme of so many poetical effusions, the residence of that illustrious nymph of Vaux,*whom Pélisson made converse with La Fontaine,—we must be spared the description of all its beauties. We will do as Despréaux*did—we will enter the park, the trees of which are of eight years' growth only, and whose summits even yet, as they proudly tower aloft, blushingly unfold their leaves to the earliest rays of the rising sun. Lenôtre had accelerated the pleasure of the Mecænas of his period; all the nursery-grounds had furnished trees whose growth had been accelerated by careful culture and rich manure. Every tree in the neighbourhood which presented a fair appearance of beauty or stature had been taken up by its roots and transplanted to the park. Fouquet could well afford to purchase trees to ornament his park, since he had bought up three villages and their appurtenances (to use a legal word) to increase its extent. M. de Scudéry*said of this palace, that, for the purpose of keeping the grounds and gardens well watered, M. Fouquet had divided a river into a thousand fountains, and gathered the waters of a thousand fountains into torrents. This same Monsieur de Scudéry said a great many other things in his *Clélie* about this palace of Valterre, the charms of which he describes most minutely. We should be far wiser to send our curious readers to Vaux to judge for themselves than to refer them to the *Clélie*; and yet there are as many leagues from Paris to Vaux as there are volumes of the *Clélie*.

This magnificent palace had been got ready for the reception of the greatest reigning sovereign of the time. M. Fouquet's friends had transported thither, some their actors and their dresses, others their troops of sculptors and artists; not forgetting others with their ready-mended pens,—floods of impromptus were contemplated. The cascades, somewhat rebellious, nymphs though they were, poured forth their waters brighter and clearer than crystal; they scattered over the bronze tritons and nereids their waves of foam, which glistened like fire in the rays of the sun. An army of servants were hurrying to and fro in squadrons in the courtyard and corridors; while Fouquet, who had only that morning arrived, walked all through the palace with a calm, observant glance, in order to give his last orders, after his intendants had inspected everything.

It was the 15th of August. The sun poured down its burning rays upon the heathen deities of marble and bronze; it raised the temperature of the water in the conch shells, and ripened on the walls, those magnificent peaches, of which the King, fifty years later, spoke so regretfully, when, at Marly,* on an occasion of a scarcity of the finer sorts of peaches being complained of, in the beautiful gardens there—gardens which had cost France double the amount that had been expended on Vaux,—the *great King* observed to someone, "You are far too young to have eaten any of M. Fouquet's peaches."

Oh! fame! Oh! the blazonry of renown! Oh! the glory of this earth! That very man whose judgment was so sound and accurate where merit was concerned—he who had swept into his coffers the inheritance of Nicholas Fouquet, who had robbed him of Lenôtre and Lebrun, and had sent him to rot for the remainder of his life in one of the state prisons—merely remembered the peaches of that vanquished, crushed, forgotten enemy. It was to little purpose that Fouquet had squandered thirty millions of francs in the fountains of his gardens, in the crucibles of his sculptors, in the writing desks of his literary friends, in the portfolios of his painters; vainly had he fancied that thereby he might be remembered. A peach—a blushing, rich-flavoured fruit, nestling in the trellis-work on the garden-wall, hidden beneath its long, green leaves,—this small vegetable production, that a dormouse would nibble up without a thought, was sufficient to recall to the memory of this great monarch the mournful shade of the last surintendant of France.*

With a perfect reliance that Aramis had made arrangements fairly to distribute the vast number of guests throughout the palace, and that he had not omitted to attend to any of the internal regulations for their comfort, Fouquet devoted his entire attention to the *ensemble* alone; in one direction Gourville showed him the preparations which had been made for the fireworks; in another, Molière led him over the theatre; at last, after he had visited the chapel, the *salons*, and the galleries, and was again going downstairs, exhausted with fatigue, Fouquet saw Aramis on the staircase. The prelate beckoned to him. The Surintendant joined his friend, and, with him, paused before a large picture scarcely finished. Applying himself heart and soul to his work, the painter, Lebrun, covered with perspiration, stained with paints, pale from fatigue and inspiration of genius, was putting the last finishing touches with his rapid brush. It was the portrait of the King, whom they were expecting, dressed in the court-suit which Percerin had condescended to show beforehand to the Bishop of Vannes. Fouquet placed himself before this portrait, which seemed to live, as one might say, in the cool freshness of its flesh, and in its warmth of colour. He gazed upon it long and fixedly, estimated the prodigious labour that had been bestowed upon it, and, not being able to find any recompense sufficiently great for this Herculean effort, he passed his arm round the painter's neck, and embraced him. The

Surintendant, by this action, had utterly ruined a suit of clothes worth a thousand pistoles, but he had satisfied, more than satisfied, Lebrun. It was a happy moment for the artist; it was an unhappy one for M. Percerin, who was walking behind Fouquet, and was engaged in admiring, in Lebrun's painting, the suit that he had had made for His Majesty, a perfect *objet d'art*, as he called it, which was not to be matched except in the wardrobe of the Surintendant. His distress and his exclamations were interrupted by a signal which had been given from the summit of the mansion. In the direction of Mélun, in the still empty, open plain, the sentinels of Vaux had perceived the advancing procession of the King and the Queens. His Majesty was entering into Mélun, with his long train of carriages and cavaliers.

"In an hour——" said Aramis to Fouquet.

"In an hour!" replied the latter, sighing.

"And the people who ask one another what is the good of these royal fêtes!" continued the Bishop of Vannes, laughing, with his false smile.

"Alas! I, too, who am not the people, ask the same thing."

"I will answer you in four-and-twenty hours, monseigneur. Assume a cheerful countenance, for it should be a day of true rejoicing."

"Well, believe me or not, as you like, d'Herblay," said the Surintendant, with a swelling heart, pointing at the *cortége* of Louis, visible in the horizon, "he certainly loves me but very little, nor do I care much for him; but I cannot tell you how it is, that since he is approaching towards my house——"

"Well, what?"

"Well, then, since I know he is on his way here, as my guest, he is more sacred than ever for me; he is my acknowledged sovereign, and as such is very dear to me."

"Dear? yes," said Aramis, playing upon the word, as the Abbé Tenay*did, at a later period, with Louis XV.

"Do not laugh, d'Herblay; I feel that if he were really to wish it, I could love that young man."

"You should not say that to me," returned Aramis, "but rather to M. Colbert."

"To M. Colbert!" exclaimed Fouquet. "Why so?"

"Because he would allow you a pension out of the King's privy purse, as soon as he becomes Surintendant," said Aramis, preparing to leave as soon as he had dealt this last blow.

"Where are you going?" returned Fouquet, with gloomy look.

"To my own apartment, in order to change my costume, monseigneur."

"Whereabouts are you lodging, d'Herblay?"

"In the blue room on the second storey."

"The room immediately over the King's room?"

"Precisely."

"You will be subject to very great restraint there. What an idea to condemn yourself to a room where you cannot stir or move about."

"During the night, monseigneur, I sleep or read in my bed."

"And your servants?"

"I have only one person with me. I find my reader quite sufficient. *Adieu*, monseigneur; do not overfatigue yourself; keep yourself fresh for the arrival of the King."

"We shall see you by-and-by, I suppose, and shall see our friend du Vallon also?"

"He is lodging next to me, and is at this moment dressing."

And Fouquet, bowing, with a smile, passed on like a commander-in-chief who pays the different outposts a visit after the enemy has been signalled in sight.

40

THE WINE OF MELUN

THE King had, in point of fact, entered Mélun with the intention of merely passing through the city. The youthful monarch was most eagerly anxious for amusements; only twice during the journey had he been able to catch a glimpse of La Vallière, and, suspecting that his only opportunity of speaking to her would be after nightfall, in the gardens, and after the ceremonial of reception had been gone through, he had been very desirous to arrive at Vaux as early as possible. But he reckoned without his captain of the musketeers, and without M. Colbert. Like Calypso,* who could not be consoled at the departure of Ulysses, our Gascon could not control himself for not having guessed why Aramis had asked Percerin to show him the King's new costumes. "There is not a doubt," he said to himself, "that my friend the Bishop of Vannes had some motive in that;" and then he began to rack his brains most uselessly. D'Artagnan, so intimately acquainted with all the court intrigues, who knew the position of Fouquet better even than Fouquet himself did, had conceived the strangest fancies and suspicions at the announcement of the fêtes, which would have ruined a wealthy man, and which became impossible

—utter madness, even,—for a man so destitute as he was. And then, the presence of Aramis, who had returned from Belle-Isle, and been nominated by Monsieur Fouquet inspector-general of all the arrangements; his perseverance in mixing himself up with all the Surintendant's affairs; his visits to Baisemeaux;—all this suspicious singularity of conduct had excessively troubled and tormented d'Artagnan during the last several weeks.

"With men of Aramis's stamp," he said, "one is never the stronger except sword in hand. So long as Aramis continued a soldier, there was hope of getting the better of him; but since he has covered his cuirass with a stole, we are lost. But what can Aramis's object possibly be?" And d'Artagnan plunged again into deep thought. "What does it matter to me, after all," he continued, "if his only object is to overthrow M. Colbert? And what else can he be after?" And d'Artagnan rubbed his forehead—that fertile land—whence the ploughshare of his nails had turned up so many and such admirable ideas in his time. He, at first, thought of talking the matter over with Colbert, but his friendship for Aramis, the oath of earlier days, bound him too strictly. He revolted at the bare idea of such a thing, and, besides, he hated the financier too cordially. Then again, he wished to unburden his mind to the King; but yet the King would not be able to understand the suspicions, which had not even a shadow of reality at their base. He resolved to address himself to Aramis, direct, the first time he met him. "I will take him," said the musketeer, "between a couple of candles, suddenly, and when he least expects it, I will place my hand upon his heart, and he will tell me——What will he tell me? Yes, he will tell me something, for, *mordioux!* there is something in it, I know."

Somewhat calmer, d'Artagnan made every preparation for the journey, and took the greatest care that the military household of the King, as yet very inconsiderable in numbers, should be well officered and well disciplined in its meagre and limited proportions. The result was that through the captain's arrangements, the King, on arriving at Melun, saw himself at the head of the musketeers, his Swiss guards, as well as a picket of the French guards. It might almost have been called a small army. M. Colbert looked at the troops with great delight; he even wished there had been a third more in number.

"But why?" said the King.

"In order to show greater honour to M. Fouquet," replied Colbert.

"In order to ruin him the sooner," thought d'Artagnan.

When this little army appeared before Melun, the chief

magistrates came out to meet the King, and to present him with the keys of the city, and invited him to enter the Hôtel de Ville, in order to partake of the wine of honour. The King, who expected to pass through the city and to proceed to Vaux without delay, became quite red in the face from vexation.

"Who was fool enough to occasion this delay?" muttered the King between his teeth, as the chief magistrate was in the middle of a long address.

"Not I, certainly," replied d'Artagnan, "but I believe it was M. Colbert."

Colbert, having heard his name pronounced, said, "What was M. d'Artagnan good enough to say?"

"I was good enough to remark, that it was you who stopped the King's progress, so that he might taste the vin de Brie. Was I right?"

"Quite so, monsieur."

"In that case, then, it was you whom the King called some name or other."

"What name?"

"I hardly know; but wait a moment—idiot, I think it was—no, no, it was fool or stupid. Yes; His Majesty said that the man who had thought of the vin de Mélun was something of the sort."

D'Artagnan, after this broadside, quietly caressed his moustache; M. Colbert's large head seemed to become larger and larger than ever. D'Artagnan, seeing how ugly anger made him, did not stop half-way. The orator still went on with his speech, while the King's colour was visibly increasing.

"*Mordioux!*" said the musketeer coolly, "the King is going to have an attack of determination of blood to the head. Where the deuce did you get hold of that idea, Monsieur Colbert? You have no luck."

"Monsieur," said the financier, drawing himself up, "my zeal for the King's service inspired me with the idea."

"Bah!"

"Monsieur, Mélun is a city, an excellent city, which pays well, and which it would be imprudent to displease."

"There, now; I, who do not pretend to be a financier, saw only one idea in your idea."

"What was that, monsieur?"

"That of causing a little annoyance to M. Fouquet, who is making himself quite giddy on his donjons yonder, in waiting for us."

This was a home-stroke, hard enough in all conscience. Colbert was completely thrown out of the saddle by it, and retired, thoroughly discomfited. Fortunately, the speech was now at an end; the King drank the wine which was presented to him, and then every one resumed the progress through the city. The King bit his lips in anger, for the evening was closing in, and all hope of a walk with La Vallière was at an end. In order that the whole of the King's household should enter Vaux, four hours at least were necessary, owing to the different arrangements. The King, therefore, who was boiling with impatience, hurried forward as much as possible, in order to reach it before nightfall. But, at the moment he was setting off again, other and fresh difficulties arose.

"Is not the King going to sleep at Mélun?" said Colbert, in a low tone of voice to d'Artagnan.

M. Colbert must have been badly inspired that day, to address himself in that manner to the chief of the musketeers; for the latter guessed that the King's intention was very far from that of remaining where he was. D'Artagnan would not allow him to enter Vaux except he were well and strongly accompanied; and desired that His Majesty would not enter except with all the escort. On the other hand, he felt that these delays would irritate that impatient character beyond measure. In what way could he possibly reconcile these two difficulties? D'Artagnan took up Colbert's remark, and determined to repeat it to the King.

"Sire," he said, "M. Colbert has been asking me if your Majesty does not intend to sleep at Mélun."

"Sleep at Mélun? What for?" exclaimed Louis XIV. "Sleep at Mélun! Who, in Heaven's name, can have thought of such a thing, when M. Fouquet is expecting us this evening?"

"It was simply," returned Colbert quickly, "the fear of causing your Majesty any delay; for, according to established etiquette, you cannot enter any place, with the exception of your own royal residences, until the soldiers' quarters have been marked out by the quarter-master, and the garrison properly distributed."

D'Artagnan listened with the greatest attention, biting his moustache to conceal his vexation; and the Queens listened attentively also. They were fatigued, and would have liked to have gone to rest without proceeding any farther; and especially, in order to prevent the King walking about in the evening with M. de Saint-Aignan and the ladies of the court; for, if etiquette required the Princesses to remain within their own rooms, the ladies of honour, as soon as they had performed the services required of them, had no restriction placed upon them, but were at liberty to walk about as they pleased. It will easily be conjectured that all these rival interests, gathering together in vapours, must necessarily produce clouds, and that the clouds would be followed by a tempest. The King had no moustache to gnaw, and therefore kept biting the handle of his whip instead, with ill-concealed impatience. How could he get out of it? D'Artagnan looked as agreeable as possible, and Colbert as sulky as he could. Whom was there he could get in a passion with?"

"We will consult the Queen," said Louis XIV., bowing to the royal ladies. And this kindness of consideration, which softened Maria Theresa's heart, who was of a kind and generous disposition when left to her own free will, replied:—

"I shall be delighted to do whatever your Majesty wishes."

"How long will it take us to get to Vaux?" inquired Anne of Austria, in slow and measured accents, and placing her hand upon her bosom, where the seat of her pain lay.

"An hour for your Majesties' carriages," said d'Artagnan, "the roads are tolerably good."

The King looked at him. "And a quarter of an hour for the King," he hastened to add.

"We should arrive by daylight?" said Louis XIV.

"But the billeting of the King's military escort," objected Colbert softly, "will make His Majesty lose all the advantage of his speed, however quick he may be."

"Double ass that you are!" thought d'Artagnan; "if I had any interest or motive in demolishing your credit, I could do it in ten minutes. If I were in the King's place," he added aloud, "I should, in going to M. Fouquet, leave my escort behind me; I should go to him as a friend; I should enter accompanied only by my captain of the guards; I should consider that I was acting more nobly, and should be invested with a still more sacred character by doing so."

Delight sparkled in the King's eyes. "That is indeed a good suggestion. We will go to see a friend as friends; those gentlemen who are with the carriages can go slowly; but we who are mounted will ride on." And he rode off, accompanied by all those who were mounted. Colbert hid his ugly head behind his horse's neck.

"I shall be quits," said d'Artagnan, as he galloped along, "by getting a little talk with Aramis this evening. And then, M. Fouquet is a man of honour. *Mordioux!* I have said so, and it must be so."

And this was the way how, towards seven o'clock in the evening, without announcing his arrival by the din of trumpets, and without even his advance guard, without out-riders or musketeers, the King presented himself before the gate of Vaux, where Fouquet, who had been informed of his royal guest's approach, had been waiting for the last half-hour, with his head uncovered, surrounded by his household and his friends.

41

NECTAR AND AMBROSIA

M. Fouquet held the stirrup of the King, who, having dismounted, bowed most graciously, and more graciously still held out his hand to him, which Fouquet, in spite of a slight resistance on the King's part, carried respectfully to his lips. The King wished to wait in the first courtyard for the arrival of the carriages, nor had he long to wait, for the roads had been put into excellent order by the Surintendant, and a stone would hardly have been found of the size of an egg the whole way from Mélun to Vaux; so that the carriages, rolling along as though on a carpet, brought the ladies to Vaux, without jolting or fatigue, by eight o'clock. They were received by Madame Fouquet, and at the moment they made their appearance, a light as bright as day burst forth from all the trees, and vases, and marble statues. This species of enchantment lasted until their Majesties had retired into the palace. All these wonders and magical effects which the chronicler has heaped up, or rather preserved, in his recital, at the risk of rivalling the creations of a romancist; these splendours, whereby night seemed conquered and nature corrected; together with every delight and luxury combined for the satisfaction of all the senses, as well as of the mind, Fouquet did in real truth offer to his sovereign in that enchanting retreat of which no monarch could at that time boast of possessing an equal. We do not intend to describe the grand banquet, at which all the royal guests were present, nor the concerts, nor the fairy-like and magical transformations and metamorphoses; it will be more than enough for our purpose to depict the countenance which the King assumed, and which, from being gay, soon wore a gloomy, constrained, and irritated expression. He remembered his own residence, royal though it was, and the mean and indifferent style of luxury which prevailed there, and which comprised only that which was merely useful for the royal wants, without being his own personal property. The large vases of the Louvre, the old furniture and plate of Henry II., of Francis I., of Louis XI.* were merely historical monuments of earlier days; they were nothing but specimens of art, the relics of his predecessors; while with Fouquet, the value of the article was as much in the workmanship as in the article itself. Fouquet ate from a gold service, which artists in his own employ had modelled and cast for himself alone. Fouquet drank wines of which the King of France did not even know the name, and drank them out of goblets each more precious than the whole royal cellar.

What, too, can be said of the apartments, the hangings, the pictures, the servants and officers of every description, of his household? What can be said of the mode of service in which etiquette was replaced by order; stiff formality, by personal, unrestrained comfort; the happiness and contentment of the guest became the supreme law of all who obeyed the host. The perfect swarm of busily engaged persons moving about noiselessly; the multitude of guests—who were, however, even less numerous than the servants who waited on them—the myriads of exquisitely prepared dishes, of gold and silver vases; the floods of dazzling light, the masses of unknown flowers of which the hot-houses had been despoiled, and which were redundant with all the luxuriance of unequalled beauty; the perfect harmony of everything which surrounded them, and which, indeed, was no more than the prelude of the promised fête,—more than charmed all who were there, and who testified their admiration over and over again, not by voice or gesture, but by deep silence and rapt attention, those two languages of the courtier which acknowledge the hand of no master powerful enough to restrain them.

As for the King, his eyes filled with tears; he dared not look at the Queen. Anne of Austria, whose pride, as it ever had been, was superior to that of any creature breathing, overwhelmed her host by the contempt with which she treated everything handed to her. The young Queen, kind-hearted by nature and curious by disposition, praised Fouquet, ate with an exceedingly good appetite, and asked the names of the different fruits which were placed upon the table. Fouquet replied that he was not aware of their names. The fruits came from his own stores; he had often cultivated them himself, having an intimate acquaintance with the cultivation of exotic fruits and plants. The King felt and appreciated the delicacy of the reply, but was only the more humiliated at it; he thought that the Queen was a little too familiar in her manners, and that Anne of Austria resembled Juno a little too much, in being too proud and haughty; his chief anxiety, however, was himself, that he might remain cold and distant in his behaviour, bordering slightly on the limits of extreme disdain or of simple admiration.

But Fouquet had foreseen all that; he was, in fact, one of those

men who foresee everything. The King had expressly declared
that so long as he remained under M. Fouquet's roof he did not
wish his own different repasts to be served in accordance with the
usual etiquette, and that he would, consequently, dine with the
rest of the society; but, by the thoughtful attention of the Surintendant, the King's dinner was served up separately, if one may so
express it, in the middle of the general table; the dinner, wonderful
in every respect, from the dishes of which it was composed,
comprised everything the King liked, and which he generally
preferred to anything else. Louis had no excuse—he, indeed, who
had the keenest appetite in his kingdom*—for saying that he was
not hungry. Nay, M. Fouquet even did better still; he certainly,
in obedience to the King's expressed desire, seated himself at the
table, but as soon as the soups were served, he rose and personally
waited on the King, while Madame Fouquet stood behind the
Queen-Mother's arm-chair. The disdain of Juno and the sulky
fits of temper of Jupiter could not resist this excess of kindly feeling
and polite attention. The Queen ate a biscuit dipped in a glass of
San-Lucar wine;* and the King ate of everything, saying to M.
Fouquet: "It is impossible, Monsieur le Surintendant, to dine
better anywhere." Whereupon the whole court began, on all
sides, to devour the dishes spread before them, with such enthusiasm
that it looked like a cloud of Egyptian locusts settling down upon
the uncut crops.

As soon, however, as his hunger was appeased, the King
became dull and gloomy again; the more so in proportion to the
satisfaction he fancied he had manifested, and particularly on
account of the deferential manner which his courtiers had shown
towards Fouquet. D'Artagnan, who ate a good deal and drank
but little, without allowing it to be noticed, did not lose a single
opportunity, but made a great number of observations which he
turned to good profit.

When the supper was finished, the King expressed a wish not
to lose the promenade. The park was illuminated; the moon, too,
as if she had placed herself at the orders of the lord of Vaux,
silvered the trees and lakes with her bright phosphoric light. The
air was soft and balmy; the gravelled walks through the thickly
set avenues yielded luxuriously to the feet. The fête was complete
in every respect, for the King, having met La Vallière in one of
the winding paths of the wood, was able to press her by the hand
and say, "I love you," without anyone overhearing him, except
d'Artagnan, who followed him, and M. Fouquet who preceded
him.

The night of magical enchantments stole on. The King having

requested to be shown his room, there was immediately a movement in every direction. The Queens passed to their own apartments, accompanied by the music of theorbos and lutes; the King found his musketeers awaiting him on the grand flight of steps, for M. Fouquet had brought them on from Mélun, and had invited them to supper. D'Artagnan's suspicions at once disappeared. He was weary, he had supped well, and wished, for once in his life, thoroughly to enjoy a fête given by a man who was in every sense of the word a king. "M. Fouquet," he said, "is the man for me."

The King was conducted with the greatest ceremony to the chamber of Morpheus, of which we owe some slight description to our readers. It was the handsomest and the largest in the palace. Lebrun had painted on the vaulted ceiling the happy, as well as disagreeable dreams with which Morpheus affects kings as well as other men. Everything that sleep gives birth to that is lovely, its perfumes, its flowers, and nectar, the wild voluptuousness or deep repose of the senses, had the painter enriched with his frescoes. It was a composition as soft and pleasing in one part as dark and gloomy and terrible in another. The poisoned chalice, the glittering dagger suspended over the head of the sleeper; wizards and phantoms with hideous masks, those half-dim shadows more terrific than the brightness of flame or the blackness of night; these, and such as these, he had made the companions of his more pleasing pictures. No sooner had the King entered the room than a cold shiver seemed to pass through him, and on Fouquet asking him the cause of it, the King replied, as pale as death,—

"I am sleepy, that is all."

"Does your Majesty wish for your attendants at once?"

"No; I have to talk with a few persons first," said the King. "Will you have the goodness to tell M. Colbert I wish to see him." Fouquet bowed and left the room.

42

A GASCON, AND A GASCON AND A HALF

D'ARTAGNAN had determined to lose no time, and in fact he never was in the habit of doing so. After having inquired for Aramis, he looked for him in every direction until he had succeeded in finding him. Besides, no sooner had the King entered into Vaux, than Aramis had retired to his own room, meditating doubtlessly some new piece of gallant attention for His Majesty's amusement. D'Artagnan desired the servants to announce him, and found on the second storey (in a beautiful room called the Blue Room, on account of the colour of its hangings) the Bishop of Vannes in company with Porthos and several of the modern Epicureans. Aramis came forward to embrace his friend, and offered him the best seat. As it was after awhile generally remarked among those present that the musketeer was reserved, and wished for an opportunity for conversing secretly with Aramis, the Epicureans took their leave. Porthos, however, did not stir; for true it is that having dined exceedingly well, he was fast asleep in his arm-chair; and the freedom of conversation therefore was not interrupted by a third person. Porthos had a deep, harmonious snore, and people might talk in the midst of its loud bass without fear of disturbing him. D'Artagnan felt that he was called upon to open the conversation.

"Well, and so we have come to Vaux," he said.

"Why, yes, d'Artagnan. And how do you like the place?"

"Very much, and I like M. Fouquet also."

"Is he not a charming host?"

"No one could be more so."

"I am told that the King began by showing a great distance in his manner towards M. Fouquet, but that His Majesty became much more cordial afterwards."

"You did not notice it, then, since you say you have been told so?"

"No; I was engaged with those gentlemen who have just left the room about the theatrical performances and the tournament which are to take place to-morrow."

"Ah, indeed! you are the comptroller-general of the fêtes here, then?"

"You know I am a friend of all kinds of amusement where the

exercise of the imagination is required; I have always been a poet in one way or another."

"Yes, I remember the verses you used to write; they were charming."

"I have forgotten them; but I am delighted to read the verses of others, when those others are known by the names of Molière, Pélisson, La Fontaine, etc."

"Do you know what idea occurred to me this evening, Aramis?"

"No; tell me what it was, for I should never be able to guess it, you have so many."

"Well, the idea occurred to me that the true King of France is not Louis XIV."

"What!" said Aramis involuntarily, looking the musketeer full in the eyes.

"No, it is Monsieur Fouquet."

Aramis breathed again and smiled. "Ah! you are like all the rest, jealous," he said. "I would wager that it was M. Colbert who turned that pretty phrase." D'Artagnan, in order to throw Aramis off his guard, related Colbert's misadventure with regard to the vin de Mélun.

"He comes of a mean race, does Colbert," said Aramis.

"Quite true."

"When I think, too," added the Bishop, "that that fellow will be your minister within four months, and that you will serve him as blindly as you did Richelieu or Mazarin——"

"And as you serve M. Fouquet," said d'Artagnan.

"With this difference, though, that M. Fouquet is not M. Colbert."

"True, true," said d'Artagnan, as he pretended to become sad and full of reflection; and then, a moment after, he added, "Why do you tell me that M. Colbert will be minister in four months?"

"Because M. Fouquet will have ceased to be so," replied Aramis.

"He will be ruined, you mean?" said d'Artagnan.

"Completely so."

"Why does he give these fêtes, then?" said the musketeer, in a tone so full of thoughtful consideration, and so well assumed, that the Bishop was for a moment deceived by it, "Why did you not dissuade him from it?"

The latter part of the phrase was just a little too much, and Aramis's former suspicions were again aroused. "It is done with the object of humouring the King."

"By ruining himself?"

"Yes, by ruining himself for the King."

"A singular calculation that."

"Necessity."

"I don't see that, dear Aramis."

"Do you not? Have you not remarked M. Colbert's daily increasing antagonism, and that he is doing his utmost to drive the King to get rid of the Surintendant?"

"One must be blind not to see it."

"And that a cabal is formed against M. Fouquet?"

"That is well known."

"What likelihood is there that the King would join a party formed against a man who will have spent everything he had to please him?"

"True, true," said d'Artagnan slowly, hardly convinced, yet curious to broach another phase of the conversation. "There are follies and follies," he resumed, "and I do not like those you are committing."

"What do you allude to?"

"As for the banquet, the ball, the concert, the theatricals, the tournaments, the cascades, the fireworks, the illuminations, and the presents—these are all well and good, I grant; but why were not these expenses sufficient? Was it necessary to have new liveries and costumes for your whole household?"

"You are quite right. I told M. Fouquet that myself; he replied, that if he were rich enough he would offer the King a newly erected château, from the vanes at the top of the house to the very cellar; completely new, inside and out; and that, as soon as the King had left, he would burn the whole building and its contents, in order that it might not be made use of by any one else."

"How completely Spanish!"

"I told him so, and he then added this: 'Whoever advises me to spare expense, I shall look upon as my enemy.' "

"It is positive madness; and that portrait too!"

"What portrait?" said Aramis.

"That of the King; and the surprise as well."

"What surprise?"

"The surprise you seem to have in view, and on account of which you took some specimens away, when I met you at Percerin's." D'Artagnan paused. The shaft was discharged, and all he had to do was to wait and watch its effect.

"That is merely an act of graceful attention," replied Aramis.

D'Artagnan went up to his friend, took hold of both his hands, and looking him full in the eyes, said, "Aramis, do you still care for me a very little?"

"What a question to ask!"

"Very good. One favour then. Why did you take some patterns of the King's costumes at Percerin's?"

"Come with me and ask poor Lebrun, who has been working upon them for the last two days and two nights."

"Aramis, that may be the truth for anybody else, but for me——"

"Upon my word, d'Artagnan, you astonish me!"

"Be a little considerate for me. Tell me the exact truth; you would not like anything disagreeable to happen to me, would you?"

"My dear friend, you are becoming quite incomprehensible. What suspicion can you possibly have got hold of?"

"Do you believe in my instinctive feelings? Formerly, you used to have faith in them. Well then, an instinct tells me that you have some concealed project on foot."

"I—a project!"

"I am convinced of it."

"What nonsense!"

"I am not only sure of it, but I would even swear it."

"Indeed, d'Artagnan, you cause me the greatest pain. Is it likely, if I have any project in hand that I ought to keep secret from you, I should tell you about it? If I had one that I could and ought to have revealed, should I not have already told it to you?"

"No, Aramis, no. There are certain projects which are never revealed until the favourable opportunity arrives."

"In that case, my dear fellow," returned the Bishop, laughing, "the only thing now is, that the 'opportunity' has not yet arrived."

D'Artagnan shook his head with a sorrowful expression. "Oh, friendship, friendship!" he said, "what an idle word you are! Here is a man, who if I were but to ask it, would suffer himself to be cut in pieces for my sake."

"You are right," said Aramis, nobly.

"And this man, who would shed every drop of blood in his veins for me, will not open the smallest corner of his heart. Friendship, I repeat, is nothing but a mere unsubstantial shadow and a lure, like everything else in this world which is bright and dazzling."

"It is not thus you should speak of our friendship," replied the Bishop, in a firm, assured voice; "for ours is not of the same nature as those you have been speaking of."

"Look at us, Aramis; three out of the old 'four.' You are deceiving me; I suspect you; and Porthos is fast asleep. An admirable trio of friends, don't you think so? A beautiful relic of former times."

"I can only tell you one thing, d'Artagnan, and I swear it on the Bible; I love you just as I used to do. If I ever suspect you, it is on account of others, and not on account of either of us. In everything I may do, and should happen to succeed in, you will find your fourth. Will you promise me the same favour?"

"If I am not mistaken, Aramis, your words—at the moment you pronounce them—are full of generous feeling."

"That is possible."

"You are conspiring against M. Colbert. If that be all, *mordioux!* tell me so at once. I have the instrument in my own hand, and will pull out the tooth easily enough."

Aramis could not restrain a smile of disdain which passed across his noble features. "And supposing that I were conspiring against Colbert, what harm would there be in that?"

"No, no; that would be too trifling a matter for you to take in hand, and it was not on that account you asked Percerin for those patterns of the King's costumes. Oh! Aramis, we are not enemies, remember, but brothers. Tell me what you wish to undertake, and upon the word of a d'Artagnan, if I cannot help you, I will swear to remain neuter."

"I am undertaking nothing," said Aramis.

"Aramis, a voice speaks within me, and seems to enlighten my darkness; it is a voice which has never yet deceived me. It is the King you are conspiring against."

"The King?" exclaimed the Bishop, pretending to be annoyed.

"Your face will not convince me; the King, I repeat."

"Will you help me?" said Aramis, smiling ironically.

"Aramis, I will do more than help you—I will do more than remain neuter—I will save you."

"You are mad, d'Artagnan."

"I am the wiser of the two, in this matter."

"You to suspect me of wishing to assassinate the King!"

"Who spoke of that at all?" said the musketeer.

"Well, let us understand each other. I do not see what any one can do to a legitimate King as ours is, if he does not assassinate him." D'Artagnan did not say a word. "Besides, you have your guards and your musketeers here," said the Bishop.

"True."

"You are not in M. Fouquet's house, but in your own."

"True; but in spite of that, Aramis, grant me, for pity's sake, but one single word of a true friend."

"A friend's word is the truth itself. If I think of touching, even with my finger, the son of Anne of Austria, the true King of this realm of France—if I have not the firm intention of prostrating myself before his throne—if in every idea I may entertain tomorrow here at Vaux will not be the most glorious day my King ever enjoyed—may Heaven's lightning blast me where I stand!" Aramis had pronounced these words with his face turned towards the alcove of his own bedroom; where, d'Artagnan, seated with his back towards the alcove, could not suspect that any one was lying concealed. The earnestness of his words, the studied slowness with which he pronounced them, the solemnity of his oath, gave the musketeer the most complete satisfaction. He took hold of both Aramis's hands, and shook them cordially. Aramis had endured reproaches without turning pale, and had blushed as he listened to words of praise. D'Artagnan, deceived, did him honour; but d'Artagnan, trustful and reliant, made him feel ashamed. "Are you going away?" he said as he embraced him, in order to conceal the flush on his face.

"Yes; my duty summons me. I have to get the watchword. It seems I am to be lodged in the King's anteroom. Where does Porthos sleep?"

"Take him away with you, if you like, for he snores like a park of artillery."

"Ah! he does not stay with you, then?" said d'Artagnan.

"Not the least in the world. He has his room to himself, but I don't know where!"

"Very good!" said the musketeer, from whom this separation of the two associates removed his last suspicion, and he touched Porthos lightly on the shoulder. The latter replied by a terrible yawn. "Come," said d'Artagnan.

"What, d'Artagnan, my dear fellow, is that you? What a lucky chance! Oh, yes—true; I had forgotten; I am at the fêtes at Vaux."

"Yes; and your beautiful dress, too."

"Yes, it was very attentive on the part of Monsieur Coquelin de Volière, was it not?"

"Hush!" said Aramis. "You are walking so heavily, you will make the flooring give way."

"True," said the musketeer; "this room is above the dome, I think."

"And I did not choose it for a fencing-room, I assure you," added the Bishop. "The ceiling of the King's room has all the sweetness and calm delights of sleep. Do not forget, therefore, that my flooring is merely the covering of his ceiling. Good-night, my friends, and in ten minutes I shall be fast asleep." And Aramis accompanied them to the door, laughing quietly all the while. As soon as they were outside, he bolted the door hurriedly; closed up the chinks of the windows, and then called out, "Monseigneur!

—monseigneur!" Philippe made his appearance from the alcove, as he pushed aside a sliding panel placed behind the bed.

"M. d'Artagnan entertains a great many suspicions, it seems," he said.

"Ah!—you recognised M. d'Artagnan, then?"

"Before you called him by his name, even."

"He is your captain of musketeers,"

"He is very devoted to *me*," replied Philippe, laying a stress upon the personal pronoun.

"As faithful as a dog; but he bites sometimes. If d'Artagnan does not recognise you before the *other* has disappeared, rely upon d'Artagnan to the end of the world; for, in that case, if he has seen nothing, he will keep his fidelity. If he sees, when it is too late—he is a Gascon, and will never admit that he has been deceived."

"I thought so. What are we to do, now?"

"You will go and take up your post at our place of observation, and watch the moment of the King's retiring to rest, so as to learn how that ceremony is performed."

"Very good. Where shall I place myself?"

"Sit down on this folding-chair. I am going to push aside a portion of the flooring; you will look through the opening, which answers to one of the false windows made in the dome of the King's apartment. Can you see?"

"Yes," said Philippe, starting as at the sight of an enemy, "I see the King!"

"What is he doing?"

"He seems to wish some man to sit down close to him."

"M. Fouquet?"

"No, no; wait a moment——"

"Look at the notes and portraits, my Prince."

"The man whom the King wishes to sit down in his presence is M. Colbert."

"Colbert sit down in the King's presence!" exclaimed Aramis, "it is impossible."

"Look."

Aramis looked through the opening in the flooring. "Yes," he said. "Colbert himself. Oh, monseigneur! what can we be going to hear—and what can result from this intimacy?"

"Nothing good for M. Fouquet, at all events."

The Prince did not deceive himself.

We have seen that Louis XIV. had sent for Colbert, and that Colbert had arrived. The conversation began between them by the King according to him one of the highest favours that he had ever done; it was true the King was alone with his subject. "Colbert," said he, "sit down."

The intendant, overcome with delight, for he feared he should be dismissed, refused this unprecedented honour.

"Does he accept?" said Aramis.

"No, he remains standing."

"Let us listen then." And the future King and the future Pope listened eagerly to the simple mortals whom they held under their feet, ready to crush them if they had liked.

"Colbert," said the King, "you have annoyed me exceedingly to-day."

"I know it, sire."

"Very good; I like that answer. Yes, you knew it, and there was courage in having done it."

"I ran the risk of displeasing your Majesty, but I risked also concealing what were your true interests from you."

"What! you were afraid of something on my account?"

"I was, sire, even if it were of nothing more than an indigestion," said Colbert; "for people do not give their sovereigns such banquets as the one of to-day except it be to stifle them under the weight of good living." Colbert waited the effect which this coarse jest would produce upon the King; and Louis XIV., who was the vainest and most fastidiously delicate man in his kingdom, forgave Colbert the joke.

"The truth is," he said, "that M. Fouquet has given me too good a meal. Tell me, Colbert, where does he get all the money required for this enormous expenditure,—can you tell?"

"Yes, I do know, sire."

"Will you be able to prove it with tolerable certainty?"

"Easily; to the very farthing."

"I know you are very exact."

"It is the principal qualification required in an intendant of finances."

"But all are not so."

"I thank your Majesty for so flattering a compliment from your own lips."

"M. Fouquet, therefore, is rich—very rich, and I suppose every man knows he is so."

"Every one, sire—the living as well as the dead."

"What does that mean, Monsieur Colbert?"

"The living are witnesses of M. Fouquet's wealth,—they admire and applaud the result produced; but the dead, wiser and better informed than we are, know how that wealth was obtained—and they rise up in accusation."

"So that M. Fouquet owes his wealth to some cause or other."

"The occupation of an intendant very often favours those who practise it."

"You have something to say to me more confidently, I perceive; do not be afraid, we are quite alone."

"I am never afraid of anything under the shelter of my own conscience, and under the protection of your Majesty," said Colbert, bowing.

"If the dead therefore were to speak——"

"They do speak sometimes, sire—read."

"Ah!" murmured Aramis, in the Prince's ear, who, close beside him, listened without losing a syllable, "since you are placed here, monseigneur, in order to learn your vocation of a king, listen to a piece of infamy of a nature truly royal. You are about to be a witness of one of those scenes which the foul fiend alone can conceive and execute. Listen attentively; you will find your advantage in it."

The Prince redoubled his attention, and saw Louis XIV. take from Colbert's hands a letter which the latter held out to him.

"The late Cardinal's handwriting," said the King.

"Your Majesty has an excellent memory," replied Colbert, bowing; "it is an immense advantage for a King who is destined for hard work to recognise handwritings at the first glance."

The King read Mazarin's letter, and, as its contents are already known to the reader, in consequence of the misunderstanding between Madame de Chevreuse and Aramis, nothing further would be learned if we stated them here again.

"I do not quite understand," said the King, greatly interested.

"Your Majesty has not yet acquired the habit of going through the public accounts."

"I see that it refers to money which had been given to M. Fouquet."

"Thirteen millions. A tolerably good sum."

"Yes. Well, and these thirteen millions are wanting to balance the total of the accounts. That is what I do not very well understand. How is this deficit possible?"

"Possible, I do not say; but there is no doubt about the fact that it really is so."

"You say that these thirteen millions are found to be wanting in the accounts?"

"I do not say so, but the registry does."

"And this letter of M. Mazarin indicates the employment of the sum, and the name of the person with whom it was deposited?"

"As your Majesty can judge for yourself."

"Yes; and the result is, then, that M. Fouquet has not yet restored the thirteen millions."

"That results from the accounts, certainly, sire."

"Well, and consequently——"

"Well, sire, in that case, inasmuch as M. Fouquet has not yet given back the thirteen millions, he must have appropriated them to his own purposes; and with those thirteen millions one could incur four times and a little more as much expenses, and make four times as great a display, as your Majesty was able to do at Fontaine-bleau, where we only spent three millions altogether, if you remember."

For a blunderer, the *souvenir* he had evoked was a very skilfully-contrived piece of baseness; for by the remembrance of his own fête he, for the first time, perceived its inferiority compared with that of Fouquet. Colbert received back again at Vaux what Fouquet had given him at Fontainebleau, and, as a good financier, he returned it with the best possible interest. Having once disposed the King's mind in that way, Colbert had nothing of much importance to detain him. He felt that such was the case, for the King, too, had again sunk into a dull and gloomy state. Colbert awaited the first word from the King's lips with as much impatience as Philippe and Aramis did from their place of observation.

"Are you aware what is the natural consequence of all this, Monsieur Colbert?" said the King, after a few minutes' reflection.

"No, sire, I do not know."

"Well, then, the fact of the appropriation of the thirteen millions, if it can be proved——"

"But it is so already."

"I mean, if it were to be declared and certified, Monsieur Colbert."

"I think it will be to-morrow, if your Majesty——"

"Were we not under M. Fouquet's roof, you were going to say, perhaps," replied the King, with something of nobleness in his manner."

"The King is in his own palace wherever he may be, and especially in houses which his own money has paid for."

"I think," said Philippe, in a low tone, to Aramis, "that the architect who constructed this dome ought, anticipating what use could be made of it, so to have contrived that it might easily be made to fall on the heads of scoundrels such as that M. Colbert."

"I thought so too," replied Aramis; "but M. Colbert is so very near the King at this moment."

"That is true, and that would open the succession."

"Of which your younger brother would reap all the advantage, monseigneur. But stay, let us keep quiet, and go on listening."

"We shall not have long to listen," said the young Prince.

"Why not, monseigneur?"

"Because if I were the King, I should not reply anything further."

"And what would you do?"

"I should wait until to-morrow morning to give myself time for reflection."

Louis XIV. at last raised his eyes, and finding Colbert attentively waiting for his next remark, said, hastily changing the conversation, "Monsieur Colbert, I perceive it is getting very late, and I shall now retire to bed. By to-morrow morning I shall have made up my mind."

"Very good sire," returned Colbert, greatly incensed, although he restrained himself in the presence of the King.

The King made a gesture of adieu, and Colbert withdrew with a respectful bow. "My attendants," cried the King; and, as they entered the apartment, Philippe was about to quit his post of observation.

"A moment longer," said Aramis to him, with his accustomed gentleness of manner; "what has just now taken place is only a detail, and to-morrow we shall have no occasion to think anything more about it; but the ceremony of the King's retiring to rest, the etiquette observed in addressing the King, that indeed is of the greatest importance. Learn, sire, and study well how you ought to go to bed of a night. Look! look!"

43

COLBERT

HISTORY will tell us, or rather history has told us, of the various events of the following day, of the splendid fêtes given by the Surintendant to his sovereign. There was nothing but amusement and delight allowed to prevail throughout the whole of the following day; there was a promenade, a banquet, a comedy to be acted, and a comedy too, in which, to his great amazement, Porthos recognised M. Coquelin de Volière, as one of the actors in the piece called *Les Fôcheux*. Full of preoccupation, however, from the scene of the previous evening, and hardly recovered from the effects of the poison which Colbert had then administered to him, the King, during the whole of the day, so brilliant in its effects, so full of unexpected and startling novelties, in which all the wonders of the *Arabian Nights' Entertainments**seemed to be reproduced for his special amusement—the King, we say, showed himself cold, reserved, and taciturn. Nothing could smooth the frown upon his face; every one who observed him noticed that a deep feeling of resentment of remote origin, increased by slow degrees, as a source becomes a river, thanks to the thousand threads of water which increase its body, was keenly alive in the depth of the King's heart. Towards the middle of the day only did he begin to resume a little serenity of manner, and by that time he had, in all probability, made up his mind. Aramis, who followed him step by step in his thoughts, as in his walk, concluded that the event that he was expecting would not be long before it was announced. This time Colbert seemed to walk in concert with the Bishop of Vannes, and had he received for every annoyance which he inflicted on the King a word of direction from Aramis, he could not have done better. During the whole of the day, the King, who, in all probability, wished to free himself from some of the thoughts which disturbed his mind, seemed to seek La Vallière's society as actively as he seemed to show his anxiety to flee that of M. Colbert or M. Fouquet. The evening came. The King had expressed a wish not to walk in the park until after cards in the evening. In the interval between supper and the promenade, cards and dice were introduced. The King won a thousand pistoles, and, having won them, put them in his pocket, and then rose, saying, "And now, gentlemen, to the park." He found the ladies of the court already there. The King, we have before observed, had won a thousand pistoles and had put them in his pocket; but M. Fouquet had somehow contrived to lose ten thousand, so that among the courtiers there was still left a hundred and ninety thousand francs profit to divide, a circumstance which made the countenances of the courtiers and the officers of the King's household the most joyous countenances in the world. It was not the same, however, with the King's face; for, notwithstanding his success at play, to which he was by no means insensible, there still remained a slight shade of dissatisfaction. Colbert was waiting for or upon him at the corner of one of the avenues; he was most probably waiting in consequence of a rendezvous which had been given him by the King, as Louis XIV., who had avoided him, or who had seemed to avoid him, suddenly made him a sign, and they then struck into the depths of the park together. But La Vallière, too, had observed the King's gloomy aspect and kindling glances; she had remarked this; and, as nothing which lay hidden or smouldering in his heart was impenetrable to her affection, she understood that this repressed wrath menaced some one; she prepared to withstand the current of his vengeance and intercede like an angel of mercy. Overcome by sadness, nervously agitated, deeply distressed at having been so long separated from her lover, disturbed at the sight of that emotion which she had divined, she accordingly presented herself to the King with an embarrassed aspect, which, in his then disposition of mind, the King interpreted unfavourably. Then, as they were alone, or nearly alone, inasmuch as Colbert, as soon as he perceived the young girl approaching, had stopped and drawn back a dozen paces—the King advanced towards La Vallière and took her by the hand: "Mademoiselle," he said to her, "should I be guilty of an indiscretion if I were to inquire if you are indisposed? for you seem to breathe as if you were oppressed by some secret cause of uneasiness, and your eyes are filled with tears."

"Oh! sire, if I be indeed so, and if my eyes are indeed full of tears, I am sorrowful only at the sadness which seems to oppress your Majesty."

"My sadness? You are mistaken, mademoiselle; no, it is not sadness I experience."

"What is it then, sire?"

"Humiliation."

"Humiliation? oh! sire, what a word for you to use."

"I mean, mademoiselle, that wherever I may happen to be, no one else ought to be the master. Well, then, look round you on every side, and judge whether I am not eclipsed—I, the King of France—before the king of these wide domains. Oh!" he continued, clenching his hands and teeth, "when I think that this king——"

"Well, sire?" said Louise terrified.

"—That this king is a faithless, unworthy servant, who becomes proud and self-sufficient with property which belongs to me, and which he has stolen. And, therefore, am I about to change this imprudent minister's fête into a sorrow and mourning, of which the nymph of Vaux, as the poets say, shall not soon lose the remembrance."

"Oh! your Majesty——"

"Well, mademoiselle, are you about to take M. Fouquet's part?" said Louis impatiently.

"No, sire; I will only ask whether you are well informed. Your Majesty has more than once learned the value of accusations made at the court."

Louis XIV. made a sign for Colbert to approach. "Speak, Monsieur Colbert," said the young Prince, "for I almost believe that Mademoiselle de la Vallière has need of your assurance before she can put any faith in the King's word. Tell mademoiselle what M. Fouquet has done; and you, mademoiselle, will perhaps have the kindness to listen. It will not be long."

Why did Louis XIV. insist upon it in such a manner? A very simple reason—his heart was not at rest; his mind was not thoroughly convinced; he imagined there was some dark, hidden, tortuous intrigue concealed beneath these thirteen millions of francs; and he wished that the pure heart of La Vallière, which had revolted at the idea of a theft or robbery, should approve—even were it only by a single word—the resolution he had taken, and which, nevertheless, he hesitated about carrying into execution.

"Speak, monsieur," said La Vallière to Colbert, who had advanced; "speak, since the King wishes me to listen to you. Tell me, what is the crime with which M. Fouquet is charged?"

"Oh! not very heinous, mademoiselle," he returned; "a simple abuse of confidence."

"Speak, speak, Colbert; and when you shall have related it, leave us, and go and inform M. d'Artagnan that I have certain orders to give him."

"M. d'Artagnan, sire!" exclaimed La Vallière; "but why send for M. d'Artagnan? I entreat you to tell me?"

"*Pardieu!* in order to arrest this haughty, arrogant Titan, who, true to his menace, threatens to scale my heaven."

"Arrest M. Fouquet, do you say?"

"Ah! does that surprise you?"

"In his own house?"

"Why not? If he be guilty, he is guilty in his own house as anywhere else."

"M. Fouquet, who at this moment is ruining himself for his sovereign."

"In plain truth, mademoiselle, it seems as if you were defending this traitor."

Colbert began to chuckle silently. The King turned round at the sound of this suppressed mirth.

"Sire," said La Vallière, "it is not M. Fouquet I am defending; it is yourself."

"Me! you defend me!"

"Sire, you would be dishonouring yourself if you were to give such an order."

"Dishonour myself!" murmured the King, turning pale with

anger. "In plain truth, mademoiselle, you show a strange persistence in what you say."

"If I do so, sire, my only motive is that of serving your Majesty," replied the noble-hearted girl; "for that I would risk, I would sacrifice my very life, without the slightest reserve."

Colbert seemed inclined to grumble and complain. La Vallière, that timid, gentle lamb, turned round upon him, and with a glance like lightning, imposed silence upon him. "Monsieur," she said, "when the King acts well, whether, in doing so, he does either myself or those who belong to me, an injury, I have nothing to say; but were the King to confer a benefit either upon me or mine, and if he acted badly, I should tell him so."

"But it appears to me, mademoiselle," Colbert ventured to say, "that I too love the King."

"Yes, monsieur, we both love him, but each in a different manner," replied La Vallière, with such an accent that the heart of the young King was powerfully affected by it. "I love him so deeply that the whole world is aware of it; so purely, that the King himself does not doubt my affection. He is my king and my master; I am the humblest of his servants. But he who touches his honour touches my life. Therefore, I repeat, that they dishonour the King who advise him to arrest M. Fouquet under his own roof."

Colbert hung down his head, for he felt that the King had abandoned him. However, as he bent his head, he murmured, "Mademoiselle, I have only one word to say."

"Do not say it, then, monsieur; for I would not listen to it. Besides, what could you have to tell me? That M. Fouquet has been guilty of certain crimes? I know he has, because the King has said so; and from the moment the King said 'I think so,' I have no occasion for other lips to say, 'I affirm it.' But, were M. Fouquet the vilest of men, I should say aloud, 'M. Fouquet's person is sacred to the King because he is the King's host. Were this house a den of thieves, were Vaux a cave of coiners or robbers, his home is sacred, his palace is inviolable, since his wife is living in it; and that is an asylum which even executioners would not dare to violate.'"

La Vallière paused and was silent. In spite of himself, the King could not but admire her; he was overpowered by the passionate energy of her voice; by the nobleness of the cause she advocated. Colbert yielded, overcome by the inequality of the struggle. At last, the King breathed again more freely, shook his head, and held out his hand to La Vallière.

"Mademoiselle," he said gently, "why do you decide against

me? Do you know what this wretched fellow will do, if I give him time to breathe again?"

"Is he not a prey which will always be within your grasp?"

"And if he escapes, and takes to flight?" exclaimed Colbert.

"Well, monsieur, it will always remain on record, to the King's eternal honour, that he allowed M. Fouquet to flee; and the more guilty he may have been, the greater will the King's honour and glory appear, when compared with such misery and such shame."

Louis kissed La Vallière's hand, as he knelt before her.

"I am lost," thought Colbert; then suddenly his face brightened up again. "Oh! no, no, not yet," he said to himself.

And while the King, protected from observation by the thick covert of an enormous lime, pressed La Vallière to his breast, with all the ardour of ineffable affection, Colbert tranquilly looked among the papers in his pocket-book, and drew out of it a paper folded in the form of a letter, slightly yellow, perhaps, but which must have been very precious, since the Intendant smiled as he looked at it; he then bent a look, full of hatred upon the charming group which the young girl and the King formed together—a group which was revealed for a moment, as the light of the approaching torches shone upon it. Louis noticed the light reflected upon La Vallière's white dress. "Leave me, Louise," he said, "for some one is coming."

"Mademoiselle, mademoiselle, some one is coming," cried Colbert, to expedite the young girl's departure.

Louise disappeared rapidly among the trees; and then, as the King, who had been on his knees before the young girl, was rising from his humble posture Colbert exclaimed, "Ah! Mademoiselle de la Vallière has let something fall."

"What is it?" inquired the King.

"A paper—a letter—something white; look there, sire."

The King stooped down immediately, and picked up the letter, crumpling it in his hand as he did so; and at the same moment the torches arrived, inundating the darkness of the scene with a flood of light as bright as day.

44

JEALOUSY

THE torches we have just referred to, the eager attention which every one displayed, and the new ovation paid to the King by Fouquet, arrived in time to suspend the effect of a resolution which La Vallière had already considerably shaken in Louis XIV.'s heart. He looked at Fouquet with a feeling almost of gratitude for having given La Vallière an opportunity of showing herself so generously disposed, so powerful in the influence she exercised over his heart. The moment of the last and greatest display had arrived. Hardly had Fouquet conducted the King towards the château, than a mass of fire burst from the dome of Vaux, with a prodigous uproar, pouring a flood of dazzling light on every side, and illumining the remotest corners of the gardens. The fireworks began. Colbert, at twenty paces from the King, who was surrounded and fêted by the owner of Vaux, seemed, by the obstinate persistence of his gloomy thoughts, to do his utmost to recall Louis's attention, which the magnificence of the spectacle was already, in his opinion, too easily diverting. Suddenly, just as Louis was on the point of holding it out to Fouquet, he perceived in his hand the paper, which, as he believed, La Vallière had dropped at his feet as she hurried away. The still stronger magnet of love drew the Prince's attention towards the souvenir of his idol; and, by the brilliant light, which increased momentarily in beauty, and drew from the neighbouring villages loud exclamations of admiration, the King read the letter, which he supposed was a loving and tender epistle which La Vallière had destined for him. But as he read it, a death-like pallor stole over his face, and an expression of deep-seated wrath, illumined by the many-coloured fires which rose brightly and soaringly around the scene, produced a terrible spectacle, which every one would have shuddered at, could they only have read into his heart, which was torn by the most stormy and most bitter passions. There was no truce for him now, influenced as he was by jealousy and mad passion. From the very moment when the dark truth was revealed to him, every gentler feeling seemed to disappear; pity, kindness of consideration, the religion of hospitality, all were forgotten. In the bitter pang which wrung his heart, he, too weak to hide his sufferings, was almost on the point of uttering a cry of alarm, and calling his guards to gather round him. This letter which Colbert had thrown down at the King's feet, the reader has doubtless guessed, was the same that had disappeared with the porter Tony, at Fontainebleau, after the attempt which Fouquet had made upon La Vallière's heart. Fouquet saw the King's pallor, and was far from guessing the evil; Colbert saw the King's anger, and rejoiced inwardly at the approach of the storm. Fouquet's voice drew the Prince from his wrathful reverie.

"What is the matter, sire?" inquired the Surintendant, with an expression of graceful interest.

Louis made a violent effort over himself, as he replied, "Nothing."

"I am afraid your Majesty is suffering."

"I am suffering, and have already told you so, monsieur; but it is nothing."

And the King, without waiting for the termination of the fireworks, turned towards the château. Fouquet accompanied him, and the whole court followed after them, leaving the remains of the fireworks burning for their own amusement. The Surintendant endeavoured again to question Louis XIV., but could not succeed in obtaining a reply. He imagined there had been some misunderstanding between Louis and La Vallière in the park, which had resulted in a slight quarrel; and that the King, who was not ordinarily sulky by disposition, but completely absorbed by his passion for La Vallière, had taken a dislike to every one because his mistress had shown herself offended with him. This idea was sufficient to console him; he had even a friendly and kindly smile for the young King, when the latter wished him good night. This, however, was not all the King had to submit to; he was obliged to undergo the usual ceremony, which on that evening was marked by the closest adherence to the strictest etiquette. The next day was the one fixed for the departure; it was but proper that the guests should thank their host, and should show him a little attention in return for the expenditure of his twelve millions. The only remark, approaching to amiability, which the King could find to say to M. Fouquet, as he took leave of him, was in these words, "Monsieur Fouquet, you shall hear from me. Be good enough to desire M. d'Artagnan to come here."

And the blood of Louis XIII., who has* so profoundly dissimulated his feelings, boiled in his veins; and he was perfectly ready to get M. Fouquet's throat cut, with the same readiness, indeed, as his predecessor had caused the assassination of Marêchal d'Ancre;*and so he disguised the terrible resolution he had formed, beneath one of those royal smiles, which are the lightning flashes indicating *coups d'état.* Fouquet took the King's hand and kissed it; Louis shuddered throughout his whole frame, but allowed M. Fouquet to touch his hand with his lips. Five minutes afterwards, d'Artagnan, to whom the royal order had been communicated, entered Louis XIV.'s apartment. Aramis and Philippe were in theirs, still eagerly attentive, and still listening with all their ears. The King did not even give the captain of the musketeers time to approach his arm-chair, but ran forward to meet him. "Take care," he exclaimed, "that no one enters here."

"Very good, sire," replied the captain, whose glance had for a long time past analysed the ravages on the King's countenance. He gave the necessary orders at the door; but, returning to the King, he said, "Is there something fresh the matter, your Majesty?"

"How many men have you here?" inquired the King, without making any other reply to the question addressed to him.

"What for, sire?"

"How many men have you, I say?" repeated the King, stamping upon the ground with his foot.

"I have the musketeers."

"Well; and what others?"

"Twenty guards and thirteen Swiss."

"How many men will be required to——"

"To do what, sire," replied the musketeer, opening his large, calm eyes.

"To arrest M. Fouquet."

D'Artagnan fell back a step. "To arrest M. Fouquet!" he burst forth.

"Are you going to tell me that it is impossible!" exclaimed the King, with cold and vindictive passion.

"I never say that anything is impossible," replied d'Artagnan, wounded to the quick.

"Very well; do it, then."

D'Artagnan turned on his heel, and made his way towards the door; it was but a short distance, and he cleared it in half a dozen paces; when he reached it he suddenly paused, and said, "Your Majesty will forgive me, but, in order to effect this arrest, I should like written directions."

"For what purpose—and since when has the King's word been insufficient for you?"

"Because the word of a king, when it springs from a feeling of anger, may possibly change when the feeling changes."

"A truce to set phrases, monsieur; you have another thought besides that?"

"Oh, I, at least, have certain thoughts and ideas, which, unfortunately, others have not," d'Artagnan replied impertinently.

The King, in the tempest of his wrath, hesitated, and drew back in the face of d'Artagnan's frank courage, just as a horse crouches on its haunches under the strong hand of a bold and experienced rider. "What is your thought?" he exclaimed.

"This, sire," replied d'Artagnan: "you cause a man to be arrested when you are still under his roof; and passion is alone the cause of that. When your anger shall have passed away you will regret what you have done; and then I wish to be in a position to show you your signature. If that, however, should fail to be a reparation, it will at least show us that the King is wrong to lose his temper."

"Wrong to lose his temper!" cried the King, in a loud, passionate voice. "Did not my father, my grandfather too, before me, lose their temper at times, in Heaven's name?"

"The King your father and the King your grandfather never lost their temper except when under the protection of their own palace."

"The King is master wherever he may be."

"That is a flattering, complimentary phrase which cannot proceed from any one but M. Colbert; but it happens not to be the truth. The King is at home in every man's house when he has driven its owner out of it."

The King bit his lips, but said nothing.

"Can it be possible?" said d'Artagnan, "here is a man who is positively ruining himself in order to please you, and you wish to have him arrested! *Mordioux!* Sire, if my name were Fouquet, and people treated me in that manner, I would swallow at a single gulp all the fireworks and other things, and I would set fire to them, and blow myself and everybody else up to the sky. But it is all the same; it is your wish, and it shall be done."

"Go," said the King; "but have you men enough?"

"Do you suppose I am going to take a whole host to help me? Arrest M. Fouquet! why that is so easy that a very child might do it! It is like drinking a glass of bitters: one makes an ugly face, and that is all."

"If he defends himself?"

"He! not at all likely. Defend himself when such extreme harshness as you are going to practise makes the man a very martyr! Nay, I am sure that if he has a million of francs left, which I very much doubt, he would be willing enough to give it in order to have such a termination as this. But what does that matter? it shall be done at once."

"Stay," said the King; "do not make his arrest a public affair."

"That will be more difficult."

"Why so?"

"Because nothing is easier than to go up to M. Fouquet in the midst of a thousand enthusiastic guests who surround him, and say, 'In the King's name, I arrest you.' But to go up to him, to turn him first one way and then another, to drive him up into one of the corners of the chess-board in such a way that he cannot escape; to take him away from his guests, and to keep him a prisoner for you, without one of them, alas! having heard anything about it,—that indeed is a real difficulty, the greatest of all, in truth; and I hardly see how it is to be done."

"You had better say it is impossible, and you will have finished much sooner. Heaven help me, but I seem to be surrounded by people who prevent me from doing what I wish."

"I do not prevent your doing anything. Are you decided?"

"Take care of M. Fouquet, until I shall have made up my mind by to-morrow morning."

"That shall be done, sire."

"And return, when I rise in the morning, for further orders; and now leave me to myself."

"You do not even want M. Colbert, then?" said the musketeer, firing this last shot as he was leaving the room. The King started. With his whole mind fixed on the thought of revenge, he had forgotten the cause and substance of the offence.

"No, no one," he said; "no, no one here! Leave me!"

D'Artagnan quitted the room. The King closed the door with his own hands, and began to walk up and down his apartment at a furious pace, like a wounded bull in an arena, dragging after him the coloured streamers and iron darts. At last he began to take comfort in the expression of his violent feelings.

"Miserable wretch that he is! not only does he squander my finances, but with his ill-gotten plunder he corrupts secretaries, friends, generals, artists, and all, and tries to rob me of the one to whom I am most attached. And that is the reason why that perfidious girl so boldly took his part! Gratitude! and who can tell whether it was not a stronger feeling—love itself?" He gave himself up for a moment to his bitter reflections. "A satyr!" he thought, with that abhorrent hate with which young men regard those more advanced in life, who still think of love. "A man who has never found opposition or resistance in any one, who lavishes his gold and jewels in every direction, and who retains his staff of painters in order to take the portraits of his mistresses in the costume of goddesses." The King trembled with passion as he continued—"He pollutes and profanes everything that belongs to me! He destroys everything that is mine. He will be my death at last, I know. That man is too much for me; he is my mortal enemy, and he shall fall! I hate him—I hate him—I hate him!" and as he pronounced these words, he struck the arm of the chair in which he was sitting violently over and over again, and then rose like one in an epileptic fit. "To-morrow! to-morrow! oh, happy day!" he murmured, "when the sun rises, no other rival will that bright orb have but me. That man shall fall so low, that when people look at the utter ruin which my anger shall have wrought, they will be forced to confess at least that I am indeed greater than he." The King, who was incapable of mastering his emotions any longer, knocked over with a blow of his fist a small table placed close to his bedside, and in the bitterness of feeling from which he was suffering, almost weeping, and half-suffocated by his passion, he threw himself on his bed, dressed as he was, and bit the sheets in the extremity of his passion, trying to find repose of body at least there. The bed creaked beneath his weight, and with the exception of a few broken sounds, which escaped from his over-burdened chest, absolute silence soon reigned in the chamber of Morpheus.

45

HIGH TREASON

THE ungovernable fury which took possession of the King at the sight and at the perusal of Fouquet's letter to La Vallière by degrees subsided into a feeling of pain and extreme weariness. Youth, invigorated by health and lightness of spirits, and requiring that what it loses should be immediately restored—youth knows not those endless, sleepless nights, which enable us to realise the fable of the vulture unceasingly feeding on Prometheus. In instances where the man of middle life, in his acquired strength of will and purpose, and the old man, in his state of exhaustion, find an incessant augmentation of their bitter sorrow, a young man, surprised by the sudden appearance of a misfortune, weakens himself in sighs, and groans, and tears, in direct struggles with it, and is thereby far sooner overthrown by the inflexible enemy with whom he is engaged. Once overthrown, his struggles cease. Louis could not hold out more than a few minutes, at the end of which he had ceased to clench his hands, and to burn up with his looks the invisible objects of his hatred; he soon ceased to attack with his violent imprecations not M. Fouquet alone, but even La Vallière herself; from fury he subsided into despair, and from despair to prostration. After he had thrown himself for a few minutes to and fro convulsively on his bed, his nerveless arms fell quietly down; his head lay languidly on his pillow; his limbs, exhausted from his excessive emotions, still trembled occasionally, agitated from slight muscular contractions; and from his breast only faint and infrequent sighs still issued. Morpheus, the tutelary deity of the apartment, towards whom Louis raised his eyes, wearied by his anger and reddened by his tears, showered down upon him the sleep-inducing poppies with which his hands were filled; so that the King gently closed his eyes and fell asleep. Then it seemed to him, as it often happens in that first sleep, so light and gentle, which raises the body above the couch, the soul above the earth —it seemed to him, we say, as if the god Morpheus, painted on the ceiling, looked at him with eyes resembling human eyes; that something shone brightly, and moved to and fro in the dome above the sleeper; that the crowd of terrible dreams which thronged together in his brain, and which were interrupted for a moment, half revealed a human face, with a hand resting against the mouth, and in an attitude of deep and absorbed meditation. And strange enough, too, this man bore so wonderful a resemblance to the King himself, that Louis fancied he was looking at his own face reflected in a mirror; with the exception, however, that the face was saddened by a feeling of the profoundest pity. Then it seemed to him as if the dome gradually retired, escaping from his gaze, and that the figures and attributes painted by Lebrun became darker and darker as the distance became more and more remote. A gentle, easy movement, as regular as that by which a vessel plunges beneath the waves, had succeeded to the immovableness of the bed. Doubtless the King was dreaming, and in his dream the crown of gold, which fastened the curtains together, seemed to recede from his vision, just as the dome, to which it remained suspended, had done, so that the winged genius which, with both its hands, supported the crown, seemed, though vainly so, to call upon the King, who was fast disappearing from it. The bed still sank. Louis, with his eyes open, could not resist the deception of this cruel hallucination. At last, as the light of the royal chamber faded away into darkness and gloom, something cold, gloomy, and inexplicable in its nature seemed to infect the air. No paintings, nor gold, nor velvet hangings, were visible any longer, nothing but walls of a dull grey colour, which the increasing gloom made darker every moment. And yet the bed still continued to descend, and after a minute, which seemed in its duration almost an age to the King, it reached a stratum of air, black and still as death, and then it stopped. The King could no longer see the light in his room, except as from the bottom of a well we can see the light of day. "I am under the influence of a terrible dream," he thought. "It is time to awaken from it. Come! let me wake up."

Every one has experienced what the above remark conveys; there is hardly a person who, in the midst of a nightmare whose influence is suffocating, has not said to himself, by the help of that light which still burns in the brain when every human light is extinguished, "It is nothing but a dream after all." This was precisely what Louis XIV. said to himself; but when he said, "Come, come! wake up," he perceived that not only was he already awake, but still more, that he had his eyes open also; he then looked all round him. On his right hand and on his left two armed men stood silently, each wrapped in a huge cloak and the face covered with a mask; one of them held a small lamp in his hand, whose glimmering light revealed the saddest picture a King could look upon. Louis could not help saying to himself that his dream still lasted, and that all he had to do to cause it to disappear was to move his arms or to say something aloud; he darted from his bed, and found himself upon the damp moist ground. Then, addressing himself to the man who held the lamp in his hand, he said,—

"What is this, monsieur, and what is the meaning of this jest?"

"It is no jest," replied in a deep voice the masked figure that held the lantern.

"Do you belong to M. Fouquet?" inquired the King, greatly astonished at his situation.

"It matters very little to whom we belong," said the phantom; "we are your masters now; that is sufficient."

The King, more impatient than intimidated, turned to the other masked figure. "If this is a comedy," he said, "you will tell M. Fouquet that I find it unseemly and improper, and that I desire it should cease."

The second masked person to whom the King had addressed himself was a man of huge stature and vast circumference. He held himself erect and motionless as a block of marble. "Well," added the King, stamping his foot, "you do not answer!"

"We do not answer you, my good monsieur," said the giant in a stentorian voice, "because there is nothing to answer."

"At least tell me what you want?" exclaimed Louis, folding his arms with a passionate gesture.

"You will know by-and-by," replied the man who held the lamp.

"In the meantime tell me where I am."

"Look."

Louis looked all around him; but, by the light of the lamp which the masked figure raised for the purpose, he could perceive nothing but the damp walls which glistened here and there with the slimy traces of the snail. "Oh! oh! a dungeon," said the King.

"No, a subterranean passage."

"Which leads——"

"Will you be good enough to follow us?"

"I shall not stir from hence!" cried the King.

"If you are obstinate, my dear young friend," replied the taller and stouter of the two, "I will lift you up in my arms, will roll you up in a cloak, and if you are stifled there, why, so much the worse for you."

And as he said this he disengaged from beneath his cloak a hand of which Milo of Crotona* would have envied him the possession, on the day when he had that unhappy idea of rending his last oak. The King dreaded violence, for he could well believe that the two men into whose power he had fallen had not gone so far with any idea of drawing back, and that they would consequently be ready to proceed to extremities, if necessary. He shook his head, and said: "It seems I have fallen into the hands of a couple of assassins. Move on, then."

Neither of the men answered a word to this remark. The one who carried the lantern walked first, and the King followed him, while the second masked figure closed the procession. In this manner they passed along a winding gallery of some length, with as many staircases leading out of it as are to be found in the mysterious and gloomy palaces of Ann Radcliff's creation.* All these windings and turnings, during which the King heard the sound of falling water over his head, ended at last in a long corridor closed by an iron door. The figure with the lamp opened the door with one of the keys he wore suspended at his girdle, where, during the whole of the time, the King had heard them rattle. As soon as the door was opened and admitted the air, Louis recognised the balmy odours which are exhaled by the trees after a hot summer's day. He paused, hesitatingly, for a moment or two; but his huge companion who followed him thrust him out of the subterranean passage.

"Another blow," said the King, turning towards the one who had just had the audacity to touch his sovereign; "what do you intend to do with the King of France?"

"Try to forget that word," replied the man with the lamp, in a tone which as little admitted of a reply as one of the famous decrees of Minos.*

"You deserve to be broken on the wheel for the word you have just made use of," said the giant, as he extinguished the lamp his companion handed to him; "but the King is too kind-hearted."

Louis, at the threat, made so sudden a movement, that it seemed as if he meditated flight; but the giant's hand was in a moment placed on his shoulder, and fixed him motionless where he stood. "But tell me, at least, where we are going," said the King.

"Come," replied the former of the two men, with a kind of respect in his manner, and leading his prisoner towards a carriage which seemed to be in waiting.

The carriage was completely concealed amid the trees. Two horses, with their feet fettered, were fastened by a halter to the lower branches of a large oak.

"Get in," said the same man, opening the carriage door, and letting down the step. The King obeyed, seated himself at the back of the carriage, the padded door of which was shut and locked immediately upon him and his guide. As for the giant, he cut the fastenings by which the horses were bound, harnessed them himself, and mounted on the box of the carriage, which was unoccupied. The carriage set off immediately at a quick trot, turned into the road to Paris, and in the forest of Sénart found a relay of horses fastened to trees in the same manner as the first horses had been, and without a postilion. The man on the box changed the horses, and continued to follow the road towards Paris with the same rapidity, and entered the city about three o'clock in the morning. The carriage proceeded along the Faubourg Saint-Antoine, and, after having called out to the sentinel "by the King's order," the driver conducted the horses into the circular enclosure of the Bastille, looking out upon the courtyard, called La Cour du Gouvernement. There the horses drew up, reeking with sweat, at the flight of steps, and a sergeant of the guard ran forward. "Go and wake the governor," said the coachman, in a voice of thunder.

With the exception of this voice, which might have been heard at the entrance of the Faubourg Saint-Antoine, everything remained as calm in the carriage as in the prison. Ten minutes afterwards, M. de Baisemeaux appeared in his dressing-gown on the threshold of the door. "What is the matter now?" he asked, "and whom have you brought me there?"

The man with the lantern opened the carriage door, and said two or three words to the one who acted as driver, who immedi-

ately got down from his seat, took up a short musk
kept under his feet, and placed its muzzle on the prison

"And fire at once if he speaks!" added aloud the n.
alighted from the carriage.

"Very good!" replied his companion, without any
remark.

With this recommendation, the person who had accompanied
the King in the carriage ascended the flight of steps, at the top
of which the governor was awaiting him. "Monsieur d'Herblay!"
said the latter.

"Hush!" said Aramis. "Let us go into your room."

"Good Heavens! what brings you here at this hour?"

"A mistake, my dear Monsieur de Baisemeaux," Aramis replied
quietly. "It appears that you were quite right the other day."

"What about?" inquired the governor.

"About the order of release, my dear friend."

"Tell me what you mean, monsieur—no, monseigneur," said
the governor, almost suffocated by surprise and terror.

"It is a very simple affair; you remember, dear M. de Baisemeaux, that an order of release was sent to you."

"Yes, for Marchiali."

"Very good! we both thought that it was for Marchiali."

"Certainly; you will recollect, however, that I would not
believe it, but that you compelled me."

"Oh! Baisemeaux, my good fellow, what a word to make use
of!—strongly recommended, that was all."

"Strongly recommended, yes; strongly recommended to give
him up to you: and that you carried him off with you in your
carriage."

"Well, my dear Monsieur de Baisemeaux, it was a mistake; it
was discovered at the ministry, so that I now bring you an order
from the King to set at liberty—Seldon, that poor Scotch fellow,
you know."

"Seldon! are you sure this time?"

"Well, read it yourself," added Aramis, handing him the order.

"Why," said Baisemeaux, "this order is the very same that has
already passed through my hands."

"Indeed!"

"It is the very one I assured you I saw the other evening.
Parbleu! I recognise it by the blot of ink."

"I do not know whether it is that or not; but all I know is
that I bring it for you."

"But, then, about the other?"

"What other?"

"Marchiali?"

"I have got him here with me."

"But that is not enough for me. I require a new order to take him back again."

"Don't talk such nonsense, my dear Baisemeaux; you talk like a child! Where is the order you received respecting Marchiali?"

Baisemeaux ran to his iron chest and took it out. Aramis seized hold of it, coolly tore it in four pieces, held them to the lamp, and burnt them. "Good Heaven! what are you doing?" exclaimed Baisemeaux, in an extremity of terror.

"Look at your position a little quietly, my dear governor," said Aramis, with his imperturbable self-possession, "and you will see how very simple the whole affair is. You no longer possess any order justifying Marchiali's release."

"I am a lost man!"

"Far from it, my good fellow, since I have brought Marchiali back to you, and it is just the same as if he had never left."

"Ah!" said the governor, completely overcome by terror.

"Plain enough, you see; and you will go and shut him up immediately."

"I should think so, indeed."

"And you will hand over this Seldon to me, whose liberation is authorised by this order. Do you understand?"

"I—I——"

"You do understand, I see," said Aramis. "Very good."

Baisemeaux clasped his hands together. "But why, at all events, after having taken Marchiali away from me, do you bring him back again?" cried the unhappy governor, in a paroxysm of terror and completely dumbfounded.

"For a friend such as you are," said Aramis,—"for so devoted a servant, I have no secrets;" and he put his mouth close to Baisemeaux's ear, as he said in a low tone of voice, "you know the resemblance between that unfortunate fellow, and——"

"And the King?—yes!"

"Very good; the very first use that Marchiali made of his liberty was to persist—— Can you guess what?"

"How is it likely I should guess?"

"To persist in saying that he was the King of France; to dress himself up in clothes like those of the King; and then pretend to assume that he was the King himself."

"Gracious Heavens!"

"That is the reason why I have brought him back again, my dear friend. He is mad, and lets every one see how mad he is."

"What is to be done, then?"

"That is very simple; let no one hold any communication with him. You understand, that when his peculiar style of madness came to the King's ears, the King, who had pitied his terrible affliction, and saw how his kindness of heart had been repaid by such black ingratitude, became perfectly furious; so that, now—and remember this very distinctly, dear Monsieur de Baisemeaux, for it concerns you most closely—so that there is now, I repeat, sentence of death pronounced against all those who may allow him to communicate with any one else but me, or the King himself. You understand, Baisemeaux, sentence of death!"

"You need not ask me whether I understand."

"And now let us go down and conduct this poor devil back to his dungeon again, unless you prefer he should come up here."

"What would be the good of that?"

"It would be better, perhaps, to enter his name in the prison-book at once."

"Of course; certainly; not a doubt of it."

"In that case have him up."

Baisemeaux ordered the drums to be beaten, and the bells to be rung, as a warning to every one to retire, in order to avoid meeting a prisoner, about whom it was desired to observe a certain mystery. Then, when the passages were free, he went to take the prisoner from the carriage, at whose breast, Porthos, faithful to the directions which had been given him, still kept his musket levelled. "Ah! is that you, miserable wretch?" cried the governor, as soon as he perceived the King. "Very good, very good." And immediately, making the King get out of the carriage, he led him, still accompanied by Porthos, who had not taken off his mask, and Aramis, who again resumed his, up the stairs, to the second Bertaudière, and opened the door of the room in which Philippe for six long years had bemoaned his existence. The King entered into the cell without pronouncing a single word; he was pale and haggard. Baisemeaux shut the door upon him, turned the key twice in the lock, and then returned to Aramis. "It is quite true," he said in a low tone, "that he has a rather strong resemblance to the King; but still, less so than you said."

"So that," said Aramis, "you would not have been deceived by the substitution of the one for the other?"

"What a question!"

"You are a most valuable fellow, Baisemeaux," said Aramis; "and now, set Seldon free."

"Oh, yes. I was going to forget that. I will go and give orders at once."

"Bah! to-morrow will be time enough."

" 'To-morrow!'—oh, no. This very minute."

"Well; go off to your own affairs, I shall go away to mine. But it is quite understood, is it not?"

"What is quite understood?"

"That no one is to enter the prisoner's cell, except with an order from the King; an order which I will myself bring."

"Quite so. *Adieu*, monseigneur."

Aramis turned to his companion. "Now, Porthos, my good fellow, back again to Vaux, and as fast as possible."

"A man is light and easy enough, when he has faithfully served his King; and, in serving him, saved his country," said Porthos. "The horses will be as light as if they had nothing at all behind them. So let us be off." And the carriage, lightened of a prisoner, who might well be—as he in fact was—very heavy for Aramis, passed across the drawbridge of the Bastille, which was raised again immediately behind it.

46

A NIGHT AT THE BASTILLE

PAIN, anguish, and suffering in human life are always in proportion to the strength with which a man is endowed. We will not pretend to say that Heaven always apportions to a man's capability of endurance the anguish with which he afflicts him; such, indeed, would not be exact, since Heaven permits the existence of death, which is, sometimes, the only refuge open to those who are too closely pressed—too bitterly afflicted, as far as the body is concerned. Suffering is in proportion to the strength which has been accorded to a person; in other words, the weak suffer more, where the trial is the same, than the strong. And, what are the elementary principles, we may ask, which compose human strength? Is it not —more than anything else—exercise, habit, experience? We shall not even take the trouble to demonstrate that, for it is an axiom in morals, as in physics. When the young King, stupefied and crushed in every sense and feeling, found himself led to a cell in the Bastille, he fancied that death itself is but a sleep; that it, too, has its dreams as well; that the bed had broken through the flooring of his room at Vaux; that death had resulted from the occurrence; and that, still carrying out his dream, as the King, Louis XIV., now no longer living, was dreaming one of those horrors, impossible to realise in life, which is termed dethronement, imprisonment, and insult towards a sovereign, who formerly wielded unlimited power. To be present at—an actual witness, too—of this bitterness of death; to float indecisively, in an incomprehensible mystery, between resemblance and reality; to hear everything, to see everything, without interfering with a single detail of agonising suffering, was—so the King thought within himself—a torture far more terrible, since it might last for ever. "Is this what is termed eternity—hell?" he murmured, at the moment the door closed upon him, which Baisemeaux had himself shut. He did not even look round him; and in the room, leaning with his back against the wall, he allowed himself to be carried away by the terrible supposition that he was already dead, as he closed his eyes in order to avoid looking upon something even worse still. "How can I have died?" he said to himself, sick with terror. "The bed might have been let down by some artificial means? But no! I do not remember to have received any contusion, nor any shock either. Would they not rather have poisoned me at one of my meals, or with the fumes of wax, as they did my ancestress, Jeanne d'Albret?" Suddenly, the chill of the dungeon seemed to fall like a cloak upon Louis's shoulders. "I have seen," he said, "my father lying dead upon his funeral couch, in his regal robes. That pale face, so calm and worn, those hands, once so skilful, lying nerveless by his side; those limbs stiffened by the icy grasp of death; nothing there betokened a sleep peopled with dreams. And yet, how numerous were the dreams which Heaven might have sent that royal corpse—him, whom so many others had preceded, hurried away by him into eternal death! No, that King was still the King; he was enthroned still upon that funeral couch, as upon a velvet arm-chair; he had not abdicated aught of his majesty. God, who had not punished him, cannot, will not punish me, who have done nothing." A strange sound attracted the young man's attention. He looked round him, and saw on the mantel-shelf, just below an enormous crucifix, coarsely painted in fresco on the wall, a rat of enormous size engaged in nibbling a piece of dry bread, but fixing, all the time, an intelligent and inquiring look upon the new occupant of the cell. The King could not resist a sudden impulse of fear and disgust; he moved back towards the door uttering a loud cry; and, as if he had but needed this cry, which escaped from his breast almost unconsciously, to recognise himself, Louis knew that he was alive and in full possession of his natural senses. "A prisoner!" he cried. "I—I, a prisoner!" He looked round him for a bell to summon some one to him. "There are no bells at the Bastille," he said, "and it is in the Bastille I am imprisoned. In what way can I have been made a prisoner? It must have been owing to a conspiracy of M. Fouquet. I have been drawn to Vaux, as into a snare. M. Fouquet cannot be acting alone in this affair. His agent——. That voice I but just now heard was M. d'Herblay's; I recognised it. Colbert was right, then. But what is Fouquet's object? To reign in my place and stead?—Impossible. Yet, who knows!" thought the King, relapsing into gloom again. "Perhaps my brother, the Duc d'Orleans, is doing that which my uncle wished to do during the whole of his life against my father. But the Queen?—My mother, too? And La Vallière? Oh! La Vallière, she will have been abandoned to Madame. Dear, dear girl! Yes, it is—it must be so. They must have shut her up, as they have me. We are separated for ever!" And at this idea of separation, the poor lover burst into a flood of tears, and sobs, and groans.

"There is a governor in this place," the King continued, in a fury of passion; "I will speak to him, I will summon him to me."

He called, but no voice replied to his. He seized hold of his chair, and hurled it against the massive oaken door. The wood resounded against the door, and awakened many a mournful echo in the profound depths of the staircase: but from a human creature, not one.

This was a fresh proof for the King of the slight regard in which he was held at the Bastille. Therefore, when his first fit of anger had passed away, having remarked a barred window, through which there passed a stream of light, lozenge-shaped, which must be, he knew, the bright orb of approaching day, Louis began to call out, at first gently enough, then louder and louder still; but no one replied to him. Twenty other attempts which he made, one after another, obtained no other or better success. His blood began to boil within him, and mount to his head. His nature was such, that, accustomed to command, he trembled at the idea of disobedience. By degrees, his anger increased more and more. The prisoner broke the chair, which was too heavy for him to lift, and made use of it as a battering ram to strike against the door. He struck so loudly, and so repeatedly, that the perspiration soon began to pour down his face. The sound became tremendous and continuous; some stifled, smothered cries replied in different directions. This sound produced a strange effect upon the King. He paused to listen to it; it was the voice of the prisoners, formerly his victims, now his companions. The voices ascended like vapours through the thick ceilings and the massive walls, and rose in accusation against the author of this noise, as doubtless their sighs and tears accused, in whispered tones, the author of their captivity. After having deprived so many people of their liberty, the King came among them to rob them of their rest. This idea almost drove him mad; it redoubled his strength, or rather his will, bent upon obtaining some information, or a conclusion to the affair. With a portion of the broken chair he recommenced the noise. At the end of an hour, Louis heard something in the corridor, behind the door of his cell, and a violent blow, which was returned upon the door itself, made him cease his own.

"Are you mad?" said a rude brutal voice. "What is the matter with you this morning?"

"This morning!" thought the King; but he said aloud, politely, "Monsieur, are you the governor of the Bastille?"

"My good fellow, your head is out of sorts," replied the voice; "but that is no reason why you should make such a terrible disturbance. Be quiet; *mordieu!*"

"Are you the governor?" the King inquired again.

He heard a door on the corridor close; the jailer had just left, not even condescending to reply a single word. When the King had assured himself of this departure, his fury knew no longer any bounds. As agile as a tiger, he leaped from the table to the window, and struck the iron bars with all his might. He broke a pane of glass, the pieces of which fell clanking into the courtyard below. He shouted with increasing hoarseness, "The governor, the governor!" This excess lasted fully an hour, during which time he was in a burning fever. With his hair in disorder and matted on his forehead, his dress torn and whitened, his linen in shreds, the King never rested until his strength was utterly exhausted, and it was not until then that he clearly understood the pitiless thickness of the walls, the impenetrable nature of the cement, invincible to all other influence but that of time, and possessed of no other weapon but despair. He leaned his forehead against the door, and let the feverish throbbings of his heart calm by degrees; it seemed as if one single additional pulsation would have made it burst.

"A moment will come when the food which is given to the prisoners will be brought to me. I shall then see some one, I shall speak to him, and get an answer."

And the King tried to remember at what hour the first repast of the prisoners was served at the Bastille; he was ignorant even of this detail. The feeling of remorse at this remembrance smote him like the keen thrust of a dagger, that he should have lived for five-and-twenty years a King, and in the enjoyment of every happiness, without having bestowed a moment's thought on the misery of those who had been unjustly deprived of their liberty. The King blushed from very shame. He felt that Heaven, in permitting this fearful humiliation, did no more than render to the man the same torture as was inflicted by that man upon so many others. Nothing could be more efficacious for reawakening his mind to religious influences than the prostration of his heart, and mind, and soul beneath the feelings of such acute wretchedness. But Louis dared not even kneel in prayer to God to entreat Him to terminate his bitter trial.

"Heaven is right," he said; "Heaven acts wisely, it would be cowardly to pray to Heaven for that which I have so often refused to my own fellow creatures."

He had reached this stage of his reflections, that is, of his agony of mind, when a similar noise was again heard behind his door, followed this time by the sound of the key in the lock, and of the bolts being withdrawn from their staples. The King bounded forward to be nearer to the person who was about to enter, but suddenly reflecting that it was a movement unworthy of a sovereign, he paused, assumed a noble and calm expression, which for him was easy enough, and waited with his back turned towards the window, in order, to some extent, to conceal his agitation from the eyes of the person who was about entering. It was only a jailer with a basket of provisions. The King looked at the man with restless anxiety, and waited until he spoke.

"Ah!" said the latter, "you have broken your chair. I said you had done so. Why, you must have become quite mad."

"Monsieur," said the King, "be careful what you say; it will be a very serious affair for you."

The jailer placed the basket on the table, and looked at his prisoner steadily. "What do you say?" he said.

"Desire the governor to come to me," added the King, in accents full of dignity.

"Come, my boy," said the turnkey, "you have always been very quiet and reasonable, but you are getting vicious, it seems, and I wish you to know it in time. You have broken your chair, and made a great disturbance; that is an offence punishable by imprisonment in one of the lower dungeons. Promise me not to begin over again, and I will not say a word about it to the governor."

"I wish to see the governor," replied the King, still controlling his passion.

"He will send you off to one of the dungeons, I tell you, so take care."

"I insist upon it, do you hear?"

"Ah! ah! your eyes are becoming wild again. Very good! I shall take away your knife."

And the jailer did what he said, quitted the prisoner, and closed the door, leaving the King more astounded, more wretched, and more isolated than ever. It was useless, though he tried it, to make the same noise again on his door, and equally useless that he threw the plates and dishes out of the window; not a single sound was heard in answer. Two hours afterwards he could not be recognised as a king, a gentleman, a man, a human being; he might, rather, be called a madman, tearing the door with his nails, trying to tear up the flooring of his cell, and uttering such wild and fearful cries that the old Bastille seemed to tremble to its very foundations for having revolted against its master. As for the governor, the jailer did not even think of disturbing him; the turnkeys and the sentinels had reported the occurrence to him, but what was the good of it? were not these madmen common enough in the fortress? and were not the walls still stronger than they? M. de Baisemeaux, thoroughly impressed with what Aramis had told him, and in perfect conformity with the King's order, hoped only that one thing might happen: namely, that the madman, Marchiali, might be mad enough to hang himself to the canopy of his bed, or to one of the bars of the window. In fact, the prisoner was anything but a profitable investment for M. Baisemeaux, and became more annoying than agreeable to him. These complications of Seldon and Marchiali—the complications, first of setting at liberty and then imprisoning again, the complications arising from the strong likeness in question—had at last found a very proper *dénouement*. Baisemeaux even thought he had remarked that M. d'Herblay himself was not altogether dissatisfied at it.

"And then, really," said Baisemeaux to his next in command, "an ordinary prisoner is already unhappy enough in being a prisoner; he suffers quite enough, indeed, to induce one to hope, charitably enough, that his death may not be far distant. With still greater reason, then, when the prisoner has gone mad, and might bite and make a terrible disturbance in the Bastille: why, in that case, it is not simply an act of mere charity to wish him dead; it would be almost a good and even commendable action quietly to put him out of his misery."

And the good-natured governor thereupon sat down to his late breakfast.

47

THE SHADOW OF M. FOUQUET

D'ARTAGNAN, still confused and oppressed by the conversation he had just had with the King, could not resist asking himself if he were really in possession of his senses; if he were really and truly at Vaux; if he, d'Artagnan, were really the captain of the musketeers and M. Fouquet the owner of the château in which Louis XIV. was at that moment partaking of his hospitality. These reflections were not those of a drunken man, although everything was in prodigal profusion at Vaux, and the Surintendant's wines had met with a distinguished reception at the fête. The Gascon, however, was a man of calm self-possession; and no sooner did he touch his bright steel blade, than he knew how to adopt morally, the cold, keen weapon as his guide of action. "Well," he said, as he quitted the royal apartment, "I seem now to be mixed up historically with the destinies of the King and of the minister; it will be written, that M. d'Artagnan, a younger son of a Gascon family, placed his hand on the shoulder of M. Nicolas Fouquet, the Surintendant of the Finances of France. My descendants, if I have any, will flatter themselves with the distinction which this arrest will confer, just as the members of the De Luynes family have done with regard to the estates of the poor Maréchal d'Ancre.* But the question is, to execute the King's directions in a proper manner. Any man would know how to say to M. Fouquet, 'Your sword, monsieur,' but it is not every one who would be able to take care of M. Fouquet without others knowing anything about it. How am I to manage, then, so that M. le Surintendant pass from the height of favour to the direst disgrace; that Vaux be turned into a dungeon for him, that, after having been steeped to his lips, as it were, in all the perfumes and incense of Assuerus,* he is transferred to the gallows of Haman; in other words of Euguerrand de Marigny?"*And at this reflection, d'Artagnan's brow became clouded with perplexity. The musketeer had certain scruples on the matter, it must be admitted. To deliver up to death (for not a doubt existed that Louis hated Fouquet mortally) the man who had just shown himself so delightful and charming a host in every way, was a real case of conscience. "It almost seems," said d'Artagnan to himself, "that if I am not a poor, mean, miserable fellow, I should let M. Fouquet know the opinion the King has about him. Yet, if I betray my master's secrets, I shall be a false-hearted, treacherous knave; a traitor, too—a crime provided for and punishable by military laws; so much so, indeed, that twenty times, in former days when wars were rife, I have seen many a miserable fellow strung up to a tree for doing, in a small degree, what my scruples counsel me to do to a greater extent now. No; I think that a man of true readiness of grit ought to get out of this difficulty with more skill than that. And now, let us admit that I do possess a little readiness of invention; it is not at all certain, though; for, after having for forty years absorbed so large a quantity, I shall be lucky if there were to be a pistole's-worth left." D'Artagnan buried his head in his hands, tore his moustache in sheer vexation, and added, "What can be the reason of M. Fouquet's disgrace? There seem to me to be three good ones: the first, because M. Colbert doesn't like him; the second, because he wished to fall in love with Mademoiselle de la Vallière; and lastly, because the King likes M. Colbert and loves Mademoiselle de la Vallière. Oh! he is a lost man! But shall I put my foot on his neck—I, of all men, when he is falling a prey to the intrigues of a set of women and clerks? For shame! If he be dangerous, I will lay him low enough; if, however, he be only persecuted, I will look on. I have come to such a decisive determination that neither King nor living man shall change my opinion. If Athos were here, he would do as I have done. Therefore, instead of going cold-bloodedly up to M. Fouquet, and arresting him off-hand and shutting him up altogether, I will try to conduct myself like a man who understands what good manners are. People will talk about it, of course, but they shall talk well of it, I am determined." And d'Artagnan, drawing by a gesture peculiar to himself his shoulder-belt over his shoulder, went straight off to M. Fouquet, who, after he had taken leave of his guests, was preparing to retire for the night and to sleep tranquilly after the triumphs of the day. The air was still perfumed or infected, whichever way it may be considered, with the odour of the fireworks. The wax-lights were dying away in their sockets, the flowers fell unfastened from the garlands, the groups of dancers and courtiers were separating in the saloons. Surrounded by his friends, who complimented him and received his flattering remarks in return, the Surintendant half-closed his wearied eyes. He longed for rest and quiet; he sank upon the bed of laurels which had been heaped up for him for so many days past; it might almost have been said that he seemed bowed beneath the weight of the new debts which he had incurred for the purpose of giving the greatest possible honour to this fête. Fouquet had just retired to his room, still smiling, but more than half dead. He could listen to nothing more, he could hardly keep his eyes open; his bed seemed to possess a fascination and irresistible attraction for him. The god Morpheus, the presiding deity of the dome painted by Lebrun, had extended his influence over the adjoining rooms, and showered down his sleep-inducing poppies upon the master of the house. Fouquet, almost entirely alone, was being assisted by his *valet-de-chambre* to undress, when M. d'Artagnan appeared at the entrance of the room. D'Artagnan had never been able to succeed in making himself common at the court; and notwithstanding he was seen everywhere and on all occasions, he never failed to produce an effect wherever and whenever he made his appearance. Such is the happy privilege of certain natures, which in that respect resemble either thunder or lightning; every one recognises them; but their appearance never fails to arouse surprise and astonishment, and whenever they occur the impression is always left that the last was the loudest or brightest and most violent. "What! M. d'Artagnan?" said Fouquet, who had already taken his right arm out of the sleeve of his doublet.

"At your service," replied the musketeer.

"Come in, my dear M. d'Artagnan."

"Thank you."

"Have you come to criticise the fête? You are ingenious enough in your criticisms, I know."

"By no means."

"Are not your men looked after properly?"

"In every way."

"You are not comfortably lodged, perhaps?"

"Nothing could be better."

"In that case I have to thank you for being so amiably disposed, and I must not fail to express my obligations to you for all your flattering kindness."

These words were as much as to say, "My dear d'Artagnan, pray go to bed, since you have a bed to lie down on, and let me do the same."

D'Artagnan did not seem to understand it.

"Are you going to bed already?" he said to the Surintendant.

"Yes; have you anything to say to me?"

"Nothing, monsieur, nothing at all. You sleep in this room, then?"

"Yes; as you see."

"You have given a most charming fête to the King."

"Do you think so?"

"Oh! beautiful!"

"Is the King pleased?"

"Enchanted."

"Did he desire you to say as much to me?"

"He would not choose so unworthy a messenger, monseigneur."

"You do not do yourself justice, Monsieur d'Artagnan."

"Is that your bed, there?"

"Yes; but why do you ask? Are you not satisfied with your own?"

"May I speak frankly to you?'

"Most assuredly."

"Well, then, I am not."

Fouquet started, and then replied, "Will you take my room, Monsieur d'Artagnan?"

"What! deprive you of it, monseigneur? Never!"

"What am I to do then?"

"Allow me to share yours with you."

Fouquet looked at the musketeer fixedly. "Ah! ah!" he said, "you have just left the King."

"I have, monseigneur."

"And the King wishes you to pass the night in my room?"

"Monseigneur——"

"Very well, Monsieur d'Artagnan, very well. You are the master here."

"I assure you, monseigneur, that I do not wish to abuse——"

Fouquet turned to his valet, and said, "Leave us." When the man had left, he said to d'Artagnan, "You have something to say to me?"

"I?"

"A man of your superior intelligence cannot have come to talk with a man like myself, at such an hour as the present, without grave motives."

"Do not interrogate me."

"On the contrary. What do you want with me?"

"Nothing more than the pleasure of your society."

"Come into the garden, then," said the Surintendant suddenly, "or into the park."

"No," replied the musketeer hastily, "no."

"Why?"

"The fresh air——"

"Come, admit at once that you arrest me," said the Surintendant to the captain.

"Never!" said the latter.

"You intend to look after me, then?"

"Yes, monseigneur, I do, upon my honour."

"Upon your honour!—ah! that is quite another thing! so I am to be arrested in my own house."

"Do not say such a thing."

"On the contrary, I will proclaim it aloud."

"If you do, I shall be compelled to request you to be silent."

"Very good! Violence towards me, and in my own house, too!"

"We do not seem to understand each other at all. Stay a moment; there is a chess-board there; we will have a game, if you have no objection."

"Monsieur d'Artagnan, I am in disgrace, then?"

"Not at all; but——"

"I am prohibited, I suppose, from withdrawing from your sight."

"I do not understand a word you are saying, monseigneur; and if you wish me to withdraw, tell me so."

"My dear Monsieur d'Artagnan, your mode of action is enough to drive me mad; I was almost sinking for want of sleep, but you have completely awakened me."

"I shall never forgive myself, I am sure; and if you wish to reconcile me with myself, why, go to sleep in your bed in my presence; I shall be delighted at it."

"I am under surveillance, I see."

"I will leave the room if you say such a thing as that."

"You are beyond my comprehension."

"Good-night, monseigneur," said d'Artagnan, as he pretended to withdraw.

Fouquet ran after him. "I will not lie down," he said. "Seriously, and since you refuse to treat me as a man, and since you finesse with me, I will try to set you at bay, as a hunter does a wild boar."

"Bah!" cried d'Artagnan, pretending to smile.

"I shall order my horses, and set off for Paris," said Fouquet, sounding the heart of the captain of the musketeers.

"If that be the case, monseigneur, it is very different."

"You will arrest me, then?"

"No, but I shall go with you."

"That is quite sufficient, Monsieur d'Artagnan," returned Fouquet, in a cold tone of voice. "It is not idly that you have acquired your reputation as a man of intelligence and full of resources; but with me that is quite superfluous. Let us two come to the point. Grant me a service. Why do you arrest me? What have I done?"

"Oh! I know nothing about what you may have done; but I do not arrest you—this evening, at least!"

"This evening!" said Fouquet, turning pale, "but to-morrow?"

"It is not to-morrow just yet, monseigneur. Who can ever answer for the morrow?"

"Quick, quick, captain! let me speak to M. d'Herblay."

"Alas! that is quite impossible, monseigneur. I have strict orders to see that you hold no communication with any one."

"With M. d'Herblay, captain—with your friend!"

"Monseigneur, is M. d'Herblay the only person with whom you ought to be prevented from holding any communication?"

Fouquet coloured, and then, assuming an air of resignation, he said: "You are right, monsieur; you have taught me a lesson that I ought not to have provoked. A fallen man cannot assert his right to anything, even from those whose fortunes he may have made; for a still greater reason, he cannot claim anything from those to whom he may never have had the happiness of doing a service."

"Monseigneur!"

"It is perfectly true, Monsieur d'Artagnan; you have always acted in the most admirable manner towards me—in such a manner, indeed, as most becomes the man who is destined to arrest me. You, at least, have never asked me anything."

"Monseigneur," replied the Gascon, touched by his eloquent and noble tone of grief, "will you—I ask it as a favour—pledge me your word, as a man of honour, that you will not leave this room?"

"What is the use of it, dear Monsieur d'Artagnan, since you keep watch and ward over me? Do you suppose that I should struggle against the most valiant sword in the kingdom?"

"It is not that at all, monseigneur; but that I am going to look for M. d'Herblay and, consequently, to leave you alone."

Fouquet uttered a cry of delight and surprise.

"To look for M. d'Herblay! to leave me alone!" he exclaimed, clasping his hands together.

"Which is M. d'Herblay's room? the blue room, is it not?"

"Yes, my friend, yes."

"Your friend! thank you for that word, monseigneur; you confer it upon me to-day, at least, even if you have never done so before."

"Ah! you have saved me."

"It will take me a good ten minutes to go from hence to the blue room and to return?" said d'Artagnan.

"Nearly so."

"And then to wake Aramis, who sleeps very soundly when he is asleep, I put that down at another five minutes, making a total of fifteen minutes' absence. And now, monseigneur, give me your word that you will not in any way attempt to make your escape, and that when I return, I shall find you here again."

"I give it you, monsieur," replied Fouquet, with an expression of the warmest and deepest gratitude.

D'Artagnan disappeared. Fouquet looked at him as he quitted the room, waited with a feverish impatience until the door was closed behind him and, as soon as it was shut, flew to his keys, opened two or three secret doors concealed in various articles of furniture in the room, looked vainly for certain papers, which doubtless he had left at Saint-Mandé, and which he seemed to regret not having found in them; then hurriedly seizing hold of letters, contracts, paper writings, he heaped them up into a pile, which he burnt in the extremest haste upon the marble hearth of the fireplace, not even taking time to draw from the interior of it the vases and pots of flowers with which it was filled. As soon as he had finished, like a man who has just escaped an imminent danger, and whose strength abandons him as soon as the danger is past, he sank down, completely overcome, on a couch. When d'Artagnan returned, he found Fouquet in the same position; the worthy musketeer had not the slightest doubt that Fouquet, having given his word, would not even think of failing to keep it, but he had thought it most likely that Fouquet would turn his (d'Artagnan's) absence to the best advantage in getting rid of all the papers, memorandums, and contracts, which might possibly render his position, which was even now serious enough, still more dangerous than ever. And so, lifting up his head like a dog who gains a scent, he perceived a certain odour resembling smoke which he fully relied upon finding in the atmosphere and, having found it, he made a movement of his head in token of satisfaction. When d'Artagnan had entered, Fouquet had, on his side, raised his head, and not one of d'Artagnan's movements had escaped him. And then the looks of the two men met, and they both saw that they had understood each other without exchanging a syllable.

"Well," asked Fouquet, the first to speak, "and M. d'Herblay?"

"Upon my word, monseigneur," replied d'Artagnan, "M. d'Herblay must be desperately fond of walks by night, and composing verses by moonlight in the park of Vaux—with some of your poets, in all probability—for he is not in his own room."

"What! not in his own room?" cried Fouquet, whose last hope had thus escaped him; for unless he could ascertain in what way the Bishop of Vannes could assist him, he perfectly well knew that in reality he could not expect assistance from anyone but him.

"Or indeed," continued d'Artagnan, "if he is in his own room, he has very good reasons for not answering."

"But surely you did not call him in such a manner that he could have heard you?"

"You can hardly suppose, monseigneur, that having already exceeded my orders, which forbade me leaving you a single moment—you can hardly suppose, I say, that I should have been mad enough to rouse the whole house and allow myself to be seen in the corridor of the Bishop of Vannes, in order that M. Colbert might state with positive certainty that I gave you time to burn your papers."

"My papers?"

"Of course; at least that is what I should have done in your place; when any one opens a door for me, I always avail myself of it."

"Yes, yes, and I thank you, for I have availed myself of it."

"And you have done perfectly right. Every man has his own peculiar secrets with which others have nothing to do. But let us return to Aramis, monseigneur."

"Well, then, I tell you, you could not have called loud enough, or Aramis would have heard you."

"However softly any one may call Aramis, monseigneur, Aramis always hears when he has an interest in hearing. I repeat what I said before—Aramis was not in his own room, or Aramis had certain reasons for not recognising my voice, of which I am ignorant, and of which you even may be ignorant yourself, notwithstanding your liege-man is his greatness the Lord Bishop of Vannes."

Fouquet drew a deep sigh, rose from his seat, made three or four turns in his room, and finished by seating himself, with an expression of extreme dejection, upon his magnificent bed with velvet hangings, and trimmed with the costliest lace. D'Artagnan looked at Fouquet with feelings of the deepest and sincerest pity.

"I have seen a good many men arrested in my life," said the musketeer sadly; "I have seen both M. de Cinq-Mars and M. de Chalais arrested, though I was very young then. I have seen M. de Condé arrested with the Princes; I have seen M. de Retz arrested; I have seen M. Broussel*arrested. Stay a moment, monseigneur; it is disagreeable to have to say, but the very one of all those whom you most resemble at this moment, was that poor fellow Broussel. You were very near doing as he did, putting your dinner napkin in your portfolio, and wiping your mouth with your papers. *Mordioux!* Monseigneur Fouquet, a man like you ought not to be dejected in this manner. Suppose your friends saw you ?"

"Monsieur d'Artagnan," returned the Surintendant, with a smile full of gentleness, "you do not understand me; it is precisely because my friends do not see me that I am such as you see me now. I do not live, exist even, isolated from others; I am nothing when left to myself. Understand that throughout my whole life I have passed every moment of my time in making friends, whom

I hoped to render my stay and support. In times of prosperity, all these cheerful, happy voices—and rendered so through and by my means—formed in my honour a concert of praises and kindly actions. In the least disfavour, these humbler voices accompanied in harmonious accents the murmur of my own heart. Isolation I have never yet known. Poverty (a phantom I have sometimes beheld, clad in rags, awaiting me at the end of my journey through life)—this poverty has been the spectre with which many of my own friends have trifled for years past, which they poetise and caress, and which has attracted me towards them. Poverty! I accept it, acknowledge it, receive it, as a disinherited sister; for poverty is not solitude, nor exile, nor imprisonment. Is it likely I shall ever be poor, with such friends as Pélisson, as La Fontaine, as Molière? with such a mistress as ——*Oh! if you knew how utterly lonely and desolate I feel at this moment, and how you, who separate me from all I love, seem to resemble the image of solitude, of annihilation, and of death itself!"

"But I have already told you, Monsieur Fouquet," replied d'Artagnan, moved to the depths of his soul, "that you exaggerate matters a great deal too much. The King likes you."

"No, no," said Fouquet, shaking his head.

"M. de Colbert hates you."

"M. de Colbert! What does that matter to me?"

"He will ruin you."

"Oh! I defy him to do that, for I am ruined already."

At this singular confession of the Surintendant, d'Artagnan cast his glance all round the room; and although he did not open his lips, Fouquet understood him so thoroughly that he added: "What can be done with such wealth of substance as surrounds us, when a man can no longer cultivate his taste for the magnificent? Do you know what good the greater part of the wealth and the possessions which we rich enjoy, confer upon us?—merely to disgust us, by their very splendour even, with everything that does not equal this splendour. Vaux! you will say, and the wonders of Vaux! What then? What boot these wonders? If I am ruined, how shall I fill with water the urns which my Naiads bear in their arms, or force the air into the lungs of my Tritons? To be rich enough, Monsieur d'Artagnan, a man must be too rich."

D'Artagnan shook his head.

"Oh! I know very well what you think," replied Fouquet quickly. "If Vaux were yours, you would sell it, and would purchase an estate in the country; an estate which should have woods, orchards and land attached, and that this estate should be made to support its master. With forty millions you might——"

"Ten millions," interrupted d'Artagnan.

"Not a million, my dear captain. No one in France is rich enough to give two millions for Vaux, and to continue to maintain it as I have done; no one could do it; no one would know how."

"Well," said d'Artagnan, "in any case, a million is not abject misery."

"It is not far from it, my dear monsieur. But you do not understand me; No; I will not sell my residence at Vaux; I will give it to you, if you like;" and Fouquet accompanied these words with a movement of the shoulders to which it would be impossible to do justice.

"Give it to the King; you will make a better bargain."

"The King does not require me to give it to him," said Fouquet; "he will take it away from me with the most perfect ease and grace, if it please him to do so; and that is the reason why I should prefer to see it perish. Do you know, Monsieur d'Artagnan, that if the King did not happen to be under my roof, I would take this candle, go straight to the dome, and set fire to a couple of huge chests of fusees and fireworks which are in reserve there, and would reduce my palace to ashes."

"Bah!" said the musketeer negligently. "At all events, you would not be able to burn the gardens, and that is the best part about the place."

"And yet," resumed Fouquet thoughtfully, "what was I saying? Great Heavens! burn Vaux! destroy my palace! But Vaux is not mine; this wealth, these wonderful creations are, it is true, the property, as far as sense of enjoyment goes, of the man who has paid for them; but as far as duration is concerned, they belong to those who created them. Vaux belongs to Lebrun, to Lenôtre, to Pélisson, to Levan, to La Fontaine, to Molière; Vaux belongs to posterity, in fact. You see, Monsieur d'Artagnan, that my very house ceases to be my own."

"That is all well and good," said d'Artagnan; "that idea is agreeable enough, and I recognise M. Fouquet himself in it. That idea, indeed, makes me forget that poor fellow Broussel altogether; and I now fail to recognise in you the whining complaints of that old Frondeur. If you are ruined, monsieur, look at the affair manfully, for you, too, *mordioux!* belong to posterity, and have no right to lessen yourself in any way. Stay a moment; look at me—I, who seem to exercise in a degree a kind of superiority over you, because I arrest you; fate, which distributes their different parts to the comedians of this world, accorded to me a less agreeable and less advantageous part to fill than yours has been; I am one of those who think that the part which Kings and powerful nobles are called upon to act are infinitely of more worth than the parts of beggars or lackeys. It is far better on the stage—on the stage I mean, of another theatre than the theatre of this world—it is far better to wear a fine coat and to talk fine language, than to walk the boards shod with a pair of old shoes, or to get one's backbone gently caressed by a sound thrashing with a stick. In one word, you have been a prodigal with money, you have ordered and been obeyed, have been steeped to the lips in enjoyment; while I have dragged my tether after me, have been commanded and have obeyed, and have drudged my life away. Well! although I may seem of such trifling importance beside you, monseigneur, I do declare to you that the recollection of what I have done serves me as a spur, and prevents me from bowing my old head too soon. I shall remain unto the very end, a good trooper; and when my turn comes, I shall fall perfectly straight, all in a heap, still alive, after having selected my place beforehand. Do as I do, Monsieur Fouquet; you will not find yourself the worse for it; that happens only once in a lifetime to men like yourself, and the chief thing is, to do it well when the chance presents itself. There is a Latin proverb,—the words have escaped me, but I remember the sense of it very well, for I have thought over it more than once, which says, 'The end crowns the work!' "

Fouquet rose from his seat, passed his arm round d'Artagnan's neck, and clasped him in a close embrace, whilst with the other hand he pressed his hand. "An excellent homily," he said, after a moment's pause.

"A soldier's, monseigneur."

"You have a regard for me, in telling me all that."

"Perhaps."

Fouquet resumed his pensive attitude once more, and then a moment after he said, "Where can M. d'Herblay be? I dare not ask you to send for him?"

"You would not ask me, because I would not do it, Monsieur Fouquet. People would learn it, and Aramis, who is not mixed up with the affair, might possibly be compromised and included in your disgrace."

"I will wait here till daylight," said Fouquet.

"Yes, that is best."

"What shall we do when daylight comes?"

"I know nothing at all about it, monseigneur."

"Monsieur d'Artagnan, will you do me a favour?"

"Most willingly."

"You guard me; I remain. You are acting in the full discharge of your duty, I suppose?"

"Certainly."

"Very good, then; remain as close to me as my shadow, if you like; and I infinitely prefer such a shadow to any one else."

D'Artagnan bowed at this compliment.

"But, forget that you are Monsieur d'Artagnan, captain of the musketeers; forget that I am Monsieur Fouquet, Surintendant of the Finances; and let us talk about my affairs."

"That is rather a delicate subject."

"Indeed?"

"Yes; but, for your sake, Monsieur Fouquet, I will do what may almost be regarded as an impossibility."

"Thank you. What did the King say to you?"

"Nothing."

"Ah! is that the way you talk?"

"The deuce!"

"What do you think of my situation?"

"Nothing."

"However, unless you have some ill feeling against me——"

"Your position is a difficult one."

"In what respect?"

"Because you are under your own roof."

"However difficult it may be, yet I understand it very well."

"Do you suppose that, with any one else but yourself, I should have shown so much frankness?"

"What! so much frankness, do you say? you, who refuse to tell me the slightest thing?"

"At all events, then, so much ceremony and consideration."

"Ah! I have nothing to say in that respect."

"One moment, monseigneur; let me tell you how I should have behaved towards any one else but yourself. It might be that I happened to arrive at your door just as your guests or your friends had left you—or, if they had not yet gone, I should wait until they were leaving, and should then catch them one after the other, like rabbits; I should lock them up quietly enough; I should steal softly along the carpet of your corridor, and with one hand upon you, before you suspected the slightest thing about it, I should keep you safely until my master's breakfast in the morning. In this way, I should just the same have avoided all publicity, all disturbance, all opposition; but there would also have been no warning for M. Fouquet, no consideration for his feelings, none of those delicate concessions which are shown by persons who are essentially courteous in their natures, whenever the decisive moment may arrive. Are you satisfied with that plan?"

"It makes me shudder."

"I thought you would not like it. It would have been very disagreeable to have made your appearance to-morrow without any preparation, and to have asked you to deliver up your sword."

"Oh! monsieur, I should have died from sheer shame and anger."

"Your gratitude is too eloquently expressed. I have not done enough to deserve it, I assure you."

"Most certainly, monsieur, you will never get me to believe that."

"Well, then, monseigneur, if you are satisfied with what I have done, and have somewhat recovered from the shock which I prepared you for as much as I possibly could, let us allow the few hours that remain to pass away undisturbed. You are harassed, and require to arrange your thoughts; I beg you, therefore, to go to sleep, or pretend to go to sleep, either on your bed, or in your bed. I shall sleep in this arm-chair; and when I fall asleep my rest is so sound that a cannon would not wake me."

Fouquet smiled. "I except, however," continued the musketeer, "the case of a door being opened, whether a secret door, or any other; or the case of any one going out of or coming into the room. For anything like that, my ear is as quick and sensitive as possible. Any creaking noise makes me start. It arises, I suppose, from a natural antipathy to anything of the kind. Move about as much as you like; walk up and down in any part of the room; write, efface, destroy, burn—nothing like that will prevent me from going to sleep, or even prevent me from snoring; but do not touch either the key or the handle of the door! for I should start up in a moment, and that would shake my nerves terribly."

"Monsieur d'Artagnan," said Fouquet, "you are certainly the most witty and the most courteous man I ever met with; and you will leave me only one regret: that of having made your acquaintance so late."

D'Artagnan drew a deep sigh, which seemed to say "Alas! you have perhaps made it too soon." He then settled himself in his arm-chair, while Fouquet, half lying on his bed, and leaning on his arm, was meditating upon his adventure. In this way, both of them, leaving the candles burning, awaited the first dawn of day; and when Fouquet happened to sigh too loudly, d'Artagnan only snored the louder. Not a single visit, not even from Aramis, disturbed their quietude; not a sound, even, was heard throughout the vast palace. Outside, however, the guards of honour on duty, and the patrols of the musketeers, paced up and down; and the sound of their feet could be heard on the gravel walks. It seemed to act as an additional soporific for the sleepers; while the murmuring of the wind through the trees, and the unceasing music of the fountains, whose waters fell tumbling into the basins, still went on uninterruptedly, without being disturbed at the slight noises and matters of trifling moment which constitute the life and death of human nature.

48

THE MORNING

IN opposition to the sad and terrible destiny of the King imprisoned in the Bastille, and tearing, in sheer despair, the bolts and bars of his dungeon, the rhetoric of the chroniclers of old would not fail to present as a complete antithesis the picture of Philippe lying asleep beneath the royal canopy. We do not pretend to say that such rhetoric is always bad, and always scatters, in places it should not, the flowers with which it embellishes and enlivens history. But we shall, on the present occasion, carefully avoid polishing the antithesis in question, but shall proceed to draw another picture as carefully as possible, to serve as a companion to the one we have drawn in the last chapter. The young Prince descended from Aramis's room, in the same way the King had descended from the apartment dedicated to Morpheus. The dome gradually and slowly sank down under Aramis's pressure, and Philippe stood beside the royal bed, which had ascended again after having deposited its prisoner in the secret depths of the subterranean passage. Alone, in the presence of all the luxury which surrounded him; alone, in the presence of his power; alone, with the part he was about to be forced to act, Philippe for the first time felt his heart, and mind, and soul expand beneath the influence of a thousand varied emotions, which are the vital throbs of a king's heart. But he could not help changing colour when he looked upon the empty bed, still tumbled by his brother's body. This mute accomplice had returned, after having completed the work it had been destined to perform; it returned with the traces of the crime; it spoke to the guilty author of that crime with the frank and unreserved language which an accomplice never fears using towards his companion in guilt; for it spoke the truth. Philippe bent over the bed, and perceived a pocket-handkerchief lying on it, which was still damp from the cold sweat which had poured from Louis XIV.'s face. This sweat-bestained handkerchief terrified Philippe as the blood of Abel had terrified Cain.

"I am now face to face with my destiny," said Philippe, with his eyes on fire, and his face lividly white. "Is it likely to be more terrifying then my captivity has been sad and gloomy? When I am compelled to follow out, at every moment, the sovereign power and authority I have usurped, shall I never cease to listen to the scruples of my heart? Yes! the King has lain on this bed; it is indeed his head that has left its impression on this pillow, his bitter tears which have stained this handkerchief; and yet, I hesitate to throw myself on the bed, or to press in my hand the handkerchief which is embroidered with my brother's arms. Away with this weakness; let me imitate M. d'Herblay, who asserts that a man's action should always be one degree above his thought; let me imitate M. d'Herblay, whose thoughts are of and for himself alone, who regards himself as a man of honour, so long as he injures or betrays his enemies only. I, I alone, should have occupied this bed, if Louis XIV.˙ had not, owing to my mother's criminal abandonment of me, stood in my way; and this handkerchief, embroidered with the arms of France, would, in right and justice, belong to me alone, if, as M. d'Herblay observes, I had been left in my place in the royal cradle. Philippe, son of France, take your place on that bed; Philippe, sole king of France, resume the blazonry which is yours! Philippe, sole heir presumptive to Louis XIII., your father, show yourself without pity or mercy for the usurper, who, at this moment, has not even to suffer the agony of the remorse of all that you have had to submit to."

With these words, Philippe, notwithstanding an instinctive repugnance of feeling, and in spite of the shudder of terror which mastered his will, threw himself on the royal bed, and forced his muscles to press the still warm place where Louis XIV. had lain, while he buried his burning face in the handkerchief still moistened by his brother's tears. With his head thrown back and buried in the soft down of his pillow, Philippe perceived above him the crown of France, suspended, as we have stated, by angels with outspread golden wings.

A man may be ambitious of lying in a lion's den, but can hardly hope to sleep there quietly. Phillippe listened attentively to every sound; his heart panted and throbbed at the very suspicion of approaching terror and misfortune; but, confident in his own strength, which was confirmed by the force of an overpowering, resolute determination, he waited until some decisive circumstance should permit him to judge for himself. He hoped that some imminent danger would be revealed for him, like those phosphoric lights of the tempests which show the sailors the altitude of the waves against which they have to struggle. But nothing approached. Silence, the mortal enemy of restless hearts, the mortal enemy of ambitious minds, shrouded in the thickness of its gloom during the remainder of the night the future King of France, who lay there sheltered beneath his stolen crown. Towards the morning a shadow, rather than a body, glided into the royal chamber. Philippe expected his approach, and neither expressed nor exhibited any surprise.

"Well, M. d'Herblay?" he said.

"Well, sire, all is done."

"How?"

"Exactly as we expected."

"Did he resist?"

"Terribly! tears and entreaties."

"And then?"

"A perfect stupor."

"But at last?"

"Oh! at last, a complete victory, and absolute silence."

"Did the governor of the Bastille suspect anything?"

"Nothing."

"The resemblance, however——"

"That was the cause of the success."

"But the prisoner cannot fail to explain himself. Think well of that; I have myself been able to do that on a former occasion."

"I have already provided for everything. In a few days, sooner, if necessary, we will take the captive out of his prison and will send him out of the country, to a place of exile so remote——"

"People can return from their exile, Monsieur d'Herblay."

"To a place of exile so distant, I was going to say, that human strength and the duration of human life would not be enough for his return."

And once more a cold look of intelligence passed between Aramis and the young King.

"And M. du Vallon?" asked Philippe, in order to change the conversation.

"He will be presented to you to-day, and confidentially will congratulate you on the danger which that conspirator has made you run."

"What is to be done with him?"

"With M. du Vallon?"

"Yes; confer a dukedom on him, I suppose."

"A dukedom," replied Aramis, smiling in a significant manner.

"Why do you laugh, Monsieur d'Herblay?"

"I laugh at the extreme caution of your idea."

"Cautious! why so?"

"Your Majesty is doubtless afraid that poor Porthos may probably become a troublesome witness, and you wish to get rid of him."

"What! in making him a duke?"

"Certainly; you would assuredly kill him, for he would die from joy, and the secret would die with him."

"Good Heavens!"

"Yes," said Aramis, phlegmatically; "I should lose a very good friend."

At this moment, and in the middle of this idle conversation, under the light tone of which the two conspirators concealed their joy and pride at their mutual success, Aramis heard something which made him prick up his ears.

"What is that?" said Philippe.

"The dawn, sire."

"Well?"

"Well, before you retired to bed last night, you probably decided to do something this morning at the break of day."

"Yes, I told my captain of the musketeers," replied the young man hurriedly, "that I should expect him?"

"If you told him that, he will certainly be here, for he is a most punctual man."

"I hear a step in the vestibule."

"It must be he."

"Come, let us begin the attack," said the young King, resolutely.

"Be cautious, for Heaven's sake; to begin the attack, and with d'Artagnan, would be madness. D'Artagnan knows nothing, he has seen nothing; he is a hundred miles from suspecting our mystery in the slightest degree; but if he comes into this room the first this morning, he will be sure to detect something which has taken place, and which he would think his business to occupy himself about. Before we allow d'Artagnan to penetrate into this room, we must air the room thoroughly, or introduce so many people into it, that the keenest scent in the whole kingdom may be deceived by the traces of twenty different persons."

"But how can I send him away, since I have given him a rendezvous?" observed the Prince, impatient to measure swords with so redoubtable an antagonist.

"I will take care of that," replied the Bishop, "and in order to begin, I am going to strike a blow which will completely stupefy our man."

"He too is striking a blow, for I hear him at the door," added the Prince, hurriedly.

And in fact, a knock at the door was heard at that moment.

Aramis was not mistaken; for it was indeed d'Artagnan who adopted that mode of announcing himself.

We have seen how he passed the night in philosophising with M. Fouquet, but the musketeer was very wearied, even of feigning to fall asleep, and as soon as the dawn illumined with its pale blue light the sumptuous cornices of the Surintendant's room, d'Artagnan rose from his arm-chair, arranged his sword, brushed his coat and hat with his sleeve like a private soldier getting ready for inspection.

"Are you going out?" said Fouquet.

"Yes, monseigneur. And you?"

"No, I shall remain."

"You give me your word?"

"Certainly."

"Very good. Besides, my only reason for going out is to try to get that reply—you know what I mean?"

"That sentence, you mean——"

"Stay, I have something of the old Roman in me. This morning when I got up, I remarked that my sword got entangled with my lace, and that my shoulder-belt had slipped quite off. That is an infallible sign."

"Of prosperity?"

"Yes, be sure of it; for every time that that confounded belt of mine sticks fast to my back, it always signified a punishment from M. de Tréville, or a refusal of money by M. de Mazarin. Every time my sword hung fast to my shoulder-belt, it always predicted some disagreeable commission or another for me to execute, and I have had showers of them all my life through. Every time, too, my sword danced about in his sheath, a duel, fortunate in its result, was sure to follow; whenever it dangled about the calves of my legs, it was a slight wound; every time it fell completely out of the scabbard, I was booked, and made up my mind that I should have to remain in the field of battle, with two or three months under the surgeon's care into the bargain."

"I never knew your sword kept you so well informed," said Fouquet, with a faint smile, which showed how he was struggling against his own weaknesses. "Is your sword bewitched, or under the influence of some charm?"

"Why, you must know that my sword may almost be regarded as part of my own body. I have heard that certain men seem to have warnings given them by feeling something the matter with their legs, or by a throbbing of their temples. With me, it is my sword that warns me. Well, it told me of nothing this morning. But, stay a moment; look here, it has just fallen of its own accord into the last hole of the belt. Do you know what that is a warning of?"

"No."

"Well, that tells me of an arrest that will have to be made this very day."

"Well," said the Surintendant, more astonished than annoyed by his frankness, "if there is nothing disagreeable predicted to you by your sword, I am to conclude that it is not disagreeable for you to arrest me."

"You! arrest you!"

"Of course. The warning——"

"Does not concern you, since you have been arrested ever since yesterday. It is not you I shall have to arrest, be assured of that. That is the reason why I am delighted, and also the reason why I said that my day will be a happy one."

And with these words, pronounced with the most affectionate graciousness of manner, the captain took leave of Fouquet in order to wait upon the King. He was on the point of leaving the room, when Fouquet said to him, "One last mark of your kindness."

"What is it, monseigneur?"

"M. d'Herblay; let me see Monsieur d'Herblay."

"I am going to try to get him to come to you."

D'Artagnan did not think himself so good a prophet. It was written that the day would pass away and realise all the predictions that had been made in the morning. He had accordingly knocked, as we have seen, at the King's door. The door opened. The captain thought that it was the King who had just opened it himself; and this supposition was not altogether inadmissible, considering the state of agitation in which he had left Louis XIV. the previous evening; but instead of his royal master, whom he was on the point of saluting with the greatest respect, he perceived the long, calm features of Aramis. So extreme was his surprise, that he could hardly refrain from uttering a loud exclamation. "Aramis!" he said.

"Good morning, dear d'Artagnan," replied the prelate coldly.

"You here," stammered the musketeer.

"His Majesty desires you to report that he is still sleeping, after having been greatly fatigued during the whole night."

"Ah!" said d'Artagnan, who could not understand how the Bishop of Vannes, who had been so indifferent a favourite the previous evening, had become in half a dozen hours the largest mushroom of fortune which had ever sprung up in a sovereign's bedroom. In fact, to transmit the orders of the King even to the mere threshold of that monarch's room, to serve as an inter-mediary of Louis XIV., so as to be able to give a single order in his name in at a couple of paces from him, he must be greater than Richelieu had ever been to Louis XIII. D'Artagnan's expressive eye, his half-opened lips, his curling moustache, said as much indeed, in the plainest language to the chief favourite who re-mained calm and perfectly unmoved.

"Moreover," continued the Bishop, "you will be good enough, captain, to allow those only to pass into the King's room this morning who have special permission. His Majesty does not wish to be disturbed just yet."

"But," objected d'Artagnan, almost on the point of refusing to obey this order, and particularly of giving unrestrained passage to the suspicions which the King's silence had aroused—"but, my Lord Bishop, His Majesty gave me a rendezvous for this morning."

"Later, later," said the King's voice, from the bottom of the alcove; a voice which made a cold shudder pass through the musketeer's veins. He bowed, amazed, confuted, and stupefied by the smile which with Aramis seemed to overwhelm him, as soon as those words had been pronounced.

"And then," continued the Bishop, "as an answer to what you were coming to ask the King, my dear d'Artagnan, here is an order of His Majesty, which you will be good enough to attend to forth-with, for it concerns M. Fouquet."

D'Artagnan took the order which was held out to him.

"To be set at liberty!" he murmured. "Ah!" and he uttered a second "ah!" still more full of intelligence than the former; for this order explained Aramis's presence with the King, and that Aramis, in order to have obtained Fouquet's pardon, must have made considerable progress in the royal favour, and that this favour explained, in its tenor, the hardly conceivable assurance with which M. d'Herblay issued the orders in the King's name. For d'Artagnan it was quite sufficient to have understood some-thing in order to understand everything. He bowed and withdrew a couple of steps, as if he were about to leave.

"I am going with you," said the Bishop.

"Where to?"

"To M. Fouquet; I wish to be a witness of his delight."

"Ah! Aramis, how you puzzled me just now!" said d'Artagnan again.

"And you understand now, I suppose?"

"Of course I understand," he said aloud; but then added in a low tone to himself, almost hissing the words through his teeth,

"No, no, I do not understand yet. But it is all the same, for here is the order for it." And then he added, "I will lead the way, monseigneur," and he conducted Aramis to Fouquet's apartments.

49

THE KING'S FRIEND

FOUQUET was waiting with anxiety; he had already sent away many of his servants and his friends, who, anticipating the usual hour of his ordinary receptions, had called at his door to inquire after him. Preserving the utmost silence respecting the danger which hung suspended over his head, he only asked them, as he did every one indeed who came to the door, where Aramis was. When he saw d'Artagnan return, and when he perceived the Bishop of Vannes behind him, he could hardly restrain his delight; it was fully equal to his previous uneasiness. The mere sight of Aramis was a complete compensation to the Surintendant for the unhappiness he had undergone in being arrested. The prelate was silent and grave; d'Artagnan completely bewildered by such an accumulation of events.

"Well, captain; so you have brought M. d'Herblay to me."

"And something better still, monseigneur."

"What is that?"

"Liberty."

"I am free!"

"Yes; by the King's order."

Fouquet resumed his usual serenity, that he might interrogate Aramis with his look.

"Oh! yes, you can thank the Bishop of Vannes," pursued d'Artagnan, "for it is indeed to him that you owe the change that has taken place in the King."

"Oh!" said Fouquet, more humiliated at the service than grateful at its success.

"But you," continued α Artagnan, addressing Aramis, "you who have become M. Fouquet's protector and patron, can you not do something for me?"

"Anything you like, my friend," replied the Bishop, in a calm voice.

"One thing only, then, and I shall be perfectly satisfied. How have you managed to become the favourite of the King, you who have never spoken to him more than twice in your life?"

"From a friend such as you are," said Aramis, "I cannot conceal anything."

"Ah! very good; tell me, then."

"Very well. You think that I have seen the King only twice, while the fact is I have seen him more than a hundred times; only we have kept it very secret, that is all." And without trying to remove the colour which at this revelation made d'Artagnan's face flush scarlet, Aramis turned towards M. Fouquet, who was as much surprised as the musketeer. "Monseigneur," he resumed, "the King desires me to inform you that he is more than ever your friend and that your beautiful fête, so generously offered by you on his behalf, has touched him to the very heart."

And thereupon he saluted M. Fouquet with so much reverence of manner, that the latter, incapable of understanding a man whose diplomacy was of so prodigious a character, remained incapable of uttering a single syllable, and equally incapable of thought or movement. D'Artagnan fancied he perceived that these two men had something to say to each other, and he was about to yield to that feeling of instinctive politeness which in such a case hurries a man towards the door, when he feels his presence is an inconvenience for others; but his eager curiosity, spurred on by so many mysteries, counselled him to remain.

Aramis thereupon turned towards him and said in a quiet tone, "You will not forget, my friend, the King's order respecting those whom he intends to receive this morning on rising." These words were clear enough, and the musketeer understood them; he, therefore, bowed to Fouquet, and then to Aramis,—to the latter with a slight admixture of ironical respect,—and disappeared.

No sooner had he left, than Fouquet, whose impatience had hardly been able to wait for that moment, darted towards the door to close it, and then returning to the Bishop, he said, "My dear d'Herblay, I think it now high time you should explain to me what has passed, for, in plain and honest truth, I do not understand anything."

"We will explain all that to you," said Aramis, sitting down, and making Fouquet sit down also. "Where shall I begin?"

"With this, first of all. Why does the King set me at liberty?"

"You ought rather to ask me what was his reason for having you arrested."

"Since my arrest, I have had time to think over it, and my idea is that it arises out of some slight feeling of jealousy. My fête put M. Colbert out of temper, and M. Colbert discovered some cause of complaint against me; Belle-Isle, for instance."

"No; there is no question at all just now of Belle-Isle."

"What is it, then?"

"Do you remember those receipts for thirteen millions which M. de Mazarin contrived to get stolen from you?"

"Yes, of course!"

"Well, you are already pronounced to be a public robber."

"Good heavens!"

"Oh! that is not all. Do you also remember that letter you wrote to La Vallière?"

"Alas, yes!"

"And that proclaims you a traitor and suborner."

"Why should he have pardoned me, then?"

"We have not yet arrived at that part of our argument. I wish you to be quite convinced of the fact itself. Observe this well: the King knows you to be guilty of an appropriation of public funds. Oh! of course *I* know that you have done nothing of the kind; but, at all events, the King has not seen the receipts, and he cannot do otherwise than believe you criminal."

"I beg your pardon, I do not see——"

"You will see presently, though. The King, moreover, having read your love-letter to La Vallière, and the offers you there made her, cannot retain any doubt of your intentions with regard to that young lady; you will admit that, I suppose?"

"Certainly. But, conclude."

"In a few words. The King is, therefore, a powerful, implacable, and eternal enemy for you."

"Agreed. But am I, then, so powerful that he has not dared to sacrifice me, not withstanding his hatred, with all the means which my weakness, or my misfortunes, may have given him as a hold upon me."

"It is clear, beyond all doubt," pursued Aramis, coldly, "that the King has quarrelled irreconcilably with you."

"But, since he absolves me——"

"Do you believe it likely?" asked the Bishop, with a searching look.

"Without believing in his sincerity of heart, I believe in the truth of the fact."

Aramis slightly shrugged his shoulders.

"But why, then, should Louis XIV. have commissioned you to tell me what you have just stated?"

"The King charged me with nothing for you."

"With nothing!" said the Surintendant, stupefied. "But that order, then——"

"Oh! yes. You are quite right. There is an order, certainly;"

and these words were pronounced by Aramis in so strange a tone, that Fouquet could not resist starting.

"You are concealing something from me, I see. What is it?"

Aramis softly rubbed his white fingers over his chin, but said nothing.

"Does the King exile me?"

"Do not act as if you were playing at the game children play at when they have to try to guess where a thing has been hidden, and are informed by a bell being rung, when they are approaching near to it, or going away from it."

"Speak then."

"Guess."

"You alarm me."

"Bah! that is because you have not guessed, then."

"What did the King say to you? In the name of our friendship, do not deceive me."

"The King has not said a word to me."

"You are killing me with impatience, d'Herblay. Am I still Surintendant?"

"As long as you like."

"But what extraordinary empire have you so suddenly acquired over His Majesty's mind?"

"Ah! that is it."

"You make him do as you like."

"I believe so."

"It is hardly credible."

"So any one would say."

"D'Herblay by our alliance, by our friendship, by everything you hold dearest in the world, speak openly, I implore you. By what means have you succeeded in overcoming Louis XIV.'s prejudices, for he did not like you, I know?"

"The King will like me *now*," said Aramis, laying a stress upon the last word.

"You have something particular then, between you?"

"Yes."

"A secret, perhaps?"

"Yes, a secret."

"A secret of such a nature as to change his Majesty's interests?"

"You are, indeed, a man of superior intelligence, monseigneur, and have made a very accurate guess. I have, in fact, discovered a secret, of a nature to change the interests of the King of France."

"Ah!" said Fouquet, with the reserve of a man who does not wish to ask any questions.

"And you shall judge of it yourself," pursued Aramis; "and you

327

shall tell me if I am mistaken with regard to the importance of this secret."

"I am listening, since you are good enough to unbosom yourself to me; only do not forget that I have asked you nothing which may be indiscreet in you to communicate."

Aramis seemed, for a moment, as if he were collecting himself.

"Do not speak!" said Fouquet; "there is still time enough."

"Do you remember," said the Bishop, casting down his eyes, "the birth of Louis XIV.?"*

"As it were yesterday."

"Have you heard anything particular respecting his birth?"

"Nothing; except that the King was not really the son of Louis XIII."

"That does not matter to us, or the kingdom either; he is the son of his father, says the French law, whose father is recognised by the law."

"True; but it is a grave matter, when the quality of races is called into question."

"A merely secondary question, after all. So that, in fact, you have never learned or heard anything in particular?"

"Nothing."

"That is where my secret begins. The Queen, you must know, instead of being delivered of one son, was delivered of two children."

Fouquet looked up suddenly, as he replied, "And the second is dead?"

"You will see. These twins seemed likely to be regarded as the pride of their mother, and the hope of France; but the weak nature of the King, his superstitious feelings, made him apprehend a series of conflicts between two children whose rights were equal; and so he put out of the way—he suppressed—one of the twins."

"Suppressed, do you say?"

"Be patient. Both the children grew up: the one on the throne, whose minister you are; the other, who is my friend, in gloom and isolation."

"Good Heavens! What are you saying, Monsieur d'Herblay? And what is this poor Prince doing?"

"Ask me rather, what he has done."

"Yes, yes."

"He was brought up in the country, and then thrown into a a fortress which goes by the name of the Bastille."

"Is it possible?" cried the Surintendant, clasping his hands.

"The one was the most fortunate of men; the other the most unhappy and most miserable of all living beings."

"Does his mother not know this?"

"Anne of Austria knows it all."

"And the King?"

"Knows absolutely nothing."

"So much the better!" said Fouquet.

This remark seemed to make a great impression on Aramis; he looked at Fouquet with the most anxious expression of countenance.

"I beg your pardon; I interrupted you," said Fouquet.

"I was saying," resumed Aramis, "that this poor Prince was the unhappiest of human beings, when Heaven, whose thoughts are over all His creatures, undertook to come to his assistance."

"Oh! in what way? Tell me?"

"You will see. The reigning King—I say the reigning King—you can guess very well why?"

"No. Why?"

"Because both of them, being legitimately entitled from their birth, ought both to have been kings. Is not that your opinion?"

"It is, certainly."

"Unreservedly so?"

"Most unreservedly; twins are one person in two bodies."

"I am pleased that a legist of your learning and authority should have pronounced such an opinion. It is agreed, then, that both of them possessed the same rights, is it not?"

"Incontestably so! but, gracious Heaven, what an extraordinary circumstance."

"We are not at the end of it yet. Patience."

"Oh! I shall find 'patience' enough."

"Heaven wished to raise up for that oppressed child an avenger, or a supporter, or vindicator, if you prefer it. It happened that the reigning King, the usurper—(you are quite of my opinion, I believe, that it is an act of usurpation quietly to enjoy, and selfishly to assume the right over, an inheritance to which a man has only the right of one half?)——"

"Yes, usurpation is the word."

"In that case, I continue. It was Heaven's will that the usurper should possess, in the person of his first minister, a man of great talent, of large and generous nature."

"Well, well," said Fouquet, "I understand; you have relied upon me to repair the wrong which has been done to this unhappy brother of Louis XIV. You have thought well; I will help you. I thank you, d'Herblay, I thank you."

"Oh, no, it is not that at all; you have not allowed me to finish," said Aramis, perfectly unmoved.

329

"I will not say another word, then."

"M. Fouquet, I was observing, the minister of the reigning sovereign was suddenly taken into the greatest aversion, and menaced with the ruin of his fortune, with loss of liberty, with loss of life even, by intrigue and personal hatred, to which the King gave too readily an attentive ear. But Heaven permits (still, however, out of consideration for the unhappy Prince who had been sacrificed) that M. Fouquet should in his turn have a devoted friend who knew this state secret, and felt that he possessed strength and courage enough to divulge this secret, after having had the strength to carry it locked up in his own heart for twenty years."

"Do not go on any farther," said Fouquet, full of generous feelings. "I understand you, and can guess everything now. You went to see the King when the intelligence of my arrest reached you; you implored him, he refused to listen to you; then you threatened him with that secret, threatened to reveal it, and Louis XIV., alarmed at the risk of its betrayal, granted to the terror of your indiscretion what he refused to your generous intercession. I understand, I understand; you have the King in your power; I understand."

"You understand nothing as yet," replied Aramis, "and again you have interrupted me. And then, too, allow me to observe that you pay no attention to logical reasoning, and seem to forget what you ought most to remember."

"What do you mean?"

"You know upon what I laid the greatest stress at the beginning of our conversation?"

"Yes; His Majesty's hate, invincible hate for me—yes; but what feeling of hate could resist the threat of such a revelation?"

"Such a revelation, do you say? that is the very point where your logic fails you. What! do you suppose that if I had made such a revelation to the King, I should have been alive now?"

"It is not ten minutes ago since you were with the King."

"That may be. He might not have had the time to get me killed outright, but he would have had the time to get me gagged and thrown into a dungeon. Come, come, show a little consistency in your reasoning, *mordieu!*"

And by the mere use of this word, which was so thoroughly his old musketeer's expression, forgotten by one who never seemed to forget anything, Fouquet could not but understand to what a pitch of exaltation the calm, impenetrable Bishop of Vannes had wrought himself. He shuddered at it.

"And then," replied the latter, after having mastered his feelings, "should I be the man I really am, should I be the true friend you regard me as, if I were to expose you, you whom the King hates already bitterly enough, to a feeling still more than ever to be dreaded in that young man? To have robbed him is nothing; to have addressed the woman he loves is not much; but to hold in your keeping both his crown and his honour, why, he would rather pluck out your heart with his own hands."

"You have not allowed him to penetrate your secret, then?"

"I would sooner, far sooner, have swallowed at one draught all the poisons that Mithridates*drank in twenty years, in order to try to avoid death, than have betrayed my secret to the King."

"What have you done, then?"

"Ah! now we are coming to the point, monseigneur. I think I shall not fail to excite a little interest in you. You are listening, I hope?"

"How can you ask me if I am listening? Go on,"

Aramis walked softly all round the room, satisfied himself that they were alone, and that all was silent, and then returned and placed himself close to the arm-chair in which Fouquet was seated, awaiting with the deepest anxiety the revelations he had to make.

"I forgot to tell you," resumed Aramis, addressing himself to Fouquet, who listened to him with the most absorbed attention—"I forgot to mention a most remarkable circumstance respecting these twins, namely, that God had formed them so startlingly, so miraculously, like each other, that it would be utterly impossible to distinguish the one from the other. Their own mother would not be able to distinguish them."

"Is it possible?" exclaimed Fouquet.

"The same noble character in their features, the same carriage, the same stature, the same voice."

"But their thoughts? degree of intelligence? their knowledge of human life?"

"There is inequality there, I admit, monseigneur. Yes; for the prisoner of the Bastille is, most incontestably, superior in every way to his brother; and if, from his prison, this unhappy victim were to pass to the throne, France would not, from the earliest period of its history, perhaps, have had a master more powerful by his genius and true nobleness of character."

Fouquet buried his face in his hands, as if he were overwhelmed by the weight of this immense secret. Aramis approached him.

"There is a further inequality," he said, continuing his work of temptation, "an inequality which concerns yourself, monseigneur, between the twins, both sons of Louis XIII., namely, the last comer does not know M. Colbert."

Fouquet raised his head immediately; his features were pale and distorted. The bolt had hit its mark—not his heart, but his mind and comprehension.

"I understand you," he said to Aramis; "you are proposing a conspiracy to me?"

"Something like it."

"One of these attempts, which, as you said at the beginning of this conversation, alters the fate of empires?"

"And of the Surintendant too—yes, monseigneur."

"In a word, you propose that I should agree to the substitution of the son of Louis XIII., who is now a prisoner in the Bastille, for the son of Louis XIII., who is now at this moment asleep in the Chamber of Morpheus?"

Aramis smiled with the sinister expression of the sinister thought which was passing through his brain, "Exactly," he said.

"Have you thought," continued Fouquet, becoming animated with that strength of talent which in a few seconds originates and matures the conception of a plan, and with that largeness of view which forsees all its consequences, and embraces all its results at a glance—"have you thought that we must assemble the nobility, the clergy, and the third estate of the realm; that we shall have to depose the reigning sovereign, to disturb by so frightful a scandal the tomb of their dead father, to sacrifice the life, the honour of a woman, Anne of Austria, the life and peace of mind of another woman, Maria Theresa; and suppose that all were done, if we succeed in doing it——"

"I do not understand you," continued Aramis slowly. "There is not a single word of the slightest use in what you have just said."

"What!" said the Surintendant, surprised; "a man like you refuse to view the practical bearings of the case! Do you confine yourself to the childish delight of a political illusion, and neglect the chances of its being carried into execution; in other words, the reality itself. Is it possible?"

"My friend," said Aramis, emphasising the word with a kind of disdainful familiarity, "what does Heaven do in order to substitute one king for another?"

"Heaven!" exclaimed Fouquet,—"Heaven gives directions to its agent, who seizes upon the doomed victim, hurries him away, and seats the triumphant rival on the empty throne. But you forget that this agent is called death. Oh! Monsieur d'Herblay, in Heaven's name, tell me if you have had the idea——"

"There is no question of that, monseigneur; you are going beyond the object in view. Who spoke of Louis XIV.'s death? who spoke of adopting the example which Heaven sets in following out the strict execution of its decrees? No; I wish you to understand that Heaven effects its purposes without confusion or disturbance, without exciting comment or remark, without difficulty or exertion; and that men inspired by Heaven succeed like Heaven itself in all their undertakings, in all they attempt, in all they do."

"What do you mean?"

"I mean, my *friend*," returned Aramis, with the same intonation on the word "friend" that he had applied to it the first time—"I meant that if there has been any confusion, scandal, and even effort in the substitution of the prisoner for the King, I defy you to prove it."

"What!" cried Fouquet, whiter than the handkerchief with which he wiped his temples, "what do you say?"

"Go to the King's apartment," continued Aramis, tranquilly, "and you who know the mystery, I defy even you to perceive that the prisoner of the Bastille is lying in his brother's bed."

"But the King?" stammered Fouquet, seized with horror at the intelligence.

"What King?" said Aramis, in his gentlest tone; "the one who hates you, or the one who likes you."

"The King——of yesterday."

"The King of yesterday! be quite easy on that score; he has gone to take the place in the Bastille which his victim has occupied for such a long time past."

"Great God! And who took him there?"

"I."

"You!"

"Yes, and in the simplest way. I carried him away last night; and while he was descending into gloom, the other was ascending into light. I do not think there has been any disturbance created in any way. A flash of lightning without thunder never awakens any one."

Fouquet uttered a thick, smothered cry, as if he had been struck by some invisible blow, and clasping his head between his clenched hands, he murmured: "You did that?"

"Cleverly enough, too; what do you think of it?"

"You dethroned the King? imprisoned him, too?"

"Yes, that has been done."

"And such an action has been committed here at Vaux?"

"Yes, here, at Vaux, in the Chamber of Morpheus. It would almost seem that it had been built in anticipation of such an act."

"And at what time did it occur?"

"Last night, between twelve and one o'clock."

Fouquet made a movement as if he were on the point of springing upon Aramis; he restrained himself. "At Vaux! under my roof!" he said, in a half-strangled voice.

"I believe so! for it is still your house, and is likely to continue so, since M. Colbert cannot rob you of it now."

"It was under my roof, then, monsieur, that you committed this crime?"

"This crime!" said Aramis stupefied.

"This abominable crime!" pursued Fouquet, becoming more and more excited; "this crime more execrable than an assassination! this crime which dishonours my name for ever, and entails upon me the horror of posterity!"

"You are not in your senses, monsieur," replied Aramis, in an irresolute tone of voice; "you are speaking too loudly; take care!"

"I will call out so loudly that the whole world shall hear me."

"Monsieur Fouquet, take care."

Fouquet turned round towards the prelate, whom he looked at full in the face. "You have dishonoured me," he said, "in committing so foul an act of treason, so heinous a crime upon my guest, upon one who was peacefully reposing beneath my roof. Oh! woe, woe, is me!"

"Woe to the man, rather, who beneath your roof meditated the ruin of your fortune, your life. Do you forget that?"

"He was my guest, my sovereign."

Aramis rose, his eyes literally bloodshot, his mouth trembling convulsively. "Have I a man out of his senses to deal with?" he said.

"You have an honourable man to deal with."

"You are mad."

"A man who will prevent you consummating your crime."

"You are mad, I say."

"A man who would sooner, oh! far sooner, die; who would kill you, even, rather than allow you to complete his dishonour."

And Fouquet snatched up his sword, which d'Artagnan had placed at the head of his bed, and clenched it resolutely in his hand. Aramis frowned, and thrust his hand into his breast as if in search of a weapon. This movement did not escape Fouquet, who, full of nobleness and pride in his magnanimity, threw his sword to a distance from him, and approached Aramis so close as to touch his shoulder with his disarmed hand. "Monsieur," he said, "I would sooner die here on the spot than survive this terrible disgrace; and if you have any pity left for me, I entreat you to take my life."

Aramis remained silent and motionless.

"You do not reply?" said Fouquet.

Aramis raised his head gently, and a glimmer of hope might be seen once more to animate his eyes. "Reflect, monseigneur," he said, "upon everything we have to expect. As the matter now stands, the King is still alive, and his imprisonment saves your life."

"Yes," replied Fouquet, "you may have been acting on my behalf, but I will not, do not accept your services. But, first of all, I do not wish your ruin. You will leave this house."

Aramis stifled the exclamation which almost escaped his broke_ . heart.

"I am hospitable towards all who are dwellers beneath my roof," continued Fouquet, with an air of inexpressible majesty; "you will not be more fatally lost, than he whose ruin you have consummated."

"You will be so," said Aramis, in a hoarse, prophetic voice; "you will be so, believe me."

"I accept the augury, Monsieur d'Herblay; but nothing shall prevent me, nothing shall stop me. You will leave Vaux—you must leave France; I give you four hours to place yourself out of the King's reach."

"Four hours?" said Aramis scornfully and incredulously.

"Upon the word of Fouquet, no one shall follow you before the expiration of that time. You will therefore have four hours advance of those whom the King may wish to despatch after you."

"Four hours!" repeated Aramis, in a thick, smothered voice.

"It is more than you will need to get on board a vessel and flee to Belle-Isle, which I give you as a place of refuge."

"Ah!" murmured Aramis.

"Belle-Isle is as much mine for you, as Vaux is mine for the King. Go, d'Herblay, go! as long as I live, not a hair of your head shall be injured."

"Thank you," said Aramis, with a cold irony of manner.

"Go at once then, and give me your hand, before we both hasten away; you to save your life, I to save my honour."

Aramis withdrew from his breast the hand he had concealed there; it was stained with blood. He had dug his nails into his flesh, as if in punishment for having nursed so many projects, more vain, insensate, and fleeting than the life of man himself. Fouquet was horror-stricken, and then his heart smote him with pity. He threw open his arms as if to embrace him.

"I had no arms," murmured Aramis, as wild and terrible in his wrath as the shade of Dido.* And then, without touching Fouquet's hand, he turned his head aside, and stepped back a pace or two. His last word was an imprecation, his last gesture a curse, which his blood-stained hand seemed to invoke, as it sprinkled on Fouquet's face a few drops of blood which flowed from his breast.

And both of them darted out of the room by the secret staircase which led down to the inner courtyard. Fouquet ordered his best horses, while Aramis paused at the foot of the staircase which led to Porthos's apartment. He reflected profoundly and for some time, while Fouquet's carriage left the stone-paved courtyard at full gallop.

"Shall I go alone?" said Aramis to himself, "or warn the Prince? Oh! fury! Warn the Prince, and then—do what? Take him with me? To carry this accusing witness about with me everywhere? War, too, would follow—civil war, implacable in its nature! And without any resource to save myself—it is impossible! What could he do without me? Oh! without me he would be utterly destroyed. Yet who knows?—let the destiny be fulfilled—condemned he was, let him remain so then! Good or evil spirit—gloomy and scornful Power, whom men call the Genius of Man, thou art a power more restlessly uncertain, more baselessly useless, than the wild wind in the mountains; Chance thou term'st thyself, but thou art nothing; thou inflamest everything with thy breath, crumblest mountains at thy approach, and suddenly art thyself destroyed at the presence of the Cross of dead wood, behind which stands another Power invisible like thyself—whom thou deniest perhaps, but whose avenging hand is on thee, and hurls thee in the dust dishonoured and unnamed! Lost!—I am lost! What can be done? Flee to Belle-Isle? Yes, and leave Porthos behind me, to talk and relate the whole affair to every one! Porthos, too, will have to suffer for what he has done. I will not let poor Porthos suffer. He seems like one of the members of my own frame; and his grief or misfortune would be mine as well. Porthos shall leave with me, and shall follow my destiny. It must be so."

And Aramis, apprehensive of meeting any one to whom his hurried movements might appear suspicious, ascended the staircase without being perceived. Porthos, so recently returned from Paris, was already in a profound sleep; his huge body forgot its fatigue, as his mind forgot its thoughts. Aramis entered, light as a shadow, and placed his nervous grasp on the giant's shoulder. "Come, Porthos," he cried, "come."

Porthos obeyed, rose from his bed, opened his eyes, even before his intelligence seemed to be aroused.

"We are going off," said Aramis.

"Ah!" returned Porthos.

"We shall go mounted, and faster than we have ever gone in our lives."

"Ah!" repeated Porthos.

"Dress yourself, my friend."

And he helped the giant to dress himself, and thrust his gold and diamonds into his pocket. Whilst he was thus engaged, a slight noise attracted his attention, and on looking up he saw d'Artagnan watching them through the half-open door. Aramis started.

"What the devil are you doing there in such an agitated manner?" said the musketeer.

"Hush!" said Porthos.

"We are going off on a mission of great importance," added the Bishop.

"You are very fortunate," said the musketeer.

"Oh, dear me!" said Porthos, "I feel so wearied; I would far sooner have been fast asleep. But the service of the King——"

"Have you seen M. Fouquet?" said Aramis to d'Artagnan.

"Yes, this very minute, in a carriage."

"What did he say to you?"

"'*Adieu*'; nothing more."

"Was that all?"

"What else do you think he could say? Am I worth anything now, since you have all got into such high favour?"

"Listen," said Aramis, embracing the musketeer; "your good times are returning again. You will have no occasion to be jealous of any one."

"Ah! bah!"

"I predict that something will happen to you to-day which will increase your importance more than ever."

"Really?"

"You know that I know all the news?"

"Oh, yes!"

"Come, Porthos, are you ready? Let us go."

"I am quite ready, Aramis."

"Let us embrace d'Artagnan first."

"Most certainly."

"But the horses?"

"Oh! there is no want of them here. Will you have mine?"

"No; Porthos has his own stud. So *adieu! adieu!*"

The two fugitives mounted their horses beneath the captain of the musketeer's eyes, who held Porthos's stirrup for him, and gazed after them until they were out of sight.

"On any other occasion," thought the Gascon, "I should say that those gentlemen are making their escape; but in these days politics seem so changed that that is what is termed going on a mission. I have no objection; let me attend to my own affairs, that is quite enough;" and he philosophically entered his apartments.

50

SHOWING HOW THE COUNTERSIGN WAS RESPECTED
AT THE BASTILLE

FOUQUET tore along as fast as his horses could drag him. On his way he trembled with horror at the idea of what had just been revealed to him.

"What must have been," he thought, "the youth of those extraordinary men, who, even as age is stealing fast upon them, still are able to conceive such plans, and can carry them out without flinching?"

At one moment he could not resist the idea that all tha. Aramis had just been recounting to him was nothing more than a dream, and whether the fable itself was not the snare; so that when Fouquet arrived at the Bastille he might possibly find an order of arrest, which would send him to join the dethroned King. Strongly impressed with this idea, he gave certain sealed orders on his route, while fresh horses were being harnessed to his carriage. These orders were addressed to M. d'Artagnan and to certain others whose fidelity to the King was far above suspicion.

"In this way," said Fouquet to himself, "prisoner or not, I shall have performed the duty which I owe to my honour. The orders will not reach them until after my return, if I should return free, and consequently they will not have been unsealed. I shall take them back again. If I am delayed, it will be because some misfortune will have befallen me; and in that case assistance will be sent for me as well as for the King."

Prepared in this manner, the Surintendant arrived at the Bastille; he had travelled at the rate of five leagues and a half the hour. Every circumstance of delay which Aramis had escaped in his visit to the Bastille befell Fouquet. It was useless his giving his name, equally useless his being recognised: he could not succeed in obtaining an entrance. By dint of entreaties, threats, commands, he succeeded in inducing a sentinel to speak to one of the subalterns, who went and told the major. As for the governor, they did not even dare to disturb him. Fouquet sat in his carriage, at the outer gate of the fortress, chafing with rage and impatience, awaiting the return of the officers, who at last reappeared with a sufficiently sulky air.

"Well," said Fouquet impatiently, "what did the major say?"

"Well, monsieur," replied the soldier, "the major laughed in my face. He told me that M. Fouquet was at Vaux, and that even were he at Paris, M. Fouquet would not get up at so early an hour as the present."

"*Mordieu!* you are a perfect set of fools," cried the minister, darting out of the carriage; and before the subaltern had had time to shut the gate Fouquet sprang through it, and ran forward in spite of the soldier, who cried out for assistance. Fouquet gained ground, regardless of the cries of the man, who, however, having at last come up with Fouquet, called out to the sentinel of the second gate. "Look out, look out, sentinel!" The man crossed his pike before the minister; but the latter, robust and active, and hurried away, too, by his passion, wrested the pike from the soldier, and struck him a violent blow on the shoulder with it. The subaltern, who approached too closely, received his part of the blows as well. Both of them uttered loud and furious cries, at the sound of which the whole of the first body of the advanced guard poured out of the guard-house. Among them there was one, however, who recognised the Surintendant, and who called out, "Monseigneur, ah! monseigneur. Stop, stop, you fellows!" And he effectually checked the soldiers, who were on the point of revenging their companions. Fouquet desired them to open the gate; but they refused to do so without the countersign; he desired them to inform the governor of his presence; but the latter had already heard the disturbance at the gate. He ran forward, followed by his major, and accompanied by a picket of twenty men, persuaded that an attack was being made on the Bastille. Baisemeaux also recognised Fouquet immediately, and dropped his sword, which he had held brandishing about in his hand.

"Ah! monseigneur," he stammered, "how can I excuse——"

"Monsieur," said the Surintendant, flushed with anger, and heated by his exertions, "I congratulate you. Your watch and ward are admirably kept."

Baisemeaux turned pale, thinking that this remark was said ironically, and portended a furious burst of anger. But Fouquet had recovered his breath, and, beckoning the sentinel and the subaltern, who were rubbing their shoulders, towards him, he said, "There are twenty pistoles for the sentinel, and fifty for the officer. Pray, receive my compliments, gentlemen. I will not fail to speak to His Majesty about you. And now, Monsieur Baisemeaux, a word with you."

And he followed the governor to his official residence, accompanied by a murmur of general satisfaction. Baisemeaux was already trembling with shame and uneasiness. Aramis's early visit, from that moment, seemed to possess consequences which a functionary such as he (Baisemeaux) was, was perfectly justified in apprehending. It was quite another thing, however, when Fouquet, in a sharp tone of voice, and with an imperious look, said, "You have seen M. d'Herblay this morning?"

"Yes, monseigneur."

"And are you not horrified at the crime of which you have made yourself an accomplice?"

"Well," thought Baisemeaux, "good so far;" and then he added, aloud, "But what crime, monseigneur, do you allude to?"

"That for which you can be quartered alive, monsieur,—do not forget that! But this is not a time to show anger. Conduct me immediately to the prisoner."

"To what prisoner?" said Baisemeaux tremblingly.

"You pretend to be ignorant? Very good—it is the best thing for you, perhaps, to do; for if, in fact, you were to admit your participation in it, it would be all over with you. I wish, therefore, to seem to believe in your assumption of ignorance."

"I entreat you, monseigneur——"

"That will do. Lead me to the prisoner."

"To Marchiali?"

"Who is Marchiali?"

"The prisoner who was brought back this morning by M. d'Herblay."

"He is called Marchiali?" said the Surintendant, his conviction somewhat shaken by Baisemeaux's cool manner.

"Yes, monseigneur; that is the name under which he was inscribed here."

Fouquet looked steadily at Baisemeaux, as if he would read his very heart; and perceived, with that clearsightedness which men possess who are accustomed to the exercise of power, that the man was speaking with the most perfect sincerity. Besides, in observing his face for a few moments, he could not believe that Aramis would have chosen such a confidant.

"It is the prisoner," said the Surintendant to him, "whom M. d'Herblay carried away the day before yesterday?"

"Yes, monseigneur."

"And whom he brought back this morning?" added Fouquet, quickly: for he understood immediately the mechanism of Aramis's plan.

"Precisely, monseigneur."

"And his name is Marchiali, you say?"

"Yes, Marchiali. If monseigneur has come here to remove him, so much the better, for I was going to write about him."

340

"What has he done, then?"

"Ever since this morning he had annoyed me extremely. He has had such terrible fits of passion, as almost to make me believe that he would bring the Bastille itself down about our ears."

"I will soon relieve you of his presence," said Fouquet.

"Ah! so much the better."

"Conduct me to his prison."

"Will monseigneur give me the order?"

"What order?"

"An order from the King."

"Wait until I sign you one."

"That will not be sufficient, monseigneur. I must have an order from the King."

Fouquet assumed an irritated expression. "As you are so scrupulous," he said, "with regard to allowing prisoners to leave, show me the order by which this one was set at liberty."

Baisemeaux showed him the order to release Seldon.

"Very good," said Fouquet; "but Seldon is not Marchiali."

"But Marchiali is not at liberty, monseigneur; he is here."

"But you said that M. d'Herblay carried him away and brought him back again."

"I did not say so."

"So surely did you say it, that I almost seem to hear it now."

"It was a slip of my tongue, then, monseigneur."

"Take care, Monsieur Baisemeaux, take care."

"I have nothing to fear, monseigneur; I am acting according to strict regulation."

"Do you dare to say so?"

"I would say so in the presence of an apostle himself. M. d'Herblay brought me an order to set Seldon at liberty; and Seldon is free."

"I tell you that Marchiali has left the Bastille."

"You must prove that, monseigneur."

"Let me see him."

"You, monseigneur, who govern this kingdom, know very well that no one can see any of the prisoners without an express order from the King."

"M. d'Herblay has entered, however."

"That is to be proved, monseigneur."

"Monsieur de Baisemeaux, once more I warn you to pay particular attention to what you are saying."

"All the documents are there, monseigneur."

"M. d'Herblay is overthrown."

"Overthrown?—M. d'Herblay! Impossible!"

"You see that he has undoubtedly influenced you."

"No, monseigneur; what does, in fact, influence me, is the King's service. I am doing my duty. Give me an order from him, and you shall enter."

"Stay, monsieur, I give you my word that if you allow me to see the prisoner, I will give you an order from the King at once."

"Give me it now, monseigneur."

"And that, if you refuse me, I will have you and all your officers arrested on the spot."

"Before you commit such an act of violence, monseigneur, you will reflect," said Baisemeaux, who had turned very pale, "that we will only obey an order signed by the King; and that it will be just as easy for you to obtain one to see Marchiali as to obtain one to do me so much injury; me, too, who am perfectly innocent."

"True, true!" cried Fouquet furiously; "perfectly true, M. de Baisemeaux," he added, in a sonorous voice, drawing the unhappy governor towards him, "do you know why I am so anxious to speak to the prisoner?"

"No, monseigneur; and allow me to observe that you are terrifying me out of my senses; I am trembling all over, and feel as if I were going to faint."

"You will stand a better chance of fainting outright, Monsieur Baisemeaux, when I return here at the head of ten thousand men and thirty pieces of cannon."

"Good Heavens, monseigneur, you are losing your senses."

"When I have raised the whole population of Paris against you and your cursed towers, and have battered open the gates of this place, and hanged you up to the bars of that tower in the corner there."

"Monseigneur! monseigneur! for pity's sake."

"I give you ten minutes to make up your mind," added Fouquet, in a calm voice. "I will sit down here, in this arm-chair, and wait for you; if, in ten minutes' time you still persist, I leave this place, and you may think me as mad as you like, but you will see."

Baisemeaux stamped his foot on the ground like a man in a state of despair, but he did not reply a single syllable; whereupon Fouquet seized a pen and ink, and wrote:—

"Order for M. le Prévot des Marchands to assemble the municipal guard and to march upon the Bastille for the King's service."

Baisemeaux shrugged his shoulders. Fouquet wrote:—

"Order for the Duc de Bouillon and M. le Prince de Condé to assume command of the Swiss guards, of the King's guards, and to march upon the Bastille for the King's service."

Baisemeaux reflected. Fouquet still wrote ;—

"Order for every soldier, citizen, or gentleman to seize and apprehend, wherever he may be found, the Chevalier d'Herblay, Bishop of Vannes, and his accomplices, who are: 1st, M. de Baisemeaux, governor of the Bastille, suspected of the crimes of high treason and rebellion——"

"Stop, monseigneur !" cried Baisemeaux ; "I do not understand a single thing of the whole matter ; but so many misfortunes, even were it madness itself that had set them at work, might happen here in a couple of hours, that the King, by whom I shall be judged, will see whether I have been wrong in withdrawing the counter-sign before so many imminent catastrophes. Come with me to the keep, monseigneur, you shall see Marchiali."

Fouquet darted out of the room, followed by Baisemeaux as he wiped the perspiration from his face. "What a terrible morning !" he said ; "what a disgrace !"

"Walk faster," replied Fouquet.

Baisemeaux made a sign to the jailer to precede them. He was afraid of his companion, which the latter could not fail to perceive.

"A truce to this child's play," he said roughly. "Let the man remain here, take the keys yourself, and show me the way. Not a single person, do you understand, must hear what is going to take place here."

"Ah !" said Baisemeaux, undecided.

"Again," cried Fouquet. "Ah ! say 'no' at once, and I will leave the Bastille and will myself carry my own despatches."

Baisemeaux bowed his head, took the keys, and unaccompanied, except by the minister, ascended the staircase. The higher they advanced up the spiral staircase, certain smothered murmurs became distinct cries and fearful imprecations. "What is that?" asked Fouquet.

"That is your Marchiali," said the governor ; "that is the way these madmen call out."

And he accompanied that reply with a glance more indicative of injurious allusions, as far as Fouquet was concerned, than of politeness. The latter trembled ; he had just recognised in one cry more terrible than any that had preceded it, the King's voice. He paused on the staircase, snatching the bunch of keys from Baise-meaux, who thought this new madman was going to dash out his brains with one of them. "Ah !" he cried, "M. d'Herblay did not say a word about that."

"Give me the keys at once !" cried Fouquet, tearing them from his hand. "Which is the key of the door I am to open?"

"That one."

A fearful cry, followed by a violent blow against the door, made the whole staircase resound with the echo. "Leave this place," said Fouquet to Baisemeaux, in a threatening voice.

"I ask nothing better," murmured the latter, "there will be a couple of madmen face to face, and the one will kill the other, I am sure."

"Go!" repeated Fouquet. "If you place your foot in this staircase before I call you, remember that you shall take the place of the meanest prisoner in the Bastille."

"This job will kill me, I am sure it will," muttered Baisemeaux, as he withdrew with tottering steps.

The prisoner's cries became more and more terrible. When Fouquet had satisfied himself that Baisemeaux had reached the bottom of the staircase, he inserted the key in the first lock. It was then that he heard the hoarse, choking voice of the King, crying out, in a frenzy of rage, "Help, help! I am the King." The key of the second door was not the same as the first, and Fouquet was obliged to look for it on the bunch. The King, however, furious, and almost made with rage and passion, shouted at the top of his voice, "It was M. Fouquet who brought me here. Help me against M. Fouquet! I am the King! Help the King against M. Fouquet!"

These cries tore the minister's heart with mingled emotions. They were followed by a shower of terrible blows levelled against the door with a part of the broken chair with which the King had armed himself. Fouquet at last succeeded in finding the key. The King was almost exhausted; he could hardly articulate distinctly as he shouted, "Death to Fouquet! death to the traitor Fouquet!" The door flew open.

51

THE KING'S GRATITUDE

THE two men were on the point of darting towards each other when they suddenly and abruptly stopped, as a mutual recognition took place, and each uttered a cry of horror.

"Have you come to assassinate me, monsieur?" said the King, when he recognised Fouquet.

"The King in this state!" murmured the minister.

Nothing could be more terrible indeed than the appearance of the young Prince at the moment Fouquet had surprised him; his clothes were in tatters; his shirt, open and torn to rags, was stained with sweat, and with the blood which streamed from his lacerated breast and arms. Haggard, ghastly pale, his hair in dishevelled masses, Louis XIV. presented the most perfect picture of despair, hunger, and fear combined, that could possibly be united in one figure. Fouquet was so touched, so affected and disturbed by it, that he ran towards him with his arms stretched out and his eyes filled with tears. Louis held up the massive piece of wood of which he had made such a furious use.

"Sire," said Fouquet, in a voice trembling with emotion, "do you not recognise the most faithful of your friends?"

"A friend—you!" repeated Louis, gnashing his teeth in a manner which betrayed his hate and desire for speedy vengeance.

"The most respectful of your servants," added Fouquet, throwing himself on his knees. The King let the rude weapon fall from his grasp. Fouquet approached him, kissed his knees, and took him in his arms with inconceivable tenderness.

"My King, my child," he said, "how you must have suffered!"

Louis recalled to himself by the change of situation, looked at himself, and ashamed of the disordered state of his apparel, ashamed of his conduct, and ashamed of the air of pity and protection that was shown towards him, drew back. Fouquet did not understand this movement; he did not perceive that the King's feeling of pride would never forgive him for having been a witness of such an exhibition of weakness.

"Come, sire," he said, "you are free."

"Free?" repeated the King. "Oh! you set me at liberty, then, after having dared to lift up your hand against me."

"You do not believe that!" exclaimed Fouquet indignantly; "you cannot believe me to be guilty of such an act."

And rapidly, warmly even, he related the whole particulars of the intrigue, the details of which are already known to the reader. While the recital continued, Louis suffered the most horrible anguish of mind; and when it was finished, the magnitude of the danger he had run struck him far more than the importance of the secret relative to his twin brother.

"Monsieur," he said suddenly to Fouquet, "this double birth is a falsehood; it is impossible—you cannot have been the dupe of it."

"Sire!"

"It is impossible, I tell you, that the honour, the virtue of my mother can be suspected. And my first minister has not yet done justice on the criminals?"

"Reflect, sire, before you are hurried away by your anger," replied Fouquet. "The birth of your brother——"

345

"I have only one brother—and that is *Monsieur*. You know it as well as myself. There is a plot, I tell you, beginning with the governor of the Bastille."

"Be careful, sire, for this man has been deceived as every one else has by the Prince's likeness to yourself."

"Likeness! Absurd!"

"This Marchiali must be singularly like your Majesty to be able to deceive every one's eye," Fouquet persisted.

"Ridiculous."

"Do not say so, sire; those who had prepared everything in order to face and deceive your ministers, your mother, your officers of state, the members of your family, must be quite confident of the resemblance between you."

"But where are these persons, then?" murmured the King.

"At Vaux."

"At Vaux! and you suffer them to remain there!"

"My most pressing duty seemed to be your Majesty's release. I have accomplished that duty; and now, whatever your Majesty may command, shall be done. I await your orders."

Louis reflected for a few moments.

"Muster all the troops in Paris," he said.

"All the necessary orders are given for that purpose," replied Fouquet.

"You have given orders!" exclaimed the King.

"For that purpose, yes, sire; your Majesty will be at the head of ten thousand men in less than an hour."

The only reply the King made was to take hold of Fouquet's hand with such an expression of feeling, that it was very easy to perceive how strongly he had, until that remark, maintained his suspicions of the minister, notwithstanding the latter's intervention.

"And with these troops," he said, "we shall go at once and besiege in your house the rebels who by this time will have established and entrenched themselves there."

"I should be surprised if that were the case," replied Fouquet.

"Why?"

"Because their chief—the very soul of the enterprise, having been unmasked by me, the whole plan seems to me to have miscarried."

"You have unmasked this false prince also?"

"No, I have not seen him."

"Whom have you seen, then?"

"The leader of the enterprise, not that unhappy young man; the latter is merely an instrument, destined through his whole life to wretchedness, I plainly perceive."

"Most certainly."

"It is M. l'Abbé d'Herblay, Bishop of Vannes."

"Your friend."

"He was my friend, sire," replied Fouquet nobly.

"An unfortunate circumstance for you," said the King, in a less generous tone of voice.

"Such friendships, sire, had nothing dishonourable in them so long as I was ignorant of the crime."

"You should have foreseen it."

"If I am guilty, I place myself in your Majesty's hands."

"Ah! Monsieur Fouquet, it was not that I meant," returned the King, sorry to have shown the bitterness of his thoughts in such a manner. "Well! I assure you that notwithstanding the mask with which the villain covered his face, I had something like a vague suspicion that it might be he. But with this chief of the enterprise there was a man of prodigious strength, the one who menaced me with a force almost herculean; what is he?"

"It must be his friend the Baron du Vallon, formerly one of the musketeers."

"The friend of d'Artagnan? the friend of the Comte de la Fère. Ah!" exclaimed the King, as he paused at the name of the latter, "we must not forget the connection that existed between the conspirators and M. de Bragelonne."

"Sire, sire, do not go too far! M. de la Fère is the most honourable man in France. Be satisfied with those whom I deliver up to you."

"With those whom you deliver up to me, you say? Very good, for you will deliver up those who are guilty to me."

"What does your Majesty understand by that?" inquired Fouquet.

"I understand," replied the King, "that we shall soon arrive at Vaux with a large body of troops, that we will lay violent hands upon that nest of vipers, and that not a soul shall escape."

"Your Majesty will put these men to death?" cried Fouquet.

"To the very meanest of them."

"Oh! sire."

"Let us understand each other, Monsieur Fouquet," said the King haughtily. "We no longer live in times when assassination was the only and the last resource which kings had in their power. No! Heaven be praised! I have Parliaments who sit and judge in my name, and I have scaffolds on which my supreme authority is carried out."

Fouquet turned pale. "I will take the liberty of observing to your Majesty, that any proceedings instituted respecting these matters would bring down the greatest scandal upon the dignity of the throne. The august name of Anne of Austria must never be allowed to pass the lips of the people accompanied by a smile."

"Justice must be done, however, monsieur."

"Good, sire; but the royal blood cannot be shed on a scaffold."

"The royal blood! you believe that!" cried the King, with fury in his voice, stamping his foot on the ground. "This double birth is an invention; and in that invention particularly, do I see M. d'Herblay's crime. It is the crime I wish to punish rather than their violence, or their insult."

"And punish it with death, sire?"

"With death; yes, monsieur."

"Sire," said the Surintendant with firmness, as he raised his head proudly, "your Majesty will take the life, if you please, of your brother Philippe of France; that concerns you alone, and you will doubtless consult the Queen-Mother upon the subject. Whatever she may command will be perfectly correct. I do not wish to mix myself up in it, not even for the honour of your crown, but I have a favour to ask of you, and I beg to submit it to you."

"Speak," said the King, in no little degree agitated by his minister's last words. "What do you require?"

"The pardon of M. d'Herblay and M. du Vallon."

"My assassins?"

"Two rebels, sire, that is all."

"Oh! I understand, then, you ask me to forgive your friends."

"My friends!" said Fouquet, deeply wounded.

"Your friends, certainly; but the safety of the State requires that an exemplary punishment should be inflicted on the guilty."

"I will not permit myself to remind your Majesty that I have just restored you to liberty, and have saved your life."

"Monsieur!"

"I will not allow myself to remind your Majesty that had M. d'Herblay wished to carry out his character of assassin, he could very easily have assassinated your Majesty this morning in the forest of Sénart, and all would have been over."

The King started.

"A pistol bullet through the head," pursued Fouquet, "and the disfigured features of Louis XIV., which no one could have recognised, would be M. d'Herblay's complete and entire justification."

The King turned pale and giddy at the idea of the danger he had escaped.

"If M. d'Herblay," continued Fouquet, "had been an assassin, he had no occasion to inform me of his plan, in order to succeed.

Freed from the real king, it would have been impossible to guess the false king. And if the usurper had been recognised by Anne of Austria, he would have been still a son for her. The usurper, as far as Monsieur d'Herblay's conscience was concerned, was still a king of the blood of Louis XIII. Moreover, the conspirator, in that course, would have had security, secrecy, and impunity. A pistol-bullet would have procured him all that. For the sake of Heaven, sire, grant me his forgiveness."

The King, instead of being touched by the picture he had drawn, so faithful in all its details, of Aramis's generosity, felt himself most painfully and cruelly humiliated by it. His unconquerable pride revolted at the idea that a man had held suspended at the end of his finger the thread of his royal life. Every word that fell from Fouquet's lips, and which he thought most efficacious in procuring his friend's pardon, seemed to pour another drop of poison into the already ulcerated heart of Louis XIV. Nothing could bend or soften him. Addressing himself to Fouquet, he said, "I really don't know, monsieur, why you should solicit the pardon of these men. What good is there in asking that which can be obtained without solicitation."

"I do not understand you, sire."

"It is not difficult, either. Where am I now?"

"In the Bastille, sire."

"Yes; in a dungeon. I am looked upon as a madman, am I not?"

"Yes, sire."

"And no one is known here but Marchiali?"

"Certainly."

"Well; change nothing in the position of affairs. Let the madman rot in the dungeon of the Bastille, and M. d'Herblay and M. du Vallon will stand in no need of my forgiveness. Their new king will absolve them."

"Your Majesty does me a great injustice, sire; and you are wrong," replied Fouquet dryly; "I am not child enough, nor is M. d'Herblay silly enough to have omitted to make all these reflections; and if I had wished to make a new king, as you say, I had no occasion to have come here to force open all the gates and doors of the Bastille, to free you from this place. That would show a want of common sense even. Your Majesty's mind is disturbed by anger; otherwise you would be far from offending, groundlessly, the very one of your servants who has rendered you the most important service of all."

Louis perceived that he had gone too far, that the gates of the Bastille were still closed upon him; whilst, by degrees, the flood-gates were gradually being opened behind which the generous-hearted Fouquet had restrained his anger. "I did not say that to humiliate you, Heaven knows, monsieur," he replied. "Only you are addressing yourself to me, in order to obtain a pardon, and I answer you according as my conscience dictates. And so, judging by my conscience, the criminals we speak of are not worthy of consideration or forgiveness."

Fouquet was silent.

"What I do is as generous," added the King, "as what you have done, for I am in your power. I will even say, it is more generous, inasmuch as you place before me certain conditions, upon which my liberty, my life, may depend; and to reject which is to make a sacrifice of them both."

"I was wrong, certainly," replied Fouquet. "Yes—I had the appearance of extorting a favour; I regret it, and entreat your Majesty's forgiveness."

"And you are forgiven, my dear Monsieur Fouquet," said the King, with a smile, which restored the serene expression of his features which so many circumstances had altered since the preceding evening.

"I have my own forgiveness," replied the minister, with some degree of persistence; "but M. d'Herblay, and M. du Vallon?"

"They will never obtain theirs as long as I live," replied the inflexible King. "Do me the kindness not to speak of it again."

"Your Majesty shall be obeyed."

"And you will bear me no ill will for it?"

"Oh! no, sire; for I anticipated it as being most likely."

"You had 'anticipated' that I should refuse to forgive those gentlemen?"

"Certainly; and all my measures were taken in consequence."

"What do you mean to say?" cried the King, surprised.

"M. d'Herblay came, as may be said, to deliver himself into my hands. M. d'Herblay left to me the happiness of saving my King and my country. I could not condemn M. d'Herblay to death; nor could I, on the other hand, expose him to your Majesty's most justifiable wrath; it would have been just the same as if I had killed him myself."

"Well; and what have you done?"

"Sire, I gave M. d'Herblay the best horses in my stables, and four hours' start over all those your Majesty might, probably, despatch after him."

"Be it so!" murmured the King. "But still, the world is wide enough and large enough for those whom I may send to overtake your horses, notwithstanding the 'four hours' start' which you have given to M. d'Herblay."

"In giving him those four hours, sire, I knew I was giving him his life, and he will save his life."

"In what way?"

"After having galloped as hard as possible, with the four hours' start, before your musketeers, he will reach my château of Belle-Isle, where I have given him a safe asylum."

"That may be! But you forget that you have made me a present of Belle-Isle."

"But not for you to arrest my friends."

"You take it back again, then?"

"As far as that goes—yes, sire."

"My musketeers will capture it, and the affair will be at end."

"Neither your musketeers, nor your whole army could take Belle-Isle," said Fouquet coldly. "Belle-Isle is impregnable."

The King became perfectly livid; a lightning flash seemed to dart from his eyes. Fouquet felt that he was lost, but he was not one to shrink when the voice of honour spoke loudly within him. He bore the King's wrathful gaze; the latter swallowed his rage, and after a few moments' silence, said, "Are you going to return to Vaux?"

"I am at your Majesty's orders," replied Fouquet, with a low bow; "but I think that your Majesty can hardly dispense with changing your clothes previous to appearing before your court."

"We shall pass by the Louvre," said the King. "Come." And they left the prison, passing before Baisemeaux, who looked completely bewildered as he saw Marchiali once more leave; and, in his helplessness, tore out the few remaining hairs he had left. It was perfectly true, however, that Fouquet wrote and gave him an authority for the prisoner's release, and that the King wrote beneath it, "Seen and approved, Louis"; a piece of madness that Baisemeaux, incapable of putting two ideas together, acknowledged by giving himself a terrible blow with his fist on his jaws.

52

THE FALSE KING

In the meantime, usurped royalty was playing out its part bravely at Vaux. Philippe gave orders for a full reception at his *petit lever.* He determined to give this order notwithstanding the absence of M. d'Herblay, who did not return, and our readers know for what reason. But the Prince, not believing that absence could be prolonged, wished, as all rash spirits do, to try his valour and his fortune when far from all protection and all counsel. Another reason urged him to do this: Anne of Austria was about to appear; the guilty mother was about to stand in the presence of her sacrificed son. Philippe was not willing, if he had a weakness, to render the man a witness of it, before whom he was bound thenceforth to display so much strength. Philippe opened his folding doors, and several persons entered silently. Philippe did not stir whilst his *valets-de-chambre* dressed him. He had watched, the evening before, all the habits of his brother, and played the king in such a manner as to awaken no suspicion. He was then completely dressed in his hunting costume, when he received his visitors. His own memory and the notes of Aramis announced everybody to him, first of all Anne of Austria, to whom Monsieur gave his hand, and then Madame with M. de Saint-Aignan. He smiled at seeing these countenances, but trembled on recognising his mother. That figure so noble, so imposing, ravaged by pain, pleaded in his heart the cause of that famous Queen who had immolated a child to reasons of State. He found his mother still handsome. He knew that Louis XIV. loved her, and he promised himself to love her likewise, and not to prove a cruel chastisement for her old age. He contemplated his brother with a tenderness easily to be understood. The latter had usurped nothing over him, had cast no shade over his life. A separate branch, he allowed the stem to rise without heeding its elevation or the majesty of its life. Philippe promised himself to be a kind brother to this Prince, who required nothing but gold to minister to his pleasures. He bowed with a friendly air to Saint-Aignan, who was all reverences and smiles, and tremblingly held out his hand to Henrietta, his sister-in-law, whose beauty struck him; but he saw in the eyes of that Princess an expression of coldness which would facilitate, as he thought, their future relations.

"How much more easy," thought he, "it will be to be the brother of that woman than her gallant, if she evinces towards me a coldness that my brother could not have for her, and which is imposed upon me as a duty." The only visit he dreaded at this moment was that of the Queen; his heart—his mind—had just been shaken by so violent a trial, that, in spite of their firm temperment, they would not, perhaps, support another shock. Happily the Queen did not come. Then commenced, on the part of Anne of Austria, a political dissertation upon the welcome M. Fouquet had given to the house of France. She mixed up hostilities with compliments addressed to the King and questions as to his health, with little maternal flatteries and diplomatic artifices.

"Well, my son," said she, "are you convinced with regard to M. Fouquet?"

"Saint-Aignan," said Philippe, "have the goodness to go and inquire after the Queen."

At these words, the first Philippe had pronounced aloud, the slight difference that there was between his voice and that of the King was sensible to maternal ears, and Anne of Austria looked earnestly at her son. Saint-Aignan left the room, and Philippe continued.

"Madame, I do not like to hear M. Fouquet ill-spoken of, you know I do not—and you have even spoken well of him yourself."

"That is true; therefore I only question you on the state of your sentiments with respect to him."

"Sire," said Henrietta, "I, on my part, have always liked M. Fouquet. He is a man of good taste—he is a superior man."

"A Surintendant who is never sordid or niggardly," added Monsieur; "and who pays in gold all the orders I have on him."

"Every one in this thinks too much of himself, and nobody for the State," said the old Queen. "M. Fouquet, it is a fact, M. Fouquet is ruining the State."

"Well, mother!" replied Philippe, in rather a lower key, "do you likewise constitute yourself the buckler of M. Colbert?"

"How is that?" replied the old Queen, rather surprised.

"Why, in truth," replied Philippe, "you speak that just as your old friend Madame de Chevreuse would speak."

"Why do you mention Madame de Chevreuse to me!" said she, "and what sort of humour are you in to-day towards me?"

Philippe continued: "Is not Madame de Chevreuse always in league against somebody? Has not Madame de Chevreuse been to pay you a visit, mother?"

"Monsieur, you speak to me now in such a manner that I can almost fancy I am listening to your father."

"My father did not like Madame de Chevreuse, and had good reason for not liking her," said the Prince. "For my part, I like her no better than he did; and if she thinks proper to come here as she formerly did, to sow divisions and hatreds under the pretext of begging money—why——"

"Well! what?" said Anne of Austria proudly, herself provoking the storm.

"Well!" replied the young man firmly, "I will drive Madame de Chevreuse out of my kingdom—and with her all who meddle with secrets and mysteries."

He had not calculated the effect of this terrible speech, or perhaps he wished to judge of the effect of it, like those who, suffering from a chronic pain, and seeking to break the monotony of that suffering, touch their wound to procure a sharper pang. Anne of Austria was near fainting; her eyes, open but meaningless, ceased to see for several seconds; she stretched out her hands towards her other son, who supported and embraced her without fear of irritating the King.

"Sire," murmured she, "you treat your mother cruelly."

"In what, madame?" replied he. "I am only speaking of Madame de Chevreuse; does my mother prefer Madame de Chevreuse to the security of the State and to the security of my person? Well, then, madame, I tell you Madame de Chevreuse is returned to France to borrow money, and that she addressed herself to M. Fouquet to sell him a certain secret."

"A certain secret!" cried Anne of Austria.

"Concerning pretended robberies that Monsieur le Surintendant had committed, which is false," added Philippe. "M. Fouquet rejected her offers with indignation, preferring the esteem of the King to all complicity with intriguers. Then Madame de Chevreuse sold the secret to Monsieur Colbert, and as she is insatiable, and was not satisfied with having extorted a hundred thousand crowns from that clerk, she has flown still higher, and has endeavoured to find still deeper springs. Is that true, madame?"

"You know all, sire," said the Queen, more uneasy than irritated.

"Now," continued Philippe "I have good reason to dislike this fury, who comes to my court to plan the dishonour of some and the ruin of others. If God has suffered certain crimes to be committed, and has concealed them in the shade of His clemency, I will not permit Madame de Chevreuse to have the power to counteract the designs of God."

The latter part of this speech had so agitated the Queen-Mother, that her son had pity on her. He took her hand and kissed it tenderly; she did not feel that in that kiss, given in spite of repulsions and bitternesses of the heart, there was a pardon for six years of horrible suffering. Philippe allowed the silence of a moment to swallow the emotions that had just developed themselves. Then, with a cheerful smile:—

"We will not go to-day," said he, "I have a plan." And, turning towards the door, he hoped to see Aramis, whose absence began to alarm him. The Queen-Mother wished to leave the room.

"Remain where you are, mother," said he, "I wish you to make your peace with M. Fouquet."

"I bear no ill will towards M. Fouquet; I only dreaded his prodigalities."

"We will put that to rights, and will take nothing of the Surintendant but his good qualities."

"What is your Majesty looking for?" said Henrietta, seeing the King's eyes constantly turned towards the door, and wishing to let fly a little poisoned arrow at his heart, supposing he was so anxiously expecting either La Vallière or a letter from her.

"My sister," said the young man, who had divined her thought, thanks to that marvellous perspicuity of which fortune was from that time about to allow him the exercise, "my sister, I am expecting a most distinguished man, a most able counsellor, whom I wish to present to you all, recommending him to your good graces. Ah! come in then, d'Artagnan."

"What does your Majesty wish?" said d'Artagnan, appearing.

"Where is monsieur the Bishop of Vannes, your friend?"

"Why, sire——"

"I am waiting for him, and he does not come. Let him be sought for."

D'Artagnan remained for an instant stupefied; but soon, reflecting that Aramis had left Vaux secretly with a mission from the King, he concluded that the King wished to preserve the secret of it. "Sire," replied he, "does your Majesty absolutely require M. d'Herblay to be brought to you?"

"Absolutely is not the word," said Philippe; "I do not want him so particularly as that; but if he can be found——"

"I thought so," said d'Artagnan to himself.

"Is this M. d'Herblay Bishop of Vannes?"

"Yes, madame."

"A friend of M. Fouquet?"

"Yes, madame, an old musketeer."

Anne of Austria blushed.

"One of the four braves who formerly performed such wonders."

The old Queen repented of having wished to bite; she broke

off the conversation, in order to preserve the rest of her teeth. "Whatever may be your choice, sire," said she, "I have no doubt it will be excellent."

All bowed in support of that sentiment.

"You will find in him," continued Philippe, "the depth and penetration of M. de Richelieu, without the avarice of M. de Mazarin."

"A prime minister, sire?" said Monsieur in a fright.

"I will tell you all about that, brother; but it is strange that M. d'Herblay is not here!" He called out:—

"Let M. Fouquet be informed that I wish to speak to him—oh! before you, before you; do not retire!"

M. de Saint-Aignan returned, bringing satisfactory news of the Queen, who only kept her bed from precaution, and to have strength to carry out all the King's wishes. Whilst everybody was seeking M. Fouquet and Aramis, the new King quietly continued his experiments, and everybody, family, officers, servants, had not the least suspicion, his air, voice, and manners, were so like the King's. On his side, Philippe, applying to all countenances the faithful notice and design furnished by his accomplice Aramis, conducted himself so as not to give birth to a doubt in the minds of those who surrounded him. Nothing from that time could disturb the usurper. With what strange facility had Providence just reversed the most elevated fortune of the world to substitute the most humble in his stead! Philippe admired the goodness of God with regard to himself, and seconded it with all the resources of his admirable nature. But he felt, at times, something like a shadow gliding between him and the rays of his new glory. Aramis did not appear. The conversation had languished in the royal family; Philippe, preoccupied, forgot to dismiss his brother and Madame Henrietta. The latter were astonished, and began, by degrees, to lose all patience. Anne of Austria stooped towards her son's ear, and addressed some words to him in Spanish. Philippe was completely ignorant of that language; and grew pale at this unexpected obstacle. But, as if the spirit of the imperturbable Aramis had covered him with his infallibility, instead of appearing disconcerted, Philippe rose. "Well! what?" said Anne of Austria.

"What is all that noise?" said Philippe, turning round towards the door of the second staircase.

And a voice was heard, saying: "This way! this way! A few steps more, sire!"

"The voice of M. Fouquet," said d'Artagnan, who was standing close to the Queen-Mother.

"Then M. d'Herblay cannot be far off," added Philippe.

356

But he then saw what he little thought to see so near to him. All eyes were turned towards the door at which M. Fouquet was expected to enter; but it was not M. Fouquet who entered. A terrible cry resounded from all corners of the chamber, a painful cry uttered by the King and all present. It is not given to men, even to those whose destiny contains the strangest elements, and accidents the most wonderful, to contemplate a spectacle similar to that which presented itself in the royal chamber at that moment. The half-closed shutters only admitted the entrance of an uncertain light passing through large velvet curtains lined with silk. In this soft shade, the eyes were by degrees dilated, and every one present saw others rather with trust than with positive sight. There could not, however, escape, in these circumstances, one of the surrounding details; and the new object which presented itself appeared as luminous as if it had been enlightened by the sun. So it happened with Louis XIV., when he showed himself pale and frowning in the doorway of the secret stairs. The face of Fouquet appeared behind him, impressed with sorrow and sternness. The Queen-Mother, who perceived Louis XIV., and who held the hand of Philippe, uttered the cry of which we have spoken, as if she had beheld a phantom. Monsieur was bewildered, and kept turning his head in astonishment from one to the other. Madame made a step forward, thinking she saw the form of her brother-in-law reflected in a glass. And, in fact, the illusion was possible. The two princes, both pale as death—for we renounce the hope of being able to describe the fearful state of Philippe—both trembling, and clenching their hands convulsively, measured each other with their looks, and darted their eyes like poniards, into each other. Mute, panting, bending forward, they appeared as if about to spring upon an enemy. The unheard of resemblance of countenance, gesture, shape, height, even to the resemblance of costume, produced by chance—for Louis XIV. had been to the Louvre and put on a violet-coloured dress—the perfect analogy of the two princes, completed the consternation of Anne of Austria. And yet she did not at once guess the truth. There are misfortunes in life that no one will accept; people would rather believe in the supernatural and the impossible. Louis had not reckoned upon these obstacles. He expected he had only to appear and be acknowledged. A living sun, he could not endure the suspicion of parity with any one. He did not admit that every torch should not become darkness at the instant he shone out with his conquering ray. At the aspect of Philippe, then, he was, perhaps, more terrified than any one round him, and his silence, his immobility were, this time, a concentration and a calm which precede violent explosions of passion.

But Fouquet! who could paint his emotion and stupor in presence of this living portrait of his master! Fouquet thought Aramis was right, that this newly-arrived was a king as pure in his race as the other, and that, for having repudiated all participation in this *coup d'état*, so skilfully got up by the General of the Jesuits, he must be a mad enthusiast unworthy of ever again dipping his hands in a political work. And then it was the blood of Louis XIII. which Fouquet was sacrificing to the blood of Louis XIII.; it was to a selfish ambition he was sacrificing a noble ambition; it was to the right of keeping he sacrificed the right of having. The whole extent of his fault was revealed to him by the simple sight of the pretender. All which passed in the mind of Fouquet was lost upon the persons present. He had five minutes to concentrate his meditations upon this point of the case of conscience; five minutes, that is to say five ages, during which the two kings and their family scarcely found time to breathe after so terrible a shock. D'Artagnan, leaning against the wall, in front of Fouquet, with his hand to his brow, asked himself the cause of such a wonderful prodigy. He could not have said at once why he doubted, but he knew assuredly that he had reason to doubt, and that in this meeting of the two Louis XIVs. lay all the difficulty which during late days had rendered the conduct of Aramis so suspicious to the musketeer. These ideas were, however, enveloped in thick veils. The actors in this assembly seemed to swim in the vapours of a confused waking. Suddenly Louis XIV., more impatient and more accustomed to command, ran to one of the shutters, which he opened, tearing the curtains in his eagerness. A flood of living light entered the chamber, and made Philippe draw back to the alcove. Louis seized upon this movement with eagerness, and addressing himself to the Queen,—

"My mother," said he, "do you not acknowledge your son, since every one here has forgotten his King!" Anne of Austria started, and raised her arms towards Heaven, without being able to articulate a single word.

"My mother," said Philippe, with a calm voice, "do you not acknowledge your son?" And this time, in his turn, Louis drew back.

As to Anne of Austria, struck in both head and heart with remorse, she lost her equilibrium. No one aiding her, for all were petrified, she sank back in her chair, breathing a weak, trembling sigh. Louis could not endure this spectacle and this affront. He bounded towards d'Artagnan, upon whom the vertigo was beginning to gain, and who staggered as he caught at the door, for support.

"Captain!" said he, "look us in the face and say which is the paler, he or I!"

This cry roused d'Artagnan, and stirred in his heart the fibre of obedience. He shook his head, and, without more hesitation, he walked straight up to Philippe, upon whose shoulder he laid his hand, saying, "Monsieur,. you are my prisoner!"

Philippe did not raise his eyes towards Heaven, nor stir from the spot, where he seemed nailed to the floor, his eye intensely fixed upon the King his brother. He reproached him by a sublime silence with all his misfortunes past, with all his tortures to come. Against this language of the soul the King felt he had no power; he cast down his eyes, dragging away precipitately his brother and sister, forgetting his mother, sitting motionless within three paces of the son whom she left a second time to be condemned to death. Philippe approached Anne of Austria, and said to her, in a soft and nobly agitated voice,—

"If I were not your son, I should curse you, my mother, for having rendered me so unhappy."

D'Artagnan felt a shudder pass through the marrow of his bones. He bowed respectfully to the young Prince, and said, as he bent, "Excuse me, monseigneur, I am but a soldier, and my oaths are his who has just left the chamber."

"Thank you, M. d'Artagnan. But what is become of M. d'Herblay?"

"M. d'Herblay is in safety, monseigneur," said a voice behind them; "and no one, while I live and am free, shall cause a hair to fall from his head."

"Monsieur Fouquet!" said the Prince, smiling sadly.

"Pardon me, monseigneur," said Fouquet, kneeling, "but he who is just gone out from hence was my guest."

"Here are," murmured Philippe, with a sigh, "brave friends and good hearts. They make me regret the world. On, M. d'Artagnan, I follow you."

At the moment the captain of the musketeers was about to leave the room with his prisoner, Colbert appeared, and, after remitting an order from the King to d'Artagnan, retired. D'Artagnan read the paper, and then crushed it in his hand with rage.

"What is it?" asked the Prince.

"Read, monseigneur," replied the musketeer.

Philippe read the following words, hastily traced by the hand of the King:—"M. d'Artagnan will conduct the prisoner to the Iles Sainte-Marguerite. He will cover his face with an iron visor, which the prisoner cannot raise without peril of his life."

"That is just," said Philippe, with resignation, "I am ready."

"Aramis was right," said Fouquet, in a low voice to the musketeer; "this one is quite as much of a king as the other."

"More!" replied d'Artagnan. "He only wants you and me."

53

IN WHICH PORTHOS THINKS HE IS PURSUING A DUCHY

ARAMIS and Porthos, having profited by the time granted them by Fouquet, did honour to the French cavalry by their speed. Porthos did not clearly understand for what kind of mission he was forced to display so much velocity; but as he saw Aramis spurring on furiously, he, Porthos, spurred on in the same manner. They had soon, in this manner, placed twelve leagues between them and Vaux; they were then obliged to change horses and organise a sort of post arrangement. It was during a relay that Porthos ventured to interrogate Aramis discreetly.

"Hush!" replied the latter; "know only that our fortune depends upon our speed."

As if Porthos had still been the musketeer, without a sou or a maille,* of 1626, he pushed forward. That magic word "fortune" always means something in the human ear. It means *enough* for those who have nothing; it means *too much* for those who have enough.

"I shall be made a duke!" said Porthos aloud. He was speaking to himself.

"That is possible," replied Aramis, smiling after his own fashion, as the horse of Porthos passed him. The head of Aramis was, notwithstanding, on fire; the activity of the body had not yet succeeded in subduing that of the mind. All that there is in raging passions, in severe toothaches, or mortal threats twisted, gnawed, and grumbled in the thoughts of the vanquished prelate. His countenance exhibited very visible traces of this rude combat. Free upon the highway to abandon himself to every impression of the moment, Aramis did not fail to swear at every start of his horse, at every inequality in the road. Pale, at times inundated with boiling sweats, then again dry and icy, he beat his horses and made the blood stream from their sides. Porthos, whose dominant fault was not sensibility, groaned at this. Thus travelled they on for eight long hours, and then arrived at Orleans. It was four o'clock in the afternoon. Aramis, on observing this, judged that nothing demonstrated pursuit to be possible. It would be without example that a troop capable of taking him and Porthos should be furnished with relays sufficient to perform forty leagues in eight hours. Thus, admitting pursuit, which was not at all manifest, the fugitives were five hours in advance of their pursuers.

Aramis thought that there might be no imprudence in taking a little rest, but that to continue would make the matter more certain. Twenty leagues more, performed with the same rapidity, twenty more leagues devoured, and no one, not even d'Artagnan, could overtake the enemies of the King. Aramis felt obliged, therefore, to inflict upon Porthos the pain of mounting on horseback again. They rode on till seven o'clock in the evening, and had only one post more between them and Blois. But here a diabolical accident alarmed Aramis greatly. There were no horses at the post. The prelate asked himself by what infernal machination his enemies had succeeded in depriving him of the means of going farther,—he who never recognised chance as a deity, he who found a cause for every result, he preferred believing that the refusal of the postmaster, at such an hour in such a country, was the consequence of an order emanating from above; an order given with a view to stopping short the king-maker in the midst of his flight. But at the moment he was about to fly into a passion, so as to procure either a horse or an explanation, he was struck with the recollection that the Comte de la Fère lived in the neighbourhood.

"I am not travelling," said he; "I do not want horses for a whole stage. Find me two horses to go and pay a visit to a nobleman of my acquaintance who resides near this place."

"What nobleman?" asked the postmaster.

"M. le Comte de la Fère."

"Oh!" replied the postmaster, uncovering with respect, "a very worthy nobleman. But, whatever may be my desire to make myself agreeable to him, I cannot furnish you with horses, for all mine are engaged by M. le Duc de Beaufort."*

"Indeed!" said Aramis, much disappointed.

"Only," continued the postmaster, "if you will put up with a little carriage I have, I will harness an old blind horse, who has still his legs left, and will draw you to the house of M. le Comte de la Fère."

"That is worth a louis," said Aramis.

"No, monsieur, that is never worth more than a crown; that is what M. Grimaud, the Comte's intendant, always pays me when he makes use of that carriage; and I should not wish the Comte de la Fère to have to reproach me with having imposed on one of his friends."

"As you please," said Aramis, "particularly as regards disobliging the Comte de la Fère; only I think I have a right to give you a louis for your idea."

"Oh! doubtless!" replied the postmaster, with delight. And he himself harnessed the old horse to the creaking carriage. In the meanwhile Porthos was curious to behold. He imagined he had discovered the secret, and he felt pleased, because a visit to Athos, in the first place, promised him much satisfaction, and, in the next, gave him the hopes of finding at the same time a good bed and a good supper. The master, having got the carriage ready, ordered one of his men to drive the strangers to La Fère. Porthos took his seat by the side of Aramis, whispering in his ear, "I understand."

"Ah! ah!" said Aramis, "and what do you understand, my friend?"

"We are going, on the part of the King, to make some great proposal to Athos."

"Pooh!" said Aramis.

"You need tell me nothing about it," added the worthy Porthos, endeavouring to place himself so as to avoid the jolting, "you need tell me nothing, I shall guess."

"Well! do, my friend; guess away."

They arrived at Athos's dwelling about nine o'clock in the evening, favoured by a splendid moon. This cheerful light rejoiced Porthos beyond expression; but Aramis appeared annoyed by it in an equal degree. He could not help showing something of this to Porthos, who replied, "Ay, ay! I guess how it is! the mission is a sec et one."

These were his last words in the carriage. The driver interrupted him by saying, "Gentlemen, you are arrived."

Porthos and his companion alighted before the gate of the little château, where we are about to meet again with Athos and Bragelonne, the latter of whom had disappeared since the discovery of the infidelity of La Vallière. If there be one saying more true than another, it is this: great griefs contain within themselves the germ of their consolation. This painful wound, inflicted upon Raoul, had drawn him nearer to his father again; and God knows how sweet were the consolations which flowed from the eloquent mouth and generous heart of Athos. The wound was not cicatrised, but Athos, by dint of conversing with his son, and mixing a little more of his life with that of the young man, had brought him to understand that this pang of a first infidelity is necessary to every human existence; and that no one has loved without meeting with it. Raoul listened often, but never understood. Nothing replaces in the deeply-afflicted heart the remembrance and thought of the beloved object. Raoul then replied to the reasonings of his father:—

"Monsieur, all that you tell me is true; I believe that no one has suffered in the affections of the heart so much as you have; but you are a man too great from intelligence, and too severely tried by misfortunes, not to allow for the weakness of the soldier who suffers for the first time. I am paying a tribute which I shall not pay a second time; permit me to plunge myself so deeply in my grief that I may forget myself in it, that I may drown even my reason in it."

"Raoul! Raoul!"

"Listen, monsieur. Never shall I accustom myself to the idea that Louise, the most chaste and the most innocent of women, has been able so basely to deceive a man so honest and so true a lover as I am. Never can I persuade myself that I see that sweet and good mask change into a hypocritical and lascivious face. Louise lost! Louise infamous! Ah! monseigneur, that idea is much more cruel to me than Raoul abandoned —Raoul unhappy!"

Athos then employed the heroic remedy. He defended Louise against Raoul, and justified her perfidy by her love. "A woman who would have yielded to a king because he is a king," said he, "would deserve to be styled infamous; but Louise loves Louis. Both young, they have forgotten, he his rank, and she her vows. Love absolves everything, Raoul. The two young people loved each other with sincerity."

And when he had dealt this severe poniard-thrust, Athos, with a sigh, saw Raoul bound away under the cruel wound, and fly to the thickest recesses of the wood, or the solitude of his chamber, whence, an hour after, he would return, pale, trembling, but subdued. Then, coming up to Athos with a smile, he would kiss his hand, like the dog, who, having been beaten, caresses a good master, to redeem his fault. Raoul redeemed nothing but his weakness, and only confessed his grief. Thus passed away the days that followed that scene in which Athos had so violently shaken the indomitable pride of the King. Never, when conversing with his son, did he make any allusion to that scene; never did he give him the details of that vigorous lecture which might, perhaps, have consoled the young man, by showing him his rival humbled. Athos did not wish that the offended lover should forget the respect due to the King. And when Bragelonne, ardent, furious, and melancholy, spoke with contempt of royal words, of the equivocal faith which certain madmen draw from promises falling from thrones, when, passing over two centuries, with the rapidity of a bird which traverses a narrow strait, to go from one world to the other, Raoul ventured to predict the time when kings would become less than other men, Athos said to him, in his serene persuasive voice, "You are right, Raoul; all that you say will happen; kings will lose their privileges, as stars which have completed their time lose their splendour. But when that moment shall come, Raoul, we shall be dead. And remember well what I say to you. In this world, all—men, women, and kings—must live for the present. We can only live for the future for God."

This was the manner in which Athos and Raoul were, as usual, conversing, and walking backwards and forwards in the long alley of limes in the park, when the bell which served to announce to the Comte either the hour of dinner or the arrival of a visitor, was rung; and, without attaching any importance to it, he turned towards the house with his son; and at the end of the alley they found themselves in the presence of Aramis and Porthos.

54

THE LAST ADIEUX

RAOUL uttered a cry, and affectionately embraced Porthos. Aramis and Athos embraced like old men; and this embrace itself being a question for Aramis, he immediately said, "My friend, we have not long to remain with you."

"Ah!" said the Comte.

"Only time to tell you of my good fortune," interrupted Porthos.

"Ah!" said Raoul.

Athos looked silently at Aramis, whose sombre air had already appeared to him very little in harmony with the good news Porthos spoke of.

"What is the good fortune that has happened to you? Let us hear it," said Raoul, with a smile.

"The King has made me a duke," said the worthy Porthos, with an air of mystery, in the ear of the young man, "a duke by brevet."

But the asides of Porthos were always loud enough to be heard by everybody. His murmurs were in the diapason of ordinary roaring. Athos heard him, and uttered an exclamation which made Aramis start. The latter took Athos by the arm, and, after having asked Porthos's permission to say a word to his friend in private, "My dear Athos," he began, "you see me overwhelmed with grief."

"With grief, my dear friend?" cried the Comte; "oh, what!"

"In two words. I have raised a conspiracy against the King;

that conspiracy has failed, and, at this moment, I am doubtless pursued."

"You are pursued!—a conspiracy! Eh! my friend, what do you tell me?"

"A sad truth. I am entirely ruined."

"Well, but Porthos—this title of duke—what does all that mean?"

"That is the subject of my severest pain; that is the deepest of my wounds. I have, believing in an infallible success, drawn Porthos into my conspiracy. He has thrown himself into it, as you know he would do, with all his strength, without knowing what he was about; and now, he is as much compromised as myself—as completely ruined as I am."

"Good God!" And Athos turned towards Porthos, who was smiling complacently.

"I must make you acquainted with the whole. Listen to me," continued Aramis; and he related the history as we know it. Athos, during the recital, several times felt the sweat break from his forehead. "It was a great idea," said he, "but a great error."

"For which I am punished, Athos."

"Therefore, I will not tell you my entire thought."

"Tell it, nevertheless."

"It is a crime."

"Capital. I know it is. *Lèse majesté.*"

"Porthos! poor Porthos!"

"What would you advise me to do? Success, as I have told you, was certain."

"M. Fouquet is an honest man."

"And I am a fool for having so ill judged of him," said Aramis. "Oh! the wisdom of man! Oh, vast millstone which grinds the world! and which is one day stopped by a grain of sand which has fallen, no one knows how, in its wheels."

"Say, by a diamond, Aramis. But the thing is done. How do you think of acting?"

"I am taking away Porthos. The King will never believe that that worthy man has acted innocently. He never can believe that Porthos has thought he was serving the King whilst acting as he has done. His head would pay for my fault. It shall not be so."

"You are taking him away; whither?"

"To Belle-Isle, at first. That is an impregnable place of refuge. Then I have the sea, and a vessel to pass over into England, where I have many relations."

"You? in England?"

"Yes, or else into Spain, where I have still more."

"But, our excellent Porthos! you ruin him, for the King will confiscate all his property."

"All is provided for. I know how, when once in Spain, to reconcile myself with Louis XIV., and restore Porthos to favour."

"You have credit, seemingly, Aramis," said Athos, with a discreet air.

"Much; and at the service of my friends."

These words were accompanied by a warm pressure of the hand.

"Thank you," replied the Comte.

"And while we are on that head," said Aramis, "you also are a malcontent; you also, Raoul, have griefs to lay to the King. Follow our example; pass over into Belle-Isle. Then we shall see, I guarantee upon my honour, that in a month there will be war between France and Spain on the subject of this son of Louis XIII., who is an Infante*likewise, and whom France detains inhumanly. Now, as Louis XIV. would have no inclination for a war on that subject, I will answer for a transaction, the result of which must bring greatness to Porthos and to me, and a duchy in France to you, who are already a grandee of Spain. Will you join us?"

"No; for my part I prefer having something to reproach the King with; it is a pride natural to my race to pretend to a superiority over royal races. Doing what you propose, I should become the obliged of the King; I should certainly be a gainer on that ground, but I should be a loser in my conscience.—No, thank you!"

"Then, give me two things, Athos,—your absolution."

"Oh! I give it you if you have really wished to avenge the weak and the oppressed against the oppressor."

"That is sufficient for me," said Aramis, with a blush which was lost in the obscurity of the night. "And now, give me your two best horses to gain the second post, as I have been refused any under the pretext of the Duc de Beaufort being travelling in this country."

"You shall have the two best horses, Aramis: and I again recommend Porthos strongly to you."

"Oh! have no fear on that head. One word more; do you think I am manœuvring for him as I ought?"

"The evil being committed, yes; for the King would not pardon him, and you have, whatever may be said, always a supporter in M. Fouquet, who will not abandon you, he being himself compromised, notwithstanding his heroic action."

"You are right. And that is why, instead of gaining the sea at once, which would proclaim my fear and guilt, that is why I remain upon French ground. But Belle-Isle will be for me whatever ground I wish it to be—English, Spanish, or Roman; all will consist, with me, in the standard I shall think proper to unfurl."

"How so?"

"It was I who fortified Belle-Isle; and whilst I defend it, nobody can take Belle-Isle from me. And then, as you have said just now, M. Fouquet is there. Belle-Isle will not be attacked without the signature of M. Fouquet."

"That is true. Nevertheless, be prudent. The King is both cunning and strong," Aramis smiled.

"I again recommend Porthos to you," repeated the Comte, with a sort of cold persistence.

"Whatever becomes of me, Comte," replied Aramis, in the same tone, "our brother Porthos will fare as I do."

Athos bowed whilst pressing the hand of Aramis, and turned to embrace Porthos with much emotion.

"I was born lucky, was I not?" murmured the latter, transported with happiness, as he folded his cloak round him.

"Come, my dear friend," said Aramis.

Raoul was gone out to give orders for the saddling of the horses. The group was already divided. Athos saw his two friends on the point of departure, and something like a mist pressed before his eyes, and weighed upon his heart.

"It is strange," thought he; "whence comes the inclination I feel to embrace Porthos once more?" At that moment Porthos turned round, and he came towards his old friend with open arms. This last endearment was tender as in youth, as in times when the heart was warm and life happy. And then Porthos mounted his horse. Aramis came back once more to throw his arms round the neck of Athos. The latter watched them along the high road, elongated by the shade, in their white cloaks. Like two phantoms, they seemed to be enlarged on departing from the earth, and it was not in the mist, but in the declivity of the ground that they disappeared. At the end of the perspective, both seemed to have given a spring with their feet, which made them vanish as if evaporated into the clouds.

Then Athos, with an oppressed heart, returned towards the house, saying to Bragelonne, "Raoul, I don't know what it is that has just told me that I have seen these two men for the last time."

"It does not astonish me, monsieur, that you should have such a thought," replied the young man, "for I have at this moment the same, and think also that I shall never see MM. du Vallon and d'Herblay again."

"Oh, you!" replied the Comte, "you speak like a man rendered sad by another cause; you see everything in black; you are young, and if you chance never to see those old friends again, it will be because they no longer exist in the world in which you have many years to pass. But I——"

Raoul shook his head sadly, and leant upon the shoulder of the Comte, without either of them finding another word in their hearts, which were ready to overflow.

All at once a noise of horses and voices, from the extremity of the road to Blois, attracted their attention that way. Flambeaux-bearers shook their torches merrily among the trees of their route, and turned round, from time to time, to avoid distancing the horsemen who followed them. These flames, this noise, this dust of a dozen richly caparisoned horses, formed a strange contrast in the middle of the night with the melancholy funeral disappearance of the two shadows of Aramis and Porthos. Athos went towards the house; but he had hardly reached the parterre, when the entrance gate appeared in a blaze; all the flambeaux stopped and appeared to enflame the road. A cry was heard of "M. le Duc de Beaufort"—and Athos sprang towards the door of his house. But the Duc had already alighted from his horse, and was looking around him.

"I am here, monseigneur," said Athos.

"Ah! good evening, dear Comte," said the Prince, with that frank cordiality which won him so many hearts. "Is it too late for a friend?"

"Ah! my dear Prince—come in!" said the Comte.

And, M. de Beaufort, leaning on the arm of Athos, they entered the house, followed by Raoul, who walked respectfully and modestly among the officers of the Prince,* with several of whom he was acquainted.

55

MONSIEUR DE BEAUFORT

THE Prince turned round at the moment when Raoul, in order to leave him alone with Athos, was shutting the door, and preparing to go with the other officers into an adjoining apartment.

"Is that the young man I have heard M. le Prince* speak so highly of?" asked M. de Beaufort.

"It is, monseigneur."

"He is quite the soldier; let him stay, Comte; we cannot spare him."

"Remain, Raoul, since monseigneur permits it," said Athos.

"*Ma foi!* he is tall and handsome!" continued the Duke. "Will you give him to me, monseigneur if I ask him of you?"

"How am I to understand you, monseigneur?" said Athos.

"Why, I call upon you to bid you farewell."

"Farewell!"

"Yes, in good truth. Have you no idea of what I am about to become?"

"Why, I suppose, what you have always been, monseigneur,— a valiant Prince, and an excellent gentleman."

"I am going to become an African Prince,—a Bedouin gentleman. The King is sending me to make conquests among the Arabs."

"What do you tell me, monseigneur?"

"Strange, is it not? I, Parisian of the Parisians,—I, who have reigned in the faubourgs, and have been called King of the *Halles*, —I am going to pass from the Place Maubert to the minarets of Gigelli ; I become from a *Frondeur* an adventurer!"

"Oh, monseigneur, if you did not yourself tell me that——"

"It would not be credible, would it? Believe me, nevertheless, and we have but to bid each other farewell. This is what comes of getting into favour again."

"Into favour?"

"Yes. You smile. Ah, my dear Comte, do you know why I have accepted this enterprise?—can you guess?"

"Because your Highness loves glory above everything."

"Oh! no; there is no glory in firing muskets at savages. I see no glory in that, for my part, and it is more probable that I shall there meet with something else. But I have wished, and still wish earnestly, my dear Comte, that my life should have that last facet, after all the whimsical exhibitions I have seen myself make during fifty years. For, in short, you must admit that it is sufficiently strange to be born the grandson of a king, to have made war against kings, to have been reckoned among the powers of the age, to have maintained my rank, to feel Henry VI. within me, to be great admiral of France—and then to go and get killed at Gigelli, among all those Turks, Saracens, and Moors."

"Monseigneur, you dwell strangely upon that subject," said Athos, in an agitated voice. "How can you suppose that so brilliant a destiny will be extinguished in that remote and miserable scene?"

"And can you believe, just and simple man as you are, that if I go into Africa for this ridiculous motive, I will not endeavour to come out of it without ridicule? Will I not give the world cause to speak of me? And to be spoken of, nowadays, when there are M.

le Prince, M. de Turenne,* and many others, my contemporaries, I, admiral of France, grandson of Henry IV., King of Paris, have I anything left but to get myself killed? *Cordieu!* I will be talked of, I tell you; I shall be killed, whether or not; if not there, somewhere else."

"Why, monseigneur, this is only exaggeration; and hitherto you have demonstrated nothing of that kind but in bravery."

"*Peste!* my dear friend, there is bravery in facing scurvy, dysentery, locusts, and poisoned arrows, as my ancestor St. Louis*did. Do you know those fellows still use poisoned arrows? And then, you know me of old, I fancy, and you know that when I once make up my mind to a thing, I do it in earnest."

"Yes, you made up your mind to escape from Vincennes."*

"Ay, but you aided me in that, my master; and, by the way, I turn this way and turn that, without seeing my old friend, M. Vaugrimaud. How is he?"

"M. Vaugrimaud is still your Highness's most respectful servant," said Athos, smiling.

"I have a hundred pistoles here for him, which I bring as a legacy. My will is made, Comte."

"Ah! monseigneur! monseigneur!"

"And you may understand that if Grimaud's name were to appear in my will——" The Duc began to laugh; then, addressing Raoul, who, from the commencement of this conversation had sunk into a profound reverie, "Young man," said he, "I know there is to be found here a certain de Vouvray wine, and I believe——" Raoul left the room precipitately to order the wine. In the meantime M. de Beaufort took the hand of Athos.

"What do you mean to do with him?" asked he.

"Nothing, at present, monseigneur."

"Ah! yes, I know; since the passion of the King for La Vallière."

"Yes, monseigneur."

"That is all true, then, is it? I think I know her, that little La Vallière. She is not particularly handsome, if I remember right?"

"No, monseigneur," said Athos.

"Do you know whom she reminds me of?"

"Does she remind your Highness of any one?"

"She reminds me of a very agreeable girl, whose mother lived in the *Halles*."

"Ah! ah!" said Athos, smiling.

"Oh! the good old times," added M. de Beaufort. "Yes, La Vallière reminds me of that girl."

"Who had a son,* had she not?"

"I believe she had," replied the Duc, with careless *naïveté*, and a complaisant forgetfulness, of which no words could translate the tone and the vocal expression. "Now, here is poor Raoul, who is your son, I believe."

"Yes, he is my son, monseigneur."

"And the poor lad has been cut out by the King, and he frets."

"Better than that, monseigneur, he abstains."

"You are going to let the boy rust in idleness; you are wrong. Come, give him to me."

"My wish is to keep him at home, monseigneur. I have no longer anything in the world but him, and as long as he likes to remain——"

"Well, well," replied the Duc. "I could, nevertheless, have soon put matters to rights again. I assure you, I think he has in him the stuff of which maréchals of France are made; I have seen more than one produced from such."

"That is very possible, monseigneur; but it is the King who makes maréchals of France, and Raoul will never accept anything of the King."

Raoul interrupted this conversation by his return. He preceded Grimaud, whose still steady hands carried the plateau with one glass and a bottle of the Duc's favourite wine. On seeing his old protégé, the Duc uttered an exclamation of pleasure.

"Grimaud! Good evening, Grimaud!" said he; "how goes it?"

The servant bowed profoundly, as much gratified as his noble interlocutor was.

"Two old friends!" said the Duc, shaking honest Grimaud's shoulder after a vigorous fashion; which was followed by another still more profound and delighted bow from Grimaud.

"But, what is this, Comte, only one glass?"

"I should not think of drinking with your Highness, unless your Highness permitted me," replied Athos, with noble humility.

"Cordieu! you were right to bring only one glass, we will both drink out of it, like two brothers in arms. Begin, Comte."

"Do me the honour," said Athos, gently putting back the glass.

"You are a charming friend," replied the Duc de Beaufort, who drank, and passed the goblet to his companion. "But that is not all," continued he, "I am still thirsty, and I wish to do honour to this handsome young man who stands here. I carry good luck with me, Vicomte," said he to Raoul; "wish for something while drinking out of my glass, and the plague stifle me if what you wish does not come to pass!" He held the goblet to Raoul, who hastily moistened his lips, and replied with the same promptitude:—

"I have wished for something, monseigneur." His eyes sparkled with a gloomy fire, and the blood mounted to his cheeks; he terrified Athos, if only with his smile.

"And what have you wished for?" replied the Duc, sinking back into his chair, whilst with one hand he returned the bottle to Grimaud, and with the other gave him a purse.

"Will you promise me, monseigneur, to grant me what I wish for?"

"*Pardieu!* That is agreed upon!"

"I wished, Monsieur le Duc, to go with you to Gigelli."

Athos became pale, and was unable to conceal his agitation. The Duc looked at his friend, as if desirous to assist him to parry this unexpected blow.

"That is very difficult, my dear Vicomte, very difficult," added he, in a lower tone of voice.

"Pardon me, monseigneur, I have been indiscreet," replied Raoul, in a firm voice; "but as you yourself invited me to wish——"

"To wish to leave me?" said Athos.

"Oh! monsieur, can you imagine——"

"Well! *mordieu!*" cried the Duc, "the young Vicomte is right! What can he do here? He will rot with grief."

Raoul blushed, and the excitable Prince continued: "War is a distraction; we gain everything by it; we can only lose one thing by it: life;—then so much the worse!"

"That is to say, memory," said Raoul eagerly; "and that is to say, so much the better."

He repented of having spoken so warmly when he saw Athos rise and open the window; which was, doubtless, to conceal an emotion. Raoul sprang towards the Comte, but the latter had already overcome his emotion, and turned to the lights with a serene and impassible countenance. "Well, come," said the Duc, "let us see! Shall he go, or shall he not? If he goes, Comte, he shall be my aide-de-camp, my son."

"Monseigneur!" cried Raoul, bending his knee.

"Monseigneur!" cried Athos, taking the hand of the Duc; "Raoul shall do just as he likes."

"Oh! no, monsieur, just as you like," interrupted the young man.

"By *la Corbleu!*" said the Prince in his turn, "it is neither the Comte nor the Vicomte that shall have his way; it is I. I will take him away. The marine offers a superb future, my friend."

Raoul smiled again so sadly, that this time Athos felt his heart penetrated by it, and replied to him by a severe look. Raoul comprehended it all; he recovered his calmness, and was so guarded, that not another word escaped him. The Duc at length rose, on observing the advanced hour, and said with much animation, "I am in great haste, but if I am told I have lost time in talking with a friend, I will reply I have gained a good recruit."

"Pardon me, Monsieur le Duc," interrupted Raoul, "do not tell the King so, for it is not the King I will serve."

"Eh! my friend, whom then will you serve? The times are past when you might have said, 'I belong to M. de Beaufort.' No, nowadays, we all belong to the King, great or small. Therefore, if you serve and board my vessels, there can be nothing equivocal in it, my dear Vicomte; it will be the King you will serve."

Athos waited with a kind of impatient joy for the reply about to be made to this embarrassing question by Raoul, the intractable enemy of the King, his rival. The father hoped that the obstacle would overcome the desire. He was thankful to M. de Beaufort, whose lightness or generous reflection had thrown an impediment in the way of the departure of a son, now his only joy. But Raoul, still firm and tranquil: "Monsieur le Duc," replied he, "the objection you make I have already considered in my mind. I will serve on board your vessels, because you do me the honour to take me with you; but I shall there serve a more powerful master than the King, I shall serve God."

"God! how so?" said the Duc and Athos together.

"My intention is to make profession, and become a knight of Malta,"*added Bragelonne, letting fall, one by one, words more icy than the drops which fall from bare trees after the tempests of winter.

Under this blow Athos staggered, and the Prince himself was moved. Grimaud uttered a heavy groan, and let fall the bottle, which was broken without anybody paying attention to it. M. de Beaufort looked the young man in the face, and read plainly, though his eyes were cast down, the fire of resolution before which everything must give way. As to Athos, he was too well acquainted with that tender, but inflexible soul; he could not hope to make it deviate from the fatal road it had just chosen. He could only press the hand the Duc held out to him.

"Comte, I shall set off in two days for Toulon," said M. de Beaufort. "Will you meet me at Paris, in order that I may know your determination?"

"I will have the honour of thanking you there, my Prince, for all your kindnesses," replied the Comte.

"And be sure to bring the Vicomte with you, whether he follows me or does not follow me," added the Duc; "he has my word, and I only ask yours."

Having thrown a little balm upon the wound of the paternal heart, he pulled the ear of Grimaud, whose eyes sparkled more than usual, and regained his escort in the parterre. The horses, rested and refreshed, set off with spirit through this beautiful night, and soon placed a considerable distance between their master and the château.

Athos and Bragelonne were again face to face. Eleven o'clock was striking. The father and son preserved a profound silence towards each other, where an intelligent observer would have expected cries and tears. But these two men were of such a nature that all emotion plunged itself where it was lost for ever when they had resolved to confine it to their own hearts. They passed, then, silently and almost breathlessly the hour which preceded midnight. The clock, by striking, alone pointed out to them how many minutes had lasted the painful journey made by their souls in the immensity of the remembrances of the past and of the fears of the future. Athos rose first, saying, "It is late—till to-morrow."

Raoul rose, and in his turn embraced his father. The latter held him clasped to his breast, and said in a tremulous voice, "In two days you will have left me, then—left me for ever, Raoul!"

"Monsieur," replied the young man, "I had formed a determination, that of piercing my heart with my sword; but you would have thought that cowardly. I have renounced that determination, and therefore we must part."

"You leave me by going, Raoul."

"Listen to me again, monsieur, I implore you. If I do not go, I shall die here of grief and love. I know how long a time I have to live thus. Send me away quickly, monsieur, or you will see me basely die before your eyes—in your house. This is stronger than my will—stronger than my strength; you may plainly see that within one month I have lived thirty years, and that I approach the end of my life."

"Then," said Athos coldly, "you go with the intention of getting killed in Africa? Oh! tell me! do not lie!"

Raoul grew deadly pale, and remained silent for two seconds, which were to his father two hours of agony. Then, all at once: "Monsieur," said he, "I have promised to devote myself to God. In exchange for this sacrifice which I make of my youth and my liberty, I will only ask of Him one thing, and that is to preserve me for you, because you are the only tie which attaches me to this world. God alone can give me the strength not to forget that I owe you everything, and that nothing ought to be with me before you."

Athos embraced his son tenderly, and said :—

"You have just replied to me on the word of honour of an

honest man; in two days we shall be with M. de Beaufort at Paris, and you will then do what will be proper for you to do. You are free, Raoul; *adieu*."

And he slowly gained his bedroom. Raoul went down into the garden, and passed the night in the alley of limes.

56

PREPARATIONS FOR DEPARTURE

ATHOS lost no more time in combating this immutable resolution. He gave all his attention to preparing, during the two days the Duc had granted to him, the proper appointments for Raoul. This labour chiefly concerned Grimaud, who immediately applied himself to it with the goodwill and intelligence we know he possessed. Athos gave this worthy servant orders to take the route to Paris when the equipments should be ready; and, not to expose himself in keeping the Duc waiting, or to delay Raoul, so that the Duc should perceive his absence, he himself, the day after the visit of M. de Beaufort, set off for Paris with his son.

For the poor young man it was an emotion easily to be understood, thus to return to Paris amongst all the people who had known and loved him. Every face recalled a suffering to him who had suffered so much, to him who had loved so much, some circumstance of his love. Raoul, on approaching Paris, felt as if he were dying. Once in Paris he really existed no longer. When he reached Guiche's residence, he was informed that Guiche was with Monsieur. Raoul took the road to the Luxembourg, and when arrived, without suspecting that he was going to the place where La Vallière had lived, he heard so much music and respired so many perfumes, he heard so much joyous laughter, and saw so many dancing shadows, that, if it had not been for a charitable woman, who perceived him so dejected and pale beneath a doorway, he would have remained there a few minutes, and then would have gone away, never to return. But, as we have said, in the first antechambers he had stopped, solely for the sake of not mixing himself with all those happy existences which he felt were moving around him in the adjacent saloons. And as one of Monsieur's servants, recognising him, had asked him if he wished to see Monsieur or Madame, Raoul had scarcely answered him, but had sunk down upon a bench near the velvet doorway, looking at a clock, which had stood for nearly an hour. The servant has passed on, and another, better acquainted with him, had come up and interrogated Raoul whether he should inform M. Guiche of his being there. This name even did not rouse the recollections of poor Raoul. The persistent servant went on to relate that Guiche had just invented a new game of lottery,* and was teaching it to the ladies. Raoul, opening his large eyes, like the absent man in Theophrastus,* had made no answer, but his sadness had increased by two shades. With his head hanging down, his limbs relaxed, his mouth half open for the escape of his sighs, Raoul remained, thus forgotten, in the antechamber, when all at once a lady's robe passed, rubbing against the doors of a lateral saloon which opened upon the gallery. A lady, young, pretty, and gay, scolding an officer of the household, entered by that way, and expressed herself with much vivacity. The officer replied in calm but firm sentences; it was rather a little love pet than a quarrel of courtiers, and was terminated by a kiss on the fingers of the lady. Suddenly, on perceiving Raoul, the lady became silent, and pushing away the officer:—

"Make your escape, Malicorne,"* said she; "I did not think there was any one here. I shall curse you, if they have either heard or seen us!"

Malicorne hastened away. The young lady advanced behind Raoul, and stretching her joyous face over him as he lay:—

"Monsieur is a gallant man," said she, "and no doubt——"

She here interrupted herself by uttering a cry: "Raoul!" said she, blushing.

"Mademoiselle de Montalais!" said Raoul, more pale than death.

He rose unsteadily, and tried to make his way across the slippery mosaic of the floor; but she had comprehended that savage and cruel grief; she felt that in the flight of Raoul there was an accusation, or at least a suspicion against herself. A woman, ever vigilant, she did not think she ought to let the opportunity slip of making a justification; but Raoul, though stopped by her in the middle of the gallery, did not seem disposed to surrender without a combat. He took it up in a tone so cold and embarrassed that if they had been thus surprised the whole court would have had no doubt about the proceedings of Mademoiselle de Montalais.

"Ah! monsieur," said she, with disdain, "what you are doing is very unworthy of a gentleman. My heart inclines me to speak to you; you compromise me by a reception almost uncivil. You are wrong, monsieur; and you confound your friends with your enemies. Farewell!"

Raoul had sworn never to speak of Louise, never even to look at those who might have seen Louise; he was going into another world, that he might never meet with anything Louise had seen, or anything she had touched. But after the first shock of his pride, after having had a glimpse of Montalais, the companion of Louise —Montalais, who reminded him of the turret of Blois and the joys of youth—all his reason faded away.

"Pardon me, mademoiselle; it enters not, it cannot enter into my thoughts to be uncivil."

"Do you wish to speak to me?" said she, with the smile of former days. "Well! come somewhere else; for here we may be surprised."

"Oh!" said he.

She looked at the clock doubting, then, having reflected:—

"In my apartment," said she, "we shall have an hour to ourselves." And, taking her course, lighter than a fairy, she ran up to her chamber, followed by Raoul. Shutting the door, and placing in the hands of her *camériste* the mantle she had held upon her arm,— "You were seeking M. de Guiche, were you not?" said she to Raoul.

"Yes, mademoiselle."

"I will go and ask him to come up here presently, after I have spoken to you."

"Do so, mademoiselle."

"Are you angry with me?"

Raoul looked at her for a moment, then, casting down his eyes, "Yes," said he.

"You think I was concerned in the plot which brought about your rupture, do you not?"

"Rupture!" said he, with bitterness. "Oh! mademoiselle, there can be no rupture where there has been no love."

"An error," replied Montalais; "Louise did love you."

Raoul started.

"Not with love, I know; but she liked you, and you ought to have married her before you set out for London."

Raoul broke into a sinister laugh, which made Montalais shudder.

"You tell me that very much at your ease, mademoiselle. Do people marry whom they like? You forget that the King then kept for himself as his mistress her of whom we are speaking."

"Listen," said the young woman, pressing the cold hands of Raoul in her own, "you were wrong in every way; a man of your age ought never to leave a woman of her's alone."

"There is no longer any faith in the world, then?" said Raoul.

"No, Vicomte," said Montalais quietly. "Nevertheless, let me tell you, that if instead of loving Louise coldly and philosophically, you had endeavoured to awaken her to love——"

"Enough, I pray you, mademoiselle," said Raoul. "I feel that you are all, of both sexes, of a different age from me. You can laugh and you can banter agreeably. I, mademoiselle, I loved Mademoiselle de——" Raoul could not pronounce her name,—"I loved her well; I put faith in her; now I am quits by loving her no longer."

"Oh, Vicomte!" said Montalais, pointing to his reflection in a mirror.

"I know what you mean, mademoiselle; I am much altered, am I not? Well! do you know why? Because my face is the mirror of my heart, the inside has changed, as the outside has."

"You are consoled, then?" said Montalais sharply.

"No, I shall never be consoled."

"I don't understand you, Monsieur de Bragelonne."

"I care but little for that. I do not too well understand myself."

"You have not even tried to speak to Louise?"

"Who! I?" exclaimed the young man, with eyes flashing fire; "I!—why do you not advise me to marry her? Perhaps the King would consent now." And he rose from his chair full of anger.

"I see," said Montalais, "that you are not cured, and that Louise has one enemy the more."

"One enemy the more?"

"Yes; favourites are but little beloved at the court of France."

"Oh! whilst she has her lover to protect her, is not that enough? She has chosen him of such a quality that her enemies cannot prevail against her." But, stopping all at once—"And then she has you for her friend, mademoiselle," added he, with a shade of irony, which did not glide off the cuirass.

"Who! I?—Oh, no! I am no longer one of those whom Mademoiselle de la Vallière deigns to look upon; but——"

Thus *but*, so big with menaces and storms; this *but*, which made the heart of Raoul beat, such griefs did it presage for her whom lately he loved so dearly; this terrible *but*, so significant in a woman like Montalais, was interrupted by a moderately loud noise heard by the speakers, proceeding from the alcove behind the wainscoting. Montalais turned to listen, and Raoul was already rising, when a lady entered the room quietly by the secret door, which she closed after her.

"Madame!" exclaimed Raoul, on recognising the sister-in-law of the King.

"Stupid wretch!" murmured Montalais, throwing herself, but

too late, before the Princess; "I have been mistaken in an hour!"*
She had, however, time to warn the Princess, who was walking
towards Raoul.

"M. de Bragelonne, madame," And at these words, the
Princess drew back, uttering a cry in her turn.

"Your Royal Highness," said Montalais, with volubility, "is
kind enough to think of this lottery, and——"

The Princess began to lose countenance. Raoul hastened his
departure, without yet divining all; but he felt that he was in the
way. Madame was preparing a word of transition to recover herself, when a closet opened in front of the alcove, and M. de Guiche
issued, all radiant, also from that closet. The most pale of the four,
we must admit, was still Raoul. The Princess, however, was near
fainting, and was obliged to lean upon the foot of the bed for
support. No one ventured to support her. This scene occupied
several minutes of terrible silence. But Raoul broke it. He went up
to the Comte, whose inexpressible emotion made his knees tremble,
and taking his hand, "Dear Comte," said he, "tell Madame I am
too unhappy not to merit my pardon; tell her also that I have
loved in the course of my life, and that the horror of the treachery
that has been practised on me renders me inexorable for all other
treachery that may be committed around me. This is why,
mademoiselle," said he, smiling, to Montalais, "I never would
divulge the secret of the visits of my friend to your apartment.
Obtain from Madame—from Madame who is so clement and so
generous—obtain her pardon for you whom she has just surprised
also. You are both free, love each other, be happy!"

The Princess felt for a moment the despair which cannot be
described; it was repugnant to her, notwithstanding the exquisite
delicacy which Raoul had exhibited, to feel herself at the mercy of
an indiscretion. It was equally repugnant to her to accept the
evasion offered by this delicate deception. Agitated, nervous, she
struggled against the double stings of the two troubles. Raoul
comprehended her position, and came once more to her aid.
Bending his knee before her: "Madame," said he in a low voice,
"in two days I shall be far from Paris; in a fortnight I shall be far
from France, where I shall never be seen again."

"Are you going away, then?" said she, with great delight.

"With M. de Beaufort."

"Into Africa!" cried Guiche, in his turn. "You, Raoul—oh!
my friend—into Africa, where everybody dies!" And forgetting
everything, forgetting that that forgetfulness itself compromised
the Princess more eloquently than his presence, "Ingrate!" said
he, "and you have not even consulted me!" And he embraced

him; during which time Montalais had led away Madame, and disappeared herself.

Raoul passed his hand over his brow, and said with a smile, "I have been dreaming!" Then warmly to Guiche, who, by degrees, absorbed him: "My friend," said he, "I conceal nothing from you, who are the elected of my heart. I am going to seek death in yonder country; your secret will not remain in my breast more than a year."

"Oh, Raoul! a man!"

"Do you know what is my thought, Guiche? This is it: 'I shall live more, being buried beneath the earth, than I have lived for this month past. We are Christians, my friend, and if such suffering were to continue, I would not be answerable for the safety of my soul."

Guiche was anxious to raise objections.

"Not one word more on my account," said Raoul; "but advice to you, dear friend; what I am going to say to you is of much greater importance."

"What is that?"

"Without doubt, you risk much more than I do, because you love."

"Oh!"

"It is a joy so sweet to me to be able to speak to you thus! Well, then, Guiche, beware of Montalais."

"What! of that kind friend?"

"She was the friend of—her you know of. She ruined her by pride."

"You are mistaken."

"And now, when she has ruined her, she would ravish from her the only thing that renders that woman excusable in my eyes."

"What is that?"

"Her love."

"What do you mean by that?"

"I mean that there is a plot formed against her who is the mistress of the King—a plot formed in the very house of Madame."

"Can you think so?"

"I am certain of it."

"By Montalais?"

"Take her as the least dangerous of the enemies I dread for—the other!"

"Explain yourself clearly, my friend; and, if I can understand you——"

"In two words. Madame has been jealous of the King."

"I know she has——"

"Oh! fear nothing; you are beloved, you are beloved, Guiche; do you feel the value of these three words? They signify that you can raise your head, that you can sleep tranquilly, that you can thank God every minute of your life. You are beloved; that signifies that you may hear everything, even the counsel of a friend who wishes to preserve your happiness. You are beloved, Guiche, you are beloved! You do not endure those atrocious nights, those nights without end, which, with the arid eye and devoured heart, others pass through who are destined to die. You will live long, if you act like the miser who, bit by bit, crumb by crumb, collects and heaps up diamonds and gold. You are beloved; allow me to tell you what you must do that you may be beloved for ever."

Guiche contemplated for some time this unfortunate young man half mad with despair, till there passed through his heart something like remorse at his own happiness. Raoul suppressed his feverish excitement to assume the voice and countenance of an impassible man. "They will make her, whose name I should wish to still be able to pronounce—they will make her suffer. Swear to me that you will not second them in anything, but that you will defend her when possible, as I would have done myself."

"I swear I will," replied Guiche.

"And," continued Raoul, "some day, when you shall have rendered her a great service, some day when she shall thank you, promise me to say these words to her: 'I have done you this kindness, madame, by the warm desire of M. de Bragelonne, whom you so deeply injured.'"

"I swear I will," murmured Guiche.

"That is all. *Adieu!* I set out to-morrow or the day after, for Toulon. If you have a few hours to spare, give them to me."

"All! all!" cried the young man.

"Thank you."

"And what are you going to do now?"

"I am going to meet M. le Comte at the house of Planchet, where we hope to find M. d'Artagnan."

"M. d'Artagnan!"

"Yes, I wish to embrace him before my departure. He is a brave man, who loves me dearly. Farewell, my friend; you are expected, no doubt; you will find me, when you wish, at the lodgings of the Comte. Farewell!"

The two young men embraced. They who might have seen them both thus, would not have hesitated to say, pointing to Raoul: "That is the happy man!"

57

PLANCHET'S INVENTORY

ATHOS, during the visit made to the Luxembourg by Raoul, had gone to Planchet's residence to inquire after d'Artagnan. The gentleman, on arriving at the Rue des Lombards, found the shop of the grocer in great confusion; but it was not the encumberment of a lucky sale, or that of an arrival of goods. Planchet was not throned, as usual, upon sacks and barrels. No. A young man with a pen behind his ear, and another with an account book in his hand, were setting down a number of figures, whilst a third counted and weighed. An inventory was being taken. Athos, who had no knowledge of commercial matters, felt himself a little embarrassed by the material obstacles and the majesty of those who were thus employed. He saw several customers sent away, and asked himself whether he, who came to buy nothing, would not be more properly deemed importunate. He therefore asked very politely if he could see M. Planchet. The reply, pretty carelessly given, was that M. Planchet was packing his trunks. These words surprised Athos. "How! his trunks!" said he, "is M. Planchet going away?"

"Yes, monsieur, directly."

"Then, if you please, inform him that M. le Comte de la Fère desires to speak to him for a moment."

At mention of the Comte's name, one of the young men, no doubt accustomed to hear it pronounced with respect, immediately went to inform Planchet. It was at this moment that Raoul, after his painful scene with Montalais and Guiche, arrived at the grocer's house. Planchet left his job directly he received the Comte's message.

"Ah! Monsieur le Comte!" exclaimed he, "how glad I am to see you! What good star brings you here?"

"My dear Planchet," said Athos, pressing the hand of his son, whose sad look he silently observed,—"we are come to learn of you—But in what confusion do I find you! You are as white as a miller; where have you been rummaging?"

"Ah, *diable!* take care, monsieur; don't come near me till I have well shaken myself."

"What for? Flour or dust only whiten."

"No, no; what you see on my arms is arsenic."

"Arsenic?"

"Yes; I am making my provision for the rats."

"Ay, I suppose in an establishment like this the rats play a conspicuous part."

"It is not with this establishment I concern myself, M. le Comte. The rats have robbed me of more here than they will ever rob me again."

"What do you mean?"

"Why, you may have observed, monsieur, my inventory is being taken."

"Are you leaving trade, then?"

"Eh! *mon Dieu!* yes. I have disposed of my business to one of my young men."

"Bah! you are rich, then, I suppose?"

"Monsieur, I have taken a dislike to the city; I don't know whether it is because I am growing old, and, as M. d'Artagnan one day said, when we grow old we more often think of the things of our youth; but for some time past I have felt myself attracted towards the country and gardening; I was a countryman formerly." And Planchet marked this confession with a little rather pretentious laugh for a man making profession of humility.

Athos made a gesture of approval, and then added:—"You are going to buy an estate then?"

"I have bought one, monsieur."

"Ah! that is still better."

"A little house at Fontainebleau,* with something like twenty acres of land round it."

"Very well, Planchet! Accept my compliments on your acquisition."

"But, monsieur, we are not comfortable here; the cursed dust makes you cough. *Corbleu!* I should not wish to poison the most worthy gentleman in the kingdom."

Athos did not smile at this little pleasantry which Planchet had aimed at him, in order to try his strength in mundane facetiousness.

"Yes," said he, "let us have a little talk by ourselves—in your own room, for example. You have a room, have you not?"

"Certainly, Monsieur le Comte."

"Upstairs, perhaps?" And Athos, seeing Planchet a little embarrassed, wished to relieve him by going first.

"It is—but——" said Planchet, hesitating.

Athos was mistaken in the cause of this hesitation, and, attributing it to a fear the grocer might have of offering humble hospitality—"Never mind, never mind," said he, still going up, "the dwelling of a tradesman in this quarter is not expected to be a palace. Come on!"

Raoul nimbly preceded him, and entered first. Two cries were heard simultaneously—we may say three. One of these cries dominated over the others; it was uttered by a woman. The other proceeded from the mouth of Raoul; it was an exclamation of surprise. He had no sooner made it than he shut the door sharply. The third was from fright; Planchet had proffered it.

"I ask your pardon!" added he, "Madame is dressing."

Raoul had, no doubt, seen that what Planchet said was true, for he turned round to go down stairs again.

"Madame——" said Athos; "Oh! pardon me, Planchet, I did not know that you had upstairs——"

"It is Trüchen," added Planchet, blushing a little.

"It is whom you please, my good Planchet; but pardon my rudeness."

"No, no; go up now, gentlemen."

"We will do no such thing," said Athos.

"Oh! madame having notice, has had time——"

"No, Planchet; farewell!"

"Eh, gentlemen! you would not disoblige me by thus standing on the staircase, or by going away without having sat down."

"If we had known you had a lady upstairs," replied Athos, with his customary coolness, "we would have asked permission to pay our respects to her."

Planchet was so disconcerted by this little extravagance, that he forced the passage, and himself opened the door to admit the Comte and his son. Trüchen was quite dressed: costume of the shopkeeper's wife, rich and coquettish; German eyes attacking French eyes. She ceded the apartment after two curtseys, and went down into the shop—but not without having listened at the door, to know what Planchet's gentlemen visitors would say of her. Athos, suspected that, and therefore turned the conversation accordingly. Planchet, on his part, was burning to give explanations, which Athos avoided, But, as certain tenacities are stronger than all others, Athos was forced to hear Planchet recite his idylls of felicity, translated into a language more chaste than that of Longus.* So Planchet related how Trüchen had charmed his ripe age, and brought good luck to his business, as Ruth did to Boaz.*

"You want nothing now, then, but heirs to your property."

"If I had one, he would have three hundred thousand livres," said Planchet.

"Humph! you must have one then," said Athos phlegmatically; "if only to prevent your little fortune being lost."

The words *little fortune* placed Planchet in his rank, like the voice of the sergeant when Planchet was but a *piqueur* in the regiment of Piedmont, in which Rochefort*had placed him. Athos perceived that the grocer would marry Trüchen, and, in spite of fate, establish a family. This appeared the more evident to him when he learned that the young man to whom Planchet was selling his business was her cousin. Having heard all that was necessary of the happy prospects of the retiring grocer, "What is M. d'Artagnan about," said he, "he is not at the Louvre?"

"Ah! Monsieur le Comte, Monsieur d'Artagnan has disappeared."

"Disappeared!" said Athos, with surprise.

"Oh! monsieur, we know what that means."

"But, I do not know."

"Whenever M. d'Artagnan disappears it is always for some mission or some great affair."

"Has he said anything to you about it?'

"Never."

"You were acquainted with his departure for England formerly, were you not?"

"On account of the speculation,'*said Planchet heedlessly.

"The speculation!"

"I mean——" interrupted Planchet, quite confused.

"Well, well; neither your affairs nor those of your master are in question: the interest we take in him alone has induced me to apply to you. Since the captain of the musketeers is not here, and as we cannot learn from you where we are likely to find M. d'Artagnan, we will take our leave of you. *Au revoir*, Planchet, *au revoir*. Let us be gone, Raoul."

"Monsieur le Comte, I wish I were able to tell you——"

"Oh, not at all; I am not the man to reproach a servant with discretion."

The word "servant" struck rudely on the ears of the demi-millionaire Planchet, but natural respect prevailed over pride. "There is nothing indiscreet in telling you, Monsieur le Comte, M. d'Artagnan came here the other day——"

"Ah! ah!"

"And remained several hours consulting a geographical chart."

"You are right, then, my friend; say no more about it."

"And the chart is there as a proof," added Planchet, who went to fetch from the neighbouring wall—where it was suspended by a twist, forming a triangle with the bar of the window to which it was fastened—the plan consulted by the captain on his last visit to Planchet. This plan, which he brought to the Comte, was a map of France, upon which the practised eye of that gentleman discovered an itinerary, marked out with small pins; wherever a pin was missing, a hole denoted its having been there. Athos, by following with his eye the pins and the holes, saw that d'Artagnan had taken the direction of the south, and gone as far as the Mediterranean, towards Toulon. It was near Cannes that the marks and the punctured places ceased. The Comte de la Fère puzzled his brains for some time, to divine what the musketeer could be going to do at Cannes, and what motive could have led him to examine the banks of the Var. The reflections of Athos suggested nothing. His accustomed perspicacity was at fault. Raoul's researches were not more successful than his father's.

"Never mind," said the young man to the Comte, who, silently and with his fingers, had made him understand the route of d'Artagnan; "we must confess that there is a Providence always occupied in connecting our destiny with that of M. d'Artagnan. There he is on the coast of Cannes, and you, monsieur, will, at least, conduct me as far as Toulon. Be assured that we shall meet with him more easily upon our route than upon this map."

Then, taking leave of Planchet, who was scolding his shopmen, even the cousin of Trüchen, his successor, the gentlemen set out to pay a visit to M. de Beaufort. On leaving the grocer's shop, they saw a coach, the future depository of the charms of Mademoiselle Trüchen and the bags of crowns of Planchet.

"Every one journeys towards happiness by the route he chooses," said Raoul, in a melancholy tone.

"Road to Fontainbleau!" cried Planchet to his coachman.

58

THE INVENTORY OF M. DE BEAUFORT

To have talked of d'Artagnan with Planchet, to have seen Planchet quit Paris to bury himself in his country retreat, had been for Athos and his son like a last farewell to the noise of the capital—to their life of former days. What, in fact, did these men leave behind them—one of whom had exhausted the past age in glory, and the other the present age in misfortune? Evidently, neither of them had anything to ask of his contemporaries. They had only to pay a visit to M. de Beaufort, and arrange with him the particulars of the departure. The Duc was lodged magnificently in Paris. He had one of those superb establishments pertaining to great fortunes,* which certain old men remembered to have seen flourish in the times of wasteful liberality in Henry III.'s reign. Then, really, several great nobles were richer than the King. They knew it, used it, and never deprived themselves of the pleasure of humiliating His Royal Majesty when they had an opportunity. It was this ego-tistical aristocracy which Richelieu had constrained to contribute, with its blood, its purse, and its duties, to what was from his time styled the King's service. From Louis XI.—that terrible mower down of the great—to Richelieu, how many families had raised their heads! How many from Richelieu to Louis XIV. had bowed their heads never to raise them again! But M. de Beaufort was born a Prince, and of a blood which is not shed upon scaffolds, unless by the decree of peoples. This Prince had kept up a grand style of living. How did he maintain his horses, his people, and his table? Nobody knew; himself less than others. Only there were then privileges for the sons of kings to whom nobody refused to become a creditor, whether from respect, devotedness, or a persuasion that they would some day be paid.

Athos and Raoul found the mansion of the Duc in as much confusion as that of Planchet. The Duc, likewise, was making his inventory; that is to say, he was distributing to his friends every-thing of value he had in the house. Owing nearly two millions—an enormous amount in those days—M. de Beaufort had calcu-lated that he could not set out for Africa without a good round sum; and, in order to find that sum, he was distributing to his old creditors plate, arms, jewels, and furniture, which was more magnificent than selling it, and brought him back double. In fact, how could a man to whom ten thousand livres were owing, refuse to carry away a present of six thousand, enhanced in merit from having belonged to a descendant of Henry IV.? And how, after having carried away that present, could he refuse ten thousand livres more to this generous noble? This, then, was what had happened. The Duc had no longer a dwelling-house—that had become useless to an admiral whose place of residence is his ship; he had no longer need of superfluous arms, when he was placed amidst his cannons; no more jewels, which the sea might rob him of; but he had three or four hundred thousand crowns fresh in his coffers. And throughout the house there was a joyous movement of people who believed they were plundering monseigneur. The Prince had, in a supreme degree, the art of making happy the credito-s the most to be pitied. Every distressed man, every empty purse, found with him patience and intelligence of his position. To some he said, "I wish I had what you have; I would give it you." And to others, "I have but this silver ewer; it is worth at least five hundred livres,—take it." The effect of which was—so truly is courtesy a current payment—that the Prince constantly found means to renew his creditors. This time he used no ceremony; it might be called a general pillage. He gave up everything. The Oriental fable of the poor Arab, who carried away from the pillage of a palace a kettle at the bottom of which was concealed a bag of gold, and whom everybody allowed to pass without jealousy,— this fable had become a truth in the Prince's mansion. Many contractors paid themselves upon the offices of the Duc. Thus, the provision department, who plundered the clothes presses and the harness-rooms, attached very little value to things which tailors and saddlers set great store by. Anxious to carry home to their wives preserves given them by monseigneur, many were seen bounding joyously along, under the weight of earthen jars and bottles, gloriously stamped with the arms of the Prince. M. de Beaufort finished by giving away his horses and the hay from his lofts. He made more than thirty happy with kitchen utensils; and thirty more with the contents of his cellar. Still further, all these people went away with the conviction that M. de Beaufort only acted in this manner to prepare for a new fortune concealed beneath the Arab tents. They repeated to each other, while devastating his hotel, that he was sent to Gigelli by the King to reconstruct his lost fortunes; that the treasures of Africa would be equally divided between the admiral and the King of France; that these treasures consisted in mines of diamonds, or other fabulous stones; the gold and silver mines of Mount Atlas did not even obtain the honour of being named. In addition to the mines to be worked,—which could not be begun till after the campaign—there would be the booty made by the army. M. de Beaufort would lay his hands upon all that the rich pirates had robbed Christendom of since the battle of Lepanto.* The number of millions from these sources defied calculation. Why, then, should he, who was going in quest of such treasures, set any store by the poor utensils of his past life? And, reciprocally, why should they spare the property of him who spared it so little himself?

Such was the position of affairs. Athos, with his investigating glance, saw what was going on at once. He found the admiral of France a little exalted, for he was rising from a table of fifty covers, at which the guests had drunk long and deeply to the prosperity of the expedition; at which, with the dessert, the remains of the meal had been given to the servants, and the empty dishes and plates to the curious. The Prince was intoxicated with his ruin and his popularity at the same time. He had drunk his old wine to the health of his future wine. When he saw Athos and Raoul,—

"There is my *aide-de-camp* being brought to me!" he cried. "Come hither, Comte; come hither, Vicomte." Athos tried to find a passage through the heaps of linen and plate.

"Ah! step over, step over!" said the Duc, offering a full glass to Athos. The latter took it; Raoul scarcely moistened his lips.

"Here is your commission," said the Prince to Raoul. "I had prepared it, reckoning upon you. You will go on before me as far as Antibes."

"Yes, monseigneur."

"Here is the order." And de Beaufort gave Raoul the order. "Do you know anything of the sea?"

"Yes, monseigneur; I have travelled with M. le Prince."

"That is well; all these barges and lighters must be in attendance to form an escort, and carry my provisions. The army must be prepared to embark in a fortnight at latest."

"That shall be done, monseigneur."

"The present order gives you the right to visit and search all the isles along the coast; you will there make the enrolments and levies you may want for me."

"Yes, Monsieur le Duc."

"And as you are an active man, and will work freely, you will spend much money."

"I hope not, monseigneur."

"But I reckon you will. My intendant has prepared orders of a thousand livres, drawn upon the cities of the south; he will give you a hundred of them. Now, dear Vicomte, begone."

Athos interrupted the Prince. "Keep your money, monseigneur; war is to be made among the Arabs with gold as well as lead."

"I wish to try the contrary," replied the Duc; "and then, you are acquainted with my ideas upon the expedition—plenty of noise, plenty of fire, and, if it must be so, I shall disappear in the smoke." Having spoken thus, M. de Beaufort began to laugh; but his mirth was not reciprocated by Athos and Raoul. He perceived this at once. "Ah," said he with the courteous egotism of his rank and his age, "you are such people as a man should not see after dinner; you are cold, stiff, and dry, when I am all fire, all suppleness. and all wine. No, devil take me! I should always see you fasting, Vicomte; and you, Comte, if you wear such a face as that. you will see me no more."

He said this pressing the hand of Athos, who replied with a smile,—"Monseigneur, do not talk so grandly because you happen to have plenty of money. I predict that within a month you will be dry, stiff, and cold, in presence of your strong box, and that then, having Raoul at your elbow, quite fasting, you will be surprised to see him gay, animated, and generous, because he will have some new crowns to offer you."

"God grant it may be so!" cried the delighted Duc. "Comte, stay with me."

"No, I shall go with Raoul; the mission with which you charge him is a troublesome and difficult one. Alone it would be too much for him to execute. You do not observe, monseigneur, you have given him a command of the first order."

"Bah!"

"And in the marine."

"That may be true. But, when people resemble him, do they not do all that is required of them?"

"Monseigneur, I believe you will find nowhere so much zeal and intelligence, so much real bravery, as in Raoul; but if he failed in your embarkation, you would only meet with what you deserve."

"Humph! you are scolding me, then?"

"Monseigneur, to provision a fleet, to assemble a flotilla, to enrol your maritime force, would take an admiral a year. Raoul is a cavalry officer, and you allow him a fortnight!"

"I tell you he will get through."

"He may; but I will help him."

"To be sure you will; I reckoned upon you, and still further believe that when we are once at Toulon you will not let him depart alone."

"Oh!" said Athos, shaking his head.

"Patience! patience!"

"Monseigneur, permit us to take our leave."

"Begone, then, and my good fortune attend you."

"*Adieu!* monseigneur; and may your good fortune attend you likewise."

"Here is an expedition admirably commenced!" said Athos to his son. "No provisions—no store flotilla! What can be done, thus?"

"Humph!" murmured Raoul; "if all are going to do as I am, provisions will not be wanted."

"Monsieur," replied Athos sternly, "do not be unjust and senseless in your egotism, or your grief, whichever you please to call it. If you set out for this war solely with the intention of getting killed in it, you stand in need of nobody, and it was scarcely worth while to recommend you to M. de Beaufort. But when you have been introduced to the Prince Commandant—when you have accepted the responsibility of a post in his army, the question is no longer about you, but about all those poor soldiers, who, as well as you, have hearts and bodies, who will weep for their country and endure all the necessities of their human condition. Remember, Raoul, that an officer is a minister as useful as a priest, and that he ought to have more charity than a priest."

"Monsieur, I know it, and have practised it; I would have continued to do so still, but——"

"You forget also that you are of a country which is proud of its military glory; go and die if you like, but do not die without honour and without advantage to France. Cheer up, Raoul! do not let my words grieve you; I love you, and wish to see you perfect."

"I love your reproaches, monsieur," said the young man mildly; "they alone may cure me, because they prove to me that some one loves me still."

"And now, Raoul, let us be off; the weather is so fine, the heavens are so pure, those heavens which we shall always find above our heads, which you will see more pure still at Gigelli, and which will speak to you of me there, as they speak to me here of God."

The two gentlemen, after having agreed upon this point, talked over the wild freaks of the Duke, convinced that France would be served in a very incomplete manner, as regarded both spirit and practice, in the ensuing expedition; and having summed up his policy under the word vanity, they set forward, in obedience to their will rather than their destiny. The sacrifice was accomplished.

59

THE SILVER DISH

THE journey passed off pretty well. Athos and his son traversed France at the rate of fifteen leagues per day; sometimes more, sometimes less, according to the intensity of Raoul's grief. It took them a fortnight to reach Toulon, and they lost all traces of d'Artagnan at Antibes. They were forced to believe that the captain of the musketeers was desirous of preserving an incognito on his route, for Athos derived from his inquiries an assurance that such a cavalier as he described had exchanged his horse for a well-closed carriage on quitting Avignon. Raoul was much affected at not meeting with d'Artagnan. His affectionate heart longed to take a farewell and receive consolation from that heart of steel. Athos knew from experience that d'Artagnan became impenetrable when

engaged in any serious affair, whether on his own account, or in
the service of the King. He even feared to offend his friend, or
thwart him by too pressing inquiries. And yet when Raoul commenced his labour of classing the flotilla, and got together the
lighters to send them to Toulon, one of the fishermen told the
Comte that his boat had been laid up to refit since a trip he had
made on account of a gentleman who was in great haste to embark.
Athos, believing that this man was telling a falsehood in order to be
left at liberty to fish, and so gain more money when all his companions were gone, insisted upon having the details. The fisherman
informed him that six days previously a man had come in the
night to hire his boat, for the purpose of visiting the island of St.
Honorat.* The price was agreed upon, but the gentleman had
arrived with an immense carriage case, which he insisted upon
embarking, in spite of all the difficulties which opposed themselves
to that operation. The fisherman had wished to retract. He had
even threatened, but his threats had procured him nothing but a
shower of blows from the gentleman's cane, which fell upon his
shoulders sharp and long. Swearing and grumbling, he had
recourse to the syndic of his brotherhood*at Antibes, who administer
justice among themselves and protect each other; but the gentleman had exhibited a certain paper, at the sight of which the
syndic, bowing to the very ground, had enjoined obedience from
the fisherman, and abused him for having been refractory. They
then departed with the freight.

"But all this does not tell us," said Athos, "how you have
injured your boat."

"This is the way. I was steering towards St. Honorat as the
gentleman had desired me; but he changed his mind, and pretended that I could not pass to the south of the abbey."

"And why not?"

"Because, monsieur, there is in front of the square tower of the
Benedictines, towards the southern point, the bank of the *Moines.*"

"A rock?" asked Athos.

"Level with the water, and below the water; a dangerous
passage, but one I have cleared a thousand times; the gentleman
required me to land him at Sainte-Marguerite's."*

"Well?"

"Well, monsieur!" cried the fisherman, with his Provençal
accent, "a man is a sailor, or he is not; he knows his course, or he
is nothing but a fresh-water lubber. I was obstinate, and wished
to try the channel. The gentleman took me by the collar, and told
me quietly he would strangle me. My mate armed himself with a
hatchet, and so did I. We had the affront of the night before to pay

him out for. But the gentleman drew his sword, and used it in such an astonishingly rapid manner, that we neither of us could get near him. I was about to hurl my hatchet at his head, and I had a right to do so, hadn't I, monsieur? for a sailor aboard is master, as a citizen is in his chamber; I was going, then, in self-defence, to cut this gentleman in two, when all at once—believe me or not, monsieur—the great carriage case opened of itself, I don't know how, and there came out of it a sort of a phantom, his head covered with a black helmet and a black mask, something terrible to look upon, which came towards me threatening with its fists."

"And that was——" said Athos.

"That was the devil, monsieur; for the gentleman, with great glee, cried out on seeing him: 'Ah! thank you, monseigneur!'"

"A strange story!" murmured the Comte, looking at Raoul.

"And what did you do?" asked the latter of the fisherman.

"You must know, monsieur, that two poor men, such as we are, could be no match for two gentlemen; but when one of them is the devil we had no chance! My companion and I did not stop to consult one another; we made but one jump into the sea, for we were within seven or eight hundred feet of the shore."

"Well, and then?"

"Why, and then, monsieur, as there was a little wind from the south-west, the boat drifted into the sands of Sainte-Marguerite's."

"Oh!—but the two travellers?"

"Bah! you need not be uneasy about them! It was pretty plain that one was the devil, and protected the other! for when we recovered the boat, after she got afloat again, instead of finding these two creatures injured by the shock, we found nothing, not even the carriage or the case."

"Very strange! very strange!" repeated the Comte. "But since that, what have you done, my friend?"

"I made my complaint to the governor of Sainte-Marguerite's, who brought my finger under my nose by telling me if I plagued him with such silly stories he would have me flogged."

"What! did the governor say so?"

"Yes, monsieur; and yet my boat was injured, seriously injured, for the prow is left upon the point of Sainte-Marguerite's, and the carpenter asks a hundred and twenty livres, to repair it."

"Very well," replied Raoul; "you will be exempted from the service. Go."

"We will go to Sainte-Marguerite's, shall we?" said the Comte to Bragelonne, as the man walked away.

"Yes, monsieur, for there is something to be cleared up; that man does not seem to me to have told the truth."

"Nor to me neither, Raoul. The story of the masked man and the carriage having disappeared may be told to conceal some violence these fellows have committed upon their passenger in the open sea, to punish him for his persistence in embarking."

"I formed the same suspicion; the carriage was more likely to contain property than a man."

"We shall see to that, Raoul. This gentleman very much resembles d'Artagnan; I recognise his mode of proceeding. Alas! we are no longer the young invincibles of former days. Who knows whether the hatchet or the iron bar of this miserable coaster has not succeeded in doing that which the best blades of Europe, balls, and bullets have not been able to do in forty years?"

That same day they set out for Sainte-Marguerite's, on board a lugger, come from Toulon under orders. The impression they felt on landing was a singularly pleasing one. The isle was full of flowers and fruits. In its cultivated part it served as a garden for the governor. Orange, pomegranate, and fig-trees bent beneath the weight of their golden or purple fruits. All around this garden, in the uncultivated parts, the red partridges ran about in coveys among the brambles and tufts of junipers, and at every step of the Comte and Raoul a terrified rabbit quitted his thyme and heath to scuttle away to his burrow. In fact, this fortunate isle was uninhabited. Flat, offering nothing but a tiny bay for the convenience of embarkation, and under the protection of the governor, who went shares with them, smugglers made use of it as a provisional depot, at the expense of not killing the game or devastating the garden. With this compromise, the governor was in a situation to be satisfied with a garrison of eight men to guard his fortress, in which twelve cannons accumulated their coats of mouldy green. The governor was a sort of happy farmer, harvesting wines, figs, oil, and oranges, preserving his citrons and lemons within his sunny casemates. The fortress, encircled by a deep ditch, its only guardian, arose like three heads upon turrets connected with each other by terraces covered with moss.

Athos and Raoul wandered for some time round the fences of the garden without finding anyone to introduce them to the governor. They ended by making their own way into the garden. It was at the hottest time of the day. Everything sought shelter beneath grass or stone. The heavens spread their fiery veils as if to stifle all noises, to envelop all existences; the rabbit under the broom, the fly under the leaf, slept as the wave did beneath the heavens. Athos saw nothing living but a soldier, upon the terrace between the second and third court, who was carrying a basket of provisions on his head. This man returned almost immediately without his basket, and disappeared in the shade of his sentry-box. Athos supposed this man must have been carrying dinner to some one, and, after having done so, returned to dine himself. All at once they heard some one call out and, raising their heads, perceived in the frame of the bars of the window something of a white colour, like a hand that was waved backwards and forwards—something shining, like a polished weapon struck by the rays of the sun. And before they were able to ascertain what it was they saw, a luminous train, accompanied by a hissing sound in the air, called their attention from the donjon to the ground. A second dull noise was heard from the ditch, and Raoul ran to pick up a silver plate which was rolling along the dry sand. The hand which had thrown this plate made a sign to the two gentlemen, and then disappeared. Athos and Raoul, approaching each other, commenced an attentive examination of the dusty plate, and they discovered, in characters traced upon the bottom of it with the point of a knife, this inscription :—

" *I am the brother of the King of France—a prisoner to-day,—a madman to-morrow. French gentlemen and Christians, pray to God for the soul and the reason of the son of your masters.*"

The plate fell from the hands of Athos whilst Raoul was endeavouring to make out the meaning of these dismal words. At the same instant they heard a cry from the top of the donjon. As quick as lightning, Raoul bent down his head and forced down that of his father likewise. A musket barrel glittered from the crest of the wall. A white smoke floated like a plume from the mouth of the musket, and a ball was flattened against a stone within six inches of the two gentlemen.

"*Cordieu!*" cried Athos. "What, are people assassinated here? Come down, cowards as you are!"

"Yes, come down!" cried Raoul, furiously shaking his fist at the castle.

One of the assailants—he who was about to fire—replied to these cries by an exclamation of surprise; and, as his companion, who wished to continue the attack, had seized his loaded musket, he who had cried out, threw up the weapon, and the ball flew into the air. Athos and Raoul seeing them disappear from the platform, expected they would come to them, and waited with a firm demeanour. Five minutes had not elapsed, when a stroke upon a drum called the eight soldiers of the garrison to arms, and they showed themselves on the other side of the ditch with their muskets in hand. At the head of these men was an officer, whom Athos and Raoul recognised as the one who had fired the first musket. The man ordered the soldiers to "make ready."

"We are going to be shot!" cried Raoul; "but, sword in hand, at least, let us leap the ditch! We shall kill at least two of these scoundrels when their muskets are empty." And, suiting the action to the word, Raoul was springing forward, followed by Athos, when a well-known voice resounded behind them—"Athos! Raoul!"

"D'Artagnan!" replied the two gentlemen.

"Recover arms! *Mordioux!*" cried the captain to the soldiers, "I was sure I could not be mistaken."

"What is the meaning of this?" asked Athos. "What! were we to be shot without warning?"

"It was I who was going to shoot you, and if the governor missed you, I should not have missed you, my dear friends. How fortunate it is that I am accustomed to take a long aim, instead of firing the instant I raise my weapon! I thought I recognised you! Ah! my dear friends, how fortunate!" And d'Artagnan wiped his brow, for he had run fast, and emotion with him was not feigned.

"How!" said Athos. "And is the gentleman who fired at us the governor of the fortress?"

"In person."

"And why did he fire at us? What have we done to him?"

"*Pardieu!* you received what the prisoner threw to you?"

"That is true."

"That plate—the prisoner has written something on the bottom of it, has he not?"

"Yes."

"Good Heavens! I was afraid he had."

And d'Artagnan, with all the marks of mortal disquietude, seized the plate to read the inscription. When he had read it, a fearful pallor spread over his countenance. "Oh! Good Heavens!" repeated he. "Silence!—Here is the governor."

"And what will he do to us? Is it our fault?"

"It is true, then?" said Athos, in a subdued voice. "Is it true?"

"Silence! I tell you,—silence! If he only believes you can read; if he only suspects you have understood; I love you, my dear friends, I will be killed for you, but——"

"But——" said Athos and Raoul.

"But, I could not save you from perpetual imprisonment, if I saved you from death. Silence, then! Silence, again!"

The governor came up, having crossed the ditch upon a plank bridge.

"Well!" said he to d'Artagnan, "what stops us?"

"You are Spaniards—you do not understand a word of French," said the captain eagerly, to his friends, in a low voice.

"Well!" replied he, addressing the governor, "I was right; these gentlemen are two Spanish captains with whom I was acquainted at Ypres, last year; they don't know a word of French."

"Ah!" said the governor sharply. "And yet they were trying to read the inscription on the plate."

D'Artagnan took it out of his hands, effacing the characters with the point of his sword.

"How!" cried the governor—"what are you doing? I cannot read them now!"

"It is a State secret," replied d'Artagnan bluntly; "and as you know that, according to the King's order, it is under the penalty of death any one should penetrate it, I will, if you like, allow you to read it, and have you shot immediately afterwards."

During this apostrophe—half serious, half ironical—Athos and Raoul preserved the coolest, most unconcerned silence.

"But is it possible," said the governor, "that these gentlemen do not comprehend at least some words?"

"Suppose they do! If they do understand a few spoken words, it does not follow that they should understand what is written. They cannot even read Spanish. A noble Spaniard, remember, ought never to know how to read."

The governor was obliged to be satisfied with these explanations, but he was still tenacious. "Invite these gentlemen to come to the fortress," said he.

"That I will willingly do. I was about to propose it to you." The fact is, the captain had quite another idea, and would have wished his friends a hundred leagues off. But he was obliged to make the best of it. He addressed the two gentlemen in Spanish, giving them a polite invitation, which they accepted. They all turned towards the entrance of the fort and, the incident being exhausted, the eight soldiers returned to their delightful leisure for a moment disturbed by this unexpected adventure.

60

CAPTIVE AND JAILERS

WHEN they had entered the fort, and whilst the governor was making some preparations for the reception of his guests— "Come," said Athos, "let us have a word of explanation whilst we are alone."

"It is simply this," replied the musketeer. "I have conducted hither a prisoner, whom the King commands shall not be seen. You came here, he has thrown something to you through the lattice of his window; I was at dinner with the governor, I saw the object thrown, and I saw Raoul pick it up. It does not take long to understand this. I understood it; and I thought you in intelligence with my prisoner. And then——"

"And then—you commanded us to be shot."

"*Ma foi!* I admit it; but if I was the first to seize a musket, fortunately I was the last to take aim at you."

"If you had killed me, d'Artagnan, I should have had the good fortune to die for the royal house of France, and it would be an honour to die by your hand—you, its noblest and most loyal defender."

"What the devil, Athos, do you mean by the royal house?" stammered d'Artagnan. "You don't mean that you, a well-informed and sensible man, can place any faith in the nonsense written by an idiot?"

"I do believe in it."

"With so much the more reason, my dear Chevalier, from your having orders to kill all those who do believe in it," said Raoul.

"That is because," replied the captain of the musketeers,— "because every calumny, however absurd it may be, has the almost certain chance of becoming popular."

"No, d'Artagnan," replied Athos promptly; "but because the King is not willing that the secret of his family should transpire among the people, and cover with shame the executioners of the son of Louis XIII."

"Do not talk in such a childish manner, Athos, or I shall begin to think you have lost your senses. Besides, explain to me how it is possible Louis XIII. should have a son in the Isle of Sainte-Marguerite?"

"A son whom you have brought hither masked, in a fishing boat," said Athos. "Why not?"

D'Artagnan was brought to a pause.

"Ah! ah!" said he; "whence do you know that a fishing boat——"

"Brought you to Sainte-Marguerite's with the carriage containing the prisoner—with a prisoner whom you styled monseigneur. Oh! I am acquainted with all that," resumed the Comte. D'Artagnan bit his moustache.

"If it were true," said he, "that I had brought hither in a boat, and with a carriage, a masked prisoner, nothing proves that this prisoner must be a prince—a prince of the house of France?"

"Oh! ask that of Aramis," replied Athos coolly.

"Of Aramis!" cried the musketeer, quite at a stand. "Have you seen Aramis?"

"After his discomfiture at Vaux, yes; I have seen Aramis, a fugitive, pursued, ruined; and Aramis has told me enough to make me believe in the complaints that this unfortunate young man cut upon the bottom of the plate."

D'Artagnan's head sank upon his breast with confusion. "This is the way," said he, "in which God turns to nothing that which men call their wisdom! A fine secret must that be of which twelve or fifteen persons hold the tattered fragments! Athos, cursed be the chance which has brought you face to face with me in this affair! for now——"

"Well!" said Athos, with his customary mild severity, "is your secret lost because I know it? Consult your memory, my friend. Have I not borne secrets as heavy as this?"

"You have never borne one so dangerous," replied d'Artagnan, in a tone of sadness. "I have something like a sinister idea that all who are concerned with this secret will die, and die unfortunately."

"The will of God be done!" said Athos, "but here is your governor."

D'Artagnan and his friends immediately resumed their parts. The governor, suspicious and hard, behaved towards d'Artagnan with a politeness almost amounting to obsequiousness. With respect to the travellers, he contented himself with offering them good cheer, and never taking his eye from them. Athos and Raoul observed that he often tried to embarrass them by sudden attacks, or to catch them off their guard; but neither the one nor the other gave him the least advantage. What d'Artagnan had said was probable, if the governor did not believe it to be quite true. They rose from table to repose awhile.

"What is this man's name? I don't like the looks of him," said Athos to d'Artagnan, in Spanish.

"De Saint-Mars," replied the captain.

"He is then, I suppose, the Prince's jailer?"

"Eh? how can I tell? I may be kept at Sainte-Marguerite for ever."

"Oh! no, not you!"

"My friend, I am in the situation of a man who finds a treasure in the midst of a desert. He would like to carry it away, but he cannot; he would like to leave it, but he dares not. The King will not dare to recall me, for fear no one else should serve him as faithfully as I should; he regrets not having me near him, from being aware that no one will be of so much service near his person as myself. But it will happen as it may please God."

"But," observed Raoul, "your not being certain proves that your situation here is provisional, and you will return to Paris."

"Ask these gentlemen," interrupted the governor, "what was their purpose in coming to Sainte-Marguerite?"

"They came from learning there was a convent of Benedictines at Sainte-Honorat which is considered curious; and from being told there was excellent shooting in the island."

"That is quite at their service as well as yours," replied Saint-Mars. D'Artagnan politely thanked him.

"When will they depart?" added the governor.

"To-morrow," replied d'Artagnan.

M. de Saint-Mars went to make his rounds, and left d'Artagnan alone with the pretended Spaniards.

"Oh!" exclaimed the musketeer, "here is a life with a society that suits me but little. I command this man, and he bores me, *mordioux!* Come let us have a shot or two at the rabbits; the walk will be beautiful, and not fatiguing. The isle is but a league and a half in length, upon a breadth of a league; a real park. Let us try to amuse ourselves."

"As you please, d'Artagnan; not for the sake of amusing ourselves, but to gain an opportunity for talking freely."

D'Artagnan made a sign to a soldier, who brought the gentlemen some guns, and then returned to the fort.

"And now," said the musketeer, "answer me the question put to you by that black-looking Saint-Mars: 'What did you come to do at the Lerin Isles?'"

"To bid you farewell."

"Bid me farewell! What do you mean by that? Is Raoul going anywhere?"

"Yes."

"Then I will lay a wager it is with M. de Beaufort?"

"With M. de Beaufort it is, my dear friend; you always guess rightly."

"From habit."

Whilst the two friends were commencing their conversation, Raoul, with his head hanging down and his heart oppressed, seated himself on a mossy rock, his gun across his knees, looking at the sea—looking at the heavens, and listening to the voice of his soul—he allowed the sportsmen to attain a considerable distance from him. D'Artagnan remarked his absence.

"He has not recovered the blow," said he to Athos.

"He is struck to death."

"Oh! your fears exaggerate, I hope. Raoul is of a fine nature. Around all hearts so noble as his, there is a second envelope which forms a cuirass. The first bleeds, the second resists."

"No," replied Athos, "Raoul will die of it."

"*Mordioux!*" said d'Artagnan, in a melancholy tone. And he did not add a word to this explanation. Then, a minute after, "Why do you let him go?"

"Because he insists upon going."

"And why do you not go with him?"

"Because I could not bear to see him die."

D'Artagnan looked his friend earnestly in the face. "You know one thing," continued the Comte, leaning upon the arm of the captain; "you know that in the course of my life I have been afraid of but few things. Well! I have an incessant, gnawing, insurmountable fear that a day will arrive in which I shall hold the dead body of that boy in my arms."

"Oh!" murmured d'Artagnan, "oh!"

"He will die, I know. I have a perfect conviction of that; but I would not see him die."

"How is this, Athos? you come and place yourself in the presence of the bravest man you say you have ever seen, of your own d'Artagnan, of that man without an equal, as you formerly called him, and you come and tell him with your arms folded that you are afraid of witnessing the death of your son, you who have seen all that can be seen in this world! Why have you this fear, Athos? Man upon this earth must expect everything, and ought to face everything."

"Listen to me, my friend. After having worn myself out upon this earth of which you speak, I have preserved but two religions; that of life, my friendships, my duty as a father—that of eternity, love and respect for God. Now I have within me the revelation that if God should decree that my friend or my son should render up his last sigh in my presence——oh! no, I cannot even tell you, d'Artagnan!"

"Speak, speak, tell me!"

"I am strong against everything, except the death of those I love. For that only there is no remedy. He who dies, gains; he who sees others die, loses. No; this is it—to know that I should no more meet upon earth him whom I now behold with joy; to know that there would nowhere be a d'Artagnan any more, nowhere again be a Raoul, oh! I am old, see you, I have no longer courage; I pray God to spare me in my weakness; but if he struck me so plainly and in that fashion, I should curse him. A Christian gentleman ought not to curse his God, d'Artagnan; it is quite enough to have cursed a king!"

"Humph!" said d'Artagnan, a little confused by this violent tempest of grief.

"Let me speak to him, Athos? Who knows?"

"Try if you please, but I am convinced you will not succeed."

"I will not attempt to console him, I will serve him."

"You will?"

"Doubtless, I will. Do you think this would be the first time a woman had repented of an infidelity? I will go to him, I tell you."

Athos shook his head, and continued his walk alone. D'Artagnan, cutting across the brambles, rejoined Raoul, and held out his hand to him. "Well, Raoul! You have something to say to me?"

"I have a kindness to ask of you," replied Bragelonne.

"Ask it then."

"You will some day return to France?"

"I hope so."

"Ought I to write to Mademoiselle de la Vallière?"

"No; you must not."

"But I have so many things to say to her."

"Come and say them to her, then."

"Never!"

"Pray, what virtue do you attribute to a letter, which your speech might not possess?"

"Perhaps you are right."

"She loves the King," said d'Artagnan bluntly; "and she is an honest girl."

Raoul started. "And you, you! whom she abandons, she, perhaps, loves better than she does the King, but after another fashion."

"D'Artagnan, do you believe she loves the King?"

"To idolatry. Her heart is inaccessible to any other feeling. You might continue to live near her, and would be her best friend."

402

"Ah!" exclaimed Raoul, with a passionate burst of repugnance for such a painful hope.

"Will you do so?"

"It would be base."

"That is a very absurd word, which would lead me to think slightly of your understanding. Please to understand, Raoul, that it is never base to do that which is imposed by a superior force. If your heart says to you, 'Go there or die,' why, go there, Raoul. Was she base or brave, she whom you loved, in preferring the King to you, the King whom her heart commanded her imperiously to prefer to you? No, she was the bravest of women. Do then as she has done. Obey yourself. Do you know one thing of which I am sure, Raoul?"

"What is that?"

"Why, that by seeing her closely with the eyes of a jealous man——"

"Well?"

"Well! you would cease to love her."

"Then I am decided, my dear d'Artagnan."

"To set off to see her again?"

"No; to set off that I may never see her again. I wish to love her for ever."

"Humph! I must confess," replied the musketeer, "that is a conclusion which I was far from expecting."

"This is what I wish, my friend. You will see her again, and you will give her a letter, which, if you think proper, will explain to her as to yourself, what is passing in my heart. Read it; I prepared it last night. Something told me I should see you to-day." He held the letter out, and d'Artagnan read it:—

"MADEMOISELLE,—You are not wrong in my eyes in not loving me. You have only been guilty of one fault towards me, that of having left me to believe you loved me. This error will cost me my life. I pardon you, but I cannot pardon myself. It is said that happy lovers are deaf to the complaints of rejected lovers. It will not be so with you, who did not love me, except with anxiety. I am sure that if I had persisted in endeavouring to change that friendship into love, you would have yielded out of a fear of bringing about my death, or of lessening the esteem I had for you. It is much more delightful to me to die, knowing you are free and satisfied. How much, then, will you love me, when you will no longer fear either my presence or my reproaches! You will love me, because, however charming a new love may appear to you, God has not made me in anything inferior to him you have chosen, and because my devotedness, my sacrifice, and my painful end will assure me, in your eyes, a certain superiority over him. I have allowed to escape, in the candid credulity of my heart, the treasure I possessed. Many people tell me that you loved me enough to lead me to hope you would have loved me much. That idea takes from my mind all bitterness, and leads me only to blame myself. You will accept this last farewell, and you will bless me for having taken refuge in the inviolable asylum where all hatred is extinguished, and all love endures for ever. *Adieu*, mademoiselle. If your happiness could be purchased by the last drop of my blood, I would shed that drop. I willingly make the sacrifice of it to my misery!

"RAOUL, VICOMTE DE BRAGELONNE."

"The letter is very well," said the captain. "I have only one fault to find with it."

"Tell me what that is?" said Raoul.

"Why, it is, that it tells everything, except the thing which exhales, like a mortal poison, from your eyes and from your heart; except the senseless love which still consumes you." Raoul grew paler, but remained silent.

"Why did you not write simply these words:—

"'Mademoiselle,—Instead of cursing you, I love you, and I die.'"

"That is true," exclaimed Raoul, with a sinister kind of joy.

And, tearing the letter he had just taken back, he wrote the following words upon a leaf of his tablets:—

"To procure the happiness of once more telling you I love you, I commit the baseness of writing to you; and to punish myself for that baseness, I die." And he signed it.

"You will give her these tablets, captain, will you not?"

"When?" asked the latter.

"On the day," said Bragelonne, pointing to the last sentence, "On the day when you can place a date under these words." And he sprang away quickly to join Athos, who was returning with slow steps.

As they re-entered the fort, the sea rose with that rapid, gusty vehemence which characterises the Mediterranean; the ill humour of the element became a tempest. Something shapeless, and tossed about violently by the waves, appeared just off the coast.

"What is that?" said Athos—"a wrecked boat?"

"No, it is not a boat;" said d'Artagnan.

"Pardon me," said Raoul, "there is a barque gaining the port rapidly."

"Yes, there is a barque in the creek, which is prudently seeking shelter here; but that which Athos points to in the sand is not a boat at all—it has run aground."

"Yes, yes, I see it."

"It is the carriage which I threw into the sea, after landing the prisoner."

"Well!" said Athos, "if you will take my advice, d'Artagnan, you will burn that carriage, in order that no vestige of it may remain, without which the fishermen of Antibes, who have believed they had to do with the devil, will endeavour to prove that your prisoner was but a man."

"Your advice is good, Athos, and I will this night have it carried out, or rather, I will carry it out myself; but let us go in, for the rain falls heavily, and the lightning is terrific."

As they were passing over the ramparts to a gallery of which d'Artagnan had the key, they saw M. de Saint-Mars directing his steps towards the chamber inhabited by the prisoner. Upon a sign from d'Artagnan they concealed themselves in an angle of the staircase.

"What is it?" said Athos.

"You will see. Look. The prisoner is returning from chapel."

And they saw, by the red flashes of the lightning against the violet fog which the wind stamped upon the bankward sky, they saw pass gravely, at six paces behind the governor, a man clothed in black, and masked by a visor of polished steel, soldered to a helmet of the same nature, which altogether enveloped the whole of his head. The fire of the heavens cast red reflections upon the polished surface, and these reflections, flying off capriciously, seemed to be angry looks launched by this unfortunate, instead of imprecations. In the middle of the gallery the prisoner stopped for a moment, to contemplate the infinite horizon, to respire the sulphurous perfumes of the tempest, to drink in thirstily the hot rain, and to breathe a sigh resembling a smothered roar.

"Come on, monsieur," said Saint-Mars, sharply to the prisoner, for he already became uneasy at seeing him look so long beyond the walls. "Monsieur, come on!"

"Say monseigneur!" cried Athos, from his corner, with a voice so solemn and terrible, that the governor trembled from head to foot. Athos insisted upon respect being paid to fallen majesty. The prisoner turned round.

"Who spoke?" asked Saint-Mars.

"It was I," replied d'Artagnan, showing himself promptly. "You know that is the order."

"Call me neither Monsieur nor Monseigneur," said the prisoner

405

in his turn, in a voice that penetrated to the very soul of Raoul;
"call me ACCURSED!" He passed on, and the iron door creaked
after him.

"That is truly an unfortunate man!" murmured the musketeer
in a hollow whisper, pointing out to Raoul the chamber inhabited
by the Prince.

61

PROMISES

SCARCELY had d'Artagnan re-entered his apartment with his
two friends than one of the soldiers of the fort came to inform him
that the governor was seeking for him. The barque which Raoul
had perceived at sea, and which appeared so eager to gain the port,
came to Sainte-Marguerite with an important despatch for the
captain of the musketeers. On opening it, d'Artagnan recognised
the writing of the King: "I should think," said Louis XIV., "you
will have completed the execution of my orders, Monsieur d'Artagnan; return then immediately to Paris, and join me at the
Louvre."

"There is the end of my exile," cried the musketeer with joy;
"God be praised, I am no longer a jailer!" And he showed the
letter to Athos.

"So then you must leave us," replied the latter, in a melancholy
tone.

"Yes, but to meet again, dear friend, seeing that Raoul is old
enough now to go alone with M. de Beaufort, and who will prefer
his father going back in company with M. d'Artagnan, to forcing
him to travel two hundred leagues solitarily to reach home at La
Fère; would you not, Raoul?"

"Certainly," stammered the latter, with an expression of tender
regret.

"No, no, my friend," interrupted Athos, "I will never quit
Raoul till the day his vessel shall have disappeared on the horizon.
As long as he remains in France, he shall not be separated from
me."

"As you please, dear friend; but we will, at least, leave Sainte-
Marguerite together; take advantage of the barque which will
convey me back to Antibes."

"With all my heart; we cannot too soon be at a distance from
this fort, and from the spectacle which saddened us so just now."

The three friends quitted the little isle, after paying their respects to the governor, and by the last flashes of the departing tempest they took their farewell of the white walls of the fort. D'Artagnan parted from his friends that same night, after having seen fire set to the carriage upon the shore, by the orders of Saint-Mars, according to the advice the captain had given him. Before getting on horseback, and after leaving the arms of Athos: "My friends," said he, "you bear too much resemblance to two soldiers who are abandoning their post. Something warns me that Raoul will require being supported by you in his rank. Will you allow me to ask permission to go over into Africa with a hundred good muskets? The King will not refuse me, and I will take you with me."

"Monsieur d'Artagnan," replied Raoul, pressing his hand with emotion, "thanks for that offer, which would give us more than we wish, either Monsieur le Comte or I. I, who am young, stand in need of labour of mind and fatigue of body; Monsieur le Comte wants the profoundest repose. You are his best friend. I recommend him to your care. In watching over him, you will hold both our souls in your hands."

"I must go; my horse is all in a fret," said d'Artagnan, with whom the most manifest sign of a lively emotion was the change of ideas in a conversation. "Come Comte, how many days longer has Raoul to stay here?"

"Three days at most."

"And how long will it take you to reach home?"

"Oh! a considerable time," replied Athos. "I shall not like the idea of being separated too quickly from Raoul. Time will travel too fast of itself to require me to aid it by distance. I shall only make half-stages."

"And why so, my friend? Nothing is more dull than travelling slowly; and hostelry life does not become a man like you."

"My friend, I came hither on post horses; but I wish to purchase two animals of a superior kind. Now, to take them home fresh, it would not be prudent to make them travel more than seven or eight leagues a day."

"Where is Grimaud?"

"He arrived yesterday morning, with Raoul's appointments; and I left him to sleep."

"That is never to come back again," d'Artagnan suffered to escape him. "Till we meet again, then, dear Athos—and if you are diligent, well I shall embrace you the sooner." So saying, he put his foot in the stirrup, which Raoul held.

"Farewell!" said the young man, embracing him.

"Farewell!" said d'Artagnan, as he got into his saddle.

His horse made a movement which divided the cavalier from his friends. This scene had taken place in front of the house chosen by Athos, near the gates of Antibes, whither d'Artagnan, after his supper, had ordered his horses to be brought. The road began to extend there, white and undulating in the vapours of the night. The horse eagerly respired the salt, sharp perfume of the marshes. D'Artagnan put him into a trot; and Athos and Raoul sadly turned towards the house. All at once they heard the rapid approach of a horse's steps, and at first believed it to be one of those singular repercussions which deceive the ear at every turn in a road. But it was really the return of the horseman. They uttered a cry of joyous surprise; and the captain, springing to the ground like a young man, seized within his arms the two beloved heads of Athos and Raoul. He held them long embraced thus, without speaking a word, or suffering the sigh which was bursting his breast to escape him. Then, as rapidly as he had come back, he set off again, with a sharp application of his spurs to the sides of his fiery horse.

"Alas!" said the Comte, in a low voice, "alas! alas!"

"Evil presage! on his side," said d'Artagnan to himself, making up for lost time. "I could not smile upon them. An evil presage!"

The next day Grimaud was on foot again. The service commanded by M. de Beaufort was happily accomplished. The flotilla, sent to Toulon by the exertions of Raoul, had set out, dragging after it in little nutshells, almost invisible, the wives and friends of the fishermen and smugglers put in requisition for the service of the fleet. The time, so short, which remained for the father and son to live together, appeared to have doubled in rapidity, as the swiftness of everything increases which inclines towards mixing with the gulf of eternity. Athos and Raoul returned to Toulon, which began to be filled with the noise of carriages, with the noise of arms, with the noise of neighing horses. The trumpeters sounded their spirited marches; the drummers signalised their strength; the streets were overflowing with soldiers, servants, and tradespeople. The Duc de Beaufort was everywhere, superintending the embarkation with the zeal and interest of a good captain. He encouraged even the most humble of his companions; he scolded his lieutenants, even those of the highest rank. Artillery, provisions, baggage, he insisted upon seeing all himself. He examined the equipment of every soldier; he assured himself of the health and soundness of every horse. It was plain that, light, boastful, egotistical, in his hotel, the gentleman became the soldier again—the high noble, a captain—in face of the responsibility he had accepted. And yet, it must be admitted that, whatever was the care with which he presided over the preparations for departure, it was easy to perceive careless precipitation, and the absence of all the precaution which make the French soldier the first soldier in the world, because in that world, he is the one most abandoned to his own physical and moral resources. All things having satisfied, or appearing to have satisfied, the admiral, he paid his compliments to Raoul, and gave the last orders for sailing, which was ordered the next morning at daybreak. He invited the Comte and his son to dine with him; but they, under a pretext of the service, kept themselves apart. Gaining their hostelry, situated under the trees of the great Place, they took their repast in haste, and Athos led Raoul to the rocks which dominate the city, vast grey mountains, whence the view is infinite, and embraces a liquid horizon, which appears, so remote is it, on a level with the rocks themselves. The night was fine, as it always is in these happy climates. The moon, rising behind the rocks, unrolled, like a silver sheet, upon the blue carpet of the sea. In the road manœuvred silently the vessels which had just taken their rank to facilitate the embarkation. The sea, loaded with phosphoric light, opened beneath the hulls of the barques which transported the baggage and munitions; every dip of the prow ploughed up this gulf of white flames; and from every oar dropped liquid diamonds. The sailors, rejoicing in the largesses of the admiral, were heard murmuring their slow and artless songs. Sometimes, the grinding of the chains was mixed with the dull noise of shot falling into the holds. These harmonies, and this spectacle, oppress the heart like fear, and dilate it like hope. All this life speaks of death. Athos had seated himself with his son, upon the moss, among the brambles of the promontory. Around their heads passed and repassed large bats, carried along in the fearful whirl of their blind chase. The feet of Raoul were across the edge of the cliff, and bathed in that void which is peopled by vertigo, and provokes to annihilation. When the moon had risen to its full height, caressing with its light the neighbouring peaks, when the watery mirror was illumined in its full extent, and the little red fires had made their openings in the black masses of every ship, Athos collected all his ideas, and all his courage, and said:—

"God has made all that we see, Raoul; He has made us also— poor atoms mixed up with this great universe. We shine like those fires and those stars; we sigh like those waves; we suffer like those great ships, which are worn out in ploughing the waves, in obeying the wind which urges them towards an end, as the breath of God blows us towards a port. Everything likes to live. Raoul; and everything is beautiful in living things."*

"Monsieur," said Raoul, "we have before us a beautiful spectacle!"

"How good d'Artagnan is!" interrupted Athos suddenly, "and what a rare good fortune it is to be supported during a whole life by such a friend as he is! That is what you have wanted, Raoul."

"A friend!" cried Raoul, "I have wanted a friend!"

"M. de Guiche is an agreeable companion," resumed the Comte, coldly, "but I believe, in the times in which you live, men are more engaged in their own interests and their own pleasures than they were in our times. You have sought a secluded life; that is a great happiness, but you have lost your strength in it. We four, more weaned from these delicate abstractions which constitute your joy, we furnished much more resistance when misfortune presented itself."

"I have not interrupted you, monsieur, to tell you that I had a friend, and that friend was M. Guiche. *Certes*, he is good and generous, and moreover he loves me. But I have lived under the guardianship of another friendship, monsieur, as precious and as strong as that of which you speak, since that is yours."

"I have not been a friend for you, Raoul," said Athos.

"Eh! monsieur, and in what respect not?"

"Because I have given you reason to think that life has but one face, because sad and severe, alas! I have always cut off for you, without, God knows, wishing to do so, the joyous buds which incessantly spring from the tree of youth; so that at this moment I repent of not having made of you a more expansive, dissipated, animated man."

"I know why you say that, monsieur. No, it is not you who have made me what I am; it was love which took me at the time when children have only inclinations; it is the constancy natural to my character, which with other creatures is but a habit. I believed that I should always be as I was; I thought God had cast me in a path quite cleared, quite straight, bordered with fruits and flowers. I had watching over me your vigilance and your strength. I believed myself to be vigilant and strong. Nothing prepared me; I fell once, and that once deprived me of courage for the whole of my life. It is quite true that I wrecked myself. Oh, no, monsieur! you are nothing in my past but a happiness—you are nothing in my future but a hope! No, I have no reproach to make against life, such as you made it for me. I bless you, and I love you ardently."

"My dear Raoul, your words do me good. They prove to me that you will act a little for me in the time to come."

"I shall only act for you, monsieur."

"Raoul, what I have never hitherto done with respect to you, I will henceforward do. I will be your friend, not your father. We will live in expanding ourselves, instead of living and holding ourselves prisoners, when you come back. And that will be soon, will it not?"

"Certainly, monsieur, for such an expedition cannot be long."

"Soon, then, Raoul, soon, instead of living moderately upon my income, I will give you the capital of my estates. It will suffice for launching you into the world till my death; and you will give me, I hope, before that time, the consolation of not seeing my race extinct."

"I will do all you shall command," said Raoul, much agitated.

"It is not necessary, Raoul, that your duty as *aide-de-camp* should lead you into too hazardous enterprises. You have gone through your ordeal; you are known to be good under fire. Remember that war with the Arabs is a war of snares, ambuscades, and assassinations."

"So it is said, monsieur."

"There is never much glory in falling in an ambuscade. It is a death which always implies a little rashness or want of foresight. Often, indeed, he who falls in it meets with but little pity. They who are not pitied, Raoul, have died uselessly. Still further, the conqueror laughs, and we Frenchmen ought not to allow stupid infidels to triumph over our faults. Do you clearly understand what I am saying to you, Raoul? God forbid I should encourage you to avoid encounters."

"I am naturally prudent, monsieur, and I have very good fortune," said Raoul, with a smile which chilled the heart of his poor father; "for," the young man hastened to add, "in twenty combats in which I have been, I have only received one scratch."

"There is in addition," said Athos, "the climate to be dreaded; that is an ugly end, that fever! King Saint-Louis prayed God to send him an arrow or the plague, rather than the fever."

"Oh, monsieur! with sobriety, with reasonable exercise——"

"I have already obtained from M. de Beaufort a promise that his despatches shall be sent off every fortnight to France. You, as his *aide-de-camp*, will be charged with expediting them, and will be sure not to forget me."

"No, monsieur," said Raoul, almost choked with emotion.

"Besides, Raoul, as you are a good Christian, and I am one also, we ought to reckon upon a more special protection of God and His guardian angels. Promise me, that if anything evil should happen to you, on any occasion, you will think of me at once."

"First and at once! Oh! yes, monsieur."

"And will call upon me?"

"Instantly."

"You dream of me sometimes, do you not, Raoul?"

"Every night, monsieur. During my early youth I saw you in my dreams, calm and mild, with one hand stretched out over my head, and that it was that made me sleep so soundly—*formerly*."

"Since we two love one another so dearly," said the Comte, "a portion of our two souls will always be together though we are separated the one from the other. Whenever you may be sad, Raoul, I feel that my heart will be drowned in sadness; and when you smile on thinking of me, be assured you will send me, from however remote a distance, a ray of your joy."

"I will not promise you to be joyous," replied the young man; "but you may be certain that I will never pass an hour without thinking of you; not one hour, I swear, unless I be dead."

Athos could contain himself no longer; he threw his arms around the neck of his son, and held him embraced with all the powers of his heart. The moon began to be now eclipsed by twilight; a golden band surrounded the horizon, announcing the approach of day. Athos threw his cloak over the shoulders of Raoul, and led him back to the city, where burdens and porters were already in motion, like a vast ant-hill. At the extremity of the plateau, which Athos and Bragelonne were quitting, they saw a dark shadow moving uneasily backwards and forwards, as if in indecision or ashamed to be seen. It was Grimaud, who, in his anxiety, had tracked his master, and was waiting for him.

"Oh! my good Grimaud," cried Raoul, "what do you want? You have come to tell us it is time to be gone, have you not?"

"Alone?" said Grimaud, addressing Athos, and pointing to Raoul in a tone of reproach, which showed to what an extent the old man was troubled.

"Oh! you are right!" cried the Comte. "No, Raoul, do not go alone; no, he shall not be left alone in a strange land, without some friendly hand to support him, some friendly heart to recall to him all he loved!"

"I?" said Grimaud.

"You, yes, you!" cried Raoul, touched to his inmost heart.

"Alas!" said Athos, "you are very old, my good Grimaud."

"So much the better," replied the latter, with an inexpressible depth of feeling and intelligence.

"But the embarkation is begun," said Raoul, "and you are not prepared."

"Yes," said Grimaud, showing the keys of his trunks, mixed with those of his young master.

"But," again objected Raoul, "you cannot leave Monsieur le Comte thus alone; Monsieur le Comte, whom you have never quitted."

Grimaud turned his dimmed eyes upon Athos and Raoul, as if to measure the strength of both. The Comte uttered not a word.

"Monsieur le Comte will prefer my going," said Grimaud.

"I should," said Athos, by an inclination of the head.

At that moment the drums suddenly rolled, and the clarions filled the air with their inspiring notes. The regiments destined for the expedition began to debouch from the city. They advanced to the number of five, each composed of forty companies. Royals marched first, distinguished by their white uniform, faced with blue. The regimental colours, quartered crosswise, violet and dead-leaf, with a sprinkling of golden fleurs-de-lis, left the white-coloured flag, with its fleur-de-lised cross, to dominate over the whole. Musketeers, at the wings, with their forked sticks and their muskets on their shoulders; pikemen in the centre, with their lances, fourteen feet in length, marched gaily towards the transports, which carried them in detail to the ships. The regiments of Picardy, Navarre, Normandy, and Royal Vaisseau, followed after. M. de Beaufort had known well how to select his troops. He himself was seen closing the march with his staff—it would take a full hour before he could reach the sea. Raoul with Athos turned his steps slowly towards the beach, in order to take his place when the Prince embarked. Grimaud, boiling with the ardour of a young man, superintended the embarkation of Raoul's baggage in the admiral's vessel. Athos, with his arm passed through that of the son he was about to lose, absorbed in melancholy meditation, was deaf to the noise around him. An officer came quickly towards them to inform Raoul that M. de Beaufort was anxious to have him by his side.

"Have the kindness to tell the Prince," said Raoul, "that I request he will allow me this hour to enjoy the company of my father."

"No, no," said Athos, "an *aide-de-camp* ought not thus to quit his general. Please to tell the Prince, monsieur, that the Vicomte will join him immediately." The officer set off at a gallop.

"Whether we part here or part there," added the Comte, "it is no less a separation." He carefully brushed the dust off his son's coat, and passed his hand over his hair as they walked along. "But, Raoul," said he, "you want money. M. de Beaufort's train will be splendid, and I am certain it will be agreeable to you to purchase horses and arms, which are very dear things in Africa. Now, as you are not actually in the service of the King, or M. de Beaufort, and are simply a volunteer, you must not reckon upon either pay or largesses. But I should not like you to want for anything at Gigelli. Here are two hundred pistoles; if you would please me, Raoul, spend them."

Raoul pressed the hand of his father, and, at the turning of a street, they saw M. de Beaufort, mounted upon a magnificent white horse, which replied by graceful curvets to the applauses of the women of the city. The Duc called Raoul, and held out his hand to the Comte. He spoke to him for some time, with such a kindly expression that the heart of the poor father even felt a little comforted. It was, however, evident to both father and son that their walk was directed to nothing less than a punishment. There was a terrible moment—that at which, on quitting the sands of the shore, the soldiers and sailors exchanged the last kisses with their families and friends; a supreme moment, in which, notwithstanding the clearness of the heavens, the warmth of the sun, the perfumes of the air, and the rich life that was circulating in their veins, everything appeared black, everything appeared bitter, everything created doubts of a God, whilst speaking by the mouth, even, of God. It was customary for the admiral and his suite to embark the last; the cannon waited to announce, with its formidable voice, that the leader had placed his foot on board his vessel. Athos, forgetful of both the admiral and the fleet, and of his own dignity as a strong man, opened his arms to his son, and pressed him, convulsively, to his heart.

"Accompany us on board," said the Duc, very much affected; "you will gain a good half-hour."

"No," said Athos, "my farewell is spoken. I do not wish to speak a second."

"Then, Vicomte, embark—embark quickly!" added the Prince, wishing to spare the tears of these two men, whose hearts were bursting. And paternally, tenderly, very much as Porthos might have done, he took Raoul in his arms and placed him in the boat; the oars of which at a signal immediately were dipped in the waves. Himself, forgetful of ceremony, he jumped into his boat, and pushed it off with a vigorous foot. "*Adieu!*" cried Raoul.

Athos replied only by a sign, but he felt something burning on his hand; it was the respectful kiss of Grimaud—the last farewell of the faithful dog. This kiss given, Grimaud jumped from the step of the mole upon the stem of a two-oared yawl, which had just been taken in tow by a barge served by twelve galley-oars. Athos seated himself on the mole, stunned, deaf, abandoned. Every instant took from him one of the features, one of the shades of the pale face of his son. With his arms hanging down, his eyes fixed, his mouth open, he remained confounded with Raoul—in one same look, in one same thought, in one same stupor. The sea, by degrees, carried away boats and faces, until at the distance at which men became nothing but points—loves, nothing but remembrances. Athos saw his son ascend the ladder of the admiral's ship, he saw him lean upon the rail of the deck, and place himself in such a manner as to be always an object in the eye of his father. In vain the cannon thundered, in vain from the ship sounded a long and loud tumult, responded to by immense acclamations from the shore; in vain did the noise deafen the ear of the father, and the smoke obscure the cherished object of all his aspirations. Raoul appeared to him up to the last moment; and the imperceptible atom, passing from black to pale, from pale to white, from white to nothing, disappeared for Athos—disappeared very long after for all the eyes of the spectators, had disappeared both gallant ships and swelling sails. Towards midday, when the sun devoured space, and scarcely the tops of the masts dominated the incandescent line of the sea, Athos perceived a soft aerial shadow rise, and vanish as soon as seen. This was the smoke of a cannon, which M. de Beaufort ordered to be fired as a last salute to the coast of France. The point was buried in its turn beneath the sky, and Athos returned painfully and slowly to his hostelry.

62

AMONG WOMEN

D'ARTAGNAN had not been able to hide his feelings from his friends so much as he would have wished. The stoical soldier, the impassible man-at-arms, overcome by fear and presentiments, had yielded, for a few minutes, to human weakness. When, therefore, he had silenced his heart and calmed the agitation of his nerves, turning towards his lackey, a silent servant, always listening, in order to obey the more promptly:—

"Rabaud," said he, "mind, we must travel thirty leagues a day."

"At your pleasure, captain," replied Rabaud.

And from that moment, d'Artagnan, accommodating his action to the pace of his horse, like a true centaur, employed his thoughts about nothing—that is to say, about everything. He asked himself why the King had sent for him back; why the Iron Mask had thrown the silver plate at the feet of Raoul? As to the first subject, the reply was negative; he knew right well that the King's calling him was from necessity. He still further knew that Louis XIV. must experience an imperious want of a private conversation with one whom the possession of such a secret placed on a level with the highest powers of the kingdom. But as to saying exactly what the King's wish was, d'Artagnan found himself completely at a loss. The musketeer had no more doubts either upon the reason which had urged the unfortunate Philippe to reveal his character and his birth. Philippe, hidden for ever beneath a mask of iron, exiled to a country where the men seemed little more than slaves of the elements; Philippe, deprived even of the society of d'Artagnan, who had loaded him with honours and delicate attentions, had nothing more to see than spectres and griefs in this world, and despair beginning to devour him,—he poured himself forth in complaints, in the belief that his revelations would raise an avenger for him. The manner in which the musketeer had been near killing his two best friends, the destiny which had so strangely brought Athos to participate in the great State secret, the farewell of Raoul, the obscurity of that future which threatened to end in a melancholy death; all this threw d'Artagnan incessantly back to lamentable predictions and forebodings, which the rapidity of his pace did not dissipate, as it used formerly to do. D'Artagnan passed from these considerations to the remembrance of the pro-scribed Porthos and Aramis. He saw them both, fugitives, tracked, ruined—laborious architects of a fortune they must lose; and, as the King called for his man of execution in hours of vengeance and malice, d'Artagnan trembled at the idea of receiving some commission that would make his very heart bleed. Sometimes, when ascending hills, when the winded horse breathed hard from his nostrils and heaved his flanks, the captain, left to more freedom of thought, reflected upon the prodigious genius of Aramis, a genius of astucity and intrigue, such as the Fronde and the civil war had produced but two. Soldier, priest, and diplomatist; gallant, avaricious, and cunning; Aramis had never taken the good things of this life but as stepping-stones to rise to bad ones. Generous in spirit, if not high in heart, he never did ill but for the sake of shining a little more brilliantly. Towards the end of his career, at the moment of reaching the goal, like the patrician Fuscus,* he had made a false step upon a plank, and had fallen into the sea. But Porthos, the good, harmless Porthos! To see Porthos hungry, to see Mousqueton without gold lace, imprisoned perhaps; to see Pierrefonds, Bracieux, razed to the very stones, dishonoured even to the timber,—these were so many poignant griefs for d'Artagnan, and every time that one of these griefs struck him, he bounded like a horse at the sting of the gadfly beneath the vaults of foliage where he had sought shade and shelter from the burning sun. Never was the man of spirit subjected to ennui, if his body was exposed to fatigue; never did the man healthy of body fail to find life light, if he had something to engage his mind. D'Artagnan, riding fast, thinking as constantly, alighted from his horse in Paris, fresh and tender in his muscles as the athlete preparing for the gymnasium. The King did not expect him so soon, and had just departed for the chase towards Meudon. D'Artagnan, instead of riding after the King, as he would formerly have done, took off his boots, had a bath, and waited till His Majesty should return dusty and tired. He occupied the interval of five hours in taking, as people say, the air of the house, and in arming himself against all ill chances. He learned that the King, during the last fortnight, had been gloomy; that the Queen-Mother was ill and much depressed; that Monsieur, the King's brother, was exhibiting a devotional turn; that Madame had the vapours; and that M. de Guiche was gone to one of his estates. He learned that M. Colbert was radiant; that M. Fouquet consulted a fresh physician every day, who still did not cure him, and that his principal complaint was one which physicians do not usually cure, unless they are political physicians. The King, d'Artagnan was told, behaved in the kindest manner to M. Fouquet, and did not allow him ever to be out of his sight; but the Surintendant, touched to the heart, like one of those fine trees which a worm has punctured, was declining daily, in spite of the royal smile, that sun of court trees. D'Artagnan learned that Mademoiselle de la Vallière had become indispensable to the King; that the King, during his sporting excursions, if he did not take her with him, wrote to her frequently —no longer verses, but, what was much worse, prose, and that whole pages at a time. Thus, as the poetical Pleiad of the day said, the *first King in the world* was seen descending from his horse *with an ardour beyond compare*, and on the crown of his hat scrawling bombastic phrases, which M. de Saint-Aignan, *aide-de-camp* in perpetuity, carried to La Vallière at the risk of foundering his horses. During this time, deer and pheasants were left to the free enjoyments of their nature, hunted so lazily, that, it was said, the art of venery ran great risk of degenerating at the court of France. D'Artagnan then thought of the wishes of poor Raoul, of that desponding letter destined for a woman who passed her life in hoping; and as d'Artagnan loved to philosophise a little occasionally, he resolved to profit by the absence of the King to have a minute's talk with Mademoiselle de la Vallière. This was a very easy affair: while the King was hunting, Louise was walking with some other ladies in one of the galleries of the Palais Royal, exactly where the captain of the musketeers had some guards to inspect. D'Artagnan did not doubt that, if he could but open the conversation upon Raoul, Louise might give him grounds for writing a consolatory letter to the poor exile; and hope, or at least consolation for Raoul, in the state of heart in which he had left him, was the sun, was life, to two men who were very dear to our captain. He directed his course, therefore, to the spot where he knew he should find Mademoiselle de la Vallière. D'Artagnan found La Vallière the centre of a circle. In her apparent solitude, the King s favourite received, like a queen, more perhaps than the Queen, a homage of which Madame had been so proud, when all the King's looks were directed to her and commanded the looks of the courtiers. D'Artagnan, although no squire of dames, received, nevertheless, civilities and attentions from the ladies; he was polite, as a brave man always is, and his terrible reputation had conciliated as much friendship among the men as admiration among the women. On seeing him enter, therefore, they immediately accosted him; and, as is not infrequently the case with fair ladies, opened the attack by questions: Where *had* he been? What *had* become of him so long? Why had they not seen him as usual make his fine horse curvet in such beautiful style, to the delight and astonishment of the curious, from the King's balcony?

He replied that he had just come from the land of oranges. This set all the ladies laughing. Those were times in which everybody travelled, but in which, notwithstanding, a journey of a hundred leagues was a problem often solved by death.

" 'From the land of oranges?' " cried Mademoiselle de Tonnay-Charente. "From Spain?"

"Eh! eh!" said the musketeer.

"From Malta?" said Montalais.

"*Ma foi!* You are coming very near, ladies."

"Is it an island?" asked La Vallière.

"Mademoiselle," said d'Artagnan; "I will not give you the trouble of seeking any further; I come from the country where M. de Beaufort is, at this moment, embarking for Algiers."

"Have you seen the army?" said several warlike fair ones.

"As plainly as I see you," replied d'Artagnan.

"And the fleet?"

"Yes; I saw everything."

"Have we any of us any friends there?" said Mademoiselle de Tonnay-Charente coldly, but in a manner to attract attention to a question that was not without a calculated aim.

"Why," replied d'Artagnan, "yes; there were M. de la Guillotière, M. de Manchy, M. de Bragelonne——"

La Vallière became pale. "M. de Bragelonne!" cried the perfidious Athenaïs.* "Eh, what!—is he gone to the wars?—he!"

Montalaïs trod upon her toe, but in vain.

"Do you know what my opinion is?" continued she, addressing d'Artagnan.

"No, mademoiselle; but I should like very much to know it."

"My opinion is, then, that all the men who go to this war are desperate, desponding men, whom love has treated ill; and who go to try if they cannot find black women more kind than fair ones have been."

Some of the ladies laughed. La Vallière was evidently confused. Montalais coughed loud enough to waken the dead.

"Mademoiselle," interrupted d'Artagnan, "you are in error when you speak of black women at Gigelli; the women there are not black; it is true, they are not white—they are yellow."

"Yellow!" exclaimed the bevy of fair beauties.

"Eh! do not disparage it. I have never seen a finer colour to match with black eyes and a coral mouth."

"So much the better for M. de Bragelonne," said Mademoiselle de Tonnay-Charente, with persistent malice. "He will make amends for his loss. Poor fellow!"

A profound silence followed these words; and d'Artagnan had time to observe and reflect that women—those mild doves—treat each other much more cruelly than tigers and bears. But making La Vallière pale did not satisfy Athenaïs; she determined to make her blush likewise. Resuming the conversation without pause, "Do you know, Louise," said she, "that that is a great sin on your conscience?"

"What sin, mademoiselle?" stammered the unfortunate girl, looking round her for support, without finding it.

"Eh!—why?" continued Athenaïs, "the poor young man was affianced to you; he loved you, you cast him off."

"Well, and that is a right every honest woman has," said Montalais, in an affected tone. "When we know we cannot constitute the happiness of a man, it is much better to cast him off."

"Cast him off! or refuse him!—that's all very well," said Athenaïs, "but that is not the sin Mademoiselle de la Vallière has to reproach herself with. The actual sin is sending poor Bragelonne to the wars; and to wars in which death is to be met with." Louise pressed her hand over her icy brow. "And if he dies," continued her pitiless tormentor, "you will have killed him. That is the sin."

Louise, half-dead, caught at the arm of the captain of the musketeers, whose face betrayed unusual emotion. "You wished to speak with me, Monsieur d'Artagnan," said she, in a voice broken by anger and pain. "What had you to say to me?"

D'Artagnan made several steps along the gallery, holding Louise on his arm; then, when they were far enough removed from the others—"What I had to say to you, mademoiselle," replied he, "Mademoiselle de Tonnay-Charente has just expressed; roughly, and unkindly, it is true, but still in its entirety."

She uttered a faint cry; and, struck to the heart by this new wound, she went on her way, like one of those poor birds which, struck to death, seeks the shade of the thicket to die in. She disappeared at one door, at the moment the King was entering by another. The first glance of the King was directed towards the empty seat of his mistress. Not perceiving La Vallière, a frown came over his brow; but as soon as he saw d'Artagnan, who bowed to him—"Ah! monsieur!" cried he, "you *have* been diligent! I am much pleased with you." This was the superlative expression of royal satisfaction. Many men would have been ready to lay down their lives for such a speech from the King. The maids of honour and the courtiers, who had formed a respectful circle round the King on his entrance, drew back, on observing he wished to speak privately with his captain of the musketeers. The King led the way out of the gallery, after having again, with his eyes, sought everywhere for La Vallière, whose absence he could not account for. The moment they were out of the reach of curious ears, "Well! Monsieur d'Artagnan," said he, "the prisoner?"

"Is in his prison, sire."

"What did he say on the road?"

"Nothing, sire."

"What did he do?"

"There was a moment at which the fisherman—who took me in his boat to Sainte-Marguerite—revolted, and did his best to kill me. The—the prisoner defended me instead of attempting to fly."

The King became pale. "Enough!" said he; and d'Artagnan bowed. Louis walked about his cabinet with hasty steps. "Were you at Antibes," said he, "when Monsieur de Beaufort came there?"

"No, sire; I was setting off when Monsieur le Duc arrived."

"Ah!" which was followed by a fresh silence. "Whom did you see there?"

"A great many persons," said d'Artagnan coolly.

The King perceived that he was unwilling to speak. "I have sent for you, captain, to desire you to go and prepare my lodgings at Nantes."

"At Nantes!" cried d'Artagnan.

"In Bretagne."

"Yes, sire, it is in Bretagne. Will your Majesty make so long a journey as to Nantes?"

"The States*are assembled there," replied the King. "I have two demands to make of them: I wish to be there."

"When shall I set out?" said the captain.

"This evening—to-morrow—to-morrow evening; for you must stand in need of rest."

"I have rested, sire."

"That is well. Then between this and to-morrow evening, when you please."

D'Artagnan bowed as if to take his leave; but, perceiving the King very much embarrassed, "Will your Majesty," said he, stepping two paces forward, "take the court with you?"

"Certainly I shall."

"Then your Majesty will, doubtless, want the musketeers?" And the eye of the King sank beneath the penetrating glance of the captain.

"Take a brigade of them," replied Louis.

"Is that all? Has your Majesty no other orders to give me?"

"No—ah—yes."

"I am all attention, sire."

"At the castle of Nantes, which I hear is very ill arranged, you will adopt the practice of placing musketeers at the door of each of the principal dignitaries I shall take with me."

"Of the principal?"

"Yes."

"For instance, at the door of M. de Lyonne?"

"Yes."

"At that of M. Litellier?"

"Yes."

"Of M. de Brienne?"

"Yes."

"And of Monsieur le Surintendant?"*

"Without doubt."

"Very well, sire. By to-morrow I shall have set out."

"Oh, yes; but one more word, Monsieur d'Artagnan. At Nantes you will meet with M. le Duc de Gesvres,* captain of the guards. Be sure that your musketeers are placed before his guards arrive. Precedence always belongs to the first comer."

"Yes, sire."

"And if M. de Gesvres should question you?"

"Question me, sire? Is it likely that M. de Gesvres should

question me?" And the musketeer, turning cavalierly on his heel, disappeared. "To Nantes!" said he to himself, as he descended the stairs. "Why did he not dare to say, from thence to Belle-Isle?"

As he reached the great gates, one of M. Brienne's clerks came running after him, exclaiming, "Monsieur d'Artagnan! I beg your pardon——"

"What is the matter, Monsieur Ariste?"

"The King has desired me to give you this order."

"Upon your cash-box?" asked the musketeer.

"No, monsieur; upon that of M. Fouquet."

D'Artagnan was surprised, but he took the order, which was in the King's own writing, and was for two hundred pistoles. "What!" thought he, after having politely thanked M. Brienne's clerk, "M. Fouquet is to pay for the journey, then! *Mordioux!* that is a bit of pure Louis XI.! Why was not this order upon the chest of M. Colbert? He would have paid it with such joy." And d'Artagnan, faithful to his principle of never letting an order at sight get cold, went straight to the house of M. Fouquet, to receive his two hundred pistoles.

63

THE LAST SUPPER

THE Surintendant had no doubt received advice of the approaching departure, for he was giving a farewell dinner to his friends. From the bottom to the top of the house, the hurry of the servants bearing dishes, and the diligence of the clerks, denoted an approaching change in both offices and kitchen. D'Artagnan, with his order in his hand, presented himself at the bureaux, when he was told it was too late to pay cash, the chest was closed. He only replied—"On the King's service."

The clerk, a little put out by the serious air of the captain, replied that that was a very respectable reason, but that the customs of the house were respectable likewise; and that, in consequence, he begged the bearer to call again next day. D'Artagnan asked if he could not see M. Fouquet. The clerk replied that M. le Surintendant did not interfere with such details; and rudely closed the outer door in d'Artagnan's face. But the latter had foreseen this stroke, and placed his boot between the door and the door-case, so that the lock did not catch, and the clerk was still nose to nose with his interlocutor. This made him change his tone, and say, with terrified politeness, "If monsieur wishes to speak to M. le Surintendant, he must go to the antechambers; these are the offices where monseigneur never comes."

"Oh! very well! Where are they?" replied d'Artagnan.

"On the other side of the court," said the clerk, delighted at being free.

D'Artagnan crossed the court, and fell in with a crowd of servants.

"Monseigneur sees nobody at this hour," he was answered by a fellow carrying a vermeil dish, in which were three pheasants and twelve quails.

"Tell him," said the captain, laying hold of the servant by the end of his dish, "that I am M. d'Artagnan, captain of His Majesty's musketeers."

The fellow uttered a cry of surprise and disappeared; d'Artagnan following him slowly. He arrived just in time to meet M. Pélisson in the antechamber: the latter a little pale, came hastily out of the dining-room to learn what was the matter—d'Artagnan smiled.

"There is nothing unpleasant, Monsieur Pélisson; only a little order I want cashed."

"Ah!" said Fouquet's friend, breathing more freely; and he took the captain by the hand, and, dragging him behind him, led him into the dining-room, where a number of friends surrounded the Surintendant, placed in the centre, and buried in the cushions of a chair. There were assembled all the Epicureans who so lately at Vaux did the honours of the mansion of wit and money of M. Fouquet. Joyous friends, for the most part faithful, they had not fled their protector at the approach of the storm, and, in spite of the threatening heavens, in spite of the trembling earth, they remained there, smiling, cheerful, as devoted to misfortune as they had been to prosperity. On the left of the Surintendant was Madame de Bellière; on his right was Madame Fouquet; as if braving the laws of the world, and putting all vulgar reasons of propriety to silence, the two protecting angels of this man united to offer him, at the moment of the crisis, the support of their intertwined arms. Madame de Bellière was pale, trembling, and full of respectful attentions for Madame le Surintendante, who with one hand on the hand of her husband, was looking anxiously towards the door by which Pélisson had gone out to bring in d'Artagnan. The captain entered at first full of courtesy, and afterwards of admiration, when, with his infallible glance, he had divined as well as taken in the expression of every face. Fouquet raised himself up in his chair.

"Pardon me, Monsieur d'Artagnan," said he, "if I did not come to receive you when coming in the King's name," and he pronounced the last words with a sort of melancholy firmness which filled the hearts of his friends with terror.

"Monseigneur," replied d'Artagnan, "I only come to you in the King's name to demand payment of an order for two hundred pistoles."

The clouds passed from every brow but that of Fouquet, which still remained overcast.

"Ah! then," said he, "perhaps you are also setting out for Nantes?"

"I do not know whither I am setting out for, monseigneur."

"But," said Madame Fouquet, recovered from her fright, "you are not going so soon, captain, as not to do us the honour to take a seat with us?"

"Madame, I should esteem that a great honour done to me, but I am so pressed for time, that, you see, I have been obliged to permit myself to interrupt your repast to procure payment of my note."

"The reply to which shall be gold," said Fouquet, making a sign to his Intendant, who went out with the order which d'Artagnan handed to him.

"Oh!" said the latter, "I was not uneasy about the payment; the house is good."

A painful smile passed over the pale features of Fouquet.

"Are you in pain?" asked Madame de Bellière.

"Do you feel your attack coming on?" asked Madame Fouquet.

"Neither, thank you both," said Fouquet.

"Your attack?" said d'Artagnan in his turn; "are you unwell, monseigneur?"

"I have a tertian fever, which seized me after the fête at Vaux."

"Caught cold in the grottos at night, perhaps?"

"No, no; nothing but agitation, that was all."

"The too much heart you displayed in your reception of the King," said La Fontaine quietly, without suspicion that he was uttering a sacrilege.

"We cannot devote too much heart to the reception of our King," said Fouquet, mildly, to his poet.

"Monsieur meant to say the too great ardour," interrupted d'Artagnan, with perfect frankness and much amenity. "The fact is, monseigneur, that hospitality was never practised as at Vaux."

Madame Fouquet permitted her countenance to show clearly that if Fouquet had conducted himself well towards the King, the

King had not rendered the like to the minister. But d'Artagnan knew the terrible secret. He alone with Fouquet knew it; those two men had not, the one the courage to complain, the other the right to accuse. The captain, to whom the two hundred pistoles were brought, was about to take his leave, when Fouquet, rising, took a glass of wine, and ordered one to be given d'Artagnan.

"Monsieur," said he, "to the health of the King, *whatever may happen.*"

"And to your health, monseigneur, *whatever may happen,*" said d'Artagnan.

He bowed, with these words of evil omen, to all the company, who rose as soon as they heard the sound of his spurs and boots at the bottom of the stairs.

"I, for a moment, thought it was me, and not my money he wanted," said Fouquet, endeavouring to laugh.

"You!" cried his friends; "and what for, in the name of Heaven?"

"Oh! do not deceive yourselves, my dear brothers in Epicurus," said the Surintendant; "I will not make a comparison between the most humble sinner on the earth and the God we adore, but remember, he gave one day to his friends a repast which is called the Last Supper, and which was nothing but a farewell dinner, like that which we are making at this moment."

A painful cry of denial arose from all parts of the table. "Shut the doors," said Fouquet, and the servants disappeared. "My friends," continued Fouquet, lowering his voice, "what was I formerly? What am I now? Consult among yourselves, and reply. A man like me sinks when he does not continue to rise. What shall we say, then, when he really sinks? I have no more money, no more credit; I have no longer anything but powerful enemies, and powerful friends."

"Quick!" cried Pélisson, rising. "Since you explain yourself with that frankness, it is our duty to be frank, likewise. Yes, you are ruined—yes, you are hastening to your ruin—stop. And, in the first place, what money have we left?"

"Seven hundred thousand livres," said the Intendant.

"Bread," murmured Madame Fouquet.

"Relays," said Pélisson, "relays, and fly!"

"Whither?"

"To Switzerland—to Savoy—but fly!"

"If monseigneur flies," said Madame Bellière, "it will be said that he was guilty, and was afraid."

"More than that, it will be said that I have carried away twenty millions with me."

"We will draw up memoirs to justify you," said La Fontaine. "Fly!"

"I will remain," said Fouquet, "And, besides, does not everything serve me?"

"You have Belle-Isle," cried the Abbé Fouquet.

"And I am naturally going there, when going to Nantes," replied the Surintendant. "Patience, then, patience."

"Before arriving at Nantes, what a distance!" said Madame Fouquet.

"Yes, I know that well," replied Fouquet. "But what is to be done there? The King summons me to the States. I know well it is for the purpose of ruining me; but to refuse to go would be to evince uneasiness."

"Well, I have discovered the means of reconciling everything," cried Pélisson. "You are going to set out for Nantes."

Fouquet looked at him with an air of surprise.

"But with friends; but in your own carriage as far as Orleans; in your barge as far as Nantes; always ready to defend yourself, if you are attacked; to escape if you are threatened. In fact, you will carry your money against all chances; and, whilst flying, you will only have obeyed the King; then, reaching the sea when you like, you will embark for Belle-Isle, and from Belle-Isle you will shoot out wherever it may please you, like the eagle which rushes into space when it has been driven from its eyrie."

A general assent followed Pélisson's words. "Yes, do so," said Madame Fouquet to her husband.

"Do so," said Madame Bellière.

"Do it! do it!" cried all his friends.

"I will do so," replied Fouquet.

"This very evening?"

"In an hour."

"Immediately."

"With seven hundred thousand livres you can lay the foundation of another fortune," said the Abbé Fouquet. "What is there to prevent our arming corsairs at Belle-Isle?"

"And if necessary we will go and discover a new world," added La Fontaine, intoxicated with projects and enthusiasm.

A knock at the door interrupted this concert of joy and hope. "A courier from the King," said the master of the ceremonies.

A profound silence immediately ensued, as if the message brought by this courier was nothing but a reply to all the projects given birth to an instant before. Every one waited to see what the master would do. His brow was streaming with perspiration, and he was really suffering from his fever at that instant. He passed

into his cabinet, to receive the King's message. There prevailed, as
we have said, such a silence in the chambers, and throughout the
attendance, that from the dining-room could be heard the voice
of Fouquet, saying, "That is well, monsieur." This voice was,
however, broken by fatigue, trembling with emotion. An instant
after, Fouquet called Gourville, who crossed the gallery amidst
the universal expectation. At length, he himself reappeared among
his guests; but it was no longer the same pale, spiritless countenance
they had beheld when he left them; from pale he had become livid;
and from spiritless, annihilated. A living spectre, he advanced with
his arms stretched out, his mouth parched, like a shade that comes
to salute friends of former days. On seeing him thus, every one cried
out, and every one rushed towards Fouquet. The latter, looking at
Pélisson, leant upon the Surintendante, and pressed the icy hand
of the Marquise de Bellière.

"Well!" said he, in a voice which had nothing human in it.

"What has happened, my God?" said some one to him.

Fouquet opened his right hand, which was clenched, humid,
and displayed a paper, upon which Pélisson cast a terrified glance.
He read the following lines, written by the King's hand:—

" 'DEAR AND WELL-BELOVED MONSIEUR FOUQUET.—Give us,
upon that which you have left of ours, the sum of seven hundred
thousand livres, of which we stand in need to prepare for our
departure.

" 'And, as we know your health is not good, we pray God to
restore you to health, and to have you in His holy keeping.

LOUIS.

" 'The present letter is to serve as a receipt.' "

A murmur of terror circulated through the apartment.

"Well!" cried Pélisson, in his turn, "you have received that
letter?"

"Received it, yes!"

"What will you do, then?"

"Nothing, since I have received it."

"But——"

"If I have received it, Pélisson, I have paid it," said the Surintendant, with a simplicity that went to the heart of all present.

"You have paid it?" cried Madame Fouquet. "Then we are
ruined!"

"Come, no useless words," interrupted Pélisson. "After money,
life. Monsieur, to horse! to horse!"

"What, leave us!" at once cried both women, wild with grief.

"Eh! monseigneur, in saving yourself, you save us all. To horse!'"

"But he cannot hold himself on. Look at him."

"Oh! if he takes time to reflect——" said the intrepid Pélisson.

"He is right," murmured Fouquet.

"Monseigneur! Monseigneur!" cried Gourville, rushing up the stairs, four steps at once. "Monseigneur!"

"Well! What?"

"I escorted, as you desired, the King's courier with the money."

"Yes."

"Well! when I arrived at the Palais Royal, I saw——"

"Take breath, my poor friend, take breath; you are suffocating."

"What did you see?" cried the impatient friends.

"I saw the musketeers mounting on horseback," said Gourville.

"There, then!" cried all voices at once; "there, then! is there an instant to be lost?"

Madame Fouquet rushed downstairs, calling for her horses; Madame de Bellière flew after her, catching her in her arms, and saying:—

"Madame, in the name of his safety, do not show anything, do not manifest any alarm."

Pélisson ran to have the horses put to the carriages. And, in the meantime, Gourville gathered in his hat all that the weeping friends were able to throw into it of gold and silver—the last offering, the pious alms made to misfortune by poverty. The Surintendant, dragged along by some, carried by others, was shut up in his carriage. Gourville took the reins and mounted the box. Pélisson supported Madame Fouquet, who had fainted. Madame de Bellière had more strength, and was well paid for it; she received Fouquet's last kiss. Pélisson easily explained this precipitate departure by saying that an order from the King had summoned the minister to Nantes.

64

IN THE CARRIAGE OF M. COLBERT

As Gourville had seen, the King's musketeers were mounting and following their captain. The latter, who did not like to be confined in his proceedings, left his brigade under the orders of a lieutenant, and set off, on his part, upon post horses, recommending his men to use all diligence. However rapidly they might travel, they could not arrive before him. He had time, in passing along the Rue des Petits-Champs,* to see a thing which afforded him plenty of food for thought and conjecture. He saw M. Colbert coming out from his house to get into his carriage, which was stationed before the door. In this carriage d'Artagnan perceived the hoods of two women and, being rather curious, he wished to know the names of the women concealed beneath these hoods. To get a glimpse of them, for they kept themselves closely covered up, he urged his horse so near to the carriage, that he drove him against the step with such force as to shake everything containing and contained. The terrified women uttered. the one a faint cry, by which d'Artagnan recognised a young woman, the other an imprecation, by which he recognised the vigour and assurance which half a century bestows. The hoods were thrown back; one of the women was Madame Vanel, the other was the Duchesse de Chevreuse. D'Artagnan's eyes were quicker than those of the ladies; he had seen and known them, whilst they did not recognise him; and as they laughed at their fright, pressing each other's hands,——

"Humph!" said d'Artagnan, "the old duchesse is not more difficult in her friendships than she was formerly. She paying her court to the mistress of M. Colbert! Poor M. Fouquet! that presages you nothing good!"

He rode on. M. Colbert got into his carriage, and this noble trio commenced a sufficiently slow pilgrimage towards the wood of Vincennes. Madame de Chevreuse set down Madame Vanel at her husband's house, and, left alone with M. Colbert, she chatted upon affairs, whilst continuing her ride. She had an inexhaustible fund of conversation, had that dear Duchesse, and as she always talked for the ill of others, always with a view to her own good, her conversation amused her interlocutor, and did not fail to leave a favourable impression behind.

She taught Colbert, who, poor man! was ignorant of it, how

great a minister he was, and how Fouquet would soon become nothing. She promised to rally around him, when he should become Surintendant, all the old nobility of the kingdom, and questioned him as to the preponderance it would be proper to allow La Vallière to take. She praised him, she blamed him, she bewildered him. She showed him the secret of so many secrets, that, for a moment, Colbert feared he must have to do with the devil. She proved to him that she held in her hand the Colbert of to-day, as she had held the Fouquet of yesterday; and as he asked her very simply the reason of her hatred for the Surintendant: "Why do you yourself hate him?" said she.

"Madame, in politics," replied he, "the differences of system may bring about divisions between men. M. Fouquet always appeared to me to practise a system opposed to the true interests of the King."

She interrupted him—"I will say no more to you about M. Fouquet. The journey the King is about to take to Nantes will give a good account of him. M. Fouquet, for me, is a man quite gone by—and for you also."

Colbert made no reply. "On his return from Nantes," continued the Duchesse, "the King, who is only anxious for a pretext, will find that the States have not behaved well—that they have made too few sacrifices. The States will say that the imposts* are too heavy, and that the Surintendant has ruined them. The King will lay all the blame on M. Fouquet, and then——"

"And then?" said Colbert.

"Oh! he will be disgraced. Is not that your opinion?"

Colbert darted a glance at the Duchesse, which plainly said: "If M. Fouquet be only disgraced, you will not be the cause of it."

"Your place, M. Colbert," the Duchesse hastened to say, "must be quite a marked place. Do you perceive any one between the King and yourself, after the fall of M. Fouquet?"

"I do not understand," said he.

"You will understand. To what does your ambition aspire?"

"I have none."

"It was useless then to overthrow the Surintendant, M. Colbert. That is idle."

"I had the honour to tell you, Madame——"

"Oh! yes, I know all about the interest of the King—but, if you please, we will speak of your own."

"Mine! that is to say the affairs of His Majesty."

"In short, are you, or are you not, ruining M. Fouquet? Answer without evasion."

"Madame, I ruin nobody."

"I cannot then comprehend why you should purchase of me the letters of M. Mazarin concerning M. Fouquet. Neither can I conceive why you have laid those letters before the King."

Colbert, half stupefied, looked at the Duchesse with an air of constraint.

"Madame," said he, "I can less easily conceive how you, who received the money, can reproach me on that head."

"That is," said the old Duchesse, "because we must will that which we wish for, unless we are not able to obtain what we wish."

"*Well!*" said Colbert, quite confounded by such coarse logic.

"You are not able, *hein!* Speak."

"I am not able, I allow, to destroy certain influences near the King."

"Which combat for M. Fouquet? What are they? Stop, let me help you."

"Do, madame."

"La Vallière?"

"Oh! very little influence; no knowledge of business; and small means. M. Fouquet has paid his court to her."

"To defend him would be to accuse herself, would it not?"

"I think it would."

"There is still another influence; what do you say to that?"

"Is it considerable?"

"The Queen-Mother, perhaps?"

"Her Majesty, the Queen-Mother, has for M. Fouquet a weakness very prejudicial to her son."

"Never believe that," said the old Duchesse, smiling.

"Oh!" said Colbert, with incredulity, "I have often experienced it."

"Formerly?"

"Very recently, madame, at Vaux. It was she who prevented the King from having M. Fouquet arrested."

"People do not always entertain the same opinions, my dear monsieur. That which the Queen may have wished recently, she would not, perhaps, to-day."

"And why not?" said Colbert, astonished.

"Oh! the reason is of very little consequence."

"On the contrary, I think it is of great consequence; for, if I were certain of not displeasing Her Majesty the Queen-Mother, all my scruples would be removed."

"Well! have you never heard talk of a certain secret?"

"A secret?"

"Call it what you like. In short, the Queen-Mother has conceived a horror for all those who have participated, in one fashion or another, in the discovery of this secret, and M. Fouquet I believe to be one of these."

"Then," said Colbert, "we may be sure of the assent of the Queen-Mother?"

"I have just left Her Majesty, and she assures me so."

"So be it, then, madame."

"But there is something further: do you happen to know a man who was the intimate friend of M. Fouquet, a M. d'Herblay, a bishop, I believe?"

"Bishop of Vannes."

"Well! this M. d'Herblay, who also knew the secret, the Queen-Mother is having him pursued with the utmost rancour."

"Indeed!"

"So hotly pursued, that if he were dead, she would not be satisfied with anything less than his head; to satisfy her he would never speak again."

"And is that the desire of the Queen-Mother?"

"An order is given for it."

"This Monsieur d'Herblay shall be sought for, madame."

"Oh! it is well known where he is." Colbert looked at the Duchesse.

"Say where, madame."

"He is at Belle-Isle-en-Mer."

"At the residence of Monsieur Fouquet?"

"At the residence of M. Fouquet."

"He shall be taken."

It was now the Duchesse's turn to smile. "Do not fancy that so easy," said she, "and do not promise it so lightly."

"Why not, madame?"

"Because M. d'Herblay is not one of those people who can be taken just when you please."

"He is a rebel, then?"

"Oh! Monsieur Colbert, we folks have passed all our lives in making rebels, and yet you see plainly, that so far from being taken, we take others."

Colbert fixed upon the old Duchesse one of those fierce looks of which no words can convey the expression, accompanied by a firmness which was not wanting in grandeur. "The times are gone," said he, "in which subjects gained duchies by making war against the King of France. If M. d'Herblay conspires, he will perish on the scaffold. That will give, or will not give, pleasure to his enemies,—that is of very little importance to *us*."

And this *us*, a strange word in the mouth of Colbert, made the Duchesse thoughtful for a moment. She caught herself reckoning inwardly with this man.—Colbert had regained his superiority in the conversation, and he was desirous of keeping it.

"You ask me, madame," he said, "to have this M. d'Herblay arrested?"

"I!—I asked you nothing of the kind!"

"I thought you did, madame. But, as I have been mistaken, we will leave him alone; the King has said nothing about him."

The Duchesse bit her nails.

"Besides," continued Colbert, "what a poor capture would this bishop be! A bishop game for a King! Oh! no, no; I will not even take the least notice of him."

The hatred of the Duchesse now discovered itself.

"Game for a woman!" said she, "and the Queen is a woman. If she wishes to have M. d'Herblay arrested, she has her reasons for it. Besides, is not M. d'Herblay the friend of him who is destined to fall?"

"Oh! never mind that," said Colbert. "This man shall be spared, if he is not the enemy of the King. Is that displeasing to you?"

"I say nothing."

"Yes—you wish to see him in prison, in the Bastille, for instance."

"I believe a secret better concealed behind the walls of the Bastille than behind those of Belle-Isle."

"I will speak to the King about it; he will clear up the point."

"And whilst waiting for that enlightenment, Monsieur the Bishop of Vannes will have escaped. I would do so."

"Escaped! he! and whither would he escape? Europe is ours, in will if not in fact."

"He will always find an asylum, monsieur. It is evident you know nothing of the man you have to do with. You do not know d'Herblay; you did not know Aramis. He was one of those four musketeers who, under the late King, made Cardinal de Richelieu tremble, and who, during the regency, gave so much trouble to Monseigneur Mazarin."

"But, madame, what can he do, unless he has a kingdom to back him?"

"He has one, monsieur."

"A kingdom, he! what, Monsieur d'Herblay?"

"I repeat to you, monsieur, that if he wants a kingdom, he either has it, or will have it."

"Well, as you are so earnest that this rebel should not escape, madame, I promise you he shall not escape."

"Belle-Isle is fortified, M. Colbert, and fortified by him."

433

"If Belle-Isle were also defended by him, Belle-Isle is not impregnable; and if Monsieur the Bishop of Vannes is shut up in Belle-Isle—well, madame, the place will be besieged, and he will be taken."

"You may be very certain, monsieur, that the zeal which you display for the interests of the Queen-Mother will affect her Majesty warmly, and that you will be magnificently rewarded for it; but what shall I tell her of your projects respecting this man?"

"That when once taken, he shall be shut up in a fortress from which her secret shall never escape."

"Very well, Monsieur Colbert, and we may say that, dating from this instant, we have formed a solid alliance; that is, you and I, and that I am perfectly at your service."

"It is I, madame, who place myself at yours. This Chevalier d'Herblay is a kind of Spanish spy, is he not?"

"More than that."

"A secret ambassador?"

"Higher still."

"Stop—King Philip III. of Spain is a bigot. He is, perhaps, the confessor of Philip III."

"You must go much higher than that."

"*Mordieu!*" cried Colbert, who forgot himself so far as to swear in the presence of this great lady, of this old friend of the Queen-Mother—of the Duchesse de Chevreuse, in short. "He must then be the general of the Jesuits."

"I believe you have guessed at last," replied the Duchesse.

"Ah! then, madame, this man will ruin us all if we do not ruin him; and we must make haste to do it, too."

"That was my opinion, monsieur, but I did not dare to give it to you."

"And it is fortunate for us that he has attacked the throne, and not us."

"But mark this well, M. Colbert. M. d'Herblay is never discouraged; and, if he has missed one blow, he will be sure to make another; he will begin again. If he has allowed an opportunity to escape of making a king for himself, sooner or later he will make another, of whom, to a certainty, you will not be prime minister."

Colbert knitted his brow with a menacing expression.

"I feel assured that a prison will settle this affair for us, madame, in a manner satisfactory for both." The Duchesse smiled again.

"Oh! if you knew," said she, "how many times Aramis has got out of prison."

"Oh!" replied Colbert, "we will take care he shall not get out this time."

"But you have not attended to what I said to you just now. Do you remember that Aramis was one of the four invincibles whom Richelieu dreaded? And at that period the four musketeers were not in possession of that which they have now—money and experience."

Colbert bit his lips.

"We will renounce the idea of the prison," said he, in a lower tone; "we will find a retreat from which the invincible will not possibly escape."

"That is well spoken, our ally!" replied the Duchesse. "But it is getting late; had we not better return?"

"The more willingly, madame, from having my preparations to make for setting out with the King."

"To Paris!" cried the Duchesse to the coachman.

And the carriage returned towards the Faubourg St. Antoine, after the conclusion of the treaty which gave up to death the last friend of Fouquet, the last defender of Belle-Isle, the ancient friend of Marie Michon, the new enemy of the Duchesse.

65

THE TWO LIGHTERS

D'ARTAGNAN had set off; Fouquet likewise was gone, and he with a rapidity which doubled the tender interest of his friends. The first moments of this journey, or better to say, of this flight, were troubled by the incessant fear of all the horses and all the carriages which could be perceived behind the fugitive. It was not natural, in fact, if Louis XIV. was determined to seize his prey, that he should allow it to escape; the young lion was already accustomed to the chase, and he had bloodhounds sufficiently ardent to allow him to depend upon them. But insensibly all the fears were dispersed; the Surintendant, by hard travelling, placed such a distance between himself and his persecutors that no one of them could reasonably be expected to overtake him. As to his position, his friends had made it excellent for him. Was he not travelling to join the King at Nantes, and what did rapidity prove but his zeal to obey? He arrived, fatigued but reassured, at Orleans, where he found, thanks to the care of a courier who had preceded him, a handsome lighter of eight oars. These lighters, in the shape of gondolas, rather wide and rather heavy, containing a small, covered chamber in shape of a deck, and a chamber in the poop formed by a tent, then acted as passage-boats from Orleans to

Nantes, by the Loire, and this passage, a long one in our days, appeared then more easy and convenient than the high road, with its post hacks or its bad, scarcely hung carriages. Fouquet went on board this lighter, which set out immediately. The rowers, knowing they had the honour of conveying the Surintendant of the Finances, pulled with all their strength, and that magic word, the *finances*, promised them a liberal gratification, of which they wished to prove themselves worthy. The lighter bounded over the tiny waves of the Loire. Magnificent weather, one of those sun risings that empurple landscapes, left the river all its limpid serenity. The current and the rowers carried Fouquet along as wings carry a bird, and he arrived before Beaugency* without any accident having signalised the voyage. Fouquet hoped to be the first to arrive at Nantes; there he would see the notables and gain support among the principal members of the States; he would make himself necessary, a thing very easy for a man of his merit, and would delay the catastrophe, if he did not succeed in avoiding it entirely. "Besides," said Gourville to him, "at Nantes you will make out, or we will make out the intentions of your enemies; we will have horses always ready to convey you to the inextricable *Poitou*, a barque in which to gain the sea and, when once in the open sea, Belle-Isle is the inviolable port. You see, besides, that no one is watching you, no one is following you." He had scarcely finished when they discovered at a distance, behind an elbow formed by the river, the masts of a large lighter, which was coming down. The rowers of Fouquet's boat uttered a cry of surprise on seeing this galley.

"What is the matter?" asked Fouquet.

"The matter is, monseigneur," replied the skipper of the barque, "that it is a truly remarkable thing—that lighter comes along like a hurricane."

Gourville started, and mounted on the deck, in order to see the better.

Fouquet did not go up with him, but he said to Gourville with a restrained mistrust: "See what it is, dear friend."

The lighter had just passed the elbow. It came on so fast, that behind it might be seen to tremble, the white train of its wake illumined with the fires of day.

"How they go," repeated the skipper, "how they go! They must be well paid! I did not think," he added, "that oars of wood could behave better than ours, but those yonder prove the contrary."

"Well, they may," said one of the rowers, "they are twelve, and we are but eight."

"Twelve rowers!" replied Gourville, "twelve! impossible."

The number of eight rowers for a lighter had never been exceeded, even for the King. This honour had been paid to Monsieur le Surintendant, much more for the sake of haste than of respect.

"What does that mean?" said Gourville, endeavouring to distinguish beneath the tent which was already apparent, travellers which the most piercing eye could not yet have succeeded in discovering.

"They must be in a hurry, for it is not the King," said the skipper.

Fouquet shuddered.

"By what do you know that it is not the King?" said Gourville.

"In the first place, because there is no white flag with fleurs de lis, which the royal lighter always carries."

"And then," said Fouquet, "because it is impossible it should be the King, Gourville, as the King was still in Paris yesterday."

Gourville replied to the Surintendant by a look which said: "You were there yourself yesterday."

"And by what do you make out they are in such haste?" added he, for the sake of gaining time.

"By this, monsieur," said the skipper; "these people must have set out a long while after us, and they have already nearly overtaken us."

"Bah!" said Gourville, "who told you that they do not come from Beaugency or from Moit, even?"

"We have seen no lighter of that shape, except at Orleans. It comes from Orleans, monsieur, and makes great haste."

Fouquet and Gourville exchanged a glance. The skipper remarked their uneasiness and, to mislead him, Gourville immediately said:—

"Some friend, who has laid a wager he would catch us; let us win the wager, and not allow him to come up with us."

The skipper opened his mouth to reply that that was impossible, when Fouquet said with much hauteur,—

"If it is any one who wishes to overtake us, let him come."

"We can try, monseigneur," said the skipper timidly, "Come, you fellows, put out your strength—row, row!"

"No," said Fouquet, "stop short, on the contrary."

"Monseigneur! what folly!" interrupted Gourville, stooping towards his ear.

"Quite short!" repeated Fouquet. The eight oars stopped, and resisting the water, they created a retrograde motion in the lighter. It was stopped. The twelve rowers in the other did not, at first, perceive this manœuvre, for they continued to urge on their boat so vigorously that it arrived quickly within musket-shot. Fouquet was short-sighted, Gourville was annoyed by the sun, which was full in his eyes; the skipper alone, with that habit and clearness which are acquired by a constant struggle with the elements, perceived distinctly the travellers in the neighbouring lighter.

"I can see them!" cried he, "there are two."

"I can see nothing," said Gourville.

"You will not be long before you distinguish them: in twenty strokes of their oars they will be within twenty paces of us."

But what the skipper announced was not realised; the lighter imitated the movement commanded by Fouquet, and instead of coming to join its pretended friends, it stopped short in the middle of the river.

"I cannot comprehend this," said the skipper.

"Nor I, neither," said Gourville.

"You who can see so plainly the people in that lighter," resumed Fouquet, "try to describe them to us, skipper, before we are too far off."

"I thought I saw two," replied the boatman, "I can only see one now, under the tent."

"What sort of man is he?"

"He is a dark man, large shoulders, short necked."

A little cloud at that moment passed across the azure of the heavens, and darkened the sun. Gourville, who was still looking, with one hand over his eyes, became able to see what he sought, and all at once, jumping from the deck into the chamber where Fouquet awaited him: "Colbert!" said he, in a voice broken by emotion.

"Colbert!" repeated Fouquet, "Oh! how strange! but no, it is impossible!"

"I tell you I recognised him, and he, at the same time, so plainly recognised me, that he is just gone into the chamber on the poop. Perhaps the King has sent him to make us come back."

"In that case he would join us, instead of lying by. What is he doing there?"

"He is watching us, without doubt."

"I do not like uncertainty," said Fouquet; "let us go straight up to him."

"Oh! monseigneur, do not do that, the lighter is full of armed men."

"He would arrest me, then, Gourville? Why does he not come on?"

"Monseigneur, it is not consistent with your dignity to go to meet your ruin."

"But to allow them to watch me like a malefactor!"

"Nothing tells us that they are watching you, monseigneur; be patient!"

"What is to be done, then?"

"Do not stop; you were only going so fast to appear to obey the King's order with zeal. Redouble the speed. He who lives will see!"

"That's just. Come!" cried Fouquet; "since they remain stock-still yonder, let us go on, on our part."

The skipper gave the signal, and Fouquet's rowers resumed their task with all the success that could be looked for from men who had rested. Scarcely had the lighter made a hundred fathoms, than the other, that with the twelve rowers, resumed its course equally. This position lasted all the day, without any increase or diminution of distance between the two vessels. Towards evening Fouquet wished to try the intentions of his persecutor. He ordered his rowers to pull towards the shore, as if to effect a landing. Colbert's lighter imitated this manœuvre, and steered towards the shore in a slanting direction. By the greatest chance, at the spot where Fouquet pretended to wish to land, a stableman from the château of Langeais,* was following the flowery banks, leading three horses in halters. Without doubt the people of the twelve-oared lighter fancied that Fouquet was directing his course towards horses prepared for his flight, for four or five men, armed with muskets, jumped from the lighter on to the shore, and marched along the banks, as if to gain ground on the horses and horseman. Fouquet, satisfied of having forced the enemy to a demonstration, considered it evident, and put his boat in motion again. Colbert's people returned likewise to theirs, and the course of the two vessels was resumed with fresh perseverance. Upon seeing this, Fouquet felt himself threatened closely, and in a prophetic voice—"Well, Gourville," said he whisperingly, "what did I say at our last repast, at my house? Am I going, or not, to my ruin?"

"Oh! monseigneur!"

"These two boats, which follow each other with so much emulation, as if we were disputing, M. Colbert and I, a prize for swiftness on the Loire, do they not aptly represent our two fortunes; and do you not believe, Gourville, that one of the two will be wrecked at Nantes?"

"At least," objected Gourville, "there is still uncertainty; you are about to appear at the States; you are about to show what sort of man you are; your eloquence and your genius for business are the buckler and sword that will serve to defend you, if not to conquer with. The Bretons do not know you; and when they shall know you your cause is won! Oh! let M. Colbert look to it well, for his lighter is as much exposed as yours to being upset! Both go quickly, his faster than yours, it is true; we shall see which shall be wrecked first."

Fouquet, taking Gourville's hand,—"My friend," said he, "everything considered, remember the proverb, 'First come, first served!' Well! M. Colbert takes care not to pass me. He is a prudent man, that M. Colbert!"

He was right; the two lighters held their course as far as Nantes, watching each other. When the Surintendant landed, Gourville hoped he should be able to seek refuge at once and have relays prepared. But, at the landing, the second lighter joined the first, and Colbert, approaching Fouquet, saluted him on the quay with marks of profoundest respect—marks so significant, so public, that the result was the bringing of the whole population upon La Fosse. Fouquet was completely self-possessed; he felt that in his last moments of greatness he had obligations towards himself. He wished to fall from such a height that his fall should crush some one of his enemies. Colbert was there—so much the worse for Colbert. The Surintendant, therefore, coming up to him, replied with that arrogant winking of the eyes peculiar to him—"What! is that you, M. Colbert?"

"To offer you my respects, monseigneur," said the latter.

"Were you in that lighter?"—pointing to the one with twelve oars.

"Yes, monseigneur."

"Of twelve rowers?" said Fouquet; "what luxury, M. Colbert. For a moment I thought it was the Queen-Mother or the King."

"Monseigneur!" —and Colbert blushed.

"This is a voyage that will cost those who have to pay for it dear, Monsieur l'Intendant!" said Fouquet. "But you have, happily, arrived——You see, however," he added, a moment after, "that I, who had but eight rowers, arrived before you." And he turned his back towards him, leaving him uncertain whether all the tergiversations of the second lighter had escaped the notice of the first. At least he did not give him the satisfaction of showing that he had been frightened. Colbert, so annoyingly attacked, did not give way.

"I have not been quick, monseigneur," he replied, "because I followed your example whenever you stopped."

"And why did you do that, Monsieur Colbert?" cried Fouquet,

irritated by this base audacity; "as you had a superior crew to mine, why did you not either join me or pass me?"

"Out of respect," said the Intendant, bowing to the ground.

Fouquet got into a carriage which the city sent to him, we know not why or how, and he repaired to *la Maison de Nantes*,* escorted by a vast crowd of people, who for several days had been boiling with the expectation of a convocation of the States. Scarcely was he installed, when Gourville went out to order horses upon the route to Poitiers and Vannes, and a boat at Paimbœuf.* He performed these various operations with so much mystery, activity, and generosity, that never was Fouquet, then labouring under an access of fever, more near being saved, except for the co-operation of that immense disturber of human projects—chance. A report was spread during the night, that the King was coming in great haste upon post horses, and that he would arrive within ten or twelve hours at latest. The people, while waiting for the King, were greatly rejoiced to see the musketeers, freshly arrived with Monsieur d'Artagnan, their captain, and quartered in the castle, of which they occupied all the posts, in quality of guard of honour. M. d'Artagnan, who was very polite, presented himself about ten o'clock, at the lodgings of the Surintendant, to pay his respectful compliments to him; and although the minister suffered from fever, although he was in such pain as to be bathed in sweat, he would receive M. d'Artagnan, who was delighted with that honour, as will be seen by the conversation they had together.

66

FRIENDLY ADVICE

FOUQUET was gone to bed, like a man who clings to life, and who economises as much as possible, that slender tissue of existence, of which the shocks and angles of this world so quickly wear out the irreparable tenuity. D'Artagnan appeared at the door of this chamber, and was saluted by the Surintendant with a very affable "good-day."

"*Bon jour!* monseigneur," replied the musketeer, "how did you get through the journey?"

"Tolerably well, thank you."

"And the fever?"

"But sadly. I drink, as you see. I am scarcely arrived, and I have already levied a contribution of cooling drinks upon Nantes."

"You should sleep first, monseigneur."

"Eh! *corbleu!* my dear Monsieur d'Artagnan, I should be very glad to sleep."

"Who hinders you?"

"Why you, in the first place."

"I? Ah, monseigneur!"

"No doubt you do. Is it at Nantes as it was at Paris; do you not come in the King's name?"

"For Heaven's sake, monseigneur," replied the captain, "leave the King alone! The day on which I shall come on the part of the King, for the purpose you mean, take my word for it, I will not leave you long in doubt. You will see me place my hand on my sword, according to the book, and you will hear me say at once in my ceremonial voice, 'Monseigneur, in the name of the King, I arrest you.'"

"You promise me that frankness?" said the Surintendant.

"Upon my honour! But we are not come to that, believe me!"

"What makes you think that, Monsieur d'Artagnan? For my part I think quite the contrary."

"I have heard speak of nothing of the kind," replied d'Artagnan.

"Eh! eh!" said Fouquet.

"Indeed, no. You are an agreeable man, in spite of your fever. The King ought not, cannot help loving you at the bottom of his heart."

Fouquet's face implied doubt. "But, M. Colbert?" said he, "does M. Colbert love me as much as you say?"

"I don't speak of M. Colbert," replied d'Artagnan. "He is an exceptional man, is that M. Colbert! He does not love you; that is very possible; but, *mordioux!* the squirrel can guard himself against the adder with very little trouble."

"Do you know that you are speaking to me, quite as a friend," replied Fouquet; "and that, upon my life! I have never met with a man of your intelligence, and your heart?"

"You are pleased to say so," replied d'Artagnan. "Why did you wait till to-day to pay me such a compliment?"

"Blind as we are!" murmured Fouquet.

"Your voice is getting hoarse," said d'Artagnan; "drink, monseigneur, drink!" And he offered him a draught, with the most friendly cordiality; Fouquet took it and thanked him by a bland smile. "Such things only happen to me," said the musketeer. "I have passed ten years under your very beard, while you were rolling about tons of gold. You were clearing an annual pension of four millions; you never observed me; and you find out there is such a person in the world, just at the moment——"

"I am about to fall," interrupted Fouquet. "That is true, my dear Monsieur d'Artagnan."

"I did not say so."

"But you thought so; and that is the same thing. Well! if I fall, take my word as truth I shall not pass a single day without saying to myself as I strike my brow, 'Fool! fool!—stupid mortal! You had a Monsieur d'Artagnan under your eye and hand, and you did not employ him, you did not enrich him!'"

"You quite overwhelm me," said the captain. "I esteem you greatly."

"There exists another man, then, who does not think as M. Colbert does," said the Surintendant.

"How this M. Colbert sticks in your stomach! He is worse than your fever."

"Oh! I have good cause," said Fouquet. "Judge for yourself." And he related the details of the course of the lighters, and the hypocritical persecution of Colbert. "Is not this a clear sign of my ruin?"

D'Artagnan became serious. "That is true," said he. "Yes; that has a bad odour, as M. de Tréville used to say." And he fixed upon M. Fouquet his intelligent and significant look.

"Am I not clearly designated in that, captain? Is not the King bringing me to Nantes to get me away from Paris, where I have so many creatures, and to possess himself of Belle-Isle?"

"Where M. d'Herblay is," added d'Artagnan. Fouquet raised his head. "As for me, monseigneur," continued d'Artagnan, "I can assure you the King has said nothing to me against you."

"Indeed!"

"The King commanded me to set out for Nantes, it is true; and to say nothing about it to M. de Gesvres."

"My friend."

"To M. de Gesvres, yes, monseigneur," continued the musketeer, whose eyes did not cease to speak a language different from the language of his lips. "The King, moreover, commanded me to take a brigade of musketeers, which is apparently superfluous, as the country is quite quiet."

"A brigade!" said Fouquet, raising himself upon his elbow.

"Ninety-six horsemen, yes, monsieur. The same number as were employed in arresting MM. de Chalais, de Cinq-Mars, and Montmorency."*

Fouquet pricked up his ears at these words, pronounced without apparent value. "And besides?" said he.

"Well! nothing but insignificant orders; such as guarding the castle, guarding every lodging, allowing none of M. de Gesvres' guards to occupy a single post—M. de Gesvres, your friend."

"And for myself," cried Fouquet, "what orders had you?"

"For you, monseigneur?—not the smallest word."

"Monsieur d'Artagnan; the safety of my honour, and, perhaps, of my life, is at stake. You would not deceive me?"

"I?—and to what end? Are you threatened? Only there really is an order with respect to carriages and boats——"

"An order?"

"Yes; but it cannot concern you—a simple measure of police."

"What is it, captain—what is it?"

"To forbid all horses or boats to leave Nantes, without a pass, signed by the King."

"Great God; but——"

D'Artagnan began to laugh. "All that is not to be put into execution before the arrival of the King at Nantes. So that you see plainly, monseigneur, the order in no wise concerns you."

Fouquet became thoughtful, and d'Artagnan feigned not to observe his preoccupation—"It is evident, by my thus confiding to you the orders which have been given to me, that I am friendly towards you, and that I endeavour to prove to you that none of them are directed against you."

"Without doubt!—without doubt!" said Fouquet, still absent.

"Let us recapitulate," said the captain, his glance beaming with earnestness. "A special and severe guard of the castle in which your lodging is to be—is it not?"

"Do you know that castle?"

"Ah! monseigneur, a true prison! The total absence of Monsieur Gesvres, who has the honour of being one of your friends. The closing of the gates of the city, and of the river, without a pass; but, only when the King shall have arrived. Please to observe, Monsieur Fouquet, that, if, instead of speaking to a man like you, who are one of the first in the kingdom, I were speaking to a troubled, uneasy conscience—I should compromise myself for ever! What a fine opportunity for any one who wished to be free! No police, no guards, no orders; the water free, the roads free, Monsieur d'Artagnan obliged .end his horses, if required! All this ought to re-assure you, Monsieur Fouquet, for the King would not have left me thus independent, if he had had any evil designs. In truth, Monsieur Fouquet, ask me whatever you like; I am at your service; and, in return, if you will consent to it, render me a service, that of offering my compliments to Aramis and Porthos, in case you embark for Belle-Isle, as you have a right to do, without changing your dress, immediately, in your *robe-de-chambre*—just as you are." Saying these words, and with a profound bow, the musketeer, whose looks had lost none of their intelligent kindness, left the apartment. He had not reached the steps of the vestibule, when Fouquet, quite beside himself, hung to the bell-rope, and shouted, "My horses!—my lighter!" But nobody answered. The Surintendant dressed himself with everything that came to hand.

"Gourville!—Gourville!" cried he, while slipping his watch into his pocket. And the bell sounded again, whilst Fouquet repeated, "Gourville!—Gourville!"

Gourville at length appeared, breathless and pale.

"Let us be gone! Let us be gone!" cried Fouquet, as soon as he saw him.

"It is too late!" said the Surintendant's poor friend.

"Too late!—why?"

"Listen!" And they heard the sounds of trumpets and drums in front of the castle.

"What does that mean, Gourville?"

"It is the King coming, monseigneur."

"The King!"

"The King, who has ridden double stages, who has killed horses, and who is eight hours in advance of your calculation."

"We are lost!" murmured Fouquet. "Brave d'Artagnan, all is over, thou hast spoken to me too late."

The King, in fact, was entering the city, which soon resounded with the cannon from the ramparts, and from a vessel which replied from the lower part of the river. Fouquet's brow darkened; he called his *valets de chambre*, and dressed in ceremonial costume. From his window, behind the curtains, he could see the eagerness of the people, and the movement of a large troop, which had followed the Prince, without its being able to be guessed how. The King was conducted to the castle in great pomp, and Fouquet saw him dismount under the portcullis, and speak something in the ear of d'Artagnan, who held his stirrup. D'Artagnan, when the King had passed under the arch, directed his steps towards the house Fouquet was in; but so slowly, and stopping so frequently to speak to his musketeers, drawn up as a hedge, that it might be said he was counting the seconds, or the steps before accomplishing his message. Fouquet opened the window to speak to him in the court.

"Ah!" cried d'Artagnan, on perceiving him, "are you still there, monseigneur?"

And that word *still* completed the proof to Fouquet of how much information, and how many useful counsels were contained in the first visit the musketeer had paid him. The Surintendant sighed deeply. "Good Heavens! yes, monsieur," replied he. "The arrival of the King has interrupted me in the projects I had formed."

"Oh! then you know that the King has arrived?"

"Yes, monsieur, I have seen him; and this time you come from him——"

"To inquire after you, monseigneur; and, if your health is not too bad, to beg you to have the kindness to repair to the castle."

"Directly, Monsieur d'Artagnan, directly?"

"Ah!" said the captain, "now the King is come, there is no more walking for anybody—no more free-will; the pass-word governs all now, you as well as me, me as well as you."

Fouquet heaved a last sigh, got into his carriage, so great was his weakness, and went to the castle, escorted by d'Artagnan, whose politeness was not less terrifying this time than it had but just before been consoling and cheerful.

67

HOW THE KING, LOUIS XIV., PLAYED HIS LITTLE PART

As Fouquet was alighting from his carriage to enter the castle of Nantes, a man of mean appearance went up to him with marks of the greatest respect, and gave him a letter. D'Artagnan endeavoured to prevent this man from speaking to Fouquet, and pushed him away, but the message had been given to the Surintendant. Fouquet opened the letter and read it, and instantly a vague terror, which d'Artagnan did not fail to penetrate, was painted upon the countenance of the first minister. Fouquet put the paper into the portfolio which he had under his arm, and passed on towards the King's apartments. D'Artagnan, through the small windows made at every landing of the donjon stairs, saw, as he went up behind Fouquet, the man who had delivered the note, look around him on the place, and make signs to several persons, who disappeared into the adjacent streets, after having themselves repeated the signals made by the person we have named. Fouquet was made to wait for a moment upon the terrace of which we have spoken, a terrace which abutted on the little corridor, at the end of which the closet of the King was established. Here d'Artagnan passed on before the Surintendant, whom, till that time, he had respectfully accompanied, and entered the royal cabinet.

"Well," said Louis XIV., who, on perceiving him, threw on to the table covered with papers a large green cloth.

"The order is executed, sire."

"And Fouquet?"

"Monsieur le Surintendant follows me," said d'Artagnan.

"In ten minutes let him be introduced," said the King, dismissing d'Artagnan again with a gesture. The latter retired; but had scarcely reached the corridor at the extremity of which Fouquet was waiting for him, when he was recalled by the King's bell.

"Did he not appear astonished?" asked the King.

"Who, sire?"

"*Fouquet*," repeated the King, without saying monsieur, a particularity which confirmed the captain of the musketeers in his suspicions.

"No, sire," replied he.

"That's well!" And a second time Louis dismissed d'Artagnan.

Fouquet had not quitted the terrace where he had been left by his guide. He reperused his note, which was thus conceived :—

"Something is being contrived against you. Perhaps they will not dare to carry it out at the castle; it will be on your return home. The house is already surrounded by musketeers. Do not enter. A white horse is waiting for you behind the esplanade!"

Fouquet recognised the writing and the zeal of Gourville. Not being willing that, if any evil happened to himself, this paper should compromise a faithful friend, the Surintendant was busy tearing it into a thousand morsels, spread about by the wind from the balustrade of the terrace. D'Artagnan found him watching the flight of the last scraps into space.

"Monsieur," said he, "the King waits for you."

Fouquet walked with a deliberate step into the little corridor, where MM. de Brienne and Rose*were at work, whilst the Duc de Saint-Aignan, seated in a little chair, likewise in the corridor, appeared to be waiting for orders with feverish impatience, his sword between his legs. It appeared strange to Fouquet that MM. Brienne, Rose, and de Saint-Aignan, in general so attentive and obsequious, should scarcely take the least notice, as he, the Surintendant, passed. But how could he expect to find it otherwise among courtiers, he whom the King no longer called anything but *Fouquet*? He raised his head, determined to look every one and every thing bravely in the face, and entered the King's apartment, where a little bell, which we already know, had announced him to His Majesty.

The King, without rising, nodded to him, and with interest: "Well! how are you, Monsieur Fouquet?" said he.

"I am in a high fever," replied the Surintendant, "but I am at the King's service."

"That is well; the States assemble to-morrow; have you a speech ready?"

Fouquet looked at the King with astonishment. "I have not, sire." replied he; "but I will improvise one. I am too well acquainted with affairs to feel any embarrassment. I have only one question to ask; will your Majesty permit me?"

"Certainly; ask it."

"Why has your Majesty not done his first minister the honour to give him notice of this in Paris?"

"You were ill; I was not willing to fatigue you."

"Never did a labour—never did an explanation fatigue me, sire; and, since the moment is come for me to demand an explanation of my King——"

"Oh! Monsieur Fouquet! an explanation upon what?"

"Upon your Majesty's intentions with respect to myself."

The King blushed. "I have been calumniated," continued Fouquet warmly, "and I feel called upon to provoke the justice of the King to make inquiries."

"You say all this to me very uselessly, Monsieur Fouquet; I know what I know."

"Your Majesty can only know things as they have been told to you; and I, on my part, have said nothing to you, whilst others have spoken many and many times——"

"What do you wish to say?" said the King, impatient to put an end to this embarrassing conversation.

"I will go straight to the fact, sire; and I accuse a man of having injured me in your Majesty's opinion."

"Nobody has injured you, Monsieur Fouquet."

"That reply proves to me, sire, that I am right."

"Monsieur Fouquet, I do not like people to be accused."

"Not when one is accused!"

"We have already spoken too much about this affair."

"Your Majesty will not allow me to justify myself?"

"I repeat that I do not accuse you."

Fouquet, with a half-bow, made a step backward. "It is certain," thought he, "that he has made up his mind. He alone who cannot go back can show such obstinacy. Not to see the danger now would be to be blind indeed; not to shun it would be stupid."

He resumed aloud: "Did your Majesty send for me for any business?"

"No, Monsieur Fouquet, but for some advice I have to give you."

"I respectfully await it, sire."

"Rest yourself, Monsieur Fouquet, do not throw away your strength; the session of the States will be short, and when my secretaries shall have closed it, I do not wish business to be talked of in France for a fortnight."

"Has the King nothing to say to me on the subject of this assembly of the States?"

"No, Monsieur Fouquet."

"Not to me, the Surintendant of Finances?"

"Rest yourself, I beg you; that is all I have to say to you."

Fouquet bit his lips and hung down his head. He was evidently busy with some uneasy thought. This uneasiness struck the King. "Are you angry at having to rest yourself, M. Fouquet?" said he.

"Yes, sire; I am not accustomed to take rest."

"But you are ill; you must take care of yourself."

"Your Majesty spoke just now of a speech to be pronounced to-morrow."

His Majesty made no reply; this unexpected stroke embarrassed him. Fouquet felt the weight of this hesitation. He thought he could read a danger in the eyes of the young Prince, which his fear would precipitate. "If I appear frightened I am lost," thought he.

The King, on his part, was only uneasy at the alarm of Fouquet. "Has he a suspicion of anything?" murmured he.

"If his first word is severe," again thought Fouquet; "if he becomes angry, or feigns to be angry for the sake of a pretext, how shall I extricate myself? Let us smooth the declivity a little. Gourville was right."

"Sire," said he suddenly, "since the goodness of the King watches over my health to the point of dispensing with my labour, may I not be allowed to be absent from the council to-morrow? I could pass the day in bed, and will entreat the King to grant me his physician, that we may endeavour to find a remedy against this cursed fever."

"So be it, Monsieur Fouquet, as you desire; you shall have a holiday to-morrow, you shall have the physician, and shall be restored to health."

"Thanks!" said Fouquet, bowing. Then opening his game:—

"Shall I not have the happiness of conducting your Majesty to my residence of Belle-Isle?"

And he looked Louis full in the face, to judge of the effect of such a proposal. The King blushed again.

"Do you know," replied he, endeavouring to smile, "that you have just said—'My residence of Belle-Isle?'"

"Yes, sire."

"Well! do you not remember," continued the King in the same cheerful tone, "that you gave me Belle-Isle?"

"That is true again, sire. Only as you have not taken it, you will come with me and take possession of it."

"I mean to do so."

"That was, besides, your Majesty's intention as well as mine; and I cannot express to your Majesty how proud and happy I have been at seeing all the King's military household come from Paris for this taking possession."

The King stammered out that he did not bring the musketeers for that alone.

"Oh, I am convinced of that," said Fouquet warmly; "your Majesty knows very well that you have nothing to do but to come alone with a cane in your hand, to bring to the ground all the fortifications of Belle-Isle."

"*Peste!*" cried the King; "I do not wish those fine fortifications, which cost so much to erect, should fall at all. No, let them stand against the Dutch and the English. You would not guess what I want to see at Belle-Isle, Monsieur Fouquet; it is the pretty peasants and women of the lands on the sea-shore, who dance so well, and are so seducing with their scarlet petticoats! I have heard great boast of your pretty tenants, Monsieur le Surintendant; well, let me have a sight of them."

"Whenever your Majesty pleases."

"Have you any means of transport? It should be to-morrow, if you like."

The Surintendant felt this stroke, which was not adroit, and replied, "No, sire; I was ignorant of your Majesty's wish; above all, I was ignorant of your haste to see Belle-Isle, and I am prepared with nothing."

"You have a boat of your own, nevertheless."

"I have five; but they are all in the port, or at Paimbœuf; and to join them, or bring them hither, we should require at least twenty-four hours. Have I any occasion to send a courier? Must I do so?"

"Wait a little; put an end to the fever,—wait till to-morrow."

"That is true; who knows but that by to-morrow we may not have a hundred other ideas?" replied Fouquet, now perfectly convinced, and very pale.

The King started, and stretched his hand out towards his little bell, but Fouquet prevented his ringing.

"Sire," said he, "I have an ague,—I am trembling with cold. If I remain a moment longer, I shall most likely faint. I request your Majesty's permission to go and conceal myself beneath the bedclothes."

"Indeed, you are all in a shiver; it is painful to behold! Come, Monsieur Fouquet, begone! I will send to inquire after you."

"Your Majesty overwhelms me with kindness. In an hour I shall be better."

"I will call some one to reconduct you," said the King.

"As you please, sire; I would gladly take the arm of any one."

"Monsieur d'Artagnan!" cried the King, ringing his little bell.

"Oh! sire," interrupted Fouquet, laughing in such a manner as made the Prince feel cold, "would you give me the captain of your musketeers to take me to my lodgings? A very equivocal kind of honour that, sire! A simple footman, I beg."

"And why, M. Fouquet? M. d'Artagnan conducts me often, and well!"

"Yes, but when he conducts you, sire, it is to obey you; whilst me——"

"Go on!"

"If I am obliged to return home supported by the leader of the musketeers, it would be everywhere said you had had me arrested."

"Arrested!" replied the King, who became paler than Fouquet himself,—"arrested! oh!"

"And why would not they say so?" continued Fouquet, still laughing, "and I would lay a wager there would be people found wicked enough to laugh at it." This sally disconcerted the monarch. Fouquet was skilful enough, or fortunate enough, to make Louis XIV. recoil before the appearance of the fact he meditated. M. d'Artagnan, when he appeared, received an order to desire a musketeer to accompany the Surintendant.

"Quite unnecessary," said the latter; "sword for sword, I prefer Gourville, who is waiting below for me. But that will not prevent me enjoying the society of M. d'Artagnan. I am glad he will see Belle-Isle, he who is so good a judge of fortifications."

D'Artagnan bowed, without at all comprehending what was going on. Fouquet bowed again, and left the apartment, affecting all the slowness of a man who walks with difficulty. When once out of the castle, "I am saved!" said he. "Oh! yes, disloyal King, you shall see Belle-Isle, but it shall be when I am no longer there!"

He disappeared, leaving d'Artagnan with the King.

"Captain," said the King, "you will follow M. Fouquet at the distance of a hundred paces."

"Yes, sire."

"He is going to his lodgings again. You will go with him."

"Yes, sire."

"You will arrest him in my name, and will shut him up in a carriage."

"In a carriage. Well! sire?"

"In such a fashion that he may not, on the road, either converse with any one or throw notes to people he may meet."

"That will be rather difficult, sire."

"Not at all."

"Pardon me, sire, I cannot stifle M. Fouquet, and if he asks for liberty to breathe, I cannot prevent him by shutting up glasses and blinds. He will throw out at the doors all the cries and notes possible."

"The case is provided for, Monsieur d'Artagnan; a carriage with a trellis will obviate both the difficulties you point out."

"A carriage with an iron trellis!" cried d'Artagnan; "but a carriage with an iron trellis is not made in half an hour, and your Majesty commands me to go immediately to M. Fouquet's lodgings."

"Therefore the carriage in question is already made."

"Ah! that is quite a different thing," said the captain; "if the carriage is ready made, very well, then, we have only to set it going."

"It is ready with the horses harnessed to it."

"Ah!"

"And the coachman, with outriders, waiting in the lower court of the castle."

D'Artagnan bowed. "There only remains for me to ask your Majesty to what place I shall conduct M. Fouquet."

"To the castle of Angers, at first."

"Very well, sire."

"Afterwards, we will see."

"Yes, sire."

"Monsieur d'Artagnan, one last word; you have remarked that for making this capture of M. Fouquet, I have not employed my guards, on which account M. de Gesvres will be furious."

"Your Majesty does not employ your guards," said the captain, a little humiliated, "because you mistrust M. de Gesvres, that is all."

"That is to say, monsieur, that I have more confidence in you."

"I know that very well, sire; and it is of no use to make so much of it."

"It is only for the sake of arriving at this, monsieur, that if, from this moment, it should happen that by any chance, any chance whatever, M. Fouquet should escape—such chances have been, monsieur——"

"Oh! very often, sire; but for others, not for me."

"And why not with you?"

"Because I, sire, have, for an instant, wished to save M. Fouquet."

The King started. "Because," continued the captain, "I had then a right to do so, having guessed your Majesty's plan, without your having spoken to me of it, and that I took an interest in M. Fouquet. Now, was I not at liberty to show my interest in this man?"

"In truth, monsieur, you do not reassure me with regard to your services."

"If I had saved him then, I was perfectly innocent; I will say more, I should have done well, for M. Fouquet is not a bad man. But he was not willing; his destiny prevailed; he let the hour of liberty slip by. So much the worse! Now I have orders, I will obey those orders, and M. Fouquet you may consider as a man arrested. He is at the castle of Angers, is M. Fouquet."

"Oh! you have not got him yet, captain."

"That concerns me; every one to his trade, sire; only, once more, reflect! Do you seriously give me orders to arrest M. Fouquet, sire?"

"Yes, a thousand times yes!"

"Write it, then."

"Here is the letter."

D'Artagnan read it, bowed to the King, and left the room. From the height of the terrace he perceived Gourville, who went by with a joyous air towards the lodgings of M. Fouquet.

68

THE WHITE HORSE AND THE BLACK HORSE

"THAT is rather surprising," said d'Artagnan, "Gourville running about the streets so gaily, when he is almost certain that M. Fouquet is in danger; when it is almost equally certain that it was Gourville who warned M. Fouquet just now by the note which was torn into a thousand pieces upon the terrace, and given to the winds by Monsieur le Surintendant. Gourville is rubbing his hands, that is because he has done something clever. Whence comes M. Gourville? Gourville is coming from the Rue aux Herbes. Whither does the Rue aux Herbes lead?" And d'Artagnan followed along the tops of the houses of Nantes dominated by the castle, the line traced by the streets, as he would have done upon a topographical plan; only, instead of the dead, flat paper, the living chart rose in relief with the cries, the movements, and the shadows of the men and things. Beyond the enclosure of the city, the great verdant plains stretched out, bordering the Loire, and appeared to run towards the empurpled horizon, which was cut by the azure of the waters and the dark green of the marshes. Immediately outside the gates of Nantes two white roads were seen diverging like the separated fingers of a gigantic hand. D'Artagnan, who had taken in all the panorama at a glance by crossing the terrace, was led by the line of the Rue aux Herbes to the mouth of one of those roads which took its rise under the gate of Nantes. One step more, and he was about to descend the stairs, take his trellised carriage, and go towards the lodgings of M. Fouquet. But chance decreed that at the moment of replunging into the staircase, he was attracted by a moving point which was gaining ground upon that road.

"What is that?" said the musketeer to himself; "a horse galloping—a runaway horse, no doubt. What a pace he is going at!" The moving point became detached from the road, and entered into the fields. "A white horse," continued the captain, who had just seen the colour thrown out luminously against the dark ground, "and he is mounted; it must be some boy whose horse is thirsty and has run away with him to the drinking-place, diagonally." These reflections, rapid as lightning, simultaneous with visual perception, d'Artagnan had already forgotten when he descended the first steps of the staircase. Some morsels of paper were spread over the stairs, and shone out white against the dirty stones. "Eh! eh!" said the captain to himself, "here are some of the fragments of the note torn by M. Fouquet. Poor man! he had given his secret to the wind; the wind will have no more to do with it, and brings it back to the King. Decidedly, Fouquet, you play with misfortune! the game is not a fair one,—fortune is against you. The star of Louis XIV. obscures yours; the adder is stronger and more cunning than the squirrel." D'Artagnan picked up one of these morsels of paper as he descended. "Gourville's pretty little hand!" cried he, whilst examining one of the fragments of the note; "I was not mistaken." And he read the word "horse." "Stop!" said he; and he examined another, upon which there was not a letter traced. Upon a third he read the word "white"; "white horse," repeated he, like a child that is spelling. "Ah! mordioux!" cried the suspicious spirit, "a white horse!" And, like to that grain of powder which, burning, dilates into a centripled volume, d'Artagnan, enlarged by ideas and suspicions, rapidly reascended the stairs towards the terrace. The white horse was still galloping in the direction of the Loire, at the extremity of which, melted into the vapours of the water, a little sail appeared, balancing like an atom. "Oh, oh!" cried the musketeer, "there is but a man who flies who would go at that pace across ploughed lands; there is but one Fouquet, a financier, to ride thus in open day upon a white horse; there is no one but the lord of Belle-Isle who would make his escape towards the sea, while there are such thick forests on the land; and there is but one d'Artagnan in the world to catch M. Fouquet, who has half an hour's start, and who will have gained his boat within an hour." This being said, the musketeer gave orders that the carriage with the iron trellis should be taken immediately to a thicket situated just outside the city. He selected his best horse, jumped upon his back, galloped along the Rue aux Herbes, taking, not the road Fouquet had taken, but the bank itself of the Loire, certain that he should gain ten minutes upon the total of the distance, and, at the intersection of the two lines, come up with the fugitive, who could have no suspicion of being pursued in that direction. In the rapidity of the pursuit, and with the impatience of the persecutor, animating himself in the chase as in war, d'Artagnan, so mild, so kind, towards Fouquet, was surprised to find himself become ferocious and almost sanguinary. For a long time he galloped without catching sight of the white horse. His fury assumed the tints of rage; he doubted of himself,—he suspected that Fouquet had buried himself in some subterranean road, or that he had changed the white horse for one of those famous black ones, as swift as the wind, which d'Artagnan, at Saint-Mandé, had so frequently admired, and envied their vigorous lightness.

At these moments when the wind cut his eyes so as to make the water spring from them, when the saddle had become burning hot, when the galled and spurred horse reared with pain, and threw behind him a shower of dust and stones, d'Artagnan, raising himself in his stirrups, and seeing nothing on the waters,—nothing beneath the trees, looked up into the air like a madman. He was losing his senses. In the paroxysms of his eagerness he dreamt of aerial ways,—the discovery of the following century; he called to his mind Dædalus and his vast wings, which had saved him from the prisons of Crete. A hoarse sigh broke from his lips, as he repeated, devoured by the fear of ridicule, "I! I! duped by Gourville! I! They will say I am growing old,—they will say I have received a million to allow Fouquet to escape!" And he again dug his spurs into the sides of his horse: he had ridden astonishingly fast. Suddenly, at the extremity of some open pasture-ground, behind the hedges, he saw a white form which showed itself, disappeared, and at last remained distinctly visible upon a rising ground. D'Artagnan's heart leaped with joy. He wiped the streaming sweat from his brow, relaxed the tension of his knees,—by which the horse breathed more freely,—and, gathering up his reins, moderated the speed of the vigorous animal, his active accomplice in this man-hunt. He had then time to study the direction of the road, and his position with regard to Fouquet. The Surintendant had completely winded his horse by crossing soft grounds. He felt the necessity of gaining a more firm footing, and turned towards the road by the shortest secant line. D'Artagnan, on his part, had nothing to do but to ride straight beneath the sloping shore, which concealed him from the eyes of his enemy; so that he would cut him off on his road when he came up to him. Then the real race would begin,—then the struggle would be in earnest.

D'Artagnan gave his horse good breathing-time. He observed that the Surintendant had relaxed into a trot, which was to say, he likewise was indulging his horse. But both of them were too much pressed for time to allow them to continue long at that pace. The white horse sprang off like an arrow the moment his feet touched firm ground. D'Artagnan dropped his hand, and his black horse broke into a gallop. Both followed the same route; the quadruple echoes of the course were confounded. Fouquet had not yet perceived d'Artagnan. But on issuing from the slope, a single echo struck the air, it was that of the steps of d'Artagnan's horse, which rolled along like thunder. Fouquet turned round, and saw behind him, within a hundred paces, his enemy bent over the neck of his horse. There could be no doubt—the shining baldrick, the red cassock—it was a musketeer. Fouquet slackened his hand likewise, and the white horse placed twenty feet more between his adversary and himself.

"Oh, but," thought d'Artagnan, becoming very anxious, "that is not a common horse M. Fouquet is upon—let us see!" And he attentively examined with his infallible eye the shape and capabilities of the courser. Round, full quarters—a thin, long tail,—large hocks—thin legs, dry as bars of steel—hoofs hard as marble. He spurred his own, but the distance between the two remained the same. D'Artagnan listened attentively; not a breath of the horse reached him, and yet he seemed to cut the air. The black horse, on the contrary, began to blow like a blacksmith's bellows.

"I must overtake him, if I kill my horse," thought the musketeer; and he began to saw the mouth of the poor animal, whilst he buried the rowels of his merciless spurs in his sides. The maddened horse gained twenty toises, and came up within pistol-shot of Fouquet.

"Courage!" said the musketeer to himself, "courage! the white horse will perhaps grow weaker, and if the horse does not fall, the master must fall at last." But horse and rider remained upright together, and gaining ground by degrees, D'Artagnan uttered a wild cry, which made Fouquet turn round, and added speed to the white horse.

"A famous horse! a mad rider!" growled the captain. "Hola! *mordioux!* Monsieur Fouquet! stop! in the King's name!" Fouquet made no reply.

"Do you hear me?" shouted d'Artagnan, whose horse had just stumbled.

"*Pardieu!*" replied Fouquet laconically; and rode on faster.

D'Artagnan was nearly mad; the blood rushed boiling to his temples and his eyes. "In the King's name!" cried he again; "stop, or I will bring you down with a pistol-shot!"

"Do!" replied Fouquet, without relaxing his speed.

D'Artagnan seized a pistol and cocked it, hoping that the noise of the spring would stop his enemy. "You have pistols likewise," said he; "turn, and defend yourself."

Fouquet did turn round at the noise, and looking d'Artagnan full in the face, opened with his right hand the part of his dress which concealed his body, but he did not even touch his holsters. There were not more than twenty paces between the two.

"*Mordioux!*" said d'Artagnan, "I will not assassinate you; if you will not fire upon me, surrender! what is a prison?"

"I would rather die!" replied Fouquet; "I shall suffer less."

457

D'Artagnan, drunk with despair, hurled his pistol to the ground. "I will take you alive!" said he; and by a prodigy of skill of which this incomparable horseman alone was capable, he threw his horse forward to within ten paces of the white horse; already his hand was stretched out to seize his prey.

"Kill me! kill me!" cried Fouquet; "it is more humane!"

"No! alive—alive!" murmured the captain.

At this moment his horse made a false step for the second time, and Fouquet's again took the lead. It was an unheard of spectacle, this race between two horses which were only kept alive by the will of their riders. It might be said that d'Artagnan rode carrying his horse along between his knees. To the furious gallop had succeeded the fast trot, and that had sunk to what might be scarcely called a trot at all. And the chase appeared equally warm in the two fatigued men. D'Artagnan, quite in despair, seized his second pistol, and cocked it.

"At your horse! not at you!" cried he to Fouquet. And he fired. The animal was hit in the quarters—he made a furious bound, and plunged forward. At that moment d'Artagnan's horse fell dead.

"I am dishonoured!" thought the musketeer; "I am a miserable wretch! for pity's sake, M. Fouquet, throw me one of your pistols that I may blow out my brains!" But Fouquet rode on.

"For mercy's sake! for mercy's sake!" cried d'Artagnan; "that which you will not do at this moment, I myself will do within an hour; but here, upon this road, I should die bravely; I should die esteemed; do me that service, M. Fouquet!"

M. Fouquet made no reply, but continued to trot on. D'Artagnan began to run after his enemy. Successively he threw off his hat, his coat, which embarrassed him, and then the sheath of his sword, which got between his legs as he was running. The sword in his hand even became too heavy, and he threw it after the sheath. The white horse began to rattle in his throat; d'Artagnan gained upon him. From a trot the exhausted animal sunk to a staggering walk— the foam from his mouth was mixed with blood. D'Artagnan made a desperate effort, sprang towards Fouquet, and seized him by the leg, saying in a broken, breathless voice, "I arrest you in the King's name! blow my brains out if you like—we have both done our duty."

Fouquet hurled far from him, into the river, the two pistols which d'Artagnan might have seized and, dismounting from his horse—"I am your prisoner, monsieur," said he; "will you take my arm, for I see you are ready to faint?"

"Thanks!" murmured d'Artagnan, who, in fact, felt the earth

moving from under his feet, and the sky melting away over his head; and he rolled upon the sand without breath or strength. Fouquet hastened to the brink of the river, dipped some water in his hat, with which he bathed the temples of the musketeer, and introduced a few drops between his lips. D'Artagnan raised himself up, looking round with a wandering eye. He saw Fouquet on his knees, with his wet hat in his hand, smiling upon him with ineffable sweetness. "You are not gone then?" cried he. "Oh, monsieur! the true king in loyalty, in heart, in soul, is not Louis of the Louvre, or Philippe of Sainte-Marguerite; it is you, the proscribed, the condemned!"

"I, who this day am ruined by a single error, M. d'Artagnan."

"What, in the name of Heaven! is that?"

"I should have had you for a friend! But how shall we return to Nantes? We are a great way from it."

"That is true," said d'Artagnan, gloomy and sad.

"The white horse will recover, perhaps; he is a good horse! Mount, Monsieur d'Artagnan; I will walk till you have rested a little."

"Poor beast! and wounded too!" said the musketeer.

"He will go, I tell you; I know him; but we can do better still, let us both get up, and ride slowly."

"We can try," said the captain. But they had scarcely charged the animal with his double load, than he began to stagger, then, with a great effort, walked a few minutes, then staggered again, and sank down dead by the side of the black horse which he had just managed to come up to.

"We will go on foot—destiny wills it so—the walk will be pleasant," said Fouquet, passing his arm through that of d'Artagnan.

"*Mordioux!*" cried the latter, with a fixed eye, a contracted brow, and a swelling heart—"A disgraceful day!"

They walked slowly the four leagues that separated them from the little wood behind which waited the carriage with the escort. When Fouquet perceived that sinister machine, he said to d'Artagnan, who cast down his eyes as ashamed of Louis XIV.. "There is an idea which is not that of a brave man, Captain d'Artagnan; it is not yours. What are these gratings for?" said he.

"To prevent your throwing letters out."

"Ingenious!"

"But you can speak if you cannot write," said d'Artagnan.

"Can I speak to you?"

"Why—certainly, if you wish to do so."

Fouquet reflected for a moment, then looking the captain full in the face, "One single word," said he; "will you remember it?"

"I will not forget it."

"Will you speak it to whom I wish?"

"I will."

"Saint-Mandé," articulated Fouquet, in a low voice.

"Well! and for whom?"

"For Madame de Bellière or Pélisson."

"It shall be done."

The carriage passed through Nantes, and took the route of Angers.

69

IN WHICH THE SQUIRREL FALLS—IN WHICH THE ADDER FLIES

IT was two o'clock in the afternoon. The King, full of impatience, went to his cabinet on the terrace, and kept opening the door of the corridor, to see what his secretaries were doing. M. Colbert, seated in the same place M. Saint-Aignan had so long occupied in the morning, was chatting, in a low voice, with M. de Brienne. The King opened the door suddenly, and addressing them, "What do you say?" asked he.

"We were speaking of the first sitting of the States," said M. de Brienne, rising.

"Very well," replied the King, and returned to his room.

Five minutes after, the summons of the bell recalled Rose, whose hour it was.

"Have you finished your copies?" asked the King.

"Not yet, sire."

"See, then, if M. d'Artagnan has returned."

"Not yet, sire."

"It is very strange!" murmured the King. "Call M. Colbert."

Colbert entered; he had been expecting this moment all the morning.

"Monsieur Colbert," said the King, very sharply; "it must be ascertained what has become of M. d'Artagnan."

Colbert, in his calm voice, replied, "Where would your Majesty desire him to be sought for?"

"Eh! monsieur! do you not know to what place I have sent him?" replied Louis acrimoniously.

"Your Majesty has not told me."

"Monsieur, there are things that are to be guessed; and you, above all others, do guess them."

"I might have been able to imagine, sire; but I do not presume to be positive."

Colbert had not finished these words when a much rougher voice than that of the King interrupted the interesting conversation thus begun between the monarch and his clerk.

"D'Artagnan!" cried the King, with evident joy.

D'Artagnan, pale and in evidently bad humour, cried to the King, as he entered, "Sire, is it your Majesty who has given orders to my musketeers?"

"What orders?" said the King.

"About M. Fouquet's house?"

"None!" replied Louis.

"Ah! ah!" said d'Artagnan, biting his moustache; "I was not mistaken, then; it was monsieur, here;" and he pointed to Colbert.

"What orders? Let me know," said the King.

"Orders to turn a house inside out, to beat M. Fouquet's servants, to force the drawers, to give over a peaceful house to pillage! *Mordioux!* these are savage orders!"

"Monsieur!" said Colbert, becoming pale.

"Monsieur!" interrupted d'Artagnan, "the King alone, understand—the King alone has a right to command*my musketeers; but, as to you, I forbid you to do it, and I tell you so before His Majesty; gentlemen who wear swords are not fellows with pens behind their ears."

"D'Artagnan! d'Artagnan!" murmured the King.

"It is humiliating," continued the musketeer; "my soldiers are disgraced. I do not command a pack of pillagers, thank you, nor clerks of the intendance, *mordioux!*"

"Well! but what is all this about?" said the King, with authority.

"About this, sire; monsieur—monsieur, who could not guess your Majesty's orders, and consequently could not know I was gone to arrest M. Fouquet; monsieur, who has caused the iron cage to be constructed for his patron of yesterday—has sent M. de Roncherat*to the lodgings of M. Fouquet, and, under pretence of taking away the Surintendant's papers, they have taken away the furniture. My musketeers have been placed round the house all the morning; such were my orders. Why did any one presume to order them to enter? Why, by forcing them to assist in this pillage, have they been made accomplices in it? *Mordioux!* we serve the King, we do, but we do not serve M. Colbert!"

"M. d'Artagnan," said the King sternly, "take care; it is not in my presence that such explanations, and made in this tone, should take place."

"I have acted for the good of the King," said Colbert, in a faltering voice; "it is hard to be so treated by one of your Majesty's officers, and that without vengeance, on account of the respect I owe the King."

"The respect you owe the King!" cried d'Artagnan, whose eyes flashed fire, "consists, in the first place, in making his authority respected, and making his person beloved. Every agent of a power without control represents that power, and when people curse the hand which strikes them, it is to the royal hand that God makes the reproach, do you hear? Must a soldier, hardened by forty years of wounds and blood, give you this lesson, monsieur? Must mercy be on my side, and ferocity on yours? You have caused the innocent to be arrested, bound, and imprisoned!"

"The accomplices, perhaps, of M. Fouquet," said Colbert.

"Who told you that M. Fouquet had accomplices, or even that he was guilty? The King alone knows that, his justice is not blind! When he shall say, 'Arrest and imprison' such and such people, then he shall be obeyed. Do not talk to me then any more of the respect you owe the King, and be careful of your words, that they may not chance to convey any menace; for the King will not allow those to be threatened who do him service by others who do him disservice; and if in case I should have, which God forbid! a master so ungrateful, I would make myself respected."

Thus saying, d'Artagnan took his station haughtily in the King's cabinet, his eyes flashing, his hand on his sword, his lips trembling, affecting much more anger than he really felt. Colbert, humiliated and devoured with rage, bowed to the King as if to ask his permission to leave the room. The King, crossed in his pride and in his curiosity, knew not which part to take. D'Artagnan saw him hesitate. To remain longer would have been an error; it was necessary to obtain a triumph over Colbert, and the only means was to touch the King so near and so strongly to the quick, that His Majesty would have no other means of extricating himself but choosing between the two antagonists. D'Artagnan then bowed as Colbert had done; but the King, who, in preference to everything else, was anxious to have all the exact details of the arrest of the Surintendant of the Finances from him who had made him tremble for a moment—the King, perceiving that the ill humour of d'Artagnan would put off for half-an-hour at least the details he was burning to be acquainted with—Louis, we say, forgot Colbert, who had nothing new to tell him, and recalled his captain of the musketeers.

"In the first place," said he, "let me see the result of your commission, monsieur; you may repose afterwards."

D'Artagnan, who was just passing through the door, stopped at the voice of the King, retraced his steps, and Colbert was forced to leave the closet. His countenance assumed almost a purple hue, his black and threatening eyes shone with a dark fire beneath their thick brows; he stepped out, bowed before the King, half drew himself up in passing d'Artagnan, and went away with death in his heart. D'Artagnan, on being left alone with the King, softened immediately, and composing his countenance: "Sire," said he, "you are a young king. It is by the dawn that people judge whether the day will be fine or dull. How, sire, will the people, whom the hand of God has placed under your law, augur of your reign, if, between them and you, you allow angry and violent ministers to act? But let us speak of me, sire, let us leave a discussion that may appear idle, and perhaps inconvenient to you. Let us speak of me. I have arrested M. Fouquet."

"You took plenty of time about it," said the King sharply.

D'Artagnan looked at the King. "I perceive that I have expressed myself badly. I announced to your Majesty that I had arrested Monsieur Fouquet."

"You did; and what then?"

"Well! I ought to have told your Majesty that M. Fouquet had arrested me; that would have been more just. I re-establish the truth, then; I have been arrested by M. Fouquet."

It was now the turn of Louis XIV. to be surprised. His Majesty was astonished in his turn. D'Artagnan, with his quick glance, appreciated what was passing in the heart of his master. He did not allow him time to put any questions. He related, with all that poetry, that picturesqueness, which perhaps he alone possessed at that period, the evasion of Fouquet, the pursuit, the furious race, and, lastly, the inimitable generosity of the Surintendant, who might have fled ten times over, who might have killed the adversary attached to the pursuit of him, and who had preferred imprisonment, and perhaps worse, to the humiliation of him who wished to ravish his liberty from him. In proportion as the tale advanced, the King became agitated, devouring the narrator's words, and knocking his finger nails against each other.

"It results from this, then, sire, in my eyes at least, that the man who conducts himself thus is a gallant man, and cannot be an enemy to the King. That is my opinion, and I repeat it to your Majesty. I know what the King will say to me, and I bow to it: reasons of state—so be it! That in my eyes is very respectable. But I am a soldier, I have received my orders, my orders are executed

—very unwillingly on my part it is true, but they are executed. I say no more."

"Where is M. Fouquet at this moment?" asked Louis, after a short silence."

"M. Fouquet, sire," replied d'Artagnan, "is in the iron cage that M. Colbert had prepared for him, and is going, as fast as four vigorous horses can drag him, towards Angers."

"Why did you leave him on the road?"

"Because your Majesty did not tell me to go to Angers. The proof, the best proof of what I advance is, that the King desired me to be sought for but this minute. And then I have another reason."

"What is that?"

"Whilst I was with him, poor M. Fouquet would never attempt to escape."

"Well!" cried the King, with stupefaction.

"Your Majesty ought to understand, and does understand certainly, that my warmest wish is to know that M. Fouquet is at liberty. I have given him one of my brigadiers, the most stupid I could find among my musketeers, in order that the prisoner might have a chance of escaping."

"Are you mad, Monsieur d'Artagnan!" cried the King, crossing his arms on his breast. "Do people speak such enormities, even when they have the misfortune to think them?"

"Ah! sire, you cannot expect that I should be the enemy of M. Fouquet, after what he has just done for you and me. No, no; if you desire that he should remain under your locks and bolts, never give him in charge to me; however closely-wired might be the cage, the bird would, in the end, fly away."

"I am surprised," said the King, in a stern tone, "you have not followed the fortunes of him whom M. Fouquet wished to place upon my throne. You had in him all you want—affection and gratitude. In my service, monsieur, you only find a master."

"If M. Fouquet had not gone to seek you in the Bastille, sire," replied d'Artagnan, with a deeply impressive manner, "one single man would have gone there, and that man would have been me— you know that right well, sire."

The King was brought to a pause. Before that speech of his captain of the musketeers, so frankly spoken, and so true, the King had nothing to offer. On hearing d'Artagnan, Louis remembered the d'Artagnan of former times;* him who, at the Palais Royal, held himself concealed behind the curtains of his bed, when the people of Paris, led on by Cardinal de Retz, came to assure themselves of the presence of the King; the d'Artagnan whom he saluted with his hand at the door of his carriag:, when repairing to Notre Dame on his return to Paris; the sollier who had quitted his service at Blois; the lieutenant whom he had recalled near his person when the death of Mazarin restored him his power; the man he had always found loyal, courageous, and devoted. Louis advanced towards the door and called Colbert. Colbert had not left the corridor where the secretaries were at work. Colbert appeared.

"Colbert, have you made a perquisition at the house of M. Fouquet?"

"Yes, sire."

"What has it produced?"

"M. de Roncherat, who was sent with your Majesty's musketeers, has remitted me some papers," replied Colbert.

"I will look at them. Give me your hand."

"My hand, sire?"

"Yes, that I may place it in that of M. d'Artagnan. In fact, M. d'Artagnan," added he, with a smile, turning towards the soldier, who, at the sight of the clerk, had resumed his haughty attitude, "you do not know this man; make his acquaintance." And he pointed to Colbert. "He has been but a moderate servant in subaltern positions, but he will be a great man if I raise him to the first rank."

"Sire!" stammered Colbert, confused with pleasure and fear.

"I have understood why," murmured d'Artagnan in the King's ear; "he was jealous."

"Precisely, and his jealousy confined his wings."

"He will henceforth be a winged serpent," grumbled the musketeer, with some remains of hatred against his recent adversary.

But Colbert, approaching him, offered to his eyes a physiognomy so different from that which he had been accustomed to see him wear; he appeared so good, so mild, so easy; his eyes took the expression of an intelligence so noble, that d'Artagnan, a connoisseur in physiognomies, was moved, and almost changed in his convictions. Colbert pressed his hand.

"That which the King has just told you, monsieur, proves how well His Majesty is acquainted with men. The inveterate opposition I have displayed up to this day, against abuses and not against men, proves that I had it in view to prepare for my King a great reign, for my country a great blessing. I have many ideas, M. d'Artagnan; you will see them expand in the sun of public peace; and if I have not the certainty and good fortune to conquer the friendship of honest men, I am at least certain, monsieur, that

I shall obtain their esteem. For their admiration, monsieur, I would give my life."

This change, this sudden elevation, this mute approbation of the King, gave the musketeer matter for much reflection. He bowed civilly to Colbert, who did not take his eyes off him. The King, when he saw they were reconciled, dismissed them. They left the room together. As soon as they were out of the cabinet, the new minister, stopping the captain, said:—

"Is it possible, M. d'Artagnan, that with such an eye as yours, you have not, at the first glance, at the first inspection, discovered what sort of man I am?"

"Monsieur Colbert," replied the musketeer, "the ray of the sun which we have in our eyes, prevents us from seeing the most ardent flames. The man in power radiates, you know; and since you are there, why should you continue to persecute him who has just fallen into disgrace, and fallen from such a height?"

"I! monsieur," said Colbert; "oh, monsieur! I would never persecute him. I wished to administer the finances and to administer them alone, because I am ambitious, and, above all, because I have the most entire confidence in my own merit; because I know that all the gold of this country will fall beneath my eyes, and I love to look at the King's gold; because, if I live thirty years in thirty years not a sou of it will remain in my hands; because, with that gold I will build granaries, edifices, cities, and dig ports; because I will create a marine, will equip navies which shall bear the name of France to the most distant peoples; because I will create libraries and academies; because I will make of France the first country in the world, and the richest. These are the motives for my animosity against M. Fouquet,* who prevented my acting. And then, when I shall be great and strong, when France is great and strong, in my turn then I will cry, 'Mercy!'"

"'Mercy,' did you say; then ask his liberty of the King. The King only crushes him on your account."

Colbert again raised his head. "Monsieur," said he, "you know that it is not so, and that the King has his personal enmities against M. Fouquet; it is not for me to teach you that."

"But the King will be tired; he will forget."

"The King never forgets, M. d'Artagnan. Hark! the King calls. He is going to issue an order. I have not influenced him, have I? Listen."

The King, in fact, was calling his secretaries. "Monsieur d'Artagnan," said he.

"I am here, sire."

"Give twenty of your musketeers to M. de Saint-Aignan, to form a guard for M. Fouquet."

D'Artagnan and Colbert exchanged looks. "And from Angers," continued the King, "they will conduct the prisoner to the Bastille, in Paris."

"You were right," said the captain to the minister.

"Saint-Aignan," continued the King, "you will have any one shot who shall attempt to speak privately with M. Fouquet, during the journey."

"But myself, sire?" said the Duke.

"You, monsieur, you will only speak to him in the presence of the musketeers." The Duke bowed, and departed to execute his commission.

D'Artagnan was about to retire likewise; but the King stopped him.

"Monsieur," said he, "you will go immediately, and take possession of the isle and fief of Belle-Isle-en-Mer."

"Yes, sire. Alone?"

"You will take a sufficient number of troops to prevent delay, in case the place should be contumacious."

A murmur of adulatory incredulity arose from the group of courtiers. "That is to be done," said d'Artagnan.

"I saw the place in my infancy," resumed the King, "and I do not wish to see it again. You have heard me? Go, monsieur, and do not return without the keys of the place."

Colbert went up to d'Artagnan. "A commission which, if you carry it out well," said he, "will be worth a marshal's baton to you."

"Why do you employ the words, 'if you carry it out well'?"

"Because it is difficult."

"Ah! in what respect?"

"You have friends in Belle-Isle, Monsieur d'Artagnan; and it is not an easy thing for men like you to march over the bodies of their friends to obtain success."

D'Artagnan hung down his head, whilst Colbert returned to the King. A quarter of an hour after, the captain received the written order from the King, to blow up the fortress of Belle-Isle, in case of resistance, with the power of life and death over all the inhabitants or refugees, and an injunction not to allow one to escape.

"Colbert was right," thought d'Artagnan; "my baton of a marshal of France will cost the lives of my two friends. Only they seem to forget that my friends are not more stupid than the birds, and that they will not wait for the hand of the fowler to extend

467

their wings. I will show them that hand so plainly, that they will have quite time enough to see it. Poor Porthos! Poor Aramis. No; my fortune shall not cost your wings a feather."

Having thus determined, d'Artagnan assembled the royal army, embarked it at Paimbœuf, and set sail, without losing a moment.

70

BELLE-ISLE-EN-MER

At the extremity of the mole, which the furious sea beats at evening tide, two men, holding each other by the arm, were conversing in an animated and expansive tone, without the possibility of any other human being hearing their words, borne away, as they were, one by one, by the gusts of wind, with the white foam swept from the crests of the waves. The sun had just gone down in the vast sheet of the reddened ocean, like a gigantic crucible. From time to time, one of these men, turning towards the east, cast an anxious, inquiring look over the sea. The other, interrogating the features of his companion, seemed to seek for information in his looks. Then, both silent, both busied with dismal thoughts, they resumed their walk. Every one has already perceived that those two men were our proscribed heroes, Porthos and Aramis, who had taken refuge in Belle-Isle since the ruin of their hopes, since the discomfiture of the vast plan of M. d'Herblay.

"It is of no use you saying anything to the contrary, my dear Aramis," repeated Porthos, inhaling vigorously the saline air with which he filled his powerful chest. "It is of no use, Aramis. The disappearance of all the fishing-boats that went out two days ago, is not an ordinary circumstance. There has been no storm at sea; the weather has been constantly calm, not even the lightest gale; and even if we had had a tempest, all our boats would not have foundered. I repeat, it is strange. This complete disappearance astonishes me, I tell you."

"True," murmured Aramis. "You are right, friend Porthos; it is true, there is something strange in it."

"And, further," added Porthos, whose ideas the assent of the Bishop of Vannes seemed to enlarge; "and, further, have you remarked, that if the boats have perished, not a single plank has been washed ashore?"

"I have remarked that as well as you."

"Have you remarked, besides, that the only two boats we had

468

left in the whole island, and which I sent in search of the others——"

Aramis here interrupted his companion by a cry, and by so sudden a movement, that Porthos stopped as if he were stupefied. "What do you say, Porthos? What!—You have sent the two boats——"

"In search of the others! Yes; to be sure I have," replied Porthos, quite simply.

"Unhappy man! What have you done? Then we are indeed lost," cried the Bishop.

"Lost!—what did you say?" exclaimed the terrified Porthos. "How lost? Aramis. How are we lost?"

Aramis bit his lips. "Nothing! nothing! Your pardon. I meant to say——"

"What?"

"That if we were inclined—if we took a fancy to make an excursion by sea, we could not."

"Very good! and why should that vex you? A fine pleasure, ma foi! For my part, I don't regret it at all. What I regret is, certainly not the more or less amusement we can find at Belle-Isle;—what I regret, Aramis, is Pierrefonds; is Bracieux; is le Vallon; is my beautiful France! Here we are not in France, my dear friend; we are—I know not where. Oh! I tell you, in the full sincerity of my soul, and your affection will excuse my frankness, but I declare to you I am not happy at Belle-Isle. No; in good truth, I am not happy!"

Aramis breathed a long but stifled sigh. "Dear friend," replied he; "that is why it is so sad a thing you have sent the two boats we had left in search of the boats which disappeared two days ago. If you had not sent them away, we would have departed."

"Departed! And the orders, Aramis?"

"What orders?"

"Parbleu! Why the orders you have been constantly and on all occasions, repeating to me—that we were to hold Belle-Isle against the usurper. You know very well!"

"That is true," murmured Aramis again.

"You see then, plainly, my friend, that we could not depart; and that the sending away of the boats in search of the others is not prejudicial to us in any way."

Aramis was silent; and his vague glance, luminous as that of a gull, hovered for a long time over the sea, interrogating space, and seeking to pierce the very horizon.

"With all that, Aramis," continued Porthos, who adhered to his idea, and that the more closely from the Bishop having found it correct—"with all that, you give me no explanation about what can have happened to these unfortunate boats. I am assailed by cries and complaints whichever way I go. The children cry at seeing the desolation of the women, as if I could restore the absent husbands and fathers. What do you suppose, my friend, and what ought I to answer them?"

"Suppose, then, my good Porthos, and say nothing."

This reply did not satisfy Porthos at all. He turned away, grumbling some words in a very ill humour. Aramis stopped the valiant soldier. "Do you remember," said he, in a melancholy tone, pressing the two hands of the giant between his own with an affectionate cordiality, "do you remember, my friend, that in the glorious days of our youth—do you remember, Porthos, when we were all strong and valiant—we, and the other two—if we had then had an inclination to return to France, do you think this sheet of salt water would have stopped us?"

"Oh!" said Porthos, "but six leagues!"

"If you had seen me get astride of a plank, would you have remained on land, Porthos?"

"No, *pardieu!* No! Aramis. But, nowadays, what sort of a plank should we want, my friend! I, in particular." And the Seigneur de Bracieux cast a proud glance over his colossal rotundity with a loud laugh. "And do you mean seriously to say you are not tired of Belle-Isle also a little, and that you would not prefer the comforts of your dwelling—of your episcopal palace at Vannes? Come, confess!"

"No," replied Aramis, without daring to look at Porthos.

"Let us stay where we are, then," said his friend, with a sigh; which, in spite of the efforts he made to restrain it, escaped with a loud report from his breast. "Let us remain!—let us remain! And yet," added he, "and yet, if we seriously wished, but that decidedly —if we had a fixed idea, one firmly taken, to return to France, and there were no boats——"

"Have you remarked another thing, my friend!—that is, since the disappearance of our barques, during the two days' absence of the fishermen, not a single small boat has landed on the shores of the isle?"

"Yes, certainly, you are right. I have remarked it also, and the observation was the more naturally made, for, before the last two fatal days, we saw barques and shallops arrive by dozens."

"I must inquire," said Aramis suddenly, and with great agitation. "And then, if I had a raft constructed——"

"But there are some canoes, my friend; shall I go on board one?"

THE MAN IN THE IRON MASK

"A canoe!—a canoe! Can you think of such a thing, Porthos? A canoe to be upset in. No, no," said the Bishop of Vannes; "it is not our trade to ride upon the waves. We will wait, we will wait."

And Aramis continued walking about with increased agitation. Porthos, who grew tired of following all the feverish movements of his friend—Porthos, who, in his calmness and belief, understood nothing of the sort of exasperation which was betrayed by his continual convulsive starts—Porthos stopped him. "Let us sit down upon this rock," said he. "Place yourself there, close to me, Aramis, and I conjure you, for the last time, to explain to me in a manner I can comprehend,—explain to me what we are doing here."

"Porthos," said Aramis, much embarrassed.

"I know that the false king wished to dethrone the true king! That is a fact I understand. Well——"

"Yes," said Aramis.

"I know that the false king formed the project of selling Belle-Isle to the English. I understand that too."

"Yes."

"I know that we engineers and captains came and threw ourselves into Belle-Isle to take the direction of the works, and the command of ten companies levied and paid by M. Fouquet, or rather the ten companies of his son-in-law. All that is plain."

Aramis arose in a state of great impatience. He might be said to be a lion importuned by a gnat. Porthos held him by the arm. "But what I cannot understand, what, in spite of all the efforts of my mind, and all my reflections, I cannot comprehend, and never shall comprehend, is, that, instead of sending us troops, instead of sending us reinforcements of men, munitions, and provisions, they leave us without boats, they leave Belle-Isle without arrivals, without help; it is that instead of establishing with us a correspondence, whether by signals, or written or verbal communications, all relations with us are intercepted. Tell me, Aramis, answer me, or rather, before answering me, will you allow me to tell you what I have thought? Will you hear what my idea is, what imagination I have conceived?"

The Bishop raised his head. "Well! Aramis," continued Porthos, "I have thought, I have an idea, I have imagined, that an event has taken place in France. I dreamed of M. Fouquet all the night, I dreamt of dead fish; broken eggs; chambers badly furnished, meanly kept. Bad dreams, my dear d'Herblay; very unlucky, such dreams!"

"Porthos, what is that yonder?" interrupted Aramis, rising

suddenly, and pointing out to his friend a black spot upon the empurpled line of the water.

"A barque!" said Porthos; "yes, it is a barque! Ah! we shall have some news at last."

"There are two!" cried the Bishop, on discovering another mast; "two! three! four!"

"Five!" said Porthos, in his turn. "Six! seven! Ah! *mon Dieu! mon Dieu!* it is a whole fleet!"

"Our boats returning, probably," said Aramis, very uneasily, in spite of the assurance he affected.

"They are very large for fishing-boats," observed Porthos, "and do you not remark, my friend, they come from the Loire?"

"They come from the Loire—yes——"

"And look! everybody here sees them as well as ourselves; look, the women and children are beginning to get upon the jetty."

An old fisherman passed. "Are those our barques yonder?" asked Aramis.

The old man looked steadily into the horizon.

"No, monseigneur," replied he, "they are lighter boats in the King's service."

"Boats in the royal service?" replied Aramis, starting. "How do you know that?" said he.

"By the flag."

"But," said Porthos, "the boat is scarcely visible; how the devil, my friend, can you distinguish the flag?"

"I see there is one," replied the old man; "our boats, or trade lighters, do not carry any. That sort of craft is generally used for the transport of troops."

"Ah!" said Aramis.

"*Vivat!*" cried Porthos, "they are sending us reinforcements; don't you think they are, Aramis?"

"Probably."

"Unless it is the English coming."

"By the Loire? That would have an ill look, Porthos, for they must have come through Paris."

"You are right; they are reinforcements decidedly, or provisions."

Aramis leant his head upon his hands and made no reply. Then, all at once,—"Porthos," said he, "have the alarm sounded."

"The alarm! do you think of such a thing?"

"Yes, and let the cannoniers mount to their batteries, let the artillerymen be at their pieces, and be particularly watchful of the coast batteries."

Porthos opened his eyes to their widest extent. He looked attentively at his friend, to convince himself he was in his proper senses.

"I will do it, my dear Porthos," continued Aramis, in his most bland tone; "I will go and have these orders executed myself, if you do not go, my friend."

"Well! I will go instantly!" said Porthos, who went to execute the orders, casting all the while looks behind him, to see if the Bishop of Vannes were not deceived; and if, on returning to more rational ideas, he would not recall him. The alarm was sounded, the trumpets brayed, the drums rolled; the great bell of the belfry was put in motion. The dikes and moles were quickly filled with the curious and soldiers; the matches sparkled in the hands of the artillerymen, placed behind the large cannon bedded in their stone carriages. When every man was at his post, when all the preparations for the defence were made: "Permit me, Aramis to try and comprehend," whispered Porthos timidly, in Aramis's ear.

"My dear friend, you will comprehend but too soon," murmured M. d'Herblay, in reply to this question of his lieutenant.

"The fleet which is coming yonder, with sails unfurled, straight towards the port of Belle-Isle, is a royal fleet, is it not?"

"But as there are two kings in France, Porthos, to which of these two kings does this fleet belong?"

"Oh! you open my eyes," replied the giant, stunned by this argument.

And Porthos, for whom the reply of his friend had just opened the eyes, or rather thickened the bandage which covered his sight, went with his best speed to the batteries to overlook his people, and exhort every one to do his duty. In the meantime, Aramis, with his eye fixed on the horizon, saw the ships continue to draw nearer. The people and the soldiers, mounted upon all the summits or irregularities of the rocks, could distinguish the masts, then the lower sails, and at last the hulls of the lighters, bearing at the masthead the royal flag of France. It was quite night when one of these vessels, which had created such a sensation among the inhabitants of Belle-Isle, was moored within cannon-shot of the place. It was soon seen, notwithstanding the darkness, that a sort of agitation reigned on board this vessel, from the side of which a skiff was lowered, of which the three rowers, bending to their oars, took the direction of the port, and in a few instants struck land at the foot of the fort. The commander of this yawl jumped on shore. He had a letter in his hand, which he waved in the air, and seemed to wish to communicate with somebody. This man was soon recognised by several soldiers as one of the pilots of the island. He was the skipper of one of the two barques kept back by Aramis, and which

Porthos, in his anxiety with regard to the fate of the fishermen who had disappeared for two days, had sent in search of the missing boats. He asked to be conducted to M. d'Herblay. Two soldiers, at a signal from the sergeant, placed him between them, and escorted him. Aramis was upon the quay. The envoy presented himself before the Bishop of Vannes. The darkness was almost complete, notwithstanding the flambeaux borne at a small distance by the soldiers who were following Aramis in his rounds.

"Well, Jonathan, from whom do you come?"

"Monseigneur, from those who captured me."

"Who captured you?"

"You know, monseigneur, we set out in search of our comrades?"

"Yes; and afterwards?"

"Well! monseigneur, within a short league we were captured by a cutter belonging to the King."

"Ah!" said Aramis.

"Of which king?" cried Porthos. Jonathan stared.

"Speak!" continued the Bishop.

"We were captured, monseigneur, and joined to those who had been taken yesterday morning."

"What was the cause of the mania for capturing you all?" said Porthos.

"Monsieur, to prevent us from telling you," replied Jonathan.

Porthos was again at a loss to comprehend. "And they have released you to-day?" asked he.

"That I might tell you they have captured us, monsieur."

"Trouble upon trouble," thought honest Porthos.

During this time Aramis was reflecting.

"Humph!" said he, "then I suppose it is the royal fleet blockading the coasts?"

"Yes, monseigneur."

"Who commands it?"

"The captain of the King's musketeers."

"D'Artagnan?"

"D'Artagnan!" exclaimed Porthos.

"I believe that is the name."

"And did he give you this letter?"

"Yes, monseigneur."

"Bring the flambeaux nearer."

"It is his writing," said Porthos.

Aramis eagerly read the following lines:—

"Order of the King to take Belle-Isle; or to put the garrison to the sword, if they resist; order to make prisoners of all the men of the garrison; signed, D'ARTAGNAN, who, the day before yesterday, arrested M. Fouquet, for the purpose of his being sent to the Bastille."

Aramis turned pale, and crushed the paper in his hands.

"What is it?" asked Porthos.

"Nothing, my friend, nothing."

"Tell me, Jonathan."

"Monseigneur?"

"Did you speak to M. d'Artagnan?"

"Yes, monseigneur."

"What did he say to you?"

"That for more ample information he would speak with monseigneur."

"Where?"

"On board his own vessel."

"On board his vessel!" and Porthos repeated, "On board his vessel!"

"The captain," continued Jonathan, "told me to take you both on board my canoe, and bring you to him."

"Let us go at once," exclaimed Porthos, "Dear d'Artagnan!"

But Aramis stopped him. "Are you mad?" cried he. "Who knows that it is not a snare?"

"Of the other King's?" said Porthos mysteriously.

"A snare in fact! That's what it is, my friend."

"Very possibly; what is to be done, then? If d'Artagnan sends for us——"

"Who assures you that d'Artagnan sends for us?"

"Yes, but—but his writing——"

"Writing is easily counterfeited. This looks counterfeited—trembling——"

"You are always right; but in the meantime, we know nothing."

Aramis was silent.

"It is true," said the good Porthos, "we do not want to know anything."

"What shall I do?" asked Jonathan.

"You will return on board this captain's vessel."

"Yes, monseigneur."

"And tell him that we beg he will himself come into the island."

"Ah! I comprehend!" said Porthos.

"Yes, monseigneur," replied Jonathan; "but if the captain should refuse to come to Belle-Isle?"

"If he refuses, as we have cannon, we will make use of them."

"What! against d'Artagnan?"

"If it is d'Artagnan, Porthos, he will come. Go, Jonathan, go!"

"*Ma foi!* I no longer comprehend anything," murmured Porthos.

"I will make you comprehend all, my dear friend; the time for it is come; sit down upon this gun-carriage, open your ears, and listen well to me."

"Oh! *pardieu!* I shall listen, no fear of that."

"May I depart, monseigneur?" cried Jonathan.

"Yes, begone, and bring back an answer. Allow the canoe to pass, you men there!" And the canoe pushed off to regain the fleet.

Aramis took Porthos by the hand, and commenced the explanations.

71

THE EXPLANATIONS OF ARAMIS

"WHAT I have to say to you, friend Porthos, will probably surprise you, but it will instruct you."

"I like to be surprised," said Porthos in a kindly tone; "do not spare me therefore, I beg. I am hardened against emotions; don't fear, speak out."

"It is difficult, Porthos, it is—difficult; for, in truth, I warn you a second time, I have very strange things, very extraordinary things, to tell you."

"Oh! you speak so well, my friend, that I could listen to you for days together. Speak, then, I beg—and—stop, I have an idea; I will, to make your task more easy, I will, to assist you in telling me such things, question you."

"I shall be pleased at your doing so."

"What are we going to fight for, Aramis?"

"If you make me many such questions as that—if you would render my task the easier by interrupting my revelations thus, Porthos, you will not help me at all. So far, on the contrary, that is precisely the Gordian knot. But, my friend, with a man like you, good, generous, and devoted, the confession must be made bravely. I have deceived you, my worthy friend."

"You have deceived me!"

"Good Heavens! yes."

"Was it for my good, Aramis?"

"I thought so, Porthos; I thought so sincerely, my friend."

"Then," said the honest seigneur of Bracieux, "you have rendered me a service, and I thank you for it; for if you had not deceived me, I might have deceived myself. In what, then, have you deceived me, say?"

"In that I was serving the usurper against whom Louis XIV., at this moment, is directing his efforts."

"The usurper!" said Porthos, scratching his head. "That is—well, I do not too clearly comprehend that."

"He is one of the two Kings who are contending for the crown of France."

"Very well! Then you were serving him who is not Louis XIV.?"

"You have hit upon the matter in a word."

"It results that——"

"It results that we are rebels, my poor friend."

"The devil! the devil!" cried Porthos, much disappointed.

"Oh! but, dear Porthos, be calm, we shall still find means of getting out of the affair, trust me."

"It is not that which makes me uneasy," replied Porthos; "that which alone touches me is that ugly word *rebels*."

"Ah but——"

"And so, according to this, the duchy that was promised me——"

"It was the usurper who was to give it to you."

"And that is not the same thing, Aramis," said Porthos majestically.

"My friend, if it had only depended upon me, you should have become a prince." Porthos began to bite his nails after a melancholy fashion.

"That is where you have been wrong," continued he, "in deceiving me; for that promised duchy I reckoned upon. Oh! I reckoned upon it seriously, knowing you to be a man of your word, Aramis."

"Poor Porthos! pardon me, I implore you!"

"So then," continued Porthos, without replying to the Bishop's prayer, "so then, it seems, I have quite fallen out with Louis XIV.?"

"Oh! I will settle all that, my good friend, I will settle all that. I will take it upon myself alone!"

"Aramis!"

"No, no, Porthos, I conjure you, let me act. No false generosity! No inopportune devotedness! You knew nothing of my projects.

You have done nothing of yourself. With me it is different. I am alone the author of the plot I stood in need of my inseparable companion : I called upon you, and you came to me, in remembrance of our ancient device, 'All for one, one for all.' My crime was being an egotist."

"Now, that is a word I like," said Porthos; "and seeing that you have acted entirely for yourself, it is impossible for me to blame you; it is natural."

And upon this sublime reflection, Porthos pressed the hand of his friend cordially.

In presence of this ingenuous greatness of soul, Aramis felt himself little. It was the second time he had been compelled to bend before real superiority of heart, much more powerful than splendour of mind. He replied by a mute and energetic pressure to the kind endearment of his friend.

"Now," said Porthos, "that we have come to an explanation, now that I am perfectly aware of our situation with respect to Louis XIV., I think, my friend, it is time to make me comprehend the political intrigue of which we are the victims—for I plainly see there is a political intrigue at the bottom of all this."

"D'Artagnan, my good Porthos, d'Artagnan is coming, and will detail it to you in all its circumstances; but, excuse me, I am deeply grieved, I am bowed down by pain, and I have need of all my presence of mind, all my reflection, to extricate you from the false step in which I have so imprudently involved you; but nothing can be more clear, nothing more plain, than your position, henceforth. The King Louis XIV. has no longer now but one enemy : that enemy is myself, myself alone. I have made you a prisoner, you have followed me, to-day I liberate you, you fly back to your prince. You can perceive, Porthos, there is not a single difficulty in all this."

"Do you think so?" said Porthos.

"I am quite sure of it."

"Then why," said the admirable good sense of Porthos, "then why, if we are in such an easy position, why, my friend, do we prepare cannon, muskets, and engines of all sorts? It seems to me it would be much more simple to say to Captain d'Artagnan : 'My dear friend, we have been mistaken; that error is to be repaired; open the door to us, let us pass through, and good-day!'"

"Ah! that!" said Aramis, shaking his head.

"Why do you say 'that'? Do you not approve of my plan, my friend?"

"I see a difficulty in it."

"What is it?"

"The hypothesis that d'Artagnan may come with orders which will oblige us to defend ourselves."

"What! defend ourselves against d'Artagnan? Folly! Against the good d'Artagnan?"

Aramis once more replied by shaking his head.

"Porthos," at length said he, "if I have had the matches lighted and the guns pointed, if I have had the signal of alarm sounded, if I have called every man to his post upon the ramparts, those good ramparts of Belle-Isle which you have so well fortified, it is for something. Wait to judge; or rather, no, do not wait——"

"What can I do?"

"If I knew, my friend, I would have told you."

"But there is one thing much more simple than defending ourselves:—a boat, and away for France—where——"

"My dear friend," said Aramis, smiling with a strong shade of sadness, "do not let us reason like children; let us be men in council and execution—But, hark! I hear a hail for landing at the port. Attention, Porthos, serious attention!"

"It is d'Artagnan, no doubt," said Porthos, in a voice of thunder, approaching the parapet.

"Yes, it is I," replied the captain of the musketeers, running lightly up the steps of the mole, and gaining rapidly the little esplanade upon which his two friends waited for him. As soon as he came towards them, Porthos and Aramis observed an officer who followed d'Artagnan, treading apparently in his very steps. The captain stopped upon the stairs of the mole, when half-way up. His companion imitated him.

"Make your men draw back," cried d'Artagnan to Porthos and Aramis; "let them retire out of hearing." The order being given by Porthos, was executed immediately. Then d'Artagnan, turning towards him who followed him:

"Monsieur," said he, "we are no longer here on board the King's fleet, where, in virtue of your order, you spoke so arrogantly to me just now."

"Monsieur," replied the officer, "I did not speak arrogantly to you; I simply, but rigorously, obeyed what I had been commanded. I have been directed to follow you. I follow you. I am directed not to allow you to communicate with any one without taking cognisance of what you do; I mix myself, therefore, with your communications."

D'Artagnan trembled with rage, and Porthos and Aramis, who heard this dialogue, trembled likewise, but with uneasiness and fear. D'Artagnan, biting his moustache with that vivacity which denoted in him the state of an exasperation closely to be followed by a terrible explosion, approached the officer.

"Monsieur," said he, in a low voice, so much the more impressive, that affecting a calm it threatened a tempest—"monsieur, when I sent a canoe hither, you wished to know what I wrote to the defenders of Belle-Isle. You produced an order to that effect; and, in my turn, I instantly showed you the note I had written. When the skipper of the boat sent by me returned, when I received the reply of these two gentlemen (and he pointed to Aramis and Porthos), you heard every word of what the messenger said. All that was plainly in your orders, all that was well executed, very punctually, was it not?"

"Yes, monsieur," stammered the officer; "yes, without doubt, but——"

"Monsieur," continued d'Artagnan, growing warm—"monsieur, when I manifested the intention of quitting my vessel to cross to Belle-Isle, you required to accompany me; I did not hesitate; I brought you with me. You are now at Belle-Isle, are you not?"

"Yes, monsieur, but——"

"But—the question no longer is of M. Colbert, who has given you that order, or of whomsoever in the world you are following the instructions: the question now is of a man who is a clog upon M. d'Artagnan, and who is alone with M. d'Artagnan upon steps whose feet are bathed by thirty feet of salt water; a bad position for that man, a bad position, monsieur! I warn you."

"But, monsieur, if I am a restraint upon you," said the officer timidly, and almost faintly, "it is my duty which——"

"Monsieur, you have had the misfortune, you or those who sent you, to insult me. It is done. I cannot seek redress from those who employ you—they are unknown to me, or are at too great a distance. But you are under my hand, and I swear that if you make one step behind me when I raise my feet to go up to those gentlemen—I swear to you by my name, I will cleave your head in two with my sword, and pitch you into the water. Oh! it will happen! it will happen! I have only been six times angry in my life, monsieur, and, on the five times which have preceded this, I have killed my man."

The officer did not stir; he became pale under this terrible threat, but replied with simplicity, "Monsieur, you are wrong in acting against my orders."

Porthos and Aramis, mute and trembling at the top of the parapet, cried to the musketeer, "Dear d'Artagnan, take care!"

D'Artagnan made them a sign to keep silence, raised his foot with a terrifying calmness to mount the stair, and turned round, sword in hand, to see if the officer followed him. The officer made a sign of the cross and stepped up. Porthos and Aramis, who knew their d'Artagnan, uttered a cry, and rushed down to prevent the blow they thought they already heard. But d'Artagnan, passing his sword into his left hand—

"Monsieur," said he to the officer, in an agitated voice, "you are a brave man. You ought better to comprehend what I am going to say to you now than that which I have just said to you."

"Speak, Monsieur d'Artagnan, speak," replied the brave officer.

"These gentlemen we have just seen, and against whom you have orders, are my friends."

"I know they are, monsieur."

"You can understand if I ought to act towards them as your instructions prescribe."

"I understand your reserves."

"Very well; permit me, then, to converse with them without a witness."

"Monsieur d'Artagnan, if I yielded to your request, if I did that which you beg me to do, I should break my word; but if I do not do it, I shall disoblige you. I prefer the one to the other. Converse with your friends, and do not despise me, monsieur, for doing for the sake of you, whom I esteem and honour; do not despise me for committing for you, and you alone, an unworthy act." D'Artagnan, much agitated, passed his arms rapidly round the neck of the young man, and went up to his friends. The officer, enveloped in his cloak, sat down on the damp weed-covered steps.

"Well!" said d'Artagnan to his friends, "such is my position; judge for yourselves." They all three embraced. All three pressed each other in their arms as in the glorious days of their youth.

"What is the meaning of all these rigours?" said Porthos.

"You ought to have some suspicions of what it is," said d'Artagnan.

"Not much, I assure you, my dear captain; for, in fact, I have done nothing, no more has Aramis," hastened the worthy baron to say.

D'Artagnan darted a reproachful look at the prelate, which penetrated that hardened heart.

"Dear Porthos!" cried the Bishop of Vannes.

"You see what has been done against you," said d'Artagnan; "interception of all that is coming to or going from Belle-Isle. Your boats are all seized. If you had endeavoured to fly, you would have fallen into the hands of the cruisers which plough the sea in all directions on the watch for you. The King wants you to be taken, and he will take you." And d'Artagnan tore several hairs from his grey moustache. Aramis became sombre, Porthos angry.

"My idea was this," continued d'Artagnan; "to make you both come on board, to keep you near me, and restore you your liberty. But now, who can say that when I return to my ship, I may not find a superior; that I may not find secret orders which will take from me my command, and give it to another, who will dispose of me and you without hopes of help?"

"We must remain at Belle-Isle," said Aramis resolutely; "and I assure you, for my part, I will not surrender easily." Porthos said nothing. D'Artagnan remarked the silence of his friend.

"I have another trial to make of this officer, of this brave fellow who accompanies me, and whose courageous resistance makes me very happy; for it denotes an honest man, who, although an enemy, is a thousand times better than a complaisant coward. Let us try to learn from him what he has the right of doing, and what his orders permit or forbid."

"Let us try," said Aramis.

D'Artagnan came to the parapet, leaned over towards the steps of the mole, and called the officer, who immediately came up. "Monsieur," said d'Artagnan, after having exchanged the most cordial courtesies, natural between gentlemen, who know and appreciate each other worthily—"monsieur, if I wished to take away these gentlemen, what would you do?"

"I should not oppose it, monsieur; but having direct orders, formal orders to take them under my guard, I should detain them."

"Ah!" said d'Artagnan.

"That's all over," said Aramis gloomily. Porthos did not stir.

"But still take Porthos," said the Bishop of Vannes; "he can prove to the King, I will help him in doing so, and you also can, Monsieur d'Artagnan, that he has had nothing to do in this affair."

"Hum!" said d'Artagnan. "Will you come? Will you follow me, Porthos? The King is merciful."

"I beg to reflect," said Porthos nobly.

"You will remain here, then?"

"Until fresh orders," cried Aramis, with vivacity.

"Until we have had an idea," resumed d'Artagnan; "and I now believe that will not be long first, for I have one already."

"Let us say *adieu*, then," said Aramis; "but in truth, my good Porthos, you ought to go."

"No!" said the latter laconically.

"As you please," replied Aramis, a little wounded in his nervous susceptibility at the morose tone of his companion. "Only I am reassured by the promise of an idea from d'Artagnan, an idea I fancy I have divined."

"Let us see," said the musketeer, placing his ear near Aramis's mouth. The latter spoke several words rapidly to which d'Artagnan replied, "That is it, precisely."

"Infallible, then!" cried Aramis.

"During the first emotion that this resolution will cause, take care of yourself, Aramis."

"Oh! don't be afraid."

"Now, monsieur," said d'Artagnan to the officer, "thanks, a thousand thanks! You have made yourself three friends for life."

"Yes," added Aramis. Porthos alone said nothing, but merely bowed.

D'Artagnan, having tenderly embraced his two old friends, left Belle-Isle with the inseparable companion M. Colbert had given him. Thus, with the exception of the explanation with which the worthy Porthos had been willing to be satisfied, nothing had changed in appearance in the fate of the one or the other. "Only," said Aramis, "there is d'Artagnan's idea."

D'Artagnan did not return on board without examining to the bottom the idea he had discovered. Now, we know that when d'Artagnan did examine, according to custom, daylight pierced through. As to the officer, become mute again, he left him full measure to meditate. Therefore, on putting his foot on board his vessel, moored within cannon-shot of the island, the captain of the musketeers had already got together all his means, offensive and defensive.

He immediately assembled his council, which consisted of the officers serving under his orders. These were eight in number: a chief of the maritime forces; a major directing the artillery; an engineer, the officer we are acquainted with, and four lieutenants. Having assembled them in the chamber of the poop, d'Artagnan arose, took off his hat, and addressed them thus:—

"Gentlemen, I have been to reconnoitre Belle-Isle-en-Mer, and I have found it a good and solid garrison; moreover, preparations are made for a defence that may prove troublesome. I therefore intend to send for two of the principal officers of the place, that we may converse with them. Having separated them from their troops and their cannon, we shall be better able to deal with them; particularly with good reasoning. Is this your opinion, gentlemen?"

The major of artillery rose.

"Monsieur," said he, with respect, but with firmness, "I have heard you say that the place is preparing to make a troublesome defence. The place is then, as you know, determined upon rebellion."

D'Artagnan was visibly put out by this reply; but he was not a man to allow himself to be subdued by so little, and resumed:—

"Monsieur," said he, "your reply is just. But you are ignorant that Belle-Isle is a fief of M. Fouquet's, and the ancient kings gave the right to the seigneurs of Belle-Isle to arm their people."

The major made a movement.

"Oh! do not interrupt me," continued d'Artagnan. "You are going to tell me that that right to arm themselves against the English was not a right to arm themselves against their king. But it is not M. Fouquet, I suppose, who holds Belle-Isle at this moment, since I arrested M. Fouquet the day before yesterday. Now the inhabitants and defenders of Belle-Isle know nothing of that arrest. You would announce it to them in vain. It is a thing so unheard-of and so extraordinary, so unexpected, that they would not believe you. A Breton serves his master, and not his masters; he serves his master till he has seen him dead. Now the Bretons, as far as I know, have not seen the body of M. Fouquet. It is not then surprising that they hold out against that which is not M. Fouquet or his signature."

The major bowed in sign of assent.

"That is why," continued d'Artagnan, "I propose to cause two of the principal officers of the garrison to come on board my vessel. They will see you, gentlemen; they will see the forces we have at our disposal; they will consequently know to what they have to trust, and the fate that attends them in case of rebellion. We will affirm to them, upon our honour, that M. Fouquet is a prisoner, and that all resistance can only be prejudicial to them. We will tell them that the first cannon that is fired, there will be no mercy to be expected from the King. Then, I hope at least, that they will no longer resist. They will yield without fighting, and we shall have a place given up to us in a friendly way, which it might cost us much trouble to subdue."

The officer who had followed d'Artagnan to Belle-Isle was preparing to speak, but d'Artagnan interrupted him.

"Yes, I know what you are going to tell me, monsieur; I know that there is an order of the King's to prevent all secret communications with the defenders of Belle-Isle, and that is exactly why I do not offer to communicate but in the presence of my staff."

And d'Artagnan made an inclination of the head to his officers, which had for its object attaching a value to that condescension.

The officers looked at each other as if to read their opinions in their eyes, with the intention of evidently acting, after they should have agreed, according to the desire of d'Artagnan. And already the latter saw with joy that the result of their consent would be sending a barque to Porthos and Aramis, when the King's officer drew from his pocket a folded paper, which he placed in the hands of d'Artagnan.

The paper bore upon its superscription the number 1.

"What! more still!" murmured the surprised captain.

"Read, monsieur," said the officer, with a courtesy that was not free from sadness.

D'Artagnan, full of mistrust, unfolded the paper, and read these words:

"Prohibition to M. d'Artagnan to assemble any council whatever, or to deliberate in any way before Belle-Isle be surrendered and the prisoners shot. Signed, Louis."

D'Artagnan repressed the movement of impatience that ran through his whole body, and, with a gracious smile,—

"That is well, monsieur," said he; "the King's orders shall be complied with."

72

RESULT OF THE IDEAS OF THE KING, AND THE IDEAS OF D'ARTAGNAN

The blow was direct. It was severe, mortal. D'Artagnan, furious at having been anticipated by an idea of the King's, did not, however, yet despair; and, reflecting upon the idea he had brought back from Belle-Isle, he augured from it a new means of safety for his friends.

"Gentlemen," said he suddenly, "since the King has charged some other than myself with his secret orders, it must be because I no longer possess his confidence, and I should be really unworthy of it, if I had the courage to hold a command subject to so many injurious suspicions. I will go then immediately and carry my resignation to the King. I give it before you all, enjoining you all to fall back with me upon the coast of France, in such a way as not to compromise the safety of the forces His Majesty has confided to me. For this purpose, return all to your posts; within an hour we shall have the ebb of the tide. To your posts, gentlemen! I suppose," added he, on seeing that all prepared to obey him, except the surveillant officer, "you have no orders to object, this time?"

And d'Artagnan almost triumphed while speaking these words. This plan was the safety of his friends. The blockade once raised, they might embark immediately and set sail for England or Spain, without fear of being molested. Whilst they were making their escape, d'Artagnan would return to the King; would justify his return by the indignation which the mistrusts of Colbert had raised in him; he would be sent back with full powers, and he would take Belle-Isle, that is to say, the cage, after the birds had flown. But to this plan the officer opposed a second order of the King's. It was thus conceived :—

"From the moment M. d'Artagnan shall have manifested the desire of giving in his resignation, he shall no longer be reckoned leader of the expedition, and every officer placed under his orders shall be held to no longer obey him. Moreover, the said Monsieur d'Artagnan having lost that quality of leader of the army sent against Belle-Isle, shall set out immediately for France, in company of the officer who will have remitted the message to him, and who will consider him as a prisoner for whom he is answerable."

Brave and careless as he was, d'Artagnan turned pale. Everything had been calculated with a depth which, for the first time in thirty years, had recalled to him the solid foresight and the inflexible logic of the great Cardinal. He leant his head on his hand, thoughtful, scarcely breathing. "If I were to put this order into my pocket," thought he, "who would know it, or who would prevent my doing it? Before the King had had time to be informed, I should have saved those poor fellows yonder. Let us exercise a little audacity! My head is not one of those which the executioner strikes off for disobedience. We will disobey!" But at the moment he was about to adopt this plan, he saw the officers around him reading similar orders which the infernal agent of the thoughts of Colbert had just distributed to them. The case of disobedience had been foreseen, as the others had been.

"Monsieur," said the officer, coming up to him, "I await your good pleasure to depart."

"I am ready, monsieur," replied d'Artagnan, grinding his teeth.

The officer immediately commanded a canoe to receive M. d'Artagnan and himself. At sight of this he became almost mad with rage.

"How," stammered he, "will you carry on the direction of the different corps?"

"When you are gone, monsieur," replied the commander of the fleet, "it is to me the direction of the whole is committed."

"Then, monsieur," rejoined Colbert's man, addressing the new leader, "it is for you that this last order that has been remitted to me is intended. Let us see your powers."

"Here they are," said the sea officer, exhibiting a royal signature.

"Here are your instructions," replied the officer, placing the folded paper in his hands; and turning towards d'Artagnan, "come, monsieur," said he in an agitated voice (such despair did he behold in that man of iron), "do me the favour to depart at once."

"Immediately!" articulated d'Artagnan feebly, subdued, crushed by implacable impossibility.

And he let himself slide down into the little boat, which started, favoured by wind and tide, for the coast of France. The King's guards embarked with him. The musketeer still preserved the hope of reaching Nantes quickly, and of pleading the cause of his friends eloquently enough to incline the King to mercy. The barque flew like a swallow. D'Artagnan distinctly saw the land of France profiled in black against the white clouds of night.

"Ah! monsieur," said he, in a low voice, to the officer, to whom, for an hour, he had ceased speaking, "what would I give to know the instructions for the new commander! They are all pacific, are they not? and——"

He did not finish; the sound of a distant cannon rolled over the waters, then another, and two or three still louder. D'Artagnan shuddered.

"The fire is opened upon Belle-Isle,"*replied the officer. The canoe had just touched the soil of France.

73

THE ANCESTORS OF PORTHOS

When d'Artagnan had quitted Aramis and Porthos, the latter returned to the principal fort to converse with the greater liberty. Porthos, still thoughtful, was a constraint upon Aramis, whose mind had never felt itself more free.

"Dear Porthos," said he suddenly, "I will explain d'Artagnan's idea to you."

"What idea, Aramis?"

"An idea to which we shall owe our liberty within twelve hours."

"Ah! indeed!" said Porthos, much astonished. "Let us see it."

"Did you remark, in the scene our friend had with the officer, that certain orders restrained him with regard to us?"

"Yes, I did remark that."

"Well! d'Artagnan is going to give in his resignation to the King, add during the confusion which will result from his absence, we will get away, or rather you will get away, Porthos, if there is a possibility of flight only for one."

Here Porthos shook his head and replied: "We will escape together, Aramis, or we will remain here together."

"You are a generous heart," said Aramis, "only your melancholy uneasiness afflicts me."

"I am not uneasy," said Porthos.

"Then you are angry with me."

"I am not angry with you."

"Then why, my friend, do you put on such a dismal countenance?"

"I will tell you: I am making my will." And while saying these words, the good Porthos looked sadly in the face of Aramis.

"Your will!" cried the Bishop. "What then! do you think yourself lost?"

"I feel fatigued. It is the first time, and there is a custom in our family."

"What is it, my friend?"

"My grandfather was a man twice as strong as I am."

"Indeed!" said Aramis; "then your grandfather must have been Samson himself."

"No; his name was Antoine.* Well! he was about my age, when setting out one day for the chase, he felt his legs weak, he who had never known this before."

"What was the meaning of that fatigue, my friend?"

"Nothing good, as you will see; for having set out, complaining still of the weakness of his legs, he met a wild boar, which made head against him; he missed him with his arquebuse, and was ripped up by the beast, and died directly."

"There is no reason in that why you should alarm yourself, dear Porthos."

"Oh! you will see. My father was as strong again as I am. He was a rough soldier, under Henry III. and Henry IV.; his name was not Antoine, but Gaspard, the same as M. de Coligny.* Always on horseback, he had never known what lassitude was. One evening, as he rose from table, his legs failed him."

"He had supped heartily, perhaps," said Aramis, "and that was why he staggered."

"Bah! A friend of M. de Bassompierre,* nonsense! No, no, he

was astonished at feeling this lassitude, and said to my mother, who laughed at him, 'Would not one believe I was going to meet with a wild boar, as the late M. du Vallon, my father, did?"

"Well?" said Aramis.

"Well! having this weakness, my father insisted upon going down into the garden instead of going to bed; his foot slipped on the first stair; the staircase was steep; my father fell against a stone angle in which an iron hinge was fixed. The hinge opened his temple; and he lay dead upon the spot."

Aramis raised his eyes to his friend: "These are two extraordinary circumstances," said he; "let us not infer that there may succeed a third. It is not becoming in a man of your strength to be superstitious, my brave Porthos. Besides, when were your legs seen to fail? Never have you been so firm, so superb; why, you could carry a house on your shoulders."

"At this moment," said Porthos, "I feel myself pretty active; but at times I vacillate, I sink; and lately this phenomenon, as you say, has occurred four times. I will not say that this frightens me, but it annoys me. Life is an agreeable thing. I have money; I have fine estates; I have horses that I love; I have also friends I love: d'Artagnan, Athos, Raoul, and you."

The admirable Porthos did not even take the trouble to dissimulate to Aramis the rank he gave him in his friendship. Aramis pressed his hand: "We will still live many years," said he, "to preserve in the world specimens of rare men. Trust yourself to me, my friend; we have no reply from d'Artagnan; that is a good sign. He must have given orders to get the vessels together and clear the seas. On my part I have just issued directions that a barque should be rolled upon rollers to the mouth of the great cavern of Locmaria,* which you know, where we have so often laid wait for the foxes."

"Yes, and which terminates at the little creek by a trench which we discovered the day that splendid fox escaped that way."

"Precisely. In case of misfortunes, a barque is to be concealed for us in that cavern; indeed, it must be there by this time. We will wait for a favourable moment, and, during the night, to sea!"

"That is a good idea; what shall we gain by it?"

"We shall gain by it—that nobody knows that grotto, or rather its issue, except ourselves and two or three hunters of the island; we shall gain by it—that if the island is occupied, the scouts, seeing no barque upon the shore, will never imagine we can escape, and will cease to watch."

"I understand."

"Well! the legs?"

"Oh! excellent, just now."

"You see then, plainly, that everything conspires to give us quietude and hope. D'Artagnan will clear the sea and make us free. No more royal fleet or descent to be dreaded. *Vive Dieu!* Porthos, we have still half a century of good adventures before us, and if I once touch Spanish ground, I swear to you," added the Bishop, with a terrible energy, "that your brevet of duke is not such a chance as it is said to be."

"We will live in hope," said Porthos, a little enlivened by the renovated warmth of his companion.

All at once a cry resounded in their ears :—"To arms! to arms!"

This cry, repeated by a hundred voices, brought to the chamber where the two friends were conversing, surprise to the one, and uneasiness to the other. Aramis opened the window; he saw a crowd of people running with flambeaux. Women were seeking places of safety, the armed population were hastening to their posts.

"The fleet! the fleet!" cried a soldier, who recognised Aramis.

"The fleet?" repeated the latter.

"Within half cannon-shot," continued the soldier.

"To arms!" cried Aramis.

"To arms!" repeated Porthos formidably. And both rushed forth towards the mole, to place themselves within the shelter of the batteries. Boats, laden with soldiers, were seen approaching; they took three directions, for the purpose of landing at three points at once.

"What must be done?" said an officer of the guard.

"Stop them; and if they persist, fire!" said Aramis.

Five minutes after the cannonade commenced. These were the shots that d'Artagnan had heard as he landed in France. But the boats were too near the mole to allow the cannon to aim correctly. They landed, and the combat commenced hand to hand.

"What's the matter, Porthos?" said Aramis to his friend.

"Nothing! nothing!—only my legs; it is really incomprehensible!—they will be better when we charge." In fact, Porthos and Aramis did charge with such vigour; they so thoroughly animated their men that the royalists re-embarked precipitately, without gaining anything but the wounds they carried away.

"Eh! but, Porthos," cried Aramis, "we must have a prisoner, quick! quick!" Porthos bent over the stair of the mole, and seized by the nape of the neck one of the officers of the royal army who was waiting to embark till all his people should be in the boat. The arm of the giant lifted up his prey, which served him as a buckler, as he recovered himself, without a shot being fired at him.

"Here is a prisoner for you," said Porthos coolly to Aramis.

"Well!" cried the latter, laughing, "have you not calumniated your legs?"

"It was not with my legs I took him," said Porthos; "it was with my arms."

74

THE SON OF BISCARRAT*

THE Bretons of the Isle were very proud of this victory; Aramis did not encourage them in the feeling.

"What will happen," said he to Porthos, when everybody was gone home, "will be that the anger of the King will be roused by the account of the resistance, and that these brave people will be decimated or shot when they are taken, which cannot fail to take place."

"From which it results then," said Porthos, "that what we have done is of no use."

"For the moment it may be of some," replied the Bishop, "for we have a prisoner from whom we shall learn what our enemies are preparing to do."

"Yes, let us interrogate the prisoner," said Porthos, "and the means of making him speak are very simple. We are going to supper; we will invite him to join us; when he drinks he will talk."

This was done. The officer was at first rather uneasy, but became reassured on seeing what sort of men he had to deal with. He gave, without having any fear of compromising himself, all the details imaginable of the resignation and departure of d'Artagnan. He explained how, after that departure, the new leader of the expedition had ordered a surprise upon Belle-Isle. There his explanations stopped. Aramis and Porthos exchanged a glance which evinced their despair. No more dependence to be placed upon the brave imagination of d'Artagnan; consequently, no more resources in the event of defeat. Aramis, continuing his interrogations, asked the prisoner what the leaders of the expedition contemplated doing with the leaders of Belle-Isle.

"The orders are," replied he, "to kill during the combat, and hang afterwards."

Porthos and Aramis looked at each other again, and the colour mounted to their faces.

"I am too light for the gallows," replied Aramis; "people like me are not hung."

"And I am too heavy," said Porthos; "people like me break the cord."

"I am sure," said the prisoner gallantly, "that we could have procured you what sort of death you preferred."

"A thousand thanks!" said Aramis seriously. Porthos bowed.

"One more cup of wine to your health," said he, drinking himself. From one subject to another the chat with the officer was prolonged. He was an intelligent gentleman, and suffered himself to be led away by the charm of Aramis's wit, and Porthos's cordial *bonhomie*.

"Pardon me," said he, "if I address a question to you; but men who are in their sixth bottle have a clear right to forget themselves a little."

"Address it!" said Porthos; "address it!"

"Speak," said Aramis.

"Were you not, gentlemen, both in the musketeers of the late King?"

"Yes, monsieur, and of the best of them, if you please," said Porthos.

"That is true; I should say even the best of all soldiers, messieurs, if I did not fear to offend the memory of my father."

"Of your father?" cried Aramis.

"Do you know what my name is?"

"*Ma foi!* no, monsieur; but you can tell us, and——"

"I am called Georges de Biscarrat."

"Oh!" cried Porthos in his turn, "Biscarrat! Do you remember that name, Aramis?"

"Biscarrat!" reflected the Bishop. "It seems to me——"

"Try to recollect, monsieur," said the officer.

"*Pardieu!* that won't take me long," said Porthos. "Biscarrat—called Cardinal—one of the four who interrupted us the day on which we formed our friendship with d'Artagnan, sword in hand."

"Precisely, gentlemen."

"The only one," cried Aramis eagerly, "we did not wound."

"Consequently, a good blade," said the prisoner.

"That's true! very true!" exclaimed both the friends together. "*Ma foi!* Monsieur Biscarrat, we are delighted to make the acquaintance of such a brave man's son."

Biscarrat pressed the hands held out to him by the two ancient musketeers. Aramis looked at Porthos as much as to say—Here is a man who will help us, and without delay,—"Confess, monsieur," said he, "that it is good to have once been a good man."

"My father always said so, monsieur."

"Confess, likewise, that it is a sad circumstance in which you find yourself, of falling in with men destined to be shot or hung, and to learn that these men are old acquaintances—old hereditary acquaintances."

"Oh! you are not reserved for such a frightful fate as that, messieurs and friends!" said the young man warmly.

"Bah! you said so yourself."

"I said so just now, when I did not know you; but now that I know you, I say—you will avoid this dismal fate, if you like."

"How—if we like?" cried Aramis, whose eyes beamed with intelligence as he looked alternately at the prisoner and Porthos.

"Provided," continued Porthos, looking, in his turn, with noble intrepidity at M. Biscarrat and the Bishop—"provided nothing disgraceful be required of us."

"Nothing at all will be required of you, gentlemen," replied the officer—"what should they ask of you? If they find you they will kill you, that is a settled thing; try, then, gentlemen, to prevent their finding you."

"I don't think I am mistaken," said Porthos with dignity; "but it appears evident to me that if they want to find us, they must come and seek us here."

"In that you are perfectly right, my worthy friend," replied Aramis, constantly consulting with his looks the countenance of Biscarrat, who was silent and constrained. "You wish, Monsieur de Biscarrat, to say something to us, to make us some overture, and you dare not—is not that true?"

"Ah! gentlemen and friends! it is because in speaking I betray my duty. But hark! I hear a voice which liberates mine by dominating over it."

"Cannon!" said Porthos.

"Cannon and musketry too!" cried the Bishop.

On hearing at a distance, among the rocks, these sinister reports of a combat which they thought had ceased, "What can that be?" asked Porthos.

"Eh! *pardieu!*" cried Aramis; "this is just what I expected."

"What is that?"

"The attack made by you was nothing but a feint; is not that true, monsieur? And whilst your companions allowed themselves to be repulsed, you were certain of effecting a landing on the other side of the island."

"Oh! several, monsieur."

"We are lost, then," said the Bishop of Vannes quietly.

"Lost! that is possible," replied the Seigneur de Pierrefonds, "but we are not taken or hung." And so saying, he rose from the table, went straight to the wall, and coolly took down his sword and

493

pistols, which he examined with the care of an old soldier who is preparing for battle, and who feels that his life, in a great measure, depends upon the excellence and the good condition of his arms.

At the report of the cannon, at the news of the surprise which might deliver up the isle to the royal troops, the terrified crowd rushed precipitately to the fort to demand assistance and advice from their leaders. Aramis, pale and downcast, between two flambeaux, showed himself at the window, which looked into the principal court, full of soldiers waiting for orders and bewildered inhabitants imploring succour.

"My friends," said d'Herblay, in a grave and sonorous voice, "M. Fouquet, your protector, your friend, your father, has been arrested by an order of the King, and thrown into the Bastille." A long cry of fury and menace came floating up to the window at which the Bishop stood, and enveloped him in a vibrating fluid.

"Avenge Monsieur Fouquet!" cried the most excited of his hearers, "and death to the royalists!"

"No, my friends," replied Aramis solemnly; "no, my friends; no resistance. The King is master in his kingdom. The King is the mandatory of God.* The King and God have struck M. Fouquet. Humble yourselves before the hand of God. Love God and the King, who have struck M. Fouquet. But do not avenge your Seigneur, do not think of avenging him. You would sacrifice yourselves in vain—you, your wives and children, your property, and your liberty. Lay down your arms, my friends—lay down your arms, since the King commands you so to do—and retire peaceably to your dwellings. It is I who ask you to do so; it is I who beg you to do so; it is I who now, in the hour of need, command you to do so, in the name of M. Fouquet."

The crowd collected under the window uttered a prolonged growl of anger and terror. "The soldiers of Louis XIV. have entered the island," continued Aramis. "From this time it would no longer be a combat between them and you—it would be a massacre. Begone, then, begone and forget; this time I command you, in the name of the Lord."

The mutineers retired slowly, submissive and silent.

"Ah! but what have you just been saying there, my friend?" said Porthos.

"Monsieur," said Biscarrat to the Bishop, "you may save all these inhabitants, but you will neither save yourself nor your friend."

"Monsieur de Biscarrat," said the Bishop of Vannes, with a singular accent of nobleness and courtesy, "Monsieur de Biscarrat, be kind enough to resume your liberty."

"I am very willing to do so, monsieur, but——"

"That would render us a service, for, when announcing to the King's lieutenant the submission of the islanders, you will perhaps obtain some grace for us on informing him of the manner in which that submission has been effected."

"Grace!" replied Porthos with flashing eyes, "what is the meaning of that word?"

Aramis touched the elbow of his friend roughly, as he had been accustomed to do in the days of their youth, when he wanted to warn Porthos that he had committed, or was about to commit a blunder. Porthos understood him, and was silent immediately.

"I will go, messieurs," replied Biscarrat, a little surprised likewise at the word "grace," pronounced by the haughty musketeer, of whom, some instants before, he had related and boasted with so much enthusiasm the heroic exploits with which his father had delighted him.

"Go, then, Monsieur Biscarrat," said Aramis, bowing to him, "and at parting receive the expression of our entire gratitude."

"But you, messieurs, you whom I take honour to call my friends, since you have been willing to accept that title, what will become of you in the meantime?" replied the officer, very much agitated at taking leave of the two ancient adversaries of his father.

"We will wait here."

"But, *mon Dieu!*—the order is formal."

"I am Bishop of Vannes, Monsieur de Biscarrat; and they no more shoot a bishop than they hang a gentleman."

"Ah! yes, monsieur—yes, monseigneur," replied Biscarrat; "it is true, you are right, there is still that chance for you. Then, I will depart, I will repair to the commander of the expedition, the King's lieutenant. *Adieu!* then, messieurs, or rather, to meet again, I hope."

The worthy officer, then jumping upon a horse given him by Aramis, departed in the direction of the sound of the cannon, and which, by bringing the crowd into the fort, had interrupted the conversation of the two friends and their prisoner. Aramis watched his departure, and when left alone with Porthos, "Well, do you comprehend?" said he.

"*Ma foi!* no."

"Did not Biscarrat inconvenience you here?"

"No; he is a brave fellow."

"Yes; but the grotto of Locmaria—is it necessary all the world should know it?"

"Ah! that is true, that is true; I comprehend. We are going to escape by the cavern."

"If you please," replied Aramis joyously. "Forward, my friend, Porthos; our boat awaits us, and the King has not caught us yet."

75

THE GROTTO OF LOCMARIA

THE cavern of Locmaria was sufficiently distant from the mole to render it necessary for our friends to husband their strength to arrive there. Besides, night was advancing; midnight had struck at the fort. Porthos and Aramis were loaded with money and arms. They walked then, across the heath, which is between the mole and the cavern, listening to every noise, and endeavouring to avoid ambushes. From time to time, on the road, which they had carefully left on their left hand, they passed fugitives coming from the interior, at the news of the landing of the royal troops. Aramis and Porthos, concealed behind some projecting mass of rock, collected the words which escaped from the poor people who fled, trembling, carrying with them their most valuable effects, and tried, whilst listening to their complaints, to draw something from them for their own interest. At length, after a rapid course, frequently interrupted by prudent stoppages, they reached the deep grottos, into which the foreseeing Bishop of Vannes had taken care to have rolled upon cylinders a good barque capable of keeping the sea at this fine season.

"My good friend," said Porthos, after having respired vigorously, "we are arrived, it seems. But I thought you spoke of three men, three servants who were to accompany us. I don't see them —where are they?"

"Why should you see them, dear Porthos?" replied Aramis. "They are certainly waiting for us in the cavern, and, no doubt, are resting for a moment, after having accomplished their rough and difficult task."

Aramis stopped Porthos, who was preparing to enter the cavern. "Will you allow me, my friend," said he to the giant, "to pass in first? I know the signal I have given to these men; who, not hearing it, would be very likely to fire upon you or slash away with their knives in the dark."

"Go on, then, Aramis! go on—go first; you are all wisdom and prudence; go on. Ah! there is that fatigue again, of which I spoke to you. It has just seized me again."

Aramis left Porthos sitting at the entrance of the grotto, and, bowing his head, he penetrated into the interior of the cavern, imitating the cry of the owl. A little plaintive cooing, a scarcely distinct cry, replied from the depths of the cave. Aramis pursued his way cautiously, and soon was stopped by the same kind of cry as he had first uttered, and this cry sounded within ten paces of him.

" Are you there, Yves ? " said the Bishop.

" Yes, monseigneur ; Goenne is here likewise. His son accompanies us."

" That is well. Are all things ready ? "

" Yes, monseigneur. "

" Go to the entrance of the grottos, my good Yves, and you will there find the Seigneur de Pierrefonds, who is resting after the fatigue of our journey. And if he should happen not to be able to walk, lift him up, and bring him hither to me."

The three men obeyed. But the recommendation given to his servants was useless. Porthos, refreshed, had already himself commenced the descent, and his heavy step resounded amongst the cavities, formed and supported by columns of silex and granite. As soon as the Seigneur de Bracieux had rejoined the Bishop, the Bretons lighted a lantern with which they were furnished, and Porthos assured his friend that he felt as strong as ever.

"Let us visit the canoe," said Aramis, "and satisfy ourselves at once what it will hold."

"Do not go too near with the light," said Yves; "for, as you desired me, monseigneur, I have placed under the bench of the poop, in the coffer you know of, the barrel of powder, and the musket charges that you sent me from the fort."

"Very well," said Aramis; and, taking the lantern himself, he examined minutely all parts of the canoe, with the precautions of a man who is neither timid nor ignorant in the face of danger. The canoe was long, light, drawing little water, thin of keel; in short, one of those which have always been so well constructed at Belle-Isle; a little high in its sides, solid upon the water, very manageable, furnished with planks, which, in uncertain weather, form a sort of bridge over which the waves glide and which protect the rowers. In two well-closed coffers, placed beneath the benches of the prow and the poop, Aramis found bread biscuit, dried fruits, a quarter of bacon, a good provision of water in leathern bottles; the whole forming rations sufficient for people who did not mean to quit the coast, and would be able to revictual, if necessity commanded. The arms, eight muskets, and as many horse pistols, were in good condition, and all loaded. There were additional oars, in case of accident, and a little lug sail, which assists the speed of the canoe at the same time the boatmen row, and is so useful when the breeze is slack. When Aramis had seen all these things, and appeared satisfied with the result of his inspection, "Let us consult Porthos," said he, "to know if we must endeavour to get the barque out by the unknown extremity of the grotto, following the descent and the shade of the cavern, or whether it be better in the open air, to make it slide upon the rollers, through the bushes, levelling the road of the little beach, which is but twenty feet high, and gives at its foot, in the tide, three or four fathoms of good water upon a sound bottom."

"It must be as you please, monseigneur," replied Yves, respectfully; "but I don't believe that by the slope of the cavern, and in the dark, in which we shall be obliged to manœuvre our boat, the road will be so convenient as in the open air. I know the beach well, and can certify that it is as smooth as a grass plot in a garden; the interior of the grotto, on the contrary, is rough; without again reckoning, monseigneur, that at the extremity we shall come to the trench which leads to the sea, and perhaps the canoe will not pass down it."

"I have made my calculations," said the Bishop, "and I am certain it would pass."

"So be it; I wish it may, monseigneur," continued the skipper; "but your greatness knows very well that to make it reach the extremity of the trench, there is an enormous stone to be lifted—that under which the fox always passes, and which closes the trench up like a door."

"That can be raised," said Porthos, "that is nothing."

"Oh! I know that monseigneur has the strength of ten men," replied Yves; "but that is giving monseigneur a great deal of trouble."

"I think the skipper may be right," said Aramis; "let us try the open-air passage."

"The more so, monseigneur," continued the fisherman, "that we should not be able to embark before day, it would require so much labour, and that as soon as daylight appears, a good vedette placed outside the grotto would be necessary, indispensable even, to watch the manœuvres of the lighters or the cruisers that are upon the look-out for us."

"Yes, yes, Yves, your reasons are good; we will go by the beach."

And the three robust Bretons went to the boat, and were beginning to place their rollers underneath it to put it in motion, when the distant barking of dogs was heard, proceeding from the interior.

Aramis darted out of the grotto, followed by Porthos. Dawn just tinted whit purple and white the waves and the plain; through the dim light the young, melancholy firs waved their tender branches over the pebbles, and long flights of crows were skimming with their black wings over the thin fields of buck-wheat. In a quarter of an hour it would be clear daylight; the awakened birds joyously announced it to all nature. The barking which had been heard, which had stopped the three fishermen engaged in moving the boat, and had brought Aramis and Porthos out of the cavern, was prolonged in a deep gorge within about a league of the grotto.

"It is a pack of hounds," said Porthos; "the dogs are upon a scent."

"Who can be hunting at such a moment at this?" said Aramis.

"And this way particularly," continued Porthos, "this way, where they may expect the army of the royalists."

"The noise comes nearer. Yes, you are right, Porthos, the dogs are on a scent. But, Yves!" cried Aramis, "Come here! come here!"

Yves ran towards him, letting fall the cylinder which he was about to place under the boat when the Bishop's call interrupted him.

"What is the meaning of this hunt, skipper?" said Porthos.

"Eh! monseigneur, I cannot understand it," replied the Breton. "It is not at such a moment that the Seigneur de Locmaria would hunt. No, and yet the dogs——"

"Unless they have escaped from the kennel."

"No," said Goenne, "they are not the Seigneur de Locmaria's hounds."

"In common prudence," said Aramis, "let us go back into the grotto; the voices evidently draw nearer; we shall soon know what we have to trust to."

They re-entered, but had scarcely proceeded a hundred steps in the darkness, when a noise like the hoarse sigh of a creature in distress resounded through the cavern, and breathless, rapid, terrified, a fox passed like a flash of lightning before the fugitives, leaped over the boat and disappeared, leaving behind it its sour scent, which was perceptible for several seconds under the low vaults of the cave.

"The fox!" cried the Bretons, with the joyous surprise of hunters.

"Accursed chance!" cried the Bishop, "our retreat is discovered."

"How so?" said Porthos, "are we afraid of a fox?"

"Eh! my friend, what do you mean by that, and why do you name the fox? It is not the fox alone, Pardieu! But don't you know,

Porthos, that after the fox come hounds, and after the hounds men?"

Porthos hung his head. As if to confirm the words of Aramis, they heard the yelping pack come with frightful swiftness upon the trail of the animal. Six foxhounds burst out at once upon the little heath, with a cry resembling the noise of a triumph.

"There are the dogs plain enough!" said Aramis, posted on the look-out behind a chink between two rocks; "now, who are the huntsmen?"

"If it is the Seigneur de Locmaria's," replied the skipper, "he will leave the dogs to hunt the grotto, for he knows them, and will not enter himself, being quite sure that the fox will come out at the other side; it is there he will go and wait for him."

"It is not the Seigneur de Locmaria who is hunting," replied Aramis, turning pale in spite of his efforts to maintain a good countenance.

"Who is it then?" said Porthos.

"Look!"

Porthos applied his eye to the slit, and saw at the summit of a hillock a dozen horsemen urging on their horses in the track of the dogs, shouting "*Taïaut! taïaut!*"

"The guards!" said he.

"Yes, my friend, the King's guards."

"The King's guards! do you say, monseigneur?" cried the Bretons, becoming pale in their turns.

"And Biscarrat at their head, mounted upon my grey horse," continued Aramis.

The hounds at the same moment rushed into the grotto like an avalanche, and the depths of the cavern were filled with their deafening cries.

"Ah! the devil!" said Aramis, resuming all his coolness at the sight of this certain, inevitable danger. "I am perfectly satisfied we are lost, but we have at least one chance left. If the guards who follow their hounds happen to discover there is an issue to the grotto, there is no more help for us, for on entering they must see both us and our boat. The dogs must not go out of the cavern. The masters must not enter."

"That is clear," said Porthos.

"You understand," added Aramis, with the rapid precision of command; "there are six dogs which will be forced to stop at the great stone under which the fox has glided—but at the too narrow opening of which they shall be themselves stopped and killed."

The Bretons sprang forward, knives in hand. In a few minutes

there was a lamentable concert of growls, and mortal howlings—
and then, nothing.

"That's well!" said Aramis, coolly, "now for the masters!"

"What is to be done with them?" said Porthos.

"Wait their arrival, conceal ourselves, and kill them."

"Kill them!" replied Porthos.

"There are sixteen," said Aramis, "at least, up at present."

"And well armed," added Porthos, with a smile of consolation.

"It will last about ten minutes," said Aramis. "To work!"

And with a resolute air he took up a musket, and placed his
hunting-knife between his teeth.

"Yves, Goenne, and his son," continued Aramis, "will pass the
muskets to us. You, Porthos, will fire when they are close. We shall
have brought down eight before the others are aware of anything—
that is certain; then, all, there are five of us; we will despatch the
other eight, knife in hand."

"And poor Biscarrat?" said Porthos.

Aramis reflected a moment—"Biscarrat the first," replied he
coolly; "he knows us."

76

THE GROTTO

In spite of the sort of divination which was the remarkable side of
the character of Aramis, the event, subject to the chances of things
over which uncertainty presides, did not fall out exactly as the
Bishop of Vannes had foreseen. Biscarrat, better mounted than his
companions, arrived the first at the opening of the grotto, and
comprehended that the fox and the dogs were all engulfed in it.
Only struck by that superstitious terror which every dark and subterraneous way naturally impresses upon the mind of man, he
stopped at the outside of the grotto, and waited till his companions
should have assembled round him.

"Well?" asked the young men, coming up, out of breath, and
unable to understand the meaning of his inaction.

"Well! I cannot hear the dogs; they and the fox must be all
engulfed in this cavern."

"They were too close up," said one of the guards, "to have lost
scent all at once. Besides, we should hear them from one side or
another. They must, as Biscarrat says, be in this grotto."

"But then," said one of the young men, "why don't they give
tongue?"

"It is strange!" said another.

"Well, but," said a fourth, "let us go into this grotto. Does it happen to be forbidden that we should enter it?"

"No," replied Biscarrat. "Only, as it looks as dark as a wolf's mouth, we might break our necks in it."

"Witness the dogs," said a guard, "who seem to have broken theirs."

"What the devil can have become of them?" asked the young men in chorus. And every master called his dog by name, whistled to him in his favourite note, without a single one replying to either the call or the whistle.

"It is perhaps an enchanted grotto," said Biscarrat; "let us see." And jumping from his horse, he made a step into the grotto.

"Stop! stop! I will accompany you," said one of the guards, on seeing Biscarrat disappear in the shade of the cavern's mouth.

"No," replied Biscarrat, "there must be something extraordinary in the place—don't let us risk ourselves all at once. If in ten minutes you do not hear of me you can come in, but not all at once."

"Be it so," said the young men, who, besides, did not see that Biscarrat ran much risk in the enterprise, "we will wait for you." And without dismounting from their horses, they formed a circle round the grotto.

Biscarrat entered then alone, and advanced through the darkness till he came in contact with the muzzle of Porthos's musket. The resistance which his chest met with astonished him. He naturally raised his hand and laid hold of the icy barrel. At the same instant, Yves lifted a knife against the young man which was about to fall upon him with all the force of a Breton's arm, when the iron wrist of Porthos stopped it half-way. Then, like low, muttering thunder, his voice growled in the darkness; "I will not have him killed."

Biscarrat found himself between a protection and a threat, the one almost as terrible as the other. However brave the young man might be, he could not prevent a cry escaping him, which Aramis immediately suppressed by placing a handkerchief over his mouth. "Monsieur de Biscarrat," said he, in a low voice, "we mean you no harm, and you must know that, if you have recognised us; but, at the first word, the first sigh, or the first breath, we shall be forced to kill you as we have killed your dogs."

"Yes, I recognise you, gentlemen," said the officer in a low voice. "But why are you here—what are you doing here? Unfortunate men! I thought you were in the fort?"

"And you, monsieur, you were to obtain conditions for us, I think?"

"I did all I was able, messieurs, but——"

"But what?"

"But there are positive orders."

"To kill us?" Biscarrat made no reply. It would have cost him too much to speak of the cord to gentlemen. Aramis understood the silence of the prisoner.

"Monsieur Biscarrat," said he, "you would be already dead if we had not had regard for your youth and our ancient association with your father; but you may yet escape from the place by swearing that you will not tell your companions what you have seen."

"I will not only swear that I will not speak of it," said Biscarrat, "but I still further swear that I will do everything in the world to prevent my companions from setting foot in the grotto."

"Biscarrat! Biscarrat!" cried several voices from the outside, coming like a whirlwind into the cave.

"Reply," said Aramis.

"Here am I!" cried Biscarrat.

"Now, begone; we depend upon your loyalty." And he left his hold of the young man, who hastily returned towards the light.

"Biscarrat! Biscarrat!" cried the voices, still nearer. And the shadows of several human forms projected into the interior of the grotto.

Biscarrat rushed to meet his friends, in order to stop them, and met them just as they were adventuring into the cave. Aramis and Porthos listened with the intense attention of men whose life depend upon a breath of air.

"Oh! oh!" exclaimed one of the guards, as he came to the light, "how pale you are!"

"Pale!" cried another, "you ought to say livid."

"I!" said the young man, endeavouring to collect his faculties.

"In the name of Heaven! what has happened to you?" exclaimed all voices.

"You have not a drop of blood in your veins, my poor friend," said one of them, laughing.

"Messieurs, it is serious," said another, "he is going to faint; does any of you happen to have any salts?" And they all laughed.

All these interpellations, all these jokes crossed each other round Biscarrat as the balls cross each other in the fire of a *mêlée*. He recovered himself amidst a deluge of interrogations.

"What do you suppose I have seen?" asked he. "I was too hot

when I entered the grotto, and I have been struck with the cold; that is all."

"But the dogs, the dogs, have you seen them again—did you see anything of them—do you know anything about them?"

"I suppose they have gone out by another way."

"Messieurs," said one of the young men, "there is in that which is going on, in the paleness and silence of our friend, a mystery which Biscarrat will not, or cannot, reveal. Only, and that is a certainty, Biscarrat has seen something in the grotto. Well! for my part, I am very curious to see what it is, even if it were the devil! To the grotto! messieurs, to the grotto!"

"To the grotto!" repeated all the voices. And the echo of the cavern carried like a menace to Porthos and Aramis, "To the grotto! to the grotto!"

Biscarrat threw himself before his companions. "Messieurs! messieurs!" cried he, "in the name of Heaven do not go in!"

"Why, what is there so terrific in the cavern?" asked several at once. "Come, speak, Biscarrat."

"Decidedly, it is the devil he has seen," repeated he who had before advanced that hypothesis.

"Well!" said another; "if he has seen him, he need not be selfish; he may as well let us have a look at him in our turns."

"Messieurs! messieurs! I beseech you," urged Biscarrat.

"Nonsense!—Let us pass!"

"Messieurs, I implore you not to enter!"

"Why, you went in yourself?"

Then one of the officers who—of a riper age than the others—had, till this time remained behind, and had said nothing, advanced. "Messieurs," said he with a calmness which contrasted with the animation of the young men, "there is in this some person, or something, that is not the devil; but which, whatever it may be, has had sufficient power to silence our dogs. We must know who this some one is, or what this something is."

Biscarrat made a last effort to stop his friends, but it was useless. In vain he threw himself before the most rash; in vain he clung to the rocks to bar the passage; the crowd of young men rushed into the cave, in the steps of the officer who had spoken last, but who had sprung in first, sword in hand, to face the unknown danger. Biscarrat, repulsed by his friends, not able to accompany them without passing in the eyes of Porthos and Aramis for a traitor and a perjurer, with painfully attentive ear and still supplicating hands leant against the rough side of a rock which he thought must be exposed to the fire of the musketeers. As to the guards, they penetrated farther and farther, with cries that grew weaker as they advanced. All at once, a discharge of musketry, growling like thunder, exploded beneath the vault. Two or three balls were flattened against the rock where Biscarrat was leaning. At the same instant, cries, howlings, and imprecations burst forth, and the little troop of gentlemen reappeared—some pale, some bleeding— all enveloped in a cloud of smoke, which the outward air seemed to draw from the depths of the cavern. "Biscarrat! Biscarrat!" cried the fugitives, "you knew there was an ambuscade in that cavern, and you have not warned us! Biscarrat, you are the cause that four of us have been killed! Woe be to you, Biscarrat!"

"You are the cause of my being wounded to death," said one of the young men, gathering his blood in his hand, and casting it into the face of Biscarrat. "My blood be upon your head!" And he rolled in agony at the feet of the young men.

"But, at least, tell us who is there?" cried several furious voices. Biscarrat remained silent. "Tell us or die!" cried the wounded man, raising himself upon one knee, and lifting towards his companion an arm bearing a useless sword. Biscarrat rushed towards him, opening his breast for the blow, but the wounded man fell back, not to rise again—uttering a groan which was his last. Biscarrat, with hair on end, haggard eyes, and bewildered head, advanced towards the interior of the cavern, saying, "You are right. Death to me, who have allowed my companions to be assassinated. I am a base wretch!" And throwing away his sword, for he wished to die without defending himself, he rushed head foremost into the cavern. The others followed him. The eleven who remained out of sixteen imitated his example; but they did not go farther than the first. A second discharge laid five upon the icy sand; and, as it was impossible to see whence this murderous thunder issued, the others fell back with a terror that can be better imagined than expressed. But, far from flying, as the others had done, Biscarrat remained safe and sound, seated on a fragment of rock, and waited. There were only six gentlemen left.

"Seriously," said one of the survivors, "is it the devil?"

"*Ma foi!* it is much worse," said another.

"Ask Biscarrat, he knows."

"Where is Biscarrat?" The young men looked round them, and saw that Biscarrat did not answer.

"He is dead!" said two or three voices.

"Oh! no," replied another; "I saw him through the smoke, sitting quietly on a rock. He is in the cavern; he is waiting for us."

"He must know who are there."

"And how should he know them?"

"He was taken prisoner by the rebels."

"That is true! Well! let us call him, and learn from him whom we have to deal with." And all voices shouted, "Biscarrat! Biscarrat!" But Biscarrat did not answer.

"Good!" said the officer who had shown so much coolness in the affair. "We have no longer any need of him; here are reinforcements coming."

In fact, a company of the guards, left in the rear by their officers, whom the ardour of the chase had carried away—from seventy-five to eighty men—arrived in good order, led by their captain and the first lieutenant. The five officers hastened to meet their soldiers; and, in a language, the eloquence of which may be easily imagined, they related the adventure, and asked for aid. The captain interrupted them: "Where are your companions?" demanded he.

"Dead!"

"But there were sixteen of you."

"Ten are dead. Biscarrat is in the cavern, and we are five."

"Biscarrat is then a prisoner?"

"Probably."

"No, for here he is—look." In fact, Biscarrat appeared at the opening of the grotto.

"He makes us a sign to come on," said the officer. "Come on!"

"Come on!" cried all the troop. And they advanced to meet Biscarrat.

"Monsieur," said the captain, addressing Biscarrat, "I am assured that you know who the men are in that grotto, and who make such a desperate defence. In the King's name I command you to declare what you know."

"Captain," said Biscarrat, "you have no need to command me; my word has been restored to me this very instant; and I come in the name of these men."

"To tell me who they are?"

"To tell you they are determined to defend themselves to the death, unless you grant them good terms."

"How many are there of them, then?"

"There are two," said Biscarrat.

"There are two—and want to impose conditions upon us."

"There are two, and they have already killed ten of our men."

"What sort of people are they—giants?"

"Better than that. Do you remember the history of the bastion aint-Gervais,* captain?"

"Yes; where four musketeers held out against an army."

"Well, these two men were of those musketeers."

"And their names?"

"At that period they were called Porthos and Aramis. Now, they are styled M. d'Herblay and M. du Vallon."

"And what interest have they in all this?"

"It is they who held Belle-Isle for M. Fouquet."

A murmur ran through the ranks of the soldiers on hearing the two words "Porthos and Aramis." "The musketeers! the musketeers!" repeated they. And among all these brave men, the idea that they were going to have a struggle against two of the oldest glories of the French army, made a shiver, half enthusiasm, half terror, run through them. In fact, those four names—d'Artagnan, Athos, Porthos, and Aramis, were venerated among all who wore a sword; as, in antiquity, the name of Hercules, Theseus, Castor, and Pollux, were venerated.

"Two men—and they have killed ten in two discharges! That in impossible, Monsieur Biscarrat!"

"Eh! captain," replied the latter, "I do not tell you that they have not with them two or three men, as the musketeers of the bastion Saint-Gervais had two or three lackeys; but, believe me, captain, I have seen these men, I have been taken prisoner by them—I know they themselves alone could suffice to destroy an army."

"That we shall see," said the Captain, "and that in a moment too. Gentlemen, attention!"

At this reply no one stirred, and all prepared to obey. Biscarrat alone risked a last attempt. "Monsieur," said he in a low voice "believe me; let us pass on our way. Those two men, those two lions you are going to attack, will defend themselves to the death. They have already killed ten of our men; they will kill double the number, and end by killing themselves rather than surrender. What shall we gain by fighting them?"

"We shall gain the consciousness, monsieur, of not having made eighty of the King's guards retire before two rebels. If I listened to your advice, monsieur, I should be a dishonoured man; and by dishonouring myself I should dishonour the army. Forward, men!"

And he marched first as far as the opening of the grotto. There he halted. The object of this halt was to give to Biscarrat and his companions time to describe to him the interior of the grotto. Then, when he believed he had a sufficient acquaintance with the places, he divided his company into three bodies, which were to enter successively, keeping up a sustained fire in all directions. No doubt, in this attack they should lose five more men, perhaps ten; but certainly, they must end by taking the rebels, since there was no issue; and, at any rate, two men could not kill eighty.

"Captain," said Biscarrat, "I beg to be allowed to march at the head of the first platoon."

"So be it," replied the captain; "you have all the honour of it. That is a present I make you."

"Thanks!" replied the young man, with all the firmness of his race.

"Take your sword, then."

"I shall go as I am, captain," said Biscarrat, "for I do not go to kill, I go to be killed."

And placing himself at the head of the first platoon with his head uncovered and his arms crossed,—"March, gentlemen!" said he.

77

AN HOMERIC SONG

IT is time to pass into the other camp, and to describe at once the combatants and the field of battle. Aramis and Porthos had gone to the grotto of Locmaria with the expectation of finding there their canoe ready armed, as well as the three Bretons, their assistants; and they at first hoped to make the barque pass through the little issue of the cavern, concealing in that fashion both their labours and their flight. The arrival of the fox and the dogs had obliged them to remain concealed. The grotto extended the space of about two hundred yards, to that little slope dominating a creek. Formerly a temple of the Celtic divinities, when Belle-Isle was still called Colonèse, this grotto had seen more than one human sacrifice accomplished in its mysterious depths. The first entrance to the cavern was by a moderate descent, above which heaped-up rocks formed a low arcade; the interior, very unequal as to the ground, dangerous from the rocky inequalities of the vault, was subdivided into several compartments which commanded each other and joined each other by means of several rough, broken steps, fixed right and left, in enormous natural pillars. At the third compartment, the vault was so low, the passage so narrow, that the barque would scarcely have passed without touching the two sides; nevertheless, in a moment of despair, wood softens and stone becomes compliant under the breath of human will. Such was the thought of Aramis, when, after having fought the fight, he decided upon flight—a flight certainly dangerous, since all the assailants were not dead; and that, admitting the possibility of putting the

508

barque to sea, they would have to fly in open day, before the conquered, so interested on recognising their small number, in pursuing their conquerors. When the two discharges had killed ten men, Aramis, habituated to the windings of the cavern, went to reconnoitre them one by one—counted them, for the smoke prevented seeing outside; and he immediately commanded that the canoe should be rolled as far as the great stone, the closure of the liberating issue. Porthos collected all his strength, took the canoe up in his arms and raised it up, whilst the Bretons made it run rapidly along the rollers. They had descended into the third compartment; they had arrived at the stone which walled up the outlet. Porthos seized this gigantic stone at its base, applied to it his robust shoulder, and gave a heave which made this wall crack. A cloud of dust fell from the vault with the ashes of ten thousand generations of sea-birds, whose nests stuck like cement to the rock. At the third shock the stone gave way; it oscillated for a minute. Porthos, placing his back against the neighbouring rock, made an arch with his foot, which drove the block out of the calcareous masses which served for hinges and cramps. The stone fell, and daylight was visible, brilliant, radiant, which rushed into the cavern by the opening, and the blue sea appeared to the delighted Bretons. They then began to lift the barque over the barricade. Twenty more yards, and it might glide into the ocean. It was during this time that the company arrived, was drawn up by the captain, and disposed for either an escalade or an assault. Aramis watched over everything, to favour the labours of his friends. He saw the reinforcements, he counted the men, he convinced himself at a single glance of the insurmountable peril to which a fresh combat would expose them. To escape by sea, at the moment the cavern was about to be invaded, was impossible. In fact, the daylight which had just been admitted to the last two compartments had exposed to the soldiers the barque being rolled towards the sea, the two rebels within musket shot, and one of their discharges would riddle the boat if it did not kill the five navigators. Besides, supposing everything—if the barque escaped with the men on board of it, how could the alarm be suppressed—how could notice to the royal lighters be prevented? What could hinder the poor canoe, followed by sea, and watched from shore, from succumbing before the end of the day? Aramis, digging his hands into his grey hair with rage, invoked the assistance of God and the assistance of the demon. Calling to Porthos, who was working alone more than all the rollers—whether of flesh or of wood—"My friend," said he, "our enemies have just received a reinforcement."

"Ah! ah!" said Porthos quietly, "what is to be done, then?"

"To recommence the combat," said Aramis, "is hazardous."

"Yes," said Porthos, "for it is difficult to suppose that out of two one should not be killed, and certainly, if one of us were killed, the other would get himself killed also." Porthos spoke these words with that heroic nature which, with him, grew greater with all the phases of the matter.

Aramis felt it like a spur to his heart. "We shall neither of us be killed if you do what I tell you, friend Porthos."

"Tell me what."

"These people are coming down into the grotto."

"Yes."

"We could kill about fifteen of them, but not more."

"How many are there in all?" asked Porthos.

"They have received a reinforcement of seventy-five men."

"Seventy-five and five, eighty. Ah! ah!" said Porthos.

"If they fire all at once they will riddle us with balls."

"Certainly they will."

"Without reckoning," added Aramis, "that the detonations might occasion fallings in of the cavern."

"Ay," said Porthos, "a piece of falling rock just now grazed my shoulder a little."

"You see, then!"

"Oh! it's nothing."

"We must determine upon something quickly. Our Bretons are going to continue to roll the canoe towards the sea."

"Very well."

"We two will keep the powder, the balls, and the muskets here."

"But only two, my dear Aramis—we shall never fire three shots together," said Porthos innocently, "the defence by musketry is a bad one."

"Find a better, then."

"I have found one," said the giant eagerly; "I will place myself in ambuscade behind the pillar with this iron bar, and invisible, unattackable if they come on in floods, I can let my bar fall upon their skulls, thirty times in a minute. Hein! what do you think of the project? You smile!"

"Excellent, dear friend, perfect! I approve it greatly; only you will frighten them, and half of them will remain outside to take us by famine. What we want, my good friend, is the entire destruction of the troop; a single man left standing ruins us."

"You are right, my friend, but how can we attract them, pray?"

"By not stirring, my good Porthos."

"Well! we won't stir, then; but when they shall be all together——"

510

"Then leave it to me! I have an idea."

"If it is thus, and your idea be a good one—and your idea is most likely to be good—I am satisfied."

"To your ambuscade, Porthos, and count how many enter."

"But you, what will you do?"

"Don't trouble yourself about me; I have a task to perform."

"I think I can hear cries."

"It is they. To your post. Keep within reach of my voice and hand."

Porthos took refuge in the second compartment, which was absolutely black with darkness. Aramis glided into the third; the giant held in his hand an iron bar of about fifty pounds weight. Porthos handled this lever, which had been used in rolling the barque, with marvellous facility. During this time, the Bretons had pushed the barque to the beach. In the enlightened compartment, Aramis, stooping and concealed, was busied in some mysterious manœuvre. A command was given in a loud voice. It was the last order of the captain commandant. Twenty-five men jumped from the upper rocks into the first compartment of the grotto, and having taken their ground, began to fire. The echoes growled, the hissing of the balls cut the air, an opaque smoke filled the vault.

"To the left! to the left!" cried Biscarrat, who, in his first assault, had seen the passage to the second chamber, and who, animated by the smell of powder, wished to guide his soldiers in that direction. The troop accordingly precipitated themselves to the left—the passage gradually growing narrower. Biscarrat, with his hands stretched forward, devoted to death, marched in advance of the muskets. "Come on! come on!" exclaimed he, "I see daylight!"

"Strike, Porthos!" cried the sepulchral voice of Aramis.

Porthos heaved a heavy sigh—but he obeyed. The iron bar fell full and direct upon the head of Biscarrat, who was dead before he had ended his cry. Then the formidable lever rose ten times in ten seconds, and made ten corpses. The soldiers could see nothing; they heard sighs and groans; they stumbled over dead bodies, but as they had no conception of the cause of all this, they came forward jostling each other. The implacable bar, still falling, annihilated the first platoon, without a single sound having warned the second which was quietly advancing, only this second platoon, commanded by the captain, had broken a thin fir, growing on the shore, and, with its resinous branches twisted together, the captain had made a flambeau. On arriving at the compartment where Porthos, like the exterminating angel, had destroyed all he touched, the first rank drew back in terror. No firing had replied to that of the guards, and yet their way was stopped by a heap of dead bodies—they literally walked in blood. Porthos was still behind his pillar. The captain, on enlightening with the trembling flame of the fir this frightful carnage, of which he in vain sought the cause, drew back towards the pillar, behind which Porthos was concealed. Then a gigantic hand issued from the shade, and fastened on the throat of the captain, who uttered a stifled rattle; his outstretched arms beating the air, the torch fell and was extinguished in blood. A second after the corpse of the captain fell close to the extinguished torch, and added another body to the heap of dead which blocked up the passage. All this was effected as mysteriously as if by magic. At hearing the rattling in the throat of the captain, the soldiers who accompanied him had turned round; they had caught a glimpse of his extended arms, his eyes starting from their sockets, and then the torch fell and they were left in darkness. From an unreflective, instinctive, mechanical feeling, the lieutenant cried,—"Fire!"

Immediately a volley of musketry flamed, thundered, roared in the cavern, bringing down enormous fragments from the vaults. The cavern was lighted for an instant by this discharge, and then immediately returned to a darkness rendered still thicker by the smoke. To this succeeded a profound silence, broken only by the steps of the third brigade, now entering the cavern.

78

THE DEATH OF A TITAN

AT the moment when Porthos, more accustomed to the darkness than all these men coming from open daylight, was looking round him to see if in this night Aramis were not making him some signal, he felt his arm gently touched, and a voice low as a breath murmured in his ear, "Come."

"Oh!" said Porthos.

"Hush!" said Aramis, if possible, still more softly.

And amidst the noise of the third brigade, which continued to advance, amidst the imprecations of the guards left alive, of the dying, rattling their last sigh, Aramis and Porthos glided imperceptibly along the granite walls of the cavern. Aramis led Porthos into the last but one compartment, and showed him, in a hollow of the rocky wall, a barrel of powder weighing from seventy to eighty pounds, to which he had just attached a match. "My friend," said he to Porthos, "you will take this barrel, the match of which I am going to set fire to, and throw it amidst our enemies; can you do so?"

"*Parbleu!*" replied Porthos; and he lifted the barrel with one hand. "Light it!"

"Stop," said Aramis, "till they are all massed together, and then, my Jupiter, hurl your thunder-bolt among them."

"Light it," repeated Porthos.

"On my part," continued Aramis, "I will join our Bretons, and help them to get the canoe to the sea. I will wait for you on the shore; launch it strongly, and hasten to us."

"Light it," said Porthos, a third time.

"But do you understand me?"

"*Parbleu!*" said Porthos again, with laughter that he did not even attempt to restrain; "when a thing is explained to me I understand it; begone, and give me the light."

Aramis gave the burning match to Porthos, who held out his arm to him, his hands being engaged. Aramis pressed the arm of Porthos with both his hands, and fell back to the outlet of the cavern where the three rowers awaited him.

Porthos, left alone, applied the spark bravely to the match. The spark,—a feeble spark, first principle of a conflagration—shone in the darkness like a fire-fly, then was deadened against the match which it enflamed, Porthos enlivening the flame with his breath. The smoke was a little dispersed, and by the light of the sparkling match, objects might, for two seconds, be distinguished. It was a short but a splendid spectacle, that of this giant, pale, bloody, his countenance lighted by the fire of the match burning in surrounding darkness! The soldiers saw him—they saw the barrel he held in his hand—they at once understood what was going to happen. Then, these men, already filled with terror at the sight of what had been accomplished—filled with terror at thinking of what was going to be accomplished, threw forth together one shriek of agony. Some endeavoured to fly, but they encountered the third brigade, which barred their passage; others mechanically took aim, and attempted to fire their discharged muskets; others fell upon their knees. Two or three officers cried out to Porthos to promise him his liberty if he would spare their lives. The lieutenant of the third brigade commanded his men to fire; but the guards had before them their terrified companions, who served as a living rampart for Porthos. We have said that the light produced by the spark and the match did not last more than two seconds; but during these two seconds this is what it illuminated— in the first place, the giant, enlarging in the darkness; then, at ten paces from him, a heap of bleeding bodies, crushed, mutilated, in the midst of whom still lived some last struggle of agony, which lifted the mass as a last respiration raises the sides of a shapeless monster expiring in the night. Every breath of Porthos, whilst enlivening the match, sent towards this heap of bodies a sulphurous hue mingled with streaks of purple. In addition to this principal group, scattered about the grotto, as the chance of death or the surprise of the blow had stretched them, some isolated bodies seemed to threaten by their gaping wounds. Above the ground, soaked by pools of blood, rose heavy and sparkling, the short, thick pillars of the cavern, of which the strongly marked shades threw out the luminous particles. And all this was seen by the tremulous light of a match attached to a barrel of powder; that is to say, a torch which, whilst throwing a light upon the dead past, showed the death to come.

As I have said, this spectacle did not last above two seconds. During this short space of time an officer of the third brigade got together eight men armed with muskets, and, through an opening, ordered them to fire upon Porthos. But they who received the order to fire trembled so, that three guards fell by the discharge, and the five other balls went hissing to splinter the vault, plough the ground, or indent the sides of the cavern.

A burst of laughter replied to this volley; then the arm of the giant swung round; then was seen to pass through the air, like a falling star, the train of fire. The barrel, hurled a distance of thirty feet, cleared the barricade of dead bodies, and fell amidst a group of shrieking soldiers, who threw themselves on their faces. The officer had followed the brilliant train in the air; he endeavoured to precipitate himself upon the barrel and tear out the match before it reached the powder it contained. Useless devotedness! the air had made the flame attached to the conductor more active; the match, which at rest might have burnt five minutes, was consumed in thirty seconds, and the infernal work exploded. Furious vortices, hissings of sulphur and nitre, devouring ravages of the fire which caught to objects, the terrible thunder of the explosion, this is what the second which followed the two seconds we have described, disclosed in that cavern, equal in horrors to a cavern of demons. The rock split like planks of deal under the axe. A jet of fire, smoke, and debris sprang up from the middle of the grotto, enlarging as it mounted. The large walls of silex tottered and fell upon the sand, and the sand itself, an instrument of pain when launched from its hardened bed, riddled the face with its myriads of cutting atoms. Cries, howlings, imprecations, and existences—all were extinguished in one immense crash.

The three first compartments became a gulf into which fell back again, according to its weight, every vegetable, mineral, or human fragment. Then the lighter sand and ashes fell in their turns, stretching like a grey winding sheet and smoking over these dismal funerals. And now, seek in this burning tomb, in this subterraneous volcano, seek for the King's guards with their blue coats laced with silver. Seek for the officers brilliant in gold; seek for the arms upon which they depended for their defence; seek for the stones that have killed them, the ground that has borne them. One single man has made of all this a chaos more confused, more shapeless, more terrible than the chaos which existed an hour before God had created the world. There remained nothing of the three compartments—nothing by which God could have known His own work. As to Porthos, after having hurled the barrel of powder amidst his enemies, he had fled as Aramis had directed him to do, and had gained the last compartment, into which air, light, and sunshine penetrated through the opening. Therefore, scarcely had he turned the angle which separated the third compartment from the fourth when he perceived at a hundred paces from him the barque dancing on the waves; there were his friends, there was liberty, there was life after victory. Six more of his formidable strides, and he would be out of the vault; out of the vault! two or three vigorous springs and he would reach the canoe. Suddenly he felt his knees give way; his knees appeared powerless, his legs to yield under him.

"Oh! oh!" murmured he, "there is my fatigue seizing me again! I can walk no farther! What is this?"

Aramis perceived him through the opening, and unable to conceive what could induce him to stop thus—"Come on, Porthos! come on!" cried he; "come quickly."

"Oh!" replied the giant, making an effort which acted upon every muscle of his body—"oh, but I cannot." While saying these words he fell upon his knees, but with his robust hands he clung to the rocks, and raised himself up again.

"Quick! quick!" repeated Aramis, bending forward towards the shore, as if to draw Porthos towards him with his arms.

"Here I am," stammered Porthos, collecting all his strength to make one step more.

"In the name of Heaven! Porthos, make haste! the barrel will blow up!"

"Make haste, monseigneur!" shouted the Bretons to Porthos, who was floundering as in a dream.

But there was no longer time; the explosion resounded, the earth gaped, the smoke which rushed through the large fissures obscured the sky; the sea flowed back as if driven by the blast of fire which darted from the grotto as if from the jaws of a gigantic chimera; the reflux carried the barque out twenty yards; the rocks cracked to their base, and separated like blocks beneath the operation of wedges; a portion of the vault was carried up towards heaven, as if by rapid currents; the rose-coloured and green fire of the sulphur, the black lava of the argillaceous liquefactions clashed and combated for an instant beneath a majestic dome of smoke; then, at first oscillated, then declined, then fell successively the long angles of rock which the violence of the explosion had not been able to uproot from their bed of ages; they bowed to each other like grave and slow old men, then prostrated themselves, embedded for ever in their dusty tomb.

This frightful shock seemed to restore to Porthos the strength he had lost; he arose, himself a giant among these giants. But at the moment he was flying between the double hedge of granite phantoms, these latter, which were no longer supported by the corresponding links, began to roll with a crash around this Titan, who looked as if precipitated from heaven amidst rocks which he had just been launching at it. Porthos felt the earth beneath his feet shaken by this long rending. He extended his vast hands to the right and left to repulse the falling rocks. A gigantic block was held back by each of his extended hands; he bent his head and a third granite mass sank between his two shoulders. For an instant the arms of Porthos had given way, but the Hercules united all his forces, and the two walls of the prison in which he was buried fell back slowly and gave him place. For an instant he appeared in this frame of granite like the ancient angel of chaos, but in pushing back the lateral rocks, he lost his point of support for the monolith, which weighed upon his strong shoulders, and the monolith, weighing upon him with all its weight, brought the giant down upon his knees. The lateral rocks, for an instant pushed back, drew together again, and added their weight to the primitive weight which would have been sufficient to crush ten men. The giant fell without crying for help; he fell while answering Aramis with words of encouragement and hope, and, thanks to the powerful arch of his hands, for an instant, he might believe that, like Enceladus,* he should shake off the triple load. But, by degrees, Aramis saw the block sink; the hands strung for an instant, the arms stiffened for a last effort, gave way, the extended shoulders sank wounded and torn, and the rock continued to lower gradually.

"Porthos! Porthos!" cried Aramis, tearing his hair. "Porthos! where are you? Speak!"

"There, there!" murmured Porthos, with a voice growing evidently weaker, "Patience! patience!"

Scarcely had he pronounced these words, when the impulse of the fall augmented the weight; the enormous rock sat down, pressed by the two others which sank in from the sides, and, as it were, swallowed up Porthos in a sepulchre of broken stones. On hearing the dying voice of his friend, Aramis had sprung to land. Two of the Bretons followed him, with each a lever in his hand—one being sufficient to take care of the barque. The last rattles of the valiant struggler guided them amidst the ruins. Aramis, animated, active, and young as at twenty, sprang towards the triple mass, and with his hands, delicate as those of a woman, raised by a miracle of vigour a corner of the immense sepulchre of granite. Then he caught a glimpse, in the darkness of that grave, of the still brilliant eye of his friend, to whom the momentary lifting of the mass restored that moment of respiration. The two men came rushing in, grasped their iron levers, united their triple strength, not merely to raise it, but to sustain it. All was useless. The three men slowly gave way with cries of grief, and the rough voice of Porthos, seeing them exhaust themselves in a useless struggle, murmured in a jeering tone those supreme words which came to his lips with the last respiration, "Too heavy."

After which the eye darkened and closed, the face became pale, the hand whitened, and the Titan sank quite down, breathing his last sigh. With him sank the rock, which, even in his agony, he had still held up. The three men dropped the levers, which rolled upon the tumulary stone. Then, breathless, pale, his brow covered with sweat, Aramis listened, his breast oppressed, his heart ready to break.

Nothing more! The giant slept the eternal sleep, in the sepulchre which God had made to his measure.

79

THE EPITAPH OF PORTHOS

ARAMIS, silent, icy, trembling like a timid child, arose shivering from the stone. A Christian does not walk upon tombs. But though capable of standing, he was not capable of walking. It might be said that something of dead Porthos had just died within him. His Bretons surrounded him; Aramis yielded to their kind exertions, and the three sailors, lifting him up, carried him into the canoe. Then having laid him down upon the bench near the rudder, they took to their oars, preferring to get off by rowing to hoisting a sail, which might betray them.

Of all that levelled surface of the ancient grotto of Locmaria, of all that flattened shore, one single little hillock attracted their eyes. Aramis never removed his from it; and, at a distance out in the sea, in proportion as the shore receded, the menacing and proud mass of rock seemed to draw itself up, as formerly Porthos used to draw himself up, and raise a smiling and invincible head towards heaven, like that of the honest and valiant friend, the strongest of the four, and yet the first dead. Strange destiny of these men of brass! The most simple of heart allied to the most crafty; strength of body guided by subtlety of mind; and in the decisive moment, when vigour alone could save mind and body, a stone, a rock, a vile and material weight, triumphed over vigour, and falling upon the body drove out the mind.*

Worthy Porthos! born to help other men, always ready to sacrifice himself for the safety of the weak, as if God had only given him strength for that purpose; when dying he only thought he was carrying out the conditions of his compact with Aramis, a compact, however, which Aramis alone had drawn up, and which Porthos had only known to suffer by its terrible solidarity. Noble Porthos! of what good are the châteaux overflowing with sumptuous furniture, the forests overflowing with game, the lakes overflowing with fish, the cellars overflowing with wealth! Of what good are the lackeys in brilliant liveries, and in the midst of them, Mousqueton, proud of the power delegated by thee! Oh! noble Porthos! careful heaper up of treasures, was it worth while to labour to sweeten and gild life, to come upon a desert shore, to the cries of sea birds, and lay thyself, with broken bones, beneath a cold stone? Was it worth while, in short, noble Porthos, to heap so much gold, and not have even the distich of a poor poet engraven upon thy monument? Valiant Porthos! He still, without doubt, sleeps, lost, forgotten, beneath the rock which the shepherds of the heath take for the mighty roof-stone of a sunken cromlech. And so many twining brambles, so many mosses, caressed by the bitter wind of the ocean, so many vivacious lichens have soldered the sepulchre to the earth, that the passenger will never imagine that such a block of granite can ever have been supported by the shoulders of one man.

Aramis, still pale, still icy, his heart upon his lips, Aramis looked, even till, with the last ray of daylight, the shore faded on the horizon. Not a word escaped his lips, not a sigh rose from his deep breast. The superstitious Bretons looked at him trembling.

That silence was not of a man, it was of a statue. In the meantime, with the first grey lines that descended from the heavens, the canoe had hoisted its little sail, which, swelling with the kisses of the breeze, and carrying them rapidly from the coast, made brave way with its head towards Spain, across the terrible gulf of Gascony, so rife with tempests. But scarcely half an hour after the sail had been hoisted, the rowers became inactive, reclining upon their benches and, making an eyeshade with their hands, pointed out to each other a white spot which appeared on the horizon as motionless as is in appearance a gull rocked by the insensible respiration of the waves. But that which might have appeared motionless to ordinary eyes was moving at a quick rate to the experienced eye of the sailor; that which appeared stationary on the ocean was cutting a rapid way through it. For some time, seeing the profound torpor in which their master was plunged, they did not dare to rouse him, and satisfied themselves with exchanging their conjectures in a low, disturbed voice. Aramis, in fact, so vigilant, so active—Aramis, whose eye, like that of the lynx, watched without ceasing, and saw better by night than by day—Aramis seemed to sleep in the despair of his soul. An hour passed thus, during which daylight gradually disappeared, but during which also the sail in view gained so swiftly on the barque, that Goenne, one of the three sailors, ventured to say aloud,—

"Monseigneur, we are being chased!"

Aramis made no reply; the ship still gained upon them. Then, of their own accord, two of the sailors, by the direction of the skipper Yves, lowered the sail, in order that that single point which appeared above the surface of the waters should cease to be a guide to the eye of the enemy who was pursuing them. On the part of the ship in sight, on the contrary, two more small sails were run up at the extremities of the masts. Unfortunately, it was the time of the finest and longest days of the year, and the moon in all her brilliancy succeeded to this inauspicious daylight. The corvette, which was pursuing the little barque before the wind, had then still half an hour of twilight, and a whole night almost as light as day.

"Monseigneur! monseigneur! we are lost!" said the skipper; "look! they see us although we have lowered our sail."

"That is not to be wondered at," murmured one of the sailors, "since they say that, by the aid of the devil, the people of the cities have fabricated instruments with which they see as well at a distance as near, by night as well as by day."

Aramis took a telescope from the bottom of the boat, arranged

it silently, and passing it to the sailor: "Here," said he, "look!"
The sailor hesitated.

"Don't be alarmed," said the Bishop, "there is no sin in it; and
if there is any sin, I will take it upon myself."

The sailor lifted the glass to his eye and uttered a cry. He believed that the vessel, which appeared to be distant about cannon-
shot, had suddenly and at a single bound cleared the distance. But,
on withdrawing the instrument from his eye, he saw that, except
the way which the corvette had been able to make during that
short instant, it was still at the same distance.

"So," murmured the sailor, "they can see us as we see them."

"They see us," said Aramis, and sank again into his impassibility.

"How—they see us!" said Yves, "impossible!"

"Well, look yourself," said the sailor. And he passed the glass to
the skipper.

"Monseigneur assures me that the devil has nothing to do with
this?" asked the skipper. Aramis shrugged his shoulders.

The skipper lifted the glass to his eye. "Oh! monseigneur," said
he, "it is a miracle—they are there; it seems as if I were going to
touch them. Twenty-five men at least! Ah! I see the captain forward. He holds a glass like this, and is looking at us. Ah! he turns
round, and gives an order; they are rolling a piece of cannon forward—they are charging it—they are pointing it. *Miséricorde!*
they are firing at us."

And by a mechanical movement, the skipper took the glass off,
and the objects, sent back to the horizon, appeared again in their
true aspect. The vessel was still at the distance of nearly a league,
but the manœuvre announced by the skipper was not less real. A
light cloud of smoke appeared under the sails, more blue then they,
and spreading like a flower opening; then, at about a mile from
the little canoe, they saw the ball take the crown off two or three
waves, dig a white furrow in the sea, and disappear at the end of
that furrow, as inoffensive as the stone with which, at play, a boy
makes ducks and drakes. That was at once a menace and a
warning.

"What is to be done?" asked the skipper.

"They will sink us!" said Goenne, "give us absolution, monseigneur!" And the sailors fell on their knees before him.

"You forget that they can see you," said he.

"That is true," said the sailors, ashamed of their weakness.
"Give us your orders, monseigneur; we are ready to die for
you."

"Let us wait," said Aramis.

"How—let us wait?"

"Yes; do you not see, as you just now said, that if we endeavour to fly, they will sink us."

"But, perhaps," the skipper ventured to say, "perhaps by the favour of the night we could escape them."

"Oh!" said Aramis, "they have, little doubt, some Greek fire to lighten their own course and ours likewise."

At the same moment, as if the little vessel wished to reply to the appeal of Aramis, a second cloud of smoke mounted slowly to the heavens, and from the bosom of that cloud sparked an arrow of flame, which described its parabola like a rainbow, and fell into the sea, where it continued to burn, illuminating a space of a quarter of a league in diameter.

The Bretons looked at each other in terror. "You see plainly," said Aramis, "it will be better to wait for them."

The oars dropped from the hands of the sailors, and the barque, ceasing to make way, rocked motionless on the summits of the waves. Night came on, but the vessel still approached nearer. It might be said it redoubled its speed with the darkness. From time to time, as a bloody-necked vulture rears its head out of its nest, the formidable Greek fire darted from its sides, and cast its flame into the ocean like an incandescent snow. At last it came within musket-shot. All the men were on deck, arms in hand; the cannoniers were at their guns, and matches were burning. It might be thought they were about to board a frigate and to combat a crew superior in number to their own, and not to take a canoe manned by four people.

"Surrender!" cried the commander of the corvette, with the aid of the speaking trumpet.

The sailors looked at Aramis. Aramis made a sign with his head. Yves waved a white cloth at the end of a gaff. This was like striking their flag. The vessel came on like a racehorse. It launched a fresh Greek fire which fell within twenty paces of the little canoe, and threw a stronger light upon them than the most ardent ray of the sun could have done.

"At the first sign of resistance," cried the commander of the corvette, "fire!" And the soldiers brought their muskets to the present.

"Did not we say we surrendered?" said Yves.

"Living! living! captain!" cried some highly excited soldiers. "They must be taken living."

"Well, yes—living," said the captain. Then turning towards the Bretons, "Your lives are all safe, my friends!" cried he, "except the Chevalier d'Herblay."

Aramis started imperceptibly. For an instant his eye was fixed upon the depths of the ocean enlightened by the last flashes of the Greek fire, flashes which ran along the sides of the waves, played upon their crests like plumes, and rendered still more dark, more mysterious and more terrible the abysses they covered.

"Do you hear, monseigneur?" said the sailors.

"Yes."

"What are your orders?"

"Accept!"

"But you, monseigneur!"

Aramis leant still more forward, and played with the ends of his long white fingers with the green water of the sea, to which he turned smiling as a friend.

"Accept!" he repeated.

"We accept," repeated the sailors; "but what security have we?"

"The word of a gentleman," said the officer. "By my rank and by my name I swear, that all but M. le Chevalier d'Herblay shall have their lives spared. I am lieutenant of the King's frigate the *Pomona*, and my name is Louis Constant de Pressigny."*

With a rapid gesture, Aramis—already bent over the side of the barque towards the sea—with a rapid gesture, Aramis raised his head, drew himself up, and with a flashing eye, and a smile upon his lips, "Throw out the ladder, messieurs," said he, as if the command had belonged to him. He was obeyed. Then Aramis, seizing the rope-ladder, instead of the terror which was expected to be displayed upon his countenance, the surprise of the sailors of the corvette was great, when they saw him walk straight up to the commander, with a firm step, look at him earnestly, make a sign to him with his hand, a mysterious and unknown sign, at the sight of which the officer turned pale, trembled, and bowed his head. Without saying a word, Aramis then raised his hand close to the eyes of the commander, and showed him the collet of a ring which he wore on the ring-finger of his left hand. And while making this sign, Aramis, draped in cold, silent, and haughty majesty, had the air of an emperor giving his hand to be kissed. The commandant, who for a moment had raised his head, bowed a second time with marks of the most profound respect. Then, stretching his hand out towards the poop, that is to say, towards his own cabin, he drew back to allow Aramis to go first. The three Bretons, who had come on board after their Bishop, looked at each other, stupefied. The crew were struck with silence. Five minutes after, the commander called the second lieutenant, who returned immediately, and gave directions for the head to be put towards Corunna.* Whilst the order was being executed Aramis reappeared upon the deck, and took a seat near the bulwarks. The night had fallen, the moon had not yet risen, and yet Aramis looked incessantly towards Belle-Isle. Yves then approached the captain who had returned to take his post in the stern, and said, in a low and humble voice, "What course are we to follow, captain?"

"We take what course monseigneur pleases," replied the officer.

Aramis passed the night leaning upon the bulwarks. Yves, on approaching him the next morning, remarked, that "the night must have been very humid, for the wood upon which the Bishop's head had rested, was soaked with dew." Who knows!—that dew was, perhaps, the first tears that had ever fallen from the eyes of Aramis!

What epitaph would have been worth that? Good Porthos!

80

THE ROUND OF M. DE GESVRES

D'ARTAGNAN was not accustomed to resistances like that he had just experienced. He returned, profoundly irritated, to Nantes. Irritation with this vigorous man vented itself in an impetuous attack, which few people, hitherto, were they King, were they giants, had been able to resist. D'Artagnan, trembling with rage, went straight to the castle, and asked to speak to the King. It might be about seven o'clock in the morning, and, since his arrival at Nantes, the King had been an early riser. But, on arriving at the little corridor with which we are acquainted, d'Artagnan found M. de Gesvres, who stopped him very politely, telling him not to speak too loud and disturb the King. "Is the King asleep?" said d'Artagnan—"well, I will let him sleep. But about what o'clock do you suppose he will rise?"

"Oh! in about two hours; the King has been up all night."

D'Artagnan took his hat again, bowed to M. de Gesvres, and returned to his own apartments. He came back at half-past nine, and was told that the King was at breakfast. "That will just suit me," said d'Artagnan, "I will talk to the King while he is eating."

M. de Brienne reminded d'Artagnan that the King would not receive anyone during his repasts.

"But," said d'Artagnan, looking askant at Brienne, "you do not know, perhaps, monsieur, that I have the privilege of entrée anywhere, and at any hour."

Brienne took the hand of the captain kindly, and said, "Not at Nantes, dear Monsieur d'Artagnan. The King in this journey has changed everything."

D'Artagnan, a little softened, asked about what o'clock the King would have finished his breakfast.

"We don't know."

"How—don't know! What does that mean? You don't know how much time the King devotes to eating? It is generally an hour; and, if we admit that the air of the Loire gives an additional appetite, we will extend it to an hour and a half; that is enough, I think. I will wait where I am."

"Oh! dear Monsieur d'Artagnan, the order is, not to allow any person to remain in this corridor; I am on guard for that purpose."

D'Artagnan felt his anger mounting a second time to his brain. He went out quickly for fear of complicating the affair by a display of ill-humour. As soon as he was out he began to reflect. "The King," said he, "will not receive me, that is evident. The young man is angry; he is afraid of the words I may speak to him. Yes; but in the meantime, Belle-Isle is besieged, and my two friends are taken or killed. Poor Porthos! As to master Aramis, he is always full of resources, and I am quite easy on his account. But, no, no; Porthos is not yet an invalid and Aramis is not yet in his dotage. The one with his arm, the other with his imagination, will find work for His Majesty's soldiers. Who knows if these brave men may not get up for the edification of His Most Christian Majesty a little bastion of Saint-Gervais! I don't despair of it. They have cannon and a garrison. And yet," continued d'Artagnan, "I don't know whether it would not be better to stop the combat. For myself alone, I will not put up with either surly looks, or treason, on the part of the King; but for my friends, rebuffs, insults, I have a right to receive everything. Shall I go to M. Colbert? Now there is a man whom I must acquire the habit of terrifying. I will go to M. Colbert." And d'Artagnan set forward bravely to find M. Colbert, but he was told he was working with the King, at the castle of Nantes. "Good," cried he, "the times are returned in which I measured my steps from M. de Tréville to the Cardinal, from the Cardinal to the Queen, from the Queen to Louis XIII. Truly is it said, that men, in growing old, become children again!—to the castle, then!" He returned thither. M. de Lyonne was coming out. He gave d'Artagnan both hands, but told him that the King had been busy all the preceding evening and all night, and that orders had been given that no one should be admitted.

"Not even the captain who takes the order," cried d'Artagnan. "I think that is rather too strong."

"Not even he," said M. de Lyonne.

"Since that is the case," replied d'Artagnan, wounded to the heart; "since the captain of the musketeers, who has always entered the King's chamber, is no longer allowed to enter it, his cabinet, or his *salle-à-manger* : either the King is dead, or his captain is in disgrace. In either case, he can no longer want him. Do me the favour then, M. de Lyonne, who are in favour, to return and tell the King plainly, I send him my resignation."

"D'Artagnan, beware of what you are doing!"

"For friendship's sake, go!" and he pushed him gently towards the cabinet.

"Well, I will go," said Lyonne.

D'Artagnan waited, walking about the corridor in no enviable mood. Lyonne returned. "Well, what did the King say?" exclaimed d'Artagnan.

"He simply answered, 'That is well,'" replied Lyonne.

"'That is well!'" said the captain, with an explosion. "That is to say, that he accepts it? Good! Now, then, I am free! I am only a plain citizen, M. de Lyonne. I have the pleasure of bidding you good-bye! Farewell, castle, corridor, antechamber! a *bourgeois*, about to breathe at liberty, takes his farewell of you."

And without waiting longer, the captain sprang from the terrace down the staircase, where he had picked up the fragments of Gourville's letter. Five minutes after, he was at the hostelry, where, according to the custom of all great officers who have lodgings at the castle, he had taken what was called his city-chamber. But when he arrived there, instead of throwing off his sword and cloak, he took his pistols, put his money into a large leather purse, sent for his horses from the castle stables, and gave orders for reaching Vannes during the night. Everything went according to his wishes. At eight o'clock in the evening, he was putting his foot in the stirrup, when M. de Gesvres appeared at the head of twelve guards in front of the hostelry. D'Artagnan saw all from the corner of his eye; he could not fail seeing thirteen men and thirteen horses. But he feigned not to observe anything, and was about to put his horse in motion. Gesvres rode up to him, "Monsieur d'Artagnan," said he, aloud.

"Ah, Monsieur de Gesvres! good evening!"

"One would say you were getting on horseback."

"More than that,—I am mounted, as you see."

"It is fortunate I have met with you."

"Were you looking for me, then?"

"*Mon dieu!* yes."

"On the part of the King, I will wager?"

"Yes."

"As I, three days ago, went in search of M. Fouquet?"

"Oh!"

"Nonsense! It is of no use being delicate with me; that is all labour lost. Tell me at once you are come to arrest me."

"To arrest you,—good heavens! no."

"Why do you accost me with twelve horsemen at your heels, then?"

"I am making my round."

"That isn't bad! And so you pick me up in that round, eh?"

"I don't pick you up; I meet with you, and I beg you to come with me."

"Where?"

"To the King."

"Good!" said d'Artagnan, with a bantering air; "the King has nothing to do at last!"

"For Heaven's sake, captain," said M. de Gesvres, in a low voice to the musketeer, "do not compromise yourself! these men hear you."

D'Artagnan laughed aloud, and replied, "March! People who are arrested are placed between the six first guards and the six last."

"But as I do not arrest you," said M. de Gesvres, "you will march behind, with me, if you please."

"Well," said d'Artagnan, "that is very polite, Duc, and you are right in being so; for if ever I had had to make my rounds near your *chambre-de-ville*, I should have been courteous to you, I assure you, by the faith of a gentleman! Now, one favour more: what does the King want with me?"

"Oh, the King is furious!"

"Very well! the King, who has thought it worth while to be furious, may take the trouble of getting calm again; that is all. I shan't die of that, I will swear."

"No, but——"

"But—I shall be sent to keep company with poor M. Fouquet. *Mordioux!* That is a gallant man, a worthy man! We shall live very sociably together, I will be bound."

"Here we are at our place of destination," said the Duc. "Captain, for Heaven's sake be calm with the King!"

"Ah, ah! you are playing the brave man with me, Duc!" said d'Artagnan, throwing one of his defiant glances over Gesvres. "I have been told that you are ambitious of uniting your guards with my musketeers. This strikes me as a capital opportunity."

"I will take devilish good care not to avail myself of it, captain."

"And why not?"

"Oh, for many reasons—in the first place, for this: If I were to succeed you in the musketeers, after having arrested you——"

"Ah! then, you admit you have arrested me?"

"No, I don't."

"Say met me, then. So, you were saying, *if* you were to succeed me, after having arrested me?"

"Your musketeers, at the first exercise with ball cartridges, would all fire towards me, by mistake."

"Ah! as to that I won't say; for the fellows do love me a little."

Gesvres made d'Artagnan pass in first, and took him straight to the cabinet where the King was waiting for his captain of the musketeers, and placed himself behind his colleague in the ante-chamber. The King could be heard distinctly, speaking aloud to Colbert, in the same cabinet where Colbert might have heard, a few days before, the King speaking aloud with M. d'Artagnan. The guards remained as a mounted piquet before the principal gate; and the report was quickly spread through the city, that the captain of the musketeers had just been arrested by order of the King. Then these men were seen to be in motion, as in the good old times of Louis XIII. and M. de Tréville; groups were formed, the staircases were filled; vague murmurs, issuing from the courts below, came rolling up to the upper storeys, like the hoarse moanings of the tide-waves. M. de Gesvres became very uneasy. He looked at his guards, who, after being interrogated by the musketeers who had just got among the ranks, began to shun them with a manifestation of uneasiness. D'Artagnan was certainly less disturbed than M. de Gesvres, the captain of the guards, was. As soon as he entered, he had seated himself on the ledge of a window, whence, with his eagle glance, he saw all that was going on, without the least emotion. None of the progress of the fermentation which had manifested itself at the report of his arrest had escaped him. He foresaw the moment when the explosion would take place; and we know that his previsions were pretty correct.

"It would be very whimsical," thought he, "if, this evening, my prætorians should make me King of France. How I should laugh!"

But, at the height, all was stopped. Guards, musketeers, officers, soldiers, murmurs and uneasinesses, all dispersed, vanished, died away; no more tempest, no more menace, no more sedition. One word had calmed all the waves. The King had desired Brienne to say, "Hush, messieurs! you disturb the King."

D'Artagnan sighed. "All is over!" said he; "the musketeers of the present day are not those of His Majesty Louis XIII. All is over."

527

"Monsieur d'Artagnan to the King's apartment," cried an usher.

81

KING LOUIS XIV.

THE King was seated in his cabinet, with his back turned towards the door of entrance. In front of him was a mirror, in which, while turning over his papers, he could see with a glance those who came in. He did not take any notice of the entrance of d'Artagnan, but laid over his letters and plans the large silk cloth which he made use of to conceal his secrets from the importunate. D'Artagnan understood his play, and kept in the background; so that, at the end of a minute, the King, who heard nothing and saw nothing but with the corner of his eye, was obliged to cry, "Is not M. d'Artagnan there?"

"I am here, sire," replied the musketeer, advancing.

"Well, monsieur," said the King, fixing his clear eye upon d'Artagnan. "what have you to say to me?"

"I, sire!" replied the latter, who watched the first blow of his adversary to make a good retort; "I have nothing to say to your Majesty, unless it be that you have caused me to be arrested, and here I am."

The King was going to reply that he had not had d'Artagnan arrested, but the sentence appeared too much like an excuse, and he was silent. D'Artagnan likewise preserved an obstinate silence.

"Monsieur," at length resumed the King, "what did I charge you to go and do at Belle-Isle? Tell me, if you please."

The King while speaking these words looked fixedly at his captain. Here d'Artagnan was too fortunate; the King seemed to place the game in his hands.

"I believe," replied he, "that your Majesty does me the honour to ask what I went to Belle-Isle to do?"

"Yes, monsieur."

"Well! sire, I know nothing about it; it is not of me that question should be asked, but of that infinite number of officers of all kinds, to whom have been given an infinite number of orders of all kinds, whilst to me, head of the expedition, nothing precise was ordered."

The King was wounded; he showed it by his reply. "Monsieur," said he, "orders have only been given to such as were judged faithful."

"And, therefore, I have been astonished, sire," retorted the musketeer, "that a captain like myself, who ranks with a marshal of France, should have found himself under the orders of five or six lieutenants or majors, good to make spies of possibly, but not at all fit to conduct warlike expeditions. It was upon this subject I came to demand an explanation of your Majesty, when I found the door closed against me, which, the last insult offered to a brave man, has led me to quit your Majesty's service."

"Monsieur," replied the King, "you still believe you are living in an age when Kings were, as you complain of having been, under the orders and at the discretion of their inferiors. You appear too much to forget that a king owes an account of his actions to none but God."

"I forget nothing at all, sire," said the musketeer, wounded by this lesson. "Besides, I do not see in what an honest man, when he asks of his King how he has ill served him, offends him."

"You have ill-served me, monsieur, by taking part with my enemies against me."

"Who are your enemies, sire?"

"The men I sent you to fight with."

"Two men the enemies of the whole of your Majesty's army! That is incredible!"

"You have no power to judge of my will."

"But I have to judge of my own friendships, sire."

"He who serves his friends, does not serve his master."

"I have so well understood that, sire, that I have respectfully offered your Majesty my resignation."

"And I have accepted it, monsieur," said the King. "Before being separated from you, I was willing to prove to you that I know how to keep my word."

"Your Majesty has kept more than your word, for your Majesty has had me arrested," said d'Artagnan, with his cold bantering air; "you did not promise me that, sire."

The King would not condescend to perceive the pleasantry, and continued seriously, "You see, monsieur," said he, "to what your disobedience has forced me."

"My disobedience!" cried d'Artagnan, red with anger.

"That is the mildest name I can find," pursued the King. "My idea was to take and punish rebels; was I bound to enquire whether these rebels were your friends or not?"

"But I was," replied d'Artagnan. "It was a cruelty on your Majesty's part to send me to take my friends and lead them to your gibbets."

"It was a trial I had to make, monsieur, of pretended servants, who eat my bread and ought to defend my person. The trial has succeeded ill, Monsieur d'Artagnan."

"For one bad servant your Majesty loses," said the musketeer, with bitterness, "there are ten who have, on that same day, gone through their ordeal. Listen to me, sire; I am not accustomed to that service. Mine is a rebel sword when I am required to do ill. It was ill to send me in pursuit of two men whose lives M. Fouquet, your Majesty's preserver, had implored you to save. Still further, these men were my friends. They did not attack your Majesty, they succumbed to a blind anger. Besides, why were they not allowed to escape? What crime had they committed? I admit that you may contest with me the right of judging of their conduct. But why suspect me before the action? Why surround me with spies? Why disgrace me before the army? Why me, in whom you have to this time showed the most entire confidence—me, who for thirty years have been attached to your person, and have given you a thousand proofs of devotedness—for it must be said, now that I am accused—why reduce me to see three thousand of the King's soldiers march in battle against two men?"

"One would say you have forgotten what these men have done to me!" said the King, in a hollow voice, "and that it was no merit of theirs that I was not lost."

"Sire, one would say that you forget I was there."

"Enough, Monsieur d'Artagnan, enough of these dominating interests which arise to keep the sun from my interests. I am founding a state in which there shall be but one master, as I promised you formerly; the moment is come for keeping my promise. You wish to be, according to your tastes or your friendships, free to destroy my plans, and save my enemies? I will thwart you or will leave you—seek a more compliant master. I know full well that another king would not conduct himself as I do, and would allow himself to be dominated over by you, at the risk of sending you some day to keep company with M. Fouquet and the others; but I have a good memory, and for me, services are sacred titles to gratitude, to impunity. You shall only have this lesson, Monsieur d'Artagnan, as the punishment of your want of discipline, and I will not imitate my predecessors in their anger, not having imitated them in their favour. And, then, other reasons make me act mildly towards you; in the first place because you are a man of sense, a man of great sense, a man of heart, and that you will be a good servant for him who shall have mastered you; secondly, because you will cease to have any motives for insubordination. Your friends are destroyed or ruined by me. These supports upon which your capricious mind instinctively relied I have made to disappear.

At this moment, my soldiers have taken or killed the rebels of Belle-Isle."

D'Artagnan became pale. "Taken or killed!" cried he. "Oh! sire, if you thought what you tell me, if you were sure you were telling me the truth, I should forget all that is just, all that is magnanimous in your words, to call you a barbarous king, and an unnatural man. But I pardon you these words," said he, smiling with pride; "I pardon them to a young prince who does not know, who cannot comprehend what such names as M. d'Herblay, M. du Vallon, and myself are. Taken or killed! Ah! ah! sire! tell me, if the news is true, how much it has cost you in men and money. We will then reckon if the game has been worth the stakes."

As he spoke thus, the King went up to him in great anger, and said, "Monsieur d'Artagnan, your replies are those of a rebel! Tell me! if you please, who is King of France? Do you know any other?"

"Sire," replied the captain of the musketeers coldly, "I very well remember that one morning at Vaux, you addressed that question to many people who did not answer to it, whilst I, on my part, did answer to it. If I recognised my King on that day, when the thing was not easy, I think it would be useless to ask it of me now, when your Majesty is alone with me."

At these words Louis cast down his eyes. It appeared to him that the shade of the unfortunate Philippe passed between d'Artagnan and himself, to evoke the remembrance of that terrible adventure. Almost at the same moment an officer entered and placed a despatch in the hands of the King, who, in his turn, changed colour while reading it.

"Monsieur," said he, "what I learn here you would know later; it is better I should tell you, and that you should learn it from the mouth of your King. A battle has taken place at Belle-Isle."

"Oh! ah!" said d'Artagnan, with a calm air, though his heart beat enough to break through his chest. "Well, sire!"

"Well, monsieur—and I have lost a hundred and ten men."

A beam of joy and pride shone in the eyes of d'Artagnan. "And the rebels?" said he.

"The rebels have fled," said the King.

D'Artagnan could not restrain a cry of triumph. "Only," added the King, "I have a fleet which closely blockades Belle-Isle, and I am certain no barque can escape."

"So that," said the musketeer, brought back to his dismal ideas, "if these two gentlemen are taken——"

"They will be hanged," said the King quietly.

"And do they know it?" replied d'Artagnan, repressing his trembling.

"They know it, because you must have told them yourself; and all the country knows it."

"Then, sire, they will never be taken alive, I will answer for that."

"Ah!" said the King negligently, and taking up his letter again. "Very well, they will be had dead then, Monsieur d'Artagnan, and that will come to the same thing, since I should only take them to have them hanged."

D'Artagnan wiped the sweat which flowed from his brow.

"I have told you," pursued Louis XIV., "that I would one day be an affectionate, generous, and constant master. You are now the only man of former times worthy of my anger or my friendship. I will not be sparing of either to you, according to your conduct. Could you serve a king, Monsieur d'Artagnan, who should have a hundred kings his equals in the kingdom? Could I, tell me, do with such weakness, the great things I meditate? Have you ever seen an artist effect solid works with a rebellious instrument? Far from us, monsieur, these old leavens of feudal abuses! The Fronde which threatened to ruin the monarchy, has emancipated it.* I am master at home, Captain d'Artagnan, and I shall have servants who, wanting, perhaps, your genius, will carry devotedness and obedience up to heroism. Of what consequence, I ask you, of what consequence is it that God has given no genius to arms and legs? It is to the head he has given it, and the head, you know, all the rest obey. I am the head."

D'Artagnan started. Louis XIV. continued as if he had seen nothing, although this emotion had not at all escaped him. "Now let us conclude between us two that bargain which I promised to make with you one day when you found me very little at Blois. Do me justice, monsieur, when you think that I do not make any one pay for the tears of shame I then shed. Look around you; lofty heads have bowed. Bow yours, or choose the exile that will best suit you. Perhaps, when reflecting upon it, you will find that this king is a generous heart, who reckons sufficiently upon your loyalty to allow you to leave him dissatisfied, when you possess a great state secret. You are a brave man; I know you to be so. Why have you judged me prematurely? Judge me from this day forward, d'Artagnan, and be as severe as you please."

D'Artagnan remained bewildered, mute, undecided for the first time in his life. He had just found an adversary worthy of him. This was no longer trick, it was calculation; it was no longer violence, it was strength; it was no longer passion, it was will; it was no longer boasting, it was council. This young man who had brought down Fouquet, and could do without d'Artagnan, deranged all the somewhat headstrong calculations of the musketeer.

"Come, let us see what stops you," said the King kindly. You have given in your resignation: shall I refuse to accept it? I admit that it may be hard for an old captain to recover his good humour."

"Oh!" replied d'Artagnan, in a melancholy tone, "that is not my most serious care. I hesitate to take back my resignation because I am old in comparison with you, and that I have habits difficult to abandon. Henceforward you must have courtiers who know how to amuse you—madmen who will get themselves killed to carry out what you call your great works. Great they will be, I feel—but, if by chance I should not think them so? I have seen war, sire, I have seen peace; I have served Richelieu and Mazarin; I have been scorched, with your father, at the fire of Rochelle; riddled with thrusts like a sieve, having made a new skin ten times, as serpents do. After affronts and injustices, I have a command which was formerly something, because it gave the bearer the right of speaking as he liked to his king. But your captain of the musketeers will henceforward be an officer guarding the lower doors. Truly, sire, if that is to be the employment from this time, seize the opportunity of our being on good terms to take it from me. Do not imagine that I bear malice; no, you have tamed me, as you say; but it must be confessed that in taming me you have lessened me; by bowing me you have convicted me of weakness. If you knew how well it suits me to carry my head high, and what a pitiful mien I shall have while scenting the dust of your carpets! Oh! sire, I regret sincerely, and you will regret as I do, those times when the King of France saw in his vestibules all those insolent gentlemen, lean, always swearing—cross-grained mastiffs, who could bite mortally in days of battle. Those men were the best of courtiers for the hand which fed them—they would lick it; but for the hand that struck them, oh! the bite that followed! A little gold on the lace of their cloaks, a fine upstanding figure, a little sprinkling of grey in their dry hair, and you will behold the handsome dukes and peers, the haughty marshals of France. But why should I tell you all this? The King is my master; he wills that I should make verses, he wills that I should polish the mosaics of his antechambers with satin shoes. *Mordioux!* that is difficult, but I have got over greater difficulties than that. I will do it. Why should I do it? Because I love money?—I have enough. Because I am ambitious? —my career is bounded. Because I love the court? No. I will remain because I have been accustomed for thirty years to go and take the orderly word of the King, and to have said to me, 'Good-evening, d'Artagnan,' with a smile I did not beg for! That smile I will beg for! Are you content, sire?" And d'Artagnan bowed his silvered head, upon which the smiling King placed his white hand, with pride.

"Thanks, my old servant, my faithful friend," said he. "As, reckoning from this day, I have no longer any enemies in France; it remains with me to send you to a foreign field to gather your marshal's baton. Depend upon me for finding you an opportunity. In the meanwhile, eat of my best bread, and sleep tranquilly."

"That is all kind and well!" said d'Artagnan, much agitated. "But those poor men at Belle-Isle? One of them, in particular—so good! so brave! so true!"

"Do you ask their pardon of me?"

"Upon my knees, sire."

"Well! then, go and take it to them, if it be still time. But do you answer for them?"

"With my life, sire!"

"Go then. To-morrow I set out for Paris. Return by that time, for I do not wish you to leave me in future."

"Be assured of that, sire," said d'Artagnan, kissing the royal hand.

And, with a heart swelling with joy, he rushed out of the castle on his way to Belle-Isle.

82

THE FRIENDS OF M. FOUQUET

THE King had returned to Paris, and with him d'Artagnan, who, in twenty-four hours, having made with the greatest care all possible inquiries at Belle-Isle, had learned nothing of the secret so well kept by the heavy rock of Locmaria, which had fallen on the heroic Porthos. The captain of the musketeers only knew what these two valiant men,—what those two friends, whose defence he had so nobly taken up, whose lives he had so earnestly endeavoured to save—aided by three faithful Bretons, had accomplished against a whole army. He had been able to see, launched on to the neigh-bouring heath, the human remains which had stained with blood the stones scattered among the flowering broom. He learned also that a barque had been seen far out at sea, and that, like a bird of prey, a royal vessel had pursued, overtaken, and devoured this poor little bird which was flying with rapid wings. But there d'Artagnan's certainties ended. The field of conjecture was thrown open at this boundary. Now, what could he conjecture? The vessel had not returned. It is true that a brisk wind had prevailed for three days; but the corvette was known to be a good sailer and solid in its timbers; it could not fear gales of wind, and it ought, according to the calculation of d'Artagnan, to either have returned to Brest, or come back to the mouth of the Loire. Such were the news, ambiguous, it is true, but in some degree reassuring to him personally, which d'Artagnan brought to Louis XIV., when the King, followed by all the court, returned to Paris.

Louis, satisfied with his success, Louis—more mild and more affable since he felt himself more powerful—had not ceased for an instant to ride close to the carriage door of Mademoiselle de la Vallière. Everybody had been anxious to amuse the two Queens, so as to make them forget this abandonment of the son and husband. Everything breathed of the future; the past was nothing to anybody. Only that past came like a painful and bleeding wound to the hearts of some tender and devoted spirits. Scarcely was the King re-installed in Paris, when he received a touching proof of this. Louis XIV. had just risen and taken his first repast, when his captain of the musketeers presented himself before him. D'Artagnan was pale and looked unhappy. The King, at the first glance, perceived the change in a countenance generally so unconcerned. "What is the matter, d'Artagnan?" said he.

"Sire, a great misfortune has happened to me."

"Good heavens! what is that?"

"Sire, I have lost one of my friends, M. du Vallon, in the affair of Belle-Isle."

And while speaking these words, d'Artagnan fixed his falcon eye upon Louis XIV. to catch the first feeling that would show itself.

"I knew it," replied the King quietly.

"You knew it, and did not tell me!" cried the musketeer.

"To what good? Your grief, my friend, is so respectable. It was my duty to treat it kindly. To have informed you of this misfortune, which I knew would pain you so greatly, d'Artagnan, would have been, in your eyes, to have triumphed over you. Yes, I knew that M. du Vallon had buried himself beneath the rocks of Locmaria; I knew that M. d'Herblay had taken one of my vessels with its crew, and had compelled it to convey him to Bayonne.* But I was willing you should learn these matters in a direct manner, in order that you might be convinced my friends are with me respected and sacred; that always in me the man will immolate himself to men, whilst the King is so often found to sacrifice men to his majesty and power."

"But, sire, how could you know?"

"How do yourself know, d'Artagnan?"

"By this letter, sire, which M. d'Herblay, free and out of danger, writes me from Bayonne."

"Look here," said the King, drawing from a casket placed upon the table close to the seat upon which d'Artagnan was leaning, "here is a letter copied exactly from that of M. d'Herblay. Here is the very letter which Colbert placed in my hands a week before you received yours. I am well served, you may perceive."

"Yes, sire," murmured the musketeer, "you were the only man whose fortune was capable of dominating the fortunes and strength of my two friends. You have used it, sire, but you will not abuse it, will you?"

"D'Artagnan," said the King, with a smile beaming with kindness, "I could have M. d'Herblay carried off from the territories of the King of Spain, and brought here alive to inflict justice upon him. But, d'Artagnan, be assured I will not yield to this first and natural impulse. He is free; let him continue free."

"Oh, sire! you will not always remain so clement, so noble, so generous as you have shown yourself with respect to me and M. d'Herblay; you will have about you counsellors who will cure you of that weakness."

"No, d'Artagnan, you are mistaken when you accuse my council of urging me to pursue rigorous measures. The advice to spare M. d'Herblay comes from Colbert himself."

"Oh, sire!" said d'Artagnan, extremely surprised.

"As for you," continued the King, with a kindness very uncommon with him, "I have several pieces of good news to announce to you; but you shall know them, my dear captain, the moment I have made my accounts all straight. I have said that I wished to make, and would make, your fortune; that promise will soon be a reality."

"A thousand times thanks, sire! I can wait. But I implore you, whilst I go and practise patience, that your Majesty will deign to notice those poor people who have for so long a time besieged your antechamber, and come humbly to lay a petition at your feet."

"Who are they?"

"Enemies of your Majesty." The King raised his head.

"Friends of M. Fouquet," added d'Artagnan.

"Their names?"

"M. Gourville, M. Pélisson, and a poet, M. Jean de la Fontaine."

The King took a moment to reflect. "What do they want?"

"I do not know."

"How do they appear?"

"In great affliction."

"What do they say?"

"Nothing."

"What do they do?"

"They weep."

"Let them come in," said the King, with a serious brow.

D'Artagnan turned rapidly on his heel, raised the tapestry which closed the entrance to the royal chamber, and directing his voice to the adjoining room, cried, "Introduce!"

The three men d'Artagnan had named soon appeared at the door of the cabinet in which were the King and his captain. A profound silence prevailed. The courtiers, at the approach of the friends of the unfortunate Surintendant of the Finances, the courtiers, we say, drew back, as if fearful of being infected by contagion with disgrace and misfortune. D'Artagnan, with a quick step, came forward to take by the hand the unhappy men who stood trembling at the door of the cabinet; he led them to the front of the chair of the King, who, having placed himself in the embrasure of a window, awaited the moment of presentation, and was preparing himself to give the supplicants a rigorously diplomatic reception.

The first of the friends of Fouquet that advanced was Pélisson. He did not weep, but his tears were only restrained that the King might the better hear his voice and prayer. Gourville bit his lips to check his tears, out of respect for the King. La Fontaine buried his face in his handkerchief, and the only signs of life he gave were the convulsive motions of his shoulders, raised by his sobs.

The King had preserved all his dignity. His countenance was impassible. He had even maintained the frown which had appeared when d'Artagnan had announced his enemies to him. He made a gesture which signified, "Speak," and he remained standing, with his eyes searchingly fixed upon these desponding men. Pélisson bowed down to the ground, and La Fontaine knelt as people do in churches. This obstinate silence, disturbed only by such dismal sighs and groans, began to excite in the King, not compassion, but impatience.

"Monsieur Pélisson," said he, in a sharp dry tone, "Monsieur Gourville, and you Monsieur——" and he did not name La Fontaine, "I cannot, without sensible displeasure, see you come to plead for one of the greatest criminals that it is the duty of my justice to punish. A king does not allow himself to be softened but by tears and remorse; the tears of the innocent, and remorse of the guilty. I have no faith either in the remorse of M. Fouquet, or the tears of his friends, because the one is tainted to the very heart, and the others ought to dread coming to offend me in my own palace. For these reasons, I beg you, Monsieur Pélisson, Monsieur Gourville, and you Monsieur—— to say nothing that will not plainly proclaim the respect you have for my will."

"Sire," replied Pélisson, trembling at these terrible words, "we have come to say nothing to your Majesty that is not the most profound expression of the most sincere respect and love which are due to a King from all his subjects. Your Majesty's justice is redoubtable; every one must yield to the sentences it pronounces. We respectfully bow before it. Far from us be the idea of coming to defend him who has had the misfortune to offend your Majesty. He who has incurred your displeasure may be a friend of ours, but he is an enemy to the State. We abandon him, but with tears, to the severity of the King."

"Besides," interrupted the King, calmed by that supplicating voice, and those persuasive words, "my Parliament will decide. I do not strike without having weighed a crime; my justice does not wield the sword without having employed the scales."

"Therefore have we every confidence in that impartiality of the King, and hope to make our feeble voices heard, with the consent of your Majesty, when the hour for defending an accused friend shall strike for us."

"In that case, messieurs, what do you ask of me?" said the King, with his most imposing air.

"Sire," continued Pélisson, "the accused leaves a wife and a family. The little property he had was scarcely sufficient to pay his debts, and Madame Fouquet, since the captivity of her husband, is abandoned by everybody. The hand of your Majesty strikes like the hand of God. When the Lord sends the curse of leprosy or pestilence into a family, every one flies and shuns the abode of the leprous or the plague-stricken. Sometimes, but very rarely, a generous physician alone ventures to approach the accursed threshold, passes it with courage, and exposes his life to combat death. He is the last resource of the dying, he is the instrument of heavenly mercy. Sire, we supplicate you, with clasped hands and bended knees, as a divinity is supplicated! Madame Fouquet has no longer any friends, no longer any support; she weeps in her poor, deserted house, abandoned by all those who besieged its doors in the hour of prosperity; she has neither credit nor hope left. At least the unhappy wretch upon whom your anger falls receives from you, however culpable he may be, the daily bread which is moistened by his tears. As much afflicted, more destitute than her husband, Madame Fouquet—she who had the honour to receive your Majesty at her table—Madame Fouquet, the wife of the ancient Surintendant of your Majesty's Finances, Madame Fouquet has no longer bread.''

Here the mortal silence which enchained the breath of Pélisson's two friends was broken by an outburst of sobs; and d'Artagnan, whose chest heaved at hearing this humble prayer, turned round towards the angle of the cabinet to bite his moustache and conceal his sighs.

The King had preserved his eye dry and his countenance severe; but the colour had mounted to his cheeks, and the firmness of his looks was visibly diminished.

"What do you wish?" said he, in an agitated voice.

"We come humbly to ask your Majesty," replied Pélisson, upon whom emotion was fast gaining, "to permit us, without incurring the displeasure of your Majesty, to lend to Madame Fouquet two thousand pistoles collected among the old friends of her husband, in order that the widow may not stand in need of the necessaries of life."

At the word *widow*, pronounced by Pélisson whilst Fouquet was still alive, the King turned very pale;—his pride fell; pity rose from his heart to his lips; he cast a softened look upon the men who knelt sobbing at his feet.

"God forbid!" said he, "that I should confound the innocent with the guilty. They know me but ill who doubt my mercy towards the weak. I strike none but the arrogant. Do, messieurs, do all that your hearts counsel you to assuage the grief of Madame Fouquet. Go, messieurs, go."

The three men arose in silence with dried eyes. The tears had been dried up by contact with their burning cheeks and eyelids. They had not the strength to address their thanks to the King, who himself cut short their solemn reverences by entrenching himself suddenly behind the chair.

D'Artagnan remained alone with the King. "Well," said he, approaching the young prince, who interrogated him with his look. "Well, my master! If you had not the device which belongs to your sun, I would recommend you one which M. Conrart should translate into Latin: 'Mild with the lowly; rough with the strong.'"

The King smiled, and passed into the next apartment, after having said to d'Artagnan, "I give you the leave of absence you must want to put the affairs of your friend the late M. du Vallon in order."

83

PORTHOS'S WILL

At Pierrefonds everything was in mourning. The courts were deserted—the stables closed—the parterres neglected. In the basins, the fountains, formerly so spreading, noisy, and sparkling, had stopped of themselves. Along the roads around the château came a few grave personages mounted upon mules or farm nags. These were country neighbours, curés, and bailiffs of adjacent estates. All these people entered the château silently, gave their nags to a melancholy-looking groom, and directed their steps, conducted by a huntsman in black, to the great dining-room, where Mousqueton received them at the door. Mousqueton had become so thin in two days that his clothes moved upon him like sheaths which are too large and in which the blades of swords dance about at each motion. His face, composed of red and white, like that of the Madonna of Vandyke, was furrowed by two silver rivulets which had dug their beds in his cheeks, as full formerly as they had become flabby since his grief began. At each fresh arrival, Mousqueton found fresh tears, and it was pitiful to see him press his throat with his fat hand to keep from bursting into sobs and lamentations. All these visits were for the purpose of hearing the reading of Porthos's will, announced for that day, and at which all the covetousness and all the friendships connected with the defunct were anxious to be present, as he had left no relation behind him.

The visitors took their places as they arrived; and the great room had just been closed when the clock had struck twelve, the hour fixed for the reading of the important document. Porthos's procureur—and that was naturally the successor of Master Coquenard—commenced by slowly unfolding the vast parchment upon which the powerful hand of Porthos had traced his sovereign will. The seal broken—the spectacles put on—the preliminary cough having sounded—every one opened his ears. Mousqueton had squatted himself in a corner, the better to weep, and the better to hear. All at once the folding-doors of the great room, which had been shut, were thrown open as if by a prodigy, and a manly figure appeared upon the threshold, resplendent in the full light of the sun. This was d'Artagnan, who had come alone to the gate, and finding nobody to hold his stirrup, he had tied his horse to a knocker and announced himself. The splendour of the daylight invading the room, the murmur of all present, and, more than all that, the instinct of the faithful dog, drew Mousqueton from his reverie; he raised his head, recognised the old friend of his master, and, howling with grief, he embraced his knees, watering the floor with his tears. D'Artagnan raised up the poor intendant, embraced him as if he had been a brother, and, having nobly saluted the assembly, who all bowed as they whispered to each other his name, he went and took his seat at the extremity of the great carved oak hall, still holding by the hand poor Mousqueton, who was suffocating and sunk down upon the steps. Then the procureur, who, like the rest, was considerably agitated, commenced the reading.

Porthos, after a profession of faith of the most Christian character, asked pardon of his enemies for all the injuries he might have done them. At this paragraph, a ray of inexpressible pride beamed from the eyes of d'Artagnan. He recalled to his mind the old soldier; all those enemies of Porthos brought to the earth by his valiant hand, he reckoned up the numbers of them, and said to himself that Porthos had acted wisely not to detail his enemies or the injuries done to them, or the task would have been too much for the reader. Then came the following enumeration:—

"I possess at this present time, by the grace of God:—

"1. The domain of Pierrefonds, lands, woods, meadows, waters, and forests, surrounded by good walls.

"2. The domain of Bracieux, château, forests, ploughed lands, forming three farms.

"3. The little estate du Vallon, so named because it is in the valley." (Brave Porthos!)

"4. Fifty farms in Touraine, amounting to five hundred acres.

"5. Three mills upon the Cher, bringing in six hundred livres each.

"6. Three fish-pools in Berry, producing two hundred livres a year.

"As to my personal or movable property, so called because it can be moved, as is so well explained by my learned friend the Bishop of Vannes——" (D'Artagnan shuddered at the dismal remembrance attached to that name)—the procureur continued imperturbably—"they consist—1. In goods which I cannot detail here for want of room, and which furnish all my châteaux or houses, but of which the list is drawn up by my intendant."

Every one turned his eyes towards Mousqueton, who was absorbed in his grief.

"2. In twenty horses for saddle and draught, which I have particularly at my château of Pierrefonds, and which are called—

Bayard, Roland, Charlemagne, Pépin, Dunois, La Hire, Ogier, Samson, Milo, Nimrod, Urganda, Armida, Falstrade, Dalilah, Rebecca, Yolande, Finette, Grisette, Lisette, and Musette.

"3. In sixty dogs, forming six packs, divide as follows: the first, for the stag; the second, for the wolf; the third, for the wild boar; the fourth, for the hare; and the two others, for setters and protection.

"4. In arms for war and the chase contained in my gallery of arms.

"5. My wines of Anjou, selected for Athos, who liked them formerly; my wines of Burgundy, Champagne, Bordeaux, and Spain, stocking eight cellars and twelve vaults, in my various houses.

"6. My pictures and statues, which are said to be of great value, and which are sufficiently numerous to fatigue the sight.

"7. My library, consisting of six thousand volumes, quite new, and have never been opened.

"8. My silver plate, which is perhaps a little worn, but which ought to weigh from a thousand to twelve hundred pounds, for I had great trouble in lifting the coffer that contained it, and could not carry it more than six times round my chamber.

"9. All these objects, in addition to the table and house linen, are divided in the residences I liked the best."

Here the reader stopped to take breath. Every one sighed, coughed, and redoubled his attention. The procureur resumed:—

"I have lived without having any children, and it is probable I never shall have any, which to me is a cutting grief. And yet I am mistaken, for I have a son, in common with my other friends: that is M. Raoul Auguste Jules de Bragelonne, the true son of M. le Comte de la Fère.

"This young nobleman has appeared to me worthy to succeed to the three valiant gentlemen, of whom I am the friend and the very humble servant."

Here a sharp sound interrupted the reader. It was d'Artagnan's sword, which, slipping from his baldric, had fallen on the sonorous flooring. Every one turned his eyes that way, and saw that a large tear had rolled from the thick lid of d'Artagnan on to his aquiline nose, the luminous edge of which shone, like a crescent enlightened by the sun.

"This is why," continued the procureur, "I have left all my property, movable or immovable, comprised in the above enumerations, to M. le Vicomte Raoul Auguste Jules de Bragelonne, son of M. le Comte de la Fère, to console him for the grief he seems to suffer, and enable him to support his name gloriously."

A long murmur ran through the auditory. The procureur continued, seconded by the flashing eye of d'Artagnan, which, glancing over the assembly, quickly restored the interrupted silence:—

"On condition that M. le Vicomte de Bragelonne do give to M. le Chevalier d'Artagnan, captain of the King's musketeers, whatever the said Chevalier d'Artagnan may demand of my property. On condition that M. le Vicomte de Bragelonne do pay a good pension to M. le Chevalier d'Herblay, my friend, if he should need it in exile. I leave to my intendant Mousqueton all my clothes, of city, war, or chase, to the number of forty-seven suits, with the assurance that he will wear them till they are worn out, for the love of and in remembrance of his master. Moreover, I bequeath to M. le Vicomte de Bragelonne my old servant and faithful friend Mousqueton, already named, providing that the said Vicomte shall so act that Mousqueton shall declare when dying he has never ceased to be happy."

On hearing these words, Mousqueton bowed, pale and trembling; his large shoulders shook convulsively; his countenance, impressed by a frightful grief, appeared from between his icy hands, and the spectators saw him stagger, and hesitate, as if, though wishing to leave the hall, he did not know the way.

"Mousqueton, my good friend," said d'Artagnan, "go and make your preparations. I will take you with me to Athos's house, whither I shall go on leaving Pierrefonds."

Mousqueton made no reply. He scarcely breathed, as if everything in that hall would from that time be foreign. He opened the door, and disappeared slowly.

The procureur finished his reading, after which the greater part of those who had come to hear the last will of Porthos dispersed by degrees, many disappointed, but all penetrated with respect. As to d'Artagnan, left alone, after having received the formal compliments of the procureur, he was lost in admiration of the wisdom of the testator, who had so judiciously bestowed his wealth upon the most necessitous and the most worthy with a delicacy that none among the most refined courtiers and the most noble hearts could have displayed more becomingly. When Porthos enjoined Raoul de Bragelonne to give d'Artagnan all he would ask, he knew well, did that worthy Porthos, that d'Artagnan would ask or take nothing; and, in case he did demand anything, none but himself could say what. Porthos left a pension to Aramis, who, if he should be inclined to ask too much, was checked by the example of d'Artagnan; and that word *exile*, thrown out by the testator, without apparent intention, was it not the most mild, the most exquisite criticism upon that conduct of Aramis which had brought about the death of Porthos? But there was no mention of Athos in the testament of the dead. Could the latter for a moment suppose that the son would not offer the best part to the father? The rough mind of Porthos had judged all these causes, seized all these shades, better than the law, better than custom, better than taste.

"Porthos was a heart," said d'Artagnan to himself, with a sigh. As he made this reflection, he fancied he heard a groan in the room above him; and he thought immediately of poor Mousqueton, whom he felt it was a pleasing duty to divert from his grief. For this purpose he left the hall hastily to seek the worthy intendant, as he had not returned. He ascended the staircase leading to the first storey, and perceived, in Porthos's own chamber, a heap of clothes of all colours and all materials, upon which Mousqueton had laid himself down after heaping them together. It was the legacy of the faithful friend. Those clothes were truly his own; they had been given to him; the hand of Mousqueton was stretched over these relics, which he kissed with all his lips, with all his face, which he covered with his whole body. D'Artagnan approached to console the poor fellow.

"My God!" said he, "he does not stir—he has fainted!"

But d'Artagnan was mistaken—Mousqueton was dead. Dead, like the dog who, having lost his master, comes back to die upon his cloak.

84

THE OLD AGE OF ATHOS

WHILE all these affairs were separating for ever the four musketeers, formerly bound together in a manner that seemed indissoluble, Athos, left alone after the departure of Raoul, began to pay his tribute to that anticipated death which is called the absence of those we love. Returned to his house at Blois, no longer having even Grimaud to receive a poor smile when he passed through the parterre, Athos daily felt the decline of the vigour of a nature which for so long a time had appeared infallible. Age, which had been kept back by the presence of the beloved object, now came on, with its attendant pains and inconveniences. Athos had no longer his son to induce him to walk firmly, with his head erect, as a good example; he had no longer, in those brilliant eyes of the young man, an ever-ardent focus at which to regenerate the fire of his looks. And then, must it be said, that nature, exquisite in its tenderness and its reserve, no longer finding anything that comprehended its feelings, gave itself up to grief with all the warmth of vulgar natures when they give themselves up to joy. The Comte de la Fère, who had remained a young man up to his sixty-second year; the warrior who had preserved his strength in spite of fatigues, his freshness of mind in spite of misfortunes, his mild serenity of soul and body in spite of malady, in spite of Mazarin, in spite of La Vallière; Athos had become an old man in a week, from the moment at which he had lost the support of his latter youth. Still handsome, though bent; noble, but sad; gentle, and tottering under his grey hairs, he sought, since his solitude, the glades where the rays of the sun penetrated through the foliage of the walks. He discontinued all the strong exercises he had enjoyed through life, when Raoul was no longer with him. The servants, accustomed to see him stirring with the dawn at all seasons, were astonished to hear seven o'clock strike before their master had quitted his bed. Athos remained in bed with a book under his pillow, but he did not sleep, neither did he read. Remaining in bed that he might no longer have to carry his body, he allowed his soul and spirit to wander from their envelope, and return to his son, or to God.

His people were sometimes terrified to see him, for hours together, absorbed in a silent reverie, mute and insensible; he no longer heard the timid step of the servant who came to the door of his chamber to watch the sleeping or waking of his master. It often occurred that he forgot that the day had half passed away, that the hours for the two first meals were gone by. Then he was awakened. He rose, descended to his shaded walk, then came out a little into the sun, as if to partake its warmth for a minute with his absent child. And then the dismal, monotonous walk recommenced, until, quite exhausted, he regained the chamber and the bed, his domicile by choice. For several days the comte did not speak a single word. He refused to receive the visits that were paid him, and, during the night, he was seen to relight his lamp, and pass long hours in writing, or examining parchments.

Athos wrote one of these letters to Vannes, another to Fontainebleau; they remained without answers. We know why Aramis had quitted France, and d'Artagnan was travelling from Nantes to Paris, from Paris to Pierrefonds. His *valet-de-chambre* observed that he shortened his walk every day by several turns. The great alley of limes soon became too long for feet that used to traverse it formerly a hundred times a day. The Comte walked feebly as far as the middle trees, seated himself upon a mossy bank which sloped towards a lateral walk, and there awaited the return of his strength, or rather the return of night. Very shortly, a hundred steps exhausted him. At length Athos refused to rise at all; he declined all nourishment, and his terrified people, although he did not complain, although he had a smile on his lips, although he continued to speak with his sweet voice—his people went to Blois in search of the ancient physician of the late Monsieur, and brought him to the Comte de la Fère in such a fashion that he could see the Comte without being himself seen. For this purpose, they placed him in a closet adjoining the chamber of the patient, and implored him not to show himself, in the fear of displeasing their master, who had not asked for a physician. The doctor obeyed; Athos was a sort of model for the gentlemen of the country; Blaisois boasted of possessing this sacred relic of the old French glories. Athos was a great seigneur compared with such nobles as the King improvised by touching with his yellow fecundating sceptre the dried trunks of the heraldric trees of the province.

People respected, we say, if they did not love Athos. The physician could not bear to see his people weep, and to see flock round him the poor of the canton, to whom Athos gave life and consolation by his kind words and his charities. He examined, therefore, from the depths of his hiding-place, the nature of that mysterious malady which bent down and devoured more mortally every day a man but lately so full of life and of a desire to live. He remarked upon the cheeks of Athos the purple of fever, which fires itself and feeds itself; slow fever, pitiless, born in a fold of the heart, sheltering itself behind that rampart, growing from the suffering it engenders, at once cause and effect of a perilous situation. The Comte spoke to nobody, we say; he did not even talk to himself. His thought feared noise; it approached to that degree of over-excitement which borders upon ecstasy. Man thus absorbed, though he does not yet belong to God, already belongs no longer to earth. The doctor remained for several hours studying this painful struggle of the will against a superior power; he was terrified at seeing those eyes always fixed, always directed towards an invisible object; he was terrified at seeing beat with the same movement that heart from which never a sigh arose to vary the melancholy state; sometimes the acuteness of pain creates the hope of the physician. Half a day passed away thus. The doctor formed his resolution like a brave man, like a man of firm mind; he issued suddenly from his place of retreat, and went straight up to Athos, who saw him without evincing more surprise than if he had understood nothing of this apparition.

"Monsieur le Comte, I crave your pardon," said the doctor,

coming up to the patient with open arms; "but I have a reproach to make you—you shall hear me." And he seated himself by the pillow of Athos, who had great trouble in rousing himself from his preoccupation.

"What is the matter, doctor?" asked the Comte, after a silence.

"Why, the matter is, you are ill, monsieur, and have had no advice."

"I! ill!" said Athos, smiling.

"Fever, consumption, weakness, decay, Monsieur le Comte!"

"Weakness!" replied Athos; "is that possible? I do not get up."

"Come, come, Monsieur le Comte, no subterfuges; you are a good Christian?"

"I hope so," said Athos.

"Would you kill yourself?"

"Never, doctor."

"Well! monsieur, you are in a fair way of doing so; to remain thus is suicide; get well! Monsieur le Comte, get well!"

"Of what? Find the disease first. For my part, I never knew myself better; never did the sky appear more blue to me; never did I take more care of my flowers."

"You have a concealed grief."

"Concealed!—not at all; I have the absence of my son, doctor; that is my malady, and I do not conceal it."

"Monsieur le Comte, your son lives; he is strong, he has all the future before him of men of his merit, and of his race; live for him——"

"But I do live, doctor; oh! be satisfied of that," added he, with a melancholy smile; "as long as Raoul lives, it will be plainly known, for as long as he lives, I shall live."

"What do you say?"

"A very simple thing. At this moment, doctor, I leave life suspended in me. A forgetful, dissipated, indifferent life would be above my strength, now I have no longer Raoul with me. You do not ask the lamp to burn when the spark has not enlightened the flame; do not ask me to live amidst noise and light. I vegetate, I prepare myself, I wait. Look, doctor; remember those soldiers we have so often seen together at the ports, where they were waiting to embark; lying down, indifferent, half upon one element, half upon the other; they were neither at the place where the sea was going to carry them, nor at the place where the earth was going to lose them; baggages prepared, minds upon the stretch, looks fixed —they waited. I repeat it—that word is the one which paints my present life. Lying down, like the soldiers, my ear on the stretch for the reports that may reach me, I wish to be ready to set out at the first summons. Who will make me that summons? life or death? God or Raoul? My baggage is packed, my soul is prepared, I await the signal—I wait, doctor, I wait!"

The doctor knew the temper of that mind; he appreciated the strength of that body; he reflected for a moment, told himself that words were useless, remedies absurd, and he left the château, exhorting Athos's servants not to leave him for a moment.

The doctor being gone, Athos evinced neither anger nor vexation at having been disturbed. He did not even desire that all letters that came should be brought to him directly. He knew very well that every distraction which should arrive would be a joy, a hope, which his servants would have paid with their blood to procure him. Sleep had become rare. By intense thinking, Athos forgot himself, for a few hours at most, in a reverie more profound, more obscure than other people would have called a dream. This momentary repose which this forgetfulness afforded the body, fatigued the soul, for Athos lived a double life during these wanderings of his understanding. One night, he dreamt that Raoul was dressing himself in a tent, to go upon an expedition commanded by M. de Beaufort in person. The young man was sad; he clasped his cuirass slowly, and slowly he girded on his sword.

"What is the matter?" asked his father tenderly.

"What afflicts me is the death of Porthos, ever so dear a friend," replied Raoul. "I suffer here of the grief you will feel at home."

And the vision disappeared with the slumber of Athos. At daybreak one of his servants entered his master's apartment, and gave him a letter which came from Spain.

"The writing of Aramis," thought the Comte; and he read.

"Porthos is dead!" cried he, after the first lines. "Oh! Raoul, Raoul! thanks! thou keepest thy promise; thou warnest me!"

And Athos, seized with a mortal sweat, fainted in his bed, without any other cause than his weakness.

THE VISION OF ATHOS

WHEN this fainting of Athos had ceased, the Comte, almost ashamed of having given way before this super-natural event, dressed himself and ordered his horse, determined to ride to Blois, to open more certain correspondence with either Africa, d'Artagnan, or Aramis. In fact, this letter from Aramis informed the Comte de la Fère of the bad success of the expedition of Belle-Isle. It gave him sufficient details of the death of Porthos to move the tender and devoted heart of Athos to its last fibres. Athos wished to go and pay his friend Porthos a last visit. To render this honour to his companion in arms, he meant to send to d'Artagnan, to prevail upon him to recommence the painful voyage to Belle-Isle, to accomplish in his company that sad pilgrimage to the tomb of the giant he had so much loved, then to return to his dwelling to obey that secret influence which was conducting him to eternity by a mysterious road. But scarcely had his joyous servants dressed their master, whom they saw with pleasure preparing himself for a journey which might dissipate his melancholy; scarcely had the Comte's gentlest horse been saddled and brought to the door, than the father of Raoul felt his head become confused, his legs give way, and he clearly perceived the impossibility of going one step farther. He ordered himself to be carried into the sun; they laid him upon his bed of moss, where he passed a full hour before he could recover his spirits. Nothing could be more natural than this weakness after the inert repose of the latter days. Athos took a basin of soup to give him strength, and bathed his dried lips in a glassful of wine he loved the best—that old Anjou wine mentioned by Porthos in his admirable will. Then, refreshed, free in mind, he had his horse brought again; but it required the aid of his servants to mount painfully into the saddle. He did not go a hundred paces; a shivering seized him again at the turning of the road.

"This is very strange!" said he to his *valet-de-chambre*, who accompanied him.

"Let us stop, monsieur—I conjure you!" replied the faithful servant; "how pale you are getting!"

"That will not prevent my pursuing my route, now I have once started," replied the Comte. And he gave his horse his head again. But suddenly, the animal, instead of obeying the thought of his master, stopped. A movement, of which Athos was unconscious, had checked the bit.

"Something," said Athos, "wills that I should go no farther. Support me," added he, stretching out his arms; "quick! come closer! I feel all my muscles relax, and I shall fall from my horse."

The valet had seen the movement made by his master at the moment he received the order. He went up to him quickly, received the Comte in his arms, and as they were not yet sufficiently distant from the house for the servants, who had remained at the door to watch their master's departure, not to perceive the disorder in the usually regular proceeding of the Comte, the valet called his comrades by gestures and voice, and all hastened to his assistance. Athos had gone but a few steps on his return, when he felt himself better again. His strength seemed to revive, and with it the desire to go to Blois. He made his horse turn round; but, at the animal's first steps, he sank again into a state of torpor and anguish.

"Well! decidedly," said he, "it is WILLED that I should stay at home." His people flocked around him; they lifted him from his horse, and carried him as quickly as possible into the house. Everything was soon prepared in his chamber, and they put him to bed.

"You will be sure to remember," said he, disposing himself to sleep, "that I expect letters from Africa this very day."

"Monsieur will no doubt hear with pleasure that Blaisois's son is gone on horseback, to gain an hour over the courier of Blois," replied his *valet-de-chambre*.

"Thank you," said Athos, with his bland smile.

The Comte fell asleep, but his disturbed slumber resembled suffering more than repose. The servant who watched him saw several times the expression of interior torture thrown out upon his features. Perhaps Athos was dreaming. The day passed away. Blaisois's son returned: the courier had brought no news. The Comte reckoned the minutes with despair; he shuddered when those minutes had formed an hour. The idea that he was forgotten seized him once, and brought on a fearful pang of the heart. Everybody in the house had given up all hopes of the courier—his hour had long passed. Four times the express sent to Blois had reiterated his journey, and there was nothing to the address of the Comte. Athos knew that the courier only arrived once a week. Here, then, was a delay of eight mortal days to be endured. He commenced the night in this painful persuasion. All that a sick man, irritated by suffering, can add of melancholy suppositions to probabilities always sad, Athos heaped up during the early hours of this dismal night. The fever rose; it invaded the chest, where the fire soon caught, according to the expression of the physician, who had been brought back from Blois by Blaisois at his last journey. It soon gained the head. The physician made two successive bleedings, which unlodged it, but left the patient very weak, and without power of action in anything but his brain. And yet this redoubtable fever had ceased. It besieged with its last palpitations the stiffened extremities; it ended by yielding as midnight struck.

The physician, seeing the incontestable improvement, returned to Blois, after having ordered some prescriptions, and declared that the Comte was saved. Then commenced for Athos a strange, indefinable state. Free to think, his mind turned towards Raoul, that beloved son. His imagination painted the fields of Africa in the environs of Gigelli, where M. de Beaufort must have landed his army. There were grey rocks, rendered green in certain parts by the waters of the sea, when it lashed the shore in storms and tempests. Beyond, the shore, strewn over with these rocks like tombs, ascended, in form of an amphitheatre, among mastick-trees and cacti, a sort of small town, full of smoke, confused noises and terrified movements. All on a sudden, from the bosom of this smoke arose a flame, which succeeded, by creeping along the houses, in covering the whole surface of the town, and which increased by degrees, uniting in its red vortices tears, cries, arms extended towards heaven.

There was, for a moment, a frightful confusion of houses falling to pieces, of swords broken, of stones calcined, of trees burnt and disappearing. It was a strange thing that in this chaos, in which Athos distinguished raised arms, in which he heard cries, sobs and groans, he did not see one human figure. The cannon thundered at a distance, musketry cracked, the sea moaned, flocks made their escape, bounding over the verdant slope. But not a soldier to apply the match to the batteries of cannon, not a sailor to assist in manœuvring the fleet, not a shepherd for the flocks. After the ruin of the village, and the destruction of the forts which dominated it —a ruin and a destruction operated magically, without the co-operation of a single human being—the flame was extinguished, the smoke began to descend, then diminished in intensity, paled, and disappeared entirely. Night then came over the scene; a night dark upon the earth, brilliant in the firmament. The large, blazing stars which sparkled in the African sky shone without lighting anything even around them.

A long silence ensued, which gave, for a moment, repose to the troubled imagination of Athos; and, as he felt that that which he saw was not terminated, he applied more attentively the looks of his understanding upon the strange spectacle which his imagination had presented. This spectacle was soon continued for him. A mild and pale moon arose behind the declivities of the coast, and streaking at first the undulating ripples of the sea, which appeared to have calmed after the roarings it had sent forth during the vision of Athos—the moon, say we, shed its diamonds and opals upon the briers and bushes of the hills. The grey rocks, like so many silent and attentive phantoms, appeared to raise their verdant heads to examine likewise the field of battle by the light of the moon, and Athos perceived that the field, entirely void during the combat, was now strewed over with fallen bodies.

An inexpressible shudder of fear and horror seized his soul when he recognised the white and blue uniform of the soldiers of Picardy, with their long pikes and blue handles, and their muskets marked with the fleur-de-lis on the butts. When he saw all the gaping, cold wounds, looking up to the azure heavens as if to demand back of them the souls to which they had opened a passage,—when he saw the slaughtered horses, stiff, with their tongues hanging out at one side of their mouths, sleeping in the icy blood pooled around them, staining their furniture and their manes,—when he saw the white horse of M. de Beaufort, with his head beaten to pieces, in the first ranks of the dead, Athos passed a cold hand over his brow, which he was astonished not to find burning. He was convinced by this touch that he was present, as a spectator, without fever, at the day after a battle fought upon the shores of Gigelli by the army of the expedition, which he had seen leave the coasts of France and disappear in the horizon, and of which he had saluted with thought and gesture the last cannon-shot fired by the Duke as a signal of farewell to his country.

Who can paint the mortal agony with which his soul followed, like a vigilant eye, the trace of those dead bodies, and examined them, one after another, to see if Raoul slept among them? Who can express the intoxication of joy with which Athos bowed before God, and thanked Him for not having seen him he sought with so much fear among the dead? In fact, fallen dead in their ranks, stiff, icy, all these dead, easy to be recognised, seemed to turn with complacency towards the Comte de la Fère, to be the better seen by him during his funeral inspection. But yet, he was astonished, while viewing all these bodies, not to perceive the survivors. To such a point did the illusion extend, that this vision was for him a real voyage made by the father into Africa, to obtain more exact information respecting his son.

Fatigued, therefore, with having traversed seas and continents, he sought repose under one of the tents sheltered behind a rock, on the top of which floated the white fleur-de-lised pennon. He looked for a soldier to conduct him to the tent of M. de Beaufort. Then, while his eye was wandering over the plain, turning on all sides, he saw a white form appear behind the resinous myrtles. This figure was clothed in the costume of an officer: it held in its hand a broken sword: it advanced slowly towards Athos, who, stopping short and fixing his eyes upon it, neither spoke nor moved, but wished to open his arms, because, in this silent and pale officer, he had just recognised Raoul. The Comte attempted to utter a cry, but it remained stifled in his throat. Raoul, with a gesture, directed him to be silent, placing his finger on his lips and drawing back by degrees, without Athos being able to see his legs move. The Comte, more pale than Raoul, more trembling, followed his son, traversing painfully briers and bushes, stones and ditches, Raoul not appearing to touch the earth, and no obstacle impeding the lightness of his march. The Comte, whom the inequalities of the path fatigued, soon stopped, exhausted. Raoul still continued to beckon him to follow him. The tender father, to whom love restored strength, made a last effort, and climbed the mountain after the young man, who attracted him by his gesture and his smile.

At length he gained the crest of the hill, and saw, thrown out in black, upon the horizon whitened by the moon, the elongated aerial form of Raoul. Athos stretched out his hand to get closer to his beloved son upon the plateau, and the latter also stretched out his; but suddenly, as if the young man had been drawn away in spite of himself, still retreating, he left the earth, and Athos saw the clear blue sky shine between the feet of his child and the ground of the hill. Raoul rose insensibly into the void, still smiling, still calling with a gesture:—he departed towards heaven. Athos uttered a cry of terrified tenderness. He looked below again. He saw a camp destroyed, and all those white bodies of the royal army, like so many motionless atoms. And, then, when raising his head, he saw still, still, his son beckoning him to ascend with him.

86

THE ANGEL OF DEATH

ATHOS was at this part of his marvellous vision, when the charm was suddenly broken by a great noise rising from the outward gates of the house. A horse was heard galloping over the hard gravel of the great alley, and the sound of most noisy and animated conversations ascended to the chamber in which the Comte was dreaming. Athos did not stir from the place he occupied; he scarcely turned his head towards the door to ascertain the sooner what these noises could be. A heavy step ascended the stairs; the horse which had recently galloped, departed slowly towards the stables. Great hesitation appeared in the steps, which by degrees approached the chamber of Athos. A door then was opened, and Athos, turning a little towards the part of the room the noise came from, cried in a weak voice:—

"It is a courier from Africa, is it not?"

"No, Monsieur le Comte," replied a voice which made the father of Raoul start upright in his bed.

"Grimaud!" murmured he. And the sweat began to pour down his cheeks. Grimaud appeared in the door-way. It was no longer the Grimaud we have seen, still young with courage and devotion, when he jumped the first into the boat destined to convey Raoul de Bragelonne to the vessels of the royal fleet. He was a stern and pale old man, his clothes covered with dust, with a few scattered hairs whitened by old age. He trembled whilst leaning against the door-frame, and was near falling on seeing, by the light of the lamps, the countenance of his master. These two men, who had lived so long together in a community of intelligence, and whose eyes, accustomed to economise expressions, knew how to say so many things silently—these two old friends, one as noble as the other in heart, if they were unequal in fortune and birth, remained interdicted whilst looking at each other. By the exchange of a single glance, they had just read to the bottom of each other's hearts. Grimaud bore upon his countenance the impression of a grief already old, of a dismal familiarity with it. He appeared to have no longer in use but one single version of his thoughts. As formerly he was accustomed not to speak much, he was now accustomed not to smile at all. Athos read at a glance all these shades upon the visage of his faithful servant, and in the same tone he would have employed to speak to Raoul in his dream,—

"Grimaud," said he, "Raoul is dead, is he not?"

Behind Grimaud, the other servants listened breathlessly with their eyes fixed upon the bed of their sick master. They heard the terrible question, and an awful silence ensued.

"Yes," replied the old man, heaving up the monosyllable from his chest with a hoarse, broken sigh.

Then arose voices of lamentation, which groaned without measure, and filled with regrets and prayers the chamber where the agonised father sought with his eyes for the portrait of his son. This was for Athos like the transition which led to his dream. Without uttering a cry, without shedding a tear, patient, mild, resigned as a martyr, he raised his eyes towards heaven, in order to there see again, rising above the mountain of Gigelli, the beloved shade which was leaving him at the moment of Grimaud's arrival. Without doubt, while looking towards the heavens, when resuming his marvellous dream, he repassed by the same road by which the vision, at once so terrible and so sweet, had led him before, for, after having gently closed his eyes, he reopened them and began to smile; he had just seen Raoul, who had smiled upon him. With his hands joined upon his breast, his face turned towards the window, bathed by the fresh air of night, which brought to his pillow the aroma of the flowers and the woods, Athos entered, never again to come out of it, into the contemplation of that paradise which the living never see. God willed, no doubt, to open to this elect the treasures of eternal beatitude, at the hour when other men tremble with the idea of being severely received by the Lord, and cling to this life they know, in the dread of the other life of which they get a glimpse by the dismal, murky torches of death. Athos was guided by the pure and serene soul of his son, which aspired to be like the paternal soul. Everything for this just man was melody and perfume in the rough road which souls take to return to the celestial country. After an hour of this ecstasy, Athos softly raised his hands, as white as wax; the smile did not quit his lips, and he murmured low, so low as scarcely to be audible, these three words addressed to God or to Raoul:

"HERE I AM!"

And his hands fell down slowly, as if he himself had laid them on the bed.

Death had been kind and mild to this noble creature. It had spared him the tortures of the agony, the convulsions of the last departure; it had opened with an indulgent finger the gates of eternity to that noble soul, worthy of every respect. God had no doubt ordered it thus that the pious remembrance of this death should remain in the hearts of those present, and in the memory of other men—a death which caused to be loved the passage from this life to the other by those whose existence upon this earth leads them not to dread the last judgment. Athos preserved, even in the eternal sleep, that placid and sincere smile—an ornament which was to accompany him to the tomb. The quietude of his features, the calm of his nothingness, made his servants for a long time doubt whether he had really quitted life. The Comte's people wished to remove Grimaud, who, from a distance, devoured the face growing so pale, and did not approach, from the pious fear of bringing to him the breath of death. But Grimaud, fatigued as he was, refused to leave the room. He sat himself down upon the threshold, watching his master with the vigilance of a sentinel, and jealous to receive either his first waking look, or his last dying sigh. The noises were all quieted in the house, and every one respected the slumber of their lord. But Grimaud, by anxiously listening, perceived that the Comte no longer breathed. He raised himself, with his hands leaning on the ground, looked to see if there did not appear some motion in the body of his master. Nothing! Fear seized him; he rose completely up, and, at the very moment, heard some one coming up the stairs. A noise of spurs knocking against a sword—a warlike sound, familiar to his ears—stopped him as he was going towards the bed of Athos. A voice still more sonorous than brass or steel resounded within three paces of him.

"Athos! Athos! my friend!" cried this voice, agitated even to tears.

"Monsieur le Chevalier d'Artagnan!" faltered out Grimaud.

"Where is he? Where is he?" continued the musketeer.

Grimaud seized his arm in his bony fingers, and pointed to the bed, upon the sheets of which the livid tint of the dead already showed.

A choked respiration, the opposite to a sharp cry, swelled the throat of d'Artagnan. He advanced on tip-toe, trembling, frightened at the noise his feet made upon the floor, and his heart rent by a nameless agony. He placed his ear to the breast of Athos, his face to the Comte's mouth. Neither noise, nor breath! D'Artagnan drew back. Grimaud, who had followed him with his eyes, and for whom each of his movements had been a revelation, came timidly, and seated himself at the foot of the bed, and glued his lips to the sheet which was raised by the stiffened feet of his master. Then large drops began to flow from his red eyes. This old man in despair, who wept, bent double without uttering a word, presented the most moving spectacle that d'Artagnan, in a life so filled with emotion, had ever met with.

The captain remained standing in contemplation before that

smiling dead man, who seemed to have kept his last thought, to make to his best friend, to the man he had loved next to Raoul, a gracious welcome even beyond life; and as if to reply to that exalted flattery of hospitality, d'Artagnan went and kissed Athos fervently on the brow, and with his trembling fingers closed his eyes. Then he seated himself by the pillow without dread of that dead man, who had been so kind and affectionate to him for thirty-five years; he fed himself greedily with the remembrances which the noble visage of the Comte brought to his mind in crowds—some blooming and charming as that smile—some dark, dismal, and icy as that face with its eyes closed for eternity.

All at once, the bitter flood which mounted from minute to minute invaded his heart, and swelled his breast almost to bursting. Incapable of mastering his emotion, he arose, and tearing himself violently from the chamber where he had just found dead him to whom he came to report the news of the death of Porthos, he uttered sobs so heart-rending that the servants who seemed only to wait for an explosion of grief, answered to it by their lugubrious clamours, and the dogs of the late Comte by their lamentable howlings. Grimaud was the only one who did not lift up his voice. Even in the paroxysm of his grief he would not have dared to profane the dead, or for the first time disturb the slumber of his master. Athos had accustomed him never to speak.

At daybreak, d'Artagnan, who had wandered about the lower hall, biting his fingers to stifle his sighs—d'Artagnan went up once more; and, watching the moment when Grimaud turned his head towards him, he made him a sign to come to him, which the faithful servant obeyed without making more noise than a shadow. D'Artagnan went down again, followed by Grimaud; and when he had gained the vestibule, taking the old man's hands, "Grimaud," said he, "I have seen how the father died; now let me know how the son died."

Grimaud drew from his breast a large letter, upon the envelope of which was traced the address of Athos. He recognised the writing of M. de Beaufort, broke the seal and began to read, walking about in the first blue rays of day, in the dark alley of old limes, marked by the still visible footprints of the Comte who had just died.

87

THE BULLETIN

THE Duc de Beaufort wrote to Athos. The letter destined for the living only reached the dead. God had changed the address.

"MY DEAR COMTE," wrote the Prince in his large, bad, schoolboy's hand,—"a great misfortune has struck us amidst a great triumph. The King loses one of the bravest of soldiers. I lose a friend. You lose M. de Bragelonne. He has died gloriously, and so gloriously that I have not the strength to weep as I could wish. Receive my sad compliments, my dear Comte. Heaven distributes trials according to the greatness of our hearts. This is an immense one, but not above your courage. Your good friend,

"LE DUC DE BEAUFORT."

The letter contained a relation written by one of the Prince's secretaries. It was the most touching recital, and the most true, of that dismal episode which unravelled two existences. D'Artagnan, accustomed to battle emotions, and with a heart armed against tenderness, could not help starting on reading the name of Raoul, the name of that beloved boy who had become, as his father had, a shade.

"In the morning," said the Prince's secretary, "monseigneur commanded the attack. Normandy and Picardy had taken position in the grey rocks dominated by the heights of the mountain, upon the declivity of which were raised the bastions of Gigelli.

"The cannon beginning to fire opened the action; the regiments marched full of resolution; the pikemen had their pikes elevated, the bearers of muskets had their weapons ready. The Prince followed attentively the march and movements of the troops, so as to be able to sustain them with a strong reserve. With monseigneur were the oldest captains and his aides-de-camp. M. le Vicomte de Bragelonne had received orders not to leave His Highness. In the meantime the enemy's cannon, which at first had thundered with little success against the masses, had regulated its fire, and the balls, better directed, had killed several men near the Prince. The regiments formed in column and which were advancing against the ramparts were rather roughly handled. There was a sort of hesitation in our troops, who found themselves ill-seconded by the artillery. In fact the batteries which had been established the evening before had but a weak and uncertain aim, on account of their position. The direction from low to high lessened the justness of the shots as well as their range.

"Monseigneur, comprehending the bad effect of this position of the siege artillery, commanded the frigates moored in the little road to commence a regular fire against the place. M. de Bragelonne offered himself at once to carry this order. But monseigneur refused to acquiesce in the Vicomte's request. Monseigneur was right, for he loved and wished to spare the young nobleman. He was quite right, and the event took upon itself to justify his foresight and refusal; for scarcely had the sergeant charged with the message solicited by M. de Bragelonne gained the sea-shore, when two shots from long carbines issued from the enemy's ranks and laid him low. The sergeant fell, dyeing the sand with his blood; observing which, M. de Bragelonne smiled at monseigneur, who said to him, 'You see, Vicomte, I have saved your life. Report that, some day, to M. le Comte de la Fère, in order that, learning it from you, he may thank me.' The young nobleman smiled sadly, and replied to the Duc, 'It is true, monseigneur, that but for your kindness I should have been killed, where the poor sergeant has fallen, and should be at rest.' M. de Bragelonne made this reply in such a tone that monseigneur answered him warmly. '*Vrai Dieu!* young man, one would say that your mouth waters for death; but, by the soul of Henry IV.! I have promised your father to bring you back alive; and please the Lord, I will keep my word.'

"Monseigneur de Bragelonne coloured, and replied in a lower voice, 'Monseigneur, pardon me, I beseech you; I have always had the desire to go to meet good opportunities; and it is so delightful to distinguish ourselves before our general, particularly when that general is M. le Duc de Beaufort.'

"Monseigneur was a little softened by this; and, turning to the officers who surrounded him, gave his different orders. The grenadiers of the two regiments got near enough to the ditches and the entrenchments to launch their grenades, which had but little effect. In the meanwhile, M. d'Estrées,* who commanded the fleet, having seen the attempt of the sergeant to approach the vessels, understood that he must act without orders, and opened his fire. Then the Arabs, finding themselves seriously injured by the balls from the fleet, and beholding the destruction and the ruins of their bad walls, uttered the most fearful cries. Their horsemen descended the mountain at the gallop, bent over their saddles, and rushed full tilt upon the columns of infantry, which, crossing their pikes, stopped this mad assault. Repulsed by the firm attitude of the battalion, the Arabs threw themselves with great fury towards the general staff, which was not on its guard at that moment.

"The danger was great; monseigneur drew his sword; his secretaries and people imitated him; the officers of the suite engaged in combat with the furious Arabs. It was then M. de Bragelonne was able to satisfy the inclination he had manifested from the commencement of the action. He fought near the Prince with the valour of a Roman, and killed three Arabs with his small sword. But it was evident that his bravery did not arise from one of those sentiments of pride natural to all who fight. It was impetuous, affected, forced even; he sought to intoxicate himself with noise and carnage. He heated himself to such a degree that monseigneur called out to him to stop. He must have heard the voice of monseigneur, because we who were close to him heard it. He did not, however, stop, but continued his course towards the entrenchments. As M. de Bragelonne was a well-disciplined officer, this disobedience to the orders of monseigneur very much surprised everybody, and M. de Beaufort redoubled his earnestness, crying, 'Stop, Bragelonne! Where are you going? Stop,' repeated monseigneur, 'I command you.'

"We all, imitating the gesture of M. le Duc, we all raised our hands. We expected that the cavalier would turn bridle; but M. de Bragelonne continued to ride towards the palisades.

"'Stop, Bragelonne!' repeated the Prince, in a very loud voice; 'stop! in the name of your father!'

"At these words M. de Bragelonne turned round; his countenance expressed a lively grief, but he did not stop; we then concluded that his horse must have run away with him. When M. le Duc had imagined that the Vicomte was not master of his horse, and had seen him precede the first grenadiers, His Highness cried, 'Musketeers, kill his horse! A hundred pistoles for him who shall kill his horse!' But who could expect to hit the beast without at least wounding his rider? No one durst venture. At length one presented himself; he was a sharp-shooter of the regiment of Picardy, named Luzerne, who took aim at the animal, fired, and hit him in the quarters, for we saw the blood redden the hair of the horse. Instead of falling, the cursed jennet was irritated, and carried him on more furiously than ever. Every Picard who saw this unfortunate young man rushing on to meet death, shouted in the loudest manner, 'Throw yourself off, Monsieur le Vicomte!—off!—off! throw yourself off!' M. le Bragelonne was an officer much beloved in the army. Already had the Vicomte arrived within pistol-shot of the ramparts; a discharge was poured upon him, and enveloped him in its fire and smoke. We lost sight of him; the smoke dispersed; he was on foot, standing; his horse was killed.

"The Vicomte was summoned to surrender by the Arabs, but he made them a negative sign with his head, and continued to march towards the palisades. This was a mortal imprudence. Nevertheless the whole army was pleased that he would not retreat, since ill chance had led him so near. He marched a few paces farther, and the two regiments clapped their hands. It was at this moment the second discharge shook the walls, and the Vicomte de Bragelonne again disappeared in the smoke; but this time the smoke was dispersed in vain; we no longer saw him standing. He was down, with his head lower than his legs, among the bushes, and the Arabs began to think of leaving their entrenchments to come and cut off his head or take his body, as is the custom with infidels. But Monseigneur le Duc de Beaufort had followed all this with his eyes, and the sad spectacle drew from him many and painful sighs. He then cried aloud, seeing the Arabs running like white phantoms among the mastick-trees, 'Grenadiers! piqueurs! will you let them take that noble body?'

"Saying these words, and waving his sword, he himself rode towards the enemy. The regiments, rushing in his steps, ran in their turns, uttering cries as terrible as those of the Arabs were wild.

"The combat commenced over the body of M. de Bragelonne, and with such inveteracy was it fought that a hundred and sixty Arabs were left upon the field, by the side of at least fifty of our troops. It was a lieutenant from Normandy who took the body of the Vicomte on his shoulders and carried it back to the lines. The advantage was, however, pursued; the regiments took the reserve with them and the enemy's palisades were destroyed. At three o'clock the fire of the Arabs ceased; the hand to hand fight lasted two hours; that was a massacre. At five o'clock we were victorious on all the points; the enemy had abandoned his positions, and M. le Duc had ordered the white flag to be planted upon the culminating point of the little mountain. It was then we had time to think of M. le Bragelonne, who had eight large wounds through his body, by which almost all his blood had escaped. Still, however, he breathed, which afforded inexpressible joy to monseigneur, who insisted upon being present at the first dressing of the wounds and at the consultation of the surgeons. There were two among them who declared M. de Bragelonne would live. Monseigneur threw his arms round their necks, and promised them a thousand louis each if they could save him.

"The Vicomte heard these transports of joy, and whether he was in despair, or whether he suffered much from his wounds, he expressed by his countenance a contradiction, which gave rise to reflection, particularly in one of the secretaries when he had heard what follows. The third surgeon was the brother of Sylvain de Saint-Cosme,* the most learned of ours. He probed the wounds in his turn, and said nothing. M. de Bragelonne fixed his eyes steadily upon the surgeon, and seemed to interrogate his every movement. The latter, upon being questioned by monseigneur, replied that he saw plainly three mortal wounds out of eight, but so strong was the constitution of the wounded, so rich was he in youth, and so merciful was the goodness of God, that perhaps M. de Bragelonne might recover, particularly if he did not move in the slightest manner. Frère Sylvain added, turning towards his assistants, 'Above everything, do not allow him to move even a finger, or you will kill him,' and we all left the tent in very low spirits. That secretary I have mentioned, on leaving the tent, thought he perceived a faint and sad smile glide over the lips of M. de Bragelonne when the Duc said to him, in a cheerful, kind voice, 'We shall save you, Vicomte, we shall save you!'

"In the evening, when it was believed the wounded man had taken some repose, one of the assistants entered his tent, but rushed immediately out again uttering loud cries. We all ran up in disorder, M. le Duc with us, and the assistant pointed to the body of M. de Bragelonne upon the ground, at the foot of his bed, bathed in the remainder of his blood. It appeared that he had had some convulsion, some febrile movement, and that he had fallen; that the fall had accelerated his end, according to the prognostic of Frère Sylvain. We raised the Vicomte: he was cold and dead. He held a lock of fair hair in his right hand, and that hand was pressed tightly upon his heart."

Then followed the details of the expedition, and of the victory obtained over the Arabs. D'Artagnan stopped at the account of the death of poor Raoul. "Oh!" murmured he, "unhappy boy! a suicide!"

And turning his eyes towards the chamber of the château in which Athos slept in eternal sleep, "They have kept their words to each other," said he, in a low voice; "now I believe them to be happy; they must be re-united." And he returned through the parterre with slow and melancholy steps. All the village—all the neighbourhood—were filled with grieving neighbours relating to each other the double catastrophe, and making preparations for the funeral.

88

THE LAST CANTO OF THE POEM

On the morrow, all the nobility of the provinces, of the environs, and wherever messengers had carried the news, were seen to arrive. D'Artagnan had shut himself up, without being willing to speak to anybody. Two such heavy deaths falling upon the captain, so closely after the death of Porthos, for a long time oppressed that spirit which had hitherto been so indefatigable and invulnerable. Except Grimaud, who entered his chamber once, the musketeer saw neither servants nor guests. He supposed, from the noises in the house, and the continual coming and going, that preparations were being made for the funeral of the Comte. He wrote to the King to ask for an extension of his leave of absence. Grimaud, as we have said, had entered d'Artagnan's apartment, had seated himself upon a joint-stool near the door, like a man who meditates profoundly; then, rising, he made a sign to d'Artagnan to follow him. The latter obeyed in silence. Grimaud descended to the Comte's bed-chamber, showed the captain with his finger the place of the empty bed, and raised his eyes eloquently towards heaven.

"Yes," replied d'Artagnan, "yes, good Grimaud—now with the son he loved so much!"

Grimaud left the chamber and led the way to the hall, where, according to the custom of the province, the body was laid out, previously to its being buried for ever. D'Artagnan was struck at seeing two open coffins in the hall. In reply to the mute invitation of Grimaud, he approached, and saw in one of them Athos, still handsome in death, and, in the other, Raoul with his eyes closed, his cheeks pearly as those of the Pallas of Virgil,* with a smile on his violet lips. He shuddered at seeing the father and son, those two departed souls, represented on earth by two silent, melancholy bodies, incapable of touching each other, however close they might be.

"Raoul here!" murmured he. "Oh! Grimaud, why did you not tell me this?"

Grimaud shook his head and made no reply; but taking d'Artagnan by the hand, he led him to the coffin, and showed him, under the thin winding-sheet, the black wounds by which life had escaped. The captain turned away his eyes, and, judging it useless to question Grimaud, who would not answer, he recollected that M. de Beaufort's secretary had written more than he, d'Artagnan, had had the courage to read. Taking up the recital of the affair which had cost Raoul his life, he found these words, which terminated the last paragraph of the letter:—

"Monsieur le Duc has ordered that the body of Monsieur le Vicomte should be embalmed, after the manner practised by the Arabs when they wish their bodies to be carried to their native land; and Monsieur le Duc has appointed relays, so that a confidential servant who brought up the young man, might take back his remains to M. le Comte de la Fère."

"And so," thought d'Artagnan, "I shall follow thy funeral, my dear boy—I, already old—I, who am of no value on earth—and I shall scatter the dust upon that brow which I kissed but two months since. God has willed it to be so. Thou hast willed it to be so, thyself. I have no longer the right even to weep. Thou hast chosen death; it hath seemed to thee preferable to life."

At length arrived the moment when the cold remains of these two gentlemen were to be returned to the earth. There was such an affluence of military and other people that up to the place of sepulture, which was a chapel in the plain, the road from the city was filled with horsemen and pedestrians in mourning habits. Athos had chosen for his resting-place the little enclosure of a chapel erected by himself near the boundary of his estates. He had had the stones, cut in 1550, brought from an old Gothic manor-house in Berry,* which had sheltered his early youth. The chapel, thus re-edified, thus transported, was pleasant beneath its wood of poplars and sycamores. It was administered every Sunday by the curé of the neighbouring bourg, to whom Athos paid an allowance of two hundred francs for this service; and all the vassals of his domain, to the number of about forty, the labourers, and the farmers, with their families, came thither to hear mass, without having any occasion to go to the city.

Behind the chapel extended, surrounded by two high hedges of nut-trees, elders, white thorns and a deep ditch, the little enclosure —uncultivated it is true, but gay in its sterility; because the mosses there were high, because the wild heliotropes and wallflowers there mixed their perfumes, because beneath the tall chestnuts issued a large spring, a prisoner in a cistern of marble, and that upon the thyme all around alighted thousands of bees from the neighbouring plains, whilst chaffinches and red-throats sang cheerfully among the flowers of the hedge. It was to this place the two coffins were brought, attended by a silent and respectful crowd. The office of the dead being celebrated, the last adieux paid to the noble departed, the assembly dispersed, talking, along the roads, of the virtues and mild death of the father, of the hopes the son had given, and of his melancholy end upon the coast of Africa.

By little and little, all noises were extinguished, like the lamps illuminating the humble nave. The minister bowed for a last time to the altar and the still fresh graves, then, followed by his assistant, who rang a hoarse bell, he slowly took the road back to the presbytery. D'Artagnan, left alone, perceived that night was coming on. He had forgotten the hour, while thinking of the dead. He arose from the oaken bench on which he was seated in the chapel, and wished, as the priest had done, to go and bid a last adieu to the double grave which contained his two lost friends.

A woman was praying, kneeling on the moist earth. D'Artagnan stopped at the door of the chapel, to avoid disturbing this woman, and also to endeavour to see who was the pious friend who performed this sacred duty with so much zeal and perseverance. The unknown concealed her face in her hands, which were white as alabaster. From the noble simplicity of her costume, she must be a woman of distinction. Outside the enclosure were several horses mounted by servants, and a travelling carriage waiting for this lady. D'Artagnan in vain sought to make out what caused her delay. She continued praying, she frequently passed her handkerchief over her face, by which d'Artagnan perceived she was weeping. He saw her strike her breast with the pitiless compunction of a Christian woman. He heard her several times proffer, as if from a wounded heart: "Pardon! pardon!" And as she appeared to abandon herself entirely to her grief, as she threw herself down, almost fainting, amidst complaints and prayers, d'Artagnan, touched by this love for his so much regretted friends, made a few steps towards the grave, in order to interrupt the melancholy colloquy of the penitent with the dead. But as soon as his step sounded on the gravel the unknown raised her head, revealing to d'Artagnan a face inundated with tears, but a well-known face. It was Mademoiselle de la Vallière! "Monsieur d'Artagnan!" murmured she.

"You!" replied the captain, in a stern voice—"you here!—oh! madame, I should better have liked to see you decked with flowers in the mansion of the Comte de la Fère. You would have wept less—they too—I too!"

"Monsieur!" she said, sobbing.

"For it is you," added this pitiless friend of the dead,—"it is you have laid these two men in the grave."

"Oh! spare me!"

"God forbid, madame, that I should offend a woman, or that I should make her weep in vain; but I must say that the place of the murderer is not upon the grave of her victims." She wished to reply.

"What I now tell you," added he coldly, "I told the King."

She clasped her hands. "I know," said she, "I have caused the death of the Vicomte de Bragelonne."

"Ah! you know it?"

"The news arrived at court yesterday. I have travelled during the night forty leagues to come and ask pardon of the Comte, whom I supposed to be still living, and to supplicate God, upon the tomb of Raoul, that he would send me all the misfortunes I have merited, except a single one. Now, monsieur, I know that the death of the son has killed the father; I have two crimes to reproach myself with; I have two punishments to look for from God."

"I will repeat to you, Mademoiselle," said d'Artagnan, "what M. de Bragelonne said of you at Antibes, when he already meditated death: 'If pride and coquetry have misled her, I pardon her while despising her. If love has produced her error, I pardon her, swearing that no one could have loved her as I have done.'"

"You know," interrupted Louise, "that for my love I was about to sacrifice myself; you know whether I suffered when you met me lost, dying, abandoned. Well! never have I suffered so much as now; because then I hoped, I desired—now I have nothing to wish for; because this death drags away all my joy into the tomb; because I can no longer dare to love without remorse, and I feel, that he whom I love—oh! that is the law—will repay me with the tortures I have made others undergo."

D'Artagnan made no reply; he was too well convinced she was not mistaken.

"Well! then," added she, "dear Monsieur d'Artagnan, do not overwhelm me to-day, I again implore you. I am like the branch torn from the trunk, I no longer hold to anything in this world, and a current drags me on, I cannot say whither. I love madly, I love to the point of coming to tell it, impious as I am, over the ashes of the dead; and I do not blush for it—I have no remorse on account of it. This love is a religion. Only, as hereafter you will see me alone, forgotten, disdained; as you will see me punished with that with which I am destined to be punished, spare me in my ephemeral happiness, leave it to me for a few days, for a few minutes. Now even, at the moment I am speaking to you, perhaps it no longer exists. My God! this double murder is perhaps already expiated!"

While she was speaking thus, the sound of voices and the steps of horses drew the attention of the captain. M. de Saint-Aignan came to seek La Vallière. "The King," he said, "was a prey to jealousy and uneasiness." Saint-Aignan did not see d'Artagnan, half concealed by the trunk of a chestnut-tree which shaded the two graves. Louise thanked Saint-Aignan, and dismissed him with a gesture. He rejoined the party outside the enclosure.

"You see, madam," said the captain bitterly to the young woman,—"you see that your happiness still lasts."

The young woman raised her head with a solemn air. "A day will come," said she, "when you will repent of having so ill-judged me. On that day it is I who will pray God to forgive you for having been unjust towards me. Besides, I shall suffer so much that you will be the first to pity my sufferings. Do not reproach me with that happiness, Monsieur d'Artagnan; it costs me dear, and I have not paid all my debt." Saying these words, she again knelt down, softly and affectionately.

"Pardon me, the last time, my affianced Raoul!" said she. "I have broken our chain; we are both destined to die of grief. It is thou who departest the first; fear nothing, I shall follow thee.* See, only, that I have not been base, and that I have come to bid thee this last adieu. The Lord is my witness, Raoul, that if with my life I could have redeemed thine, I would have given that life without hesitation. I could not give my love. Once more, pardon!"

She gathered a branch and stuck it into the ground; then, wiping the tears from her eyes, she bowed to d'Artagnan, and disappeared.

The captain watched the departure of the horses, horsemen, and carriage, then crossing his arms upon his swelling chest, "When will it be my turn to depart?"* said he, in an agitated voice. "What is there left for man after youth, after love, after glory, after friendship, after strength, after riches? That rock, under which sleeps Porthos, who possessed all I have named; this moss, under which repose Athos and Raoul, who possessed still much more!"

He hesitated a moment, with a dull eye; then, drawing himself up: "Forward! still forward!" said he. "When it shall be time, God will tell me, as he has told the others."

He touched the earth, moistened with the evening dew, with the ends of his fingers, signed himself as if he had been at the font of a church, and retook alone—ever alone—the road to Paris.

EPILOGUE

Four years after the scene we have just described, two horsemen, well mounted, traversed Blois early in the morning, for the purpose of arranging a birding party which the King intended to make in that uneven plain which the Loire divides in two, and which borders on the one side on Meung, on the other on Amboise. These were the captain of the King's harriers and the governor of the falcons, personages greatly respected in the time of Louis XIII., but rather neglected by his successor. These two horsemen, having reconnoitred the ground, were returning, their observations made, when they perceived some little groups of soldiers here and there whom the sergeants were placing at distances at the openings of the enclosures. These were the King's musketeers. Behind them came, upon a good horse, the captain, known by his richly embroidered uniform. His hair was grey, his beard was becoming so. He appeared a little bent, although sitting and handling his horse gracefully. He was looking about him watchfully.

"M. d'Artagnan does not get any older," said the captain of the harriers to his colleague the falconer; "with ten years more than either of us, he has the seat of a young man on horseback."

"That is true," replied the falconer. "I don't see any change in him for the last twenty years."

But this officer was mistaken; d'Artagnan in the last four years had lived twelve years. Age imprinted its pitiless claws at each angle of his eyes; his brow was bald; his hands, formerly brown and nervous, were getting white as if the blood began to chill there.

D'Artagnan accosted the officers with the shade of affability which distinguishes superior men, and received in return for his courtesy two most respectful bows.

"Ah! what a lucky chance to see you here, Monsieur d'Artagnan!" cried the falconer.

"It is rather I who should say that, messieurs," replied the captain, "for nowadays, the King makes more frequent use of his musketeers than of his falcons."

"Ah! it is not as it was in the good old times," sighed the falconer. "Do you remember, Monsieur d'Artagnan, when the late King flew the pie* in the vineyards beyond Beaugence? Ah! you were not captain of the musketeers at that time, Monsieur d'Artagnan."

"And you were nothing but under-corporal of the tiercelets,"* replied d'Artagnan, laughing. "Never mind that; it was a good time, seeing that it is always a good time when we are young. Good day, monsieur the captain of the harriers."

"You do me honour, Monsieur le Comte," said the latter. D'Artagnan made no reply. The title of Comte had not struck him; d'Artagnan had been a Comte for four years.

"Are you not very much fatigued with the long journey you have had?" continued the falconer. "It must be full two hundred leagues from hence to Pignerol."

"Two hundred and sixty to go, and as many to come back," said d'Artagnan quietly.

"And," said the falconer, "is *he* well?"

"Who?" asked d'Artagnan.

"Why, poor M. Fouquet," continued the falconer, still in a low voice. The captain of the harriers had prudently withdrawn.

"No," replied d'Artagnan, "the poor man frets terribly; he cannot comprehend how imprisonment can be a favour; he says that the parliament had absolved him by banishing him, and that banishment is liberty. He cannot imagine that they had sworn his death, and that to save his life from the claws of the parliament was to have too much obligation to God."

"Ah! yes; the poor man had a near chance of the scaffold;" replied the falconer; "it is said that M. Colbert had given orders to the governor of the Bastille, and that the execution was ordered."

"Enough!" said d'Artagnan pensively, and with a view of cutting short the conversation.

"Yes," said the captain of the harriers, drawing towards them, "M. Fouquet is now at Pignerol; he has richly deserved it. He has had the good fortune to be conducted there by you; he had robbed the King enough."

D'Artagnan launched at the master of the dogs one of his evil looks, and said to him,—"Monsieur, if any one told me that you had eaten your dogs' meat, not only would I refuse to believe it; but, still more, if you were condemned to the whip or the jail for it, I should pity you, and would not allow people to speak ill of you. And yet, monsieur, honest man as you may be, I assure you that you are not more so than poor M. Fouquet was."

After having undergone this sharp rebuke, the captain of the harriers hung his head, and allowed the falconer to get two steps in advance of him, nearer to d'Artagnan.

"He is content," said the falconer, in a low voice to the musketeer; "we all know that harriers are in fashion nowadays; if he were a falconer he would not talk in that way."

D'Artagnan smiled in a melancholy manner at seeing this great political question resolved by the discontent of such humble interests. He for a moment ran over in his mind the glorious existence of the Surintendant, the crumbling away of his fortunes, and the melancholy death that awaited him; and, to conclude,— "Did M. Fouquet love falconry?" said he.

"Oh! passionately, monsieur!" replied the falconer, with an accent of bitter regret, and a sigh that was the funeral oration of Fouquet.

D'Artagnan allowed the ill-humour of the one and the regrets of the other to pass, and continued to advance into the plain. They could already catch glimpses of the huntsmen at the issues of the wood, the feathers of the outriders passing like shooting-stars across the clearings, and the white horses cutting with their luminous apparitions the dark thickets of the copses.

"But," resumed d'Artagnan, "will the sport be long? Pray give us a good swift bird, for I am very tired. Is it a heron or a swan?"

"Both, Monsieur d'Artagnan," said the falconer; "but you need not be alarmed; the King is not much of a sportsman; he does not sport on his own account; he only wishes to give amusement to the ladies."

The words "to the ladies," were so strongly accented, that it set d'Artagnan listening.

"Ah!" said he, looking at the falconer with surprise.

The captain of the harriers smiled, no doubt with a view of making it up with the musketeer.

"Oh! you may safely laugh," said d'Artagnan; "I know nothing of current news; I only arrived yesterday, after a month's absence. I left the court mourning the death of the Queen-Mother.* The King was not willing to take any amusement after receiving the last sigh of Anne of Austria; but everything has an end in this world. Well! then he is no longer sad? So much the better."

"And everything commences as well as ends," said the captain of the dogs, with a coarse laugh.

"Ah!" said d'Artagnan a second time—he burned to know, but dignity would not allow him to interrogate people below him,— "there is something beginning, then, it appears?"

The captain gave him a significant wink; but d'Artagnan was unwilling to learn anything from this man.

"Shall we see the King early?" asked he of the falconer.

"At seven o'clock, monsieur, I shall fly the birds."

"Who comes with the King? How is Madame? How is the Queen?"

"Better, monsieur."

"Has she been ill, then?"

"Monsieur, since the last chagrin she had, Her Majesty has been unwell."

"What chagrin? You need not fancy your news is old. I am but just returned."

"It appears that the Queen, a little neglected since the death of her mother-in-law, complained to the King, who replied to her,— 'Do I not sleep with you every night, madame? What more do you want?'"

"Ah!" said d'Artagnan,—"poor woman! She must heartily hate Mademoiselle de la Vallière."

"Oh, no! not Mademoiselle de la Vallière," replied the falconer.

"Who then——?" The horn interrupted this conversation. It summoned the dogs and the hawks. The falconer and his companion set off immediately, leaving d'Artagnan alone in the midst of the suspended sentence. The King appeared at a distance, surrounded by ladies and horsemen. All the troop advanced in beautiful order, at a foot's pace, the horns of various sorts animating the dogs and the horses. It was a movement, a noise, a mirage of light, of which nothing now can give an idea, unless it be the fictitious splendour or false majesty of a theatrical spectacle. D'Artagnan, with an eye a little weakened, distinguished behind the group three carriages. The first was intended for the Queen; it was empty. D'Artagnan, who did not see Mademoiselle de la Vallière by the King's side, on looking about for her, saw her in the second carriage. She was alone with two of her women, who seemed as dull as their mistress. On the left hand of the King, upon a high-spirited horse, restrained by a bold and skilful hand, shone a lady of the most dazzling beauty. The King smiled upon her, and she smiled upon the King. Loud laughter followed every word she spoke.

"I must know that woman," thought the musketeer; "who can she be?" And he stooped towards his friend the falconer, to whom he addressed the question he had put to himself. The falconer was about to reply, when the King, perceiving d'Artagnan, "Ah, Comte?" said he, "you are returned, then! why have I not seen you?"

"Sire," replied the Captain, "because your Majesty was asleep when I arrived; and not awake when I resumed my duties this morning."

"Still the same!" said Louis in a loud voice, denoting satisfaction. "Take some rest, Comte; I command you to do so. You will dine with me to-day."

A murmur of admiration surrounded d'Artagnan like an immense caress. Every one was eager to salute him. Dining with the King was an honour His Majesty was not so prodigal of as Henry IV. had been. The King passed a few steps in advance, and d'Artagnan found himself in the midst of a fresh group, among whom shone Colbert.

"Good day, Monsieur d'Artagnan," said the minister, with affable politeness; "have you had a pleasant journey?"

"Yes, monsieur," said d'Artagnan, bowing to the neck of his horse.

"I heard the King invite you to his table for this evening," continued the minister; "you will meet an old friend there."

"An old friend of mine?" asked d'Artagnan, plunging painfully into the dark waves of the past, which had swallowed up for him so many friendships and so many hatreds.

"M. le Duc d'Alméda, who is arrived this morning from Spain."

"The Duc d'Alméda?" said d'Artagnan, reflecting in vain.

"I!" said an old man, white as snow, sitting bent in his carriage, which he caused to be thrown open to make room for the musketeer.

"Aramis!" cried d'Artagnan, struck with perfect stupor. And he left, inert as it was, the thin arm of the old nobleman hanging round his neck.

Colbert, after having observed them in silence for a minute, put his horse forward, and left the two old friends together.

"And so," said the musketeer, taking the arm of Aramis, "you the exile, the rebel, are again in France!"

"Ah! and I shall dine with you at the King's table," said Aramis, smiling. "Yes; will you not ask yourself what is the use of fidelity in this world? Stop! let us allow poor La Vallière's carriage to pass. Look, how uneasy she is! How her eye, dimmed with tears, follows the King, who is riding on horseback yonder!"

"With whom?"

"With Mademoiselle de Tonnay-Charente, now become Madame de Montespan," replied Aramis.

"She is jealous; is she then deserted?"

"Not quite yet, but it will not be long."

They chatted together, while following the sport, and Aramis's coachman drove them so cleverly that they got up at the moment when the falcon, attacking the bird, beat him down, and fell upon him. The King alighted, Madame de Montespan followed his example. They were in front of an isolated chapel, concealed by large trees, already despoiled of their leaves by the first winds of autumn. Behind this chapel was an enclosure, closed by a latticed gate. The falcon had beat down his prey in the enclosure belonging to this little chapel, and the King was desirous of going in to take the first feather, according to custom. The *cortége* formed a circle round the building and the hedges, too small to receive so many. D'Artagnan held back Aramis by the arm, as he was about, like the rest, to alight from his carriage, and in a hoarse, broken voice, "Do you know, Aramis," said he, "whither chance has conducted us?"

"No," replied the Duke.

"Here repose people I have known," said d'Artagnan, much agitated.

Aramis without divining anything, and with a trembling step, penetrated into the chapel by a little door which d'Artagnan opened for him. "Where are they buried?" said he.

"There, in the enclosure. There is a cross, you see, under that little cypress. The little cypress is planted over their tomb; don't go to it; the King is going that way; the heron has fallen just there."

Aramis stopped and concealed himself in the shade. They then saw, without being seen, the pale face of La Vallière, who, neglected in her carriage, had at first looked on, with a melancholy heart, from the door, and then, carried away by jealousy, she had advanced into the chapel, whence, leaning against a pillar, she contemplated in the enclosure the King smiling and making signs to Madame de Montespan to approach, as there was nothing to be afraid of. Madame de Montespan complied; she took the hand the King held out to her, and he, plucking out the first feather from the heron, which the falconer had strangled, placed it in the hat of his beautiful companion. She, smiling in her turn, kissed the hand tenderly which made her this present. The King blushed with pleasure; he looked at Madame de Montespan with all the fire of love.

"What will you give me in exchange?" said he.

She broke off a little branch of cypress and offered it to the King, who looked intoxicated with hope.

"Humph!" said Aramis to d'Artagnan; "the present is but a sad one, for that cypress shades a tomb."

"Yes, and the tomb is that of Raoul de Bragelonne," said d'Artagnan aloud; "of Raoul, who sleeps under that cross with his father."

A groan resounded behind them. They saw a woman fall fainting to the ground. Mademoiselle de la Vallière had seen all, and heard all.

"Poor woman!" muttered d'Artagnan, as he helped the attendants to carry back to her carriage her who from that time was to suffer.

That evening d'Artagnan was seated at the King's table, near M. Colbert and M. le Duc d'Alméda. The King was very gay. He paid a thousand little attentions to the Queen, a thousand kindnesses to Madame, seated at his left hand, and very sad. It might have been supposed to be that calm time when the King used to watch the eyes of his mother for the avowal or disavowal of what he had just done.

Of mistresses there was no question at this dinner. The King addressed Aramis two or three times, calling him M. l'Ambassadeur, which increased the surprise already felt by d'Artagnan at seeing his friend the rebel so marvellously well received at court.

The King, on rising from table, gave his hand to the Queen, and made a sign to Colbert, whose eye watched that of his master. Colbert took d'Artagnan and Aramis on one side. The King began to chat with his sister, whilst Monsieur, very uneasy, entertained the Queen with a preoccupied air, without ceasing to watch his wife and brother from the corner of his eye. The conversation between Aramis, d'Artagnan, and Colbert, turned upon indifferent subjects. They spoke of preceding ministers; Colbert related the feats of Mazarin, and required those of Richelieu to be related to him. D'Artagnan could not overcome his surprise at finding this man, with heavy eyebrows and a low forehead, contain so much sound knowledge and cheerful spirits. Aramis was astonished at that lightness of character which permitted a serious man to retard with advantage the moment for a more important conversation, to which nobody made any allusion, although all three interlocutors felt the imminence of it. It was very plain from the embarrassed appearance of Monsieur, how much the conversation of the King and Madame annoyed him. The eyes of Madame were almost red; was she going to complain? Was she going to commit a little scandal in open court? The King took her on one side, and in a tone so tender that it must have reminded the Princess of the time when she was loved for herself,—

"Sister," said he, "why do I see tears in those beautiful eyes?"

"Why—sire——" said she.

"Monsieur is jealous, is he not, sister?"

She looked towards Monsieur, an infallible sign that they were talking about him.

"Yes," said she.

"Listen to me," said the King; "if your friends compromise you, it is not Monsieur's fault."

He spoke these words with so much kindness, that Madame, encouraged, she who had had so many griefs for so long a time, was near bursting, so full was her heart.

"Come, come, dear little sister," said the King, "tell me your griefs; by the word of a brother, I pity them; by the word of a King, I will terminate them."

She raised her fine eyes, and in a melancholy tone,—

"It is not my friends who compromise me," said she; "they are either absent or concealed; they have been brought into disgrace with your Majesty; they, so devoted, so good, so loyal!"

"You say this on account of Guiche, whom I have exiled,* at the desire of Monsieur?"

"And who, since that unjust exile, has endeavoured to get himself killed every day!"

"Unjust, do you say, sister?"

"So unjust, that if I had not had the respect mixed with friendship that I have always entertained for your Majesty——"

"Well?"

"Well! I would have asked my brother Charles,* upon whom I can always——"

The King started. "What then?"

"I would have asked him to have represented to you that Monsieur and his favourite, M. le Chevalier de Lorraine,* ought not with impunity to constitute themselves the executioners of my honour and my happiness."

"The Chevalier de Lorraine," said the King; "that dismal face?"

"Is my mortal enemy. Whilst that man lives in my household, where Monsieur retains him and delegates his powers to him, I shall be the most miserable woman in this kingdom."

"So," said the King slowly, "you call your brother of England a better friend than I am?"

"Actions speak for themselves, sire."

"And you would prefer going to ask assistance there."

"To my own country!" said she, with pride; "yes, sire."

"You are the grandchild of Henry IV. as well as myself, my friend. Cousin and brother-in-law, does not that amount pretty well to the title of brother-germain?"

"Then," said Henrietta, "act!"

"Let us form an alliance."

"Begin."

"I have, you say, unjustly exiled Guiche."

"Oh! yes," said she, blushing.

"Guiche shall return."

"So far, well."

"And now you say that I am wrong in having in your household the Chevalier de Lorraine, who gives Monsieur ill-advice respecting you."

"Remember well what I tell you, sire; the Chevalier de Lorraine some day——Observe, if ever I come to an ill end, I beforehand accuse the Chevalier de Lorraine; he has a soul capable of any crime."

"The Chevalier de Lorraine shall no longer annoy you—I promise you that."

"Then that will be a true preliminary of alliance, sire—I sign; but since you have done your part, tell me what shall be mine."

"Instead of embroiling me with your brother Charles, you must make him my more intimate friend than ever."

"That is very easy."

"Oh! not quite so much so as you may think, for, in ordinary friendship people embrace or exercise hospitality, and that only costs a kiss or a return—easy expenses; but in political friend-ship——"

"Ah! it's a political friendship, is it?"

"Yes, my sister; and then, instead of embraces and feasts, it is soldiers, it is soldiers all living and well equipped, that we must serve up to our friend; vessels we must offer, all armed with cannon and stored with provisions. It hence results that we have not always our coffers in a fit state to form such friendships."

"Ah! you are quite right," said Madame; "the coffers of the King of England have been very sonorous for some time."

"But you, my sister, who have so much influence over your brother, you can obtain more than an ambassador could ever obtain."

"To the effect that I must go to London, my dear brother."

"I have thought so," replied the King eagerly; "and I have said to myself that such a voyage would do your spirits good."

"Only," interrupted Madame, "it is possible I should fail. The King of England has dangerous counsellors."

"Counsellors, do you say?"

"Precisely. If, by chance, your Majesty had any intention—I am only supposing so—of asking Charles II. his alliance for a war——"

"For a war?"

"Yes; well! then the counsellors of the King, who are to the number of seven—Mademoiselle Stewart, Mademoiselle Wells, Mademoiselle Gwyn, Miss Orchay, Mademoiselle Zunga, Miss Davies, and the proud Countess of Castlemaine*—will represent to the King that war costs a great deal of money; that it is better to give balls and suppers at Hampton Court than to equip vessels of the line at Portsmouth and Greenwich."

"And then your negotiation will fail?"

"Oh! those ladies cause all negotiations to fail that they don't make themselves."

"Do you know the idea that has struck me, sister?"

"No; tell me what it is."

"It is that by searching well around you, you might perhaps find a female counsellor to take with you to your brother whose eloquence might paralyse the ill-will of the seven others."

"That is really an idea, sire, and I will search."

"You will find what you want."

"I hope so."

"A pretty person is necessary; an agreeable face is better than an ugly one, is it not?"

"Most assuredly."

"An animated, lively, audacious character."

"Certainly."

"Nobility; that is, enough to enable her to approach the King without awkwardness; little enough, so as not to trouble herself about the dignity of her race."

"Quite just."

"And who knows a little English."

"*Mon Dieu!* why, some one," cried Madame, "like Mademoiselle de Kéroualle," for instance!"

"Oh! why, yes!" said Louis XIV.; "you have found—it is you who have found, my sister."

"I will take her; she will have no cause to complain, I suppose."

"Oh! no; I will name her *séductrice plénipotentiaire* at once, and will add the dowry to the title."

"That is well."

"I fancy you already on your road, my dear little sister, and consoled for all your griefs."

"I will go, on two conditions. The first is, that I shall know what I am negotiating about."

"This is it. The Dutch, you know, insult me daily in their gazettes, and by their republican attitude. I don't like republics."

"That may easily be conceived, sire."

"I see with pain that these kings of the sea—they call themselves so—keep trade from France in the Indies, and that their vessels will soon occupy all the ports of Europe. Such a power is too near me, sister."

"They are your allies, nevertheless."

"That is why they were wrong in having the medal you have heard of struck; a medal which represents Holland stopping the sun as Joshua did, with this legend, *The sun has stopped before me.*

577

There is not much fraternity in that, is there?"

"I thought you had forgotten that miserable affair."

"I never forget anything, my sister. And if my true friends, such as your brother Charles, are willing to second me——" The Princess remained pensively silent.

"Listen to me; there is the empire of the seas to be shared," said Louis XIV. "For this partition, which England submits to, could I not represent the second party as well as the Dutch?"*

"We have Mademoiselle de Kéroualle to treat that question," replied Madame.

"Your second condition for going, if you please, sister?"

"The consent of Monsieur, my husband."

"You shall have it."

"Then consider me gone, my brother."

On hearing these words, Louis XIV. turned round towards the corner of the room in which d'Artagnan, Colbert and Aramis stood, and made an affirmative sign to his minister. Colbert then broke the conversation at the point it happened to be at, and said to Aramis,—

"Monsieur l'Ambassadeur, shall we talk about business?"

D'Artagnan immediately withdrew, from politeness. He directed his steps towards the chimney, within hearing of what the King was going to say to Monsieur, who, evidently very uneasy, had gone to him. The face of the King was animated. Upon his brow was stamped a will, the redoubtable expression of which already met with no more contradiction in France, and was soon to meet with no more in Europe.

"Monsieur," said the King to his brother, "I am not pleased with M. le Chevalier de Lorraine. You, who do him the honour to protect him, must advise him to travel for a few months." These words fell with the crush of an avalanche upon Monsieur, who adored this favourite, and concentrated all his affections in him.

"In what has the Chevalier been able to displease your Majesty?" cried he, darting a furious look at Madame.

"I will tell you that when he is gone," replied the impassible King. "And also when Madame, here, shall have crossed over into England."

"Madame! into England!" murmured Monsieur, in a perfect state of stupor.

"In a week, my brother," continued the King, "whilst we two will go whither I will tell you." And the King turned upon his heel, after having smiled in his brother's face, to sweeten a little the bitter draught he had given him.

During this time Colbert was talking with the Duc d'Alméda.

"Monsieur," said Colbert to Aramis, "this is the moment for us to come to an understanding. I have made your peace with the King, and I owed that clearly to a man of your merit; but as you have often expressed friendship for me, an opportunity presents itself for giving me a proof of it. You are, besides, more a French-man than a Spaniard. Shall we have, answer me frankly, the neutrality of Spain, if we undertake anything against the United Provinces?"

"Monsieur," replied Aramis, "the interest of Spain is very clear. To embroil Europe with the United Provinces,* against which subsists the ancient malice of their conquered liberty, is our policy, but the King of France is allied with the United Provinces. You are not ignorant, besides, that it would be a maritime war, and that France is not in a state to make such a one with advantage."

Colbert, turning round at this moment, saw d'Artagnan, who was seeking an interlocutor, during the "aside" of the King and Monsieur. He called him, at the same time saying in a low voice to Aramis, "We may talk with M. d'Artagnan, I suppose?"

"Oh! certainly," replied the ambassador.

"We were saying, M. d'Alméda and I," said Colbert, "that war with the United Provinces would be a maritime war."

"That's evident enough," replied the musketeer.

"And what do you think of it, Monsieur d'Artagnan."

"I think that to carry that war on successfully, you must have a very large land army."

"What did you say?" said Colbert, thinking he had ill-understood him.

"Why such a land army?" said Aramis.

"Because the King will be beaten by sea if he has not the English with him, and that when beaten by sea, he will soon be invaded, either by the Dutch in his ports, or by the Spaniards by land."

"And Spain neutral?" asked Aramis.

"Neutral as long as the King shall be the stronger," rejoined d'Artagnan.

Colbert admired that sagacity which never touched a question without enlightening it thoroughly. Aramis smiled, as he had long known that in diplomacy d'Artagnan acknowledged no master. Colbert, who, like all proud men, dwelt upon his fantasy with a certainty of success, resumed the subject: "Who told you, M. d'Artagnan, that the King had no navy?"

"Oh! I have taken no heed of these details," replied the captain. "I am but a middling sailor. Like all nervous people, I hate the

579

sea; and yet I have an idea that with ships, France being a seaport with two hundred heads, we might have sailors."

Colbert drew from his pocket a little oblong book, divided into two columns. On the first were the names of vessels, on the other the figures recapitulating the number of cannon and men requisite to equip these ships. "I have had the same idea as you," said he to d'Artagnan, "and I have had an account drawn up of the vessels we have altogether—thirty-five ships."

"Thirty-five ships! that is impossible!" cried d'Artagnan.

"Something like two thousand pieces of cannon," said Colbert. "That is what the King possesses at this moment. With thirty-five vessels we can make three squadrons, but I must have five."

"Five!" cried Aramis.

"They will be afloat before the end of the year, gentlemen; the King will have fifty ships of the line. We may venture on a contest with them, may we not?"

"To build vessels," said d'Artagnan, "is difficult, but possible. As to arming them, how is that to be done? In France there are neither foundries nor military docks."

"Bah!" replied Colbert, with a gay tone, "I have instituted all that this year and a half past. Did you not know it? Don't you know M. d'Imfreville?"

"D'Imfreville?" replied d'Artagnan; "no."

"He is a man I have discovered; he has a speciality; he is a man of genius—he knows how to set men to work. It is he who has founded cannon and cut the woods of Bourgogne. And then, Monsieur l'Ambassadeur, you may not believe what I am going to tell you, but I have a further idea."

"Oh, monsieur!" said Aramis civilly, "I always believe you."

"Figure to yourself that, calculating upon the character of the Dutch, our allies, I said to myself, 'They are merchants, they are friends with the King; they will be happy to sell to the King what they fabricate for themselves; then, the more we buy'—Ah! I must add this: I have Forant*—do you know Forant, d'Artagnan?"

Colbert in his warmth, forgot himself; he called the captain simply *d'Artagnan*, as the King did. But the captain only smiled at it.

"No," replied he, "I don't know him."

"That is another man I have discovered, with a genius for buying. This Forant has purchased for me 350,000 pounds of iron in balls, 200,000 pounds of powder, twelve cargoes of Northern timber, matches, grenades, pitch, tar—I know not what! with a saving of seven per cent. upon what all those articles would cost me fabricated in France."

"That is a good idea," replied d'Artagnan, "to have Dutch balls founded, which will return to the Dutch."

"Is it not, with loss too?" And Colbert laughed aloud. He was delighted with his own joke.

"Still further," added he; "these same Dutch are building for the King at this moment, six vessels after the model of the best of their marine. Destouches—Ah! perhaps you don't know Destouches?"

"No, monsieur."

"He is a man who has a glance singularly sure to discern, when a ship is launched, what are the defects and qualities of that ship—that is valuable, please to observe! Nature is truly whimsical. Well, this Destouches appeared to me to be a man likely to be useful in port, and he is superintending the construction of six vessels of 78,* which the Provinces are building for His Majesty. It results from all this, my dear Monsieur d'Artagnan, that the King, if he wished to quarrel with the Provinces, would have a very pretty fleet. Now, you know better than anybody else if the land army is good."

D'Artagnan and Aramis looked at each other, wondering at the mysterious labours this man had effected in a few years. Colbert understood them, and was touched by this best of flatteries.

"If we in France were ignorant of what was going on," said d'Artagnan, "out of France still less must be known."

"That is why I told Monsieur l'Ambassadeur," said Colbert, "that Spain promising its neutrality, England helping us——"

"If England assists you," said Aramis, "I engage for the neutrality of Spain."

"I take you at your word," hastened Colbert to reply with blunt good humour. "And talking of Spain, you have not the *Golden Fleece*, Monsieur d'Alméda. I heard the King say the other day that he should like to see you wear the Grand Cordon of St. Michael."*

Aramis bowed. "Oh!" thought d'Artagnan, "and Porthos is no longer here! What ells of ribbon would there be for him in these decorations! Good Porthos!"

"Monsieur d'Artagnan," resumed Colbert, "between us two, you will have, I would wager, an inclination to lead your musketeers into Holland. Can you swim?" And he laughed like a man in a very good humour.

"Like an eel," replied d'Artagnan.

"Ah! but there are some rough passages of canals and marshes yonder, and the best swimmers are sometimes drowned there."

"It is my profession to die for His Majesty," said the musketeer.

"Only, as it is seldom that in war much water is met without a little fire, I declare to you beforehand that I will do my best to choose fire. I am getting old; water freezes me—fire warms, Monsieur Colbert."

And d'Artagnan looked so handsome in juvenile vigour and pride as he pronounced these words, that Colbert, in his turn, could not help admiring him. D'Artagnan perceived the effect he had produced. He remembered that the best tradesman is he who fixes a high price upon his goods when they are valuable. He prepared then his price in advance.

"So then," said Colbert, "we go into Holland?"

"Yes," replied d'Artagnan; "only——"

"Only?" said M. Colbert.

"Only," repeated d'Artagnan, "there is in everything the question of interest and the question of self-love. It is a very fine title, that of captain of the musketeers; but observe this: we have now the King's guards and the military household of the King. A captain of musketeers ought either to command all that, and then he would absorb a hundred thousand livres a year for expenses of representation and table——"

"Well! but do you suppose, by chance, that the King would haggle with you?" said Colbert.

"Eh! monsieur, you have not understood me," replied d'Artagnan, sure of having carried the question of interest; "I was telling you that I, an old captain, formerly chief of the King's guard, having precedence* of the marshals of France—I saw myself one day in the trenches with two other equals, the captain of the guards and the colonel commanding the Swiss. Now, at no price will I suffer that. I have old habits; I will stand to them."

Colbert felt this blow, but he was prepared for it.

"I have been thinking of what you said just now," replied he.

"About what, monsieur?"

"We were speaking of canals and marshes in which people are drowned."

"Well?"

"Well! if they are drowned, it is for want of a boat, a plank, or a stick."

"Of a stick, however short it may be," said d'Artagnan.

"Exactly," said Colbert. "And, therefore, I never heard of an instance of a marshal of France being drowned."

D'Artagnan became pale with joy, and in a not very firm voice: "People would be very proud of me in my country," said he, "if I were a marshal of France; but a man must have commanded an expedition in chief to obtain the baton."

"Monsieur!" said Colbert, "here is in this pocket-book, which you will study, a plan of a campaign you will have to lead a body of troops to carry out in the next spring."

D'Artagnan took the book tremblingly, and his fingers meeting with those of Colbert, the minister pressed the hand of the musketeer loyally.

"Monsieur," said he, "we had both a revenge to take, one over the other. I have begun; it is now your turn."

"I will do you justice, monsieur," replied d'Artagnan, "and implore you to tell the King that the first opportunity that shall offer, he may depend upon a victory, or seeing me dead."

"Then I will have the fleur-de-lis for your marshal's baton prepared immediately," said Colbert.

On the morrow of this day, Aramis, who was setting out for Madrid, to negotiate the neutrality of Spain, came to embrace d'Artagnan at his hotel.

"Let us love each other for four," said d'Artagnan; "we are now but two."

"And you will, perhaps, never see me again, dear d'Artagnan," said Aramis;—"if you knew how I have loved you! I am old, I am extinguished, I am dead."

"My friend," said d'Artagnan, "you will live longer than I shall: diplomacy commands you to live; but for my part, honour condemns me to die."

"Bah! such men as we are, Monsieur le Marshal," said Aramis, "only die satiated with joy or glory."

"Ah!" replied d'Artagnan, with a melancholy smile, "I assure you, Monsieur le Duc, I feel very little appetite for either."

They once more embraced, and, two hours after, they were separated.

THE DEATH OF D'ARTAGNAN

CONTRARY to what always happens, whether in politics or morals, each kept his promise, and did honour to his engagements.

The King recalled M. de Guiche, and banished M. le Chevalier de Lorraine; so that Monsieur became ill in consequence. Madame set out for London, where she applied herself so earnestly to make her brother, Charles II., have a taste for the political councils of Mademoiselle de Kéroualle, that the alliance between England and France was signed, and the English vessels, ballasted by a few millions of French gold, made a terrible campaign against the fleets of the United Provinces. Charles II. had promised Mademoiselle de Kéroualle a little gratitude for her good councils; he made her Duchess of Portsmouth.* Colbert had promised the King vessels, munitions, and victories. He kept his word, as is well known. At length Aramis, upon whose promises there was least dependence to be placed, wrote Colbert the following letter, on the subject of the negotiations which he had undertaken at Madrid :—

"MONSIEUR COLBERT,—I have the honour to expedite to you the R. P. d'Oliva, general *ad interim* of the Society of Jesus, my provisional successor.* The reverend father will explain to you, Monsieur Colbert, that I preserve to myself the direction of all the affairs of the Order which concern France and Spain; but that I am not willing to retain the title of general, which would throw too much light upon the march of the negotiations with which His Catholic Majesty wishes to entrust me. I shall resume that title by the command of His Majesty, when the labours I have undertaken in concert with you, for the great glory of God and his Church, shall be brought to a good end. The R. P. d'Oliva will inform you likewise, monsieur, of the consent which His Catholic Majesty gives to the signature of a treaty which assures the neutrality of Spain, in the event of a war between France and the United Provinces. The consent will be valid, even if England, instead of being active, should satisfy herself with remaining neutral. As to Portugal, of which you and I have spoken, monsieur, I can assure you it will contribute with all its resources to assist the most Christian King in his war. I beg you, Monsieur Colbert, to preserve to me your friendship, as also to believe in my profound attachment, and to lay my respect at the feet of His Most Christian Majesty.

(Signed) LE DUC D'ALMÉDA."

Aramis had then performed more than he had promised; it remained to be known how the King, M. Colbert, and d'Artagnan would be faithful to each other. In the spring,* as Colbert had predicted, the land army entered on its campaign. It preceded, in magnificent order, the court of Louis XIV., who, setting out on horseback, surrounded by carriages filled with ladies and courtiers, conducted the *élite* of his kingdom to this sanguinary fête. The officers of the army, it is true, had no other music but the artillery of the Dutch forts; but it was enough for a great number, who found in this war honours, advancement, fortune, or death.

M. d'Artagnan set out commanding a body of twelve thousand men, cavalry and infantry, with which he was ordered to take the different places which form the knots of that strategic network which is called La Frise.* Never was an army conducted more gallantly to an expedition. The officers knew that their leader, prudent and skilful as he was brave, would not sacrifice a single man, nor yield an inch of ground without necessity. He had the old habits of war, to live upon the country, keep his soldiers singing and the enemy weeping. The captain of the King's musketeers placed his coquetry in showing that he knew his business. Never were opportunities better chosen, *coups de main* better supported, errors of the besieged taken better advantage of.

The army commanded by d'Artagnan took twelve small places within a month. He was engaged in besieging the thirteenth, which had held out five days. D'Artagnan caused the trenches to be opened without appearing to suppose that these people would ever allow themselves to be taken. The pioneers and labourers were, in the army of this man, a body full of emulation, ideas, and zeal, because he treated them like soldiers, knew how to render their work glorious, and never allowed them to be killed if he could prevent it. It should have been seen then, with what eagerness the marshy glebes of Holland were turned over. Those turf-heaps, those mounds of potter's clay melted at the word of the soldiers like butter in the vast frying-pans of the Friesland housewives.

M. d'Artagnan despatched a courier to the King to give him an account of the last successes, which redoubled the good humour of His Majesty and his inclination to amuse the ladies. These victories of M. d'Artagnan gave so much majesty to the Prince, that Madame de Montespan no longer called him anything but

Louis the Invincible. So that Mademoiselle de la Vallière, who only called the King Louis the Victorious, lost much of His Majesty's favour. Besides, her eyes were frequently red, and for an Invincible nothing is more disagreeable than a mistress who weeps while everything is smiling around her. The star of Mademoiselle de la Vallière was being drowned in the horizon in clouds and tears. But the gaiety of Madame de Montespan redoubled with the successes of the King, and consoled him for every other unpleasant circumstance. It was to d'Artagnan the King owed this; and His Majesty was anxious to acknowledge these services; he wrote to M. Colbert:—

"Monsieur Colbert, we have a promise to fulfil with M. d'Artagnan, who so well keeps his. This is to inform you that the time is come for performing it. All provisions for this purpose you shall be furnished with in due time.—LOUIS."

In consequence of this, Colbert, who detained the envoy of d'Artagnan, placed in the hands of that messenger a letter from himself for d'Artagnan, and a small coffer of ebony inlaid with gold, which was not very voluminous in appearance, but which, without doubt, was very heavy, as a guard of five men was given to the messenger, to assist him in carrying it. These people arrived before the place which d'Artagnan was besieging, towards daybreak and presented themselves at the lodgings of the general. They were told that M. d'Artagnan, annoyed by a sortie which the governor, an artful man, had made the evening before, and in which the works had been destroyed, seventy-seven men killed, and the reparation of the breaches commenced, had just gone, with half a score companies of grenadiers, to reconstruct the works.

M. Colbert's envoy had orders to go and seek M. d'Artagnan wherever he might be, or at whatever hour of the day or night. He directed his course, therefore, towards the trenches, followed by his escort, all on horseback. They perceived M. d'Artagnan in the open plain with his gold-laced hat, his long cane, and his large gilded cuffs. He was biting his white moustache, and wiping off, with his left hand, the dust which the passing balls threw up from the ground they ploughed near him. They also saw, amidst this terrible fire, which filled the air with its hissing whistle, officers handling the shovel, soldiers rolling barrows, and vast fascines, rising by being either carried or dragged by from ten to twenty men, cover the front of the trench, re-opened to the centre by this extraordinary effort of the general animating his soldiers. In three hours, all had been reinstated. D'Artagnan began to speak more mildly; and he became quite calm, when the captain of the pioneers approached him, hat in hand, to tell him that the trench was again lodgeable. This man had scarcely finished speaking when a ball took off one of his legs, and he fell into the arms of d'Artagnan. The latter lifted up his soldier; and quietly, with soothing words, carried him into the trench, amidst the enthusiastic applause of the two regiments. From that time, it was no longer ardour: it was delirium; two companies stole away up to the advanced posts, which they destroyed instantly.

When their comrades, restrained with great difficulty by d'Artagnan, saw them lodged upon the bastions, they rushed forward likewise; and soon a furious assault was made upon the counterscarp, upon which depended the safety of the place. D'Artagnan perceived there was only one means left of stopping his army, and that was to lodge it in the place. He directed all his force to two breaches, which the besieged were busy in repairing. The shock was terrible; eighteen companies took part in it, and d'Artagnan went with the rest, within half cannon-shot of the place, to support the attack by *échelons*. The cries of the Dutch who were being poniarded upon their guns by d'Artagnan's grenadiers, were distinctly audible. The struggle grew fiercer with the despair of the governor, who disputed his position foot by foot. D'Artagnan, to put an end to the affair, and silence the fire, which was unceasing, sent a fresh column, which penetrated like a wimble* through the posts that remained solid; and he soon perceived upon the ramparts, through the fire, the terrified flight of the besieged, pursued by the besiegers.

It was at this moment, the general, breathing freely and full of joy, heard a voice behind him, saying, "Monsieur, if you please, from M. Colbert."

He broke the seal of a letter which contained these words:—

"MONSIEUR D'ARTAGNAN,—The King commands me to inform you that he has nominated you Marshal of France, as a reward of your good services, and the honour you do to his arms. The King is highly pleased, monsieur, with the captures you have made; he commands you in particular, to finish the siege you have commenced, with good fortune to you and success for him."

D'Artagnan was standing with a heated countenance and a sparkling eye. He looked up to watch the progress of his troops upon the walls, still enveloped in red and black volumes of smoke. "I have finished," replied he to the messenger; "the city will have surrendered in a quarter of an hour." He then resumed his reading:—

"The accompanying box, Monsieur d'Artagnan, is my own present. You will not be sorry to see that, whilst you warriors are drawing the sword to defend the King, I am animating the pacific arts to ornament the recompenses worthy of you. I commend myself to your friendship, Monsieur le Marshal, and beg you to believe in all mine.—COLBERT."

D'Artagnan, intoxicated with joy, made a sign to the messenger, who approached, with his box in his hands, But at the moment the marshal was going to look at it, a loud explosion resounded from the ramparts, and called his attention towards the city. "It is strange," said d'Artagnan, "that I don't see the King's flag upon the walls, or hear the drums beat." He launched three hundred fresh men, under a high-spirited officer, and ordered another breach to be beaten. Then, being more tranquil, he turned towards the box which Colbert's envoy held out to him. It was his treasure, he had won it.

D'Artagnan was holding out his hand to open the box, when a ball from the city crushed the box in the arms of the officer, struck d'Artagnan full in the chest, and knocked him down upon a sloping heap of earth, whilst the fleur-de-lised baton, escaping from the broken sides of the box, came rolling under the powerless hand of the marshal. D'Artagnan endeavoured to raise himself up. It was thought he had been knocked down without being wounded. A terrible cry broke from the group of his terrified officers; the marshal was covered with blood; the paleness of death ascended slowly to his noble countenance. Leaning upon the arms which were held out on all sides to receive him, he was able once more to turn his eyes towards the place, and to distinguish the white flag at the crest of the principal bastion; his ears, already deaf to the sounds of life, caught feebly the rolling of the drum which announced the victory. Then, clasping in his nerveless hand the baton ornamented with its fleur-de-lis, he cast down upon it his eyes, which had no longer the power of looking upwards towards heaven, and fell back, murmuring those strange words, which appeared to the soldiers cabalistic words,—words which had formerly represented so many things upon earth, and which none but the dying man longer comprehended.

"Athos—Porthos, farewell till we meet again! Aramis, *adieu* for ever!"

Of the four valiant men whose history we have related, there now no longer remained but one single body; God had resumed the souls.

EXPLANATORY NOTES

1   *Place de Grève . . . Place Baudoyer . . . Rue Saint-Jean*: the Place de Grève had been in use as a place of public execution since 1310: the guillotine was first used there in April 1792. Called the Place de l'Hôtel de Ville since 1806, the site is on the right bank of the Seine, opposite the pont d'Arcoli. The Place Baudoyer still exists but the rue Saint-Jean was absorbed into the present rue Lubau in 1838. Exact topographical references of this sort form part of Dumas's realism.

Ninon de l'Enclos: Ninon de Lenclos (1620–1705), a woman of great wit and influence, retained her beauty into old age. Her *salon* attracted the most famous men of the century.

my dear Duchesse: Marie de Rohan-Montbazon (1600–79), widow of the Duke de Luynes, married Claude de Lorraine, Duke de Chevreuse in 1622. For plotting against Richelieu, she was confined in the prison at Loches, near Tours, but after the Cardinal's death in 1642 she was readmitted to the court of her friend the Queen. Politically active during the Fronde, she later intrigued against Mazarin, for which she was exiled. Though the Duchess de Chevreuse does not appear in *The Three Musketeers*, she figures off-stage as Marie Michon of Tours, Athos's great love and secret ally at court: Raoul de Bragelonne (born *c.*1633) is their son. According to *Twenty Years After* (chap. 22), she was in 1648 'still considered a handsome woman. Indeed, though she was at that time forty-four or forty-five, she looked no more than thirty-eight or -nine; she still had her blond hair, the same large, flashing, intelligent eyes which had so often been opened wide by intrigue and closed by love, and the same nymph-like waist, so that from behind she looked like a young girl . . . She was still the same wild creature . . .' The action of *The Man in the Iron Mask* begins in 1661 and the Duchess, a redoubtable enemy and elusive ally, is as old as the century.

the Franciscan's death: the mysterious Franciscan friar who arrived at the Blue Peacock Inn at Fontainebleau to undertake secret negotiations designed to destabilize Germany and kill the Pope (*The Vicomte de Bragelonne* (Routledge, 1896, vol. iii, chaps. 17–18), was no less than the Vicar-General of the Jesuits. When

Aramis, Bishop of Vannes, reveals to him the true identity of the Prisoner in the Iron Mask, information which could prove most useful to the Order, the 'Franciscan', who is close to death, nominates him as his successor: this is the 'initiation into certain secrets' to which the Duchess refers. At a stroke, Aramis becomes immensely powerful and as wealthy as Monte Cristo, and much of his subsequent political plotting is intended to further Jesuit interests. The 'Franciscan' was buried at Fontainebleau and Aramis and Madame de Chevreuse met at night at his graveside (*Bragelonne*, iii, chap. 36). Their meeting was observed by d'Artagnan, but only now does the reader learn exactly what the plotters had plotted.

2   *Madame de Longueville*: Anne-Geneviève, Duchess de Longueville (1619–79), was the sister of the Grand Condé. A bitter opponent of Mazarin, she played an important role in the Fronde. Dumas made extensive use of her Memoirs for the historical background to the d'Artagnan cycle.

Marie Michon: see note to p. 1.

3   *a friend of M. Fouquet's*: a protégé of Mazarin, Nicolas Fouquet (1615–80) was still, in 1661, Surintendant of France's finances and the master of vast wealth acquired through abuse of power. He built the magnificent château at Vaux (1658) and was a generous patron of art and literature. He was admired for his munificent style of management, but resented by sections of the court and the bourgeoisie for his unashamed corruption. It has been argued that Louis turned against him out of jealousy for his wealth, but it is more likely that he feared the influence of Fouquet who, in 1658, acquired the Breton island of Belle-Isle from which he might have led a campaign against the throne at a time when Louis had yet to command the obedience of all the provinces of France. A cabal was formed to ruin him. Fouquet was arrested in September 1661 and remained in prison until his death in 1680. Dumas, himself a reckless man who admired lavish style, gives him a noble and sympathetic persona in *The Vicomte de Bragelonne*. It was Fouquet who appointed Aramis Bishop of Vannes and promised him a cardinal's hat. On his order, Aramis fortified Belle-Isle, using the skills of Porthos who remained ignorant of his plans, and the new Jesuit General threw the inexhaustible resources of the Order behind his protector and against the wily Colbert who, by means of purloined letters, had amassed enough evidence to convince the King of his corruption.

Dumas viewed Fouquet as a dashing Cavalier who possessed all the flair and imagination he found lacking in the grim and devious Roundhead, Colbert.

le Comte de la Fère: i.e. Athos.

Queen-Mother: Anne of Austria (1601–66), daughter of Philip III of Spain, wife of Louis XIII, and Regent during the minority of Louis XIV when she ruled France with Mazarin who was her lover and perhaps her husband (Mazarin, though a cardinal, was not an ordained priest). It was to recover the diamond tags which she had given to Buckingham that d'Artagnan first took on the wicked Milady in *The Three Musketeers*. Madame de Chevreuse had been close to Anne in the 1620s, returned to court favour in 1643, but fell from grace for her part in the Fronde between 1648 and 1650. Anne's 'grievances' against her include Chevreuse's part in the Fronde and the fact that she was one of the few people privy to the secret of the identity of the Man in the Iron Mask.

d'Artagnan: of the four friends, only d'Artagnan, the youngest, was still a Musketeer.

Baisemeaux: François de Montlézun (*c.*1613–97), joined the King's Musketeers in 1634 in which he served with the real d'Artagnan (and Dumas's fictitious quartet). He saw active service in Italy during the 1640s and was appointed Captain of Mazarin's Guards in 1649. In 1655 he became *seigneur* de Besmaus, a family property in the Gers in south-west France, and was named Governor of the Bastille in 1658, a post which he held until 1664. As part of a long-term strategy designed to give him easy access to the Bastille, Aramis had earlier advanced him the money required to buy his governorship (*Bragelonne*, ii, chap. 40).

4 *M. de Laicques*: i.e. Geoffroy de Laigues (1614–74), Gaston d'Orléans's Captain of Guards, who fought in the Italian campaigns of the 1640s and distinguished himself at the battle of Lens (1648). His association with Madame de Chevreuse dated from the Fronde (see note to p. 7) in which he took a prominent part.

King of Spain: Philippe IV (1605–65).

5 *general of the Jesuits*: the General of the Society of Jesus (founded in 1534 by Ignatius Loyola) is elected by a congregation of professed members and holds office for life. The history of the Society is broadly the same in all countries (brilliant rise,

followed by repression and finally restoration), a cycle several times repeated in France from which the Jesuits were expelled in 1598, 1762, and 1901 for activities frequently regarded as conspiratorial and subversive. In 1661 they were still reeling from Pascal's scathingly witty *Lettres provinciales* (1656–7). A German named Nickel was General between 1652 and 1664.

5 *Dampierre*: the Château of Dampierre, near Rambouillet, was built in 1660. It was acquired by the Luynes family, to which the Duchess de Chevreuse was related by her first marriage, in 1664.

forgotten everything: i.e. Anne of Austria had forgotten the role once played by 'Marie Michon', the indispensable go-between of *The Three Musketeers*. The Duchess seems to overlook the fact that her part in the Fronde was scarcely calculated to endear her to her former friend, now Queen Mother.

7 *the Fronde*: the Fronde was the civil war which divided France between 1648 and 1653 during the minority of Louis XIV. The first phase (to 1649) set the Paris *parlement*, supported by the Prince de Conti and the Cardinal de Retz, against the Queen's party led by Mazarin: the respected *parlementaire* Broussel was arrested, barricades were set up by Parisians, and the court withdrew to Saint-Germain-en-Laye. During the second phase (to 1652), Condé, Beaufort, and Mme de Longueville, with Spanish support, led a campaign against royal forces led by Turenne. It was during this second phase that Madame de Chevreuse was a particularly active *frondeuse*.

8 *Cardinal Mazarin*: Jules Mazarin (1602–61), an Italian who was naturalized French in 1639, was named by Richelieu as his successor in 1642. He ruled France during the regency of Anne of Austria, ended the Thirty Years War in 1648, and assured the Spanish succession by arranging the marriage of Louis XIV with the Infanta, Maria-Teresa, in 1660. The avarice, wiliness, and habit of deception which Dumas imputes to him in earlier instalments of *The Vicomte de Bragelonne* are well attested. Like most representatives of established authority in the novel, he is portrayed as odious. The letters in question furnished proof of Fouquet's corruption.

9 *Signor Mazarini*: Mazarin's Italian origins were frequently held against him. It is now accepted that he was the lover of Anne of Austria, but there is no documentary proof that he was her husband, as Dumas roundly states here.

13 *Colbert*: Jean-Baptiste Colbert (1619–83), a draper's son and Mazarin's confidant, worked indefatigably in partnership with Louis XIV to build up the economic and administrative life of the State. He did not live in the rue Croix-des-Petits-Champs (which runs from the rue Saint-Honoré to the Place des Victoires), though in 1665 he rented a house in the rue des Petits-Champs which lies between the Palais-Royal and the Bibliothèque Nationale. Between 1661 and 1669, he also built a number of houses nearby, in the rue Vivienne. Though he later gives a fair estimate of Colbert's achievements (see p. 466), Dumas portrays him as devious, 'rough and uncouth' (p. 14): he is another authority figure who is painted in thoroughly unsympathetic colours.

14 *Louis XIII. . . . great Cardinal*: perhaps the greatest achievement of Louis XIII (1601–43) was to have allowed Armand-Jean du Plessis, Cardinal de Richelieu (1585–1642), a free hand to create the centralized monarchy which Louis XIV inherited and completed. The Richelieu of *The Three Musketeers* is a ruthless and unfeeling machine as much dedicated to his own power as to extending that of the King.

15 *Surintendant*: when Mazarin died in March 1661 (a few months before Aramis and Chevreuse meet) the Surintendant of Finances was Fouquet who confidently expected to become Louis XIV's chief minister in succession to the Cardinal. By May, however, Louis had decided that he would take personal charge of the nation's affairs. He persuaded Fouquet, still expecting to be made Chancellor, to resign his post of *procureur-général* which had made him answerable only to the Paris *parlement*. Abetted by the ambitious Colbert, he set out to ruin and discredit Fouquet, as we shall see. Colbert became Controller of Finances in 1664.

Voiture: Vincent Voiture (1598–1648), poet, letter writer, and one of the arbiters of grammar and refined language.

Conrart: Valentin Conrart (1603–75), first secretary of the French Academy created by Richelieu in 1635, and occasional poet—so occasional that Boileau went out of his way to admire his 'prudent silence'. The Colossus of Rhodes, a huge statue of the sun, was destroyed by an earthquake in 227 BC, fifty-six years after its completion. It was said to bestride the harbour and that a ship could sail between its legs.

16 *Cinq-Mars*: Henri Coiffier de Ruzé, Marquis de Cinq-Mars

(1620–42), was executed along with his friend de Thou for plotting with the Spaniards against Richelieu. The Duchess's sympathy for Cinq-Mars is genuine, for she too had sought to overthrow the Cardinal. See note to p. 1.

18 *the Parliament*: the *parlement* was a body of magistrates charged with administering the law. However, it had the right to pass judgment on any matters submitted for its consideration by the King. On occasions, it refused to approve royal edicts and was then generally supported by the Third Estate which viewed it as a rather flimsy constitutional check on the monarchy. As *procureur-général*, a post to which he was appointed in 1654, Fouquet's allegiance was to the *parlement*. As long as he held the post, he was beyond the reach of the royal jurisdiction.

19 *paroxysms of her disease*: according to the *Mémoires* of Mme de Motteville (Paris, 1824, v. 198), the Queen Mother's cancer did not declare itself until the spring of 1664.

Béguines: an order of lay nuns, originating in the Netherlands, who take no vows but live in religious communities. On p. 22, Chevreuse is a 'béguine' in the popular sense of the word: a bigot, a hypocrite.

22 *Vanel*: Claude Vanel (d. *c*.1687), later the Duke d'Orléans's Controller of Finances, was a magistrate of the *parlement* and author of histories of court gallantry. Dumas's Vanel bears little relationship to the real Vanel whose name he borrows. The post of *procureur-général* was bought on 8 August 1661, when Fouquet resigned it, by Achille de Harlay, Comte de Beaumont (1606–71), for 1.4 million *livres*.

25 *M. de Gourville, M. Pélisson, and others*: Fouquet inspired keen loyalty among the administrators, writers, and artists who formed a côterie known as 'the Epicureans'. Jean Hérault de Gourville (1625–1703) had been a *frondeur* before becoming Fouquet's agent: after Fouquet's arrest, he was sentenced to death but escaped to Brussels where he lived on money not entirely honestly come by. Paul Pellisson (1624–93) wrote spiritedly in Fouquet's defence and spent five years in the Bastille before regaining favour by his appointment as Historiographer Royal. On Valentin Conrart, see note to p. 15. Jean Loret, the author of a weekly verse gazette which commented upon public events and figures, also spoke in Fouquet's defence: for his pains, Colbert stopped his small pension, but Fouquet arranged for a

sum of money to be paid to him anonymously. He died in 1665. Both Jean de La Fontaine (1621–95), known primarily as the author of the *Fables* (1668–94), and Molière (1622–73), France's greatest comic playwright, acknowledged their debts to the generosity of their patron.

26 *Verses to my wife*: Madame Vanel, libelled here by Dumas, was never Fouquet's mistress nor did La Fontaine (then carrying on his affair with Madame Colletet) write verses to her.

28 *Madame de Motteville and the Senora Molena*: Françoise Bertaut (*c.*1619–89), widow of Nicolas Langlois, *seigneur* de Motteville, was lady-in-waiting to Anne of Austria; Dumas used her *Mémoires* extensively as a source of background information. Doña Molina was Anne's devoted and unfailingly discreet duenna. The 'estos hijos' episode was taken from the *Journal* (Paris, 1860–1, ii. 144) of Olivier d'Ormesson (1616–86) who also reported Fouquet's trial in considerable detail.

the Queen: i.e. Maria-Teresa, the Spanish Infanta, whom Louis had married in 1660.

Mademoiselle de la Vallière: Louise de La Baume Le Blanc, Duchess de la Vallière (1644–1710). *The Vicomte de Bragelonne* has previously related how Raoul, who lived near her at Blois, loved her when they were both children but lost her to Louis XIV whose mistress she was from 1661 until 1667 when she was replaced in the King's affections by Madame de Montespan. As the 'imprecations' suggest, the ladies much resented Louise's influence.

29 *Vallot*: Antoine Vallot (1594–1671), doctor to Anne of Austria before becoming the King's chief medical adviser in 1652. He regularly prescribed an emetic wine of his own invention.

30 *your ... son, was born*: Louis XIV (1638–1715) was born at Saint-Germain-en-Laye on 5 September 1638. Dumas's chronology is again faulty here, since the action is set in early August 1661.

34 *Bouvard ... Honoré*: Charles Bouvard (1572–1658) was doctor to Louis XIII whom he once bled forty-seven times in one year. He was a celebrated examiner of medical theses which he failed when they did not coincide with his own views. As a physician, he was in fierce competition with the surgeon Honoré who attended Anne of Austria at her confinement in September 1638: the two

branches of medicine were not joined until the end of the
eighteenth century.

Péronne ... Laporte: Dumas borrowed Mme Péronne or
Péronnette from the account of the birth of Anne of Austria's
'twins' given by Soulavie in his highly fanciful *Memoirs of the Duke
de Richelieu* (Paris, 1790) which Dumas knew and quoted in his
Crimes célèbres (1839–40). Soulavie attributed the story to an
unidentified courtier whom Dumas names as Pierre de La Porte
(1603–80) who entered the service of Anne of Austria in 1621.
Unfortunately for Dumas, La Porte was imprisoned in the
Bastille in 1637 and was not therefore on hand for the
double-birth in 1638. He returned to favour only after the death
of Louis XIII in 1643 and thereafter served the Queen loyally.
La Porte's *Memoirs* were one of Dumas's sources for the period.
Earlier in *Bragelonne* (ii, chap. 44), the Man in the Iron Mask
informed Aramis that he was raised by a nurse and a valet—here
revealed as Péronne and La Porte—who died, doubtless
poisoned, in about 1653.

Madame de Hausac: in fact, Mme de Lansac, later governess to
Louis XIV.

37 *Albert de Luynes*: Louis-Charles d'Albert, Duke de Luynes
(1620–90), son of Madame de Chevreuse by her first husband,
was a man of studious disposition who was thrown against his
inclination into army service where he won distinction at the siege
of Arras in 1653.

42 *Saint-Mandé*: now part of Paris's eastern suburb, Saint-Mandé, in
the Bois de Vincennes, was in 1661 a small rural community
dominated by the country house where Fouquet's artistic
entourage and political associates met regularly.

Vatel: Vatel was Fouquet's steward and it was he who organized
the fête at Vaux. His professional standards were legendary. In
1671, as Condé's *maître d'hôtel*, he was responsible for a ceremonial
supper for Louis XIV: there was not enough meat and the
fireworks were spoiled by mist. For failing in his duty, Vatel
committed suicide.

Abbé Fouquet: Basile Fouquet (1622–80), brother of Nicolas, was a
lay priest with devious talents whom Mazarin placed at the head
of his secret service. He had a hand in most of the political
intrigues of the 1640s and 1650s: it was he who negotiated the
submission of Madame de Chevreuse after the Fronde, and his

intrigues helped his brother to achieve high office. From about 1657, he turned against Fouquet and quarrelled publicly with him in January 1661. After Fouquet's fall, he was exiled to Tours on 8 September.

45 *Boccacio, Arétin*: Boccaccio (1313–75), author of *The Decameron*, and Pierre Aretino (1492–1556), a satirist known mainly for his licentious verve, are used by Dumas to characterize not La Fontaine's fables but his tales which appeared between 1665 and 1674. Though La Fontaine borrowed from Aretino 'and others', his major sources are indicated in the title of his first collection: *Verse Tales taken from Boccaccio and Ariosto, by Monsieur de La F.* Dumas took a keen professional interest in the earnings of other writers.

46 *the Academy*: i.e. the French Academy, founded by Richelieu in 1635.

47 *Fugiunt risus leporesque*: members of the *parlement* wore a robe (or gown) of office which was associated with a certain dourness of purpose, which is why those who wear it 'flee from the smiles and the graces'. Pélisson's remark puns on *lepos* (good humour) and *lepus* (a hare).

Quo non ascendant: Fouquet's motto, meaning 'To what heights may he not aspire?' was *Quo non ascendet*.

Indian fable: from time to time Dumas alludes to 'Indian' or 'Oriental' fables usually taken from the *Arabian Nights* which he believed, erroneously, to have been current in the seventeenth century. See note to p. 280.

48 *Eschylus*: by one account, Aeschylus the tragic playwright died when a bird dropped a tortoise on his head.

Rara avis interris!: read *in terris*: 'a creature rare on earth' (Juvenal, *Satires*, vi. 165).

50 *Semper ad eventum*: Horace's recommendation to all epic poets (*Ars poetica*, line 148): 'With always an eye to the climax.' It was advice of which Dumas, the natural romancer, had no need.

51 *Madame de Bellière*: Suzanne de Bruc, Marquise Du Plessis-Bellière, who died in 1705 aged 'almost a hundred' Courted by Mazarin after her husband's death in 1654, she became close to Fouquet. When he was arrested in 1661, she remained under house-detention at Montbrison until 1665. Dumas makes her the sister of Mary Grafton (*Bragelonne*, iv,

chap. 15) and measures her love for Fouquet by the gift of her plate (ii, chaps. 45–6) which temporarily staved off his ruin: see note to p. 69.

54 *Palissy Ware ... Benvenuto*: Bernard Palissy (1510–90), scientist and the greatest maker of earthenware of his age. Benvenuto Cellini (1500–71), Florentine goldsmith, sculptor, and engraver, and author of an autobiography which served Dumas as the basis for his *Ascanio* (1843).

Gorgny wine: a fortified wine, flavoured with herbs, in the manner of vermouth.

57 *the Valtelline*: i.e. the Valteline, between Lake Como and the River Adda. In 1626, during the Thirty Years War, Richelieu denied Spain a passage to southern Germany through this area of north Italy.

58 *Montfauçon*: i.e. Montfaucon, now absorbed into Paris between La Villette and the Buttes Chaumont, which was the notorious site of a gallows installed by Enguerrand de Marigny (1260–1315) who, having served as first minister to Philip the Fair, was convicted of corruption and hanged on his own gibbet: his body remained there for two years. Jacques de Beaune, *seigneur* de Semblançay (*c.*1457–1527), minister to Louis XII and François I, was also found guilty of embezzling State monies and was hanged at Montfaucon, the French equivalent of Tyburn, for his crimes.

68 *a lecture divided into three heads*: the anecdote is more reminiscent of the Pangloss of Voltaire's *Candide* (1759) than of any recognizable fable or tale by La Fontaine.

69 *with one million only*: earlier in *The Vicomte de Bragelonne* (ii, chap. 41), the King, implementing Colbert's policy of ruining Fouquet, had asked him to provide 4 million francs for a fête to be held at Fontainebleau. On that occasion, he was saved by Madame de Bellière's offer of her plate and jewels which amounted to the million francs which Aramis did not then possess, though his appointment as General of the Society of Jesus now gives him unlimited funds to draw upon.

71 *Ruysdaël*: Jakob van Ruysdaël (1628–82), a Dutch landscape painter noted for his acute observation, rich colour, and strong line.

Raoul: Louis XIV, seeing Raoul as a rival for the affections of

Louise de la Vallière, had sent him to the court of Charles II of England (*Bragelonne*, iv, chaps. 15–17) where he had orders to remain indefinitely. The Duchess d'Orléans, Henrietta, sister to the English King, jealous of Louise's growing influence over Louis, had written secretly to her brother requesting that Raoul be sent back to Paris. Louis and Louise are exchanging their first kiss when Raoul, abetted by Louise's childhood friend, the devious Montalais, bursts in upon them—which is why in the next paragraph he flees 'in a state of frenzy and dismay'.

Guiche: Armand de Gramont, Comte de Guiche (1638–73), famous for his military and amorous conquests which included Henrietta, Duchess d'Orléans. Dumas makes him Raoul's closest friend. Earlier in the story (*Bragelonne*, ii, chaps. 42–3), Guiche takes exception to ungallant remarks made about Louise by the despicable Comte de Wardes at Fontainebleau and fights a duel in which he is badly wounded.

74 *the adventure of the oak*: strolling beneath the royal oak with Mademoiselle de Montalais and Mademoiselle de Tonnay-Charente during the fête at Fontainebleau, Louise innocently reveals that she loves the King. To her chagrin, she discovers that she has been overheard by Louis who thereafter returns her love (*Bragelonne*, iii, chap. 5).

75 *his friend's son*: Raoul is the son of Athos and Mme de Chevreuse. The circumstances of his conception are related in chaps. 10 and 22 of *Twenty Years After*.

the Captain: Dumas makes d'Artagnan Captain of the King's Musketeers as a reward for services rendered in *Twenty Years After*.

I have been in England: but not as a tourist. D'Artagnan travelled to England in *The Three Musketeers* to recover the diamond tags given to Buckingham by Anne of Austria, thus upsetting the dastardly plot hatched by Richelieu and Milady. In *Twenty Years After*, he is on hand in London to foil the villainous Mordaunt, son of Milady, though not before Charles I is beheaded. In the first volume of *The Vicomte de Bragelonne*, d'Artagnan kidnaps General Monk at Newcastle and helps restore the English monarchy.

76 *Porthos*: after the adventures described in *The Three Musketeers*, Porthos—M. du Vallon—had married Mme Coquenard, a rich lawyer's widow, thereby acquiring lands which allowed him to

become 'Monsieur du Vallon de Bracieux de Pierrefonds'. 'The Titan' has a taste for titles and was created Baron for his role in *Twenty Years After*. Earlier in *The Vicomte de Bragelonne*, we learn that Aramis had plucked him from retirement and entrusted him with the secret mission of fortifying Belle-Isle, in Quiberon Bay, which Fouquet had bought in 1658 on the orders of Mazarin.

80 *Madame*: by custom, the King's brother, the Duke d'Orléans, was known as 'Monsieur' and his wife as 'Madame'.

81 *de Wardes*: the son of the de Wardes killed at Calais by d'Artagnan in *The Three Musketeers*. One of Dumas's series of evil characters (which includes Milady and her son Mordaunt), de Wardes seeks vengeance for his father's death. He challenges Raoul, kills the son of Buckingham, and wounds Guiche (see note to p. 71). Several de Vardes are to be found in the memoirs of the period, but none matches the villainy of Dumas's invented de Wardes.

82 *letter to Charles II.*: see not to p. 71.

83 *flight to Chaillot*: these stages in Louis's courtship of Louise are enacted earlier in *The Vicomte de Bragelonne*. Historically, Louise's flight to the convent at Chaillot did not occur until February 1662, almost a year after the events recounted here.

85 *Saint-Aignan's apartment*: François de Beauvillier, Comte de Saint-Aignan (1610–87), was appointed Gaston d'Orléans's Captain of Guards in 1644 and First Gentleman of the Bedchamber to the King in 1649. This office made him responsible for organizing ballets and fêtes at court. He was a patron of the arts and an occasional versifier (see p. 98). A confidant of Louis XIV, he occupied rooms in the Palais-Royal immediately below Louise's apartment. He had paid the carpenter to whom d'Artagnan has referred (p. 78) to install a staircase connecting the two chambers (*Bragelonne*, iv, chaps. 10–13), thus enabling Louise to meet the King in secret. He had further commissioned the painter Charles Lebrun (1619–90) to paint her portrait which was kept there.

88 *Amadis*: the eponymous hero of Montalvo's *Amadis de Gaule* (1508) became the type of the constant, respectful lover of the chivalric tradition. Though in Dumas's mind Raoul was quite different from the excessively sentimental hero of seventeenth-century pastoral romance, the son of Athos in fact cuts a not dissimilar figure—but as an exemplar of the extravagant sensibility of Dumas's own Romantic age.

89 *Montalais ... Tonnay-Charente*: like Louise, Françoise de
Montalais had been a maid of honour at the marriage of Louis's
brother and Henrietta of England. A considerable schemer, she
had a hand in sending the 'Spanish letter' in 1664 which
informed the Queen, Maria-Teresa, of Louis's infatuation with
Louise, her erstwhile friend. Françoise-Athenaïs de Roche-
chouart de Mortemart (1641–1707) was born at the Château
de Tonnay-Charente. As Mme de Montespan, she was to oust
Louise from the affections of Louis XIV by 1667.

91 *Porthos*: Porthos had been introduced to court by Aramis at the
fête at Fontainebleau where he warmed the King's heart by his
good humour and solid trenchermanship.

Mouston: Mousqueton, Porthos's former servant but now steward
of his master's estates, had abbreviated his name to a form which
he believes to be more dignified than the 'blunderbuss' by which
he was known in *The Three Musketeers*.

Messrs. de Tréville ... Bouillon-Turenne: Jean-Arnaud du Peyrer,
Comte de Troisvilles (pronounced 'Tréville') (1599–1672), was
Captain-Lieutenant of the King's Musketeers when Dumas first
brought d'Artagnan to Paris in 1625. He lost his post in 1646 and
was later appointed Governor of Foix. Charles de Schomberg
(1601–56), Duke d'Halluin, achieved the rank of Marshall of
France. Charles, Duke de La Vieuville (*sic*) (1582–1653),
appointed Surintendant of Finances in 1623, introduced fiscal
reforms which antagonized the nobility; an opponent of
Richelieu, he was later recalled by Mazarin to administer the
nation's finances. The Condé family, a branch of the Bourbons,
furnished France with many generals: Dumas here refers to Louis
de Bourbon, Prince de Condé (1621–86), known as 'Monsieur le
Prince', who fought with valour in the battles of Rocroi (1643)
and Lens (1648), rebelled during the Fronde but returned to
favour in 1659. Henri de la Tour d'Auvergne (1555–1623) was
Vicomte de Turenne before becoming Duke de Bouillon;
diplomat and soldier, he was the father of Louis XIV's great
general, 'le Grand Turenne'.

Truchen and Planchet: Planchet, d'Artagnan's servant in *The Three
Musketeers*, subsequently bought a confectioner's shop in the rue
des Lombards and prospered. Whenever crises loom, d'Artagnan
coaxes him out of retirement, though he now longs to sell his
business and live quietly in the house he has bought at
Fontainebleau with the motherly Trüchen who goes with it. It

was from this house that d'Artagnan observed the meeting between Aramis and Madame de Chevreuse in the cemetery which was evoked in Chapter 1. Porthos stayed at Planchet's house during the Fontainebleau fête and consumed everything in sight.

96 *Minimes*: i.e. the convent of the Order of Minimes, founded in 1435.

100 *Fiesque ... de las Fuentès*: Dumas was fond of using authentic names as local colour. Charles-Léon, Comte de Fiesque (1613–58), sentenced to death for his part in the Fronde, had escaped to Spain where he died poor. Mme de Laferté was the wife of Henri de La Ferté de Saint-Nectaire (1600–81), Marshall of France, who had fought against the *frondeurs*. The Marquis de Las Fuentes was Governor of Milan.

111 *"Mercury"*: as Louis's go-between, Saint-Aignan qualifies as a messenger of the gods.

112 *Styx*: according to classical mythology, the river of Death which circled hell seven times.

sink from Apollo to Phœbus: a rather obscure jest by which the King (himself 'the Sun King') distinguishes between Apollo in his later manifestation as Helios, the sun-god, and Phoebus, the name first used to describe his 'purity' and 'brightness'.

116 *Ovidius Naso*: Ovid (43 BC–AD 17) was banished by the Emperor Augustus in AD 9. He admitted to deserving his punishment but claimed that he was a witness to, rather than the perpetrator of, an event which still remains shrouded in mystery.

119 *you refused*: when asked for his opinion (*Bragelonne*, ii, chap. 37), Louis XIV had considered Louise neither rich enough nor pretty enough for a man of the rank of the Vicomte de Bragelonne. At the time, the Comte de la Fère (Athos) shared his view.

130 *Heu! Miser!*: i.e. 'O Miserere!'

131 *as I have just been tried myself*: a reference to Athos's love for the predatory Madame de Chevreuse.

140 *Grimaud*: Athos's faithful and resourceful servant since the time of *The Three Musketeers* and for some time now steward of his master's estate near Blois. It was the resourceful Grimaud, a man of few words, who had enabled the Duke de Beaufort to escape from the prison of Vincennes at the beginning of *Twenty Years After*.

141 *Bastille*: the Bastille was a fortified gaol built in the fourteenth century at the Porte Saint-Antoine in the east of Paris. It was extended at various times and in Louis XIV's day was equipped with four towers each five storeys high. Prisoners entered a courtyard overlooked by the Governor's quarters (the 'Cour du Gouvernement'), and passed through a guarded portcullis before being taken to a dungeon or, in the case of convicted persons of rank, to a room in one of the towers: Dumas later mentions the Tour de la Bertaudière and the Tour de la Bazinière, both in the south-west corner. The Bastille held many notable historical and literary prisoners—though it could contain eighty inmates, it averaged forty at any time during Louis XIV's reign—and eventually came to symbolize the repressive character of the *ancien régime*.

Cours-la-Reine: Paris, which still had the character of a walled city, was ringed by about eighty gates at which internal customs duties were levied on goods entering and leaving the capital. The gate Dumas refers to here was a 'barrier' designed for river-traffic and was situated at the western end of the present Cours la Reine which runs from the Place de la Concorde to the Place du Canada. Another river 'barrier', the 'Barrière de la Conférence', mentioned on p. 150, was sited further east on the present Quai de la Conférence opposite the Invalides.

M. Monk: General George Monk (1608–70), Duke of Albemarle, restored the English monarchy to Charles II in 1660. In the first part of *The Vicomte de Bragelonne*, Dumas gives d'Artagnan a major role in events, which included kidnapping Monk and transporting him to Holland in a sealed chest. For services rendered, Monk rewarded him with 'a little house in a grove' to which are attached a hundred acres 'on the banks of the Clyde' (i, chap. 36). Dumas's knowledge of British geography was somewhat sketchy.

145 *de Louvière . . . de Tremblay*: when the Fronde began in 1648, the Governor of the Bastille was Charles Le Clerc du Tremblay who capitulated to the *frondeurs* in January 1649. He was replaced by Pierre Broussel, a respected member of the Paris *parlement*, whose arrest in August 1648 had triggered the Fronde. Broussel's functions as governor were carried out by his son Jérôme, *seigneur* de Louvières.

148 *the Dowager Madame*: Marguerite de Lorraine, Dowager Duchess

d'Orléans, the second wife of Gaston d'Orléans, withdrew to
Blois after the Fronde. Between 1654 and 1659, five or six girls of
good family (including Louise and Mademoiselle de Montalais)
kept her own three daughters company.

149 *his mother ... the Queen ... Madame*: Louis's mother was Anne of
Austria. The Queen was his wife, Maria-Teresa. Madame was
Henrietta of England, Duchess d'Orléans and sister of the
English King Charles II.

Baradas ... Cinq-Mars: François, Chevalier de Barradat (*sic*)
(1604–82), one of Louis XIII's 'mignons', plotted against
Richelieu with Cinq-Mars (see note to p. 16) but was
subsequently reinstated.

152 *my resignation*: at the beginning of *The Vicomte de Bragelonne* (i,
chap. 14), d'Artagnan resigned his commission because, in his
view, Louis had not acted like a true king in refusing Charles of
England the million francs he needed to recover his throne from
Cromwell's rebels. The Comte de la Fère did not finance Charles
out of his own pocket. More accurately, he told him that a secret
cache amounting to a million was hidden in a vault in Newcastle
and then helped him to set hands on it.

155 *his own individual profit*: all public offices during the *ancien régime*
were bought and sold by their incumbents who had a free hand to
exploit their posts financially. The Governor of the Bastille was
paid 50 francs a day for royal prisoners, 30 francs for aristocrats
and generals, from 15 to 5 francs for inmates of lesser social
distinction, and 3 francs for poets, tradesmen, and bailiff's clerks.
When Besmaus died in 1697, he was worth 2 million francs.

157 *on the banks of the Loire*: Dumas situated Athos's modest—and
fictitious—property of La Fère in the Loire valley, somewhere
west of Blois, in order that Raoul and Louise be childhood
sweethearts. La Vallière, which Dumas places 'nearby', is a small
estate at Reugny, some 25 kilometres west of Amboise. As a girl,
the historical Louise was on close terms with the son of a family in
the locality named Bragelonne or Bragelongne. Raoul's character
and role, however, are of Dumas's invention.

159 *a drama in five acts*: Dumas, the author of about sixty plays, was a
sound judge of dramatic material.

161 *gigantic stature*: according to *Twenty Years After*, Porthos is 'slightly
under six feet tall', Mouston a foot and a half shorter, and

d'Artagnan 'just over 5 feet'. The French foot ('le pied de roi') was the equivalent of 12.8 English inches, which means that in British terms Porthos measured around 6 feet 4 inches and d'Artagnan 5 feet 6 inches which was about average for the period. Later (p. 218), Dumas notes that Louis XIV, like Mouston, was 'a foot and a half shorter' than Porthos, though much earlier (*Bragelonne*, i, chap. 8) he had noted that the King, who was 'short of stature', 'was scarcely five feet two inches'—or in English about 5 feet 6, like d'Artagnan. Charles I of England had measured a good 2 inches over 6 feet and was regarded as very tall indeed.

163   *little street Jean-Beausire*: the rue Jean-Beausire, which still exists, led off the Faubourg Saint-Antoine at the northern end of the prison.

    the Faubourg St. Antoine: instead of heading for the centre of Paris, where Athos has lodgings, the coach follows the road to Melun before turning west for Blois.

164   *Do you recollect Baisemeaux, Porthos?*: as a former Musketeer, Besmaus had served with Porthos and company during the 1630s.

168   *secret society*: i.e. the Society of Jesus, of which Aramis is General.

174   *I have seen you before*: readers of earlier parts of the novel will recall that Aramis, by feigning an interest in a prisoner named Seldon, had already visited no. 12 (*Bragelonne*, ii, chaps. 42–4) who is entered in the register as 'Marchiali' as a 50 franc or royal prisoner, a figure later corrected by Mazarin to 15, the rate for commoners. He is not tall, has short hair, and is dressed in cambric and black velvet. See note to p. 228.

179   *Noisy-le-Sec*: after the adventures recounted in *The Three Musketeers*, Aramis, who had already shown an interest in religion, became the abbé d'Herblay and retired to a monsatery at Noisy-le-Sec, 6 kilometres from the Porte des Lilas on Paris's north-eastern rim, where d'Artagnan found him at the start of *Twenty Years After*.

180   *the only persons I have ever seen*: the lady is Mme de Chevreuse and her companion in black is Anne of Austria. The 'gentleman about forty-five years old' is possibly Mazarin. His master, who also acted as his tutor, was La Porte. On Perronnette and La Porte see note to p. 34.

190   *Gaston d'Orléans*: Gaston-Jean-Baptiste de France, Duke d'Orléans

(1608–60), younger brother of Louis XIII, had a hand in all intrigues directed against Richelieu, became Lieutenant-Governor of the kingdom, and supported Anne of Austria during the Fronde. Aramis's harsh judgement of him was shared by his contemporaries. The Cardinal de Retz remarked that Gaston 'had everything a gentleman should have, except courage' (*Mémoires*, Paris, 1779, ii. 306).

195 *one hundred and fifty thousand livres*: this was the sum advanced to Baisemeaux by Aramis for the purchase of the governorship of the Bastille: see note to p. 3.

196 *His Majesty's society*: see note to p. 91.

La Fontaine's hare: in *The Hare and the Frogs* (Fables, bk. II. xiv), the hare sits sad and reflective until he stirs and scatters a group of frogs: their reaction makes him realize that there are creatures even more nervous and timid than he.

198 *the Roman general Antony*: Mark Antony (83–30 BC), whose extravagance was legendary.

199 *fortified Belle-Isle*: see note to p. 76.

the late Madame du Vallon: see note to p. 76.

200 *Costar*: Pierre Costar (1603–60), son of a Paris hatmaker and renowned for his vanity, was the author of minor works in the currently fashionable verbose, 'precious' style

202 *Percerin*: there was a succession of court tailors—Ourdault, Barthélemy Audran, and Baraillon (who invented French breeches)—but the Percerin family appears not to occur in the memoirs of the period nor in the street where Dumas situates their shop (though it did house François Barnom, the King's barber).

Ambrose Paré: Ambroise Paré (1510–90), surgeon to four kings, who replaced cauterization by the tourniquet during amputation. The religious wars of the sixteenth century involved considerable persecution of the Huguenots which was ended by the Edict of Nantes published by Henri IV in 1598.

203 *the Queen of Navarre*: Marguerite de Navarre (1492–1549) (also known as Marguerite d'Angoulême) was the sister of François I. She protected the Huguenots and was a lover of literature and the arts: her *Heptameron* (1559) was a collection of tales modelled on Boccaccio's *Decameron*.

Queen Catherine: Catherine de Medici (1519–89), wife of Henri II, mother of three French kings, was a ruthless political manipulator who played a major role in the St Bartholomew's Day Massacre of Protestants in 1572.

Henri III.: son of Catherine de Medici, Henri III (1551–89) became King of France in 1574. A man of dissolute habits—and 'gay' in the modern sense—he pursued the Huguenots relentlessly. He was assassinated in 1589 and with him the male line of the house of Valois became extinct.

The marriage of Henri IV. and Marie de Medici: Henri of Navarre (1553–1610) inherited the French crown by Salic law in 1589. A Protestant, he converted to catholicism in 1593. He revived French fortunes abroad and at home ended the civil wars with the Edict of Nantes which guaranteed Protestants freedom of conscience and impartial justice. He divorced Marguerite de France in 1599. On 14 May 1610, the day after the coronation of his second wife, Marie de' Medici, he was assassinated by a fanatic named Ravaillac. It was the twentieth attempt on his life.

Bassompière: François de Bassompierre (1579–1646), diplomat and Marshall of France. For plotting against Richelieu he was detained in the Bastille between 1631 and 1643.

Concino Concini: a Florentine adventurer who, abetted by his wife Laure Galigaï, gained considerable power through his influence over Marie de' Medici. A weak but ambitious man, he acquired the title of Maréchal d'Ancre. He died on 24 April 1617 when resisting an order for his arrest issued by Louis XIII: he was shot on the Pont du Louvre by Nicolas de Vitry (1581–1644), Captain of the King's Guard, who was made Marshall of France for his efforts.

204 *Anne of Austria ... Marion de Lorme*: Anne of Austria married Louis XIII in 1615. According to a rumour, recorded in various seventeenth-century memoirs, Richelieu, besotted with the Queen, once danced a saraband before her, dressed in the costume of a clown.

Mirame (1641), by Desmarets de Saint-Sorlin (1595–1676), inaugurated the new theatre in the Palais-Cardinal, renamed the Palais-Royal after the death of Richelieu. George Villiers, Duke of Buckingham (1592–1628)—the Buckingham of *The Three Musketeers*—became through influence and marriage the richest man in England: Dumas's usual sources do not seem to mention his casual way with pearls, though if the incident occurred at all, it happened in 1625 when Buckingham was paying unsuccessful court to Anne of Austria at the Palace of the Louvre. On Cinq-Mars and Mademoiselle Ninon, see notes to pp. 16 and 1. François de Vendôme, Duke de Beaufort (1616–69), was the grandson of Henri IV and his royal mistress Gabrielle d'Estrées; jailed for plotting with Madame de Chevreuse against Mazarin, he escaped from the prison of Vincennes with the help of a valet (Grimaud, according to *Twenty Years After*) and, called 'the King of Les Halles' on account of his popularity, played a prominent part in the Fronde; subsequently, as we shall see, he returned to power and died a hero at the siege of Candia in 1669. His body was never found and some have identified him with the Man in the Iron Mask. Marion Delorme (1611–50), a woman of brilliant wit and great beauty, was loved by many men but loved only Cinq-Mars. Her fame had recently been revived by Victor Hugo who, in a play bearing her name (1831), demonstrated that even a fallen woman may be saved by love.

MM. de Lyonne and Letellier: i.e. Hugues de Lionne (1611–71), Minister of State and Secretary for Foreign Affairs, who concluded the Treaty of the Pyrenees with Spain in 1659. Michel Le Tellier (1603–85) was Secretary of State for War between 1643 and 1666. Later, as Minister of Justice, he signed the revocation of the Edict of Nantes in 1685.

Monsieur ... Madame: i.e. the Duke and Duchess d'Orléans. 'Monsieur le Prince', a few lines further on, is the Prince de Condé.

205 *the Halles*: the main Paris market had occupied a site just south of the church of Saint-Eustache since the thirteenth century. D'Artagnan and Porthos head south towards the rue Saint-Honoré from which the rue de l'Arbre-Sec led down to the Seine.

hotel de Bourgogne: for over a century, the site of the former residence of the Dukes of Bourgogne had housed successive troups of actors granted the monopoly of staging plays, a privilege bitterly resented by other companies which were forced to tour the provinces. In 1600, however, Mondory's rival players set up the Théâtre du Marais and in 1658 Molière moved into the Petit-Bourbon and thence, in 1661, to the Palais-Royal. When Louis XIV merged rival troups into the Comédie-Française in

1680, the Hôtel de Bourgogne (now no. 29 rue Étienne-Marcel in the second *arrondissement*) became for a century the home of the Comédie-Italienne.

206   *Blue Ribands*: i.e. members of the traditional landed aristocracy who were entitled to wear the *cordon bleu* of rank.

207   *Monsieur Molière*: Jean-Baptiste Poquelin, known as Molière (1622–73), was an actor-manager as well as playwright. For the fête at Vaux given by Fouquet to honour the King on 17 August 1661, he was commissioned to write a comedy-ballet, *Les Fâcheux*, a series of satirical portraits much admired by La Fontaine, by which Molière first attracted the attention of Louis XIV.

211   *do we write no more poems now, neither?*: readers of *The Three Musketeers* will recall that in his youth Aramis wrote verses, among others a poem written in words of one syllable.

     Lebrun: Charles Le Brun (1619–90), a protégé of Fouquet and later of Colbert, became Painter Royal in 1662, director of the Gobelins pottery in 1663, and oversaw the decoration of the Palace of Versailles.

216   *The Bourgeois Gentilhomme*: Monsieur Jourdain, the 'would-be gentleman' of one of Molière's finest satires (1670), acts on the principle that clothes make the man. His sartorial vanity is particularly emphasized in the scene with his tailor (II. v) and the ceremony in Act IV which confers upon him the title of Mamamouchi. In offering a character of his own creation as a 'model' exploited by Molière, Dumas can scarcely be thought modest.

219   *Madame Coquenard*: Porthos's first wife: see note to p. 76.

221   *the gazetteers*: Dumas himself was never aloof from the kind of invention he archly criticizes here.

222   *Madame de Sevigné*: Marie de Rabutin-Chantal, Marquise de Sévigné (1626–96) whose correspondence with her daughter (which she called 'conversation at a distance') combines shrewd observation with imagination and spontaneity.

     You rhyme in a slovenly manner: La Fontaine's verse, which sought supple rhythms, was frowned on by the formal purists but much admired in other quarters for its fluidity: *lumière* rhymes with *ornière* (like *fâcheux* with *heureux* on p. 225) but is not a 'rich' rhyme suitable for noble, end-stopped classical verse. Though La

Fontaine's foolishness is rather overdone, his position in Fouquet's côterie was in fact that of court-jester.

223   *run away with my wife*: in 1647 La Fontaine, then 26, married Marie Héricart who was 14 and a distant relative of Racine. The marriage was not happy and husband and wife went their separate ways in 1658, though they remained on friendly terms until about 1672. Mme La Fontaine's unwifely conduct has been much exaggerated and La Fontaine's fight with a lieutenant has no basis in fact, though tradition has it that he crossed swords at some time during the 1650s with a retired army officer named Poignan who had made advances to Madame La Fontaine.

a moralist . . . not a philosopher: to English eyes, Molière's shrewd observation of people and manners may seem 'philosophical' enough. By French standards, however, his views are neither sufficiently abstract nor systematic to qualify as 'philosophy'. His taste for psychological and social analysis places him squarely in the tradition of French *moralistes*.

224   *Chaplain*: Jean Chapelain (1595–1674), thankfully a reticent poet, maintained his literary reputation with the promise of an epic poem on the subject of Joan of Arc. He kept the public waiting twenty-five years before producing *La Pucelle* (1656) which was quite awful.

226   *Xenocrates*: Xenocrates (396–314 BC) studied with Aristotle under Plato. He was so sober and serious that Plato urged him unavailingly 'to sacrifice to the Graces'. But even Phryné, the courtesan, who had wagered that she could seduce him, failed to provide enough 'graces' to secure his attention.

228   *Lyonne*: on Hugues de Lionne, see note to p. 204.

Lettre de cachet!: an order granted by the King for the arrest and detention 'during his Majesty's pleasure', normally at the Bastille, of subjects who were troublesome to the state or to private families (who applied for these sealed warrants as a means of bringing errant relatives to their senses or of getting them out of the way). Some prisoners thus detained were simply forgotten.

Seldon: it was by pretending to take an interest in Seldon—a poor young student sent to the Bastille for writing a couplet against the Jesuits (*Bragelonne*, ii, Chap. 42)—that Aramis had succeeded in obtaining his first interview with 'Marchiali'. Dumas, always careful to use 'authentic' names for his invented characters, may have chosen 'Seldon' (who is Irish on p. 236 and 'Scotch' on p. 295 and plays no active part in the plot) by analogy with John Felton (1595–1628) who assassinated the Duke of Buckingham in Portsmouth in 1628 (*The Three Musketeers*, chap. 59). He may also be a vague memory of John Selden (1584–1654), an English scholar and jurist: Dumas was always freer with the facts of the history of England than of France. However, the student was taken from an episode of Courtilz's *L'Inquisition française ou l'Histoire de la Bastille* (Paris, 1715) which relates how a 'schoolboy of twelve or thirteen' was jailed in about 1674 for writing satirical verses against the Jesuits.

229 *The timepiece of the Bastille*: the clock in question was replaced in the early eighteenth century, when Marc-René D'Argenson (1652–1721) was Lieutenant-General de Police, by an even more famous one showing a man and a woman chained at the neck, waist, hands, and feet.

230 *the idea of a cardinal*: Fouquet had promised Aramis a cardinal's hat.

235 *Bertaudière*: see note to p. 141.

Marchiali: see notes to pp. 174 and 228. Du Junca's register (see introduction) gives the name as 'Marchiel'. The entry recording his burial the following day gives 'Marchioly'. Dumas was not alone in writing 'Marchiali'.

241 *Rue St Antoine ... Senarl*: the carriage heads south through the Porte de Bercy, across the Seine at Charenton, and thence past Villeneuve-Saint-Georges in the Val-de-Marne. Though the English text is garbled at this point, the reference is to the forest of Senart (*sic*) which lies along the road to Melun and Vaux-le-Vicomte.

243 *Louis XI. or Charles IX.*: Louis XI (1423–83) strove with a notable lack of scruples to unify France. Charles IX (1550–74) presided over four religious wars and the Massacre of St Bartholomew's Day in 1572.

'Patiens quia æternus': Saint Augustine thus described God's unshakeable tolerance of a wicked world: 'he is patient because he is eternal' (æternus). The expression is sometimes applied to the Papacy but not to the Jesuits whose motto remains *Ad majorem Dei gloriam* ('To the greater glory of God'). Aramis sees himself as

the instrument of Providence, a mistake also made by Edmond Dantès, Count of Monte Cristo.

247 *Bas-Poiton*: i.e. Bas-Poitou, an old province lying inland from the Atlantic coast between La Rochelle and the limit of Lower Brittany.

251 *Your second brother?*: i.e. 'Monsieur', Philippe, Duke d'Orléans, who, according to Dumas (*Bragelonne*, ii. chap. 53), had inherited his father's 'uncertain, irresolute, character; impulsively good, indifferently disposed at bottom' and 'not very passionately inclined towards women'. His wife, Henrietta of England, had been the object of the King's attentions before Louise de la Vallière appeared at court.

252 *He who escorted La Vallière ... served my mother*: this partial list of d'Artagnan's services spans the thirty-five years of the Musketeer cycle: he accompanied Louise to the convent at Chaillot earlier in *The Vicomte de Bragelonne* (iv, chap. 4); the previous year (i. chaps. 29–31), he had kidnapped General Monk (see note to p. 141); and his faithful service to Anne of Austria dates back to his battle of wits with Richelieu and Milady on her behalf in *The Three Musketeers*.

254 *Charles the Fifth ... Charlemagne*: the empire of Charles V (Charles Quint) (1500–58) included Spain and her colonies, Flanders, Austria, and Germany. Charlemagne (742–814) was crowned Emperor of the West in 800.

256 *Vaux-le-Vicomte*: work had begun on Fouquet's house at Vaux, 6 kilometres from Melun, in 1654.

Levan ... Lenôtre ... Lebrun: i.e. Louis Le Vau (1612–70), who had built the Louvre and the Tuileries in Paris. André Le Nôtre (1613–1700) planned and oversaw the creation of the classical gardens at Vaux, Versailles, and Chantilly. On Le Brun, who later supervised the decoration of Versailles, see note to p. 211.

Wolsey: Thomas Wolsey (1471–1530), who was Henry VIII's unpopular Prime Minister between 1515 and his execution. Among the 'royal residences' mentioned here, Dumas had especially in mind Raoul's earlier stay at Hampton Court, built by Wolsey and presented by him to the King in 1526.

257 *that illustrious nymph of Vaux*: Dumas may be thinking of an '*Elegy to the Nymphs of Vaux*' published anonymously in 1662, written in

defence of Fouquet by La Fontaine but attributed, among others, to Pellisson.

Despréaux: Nicolas Boileau-Despréaux (1636–1711), satirist, friend of Molière and Racine, and theorist-practitioner of French classicism.

M. de Scudéry: Georges de Scudéry (1601–67), playwright and poet in the style of the fashionable 'preciosity'. The author of *Clélie*, which appeared between 1656 and 1660 in ten volumes, was Scudéry's sister Madeleine (1607–1701). The palace of Valterre is described in the last volume, though few readers ever get that far.

Marly: when Louis XIV later built a retreat at Marly-le-Roi, at a cost of 4.5 million *livres*, he installed a famous 'hydraulic machine' which, driven by the current of the Seine, supplied Versailles with water. The fruit-trees at Vaux were famous and Louis subsequently transferred many of them to Versailles. Dumas moved into his own extravagant and eccentric 'Château de Monte-Cristo' near Marly in 1846.

258 *the last surintendant of France*: as others have done, Dumas suggests that Louis's hatred of Fouquet was based on jealousy of his wealth. Modern historians believe that Louis feared Fouquet's power and influence and viewed him as a political threat. But hate him he did: after Fouquet's trial in 1664, Louis intervened and increased the sentence of the court from banishment to imprisonment for life. Fouquet was kept in a number of prisons before being sent to Pignerol where he died in 1680.

259 *Abbé Tenay*: i.e. the abbé Joseph-Marie Terray (1715–78). Appointed Louis XV's controller of finances in 1769, he complained that his high-spending King was dear to him in more than one sense of the word.

260 *Calypso*: Homer's *Odyssey* tells how Calypso, daughter of Atlas, lived alone on the island of Ogygia. When Ulysses was shipwrecked there, she fell in love with him and offered him immortality if he would marry her. She detained him for seven years and on his departure died of grief.

265 *Henry II. . . . Francis I. . . . Louis XI.*: Henri II (1547–59), François I (1515–47), and Louis XI (1461–83) had been particularly successful in surrounding the monarchy with the suitable trappings of royal magnificence.

267   *the keenest appetite in his kingdom*: as a baby, Louis required the services of several wet-nurses. In later life, he was in the habit of having a cold chicken and other comestibles placed at his bedside as a precaution against night-starvation.

     San-Lucar wine: Sanlucar, near Cadiz, was already famous for its Manzanilla.

279   *Les Fôcheux*: i.e. *Les Fâcheux*.

280   *Arabian Nights' Entertainments*: the *Mille et une Nuits* (*The Arabian Nights*) did not begin to appear until 1704, in a translation by the orientalist Antoine Galland (1646–1715).

286   *the porter Tony*: before he realized that the King was interested in Louise de la Vallière, Fouquet had written her an undated note offering his protection and his heart. Entrusted to Toby (*sic*), who proves to be a spy (*Bragelonne*, ii, chap. 28), the letter falls into the hands of Colbert who here uses it to turn the King against Fouquet.

     who has: read 'who *had*'.

     Maréchal d'Ancre: i.e. Concino Concini, Marshall of France: see note to p. 203.

293   *Milo of Crotona*: Milo of Crotona (sixth century BC) was six times Olympic wrestling champion. It was said that he once carried a live ox for a hundred yards, slew it with one hand, and ate it all up in a single day. Vegetarians with a sense of fair play may be reassured (*a*) by a marble by Pierre Puget (1620–94) which shows him being devoured by a lion, and (*b*) by a mythological report which claims that he was held fast by a tree which he had failed to split with his bare hands and was there eaten by wolves.

     Ann Radcliff's creation: the Gothic romances of Ann Radcliffe (1764–1823)—*The Mysteries of Udolpho* (1794), in particular—fuelled the Romantic taste for terror and the *roman noir* throughout Europe.

294   *Minos*: Minos (grandson of the Minos who was said to be the son of Europa and Zeus) was King of Crete who, with the help of Zeus, formulated the Laws of Minos.

299   *Jeanne d'Albret*: Jeanne d'Albret (1528–72), Queen of Navarre and mother of Henri IV, was a patron of the arts and a defender of the Huguenots. Though there is no proof, it was widely believed that she was murdered—by a variety of highly ingenious

methods which also included a gift of poisoned gloves—by Catherine de Medici.

300 *Perhaps my brother*: Louis's younger brother Philippe, Duke d'Orléans. Their uncle, Gaston d'Orléans, next in line to the French throne for as long as his brother, Louis XIII, remained childless, had consistently intrigued against the King and Richelieu. See note to p. 190.

304 *Maréchal d'Ancre*: Charles, Marquis d'Albert, Duke de Luynes (1578–21), first husband of Madame de Chevreuse, was instrumental in turning Louis XIII against Concini. The family was suitably rewarded.

Assuerus: according to the book of Esther, Haman, grand vizier of Persia, angry at the refusal of the Jew Mordecai to pay him due homage, ordered his death as a first step in a plan to exterminate all the nation's Jews. King Ahasuerus (perhaps Xerxes, Darius I, or Ataxerxes) was persuaded by Esther to repeal the order and Haman was hanged on the gallows erected for Mordecai. Racine used the incident as the basis for his *Esther* (1689).

Enguerrand de Marigny: see note to p. 58.

311 *Cinq-Mars ... Broussel*: Cinq-Mars was executed for treason in 1642 (see note to p. 16) and Henri de Talleyrand, Comte de Chalais (1599–1626), was decapitated for plotting against Richelieu. Louis de Bourbon, Prince de Condé (1621–86), and Paul de Gondi, Cardinal de Retz (1613–79) were imprisoned for their roles in the Fronde: both were subsequently rehabilitated. The arrest in 1648 of Pierre Broussel, a leading member of the Paris *parlement*, was the spark which began the Fronde: see the first volume of *Twenty Years After*.

312 *such a mistress as* ——: i.e. Mme de Bellière.

328 *the birth of Louis XIV*: Anne of Austria and Louis XIII had been married for twenty-three years before producing an heir in 1638. Though there was general rejoicing, doubts were cast—discreetly—on the King's paternity.

331 *Mithridates*: it was said of Mithridates VI (*c*.132–63 BC), King of Pontus, that, as a defence against assassins, he had since youth so accustomed himself to poisons that none proved effective when he came finally to take his life. He was obliged to ask a guard to run him through with a sword.

335 *the shade of Dido*: in the *Aeneid*, Virgil tells how Dido, Queen of Carthage, stabbed herself to death when Aeneas failed to return her love. Passing through the Underworld in book vi, he is understandably unnerved to encounter her, with her wounds still gaping wide, standing like a block of Parian marble. She glares grimly at him before rushing furiously away into a dark wood.

352 *petit lever*: whereas the *grand lever*, the first appearance of the day of royal personages, was a court occasion, the *petit lever* was a more intimate ceremony: only specially invited courtiers were allowed to be present when the King or his close relatives rose and dressed.

359 *iron visor*: the masks later worn by certain prisoners were made of black velvet with, at most, a frame of metal struts. See Introduction.

360 *maille*: a small copper coin, worth half a *denier*: the lowest current denomination.

361 *M. le Duc de Beaufort*: see note to p. 204.

366 *who is an Infante*: i.e. the prisoner in the mask is potentially as dangerous to relations between France and Spain as had been the Infanta, Maria-Teresa, whom Louis XIV had married as a means of settling the question of the Spanish succession.

368 *M. le Prince*: i.e. Louis de Bourbon, Prince de Condé.

369 *from the Place Maubert to ... Gigelli*: during the Fronde, Beaufort, appointed Admiral of the Fleet in 1650, was known as 'the King of the Halles' and 'the Admiral of the Haymarket' because of his popularity with the people of Paris. After the Fronde, he feared for his life—the Place Maubert was a place of public execution from the time of François I until the mid-eighteenth century—but was subsequently reinstated. Beaufort saw service in North Africa and in 1664 took Djidjelli, 130 kilometres north-west of Constantine in Algeria, the garrison of which was massacred after his departure.

Henry VI.: read Henri IV. Beaufort was the illegitimate grandson of Henri IV and Gabrielle d'Estrées.

370 *M. de Turenne*: Henri de la Tour d'Auvergne, Vicomte de Turenne (1611–75), was the greatest French general of the period.

St. Louis: Louis IX (1214–70) died of the plague at Carthage during his eighth and, of course, final Crusade.

escape from Vincennes: jailed by Mazarin in 1643, he escaped from the prison at Vincennes in 1648, a feat engineered, according to *Twenty Years After*, by Athos and Grimaud.

Who had a son: perhaps Dumas intends to suggest that the Puritan Mordaunt, the villain of *Twenty Years After*, was Beaufort's son by Milady de Winter who, however, was not 'agreeable' nor did she live near the Halles. On the other hand, the girl might symbolize the Fronde and the 'son' its legacy. This loop of the conversation is somewhat obscure.

373 *knight of Malta*: the Knights Hospitallers, who were dedicated to the defence of the Holy Sepulchre, formed the oldest of the military and religious orders bequeathed by the Crusades. There were three ranks: Knight, Chaplain, and fighting Squire. After the Reformation, the Order's influence declined, though it was as popular with novelists of the *ancien régime* as the Foreign Legion was later to be: younger sons and love-thwarted heroes were sent off to fight or die or disappear in some vaguely Middle Eastern country as *Chevaliers de Malte*. Raoul's entry to the Order committed him to a vow of chastity and to service outside France: hence the consternation of Athos.

376 *a new game of lottery*: public and private lotteries were extremely popular in France and other European countries, and governments used them as a supplementary means of financing national projects. During the reign of Louis XIV, five kinds were permitted: in addition to State lotteries, there were lotteries which raised money for public works, for charity, for private profit, and for financing business ventures. Guise's new entertainment probably involved drawing lots for some gallant society game.

Theophrastus: Theophrastus (372–287 BC), naturalist, philosopher, and author of a series of thirty satirical portraits of moral types, which served as a model for La Bruyère's *Characters from Theophrastus, translated from the Greek, showing the Characters or Manners of the present century* (1688), Dumas's immediate source for this remark.

Malicorne: Malicorne, one of Guise's squires, had been Anne of Austria's lover in 1648, as the memoirs of the period reveal. He figures in the entourage of Saint-Aignan upstream in *The Vicomte de Bragelonne* as the lover of Françoise de Montalais and a somewhat oily go-between. With Montalais's help, he was instrumental in furthering the King's affair with Louise: see note to p. 85.

379 *mistaken in an hour!*: i.e. Montalais has miscalculated the time.

383 *A little house at Fontainebleau*: see note to p. 91.

384 *Longus*: late second-early third-century AD. Author of *Daphnis and Chloe*, a pastoral novel much admired in the seventeenth century for its elegance of expression.

 as Ruth did to Boaz: the story is told in the Old Testament, in the book of Ruth. Hugo's famous poem *Booz endormi*, one of the finest of the collection *La Légende des siècles*, did not appear until 1859.

385 *Rochefort*: Rochefort, Richelieu's evil right hand and the man with the scar who insulted d'Artagnan at the beginning of *The Three Musketeers*, subsequently became his close friend. When Rochefort attempts to shoot Louis XIV during the Fronde in *Twenty Years After*, d'Artagnan kills him: though they are political enemies, they remain friends in death. In Courtilz's pseudo-*Memoirs of d'Artagnan*, a fictitious character called Rosnay plays the role given to Rochefort by Dumas who may have taken the name from another romance by Courtilz entitled *Mémoires de M.L.C.D.R.* [*Monsieur le Comte de Rochefort*] (1678).

 the speculation: d'Artagnan's role in restoring the English monarchy in May 1660 had been financed, not by the miserly Mazarin, but with his own money plus a large contribution from Planchet, who regarded his participation in their partnership as a sound investment. The gratitude of those who gained from d'Artagnan's success would, he believed, be translated into handsome rewards.

387 *great fortunes*: the long struggle to subordinate aristocratic power to the throne was maintained by Louis XIV who centralized political authority. Noble privilege was broken by the French Revolution, but the matter had still finally to be resolved in the post-Napoleonic world inhabited by Dumas who, though a natural democrat, dearly loved the company of the great.

388 *Lepanto*: John of Austria, commanding a large Spanish force, had broken the Turks at the battle of Lepanto in 1571 during which Cervantes lost an arm. In the 1660s Beaufort, commanding a French force, fought the Barbary pirates who infested the Mediterranean.

392 *St. Honorat*: i.e. Saint-Honnorat, the smaller of the two main Lerin islands, off Cannes, and site of a seventh-century mon-

astery, now abandoned, and a fortified castle dating from the twelfth century.

syndic of his brotherhood: until the end of the *ancien régime*, trades and avocations (builders, printers, etc.) were carried out under the auspices of organized guilds. Elected officers (*syndics*, and *échevins*) dealt with the State and with other bodies, their main goal being to protect their corporate monopoly.

Sainte-Marguerite's: a fortified prison had recently been built on the island to accommodate high security prisoners. The Man in the Iron Mask was detained there between 1687 and 1698.

395 *a silver plate*: the incident of the message scratched on a silver plate was first recorded by Voltaire in chap. 25 of his *History of the Century of Louis XIV* published in 1751.

400 *Saint-Mars*: the governor may have been 'a happy farmer' (p. 394), but he was not, in 1661, Bénigne d'Auvergne, *sieur* de Saint-Mars (*c.*1622–1708). After Fouquet's trial ended in November 1664, Saint-Mars was appointed Governor of the prison of Pignerol in Piedmont previously directed by a functionary named Roncherolles. He was charged with keeping the Surintendant in conditions of absolute security. Saint-Mars had only a few days to prepare before Fouquet, escorted by Charles de Batz-Castelmore d'Artagnan, arrived on 16 January 1665. Saint-Mars, along with his masked prisoner, was transferred to Saint-Marguerite only in 1687.

409 *everything is beautiful in living things*: Athos's philosophy, like his later 'doubts of a God' (p. 414), is much closer to Romantic pantheism than to ideas current in the seventeenth century which both mistrusted nature and professed doctrinaire theological ideas.

411 *war with the Arabs*: a remark which was particularly topical in the 1840s when France was embarked upon a policy of colonial expansion in North Africa.

413 *forked sticks*: i.e. the rests required for firing the long-barrelled flintlock muskets then in use.

416 *Fuscus*: Cornelius Fuscus, former commander of the guards of Domitian (AD 51–96), last of the Twelve Caesars, died in AD 86 during a punitive expedition against the Dacians in what is now Romania.

418 *Mademoiselle de Tonnay-Charente*: see note to p. 89.

M. de la Guillotière, M. de Manchy: further examples of Dumas's habit of borrowing 'authentic' names, not all of which are identifiable in his usual sources.

419 *the perfidious Athenaïs*: i.e. Athenaïs de Tonnay-Charente.

421 *The States*: not the States General (which did not meet between 1614 and 1789), but a meeting of the 'States of Britanny'. Periodically, provincial assemblies or 'States', to which the clergy, aristocracy, and the 'third estate' sent representatives, were held to hear the King's will, which increasingly meant calls for money to be raised through taxation.

Lyonne ... Litellier ... Brienne ... Surintendant: on Lionne and Le Tellier, see note to p. 204. Henri-Auguste de Loménie, Comte de Brienne (1596–1666) had been ambassador to England and minister for foreign affairs. The Surintendant was, of course, Fouquet.

M. le Duc de Gesvres: Léon Potier (1620–74), as the Marquis de Gesvres, was appointed Captain of the King's Guards in 1646. He became a Duke in 1669.

429 *Rue des Petits-Champs*: where Colbert lived: see note to p. 13.

430 *imposts*: i.e. taxes. On 4 September 1661 Fouquet succeeded in forcing the States of Brittany to contribute 4 million *livres* to the Royal Exchequer.

435 *distance between himself and his persecutors*: on 26 August Fouquet travelled to Nantes in the company of Le Tellier and Colbert: the chase described by Dumas is an invention. The King arrived at Nantes on 31 August.

436 *Beaugency*: 25 kilometres downstream from Orléans and 31 from Blois.

439 *château of Langeais*: 25 kilometres downstream from Tours.

440 *La Fosse*: i.e. the Quai de la Fosse on the right bank of the Loire at Nantes.

441 *la Maison de Nantes*: the Château of Nantes, founded in 938 and rebuilt in 1466, was the occasional residence of French kings. Henri IV's Edict giving freedom of worship to French Protestants was signed there in 1598.

Paimbœuf: on the left bank of the Loire, 11 kilometres from Saint-Nazaire.

443 *Montmorency*: Henri, Duke de Montmorency (1595–1632), Marshall of France, arrested for rebelling with Gaston d'Orléans,

was decapitated at Toulouse. On Chalais and Cinq-Mars, see note to p. 311.

447 *MM. de Brienne and Rose*: on Brienne, see note to p. 421. Toussaint Rose (or Roze) (1615–1701), was secretary to Mazarin and Louis XIV.

452 *the castle of Angers*: Fouquet was arrested by Charles de Batz-Castelmore d'Artagnan outside Nantes cathedral on 5 September 1661, and not in the fanciful circumstances Dumas describes in the next chapter. He was transferred to the castle at Angers and, in December, to Amboise. On 30 May 1663 he was taken to the Bastille and thence briefly to the castle of Moret in 1664. After sentence was pronounced in November 1664, de Batz the Musketeer escorted Fouquet to Pignerol where he was handed into the care of Saint-Mars: see note to p. 400. He was closely guarded and was forbidden to communicate with the outside world.

461 *the King alone has a right to command*: although d'Artagnan was the effective commander of the King's Musketeers, his rank was 'Captain-Lieutenant'. The rank of 'Captain' belonged to the King.

M. de Roncherat: Dumas, who used authentic names whenever possible, here confuses the name and role of Roncherolles: see note to p. 400.

464 *the d'Artagnan of former times*: Dumas refers to events spanning a dozen years which are recounted in *Twenty Years After* and earlier volumes of *The Vicomte de Bragelonne*.

466 *the motives for my animosity against M. Fouquet*: this is a fair estimate of Colbert's subsequent services to France.

487 *The fire is opened upon Belle-Isle*: there was no action at Belle-Isle, though Louis ordered several companies of Guards to be ready to march against the castle should Fouquet make a show of resistance there.

488 *his name was Antoine*: this account of Porthos's ancestry is as fictitious as the character himself.

Coligny: Gaspard de Coligny (1519–72), one of France's greatest admirals, converted to Protestantism and was one of the first victims of the St Bartholomew's Day Massacre of 1572. His corpse was displayed on the gallows at Montfaucon.

Bassompierre: see note to p. 203.

489 *Locmaria*: a village at the eastern tip of Belle-Isle. The famous caves are situated at the other end of the island. Dumas's topography is again somewhat hazy.

491 *Biscarrat*: in chap. 5 of *The Three Musketeers*, Richelieu's guards are routed, with the exception of Biscarrat, a Gascon, whose gallantry earns the respect of the victors. Dumas may have had in mind Jacques de Rotondis de Biscarat who became a lieutenant of light horse and was killed in action in 1641. His son, equally gallant, proves not to have his steely qualities and confirms Dumas's general view that the new generation did not match up to the old.

494 *the mandatory of God*: according to the still orthodox view (which had, however, been challenged by other theories of kingship), the monarch sat on his throne by Divine Right. The Pope was God's spiritual lieutenant and kings his temporal representatives.

506 *the bastion Saint-Gervais*: in a purely invented episode of *The Three Musketeers* (chap. 46), d'Artagnan and his three friends take and hold a position on the enemy's lines during the siege of La Rochelle in 1628.

516 *Enceladus*: according to Greek myth, Enceladus was one of the giants who attacked Mount Olympus. He was engulfed by Mount Etna by order of Athena.

518 *drove out the mind*: the sensibility which dictated this passage had little to do with the seventeenth century and expresses essentially Romantic ideals.

519 *gulf of Gascony*: i.e. the Bay of Biscay.

     longest days of the year: Dumas seems to forget that events take place in early September and not, as this suggests, at midsummer.

522 *Constant de Pressigny*: another name which Dumas exploits for its authenticity value.

     Corunna: in Galicia, on the north-west coast of Spain.

526 *uniting your guards with my musketeers*: the rivalry between Richelieu's (later Mazarin's) Guards and the King's Musketeers was intense. When Tréville was disgraced in 1646, the Musketeers were disbanded and reformed only in 1657. Gesvres's 'ambition' to combine his Guards with the Musketeers has no basis in fact, but does reflect the continuing rivalries between the two groups.

529 *a captain like myself*: Dumas consistently upgrades d'Artagnan's rank. See note to p. 461.

532 *The Fronde ... emancipated it*: this estimate of the political significance of the Fronde, though it requires qualification, is substantially fair. After 1653 the political power of the nobility was much reduced and the monarchy under Louis XIV was to achieve absolute, centralized control of the State.

535 *Bayonne*: Bayonne, at the mouth of the Adour in south-west France, was a fortified town which had several times resisted Spanish sieges. After setting a course for Corunna (p. 522), Aramis did not land in Spain, where he has influence, but at a convenient frontier port.

559 *M. d'Estrées*: Jean d'Estrées (1624–1707), Marshall of France, appointed Vice-Admiral in 1669. In 1670 he saw action in North Africa and in 1671 returned to serve France in her European wars.

562 *Sylvain de Saint-Cosme*: there appears to be no trace of Sylvain de Saint-Cosme or of his brothers in Dumas's usual sources or elsewhere. Saint-Côme was the patron saint of surgeons.

563 *the Pallas of Virgil*: son of Evander and companion of Aeneas in the *Aeneid*. Pallas was killed in battle by Turnus (bk. x) and his body, its face as white as snow, was committed to an honourable pyre (bk. xi).

564 *an old Gothic manor-house in Berry*: the house, like its owner, is an invention. The Armand de Sillègue d'Athos whose name may have been appropriated for Dumas's Athos, was born in the Béarn.

567 *I shall follow thee*: she did, of course, but later rather than sooner: Louise de la Vallière died 1710, aged 66.

When will it be my turn to depart?: again Dumas strikes a Romantic attitude: there are echoes here of Vigny's *Moïse* (1826) in which Moses, 'powerful and lonely', asks God for eternal rest.

568 *flew the pie*: an instance of translator fatigue. The French has *voler de la pie* which means to hunt magpies with falcons. Louis, an enthusiastic huntsman, pursued various kinds of game in the woods around Versailles and Paris, Compiègne and, as here, on the banks of the Loire.

the tiercelets: the name given by falconers to the male young of certain birds of prey such as the sparrow-hawk.

569 *the long journey you have had*: Charles de Batz-Castelmore had indeed been responsible for escorting Fouquet to his final prison

at Pignerol in Piedmont where guard and prisoner had arrived in January 1665.

570 *the death of the Queen-Mother*: Anne of Austria died on 20 January 1666. Dumas's chronology is again faulty.

572 *Mademoiselle de Tonnay-Charente, now become Madame de Montespan*: Mademoiselle de Tonnay-Charente had married the complaisant Duke de Montespan et d'Antin in 1663.

575 *Guiche, whom I have exiled*: the Comte de Guiche was exiled in 1664 for attempting to distance Louise from the King. He fought for the Dutch against the English and returned to France in 1669, though he did not reappear at court until 1671.

my brother Charles: Madame, Duchess d'Orléans, was the sister of Charles II of England.

M. le Chevalier de Lorraine: Charles (1643–90), whom Dumas has shown as the friend of the homosexual Duke d'Orléans, was heir to the Duchy of Lorraine. In 1662 he was stripped of his entitlement by the Treaty of Montmartre which gave France rights over Lorraine. He protested but was ordered to leave the country within four days. Thereafter, he expressed hatred of France. He assumed the title of Duke in 1675 and was acknowledged by all European nations save France.

576 *Mademoiselle Stewart ... Countess of Castlemaine*: of this list of Charles II's mistresses, the most influential were Frances Stewart, Duchess of Richmond; 'pretty, witty' Nell Gwyn (1650–87); and Barbara Villiers (1640–1709), who was made Countess of Castlemaine in 1661 and Duchess of Cleveland in 1670. To Winifred Wells, Mary 'Moll' Davies, and the rest might be added Lucy Walters, Mrs Jane Roberts, Mrs Knight, Mary Killigrew ...

577 *Mademoiselle de Kéroualle*: Louise de la Penancoët de Kéroualle (1649–1734)—'of a childish, simple and baby face' according to John Evelyn—was born at Brest. A keen promoter of French interests, 'Madame Carwell' was one of Charles II's many mistresses. She was made Duchess of Portsmouth in 1672: see p. 584.

The Dutch ... insult me daily: in 1665 Louis XIV laid claim to the Spanish Netherlands by the Law of Devolution, a local law which awarded inherited property to the female children of a first marriage (in this case, to Maria-Teresa, Louis's Queen) rather than to the male children of the second (thus disinheriting Spain). By 1667 Charleroi, Tournay, and Lille had become French. It was French expansionism and not, as Dumas suggests, Dutch 'insults' which led to the War of Devolution. In 1661, according to an earlier incident (*Bragelonne*, iv, chap. 6), Louis had been enraged by the appearance of Dutch pamphlets which made slighting reference to the 'Sun-King'. One medal bore the legend: *in conspectu meo stetit sol* ('on beholding me the sun stood still') which Dumas translates at the foot of the page by quoting Joshua 10: 13: 'And the sun stood still, and the moon stayed, until the people had avenged themselves upon their enemies...'

578 *could I not represent ... as well as the Dutch?*: negotiations began in November 1667 but within a month it was clear that the English would not tolerate an alliance with France. The Triple Alliance (England, Holland, and Sweden) was formed to counter the threat of growing French power, though it guaranteed the gains of the War of Devolution. France made further advances at the expense of Spanish interests by the Treaty of Aix-la-Chapelle (1668) which secured what was later to be considered France's 'natural' north-eastern frontier. The acquiesence of England was guaranteed by the secret Treaty of Dover (1670) which was finally effected by the Duchess d'Orléans who here prepares to set off to meet her brother, Charles II. Louis's hatred of Holland finally turned into war in October 1672 and the campaign of 1673 was to prove decisive.

579 *To embroil Europe with the United Provinces*: Dumas's chronology of events is somewhat confused here and his loyalties mixed. Though he clearly admires Louis's energy, he was far from being a supporter of absolute royal power—as the sympathetic portrait drawn of John de Witt, the Dutch Prime Minister assassinated in 1672 at the beginning of *The Black Tulip* (1850), clearly indicates.

580 *Forant*: Job Forant (1630–92), naval engineer and armourer, who rose through the ranks of Louis's navy and was given his own command in 1665. In 1666 the King sent him to Holland to supervise the construction of six men-of-war. He fought at Candia with Beaufort in 1669. His later career was impeded by his refusal to renounce Calvinism, and resumed only after he turned Catholic in 1685. D'Imfreville and Destouches (p. 581) were also naval engineers and armourers.

581 *vessels of 78*: i.e. of 78 guns.

the Golden Fleece ... Grand Cordon of St. Michael: the Order of the Golden Fleece, the highest of the Spanish Orders of Chivalry, was founded by Philip the Good in 1429, passed first to Austria, through Charles the Bold, and thence to Spain through Charles V. The Order of Saint Michael was a military Order created by Louis XI in 1469.

582 *precedence*: to the end, Dumas insists on enhancing the influence of d'Artagnan's rank.

584 *The King recalled ... Duchess of Portsmouth*: Guiche was recalled in 1671 and the Chevalier de Lorraine was exiled in 1662. Madame helped secure the Treaty of Dover in 1670 and Kéroualle became Duchess of Portsmouth in 1672 ... Dumas's list of significant events is again chronologically confused.

d'Oliva ... provisional successor: there was nothing provisional about the generalship of the Italian Jean-Paul Oliva who headed the Society of Jesus between 1664 and 1681.

585 *In the spring*: of 1673, the year of Louis's major and decisive push against the Dutch.

La Frise: i.e. Friesland, a northern province of the Netherlands.

587 *a wimble*: a gimlet: the column 'bores a hole' in the enemy defences.

588 *God had resumed the souls*: later, lightly corrected editions of the translation express Dumas's parting words rather more clearly: 'Of the four valiant men whose history we have related, there now no longer remained but one. Heaven had taken to itself three noble souls.'